MAXIMUM EFFORT

Maximum Effort

By

Vincent Formosa

2020

Copyright © 2020 by Vincent Formosa.

1st Edition created 2020.

This is a novel. The characters, situations and military organisations are an invention of the author, except where they can be identified historically. Any other resemblance to actual persons, living or dead is purely coincidental. Likewise, names, dialogue and opinions expressed are products of the author's imagination to fit the story and not to be interpreted as real.

ISBN: 9798614369668

3D of Lancaster created by EGPJET3D and purchased from Tubrosquid under royalty free licence for commercial use. Adaptations to mesh and texture created by Vincent Formosa. Cover layout by Vincent Formosa.

All rights reserved under International and Pan-American Copyright Conventions.

No part of this book may be reproduced in any form or by any electronic or mechanical means, ; this includes but is not restricted to information storage and retrieval systems, without written permission from the author or publisher, except by a reviewer who may quote passages in a review.

This book would not exist if it were not for the help and hard work of a number of people. Particular thanks go to my diligent beta readers, Jon Hayden, Barbara Boon, Caroline Edink-Koppelaar and Claire Hack for spending many hours going over my manuscript, making suggestions and discussing their ideas with me for which I am truly grateful.

I am also especially grateful to Dom Howard for providing copies of the official Bomber Command Night Raid Reports covering the period the novel took place, they were invaluable for helping to make details on the raids as accurate as possible.

Other titles by the same author

The Eagles Of Peenemunde
Run The Gauntlet
Prototype
Callicoe RNVR

Available in both Kindle and paperback formats on Amazon.

Contents

01 - Going Home	1
02 - A Stranger, In A Strange Land	10
03 - Here We Go Again	23
04 - Busman's Holiday	27
05 - Gardening, A Very British Past Time	33
06 - We're H-A-P-P-Y	39
07 - It's Always The Little Things	50
08 - Deep And Crisp And Even	56
09 - One Of Those Months	61
10 - Tremors	74
11 - The Big City	82
12 - Lost Souls	94
13 - The Stuff That Dreams Are Made Of	102
14 - Chance Meetings	113
15 - Back In The Saddle	120
16 - On Their Way	130
17 - Pushing Your Luck	136
18 - Bah, Humbug!	144
19 - Under A Wandering Star	154
20 - Milk Runs	161
21 - Silver Screen	170
22 - Take A Chance On Me	176
23 - Again, Again, Again	191
24 - Love And War	206
25 - Hoodoo Boy	216
26 - All The Fun Of The Fair	232
27 - London's Burning	241
28 - On The Fence	252
29 - Two Down, One To Go	264
30 - Best Laid Plans And All That	278
31 - Elan And Greek Myth	285
32 - Left Hand, Right Hand	289
33 - New Broom	300
34 - When Luck Finally Runs Out	303
35 - Without Which Not	309
36 - Send In The Heavies	315
37 - Fingernails	321
38 - Paraskevi	336
39 - To Shelter For A While	342
40 - Humpty Dumpty	354
41 - It's So Bracing	361
42 - To Fight Another Day	367
43 - New Lease	374

44 - Waltz The Light Fantastic	378
45 - With Great Power	384
46 - Baby Steps	395
47 - Teething Troubles	401
48 - Picking Up The Pieces	408
49 - Flogging A Dead Horse	413
50 - Bull And Brass	424
51 - Monkey And The Grinder	430
52 - Joyride	434
53 - Unreasonable Haste Is The Direct Road To Error	444
54 - One Of Our Aircraft Is Missing	448
55 - Hold Them By The Hand	456
56 - Command Decisions	462
57 - The Measure Of A Man	468
58 - The Politics Of War	477
59 - Trout	481
60 - Crucible	489
61 - World Enought And Time	501

1 – Going Home

The war that had engulfed Europe seemed far away in Scotland. The Germans hadn't ventured so far north since 1940 and the nearest the rolling hills and lochs got to the war was the sound of engines reverberating off the heather. Aircraft flew up and down, the men on board doing what they could to prepare for war.

They went out for hours at a time, flying their aircraft around northern Scotland at operational weight, dropping practice bombs on the ranges and then coming home. Sometimes, those close to finishing their course would go on an actual op, laying mines off the coast or dropping leaflets telling the Germans how nasty the war was and they should all pack it in. Relatively easy jobs like this could give a crew more learning than any number of hours in a classroom or on a training flight.

They had come from all over the world. Trained abroad in Canada, South Africa and Australia as part of the Empire training program, these men had crossed vast oceans to get the final polish at Operational Training Units before being posted to an operational squadron down south.

Overseeing this training were men who had already been through the crucible. One of them was Flight Lieutenant Alexander Carter. His experience was worth more than gold. It had been won with blood and guts and raw courage during seven long months flying Hampdens over Germany. Then one day, someone decided he'd done enough trips and he was screened, given some leave and packed off to a Flying Instructors School in the Cotswolds.

Now it was his job to pass on these lessons to the next generation. A stickler for detail, he held his pupils to a high standard and he expected them to excel. War was a serious business. Too often on his old squadron, he'd often seen mediocre aircrew take off into the inky night never to return.

No one would ever know for sure why they didn't come back. Some obviously fell to flak, some fell to fighters but a lax attitude could kill you just as easily as the enemy could. He knew of gunners who'd have a casual fag on the way home after a long op. Then there was the crew who would listen to the radio when they got over the channel, like it was a summer outing. He had no time for someone who was here to play. A navigator who got you lost on a clear day with no wind would be next to useless over Germany in the dark. One man's lack of skill could kill six or seven other poor sods that deserved better.

Carter found he had to balance his own personal standard with that of requirement. Squadrons were crying out for men, so he couldn't bin everyone he felt was lacking, but he could do what he could to help them survive. If that meant he was harsh sometimes, then so be it. He knew some sprogs called him flak happy, regarding his dour demeanour as pessimism or even a lack of nerve. One pilot he'd washed out had told him to his face he was round the bend. His conscience could live with that.

Today, he was giving one of his crews their final assessment to see how much they had learned and absorbed from him. He stood in the cockpit just by the right shoulder of a smooth faced twenty year old Pilot Officer who was doing his best under his instructor's beady gaze. The aircraft dipped on a swell of air and then bounded up again. The airframe of the Vickers Wellington creaked in protest at this sudden shift in height. Carter gripped the back of the pilot's seat hard to maintain his balance.

Behind him, the navigator was busy plotting their course and he gave his pilot a course correction over the R/T. The twin engine bomber turned left, the pilot doing his best to maintain the same height through the turn, riding the controls as he fought the gusting winds.

It was what Carter called a medium day. Heavy clouds were being turned into fluffy big balls of cotton by high winds, giving them a bumpy ride and an interesting challenge. This was good weather for a raid at night. Cloudy conditions made it harder for searchlights and nightfighters to find you. Darkness was your friend, to be embraced and fondled like a lover.

Nothing could prepare you for that first time when an enemy searchlight speared you in its white hard glare and the flak started to zero in on you. Your stomach would coil and churn, your eyes would go wide; your mouth would go dry as your aircraft shook from the exploding shells. If you were good enough or lucky enough or reacted quick enough, you'd shake them off and lose yourself in the inky black.

The Wellington lurched again and Carter smiled. High winds threw off dead reckoning. Turbulence made things difficult for the crew. He made it harder by announcing that their radio had packed up. Now it was all down to their navigator so it was up to the rest of the crew to help him. Soon, gunners were passing sightings of landmarks, lakes, rivers and villages as they spotted them. It was all good stuff at getting them to work together as a team. They had to learn that they relied on one another to survive. It was better they realised that now rather than at a moment of crisis when it was too late to make a difference.

They held this course for another half an hour, ever westwards.

Weaving in and out of the clouds, the bomber flew on sedately. Carter liked the Wellington. On the ground she looked like a pregnant cow, squatting on her main undercarriage. In the air, she was just a little bit tubby around the middle, but she had the strength to get you home. He'd heard more than one tale of Wellingtons coming back with their canvas torn to shreds and the geodetic frames shot through.

The ones they had at the OTU were tired and had seen better days, but even that was a lesson he could use to his advantage. Pilots needed to have the confidence that their plane would hold together. Minor defects were not things to scrub an op for. You worked around those and you shoved, cajoled and pleaded with the gremlins to cooperate. If that didn't work, you ignored them and just got on with it.

East of Inverness on the picturesque shore of the Moray Firth, six miles north of Elgin, was RAF Lossiemouth. The station wouldn't win any beauty prizes, but it was a wonderful location to fly from. Built on over five hundred acres of rough farm land, it had been completed in May 1939, not long before the outbreak of war. It wasn't as fancy as the more permanent stations down south, but Lossiemouth still had a lot going for it. The land was flat for miles around, perfect to stop raw crews from wrapping themselves around any odd tree or hill that took their fancy. That was not to say that accidents didn't happen, but it certainly made the odds of surviving the day better.

To the south was the hilly expanse of the Cairngorms. Many an escape and evasion exercise had been run in the gorse and heather of the Cairngorms. The local soldiers got to hunt RAF types and throw around a lot of thunderflashes. It was all thrilling stuff, right out of the boy's own papers. Biggles would have been proud.

Coming in from the north over the sea, the Wellington broke into the circuit and waited for their turn to land. Despite the weather and whatever niggles Carter had decided to throw their way, their navigator had managed to stay on track and bring them back on time. He watched intently as the pilot went through the landing routine. Gear down, flaps down, a confident hand slowly closing the throttles as the big bomber descended. Yes, this crew would make the grade, he decided. He'd cast a critical eye over everything and they'd handled it with aplomb. Short of shooting at them, he'd pushed them as much as he could.

The Wellington kissed the ground for a perfect three pointer and taxied smartly off the runway to dispersal. A final touch of the brakes, full rudder and a quick burst of throttle from the starboard engine and the bomber swung around and came to a stop. The engines were shut down and for the first time in three hours there was peace and quiet.

The pilot dragged the leather helmet off his head and ran his fingers through his blonde hair. Ears ringing from the engine noise he worked his jaw, trying to make them go pop. Carter crouched down and went into the nose as the bomb aimer opened the hatch. A ladder was hooked on and they got down to stand once more on terra firma. The pilot signed the aircrafts form 700 and then turned an expectant look on Carter. The whole crew did.

"You'll do," Carter said with a smile. He remembered when he'd been on an OTU himself, that curious feeling of expectation and worry, nervousness and excitement while you waited to be told that you had made it. The pilot extended a hand towards him.

"Thank you, sir," he said, his voice full of plummy vowels and cut glass enunciation.

"No need to thank me, Andrews, all of you," replied Carter, addressing the whole crew. "You've worked hard to get this far. I just helped polish the rough edges. I'll see you in the Mess later to celebrate."

Going their separate ways, Carter went to the instructors Nissen hut next to one of the hangars. He sat down at his desk and started writing up some notes on the flight. He was still at it half an hour later when Arthur 'Askey' Burton came in. Carter grunted in response to a question as he carried on writing. Burton tutted as he dumped his flying gear on a vacant armchair.

"All work and no play makes, Carter a dull boy," commented Burton. He'd just got in from a check flight of his own and was now done for the day. With the course drawing to a close there was almost a holiday air about the place. Burton was looking forward to the forty eight hour pass the instructors would have to relax before the next batch of pupils arrived.

"Figured out where you're going?" he asked Carter.

There was a pause while Carter finished off a sentence before replying.

"I thought I might drift over to Loch Ness, walk around the hills a bit, stroll by the water."

Burton snorted.

"Haggis hunting?"

Carter grinned, showing an even row of teeth.

"The quiet appeals to me." They both looked up as the thunder of a Whitley passed overhead. "After this madhouse? A few days with some peace and quiet sounds like heaven."

Burton made a face, it was civilisation for him and a quick train to Inverness. His needs were simple. He wanted a hotel with a warm room, a comfy bed and some decent booze. He thought about the graduation knees up in the Mess that evening. He was in the mood for a few jars to finish off the day before going off on leave.

He hovered over Carter, watching quietly as his friend continued to write his report. He shook his head and tutted as Carter wrote a particular sentence.

"What's three down, ends in 'S', another name for a donkey?" asked Carter without looking up, his voice distant and distracted.

"Ass," answered Burton quickly.

"Well you're being one," said Carter tartly. "I'll be done in a minute."

Burton made a face and stuck out his tongue. He shoved his gear off the armchair and collapsed onto it, his long legs stuck out in front of him. He rubbed a hand up and down his face and yawned. He found assessing someone else's flying tiring. It took a lot of mental energy to just stand there and watch when you wanted to yank the controls out of their hands and do it yourself.

A salt of the earth type, Burton had come up the hard way. He'd been a Sergeant pilot on the first daylight raids of the war and watched as his friends got cut to pieces. After surviving that bloodbath, he'd been switched over to night bombing. Like the rest of them, he had groped over northern Europe at six and seven thousand feet in the dark, learning how to do his job all over again.

After eight trips, he got his own aircraft. On his ninth op, he came back with two dead crew and a skeletal bomber. A fire had broken out and burned off all the canvas from the rear fuselage all the way back to the tail. He got a DFM for that. He got his commission not long afterwards and when his tour was over, he was sent to Lossiemouth; a rare survivor.

Burton picked up a stray newspaper and scanned the gloomy headlines. There'd been very little good news in 1941. They were hanging on but people were starting to ask just how many reverses and disasters they could withstand. Europe was under the Nazi jackboot after the cockup in France and the Low Countries. It was a mess in the Med and now the Russians were catching it.

He looked over the top of the paper at Carter who was still writing away. He may have been a stick in the mud sometimes, but he could be quite good fun when he was in the mood. Burton remembered when Carter had first arrived at Lossie. He'd been like a coiled spring after months on ops and it took him a good few weeks to unwind. Burton knew what that felt like.

Carter nibbled on the end of a pencil as he pondered how to word a certain phrase in his assessment. After a few months, Burton had developed the knack to rattle off his reports, but Carter took the time to make them particular to each candidate. This prissy attitude had brought him some stick at times but Burton rather liked this pernickety aspect of Carters character. He didn't suffer fools gladly but he also gave credit where it was due. That was a nice trait to have

Burton thought.

Carter absently scratched at a thin scar that followed the line of his left cheekbone as he signed off the report. He shoved the paper into an envelope with a bundle of other reports and left it on his desk.

"There, done," he announced.

"Good, can we go to the bar now?"

Laughing, Carter picked up his cap and held the door open for Burton. The tall man uncoiled from the armchair and loped towards the exit.

"Ah thang yah," he said in a slow drawl as he went past. "Gods teeth," he hissed as he got outside. The weather had turned. On the north east horizon, a bank of dark clouds was looming over the lead grey waters of the Moray Firth and coming in quickly. There was rain in those clouds, or Burton was no judge and he quickened his pace. The wind increased in the time it took them to get to the Mess and their greatcoats were whipping around their ankles when they went inside.

Cheeks tingling from the cold, they hung their coats on some spare hooks and went through to the bar. The mood was buoyant. This intake had come to the end of their course and it was a chance to have a good knees up before they scattered to different squadrons and Groups around the country. Andrews came over. His cheeks were pink and it wasn't from the cold.

"What can I get you, sir?" he asked Carter.

"A pint if that's okay," replied Carter. He spied two more of his pilots by the piano and he knew he would have to pace himself if he was going to get through the evening. Andrews disappeared towards the crowd around the bar and returned a few minutes later carrying three tankards. He handed one to Carter and another to Burton.

"For you, sir," said Andrews, handing them over. "Cheers," he clinked his tankard against each of theirs and drank deep.

"Do you know where you're going?" asked Carter.

"They posted the list earlier," said Andrews with some enthusiasm. "I'm going to 5 Group, 363 Squadron." He may as well have added, "I can't wait," at the end, such was his obvious pleasure at finally going onto ops.

"I'm sure you'll do fine," said Carter. Nodding his thanks, Andrews drifted off to join some of his classmates. Carter and Burton watched him go.

"Crawler," commented Burton, his tone light.

"I've already written his report up," said Carter, licking the froth off his top lip. They moved into the room, joining in some of the songs. Tonight, was one of those nights where the division between the old hands and the new boys mattered little.

The following morning, Carter was reading the newspaper over some toast and marmalade. He slurped on his tea as he digested another gloomy headline. He was marshaling his thoughts about how Rommel might be brought to book when a steward hovered at his shoulder and politely coughed behind one hand.

"I'm sorry to bother you, sir, but Wing Commander, Grant would like a word with you."

"Now?" Carter was surprised. He didn't recall doing anything particularly egregious the night before in the bar. He remembered being disqualified after crashing into a rival rider during a race around the Mess on some bicycles. Snagging a piece of toast with a lump of marmalade on, he munched on it as he went across to the CO's office in one of the admin huts.

It had rained overnight and the grass was damp but the wind had gone and it was a relatively still morning. He listened to the sounds of the sea as he walked along. He caught the Adjutant's eye as he came into the room before the CO's office.

"Go right in, sir," said the Adjutant. Carter knocked briefly on the door, heard a rumbled assent and went in. Wing Commander Grant looked up from his desk and smiled as he saw Carter. He gestured to a chair in front of his desk with his scarred left hand. "Carter, do come in, have a seat." he said warmly.

Carter sat down, still mystified as to the reason for the summons.

Grant leaned back, in apparent good mood. He smiled and reached for a cigarette. He stuck it between his lips and then went for the lighter, his motions precise, his thumb fumbling with the striker. Carter's eyes were drawn as they always were to the left hand that was missing the top digit of the index finger and the empty right sleeve that was folded and pinned to the side of his uniform jacket. A flying accident before the war had robbed Grant of his right arm but had done little to dull his drive and determination.

"You had a pretty good day yesterday," Grant observed. Carter had no idea if the CO was talking about his pupils or the Mess party, so he stuck to talking shop.

"Not bad, sir. I think this bunch make the grade." Grants mouth quirked in good humour.

"I'm glad to hear it; I'd hate to think you would be washing out someone at the end of a course."

"Yes, sir. Andrews will do okay. Bishop as well. He lacks a bit of confidence but I'm sure that'll change with time." Neither of them uttered the unspoken question, *if he lives long enough to get the time.*

"Anyway, we'll have the new intake coming in next week. Not that they'll be any of *your* concern," Grant said pointedly. Carter frowned in confusion, the scar on his cheek rippling.

7

"Sir?"

"Your orders have come through, Carter. You're going back to the coal face." Carter blinked. "Ops." The CO's voice seemed to come from far away as Carter tried to focus on what he'd said. Grant let him absorb the news and watched the reaction.

Carter rubbed his hand through short dark brown hair. His blue eyes glittered in intensity as his mouth went dry at the prospect of ops. Grant had seen those eyes cut a candidate stone dead when they made a mistake, but he'd also seen them soften in sympathy when words of encouragement were required. Average in height, Carter was slight in build but had filled out a little bit during his time at Lossiemouth. After months of operations, a man got thin living on a diet of cigarettes and adrenalin.

"I'll be sorry to lose you, but you're going home. 5 Group." Grant tapped a bundle of papers on his desk. "Your orders are in there. You don't need to report to your new squadron until the 23rd October so you've got a week's leave. Uncle will sort out your travel warrant for you later."

He handed over the envelope. Carter was surprised his hands were so steady when he took it. His whole world had been turned on its head. He always knew that he'd go back on ops sooner or later; he just thought he would get a bit more notice. At least with some leave he could see his family.

He thrilled at the chance to see Mary again. It had been two months since he'd last seen her and in the intervening period, he thought there'd been a cooling in her regard for him. Her letters to him had become more infrequent and shorter and far less personal.

"I realise this is something of a surprise, but you have been here nearly six months. We'll have a bit of a send off tonight and then you can get away on your leave."

"Thank you, sir," Carter replied woodenly, only part of his attention in the room. Grant came round from his desk and Carter stood up; the envelope clasped tightly in his hands.

"I just wanted to thank you for your efforts," Carter shook his hand warmly.

Carter was just trying to close the lid on his suitcase when Burton stormed through the door of the billet like a hurricane. He took in the scene in a half second.

"Bloody hell, so it's true."

"It is," said Carter. He put a knee on the suitcase and strained to get the clasp to click shut. "That got around quick."

Burton shrugged and moodily shoved his hands into his pockets as he leaned against the door frame.

"You know what the village tom toms are like. Nothing stays

secret for very long. Where are you headed?"

Carter nodded to the envelope Grant had given him on the chair by the bedside. Burton picked it up and pulled out the top sheet. He muttered under his breath as he read the bald language.

"Who's 363 squadron when they're at home?" he asked. Carter shrugged.

"Not a clue. I've never heard of them. They weren't in 5 Group the last time I was there."

"Hmmm, rum," muttered Burton. "Drop me a line, when you get there?"

"I'll do you one better," said Carter, "you can go in my place." He shoved the remaining clothes in his kit bag and stood up. He cast an appraising eye around the room to see if he'd missed anything and then clapped Burton on the shoulder. "Come on, you can get me a drink before I go and tidy up my paperwork."

When the goodbyes had been said and the last songs sung, Carter had lain awake for some hours. He lay on the bed, arm behind his head as he stared at the ceiling. He worked his way through a few cigarettes in the dark. This was one of those occasions he was grateful instructors got a room to themselves.

He cast his mind back to his first op as captain of a Hampden. It had been a milk run to Brest. Even so, the flak had been terrifying. The sharp *pock* as shells burst nearby which you felt rather than heard. A Hampden up ahead had been bracketed by searchlights and he watched, fascinated as it gyrated around the sky, trying to shake off the cones of light. The flak crept up to meet it and the aircraft was changed into a flaming comet that streaked for the ground.

When they finally got to their target, the port was covered by cloud and Carter had criss crossed over the city three times before they let their bombs go. He had no idea if they ever hit anything. There had been many more operations after that, but the first one never left you.

He blinked away tears as he smoked in the dark. He tried to convince himself it was the smoke from the cigarettes irritating his eyes that caused it.

2 – A Stranger, In A Strange Land

The Adjutant, Flight Lieutenant Harold Saunderson showed Carter to his new billet. Strictly a ground bird, Saunderson had been an insurance salesman in civvy street. He had that homely trustworthy face that oozed sincerity, just the kind of trait you needed to have, sitting on an armchair in someones living room to flow them pensions and life insurance. Like most Adjutants, he was the mother hen that fussed around behind the scenes, seeing to the squadrons needs and being the touchstone that the CO could tap to gauge the mood of the men when required.

Saunderson stood at the door as Carter went in and dumped his bags on the floor. He had the bed on the left in a two person room in a fairly tatty run down Nissen hut. There were two beds, a chest of drawers and a small bedside cabinet. A communal desk and chair were in the corner to the left. A wardrobe occupied the space to the right of the door. Carter bounced up and down experimentally on a corner of the bed. The springs creaked and squealed with every movement, setting his teeth on edge.

"Not much I know, but I'm sure you'll make the best of it," Saunderson commented smoothly. Carter said nothing. He wrinkled his nose at the smell emanating from the other side of the room. Clothes were screwed up and shoved under the bed.

"The CO will see you at 2pm. You know, you've thrown us for a bit of a loop old boy, we weren't expecting you until tomorrow."

"What can I say? I couldn't wait to get here."

Senses twitching, Saunderson knew there was more to that statement but he also knew there was no point asking. When he'd met Carter at the gatehouse, he had seen the simmering anger in every aspect of his frame. Whether that was because of the posting or something else, time would tell.

"You'll find the boys to be a friendly lot. There are no ops on today and the forecast is pretty grim, I'm sure you'll find most of them laagered up in the Mess." When that elicited no response, Saunderson took the hint. "I'll leave you to get settled," he said as he closed the door behind him.

It was a gloomy day, so Carter switched the light on. That made little difference, the low watt bulb barely lighting the corners. Sighing heavily, he began unpacking his kit. He slung his sponge bag onto the bed. He hung up his shirts and shoved his flying gear in the wardrobe. His underwear and small personal things went in the top drawer. He chucked his boots under the bed along with the suitcase.

He ruminated on his leave as he unpacked and put his things in order. Four days at the family home in Harrogate with his mother fluttering around and making a fuss of him had been marvellous. He'd caught up on the family news as his mother gave him some letters from his brother and sister to read. His sister Margaret was a nurse at a hospital in Manchester. His brother, Arthur, was a Captain in a tank regiment and had been shipped overseas. He didn't say where he was going but considering what was going on, Carter thought Egypt was the most likely destination.

His mother seemed to be coping with it all. She was keeping herself busy, helping some of the local families who had taken in evacuee children from London. A number of his childhood toys had been pressed back into service. Carter didn't mind, it was better they were used rather than gathering dust in some box in the attic.

The second half of his leave had been a monumental disaster. Once his family duties had been completed, he'd caught a train to London and turned up at Mary's flat. When she opened the door, she'd seemed to be more shocked than surprised. She hugged him and kissed him but there was something not quite right in her reaction.

A stunning blonde, Mary stirred his blood as much now as the day they had first met. He'd always been mystified that she was interested in him when they first got together. On leave in London with his crew, they'd literally bumped into each other on the dance floor. Helping her to her feet, she'd smoothed down her blue dress as he apologised for knocking her over. She was tall, lithe and moved with a fluid grace, like a cat does when it prowls across a room. Her blonde hair was cut in a fashionable short bob that framed her oval face and her green eyes were like two emerald pools you could drown in.

When her group abandoned the club, Carter and his navigator Ducky Webb were invited along. They all went to a plush Grosvenor flat with lots of rooms. Webb disappeared with a gorgeous redhead not long after and as the rest drifted away, Carter had found himself alone with her.

She literally tore his clothes off that first night. Maybe it was the attraction of a man in uniform but Carter was not entirely convinced by that argument. Her father was some high up type in the Air Ministry and she had travelled a lot before the war so she'd had no shortage of suitors more senior than him vying for her attention.

She had been his lifeline during his tour, bucking him up when his spirits were down. She moved to Lincoln to be closer to him and he saw her as often as he could when the squadron was stood down. At the end of his tour they had gone to North Wales and spent some proper time together. Everything had been fine then. She moved back to London when he was posted to Scotland and that was when things changed. The distance between them had become emotional as well as physical.

Carter had been hoping to do something about that when he got to London. The good thing about being in the middle of nowhere in Scotland was that there wasn't much to spend your money on and he was never a heavy drinker. They had tea and sandwiches at Claridges and then a bottle of Chenin Blanc, the price of which made Carter wince. She looked at him over the top of her wine glass but it was like a stranger staring back at him.

They went for a walk around Hyde Park. She drew plenty of admiring glances in her turquoise dress as she looped her arm in his. Their shoulders bumped as they walked along but he could feel the gulf between them. When they were together in the past, she had always been quite chatty, pointing places out to him or talking with animation about things that caught her attention. This time she was more reserved and introspective.

When he told her he was going back on ops she had visibly tightened. It was the one time he had noticed genuine worry in her eyes. She had weathered three months of waiting when he was part way through his tour the last time. He had thought that his being safe in Scotland would have made her happier but clearly the distance apart had been a bigger obstacle than he realised. Out of sight, out of mind seemed to fit the bill.

Their lovemaking that night had seemed almost perfunctory. He had marvelled at her beauty but noticed the reserve in her eyes. Afterward, he had lain awake for a while, wondering where it had all gone wrong. His reception was no warmer the following day. She was civil, but the spark had gone, drifted away like smoke on the wind.

"I am fond of you, you know that," she'd told him over dinner.

"But you don't love me?" he finished for her; his tone curt.

"It's more complicated than that," she protested. "When you were on operations, do you have any idea how much agony it was for me? Every night I'd hear the bombers going overhead never know if you were alive or dead or coming back. I would listen to the radio." She laughed just the safe side of hysterical. "I even listened to that idiot, Haw Haw." Her hands fidgeted in her lap. "I don't think I can go through that again."

"Can't, or don't want to?" he asked her.

"*Can't,* darling," she protested, the strain evident in her voice. She stared off to the left, not wanting to meet his eye. After that there was little point in staying. She made a half hearted attempt to persuade him but he could tell she was grateful when he went.

"Look after yourself," she'd told him as they stood together at the door to her flat. She smoothed down the lapels on his battledress, her fingers lingering over the wings on his left breast and the purple and white ribbon of his DFC.

"I always do," he answered with an air of finality. He went straight to Lincoln overnight on the train and had a long hard think. She'd helped him get through his first tour and he was grateful for that; maybe that was enough.

Once he had everything squared away, he jammed his battered peaked cap on his head and went for an explore. On his last tour, he'd been spoilt; flying from one of the pre-war stations with all the comforts of home. The officer's quarters had been a splendid red brick building next to an equally splendid Mess.

Seven miles from Lincoln, he found RAF Amber Hill was every bit as basic as Lossiemouth. He passed row upon row of Nissen huts with muddy paths leading from one hut to another. There were a few duck boards down, but he imagined this place would turn into a swamp once it got wet in the winter. The control tower was a squat, boxey building and he could see the dark shapes of three large T2 Hangars on the horizon but that was about it.

The wind tugged at his trousers as he walked. The sky was darkening to the east and there was every indication it would rain later on. Tucking his chin into the top of his greatcoat he quickened his pace as he followed the signs to the admin buildings.

The interview with the CO was short. Wing Commander Asher occupied a small office in the ops building. A blackboard was on the wall to the left, filled with names and dates. Carter saw the squadron was split into two flights, with enough room on the board for over twenty crews to be listed. He also saw a number of rows were blank, the names rubbed off.

Also present in the room was 'B' Flights commander, Squadron Leader Dickinson. A short, compact New Zealander; Carter warmed to him immediately. Brown eyes gave Carter an appraising stare and when he smiled, Dickinson revealed a prominent gap between his two front teeth.

Both Asher and Dickinson had seen action and had the DFC for their troubles. Asher had flown Blenheims during the withdrawal from France. When he was wounded, he got posted to a staff job at 2 Group Headquarters for a time before transferring to the heavies.

Dickinson had risen through the ranks swiftly and he'd temporarily commanded his previous squadron for a time when the CO had been lost on ops. He anticipated getting a unit of his own in due course.

Asher was pleased to see Carter. The squadron had only been

formed six months before and in some respects was still finding its feet. Created from the nucleus of another squadron, the few veterans had done their best to bring on the new men, but attrition from ops and training accidents had only thinned out the old hands further. No one on the squadron had done a full tour like Carter had. Carter's roommate was on nine. Dickinson and Asher had fifteen and fourteen respectively. 'A' Flights commander, Squadron Leader Church had done eight. An experienced officer was a boon he didn't intend to waste.

"I know you've had six months out, but I'm sure it won't take you long to find your feet again," said Asher, his accent displaying a hint of a midlands lilt.

"I hope not, sir."

"I'll see if we can get you something easy first time out, but we are rather at the mercy of what Group sends our way as you can imagine."

"I understand, sir. I'll have a chat to some of the lads later on. I'll just have to learn on the job as it were." Dickinson produced a pack of cigarettes from a breast pocket and offered one to Carter. Carter shook his head so Dickinson lit one for himself and leaned back, relaxed.

"I'd rather hoped to give you the opportunity to pull together a crew for yourself but I'm afraid that will have to wait for now. A few of the squadron have come down with chickenpox. The MO's quarantined them but it's left me short of a few pilots for the time being until they've recovered. I realise it's far from ideal but for now I'd like you to take over Pilot Officer Lambert's crew. They've done four ops already so they have *some* experience which is better than none at all. Squadron Leader, Dickinson can make the introductions later."

Carter kept his face impassive but his stomach clenched when he heard that. Coming into an established crew could be very hard work, particularly as their new pilot.

In Bomber Command, there was no set method of how crews were formed. No one was ordered to crew up, it was just something that happened at OTU's. A gunner might hear that such and such needed someone as tail end charlie. A pilot might be told that so and so was a very good navigator. It was an organic process as people tried each other on for size to see how they fitted together. Carter was very conscious that despite his experience, he would be the outsider and therefore viewed with suspicion.

"We'll get you checked out when the weather clears tomorrow. I'm sure you'll want to go up with your new crew as soon as possible so you can get to know each other better." Carter nodded in agreement. "I won't keep you. Welcome to 363, Mister Carter."

Carter saluted and exited the office. He waited in Saunderson's office until Dickinson appeared a few minutes later and told him to follow him. Carter gasped as they went outside. The wind had gotten colder in the intervening time and they walked over to the Sergeants Mess. Dickinson tracked down Lambert's crew and made the introductions. Carter reserved judgement for later, but he wasn't encouraged by the first encounter.

The following day was hectic. Dickinson took Carter up himself first thing in the morning to see how he did. He had read Carters record, but he wanted to see the substance, not just the gloss. He had no concerns, and was happy to let him loose on his crews.

After lunch, Carters new crew were waiting for him at dispersal as he had requested. Lambert's Manchester was coded P for Peter but the crew referred to the bomber as Popsie. There was no art adorning the nose, no name, but the ground crew had painted four little yellow bombs under the pilot's window.

While he walked around doing his preflight check, Carter sorted through his feelings about the Manchester. Having flown them at OTU, he knew their reputation at first hand. A modern design, the Manchester was a mid wing monoplane with an all metal stressed skin. The fuselage had three power operated turrets to give a good all round field of fire. Two guns were in the nose turret, two in the mid upper turret halfway along the top of the fuselage and the rear turret housed four .303 machine guns. The bomb bay ran most of the length of the fuselage and it could carry a fairly respectable load into the heart of Germany.

The flying characteristics on the other hand were a mixed bag. The Manchester was a rock steady bombing platform and the ailerons were light and responsive, but the elevators were heavy and it needed a lot of effort to make the aircraft do what you wanted. A lack of longitudinal stability in early Manchester's had been cured with the modification of larger tail control surfaces and the addition of a third vertical fin to the fuselage but it was still hard work.

It was the engines however that really let the Manchester down. On paper, it had seemed a good idea. Bolt two V12 engines onto a single crankcase to make a more powerful engine. In practice, the Vultures were prone to overheating, seizing up and throwing connecting big end bearings whenever they felt like it. The problems were bad enough that the engines had actually been derated so they could only deliver eighty five to ninety percent of their designed maximum. In real terms that meant when an engine decided to spit its dummy out and quit for the day, there wasn't enough power to maintain height and the only direction you were going was down.

Once he was happy this particular Manchester was as ready as it was ever going to be, he went round to the nose to climb up the ladder. Before he could put a foot on the bottom rung, the navigator, a Flight Sergeant called Tinsley barged past and chucked his parachute pack up through the hatch. He followed it in and went past the cockpit, settling himself at his navigator's table.

Carter clicked his tongue but stopped himself from saying anything. It was his rule to be the one to board first. It was partly a rank thing, partly a superstition. On every op, he'd boarded first and they all made it home; that was the way it was. The rules didn't change just for an air test.

The second pilot, a blonde Flight Sergeant called Forrester got in next. Carter tapped his foot in annoyance but kept quiet. Steaming, he waited until the wireless op, Fitzgerald went up the ladder before getting on board himself.

Coming up into the cockpit, Carter enjoyed the spacious interior. The view was excellent with a spacious cockpit and canopy. He thought the layout of the instruments was very good and anything was better than the cramped cockpit of his Hampden. Popularly known as the flying suitcase, the Hampden was only wide enough for a single person. If the pilot was hit, there was virtually nothing the rest of the crew could do about it.

In comparison, the Manchester was huge and even had dual controls in the cockpit. Carter occupied the pilots seat on the left and Forrester had a folding seat to the right. When he wasn't flying, the second pilot had to monitor the engines and help the pilot with the throttles. Second Dicky's like Forrester would do a few trips to learn the ropes from a more experienced pilot and eventually progress to having their own crew.

Carter stowed his parachute behind his seat and started getting settled. Forrester was already going through the start up sequence. Carter watched him smoothly get things ready and was mollified somewhat that at least one crew member seemed to know what he was doing.

Once the engines were started, they taxied round the perimeter track and lined up on the runway. The tower gave them a green and they were off. Carter advanced the throttles and Forrester was right next to him, his own hand following his pilots, ready to take over when Carter put both hands on the yoke.

Carter got the tail up as soon as possible as Forrester put the throttles to the max. As the airspeed passed 100mph, Carter kept the aircraft balanced on its main wheels, using the rudders to keep it straight. Forrester glanced across at Carter but his pilot kept his gaze focused forwards. At 110, Carter pulled the yoke back in one smooth pull. With no bombs on board and only a limited amount of fuel, the Manchester practically bounded into the air. At five hundred feet, Forrester raised the flaps and the undercarriage. Carter felt the slight thump as the wheels came to rest in their nacelles.

Carter levelled off at three thousand feet, cruising over an ocean of thick clouds. As soon as they stopped climbing the chat started.

"Hey, Fitz, you seeing your WAAF tonight?" asked the tail gunner, a short pugnacious type called Smith.

"I am," said Fitzgerald. "And I'd kindly ask you to not follow me on the bus like last time. A fellow needs space to work."

"Hark at you," chipped in Tinsley. "What about what you did at the dance? Telling my date I had a medical condition. She wouldn't let me touch her after that."

"Don't worry about it, ducks," laughed Fitzgerald. "I'll get you a nice certificate done up from the MO giving you a clean bill of health."

"When you're quite ready?" Carter asked coldly, cutting across the banter, his tone glacial. Conversation came to a crashing halt. Forrester winced at the interplay over the R/T. Tinsley leaned back in his seat and looked up the fuselage towards the cockpit glowering at their new pilots back.

Carter took them up to twelve thousand feet and they went on oxygen. He checked each man in turn, getting a feeling for how they responded to calls. He then put the crew through the same series of tests he put the trainees through at the OTU's. He wanted to see what they could do and how this particular Manchester performed. All aircraft had their little ways and it was better to find out any peculiarities now rather than over Germany.

At fourteen thousand the Manchester was wallowing but there was no sloppiness in the yoke. The control cables were nice and tight and gave good response. He had Forrester feather the starboard engine and then Carter fought the aircraft for five minutes.

He went to full power on the remaining engine but it needed quite a lot of rudder to keep the nose pointing straight. His leg started to go numb from the effort. Even though they weren't weighed down with bombs, there was only a thin margin of reserve power to spare. He found he could just about maintain height but it was hard work. God help them if an engine went out when they had a full bombload.

They restarted the starboard engine and ambled along for a while, letting the temperatures on the port engine settle back down. They had shot up alarmingly fast and Carter saw there was going to be little leeway in the event of an emergency.

"Pilot to navigator," he called over the intercom.

"Yes, sir."

"Can I have a course for home, please?" There was a long pause. "Course please, navigator," Carter repeated his demand when a response was not forthcoming, his tone peremptory.

"One moment, sir."

"Don't you know?" Carter asked sharply.

Fitzgerald looked round at Tinsley who was sitting at his small desk, rapidly turning his map every which way.

17

"Steer two four three, magnetic," the hapless navigator said, plucking a figure out of thin air.

Distinctly unimpressed, Carter turned onto the course given. Fitzgerald rapidly used his equipment to get a bearing on the station's transmitter. He wrote it down on a slip of paper and held it round the bulkhead, waving his hand to get Tinsley's attention. Tinsley took it and gratefully found it was only a few degrees off the course he had given. He started figuring out where they could be and issued a correction a few minutes later, explaining that the wind had veered, pushing them off course. That seemed to satisfy their pilot and nothing more was said.

On the run back to Amber Hill, a flight of Spitfires sauntered past overhead. They were a good two or three thousand feet above them heading west. The fighters stayed well clear. They'd had too many experiences where a bored gunner opened up on them. The R/T stayed quiet so Carter was not one to turn down an opportunity.

"Fighters! Fighters! Corkscrew to port, GO!"

The Manchester lurched into a bank to port. Carter stamped on the rudder pedal and then rammed the starboard throttle to the stops. The bomber fell out of the sky. The fuselage creaked; the engines screamed. The Manchester was close to ninety degrees of bank and heading down fast.

Carter evened out the throttles and then gritted his teeth as he hauled the yoke to the right. The roll reversed and he pulled back on the controls, hugging them to his stomach. It took every ounce of strength to keep that yoke back. He grunted as his weight increased and he fought to keep his head against the back of the pilot's seat. He stood the Manchester on her other wing tip as she swooped back up.

The nose pointed to the sky and Carter could feel the buffet in the controls as the airspeed bled off. Not wanting to stall, he let the nose fall away, keeping a firm grip on the controls to stop her rolling onto her back. As they descended again, he let the airspeed build back up before resuming level flight.

"You take her," he told Forrester. He breathed heavily. That had been very hard work. His arms were like lead and he reflected that it would take a lot to make the Manchester behave if there was a sustained nightfighter attack.

The R/T burst into life again. Protest piled upon protest as the crew recovered from having the shock of their lives. There had been a moment of stomach clenching terror as the word 'fighter' burned into their brains and then the Manchester had careened across the sky. Smith fished out a hanky from up his sleeve and held it against his nose. During that first dive, he had banged his face against the turret control yokes. He was still seeing stars when they'd levelled off.

Tinsley was on the floor, picking up his pencils and maps. He shot a venomous glare at Carters back while he scrabbled around, feeling for the other things that had gone flying. In the cockpit, Forrester had hung on for grim life as he was treated to a grandstand view of the earth and then the sky and then the earth again. They had corkscrewed once before on a raid, but that had been in the dark. When they had done it at OTU it had been a cloudy day and they had never seen the ground. He wasn't sure which was better, at least in the dark you had no idea what was going on.

Carter let them vent for a few more minutes and then cracked the whip. The crew went quiet, shocked at being spoken to like that. They stewed for the remainder of the flight. No one was particularly bothered when Carter brought it in as light as a feather and taxied back to their starting point.

After they'd got down from the bomber, Carter gathered them together by the tail. They clumped together as a group, as Carter stood in front of them, his arms crossed, the outsider.

"That was an interesting start," he said, his tone crisp, clipped. "I won't lie; I can't say I was particularly impressed today. R/T procedure was lax. There was far too much chatter up there. Training flights are not a social occasion." He turned a withering gaze on Tinsley. "I expect my navigator's to know where they are at all times and when I ask for a course, I want it. Not in five minutes, not in an hour, I want it fast!" He clicked his fingers for emphasis. "And why did no one tell me about the Spitfires coming up from astern?" he asked the group as a collective whole, although the question was firmly aimed at the two gunners. Smith glared back at him over the top of a bloody hanky; his eyes wild with anger. Jones shrugged.

"They were only Spitfires, sir. Nothing to worry about." It sounded feeble and was said with little conviction. Forrester bit his lip.

"I expect to be told when anything is in the sky near us," Carter replied curtly. He could see a great deal of anger and indignation stood before him so he tried to pour some oil on the troubled waters he had stirred up.

"When we go up in the air, you have every right to expect me to be able to do my job. That means I've got to fly us there and get us back and if it means throwing her around the sky to do it, I will. In return, I have every right to expect that you can do your jobs too. Bear that in mind before we go up again." Speech over, he walked off before he said something he regretted.

Coming into an established crew, he didn't have the time to have the *'with our old skipper we did, this, that, the other'* types of conversation. They would just have to fit themselves to him as far as he was concerned. He'd been close with his last crew. That was an inevitable fact of life after flying thirty ops together. Some were dead now; he wasn't ready to join them just yet.

Dickinson found him later in the Officers Mess, reading a copy of the pilots notes while he was nursing a pint. His Flight Commander gestured to the other armchair.

"May I?"

Carter looked up and put the notes aside.

"Of course, sir."

Dickinson slid in to the beat up armchair and put his own pint on the side table between them.

"How did the first meeting go?"

Carter shrugged. He had no doubt Dickinson had heard things through the usual sources that any operational unit had.

"I don't think I'll be winning a popularity contest," he said ruefully. Dickinson gave him a wry smile. He thought it would be something like that.

When he had seen Carter in the CO's office, he had seen the tension in him. Carter was sitting slightly hunched forward in his chair; his arms balanced on the tops of his legs. Dickinson was quite sure that if he had mentioned this to Carter, he would have had no recollection of it. The New Zealander had written that off to first day nerves. He could not say the same for the air test.

Carter flew competently enough. He was smooth on the controls and precise in how he set up the aircraft for landing, but there had been a brittleness there as well. His eyes were bright, the gaze just that little bit too fixed and intense. Dickinson knew what this was of course. He had seen other men under severe strain, men who had been pushed to the limit.

It was a rough deal, coming back to ops. When he completed his own tour and had a rest, Dickinson was sure he would be feeling the same way. It was hard enough as it was, screwing up the courage to go up night after night with the knowledge that there was a four or five percent chance he wouldn't be coming back. To return and face down those demons or a second time must be a daunting prospect for any man.

"Give them some time," he counselled. "They've been with Lambert since OTU and done a few ops with him, it was a bit of a jolt being told they'd be carrying on their tour without him."

Carter could hear where Dickinson was coming from. He would have to bend, for now, but not too much.

"I'll try, sir."

Carter's crew had an impromptu conference that evening in the tap room of *The Duck and Drake*. It was one of the local pubs around Amber Hill frequented by air crew and the walls were adorned with souvenirs. Being ex-RAF, the landlord was quite well disposed to the crews in their off duty hours and you could always get a good game of darts there.

Hunched around a small circular table, the mood was ugly while they dissected the day's events. Smith opened the batting for the prosecution.

"I say we go in to the CO and ask for a new pilot," he said angrily, but it was hard to take him seriously with two wads of cotton wool up his nostrils. There was a gash scabbing quite nicely on the bridge of his nose. Jones murmured agreement with him, but the rest of them looked distinctly uncomfortable at the suggestion.

"Don't be bloody daft," said Forrester. "How will that look? A bunch of nobodies like us go strolling in to see the old man and think our word is going to count over that of a DFC on his second tour." He looked at each of them. "We'll look like idiots." He leaned back in his chair and sipped moodily from his pint.

"Then what do we do?" asked Tinsley. He looked at Smith, then Jones. The young lad looked away, distinctly uncomfortable.

"We put up with it," said Forrester. He didn't entirely agree with Carters way of putting his point across but there was something in what he was trying to do that afternoon. Tinsley snorted.

"Spoken like a true believer," he said with a snide lilt to his Norfolk accent. Forrester immediately shot back at him.

"Hey, I'm not the one who couldn't even come up with a course when he was asked for it," he replied, dabbing Tinsley in the chest with his forefinger. The rest of the crew turned on their navigator. Some of them secretly thought the whole thing with the corkscrew was to get back at Tinsley for being slow on providing a course.

"Yeah, what was that about?" asked Fitzgerald.

"So I didn't have a course ready, so what?" Tinsley was bullish at this sudden hostility, his cheeks flushing red with embarrassment.

"I saw you fiddling with the map," Fitzgerald accused him. "You didn't have a clue where we were."

"Because-we-were-on-an-air-test," Tinsley replied slowly, enunciating each word. "Lambert just circles the airfield," he protested. He threw up his hands in frustration. "I figured this guy would do the same."

"Well you figured wrong, didn't you, ducky?" Smith told him.

"Thank you very much," said Tinsely in a sulk, pissed off he was being made the scapegoat. There had been a lot more mistakes than just him. On ops, they worked well together and he was annoyed that after just one test flight, that unity was starting to unravel.

"Look, there's a lot we could learn from this guy," suggested Forrester, trying to pour oil on troubled waters.

"Not if he keeps nagging us, we won't," said Fitzgerald. "I had a nanny as bad as him."

"He can fly though," said Forrester.

"So he held her up while he feathered an engine, big deal," complained Tinsley.

Forrester shrugged. They hadn't seen Carter in the cockpit like he had, fighting the controls to maintain height on one engine, using the trim tabs and force of will to hold it there. Forrester doubted he'd have been able to do the same.

Jones thought about Carter. One look told you that their new pilot was a time served veteran. His officers peaked cap was this squashed shape that perched on his head at a rakish angle. The leather flying jacket slung over one shoulder was stained and worn and his blue battledress and pants looked like they had been dragged up and down a field. The white and purple ribbon of his DFC and his pilot wings were stained and blackened.

"I want to know where he got his scar from," he asked aloud, thinking about that livid pink line on his cheek that moved when he spoke.

"Why don't you ask him?" suggested Smith, deadpan. He could imagine what response that kind of question would provoke.

3 – Here We Go Again

When the word got out they were on that night, heads craned to read the list posted on the notice board in the Mess. With more crews than operational aircraft, it was always a bit of a battle to be one of the chosen few. Carter saw his name near the top, right under Dickinson's. Briefing was 3pm, take off at 6pm. With the long winter nights, they could get away earlier and be home in the early hours the following morning. It was to be another maximum effort, all squadrons in the Group to attack with heavy loads. Wrestling with the usual servicing problems, 363's ground crew managed to put nine aircraft on the line.

There were lively discussions over lunch about what and where the target might be. The Mess staff asked who were flying that night and served them the symbolic eggs and bacon. Carter thought about the coming operation while he worked his way through his helping of sponge and custard, mentally ticking off what needed to be done.

After lunch, Carter rounded up his crew and had a short air test. They were good little boys this time and seemed to do their jobs competently enough. The port engine ran a little rough but the ground crew checked the cooling system and that seemed to cure it when Carter took it up a second time to see.

The squadron gathered for briefing in a big Nissen hut. At the far end there was a stage twelve feet deep with two steps up to the main platform at either side. On the left side of the stage was a six foot long table and behind that a blackboard on a wheeled base, the kind you saw in small village schools. Five chairs occupied centre stage and behind all of it was a large map of Europe. Rows of seats filled the rest of the hut with an aisle down the middle. All the windows had their blackout curtains drawn and the room had the air of a cinema on the Saturday matinee showing.

Carter was seated with his crew in the middle of the hall, surrounded by the hubbub of friendly chatter and banter. His crew talked quietly amongst themselves but no one involved him in the conversation. The ice had not yet fully thawed it seemed.

Sent to Coventry, he looked around the hall. Some enterprising soul had hung wooden models of RAF and Luftwaffe types from the ceiling. Propaganda posters were pinned to the curved walls, preaching their warnings about security with the familiar lines, 'keep mum, she's not so dumb' and, 'loose lips sink ships'.

"Room, attention!" barked Dickinson from the back of the room. Chairs scraped and squealed on the lino as one hundred men got to their feet and braced to attention.

Asher strode down the central aisle followed by Dickinson. The met officer, Linkletter, the squadrons intel officer, a Flight Lieutenant called Donovan Kent followed behind. Dickinson's navigator and bomb aimer, John Blackthorne, or Black Jack as he was known amongst the men was the squadrons bombing leader and he brought up the rear. They mounted the stage and occupied the chairs. Asher motioned for the men to sit. Saunderson stood at the back of the room which was now guarded outside by MP's. Asher went first, striding to the front of the stage, hands on hips. He looked around the room, each man feeling as if he was talking to them directly.

"Now you've had the chance to enjoy your few days off, it's back to business." A good humoured laugh rippled around the room with this opening comment. "Tonight, over one hundred bombers are going to attack Germany." That remark brought a rumble of interest. Asher picked up a long stick leaning against the blackboard. He walked over to the large map and slapped it with the tip of the stick.

"There it is," the stick circled a city. "Kiel. We'll take a northerly track out over the water and then head east towards the target. Navigator's, don't forget Heligoland to get a pinpoint. Don't stray too far south otherwise you'll blunder into the guns near Wilhelmshaven and Cuxhaven."

He went on to detail the route in more depth. Carter made a few salient notes, fixing the broad strokes in his head. Kiel should be relatively easy to find. A sprawling port city, any navigator should be able to find a town along a coastline.

Linkletter got up next and went over to the blackboard. Bookish, with horn rimmed glasses and thinning dark hair, he was swamped by his uniform which hung off his gangling frame. Linkletter was well liked. He spoke with enthusiasm and cared deeply about helping the crews as much as he could.

"The low pressure front of the last few days has moved on further east. We should experience a period of clear weather." There was a small cheer. He circled some white lines that covered the board. Gibberish to most people, it was like music to Linkletter. He could read those lines as others might read Mozart.

"Winds over central Europe will be mainly easterly between twenty and thirty knots. Cloud cover will be patchy but clear over the target. On your return journey, that easterly wind will help push you home until you're all tucked up in bed. It's a dim moon tonight, enough light for you navigator's to get a good sight over water."

Kent talked about the known areas of flak to avoid and pointed out a few new airfields where the German nightfighters were thought to be operating from. Carter noticed that two in particular were quite close to their easterly track but there was a flak belt further south that made things tricky. It would take some delicate navigating to thread through the gap.

Black Jack jumped up next. An energetic Welshman, he was a reservist who had embraced the war whole heartedly from day one. He had survived some of the early raids flown during the summer of 1940. Wounded in the arm and leg on a raid over Bremen he had fought tooth and nail to come back to an operational squadron to do another tour.

He described the target, the Deutsche Werke U-boat yard. Not far away was the naval base so there was plenty to aim at. He pointed out the dry docks and slipways where the submarines were built and serviced. Blackthorne used the CO's stick to point at a crude chalk outline of the city on the other side of the blackboard.

"Kiel has a long canal just to the north west. That's a good pinpoint for your run in and you should see it easily. The last bit of it runs almost west to east straight to the city. The boat yard is here," he pointed out the western side of the channel, "Pay attention to the canal, Eckenforde is just to the north and it's easy to get confused between the two. Watch out for dummy targets. It would be a shame to go all that way and drop them on open countryside."

Asher stood up at the end for the final speech. The trick was finding the right balance between giving them the propaganda line and some encouragement. The station commander, Group Captain Etheridge normally gave the boys a pep talk but he was currently on leave so it was up to Asher to fill in.

"This war won't be won at full speed lads. I'd rather be the tortoise than the hare if it means we make it to the finish line. I don't relish the thought of coming back here to finish the job some other time so let's do it right the first time. I want to see all of you back in the Mess later. Good luck to you all."

The men got to their feet as Asher jumped down off the stage and walked down the central aisle. As soon as he left the room, the chatter started again. Carter noticed the mood was buoyant, there seemed to be a good press on attitude despite the distance to the target.

Carters crew scattered after briefing, each to their own. Carter went back to his room and got himself ready. Forrester did his best to get some sleep. Laid out on his bed he tried to relax while Fitzgerald wrote a letter. When he was finished, he licked the envelope and then left it propped up against his travel clock.

They went out to the aircraft at five. Squashed into a truck, the WAAF driver drove around the peri track, dropping the crews off as she went. The ground crew were waiting for them by their aircraft.

One man was up a ladder polishing the bomb aimers nose blister with some cotton waste while the remainder gathered by a hut they had built from salvaged bits of Nissen hut.

It was an old joke that aircrew were only borrowing an aircraft from the ground crew. In the case of the Manchester that was more accurate. They spent the most time with it, showering those delicate engines with love and care and tinkering with the troublesome hydraulic system.

Carter did his walk around with Forrester, showing him what he thought should be checked. They finished by looking in the bomb bay which was filled with a mixed load of 500lb bombs and containers stuffed with 4lb incendiary sticks.

Twenty minutes to start up time, Carter had them board. The Manchester was icy inside, the winter cold penetrating the metal. Carter worked the yoke while Forrester looked out of the canopy to see the control surfaces were moving properly. Fitzgerald tested his radio. Tinsley spread his maps and pencils and log book out on the small table. Carter asked him for the course changes on a piece of paper. He'd learned from bitter experience what could happen if something happened to your navigator. He tucked the paper into the top of his flying boot.

They assumed positions for take off. Smith, Jones and Fitzgerald were sitting with their backs resting against the main spar. No one was up front in the nose in case of accidents.

Ten minutes to take off time, the quiet was shattered as a Manchester along the line started their engines. The roar intensified as plane after plane started up. The ground crew came out of their little hut and Carter got their attention by circling a bunched fist above his head. The Sergeant pointed at the port engine.

"Starting one," Carter announced. The starter motor whined. The engine coughed once, twice and then the big propeller span into a glittering disc. The noise was terrific. Carter closed the sliding window on the canopy but it made little difference in dimming the racket. Forrester watched the dials as the temperature started to rise.

They started the starboard engine. Again, the prop started turning and within a few seconds, the engine burst into life. For all its faults, the Vulture started far easier than the engines ever did on the old Hampdens. They let them run for a few minutes to get warm and settle down. Carter then ran them up, the big mainwheels squashing up against the yellow wooden chocks. The bomber strained for the off, airframe vibrating as the engines roared.

At his signal, the chocks were pulled clear and the Manchester moved forwards. Turning right onto the perimeter track, they headed round to the runway. Carter was going back to war.

4 – Busman's Holiday

It was a dark night. Even with half light from the moon, the thick clouds made it hard to see very far. At twelve thousand feet, Carter was finding his work cut out for him. Topped off to the brim with petrol to get there and back, the Manchester was very close to its maximum all up weight. It had taken them an age to get up to ten thousand, but the further they went, the more fuel they burned so there was less strain on the engines.

The take off had been hairy. Fully loaded, the lack of power was painfully obvious as the Manchester had trundled along, slow to accelerate to take off speed. Towards the end of the runway, they had finally come unstuck but then Carter found it almost impossible to climb. Raising the wheels and flaps at five hundred feet, he had begun an almost constant battle to coax the big bomber into the sky.

Over the channel he had the gunners test their guns. Jones had wormed into the front turret and fired some short bursts, watching the bullets go arcing over the water before going back and doing the same in the mid upper turret.

In the tail, Smith muttered as he moved his turret side to side, his eyes quartering the sky. His nose still hurt from the day before but he hadn't been to see the MO about it. The last thing he wanted was to be grounded and miss a trip with his crew.

Carter settled down for the long haul. He yawned and rolled his shoulders, trying to keep awake. That was something he had forgotten after months at the OTU. The cold he could deal with. His trouble had been keeping himself alert on the long outward leg.

Staring into the inky black was tiring but it had to be done. Out there were lots of other aircraft, all heading in the same direction as a loose gaggle towards Kiel. On particularly filthy nights, another aircraft was just a dark smudge tired eyes could scarcely distinguish. The only warning might be a jolt from crossing the turbulent air of its propeller wash, then a pilot would have to react quickly, diving away before running into the back of someone else.

Carter alternated looking outside with roving his eyes over the instrument in a set order. It was a constant routine of watching his turn and slip indicator, the airspeed indicator, the artificial horizon and the compass. It would be very easy to wander a few degrees off course or lose a few hundred feet in valuable height if you weren't paying attention.

He looked out over an undulating sea of grey clouds. Linkletter's prediction had been off. The cloud was not patchy, it was a thick grey blanket and Carter would have bet money that the winds were higher than predicted too.

Tinsley had them behind schedule at the last checkpoint by fifteen minutes. Of course, that was assuming they were even close to their checkpoint in the first place. They could easily have been blown off course and Carter remained to be convinced of Tinsley's abilities as a navigator.

They hit a patch of clear skies and they could see some Hampden's below them. Carter was comforted by the fact that quite a few aircraft lower than he was. To someone on the outside that might sound brutal, but it was accepted that you tried to get as much height as possible on the outward leg. If someone else was lower than you and made a more tempting target, too bad.

South of Rendsburg the anti aircraft gunners woke up. Their range finding was very accurate and there was an uncomfortable few minutes flying through a storm of flak bursts. They wove from side to side, always heading eastwards. Just as the flak batteries were getting the range they abruptly stopped. The hairs on the back of Carters neck stood on end. Every sense came alive and he broke out in a cold sweat.

"Pilot to crew, keep an eye out for nightfighters," he called on the R/T. Smith and Jones acknowledged promptly.

They crept on, every minute seeming like an hour. Carter hunched forward in his seat, almost leaning over the yoke. Any second, he expected to hear a panicked warning and he was ready to throw his aircraft around the sky.

"One of ours catching it behind," shouted Jones, his thin and reedy voice further distorted by the R/T. "Four o'clock, our level a mile or so back."

Eyes snapped to the right. Forrester peered over the lip of the canopy. Slightly behind them, lines of tracer were reaching out. The target was a Hampden, its long slender fuselage limned by orange flames on the starboard side. Closing in for the kill, the German pilot sent a final squirt into the blazing wing tanks and then broke right, not even bothering to admire his handiwork as he hunted for more prey.

A small shape fell from the doomed bomber, then another. The crew were bailing out. The nose went down as it started its death dive. The clouds were illuminated from within for a moment as the burning aircraft plunged to the ground.

No one commented on the chain of events. Jones was just relieved it wasn't them. Smiths finger twitched over the triggers for his guns. With a snarl he went back to quartering the sky. Tinsley marked the location on his chart.

"Keep your eyes open, where there's one, there may be more," Carter cautioned. Smith swallowed a retort. He was not fresh off the boat and resented being told the obvious.

Adjusting for wind drift, Tinsley called out a course change to port. Comparing his map with what little he could see on the ground; he figured the wind had veered. It had changed from easterly to a more north easterly bearing and was pushing them south. Carter made the change to get them back on track.

The rest of the leg was uneventful and they got ready for the run in to the target. Ahead, the sky was glowing. Searchlights dodged left and right illuminating the clouds like some sort of shadow puppet theater. Fires on the ground were scattered far and wide which was not a good sign.

Tinsley came forward from the navigator's position and settled himself on his cushion to peer through the bombsight. It was his show. On the run in, he opened the bomb bay doors. Carter felt the drag on the controls and did his best to keep the Manchester steady for the bomb run.

Tinsley couldn't see very much. The clouds had drifted in on that easterly wind. He caught the flash of weak moonlight on water and followed the silvery line through the thick cotton. It ran roughly north to south, undulating left and right and before curling away. He tried to picture the run of the river on his chart as he looked at the countryside below but the cloud cover was making it difficult. There were a few fires below but nothing particularly concentrated, the flak wasn't very heavy either. Black Jack and Kent had told them to expect heavy defences over the target.

"This doesn't look so good," he said ominously. The curl to the water seemed right but nothing else seemed to fit.

"What's up?" asked Carter.

"I'm not sure. I don't think we're where we're supposed to be."

"It's your call," said Carter. "Tell me what you want."

"The are fires further north west, twenty odd miles away?"

"I see them." Carters lips pulled thin. With his old crew he could have this conversation with Dobson and almost know what he was thinking. He also had confidence that Dobson had got them to the right place. He drummed his fingers on the yoke and did an orbit while Tinsley discussed back and forth what to do.

Tinsley thought they could be over Lübeck and Carter had to agree. The wind must have pushed them much further east and it had been Neumünster they had passed over, not Rendsburg. Last year he might have gone lower for a look see but not now. In the Manchester, height meant everything if there were problems with the engines.

They closed the bombs doors and headed north. It wasn't long before Tinsley knew he'd been right. Heavy flak started as soon as they got close to Kiel but there was little Carter could do about that. He needed to hold it as steady as he could for Tinsley, keeping the inputs small.

Tinsley peered through the sight and cursed. Smoke rose into the sky from the scattered fires which only made the poor visibility worse. He wiped sweat from his face. There was very little that seemed to look like a shipyard but there was no way he was asking Carter to go around again. He picked up the coastline and followed it down, looking for the dry docks and slipways. He spotted a big crane and some buildings that looked like workshops and asked Carter for a final correction. He waited a few seconds for the plane to steady and then he hit the release.

"They're off!"

The Manchester almost leapt upwards as the bombs fell away. Smith peered down hoping to see the bombs go off but there were too many flashes from the guns firing up at them. He carried on watching the sky, looking for those little tell tales that would show someone creeping up on them.

The German flak gunners suddenly seemed to wake up. The big bomber rocked as flak burst much closer. Carter fought to get her back under control as the starboard wing lifted. Shrapnel pinged off the canopy and the stench of smoke filled his nostrils. He pushed the oxygen mask to his face and breathed deep, the tang of rubber on his tongue.

Carter took them down, diving under the wall of explosions. He then cut the corner on their exit out of the target area, going to port. They were disappearing into the darkness as the Manchester jolted again.

"Strewth, that was close," said Jones. There had been a massive bang to port and there was a huge draught somewhere below because he could feel the cold air rushing on his legs. He ducked down out of the turret for a look and was horrified to see sparks and flames.

"FIRE! Fire, in the tail!"

He rushed for an extinguisher clipped to the side of the fuselage. Flames licked around a box and sparks flew as acrid smoke began to fill the air. The extinguisher made short work of the fire and he was just putting the last of it out when Forrester got over the main spar to help him.

"I've done it," Jones panted. Forrester clapped him on the shoulder and pointed to the mid upper turret. Jones nodded and went back to his position. Forrester gave the smouldering box a few more squirts from his own extinguisher before having a look. Wisps of smoke issued out of the torn metal casing and there was a puddle of molten metal on the floor. He used a torch to check for any other damage. He went down to the tail and saw the turret rotating left and right so the hydraulics seemed fine. He went up to the cockpit and plugged back in to the R/T.

"It's a bit draughty back there but I think we're all right. The IFF box took a hit though. The fire was the thermite charge going up."

"We're lucky it didn't burn the tail off."

"We get lucky sometimes," Forrester smiled behind his mask, his eyes crinkling in good humour.

"Crew, check in." They called out their names one after the other, prompt, as he liked. "We've still got two engines, nothing majors fallen off, but we've got a long way to go so be on the ball."

Tinsley gave him the next course to steer and they hunkered down for the long haul back, Linkletters tail wind shoving them along.

"Bloody hell," said Forrester as they stood looking at the damage on the port side. Just behind the roundel there was a jagged three foot gash and there were at least ten other holes of varying size punctured in the thin metal. Paint had blistered off from the heat of the thermite charge, the shine of the aluminium bright against the flat black paint around it.

The ground crew tutted and whistled as they fussed around the Manchester. There were a few other holes here and there in the wings and tail but nothing to worry about. They would have them patched in no time. The Sergeant wiped his hand on a rag as he walked up to Carter.

"A few days to sort this out I think, sir. Were the engines okay?"

"Fine, Sarge. Didn't miss a beat." The erks stood a little straighter, pleased their hard work had paid off.

Leaving the erks to it, they hopped on the truck and were driven to debriefing. They were one of the last to get back and the room was full. Carter saw Dickinson at the far end of the room, leaning against a radiator while he nibbled on a biscuit.

"Good trip, Carter?" he asked, his tone amiable.

"We made out okay, sir." Carter shrugged as he spoke, which spoke volumes. Nothing to worry about, piece of cake. "Took a bit of damage."

Dickinson examined Carter for the little tell tale signs he had seen before but was pleased to see they had vanished like smoke in the wind. All it had taken was one good op for him to settle down and relax and get back in the groove again.

"How about the rest of the boys?" Carter asked.

"Everyone made it back. One wounded and Granville made it in with one engine out. Apart from that, a pretty good show all round."

Chairs scraped as a crew finished debriefing and Carters crew took their place. The WAAF officer looked to each of them, waiting for an indication of who was the captain. Forrester pulled out a chair for him and Carter joined them.

"Sorry I'm late," he muttered. She caught a glimpse of pilot's wings on his battledress where his leather jacket was open and asked him what aircraft they were. "P-Popsie," he told her. She wrote that at the top and waited for him to continue, pen poised.

5 - Gardening, A Very British Past Time

Over the next few days, Carter got to know some of the other members of the squadron and there were a few individuals who stood out from the crowd. By general agreement, his room mate, was a decent sort. He was a bluff little Liverpudlian pilot called William Walsh, 'Billy' for short, "it matches my height," he'd said in his thick Scouse accent. He smoked like a chimney, drank his pints quickly and was a constant ball of energy.

There was 'Fish' Salmon, a rail thin Scot. He was reputed to have been an Olympic swimmer before the war and he certainly fit the part. Long of limb and large of foot, he was someone who had obviously shot up in his youth and just kept on going. He had a narrow face, thin aquiline nose and sad watery eyes.

Another stand out was Archer, a tall blonde rower from Cambridge who had acquired a press on reputation. He had a dazzling smile that Carter was sure worked wonders on the ladies. On the ground he played as hard as he flew. When he wasn't drinking his way through the bar supplies, he could be found roaring round the countryside in a natty little lemon yellow sports car. Inherited from a former member of the squadron, an engine fitter had tweaked the engine to like aviation fuel without blowing the spark plugs through the bonnet.

A Flight Lieutenant called Everett rounded out the field. One of the other DFC's on the squadron, he'd done half a tour on Whitley's before being posted to 363. He was never seen without a cigarette in his hands and would sit quietly, watching what was going on around him, his eyes constantly moving, ever watchful. The rest of the squadron, Carter would get to know in time, if the fates allowed.

The remainder of October was a frustrating month. In the week following the raid on Kiel the squadron was alerted twice and scrubbed twice. The first time due to weather conditions over the target, the second because of weather conditions at home. It had been slightly misty at take off time, but the forecast for their return had been thick fog. The AOC was willing to accept some casualties on a raid but even he wasn't mad enough to risk his force being unable to get home afterwards.

It wasn't all bad news. The ground crew had time to patch Popsie up and five days after they got back from Kiel, Carter took her up for an air test. Where the gash had been, they had reskinned the fuselage with a new panel. The other holes had been patched with small flush riveted plates. Everything had been given a fresh coat of paint and the ID letters had been refreshed as well.

Even though there was little operational flying, there were still casualties of one sort or another. One of the crews got a scare on an air test when their starboard engine packed up and then promptly caught fire. They managed to get down at Coningsby, but it was a nasty reminder that the Manchester was not as docile as she sometimes made out to be.

Another crew was lost on a navigational exercise. Getting lost in heavy cloud, they let down expecting to find themselves over the Irish sea and instead discovered they were in the Lake District. The Manchester ploughed into the side of a steep hill and the flaming wreckage spilled down the side of the rock face.

When they weren't flying, the men spent their time as aircrew always did, in the pub or the Mess. On full stand downs they ventured as far as Lincoln congregating in the pubs, living life fast and hard.

Every day, Forrester, Tinsley and the rest of the crew asked the MO how their *proper* pilot was doing. Despite Carters best efforts, he knew he was still the interloper and he couldn't really blame them. They had come through OTU with Lambert, it was only natural their loyalties would lie with him. The MO assured them Lambert was doing well. He was still as spotty as a plum duff, but he was no longer the angry red he'd been a few days before and he was keen to get back out there. That cheered them up no end.

Carters room mate returned from leave and Walsh introduced him to his second dicky over breakfast in the Mess. Softly spoken, Eddie Nicol was a quiet, reserved lad from Bristol, a perfect foil to Walsh's bubbling enthusiasm. Carter liked him very much and it was good to make some new connections in the squadron.

Despite the best efforts of the ground crew, 363's serviceability continued to be a problem. Since July, aircraft availability had been shocking, averaging only eight or nine out of a squadron strength of eighteen. Some of it was down to the usual niggles of getting to used to a new type of aircraft, but the engines continued to be the main source of woe.

363 had inherited their Manchester's from 207 and 61 squadrons as they in turn received new aircraft. There was nothing particularly wrong with the planes they received but like the Manchester's Carter had seen at Lossie, some of them were just a little tired.

One day, they gathered in the hangar to look at a new one which had been delivered fresh from the factory, its fuselage bare of squadron ID letters. There was spirited debate over who would be assigned the aircraft. The sure bet was one of the Flight Commanders, but here people did Dickinson and Church a disservice. They had their plane, they were used to its foibles and quirks and trading it in for an unknown held little appeal.

Two days after the new kite was delivered, six aircraft were tasked to lay mines off the Baltic coast. Enemy shipping went up and down the coast of occupied Europe delivering cargo. By day, Bristol Blenheim's from 2 Group went out to attack this shipping. Nightly, the Royal Navy ventured across the water to play merry hell with the coastal traffic in MTB's and other small craft. Dropping mines, or Gardening as it was called, was the other half of the RAF's contribution to this effort.

When Carter's crew found out where they were going, they weren't that bothered. A short hop over the water to drop a bunch of mines sounded easy; easier than threading their way through the flak and fighters over Germany at any rate. Carter knew otherwise, they'd learn soon enough.

Dropping mines was a precise exacting job. You had to fly low and slow in a straight line which made you a ripe little target for the enemy. While there was less chance of running into a night fighter off the coast, the Germans had gotten very good at siting flak ships along the sea lanes, ready to catch the unwary napping. Your navigator needed to get things right as well. After a long run over water in the dark with unpredictable winds, it was all too easy to drift off track. Precious time could be spent circling to try and pick up a fix before dropping your mines in the right place.

A Manchester could carry four mines and Carter glared at the malevolent lumps as he watched them being winched up into the cavernous bomb bay. Each mine was nearly ten feet long and weighed 1500lbs. A parachute pack at the rear would deploy when it was dropped and would detach itself once the mine hit the water.

From the beginning, Carter knew it was going to be one of those nights. If Popsie had been a dog on the last op, she was no better this time. Even with the throttles to the stops, they had been lucky to clear the trees at the end of the runway and she made them work for every foot of height on the outward leg. During the climb, it was a constant debate between Carter and Forrester over the engine temperatures. Forrester tapped gauges, they juggled the throttles, anything and everything to coax the bomber to perform.

For a while, the port engine ran very rough indeed. Carter could feel the vibration through the yoke and near the main spar, Tinsley felt his teeth rattling. Then, as mysteriously as it had started, the engine settled down and was smooth as silk. Forester began to relax and that was when Popsie reminded them to never take her for granted.

A gout of sparks shot back from the port engine and it started to surge, giving varying amounts of power. For a brief instant, Jones and Smith thought they were being shot at and they looked frantically round the sky for an attacking fighter. Another spray of sparks issued from the engine and lit up the night sky.

Carter debated calling it a day. If the engine gave up on them off the European coast then that was them headed for the bag, no two ways about it. He glanced at the altimeter. They had clawed up to eight thousand feet so he levelled off and closed the throttles slightly to give the engines a chance to settle down. Forrester stared at him and Carter shrugged in response, there wasn't much else they could do.

Briefed to drop their load in the channels north of Kiel, Tinsley did a good job at making landfall close to their planned track. Although it was a simple task of almost repeating their route from the last raid, chastened by his last performance, Tinsley had studied the maps hard to avoid any mistakes this time.

They threaded their way through the clouds as they continued to head east. They began their descent as they hit open water again. The wave tops glittered as the moonlight caught them. Their target was the narrow channel between the islands of Langeland and Lolland but Carter had no intention of offering himself up on a plate to the German gunners. Rather than fly up the channel itself, he was going to cut diagonally across the stretch of water and cover its width.

A long thin island that ran roughly north to south, Langelland was a narrow strip of land and Carter throttled back as they passed over it. With the wind coming from the east, there was a slim chance the Germans may not even hear them coming. He levelled off at three hundred feet and prepared for the run in. If the mines were dropped from too high, they broke up on contact with the water. Drop them too fast and the parachute would tear off when it deployed.

The water flashed below Tinsley in the nose. Low flying on air tests and training was generally frowned upon due to the high accident rate so any chance to indulge was exciting. Forrester called off the height and speed as they settled at 120mph, a big fat target while they had the mines on board.

Tinsley opened the bomb doors and dropped the first mine. He counted off ten seconds and dropped the next one and so on until all four were away. Smith saw the mines fall away, drifting for a few seconds under their parachutes before slicing into the dark water.

As the bomb doors closed, Forrester rammed the throttles forward and Carter went lower, skimming the surface of the sea. If it had been exciting before, Tinsley was terrified now. One hiccup and they would make an enormous splash. In the tail, Smith could see their slipstream stirring up the surface of the water.

"What's that?" Forrester asked as he pointed ahead of them to the right. Just off the western shoreline of Lolland island there was a sandbar. A black shape blotted out some of the white capped waves as they crashed over the bar.

Carter knew what it was. He clung grimly to his course, relying on their speed to get them out of this.

"Flak ship to starboard!" he shouted. "Give them a squirt as we go past!" he told his gunners. Jones and Smith didn't need telling twice. Both sides opened up at the same time.

The dark was split apart by bright flashes of gunfire. The sea around the Manchester churned to froth as tracer fell around them. Smith blazed away in return but he had no idea if he was hitting anything. In moments they were through, hugging the waves and heading north, melting into the dark.

After putting some distance between them and the flak ship, Carter turned to port and circled round Fyn island, a large, almost circular clump of land just off the Danish coast. Ground fire chased them all the way round. One or two searchlights switched on and Smith reported flak going up over Kiel as the German gunners entertained themselves, chasing after phantom bombers.

Carter had the crew to check in, then had Forrester go looking for any damage. He found one hole on the starboard side, but it was an awkward one. A cannon shell had come in on a low angle and smashed through the Elsan chemical toilet. The back of the fuselage was quite fragrant where the liquid was sloshing around on the floor.

"I thought we were done for," Forrester commented after resuming his seat.

"No sweat," said Carter with some small amount of bravado. "We were on top of them before they knew we were there." He took Popsie back up to three thousand feet and they headed west for home.

On the way back across the North Sea, the port engine started to play up again. Forrester reduced speed and that helped a bit but no one relaxed. Just after they passed Withensea, Carter looked to his left, glaring at the recalcitrant engine, daring it to cross him. It duly obliged.

There was a final shower of sparks and then the engine decided that was it for the evening. There was a massive bang and a shudder and the prop started to windmill. The Manchester lurched to the left with the loss of power and Carter stamped on the rudder pedal to get her back. Forrester cut the switches to the port engine and feathered the prop and Popsie started to descend.

"If anybody wants to jump, you'd better get going," Carter informed the rest of the crew as the altimeter wound down.

Jones was sorely tempted but he didn't fancy the idea of baling out of the mid upper turret. The turret was fitted with doors at the back, so a gunner could open them and go over the side, but Jones had visions of being cut up by the tail plane. He clung on as the airframe rattled. Carter flattened out at six thousand feet, using the speed gained in the dive to hold her steady.

"I'm staying, sir," said Tinsley, Fitzgerald said the same, as did Jones and Smith. Carter looked at Forrester.

"Looks like you're stuck with us," said his second pilot simply. He went back to staring at the temperatures intently, hoping the other engine didn't crack up.

"Gawd save us," muttered Carter. "How long to base?" he asked Tinsley.

"About fifteen minutes?"

Carter did some maths quickly in his head as he eyed the altimeter. Fifteen minutes flying time, it would be touch and go to make it.

Reaching Amber Hill, Carter went straight in. Crossing the threshold at one hundred feet, they floated down the runway with full flaps and tons of opposite rudder to counteract the dead engine. Just before touchdown, he eased off on the rudder to let the wheels straighten up and then thumped it down.

The tyres squealed as they kissed the tarmac. The Manchester bounced and Carter kept a firm grip on the controls. The bomber touched back down and stayed down. He kept the yoke pulled back to keep the nose up and then turned off the runway.

Wrung out after nearly seven hours in the air, Carter was grateful when his feet touched the ground. He joined the rest of the crew round the front to find them all starting up at the port engine. There was a hole in the outer panel where a thrown con-rod had made a smart exit. Oil dripped out of the hole like blood from a ragged chest wound.

6 - We're H-A-P-P-Y

That sortie marked the end of Carters involvement with Lambert's crew. The MO let Lambert out of the ward the following morning and he was given a clean bill of health to resume operational flying. Carter got five hours sleep and woke at nine. It was a miserable day and he lay for a while listening to the rain lashing the glass. One of the panes in the wooden frame was loose and it rattled as the wind battered the hut. The curtains swayed in time to the gale.

During interrogation, Tinsley had produced his chart and log showing where they had laid the mines. Carter filled in the blanks where some of the flak sites had been. The Intel WAAF was particularly keen to pin down the location where the flak ship had been moored and wanted a better description of it.

Carter was pretty good on its location but the description he left to the crew. The WAAF was met by blank looks all round. She clicked her tongue in annoyance but Smith wasn't phased. He'd aimed at flashes in the dark, so had Jones. Fine detail was the last thing on their minds at that point.

Carter got dressed and and went for breakfast. He seated himself across from two of the other pilots that had laid mines off the Texel the previous night. One was slurping his tea while reading a letter from home. The other was wiping the last of the egg yolk from his plate with a bit of fried bread. A steward came over to Carter bearing a plate of crispy bacon and a fried egg. He asked for a tomato and the steward pointed him towards the toast on the rack in the middle of the table before gliding off to get one for him. Carter buttered a slice of bread while the others asked him how he'd got on. He shrugged.

"All right. Buggers had put a flak ship in the channel but he saw us too late. Engine packed up on the way home."

"Lucky you," murmured the tea drinker, his tone almost disinterested. The other pilot popped the yolk smothered bread into his mouth and started chewing.

"I ran into one too," he said, his voice muffled from food. He chewed a bit faster. "He got the chap ahead of us." He shuddered at the memory burned onto his brain.

He had just got to the chain of islands just off the Dutch coastline to make his run in when the sky had been torn into a kaleidoscopic light show. An F-lighter had been moored in the shallows. Bristling with guns, they were large concrete lined barges that the Germans used to move cargo around. Due to the aggressive MTB activity, they were also used sometimes to beef up the escort on the coastal convoys. Some F-lighters were very well armed, having everything up to an 88mm on the deck.

The Manchester in front had just dropped its last mine when a blizzard of fire had arced across the water from the port side. At two hundred feet, it was almost like going clay pigeon shooting. Golf ball sized gobs of light turned the twin engined bomber into a shredded mess. The wing tanks brewed up and the Manchester nosed into the water, a large plume of water to mark its passing.

Breaking off his run to the right, he disappeared into the dark to get as far from the F-lighter as possible. Circling round, he dropped his mines further up the channel and then made for home, pondering the random nature of war. Ten more seconds and he would have run right into that himself. He broke into a smile when a new arrival traipsed into the Mess.

"Well, well, so you aren't dead after all."

Carter turned to see who had come in and he saw a Pilot Officer striding towards them. Thin, about five feet ten with fine blonde hair, he had a pale face and drawn cheeks with dark smudges under his eyes. Faded red marks on his face and hands showed he must have been one of the squadrons diseased members. The sickly pallor made him look barely eighteen.

"Shouldn't you be ringing a bell, shouting, *'unclean, unclean'* as you go along, old man?" asked the tea drinker in good humour.

"Very funny," the new arrival said as he sat down next to Carter. "After being confined to bed for two weeks while a bunch of doctors poke and prod you was long enough."

"My heart bleeds," tea drinker responded deadpan. He rather liked the idea of two weeks in bed. It was better than flying three ops and slogging across flak filled countryside.

"Are you, Carter?" asked the new man, glancing at Carter's chest and noting the scruffy DFC ribbon below his wings.

"I am." He held out his hand. The new man took it, shaking firmly.

"I'm, Lambert. Dicko told me you've been looking after my mob."

"If you can call it that," replied Carter, trying to keep his voice upbeat. "I like to think we were looking after each other."

The steward came back with a small side plate, bearing the requested tomato. It was slid onto Carter's plate. Lambert asked for some porridge.

"I don't think my tummy would tolerate anything else at the

moment," he said, jealously eyeing Carter's egg and bacon. His mouth watered at the prospect of crispy bacon. He'd barely eaten the first week when he'd been laid up in hospital. While Chickenpox in youth might be something that made you a bit uncomfortable for a week, for an adult it was much more serious.

Lambert had been rubbed all over with Calamine lotion, repeatedly told not to scratch or pick at the blisters and they had funnelled so many aspirin down his throat he could be a pill dispenser. The worst thing had been the scratching. Morning noon and night, his skin had itched like crazy and sleep had been hard to come by.

His porridge placed in front of him. Lambert dumped a load of sugar on top and mixed it in by stirring his spoon.

"I hope everything's gone okay?" he asked as he started into the porridge.

"As it can be," Carter responded. "I'm not so sure you'll be pleased with me after you see what I did to your kite." Lambert arched an eyebrow as Carter reeled off the litany of woes, "had a fire, broke the loo, bust an engine."

"I heard," said Lambert. He shrugged as he shoved a big spoonful of porridge into his mouth. "Nothing the erks can't put right. It's just a bit of metal at the end of the day. As long as everyone made it home, that's the main thing." He stopped himself from itching around the collar of his shirt where it was bothering him. "What are you going to do now?"

"I'm not sure," said Carter. He knew flying with Lambert's crew had only been temporary, but a few days had stretched to a week. He'd not thought about having to go shopping for a crew of his own. He talked with Lambert while he finished his breakfast and then went looking for Dickinson.

He found his flight commander in his office, fiddling with some memos from Group. Carter provided a welcome distraction and Dickinson waved him in as he knocked on the door. Carter came in, spinning his peaked cap on his left index finger as he parked himself on a chair in front of Dickinson's desk. There was a pile of files to the right, on the left some wooden In and Out trays. A telephone occupied one corner; a bible was on the other. Dickinson put the memo's back in their tray and turned his attention to his pilot.

"What can I do for you, Mr Carter?"

"Lamberts out of the infirmary so I need a new crew, sir."

Dickinson leaned back in his chair, sucking on his lower lip. Air whistled through the gap in his teeth while he pondered the possibilities.

"I don't have complete crews lying around you know," he said, his tone light. He glanced to his right. There was a chest of drawers against the wall and on top was a bundle of personnel files. He could go thumbing through it and make suggestions but he always thought that the tried and true methods worked best. "There's a few odds and sods floating around that might fit the bill. I'd rather you found some people rather than ordering someone to do it."

Carter nodded his understanding. There were always a few men on a squadron looking to get on a crew. They might have been wounded or gone on a course and come back to find the rest of their crew gone. Some might have been dumped because they were not so good at their jobs. He would have to form his crew from a limited pool and hope he got a few good 'uns in the mix.

"Give it a few days, put some feelers out," Dickinson suggested.

"I'll give it a go, sir."

The first member of his new crew appeared that evening. Carter was lazing on his bed. He'd snaffled one of the magazines from Walsh's side of the room and was thumbing through the pages when there was a knock on his door.

"Come," he said, his voice far away while he focused on an article. A dark head appeared round the door jamb.

"Could I come in, sir?"

Carter sat up. The visitor was a short dark haired Flight Sergeant.

"By all means."

The man came into the room. He was about five foot four, broad shouldered and had an AG brevet on his left breast. His uniform was the darker blue of the Royal Australian Air Force. He cast a glance around the room, gauging his surroundings.

"I'm, George Todd, I heard you're looking for a new crew, sir," he said, his voice pure Aussie twang.

"I am, where'd you hear about that?" replied Carter, his tone cautious as he considered how to play this. He couldn't just accept someone straight off the bat without getting a feel for them first, but if he said no, word might get around he was being a bit of a snob.

"People talk. I thought I'd pay you a visit."

Carter nodded. No doubt, Smith and the others had been crowing about getting their pilot back in the Sergeants Mess. He grabbed his peaked cap and made for the door.

"Let's take a walk and have a chat."

They went past the NAAFI and headed towards the hangars. Carter offered the man a cigarette which was gratefully accepted.

"Tell me about yourself," he said.

"Not much to tell, sir. It was only ever me and me mum. I did a few bum jobs for a while and then one day I saw a poster on the bus." Todd remembered it well. He'd been on the bus after another hard day at the mill, sweat streaking his face, when the poster had caught his eye. Aircrew seemed a lot better than flogging your guts out in some factory job.

"I figured it was better to volunteer than waiting around to get conscripted as a footslogger. I joined up in Melbourne, did some initial training at home and then got shipped over here."

"How many trips have you done?" asked Carter, getting to the nub of the issue straight away. Any man who was willing to come thousands of miles to fight already had his respect.

"Seven, and I got one kill on my fourth trip out. Then I got sent on a gunnery course and the rest of my crew left me behind. I've had to pick up the odd trip here and there after that." Carter noticed that Todd had hesitated before mentioning the course. There was more to that story than a glib one liner but there would be time to hear the full reason later. Seven ops was a respectable number and Carter had to admit, anyone with the nerve to come and seek out an officer and ask, rather than be approached himself deserved consideration.

In fact, Todd had beaten a path to Carters door as soon as he'd heard he needed to form a new crew. A few days before he had overheard Smith moaning about *Nanny* Carter and his strict ways in the Sergeants Mess. Todd took that with a pinch of salt.

Firstly, Smith had drunk too many pints and secondly, he was a bit of a blowhard anyway. He had a belligerent streak that needed careful handling and Todd knew it wouldn't take much for him to take a dislike to someone. In addition, the fact that Carter was on his second tour counted for a lot more than Smith's *expert* opinion as far as Todd was concerned. A second tour man would know what he was doing. Todd rated his chances of getting through his own first tour a lot more highly if he was flying with someone who had seen it and done it once already.

His own crew had been very good. His pilot had been an experienced second dicky who had done five trips before being bumped up to first pilot. Then Todd had been sent off on an advanced gunnery course at Sutton Bridge. For a few weeks he had flown around in clapped out Hampdens and Wellingtons in a remote corner of the fen country.

When he got back to Amber Hill, he was informed in fairly bald terms that his crew had got the chop while he'd been away. They'd gone out on a trip to Cologne and failed to return. Posted as missing, Todd knew that was just a euphemism for the bits that were left being too small to identify.

Their walk had taken them to the hangar where Popsie was being worked on. Popsie had been wheeled into the hangar and the mechanics had already pulled off the wrecked port engine.

During the walk, Carter had asked Todd about his kill and the

Australian had been honest enough to admit it was ninety percent luck. He had been flying along, skipping over the tops of the clouds when a 110 had suddenly appeared right behind him. It was over in a matter of seconds. No more than fifty yards away, his four .303's had skewered the sleek nightfighter from nose to tail before it disappeared back into the clouds, streaming a banner of flame.

Carter found this admission to be a good measure of the man. It would have been easy to shoot a line about it. He made his decision. He offered Todd his hand and the Australian took it.

"First come, first served, Todd, welcome aboard."

"We'll need some good lads to make up the rest of the crew, sir." Todd said, grinning from ear to ear.

"I'm open to suggestions," Carter replied.

Over the next two days, Carter accumulated the rest of his crew and a mixed bag it proved to be. None of them had done more than one or two trips, but personal recommendations and direct approaches mollified any concerns Carter may have had. His new navigator had collared him over breakfast in the officers Mess.

A large figure loomed over him, in actual fact, blocking the light. Carter glanced up to see a mountain of a man looking down at him with brown eyes. His chest was bulging fit to pop the buttons off his battledress jacket. He had the Canada flash on his shoulders and Pilot Officer rings on his epaulettes. After a short conversation, Paul Woods became his navigator.

Woods was a double act. He brought with him a wireless operator; a Pilot Officer called Christophe Vos. The pair of them had come from Canada under the Commonwealth Air Training Plan. Belgian, Vos had got out of his homeland in 1940 with the shirt on his back and little else. He had joined the RAF with the fire of revenge burning in his heart.

His second pilot came via Forrester. A quiet type, White said little, but in the air, he was all business, his tone brisk and his attention focused. He flew with a confident hand, his control inputs were small but well judged, enough to keep a Manchester under firm control. He would do.

Todd provided their mid upper gunner. Where Todd was dark and compact, Murphy was blonde and tall. Todd came from the outskirts of Melbourne, Murphy from Barnsley; a scruffy mining town just outside of Sheffield. The two of them had met on their gunnery course and hit it off right away.

Off duty, they were a double act. Going regularly into Lincoln, they had made the *Blue Anchor* their pub of choice and did their best to cut a swathe through the female inhabitants of the city, using the glamour of the uniform and their limited charm to great affect.

Walsh loaned Carter his Manchester and they went up as a crew for the first time on the Tuesday afternoon. Woods proved to be a good navigator, confidently taking them north east to the coast before looping back to the bombing range at Wainfleet. They dropped a bunch of practice bombs from different heights and Carter spelled out what he expected from his crew. Wireless Op's would keep watch for fighters out of the astrodome. Gunners would call out pinpoints to help the navigator. He would do regular checks on the intercom and he expected prompt responses. He wasn't bothered if they said Captain, skip or, sir as long as it was on the button. The one thing he would not tolerate was idle gossip. Too much chatter meant people were distracted from their jobs.

The other golden rule he wanted to impress upon them was that no one took a break until they were back on the ground. He'd never done it on his first tour, he was not about to start now.

When they got back, he gathered them together and gave them the out. If anyone felt they would not be a good fit, now was the time to say so. No one moved. He had his crew. That evening he went to see Dickinson and gave him the good news.

The following day Dickinson assigned them a Manchester and they went over to the hangar to see it. It was a brand new one which had been flown in the day before. The code letters 'L' had been painted on either side of the roundels. They spent a good hour crawling over her, trying out their respective stations. Carter fiddled around until he had the pilots seat adjusted like he wanted.

This Manchester wasn't fitted with a mid upper turret so Todd and Murphy argued over who would have to be up front and the other in the tail. They flipped for it, Murphy won so he picked the front turret. Close to six feet, he hated folding himself into the rear turret, finding it too cramped for his legs. At least up front he could let his feet dangle and enjoy some comfort on these long trips. After lunch they went up on another air test, starting to click as a team.

It was starting to snow when they got back to Amber Hill. The weather had changed quickly and Carter had to descend to eight hundred feet to keep the ground in sight. The clouds had thickened and a chill wind started to blow from the east. It bit into them when they got back on the ground.

"Gods," said Vos through clenched teeth. "Let's get inside quick before we freeze up." He fastened up his jacket and huddled into the furry collar. On the ride back to the crew room in the three tonner they decided to head into Lincoln for a drink to celebrate. They rounded up Walsh and his crew along the way. As Walsh said, "We can't let you boys celebrate all alone now, can we?"

They caught a Bedford for the seven mile run into Lincoln. The motor pool had a few trucks running most evening's between the station and town. Alternatively, a one mile trudge got you to the nearest bus route which was a little unreliable. If worst came to the worst, a fellow could walk or cycle there and back but that was a last resort as the winter weather continued to be deeply unpleasant.

They wrapped up with scarves and gloves against the cold. Vos went one further and wore his flying jacket on top of his battledress for which he was ribbed mercilessly on the ride in. Carter reflected it wasn't as severe as being on the coast of north eastern Scotland, feeling the wind coming in off the North Sea.

The truck dropped them at the bottom end of the high street. After six months away in the north of Scotland, Carter found himself back in familiar territory. Things in town hadn't changed very much. With so many airfields around the city, Lincoln was awash with uniforms. Men wandered from pub to pub, living life like blazing comets because tomorrow, they may not be around to enjoy it.

For all the bonhomie between crews, there were still distinct class divisions of where they socialised. The officers main watering hole was the *Saracen's Head*. In the centre of town it was at the top of the High Street, right across from the Guildhall. Until the railways had arrived it had been a main stop for coaches running north and south, east to west. The original pub dated back to the middle ages but in the 1800's it had been rebuilt and had a splendid Victorian facade. The front of the pub was deceptive. Most of the building was hidden behind shops either side of it and there was another entrance on Salter gate, handy if the MP's ever showed up and you needed to make a quick exit.

The NCO's hung out at the *The Crown* and never the twain would meet. On those occasions when an officer wanted to hang out with the rest of his crew, both sides would meet on neutral ground at pubs like the *Linden* or the *Blue Anchor* or anywhere else that took their fancy. Carter had gone for many pints with his old crew at the *Blue Anchor* but this night, they stopped at a modest little pub called *The Tarleton* on Portland Street.

The sign had a painting of a light cavalryman from the Napoleonic period. He was riding a white horse with a red shabraque. The artist had made him very dashing in his blue uniform with a pelisse slung over his left shoulder and black Tarleton hat on his head with a white plume. Murphy peered in the tap room window though a gap in the blackout curtain and announced that it would do and they piled in.

A few figures in RAF blue propped up the bar, two army officers occupied a small table off to the right near a blazing fire. The new arrivals commandeered two tables and shouted for beer. The barmaid acknowledged their presence and started putting pint glasses on the bar.

As the new boy, Carter got the beers in and splashed the cash a little. Nicol and Walsh attacked theirs. Murphy and White sipped pints of mild. Vos nursed a ginger beer which drew odd looks but no comment. Walsh waited until everyone had a drink and then tapped his pint glass with a key. He waited until there was hush and all eyes turned in his direction.

"I suppose it falls to me to welcome into the fold the squadrons latest crew. Now I've watched Carter here for a while, and I must admit, I saw greatness there, a leader." Fists thumped the tables in good humour. Walsh swept his hand from left to right encompassing Carters men. "And let's face it, with a bunch like this, he's going to need every bit of inspiration he can muster to keep them going." There was a howl of protest and then laughter. He raised his pint glass. "I give you, the crew of L for London." They raised their glasses and said, 'Cheers'.

"Nice speech," said Carter. He finished off his pint and was about to rise to get another one when Walsh put his hand across Carter's chest.

"I'll get this," said his room mate. He sauntered off to the bar and gave the bar maid his best smile. "Two Burton's please my darling."

"Darling my eye," she said, distinctly unimpressed by Walsh's approach. She shook her head to herself as she pulled a pint for someone else. "You'll have to wait a minute," she told him as she sashayed back down the bar to an army officer. Walsh admired the line of her calves as she exchanged pleasantries with the Captain. A large figure lurched across his view and leaned on the handles of the beer pumps.

"And what can I get for you, sir?" he asked, his voice tinged with just enough menace for daring to leer at the legs of his staff.

"Two Burton's please," said Walsh, suitably repentant in look. The landlord grunted and picked up two glasses from the shelf above the bar. Walsh took the glasses back to their table. "My oath, there's a corker serving behind the bar," he announced.

"Why do you think I wanted to come in here?" Todd said sagely as he sipped on his pint. Nicol thought Todd was joking but the Australian was deadly serious. Ever the keen eye for the ladies, he had spotted her through the window when they were deciding where to go. Tall, lithe, with flame red hair, pale skin and bumps in all the right places she had immediately caught his attention.

The crews started talking shop so Woods ambled over to the bar and struck up conversation with the barmaid. She patted her hair and stared up at him, charmed by his easygoing manner. He bashfully answered her questions about his home while she held his big paw. Todd glanced over and was annoyed someone had beaten him to it. He was convinced it was Woods soft Canadian accent that did it.

White challenged Carter to a game of darts. Carter couldn't throw a dart for toffee, but then that was not the point of the exercise.

"Best of three?" he asked his second pilot.

They were there an hour when a noisy crowd of RAF blue streamed in. At their head was Archer, who was leading his crew on a crawl around Lincoln. This was not their first stop and most of them were three sheets to the wind. A Pilot Officer with big broad shoulders and beefy hands, Archer thumped the bar top for attention.

Carter saw Walsh's face twist into a scowl when they came in and he arched an eyebrow in question. Walsh jerked his chin towards their table and Carter drifted away from keeping score on White and Murphy's game of darts.

"What's the story?" he asked, sitting down next to Walsh.

The Liverpudlian glared at the tall figure in the midst of the new arrivals.

"Glory boy and I don't get on," he muttered in a low voice.

"Glory boy?" Carter looked at him with renewed interest. For all his outward brashness, Walsh was quite level headed when it came to ops. To hear him comment so directly on another pilot spoke of some past transgression that offended even Walsh's standards.

Walsh fished a pack of cigarettes out of his top pocket and lit one while he thought about how to phrase a response to Carter's query.

"You'll have heard he's a press on type?" Carter nodded and Walsh continued. "On his second trip, they were hit by flak, two crew killed. God knows how they got home." He could still picture Archer's Manchester when they'd got back. The whole rear of the fuselage had been like a colander, the rudders mere skeletons and one elevator ripped off. Archer had earned himself a mention in dispatches for that.

Walsh picked a flake of tobacco from between his teeth and stared at the table top. His eyes followed a gouge in the wood where somewhere had carved a random pattern with a coin while he marshaled his thoughts.

"The next time out, he lost the intercom on the outward leg, well before they reached the coast but he carried on anyway. They made it to the target, dropped the bombs and made it back," Walsh stubbed out the cigarette and moodily grabbed his pint glass, his hand gripping it tight, his knuckles turning white. "Yeah, they made it back, but not before a night fighter had stalked them for a while and killed the rear gunner. The mid upper managed to drive it away before it finished them off." Walsh glared at Archer. "*He* just said it was the luck of the game."

Carter listened in silence. If something went wrong on an op you were expected to carry on regardless but there were a few accepted reasons to abort. Losing the intercom was one of them. No intercom meant no warning in case of attack. To push on in those kinds of circumstances was foolhardy at best, reckless at worst.

He glanced up from this conspiratorial chat to look again at the man by the bar. He thought long and hard on what Walsh had told him but found it hard to condemn the desire to press on. Clearly Walsh and Archer did not get on, but Carter wasn't about to judge someone on second hand information. It was easy second guessing decisions when you weren't there to judge. As far as he was concerned, everyone had a fresh slate until he was shown otherwise, but it certainly seemed like there was some reason for caution.

Once they were served, Archers crew drifted over to them and space was made for them around the tables. Walsh stayed mum and didn't involve himself in conversation if he could help it. Up close, Carter was surprised how young Archer appeared. Hazel green eyes stared back at him from a smooth, pale skinned face. He considered his own scarred appearance in comparison and felt like an old man.

"Must be nice to have your own crew finally," Archer said in an Essex accent.

"Yes," Carter replied, his tone neutral. "It's not the same when you borrow someone else's."

"I can imagine," said Archer, his tone dismissive. "Of course, when someone buys it you have to help the new men settle in. That's why we should drink and make merry while we can." There was a pause while those words were digested and then it hit Carter, that was as much eulogy as Archer's previous crew members were going to get.

For Archer, it never even registered for one second that it could have been him. He firmly believed you made your own luck. Flak was something that happened to other people, the same thing went for nightfighters too. If his crew had been more alert, they wouldn't have got the chop. Carter looked at him askance, wondering how much of this persona was for show.

7 - It's Always The Little Things

L-London was on the final leg back to Amber Hill. Aside from a few holes in the starboard wing, their brand new Manchester had performed well. Even the engines had behaved although Carter was never going to trust them like he did with his old Hampden.

The squadron had been sent to Cologne. In the heart of the Ruhr, it was a vital industrial centre and was a veteran from Bomber Commands frequent visits. The inhabitants went to their shelters in good order, the defences of heavy guns and searchlight batteries were well organised.

When the tannoy had called the crews to briefing late in the afternoon, Carter already knew they would be flying. Despite the general servicing problems, with a brand spanking new plane, there was no way they weren't going to be on the list. Most of Bomber Command was going to Berlin tonight, but 5 Group were going to bomb Cologne instead. Air Vice Marshal Slessor had seen the weather reports and objected to the plan. The AOC didn't press the issue and allowed 5 Group to withdraw to do their own thing.

Church was upbeat about it at briefing. With over two hundred aircraft going to the big city, all eyes would be on them. That should leave the way relatively clear for 5 Group and 363 to nip over, bomb Cologne and get home again without attracting too much attention.

Carter tried to quell his nerves as he wiled away the hours until take off. He went back to his room and found Walsh asleep when he came in. The man had the uncanny knack of being able to sleep on demand. The fact he was also flying didn't seem to worry him in the slightest. Carter caught up on his correspondence. His sister had sent him two letters since he'd come to Amber Hill and he knew he should have responded before, but now he had something to tell her.

The rest of his crew dealt with their nerves in their own way. Woods dug out his charts and went over a few things, trying to anticipate any problems he might encounter. He sorted out his navigator's' bag, sharpening pencils, checking his log and making sure his stop watch was working. He found solace in routine.

Vos *borrowed* a bicycle and went for a ride around the airfield. He was restless, waiting for the off. He got up some speed, panting as his legs pumped. The spokes rattled; the frame creaked as it swayed from side to side. He went faster, trying to outrun the ghosts that lingered.

Murphy went for a walk and was surprised when his feet took him to dispersal and their Manchester. The armourers were busy bombing up while the erks crawled over the bomber, getting her ready. Trolleys were parked under the bomb bay and a mix of incendiary containers and 1,000lb bombs were being winched into place.

The erks were giving him odd looks so he climbed inside and went up to his turret in the nose. He filched a wad of cotton waste from the instrument basher in the cockpit and kept himself busy industriously polishing the perspex in his turret. With the power off he tried the manual traversing mechanism, then he just sat there for a bit until he got bored, so he got down.

Feeling foolish, he left the ground crew to it and went back to the Sergeants Mess. Todd was having a game of darts with White. He was two shillings down and determined to win his money back. He noticed Murphy's pensive look.

"Where did you get to?" he asked. "You weren't going to duck out, were you?"

Murphy shrugged. He pinched some toast off Todd's plate.

"I was just making sure our ride was ready."

Todd nudged his partner in crime on the shoulder.

"We'll be fine mate. Don't worry about it."

Dickinson led the way on this one. Lambert was eager to get back to the coal face and with Popsie repaired, he was ready to go. Seven other crews rounded out the field and it had been a fair sized crowd at briefing.

The whole trip had been pretty straightforward. Flak had been scattered and the nightfighters had left them alone. The weather had been a mixed bag. They flew through banks of hail over the Channel and rain had lashed them as they crossed the Dutch coast. Carter had to peer through the canopy as visibility dropped almost to nothing. Eventually he managed to wring a bit more altitude out of their new Manchester and get above it.

Scattered clouds obscured the ground but Woods got them to the target without too many problems. There was some debate when they reached Cologne as the Fires on the ground were scattered all over the shop. They argued back and forth while they tried to identify landmarks and the flak intensified as they followed the line of the river.

Peering through his sight, Woods saw a big cluster of factory buildings arranged in a linear pattern. He lined up on it and asked for one final correction before hitting the release.

"They're away!" he shouted.

Carter held her for the photograph and then dived, letting the speed build up and taking them further away from the city. Leveling off at four thousand, they headed north west for home and he handed over to White for a while, giving him a chance to fly the plane. Crossing the coast, Carter reminded everyone to stay alert. Just because they were almost home was no reason not to pay attention to their jobs. He was conscious it verged on nagging, but first time out, he wanted to make sure his rules were clear.

Woods kept checking his maps but he was finding it difficult as they flew over the darkened English countryside. Occasionally a badly shaded light would show on the ground, but otherwise, the land below was in total darkness. Learning to navigate in Canada had been far easier than ops over England. In Canada it was wide open countryside as far as the eye could see, with big mountains, wide plains and large rivers. The winds were also fairly mild and the weather was quite predictable. Training had been a doddle compared to this.

After checking his figures for the umpteenth time, Woods was sure the predicted winds had been wrong. He asked Vos for help and the Belgian duly obliged. The DF bearing proved him right when he found he was thirty miles or so off track to the south. He gave Carter the correction and the bomber changed course as directed.

Arriving back at Amber Hill, the weather was starting to close in. An ugly bank of clouds was looming on the horizon. It would rain in the morning, Murphy thought.

As they went around the circuit, he saw another Manchester was ahead of them. The wings glinted as the weak moonlight caught them. They followed them all the way round as the other bomber shaped up for a landing. The undercarriage came down, then the flaps. He saw the bods on the ground had lit the flare path but they hadn't don't it very well. Quite a few lights weren't lit at all.

In the cockpit, White and Carter thought there was something strange about the lights. They were pondering what was going on when another aircraft muscled into the circuit in front of them. It was so close; their Manchester shook from the slipstream.

"Cheeky sod," said Carter, unimpressed at having to break off to go round again. He was just about to pull back on the yoke when the newcomer opened fire on the bomber going in to land.

"What the-" exclaimed Murphy in surprise as the German intruder broke off.

The Manchester ahead of them stood no chance. Low and slow, with the flaps and wheels down, it was a sitting duck. The rear gunner was caught napping as golf ball size cannon shells went whipping past him and chewed into the wings and fuselage. The bomber lurched, dropped its left wing and piled in from one hundred feet.

The Manchester ploughed into the ground, short of the runway. The nose crumpled and the rest of the aircraft folded around it. The night sky was lit up by orange flame as the tanks touched off. Gobs of burning petrol skittered across the grass, chased by lumps of engine and pieces of fuselage. The crash crews went charging across the field. The pealing wail of the bell on the fire engine split the night. The ambulance brought up the rear.

Carter circled well wide of Amber Hill. Somewhere out there was something with black crosses on the wing, prowling around in the dark and looking for game. He felt himself straining against his harness, wishing he could wring a few hundred extra miles an hour out of the engines. Everyone was alert, their senses twitching like crazy. If Todd even saw a dark smudge coming towards them, he was giving it the lot before shouting out a warning.

Finally, the tower came on the line, the remaining aircraft were to divert to Waddington. Before Woods figured out the new course Carter already had them on the way. He knew this area like the back of his hand and could fly there blindfolded. It wasn't even ten minutes and they were lining up on the east west runway. They got an all clear and went straight in.

"For gods sake keep your eyes skinned," he warned everyone. He would laugh if a German intruder caught them out now.

He deliberately kept his approach fast and White had his hand behind the throttles, ready to ram them forwards if necessary. Carter skimmed over the perimeter fence with the flaps and wheels down. Now was the dangerous time. If anybody was to attack there wouldn't be much he could do about it. He thumped his bomber down with no finesse and let her roll, running half the length of the runway before slowing down and turning off onto the grass. When he finally shut the engines down, he was exhausted.

A truck came to pick them up and take them to interrogation. They kept it short and sweet and went for their bacon and eggs. White ate like a starving man. Such a close reminder of his own mortality had made him exceedingly hungry. When they were shown to a hut with some beds, he asked someone to wake him when the sun came up, "I want to see it," he said, glad to be alive.

They flew back to Amber Hill at nine in the morning. Half of them were still punchy from the op, but a quick sniff of oxygen helped clear their heads. Coming in to land, they flew over the still smoldering remains. A dark scar had been carved in the grass and the blackened bits of airframe had a lonely figure standing guard over them.

They shut down at dispersal and were whisked back to their billets. After getting changed, Carter headed to the Mess to find energetic discussion of the previous night's events. Carter quickly looked around, searching for the missing face but had to admit defeat. He sought out Dickinson, finding him in an armchair nursing a cup of tea.

"Carter, good to see you back. Shaky do last night," he murmured. He gestured to the armchair next to him and Carter sank into it.

"I saw it all, I was right behind them," Carter replied, his voice neutral. "They came right up behind them and just blew them away," he shuddered, as if someone had walked over his grave.

"Bad show," said Dickinson, "sneaky bloody Huns." His eyes were red rimmed. He'd not been to bed yet and he was dog tired. "His first op back as well. Such a bloody waste," he muttered. Carter's head turned very slowly to look at Dickinson as the words clicked into place.

"Do you mean it's Lambert who's spread across the field?"

It took a moment for Carter's question to register in Dickinson's brain.

"I'm sorry. I forgot; how could you have known? Yes, it was Lambert. Bad luck, just bad luck."

Dickinson stared off into the distance as he remembered the crash scene. He had started running towards the crash, his flying boots slipping as he clumped across the grass. Almost out of breath, he'd flagged down the fire engine as it went past. Clinging to the running board, he shouted at the driver to go faster as they bumped across the ground and then slithered to a halt.

Wreckage was scattered all over the place. What was left of the fuselage lay on its port side, the stump of the starboard wing pointing to the sky. Bits of twisted metal lay amongst the bushes and trees that grew at the edge of the field. Fires were scattered all around, blazing puddles of petrol that had spilled from the split tanks.

Skirting round an undercarriage leg and large mainwheel which lay smoking, Dickinson had stopped in his tracks as he saw a figure hobbling away from the flames.

"Good god," he breathed, as the grim apparition of Smith appeared, struggling as he walked backwards, dragging a body across the grass. His face was covered in blood, his eyes wild. His jacket was ripped open on one arm, his Mae West blackened and scorched.

Smith's turret had broken free from the fuselage on impact and thrown him clear of the crash. Head ringing, some primal instinct had kicked in and he had forced his way out of the smashed turret and crawled back towards the wreckage. Eyes stinging from the smoke, in a daze; he had fumbled around, almost blind until his flailing hand had latched onto clothing. Clamping his hands tight he had pulled, doggedly putting one foot in front of the other, sheer will alone keeping him going.

"It's all right mate, I'll get you home," he kept repeating like a mantra as he dragged Jones from the flames. It was wasted effort. He was so dazed by the crash he'd not seen that Jones had a hole in his chest so big you could shove a fist through it. Jones had been dead before the crash, shot up by the intruder in their first burst.

Smiths strength finally gave out as Dickinson got up to him and he collapsed onto the grass. Friendly hands hustled him away and he was carted off to hospital with a suspected fractured skull and burns. The rest of the crew were dead. Forrester, Fitzgerald, Tinsley, Jones and Lambert, all dead, just like that. That was the way it was on ops. The way it had always been.

"Sneaky bloody Huns," Dickinson repeated to himself as he stared off into the distance.

8 - Deep And Crisp And Even

After a recent run of bad weather and poor bombing results, nearly four hundred aircraft that night. Half went to Berlin. The remainder had gone to Cologne, Mannheim and Essen. Officially, Bomber Command had delivered a blow to the Big City. Half the aircraft dispatched had made the target and bombed all over the city, setting a large number of fires. Lord Haw Haw said otherwise, claiming that the sky had rained bombers brought down by accurate flak but no one paid much attention to him. The raid on Cologne barely merited a mention, Asher's prediction about everyones attention being diverted north seemed to have been accurate.

A dark pall hung over Carter for the rest of the day. Lambert's Manchester had been the squadrons only casualty and the fact that it had happened on their own doorstep upset him greatly. The thought played in his head that it was his fault. He'd flown two ops with them, he'd had plenty of time to pour his knowledge and experience into them. Throughout his first tour he had never lost a crew member. Two had been wounded, he himself had been wounded; but he'd never lost one.

He sulked in his room for a while. Coming back from Waddington had cost him three or four hours sleep. After the news about Lambert's crew, he was more awake than ever and sleep eluded him as he replayed events in his head, seeing Lambert's Manchester go in and tearing itself apart.

By late morning, bitterly cold winds howled across the land and heavy clouds rolled in, dumping snow on the airfield. The scars in the earth disappeared under a layer of white and the twisted wreckage of the Manchester softened under its death shroud. Visibility dropped to a few hundred yards as big fat flakes of snow continued to fall for the rest of the day. The winter of 1940 had been one of the worst on record, it looked like the winter of 1941 was going to give it a good run for its money.

There would be no ops that day but that's not to say there was no work. Just because the aircrew weren't flying didn't mean everything came to a crashing halt. Ground crew continued to work on the aircraft in the cold. Exposed to the elements on work platforms to get to the engines, fingers soon went numb. The holes on the wing of

Carter's Manchester were patched, then the wind strength increased and the erks retired to their little makeshift hut. They hunkered down and got a good blaze going and drank some tea as they watched the snow coming down.

Carter finally stirred himself out of his funk in the early afternoon and willed himself to get up. In the intervening hours he'd discovered that Walsh could snore quite loudly. Thankfully, throwing something at him made him turn over and the noise would stop for a while. Carter was dog tired but it was no good continuing to lie there. What he needed was a brisk walk to blow away the cobwebs, some food and a good cup of tea.

He shrugged on his greatcoat and crammed his battered cap on his head as he went out the door to the hut. His breath caught in his throat as the biting cold blasted him. His cheeks stung from the driving wind and he sank into his greatcoat, his nose poking out over the collar.

He inevitably drifted over to the Mess. There was a good blaze going in the hearth and Carter thawed himself out as he pawed idly at the newspapers and training manuals that were lying around. He sprawled sideways on an armchair, his feet towards the fire as he thumbed through the reading material. He got half an hour without interruption when the station tannoy burst into life.

"The Station Snow Plan is now in operation. Any personnel not on duty are to report to their sections for work detail."

There was a collective groan around the room. The message repeated over the tannoy and then bodies began to move. Feet dragged as they went out into the hall as they threw on their greatcoats and hats. Gloves were dug out of pockets and pulled on as they clumped outside. Seeing no way out of this, Carter got up and followed the herd.

For the rest of the day they shovelled snow. Split up into groups, they joined hundreds of other station personnel to keep the taxiways and runway clear while the snow continued to come down. This annoyed Carter but there was no way round it. It wasn't realistic to wait for the snow to stop before doing anything, but it stung to shovel snow, only to see the ground turn white again before they were finished.

NAAFI vans did the rounds on a regular basis, delivering welcome hot mugs of tea and sandwiches. Cold hands cupped the mugs, trying to get feeling back into numb fingers. They were kept at it until five when the light began to go but they were under no illusions that they would probably be doing it again the following day.

Carter's feet were like blocks of ice when he shuffled back into his billet. He promised himself that he'd put on an extra pair of long johns and socks in the morning. After the previous night's operation and the days exertion he just flopped into bed fully dressed. Walsh turned up twenty minutes later. He looked like some sort of abominable snowman. Snow covered his shoulders and his greatcoat was stiff from the cold. He had been out at the bomb dump on the far end of the field for most of the day keeping the road clear.

He stamped the snow off his boots and then perched on the end of his bed. He put one foot in front of the other and put the heel to the toe. Slowly the boot on his left foot came off. He slumped over his knees and dragged his right boot off. He slung them both towards a corner and lay back on his bed like Carter, fully dressed. He groaned and rubbed his face, trying to get some feeling back into his cheeks.

"Much more of this and we'll all be coming down with pneumonia," Carter said, his voice dull and listless.

"Much more of this," Walsh told him, his voice muffled behind his hands, "and I'll be breaking into the hospital to get the pox. I could do with a few weeks off."

Suddenly that sounded like a viable plan. Get chickenpox, get quarantined in the hospital. It would be a diet of warm beds, good food and lots of rest.

"Ah, but you might scar that pretty face of yours," Carter warned him, wagging an admonishing finger. Walsh was unconcerned.

"Better a few scars than be so cold that my little chap drops off." Carter laughed, his voice a braying neigh, his jaw tight from the cold. "No point getting myself a woman then," Walsh continued, "I won't be able to do anything to her."

"It won't be that bad," Carter got out between gasps of laughter.

"I hope not," Walsh replied, his tone serious.

Asher had them out shoveling snow the following day. Half dead, they trailed into the Mess at first light, loaded up with porridge laced with sugar and then shuffled outside. The more forward thinking individuals dug out their hip flasks and added a little extra kick in their porridge. Wrapped in as many layers as possible, Carter had lined up with the rest outside as they were divided up into work parties.

They shouldered their tools and got ready to move off. Stood next to him, Walsh nearly brained him with a shovel when they did a smart right turn and marched off to hangar one. A good couple of inches had come down overnight and snow covered the tops of their boots. They got busy shifting the snow into heaps by the hangar doors.

The good thing with being by the hangar is they could periodically nip inside for a warm. They could also go for a wee in a proper toilet without the risk of getting their boy frostbitten in the outside air. Miserable groups huddled behind the hangar walls to get out of the wind so they could have a smoke.

The snow stopped at lunchtime. By one o'clock the sun decided to peek out from behind the iron grey clouds. Cheeks welcomed the little bit of heat. After clearing the front of the hangar they were taken by Bedford out to the peri-track and were put to work clearing a section. Out in the open, the wind flailed them, the cold cutting them to the bone and numbing their senses.

Asher called time at four. No more snow was forecast and most of the important areas on the airfield had been cleared. Anything left over that needed finishing could be dealt with by the usual crop of defaulters over the next few days.

With no flying due to the weather, they were at liberty to go drinking. No one went very far. After a day in the cold, even the thought of slogging through the snow to the local pubs held little attraction. Most went to bed, a few stumbled to their respective Messes but it was a very subdued evening. Walsh had persuaded Carter to have a couple of drinks before turning in.

"If we go to bed too early, we'll only end up staring at the ceiling in the wee small hours," he had said.

"No," Carter corrected him. "I'll be staring at the ceiling, you'll be the one snoring, giving me a headache."

Walsh paused as he drank from his pint and looked at him over the top of the glass.

"Do I?" he asked, quite serious.

"You do. Loudly."

The following day was cold but the snow stayed away. The crews went out to the kites and ran them up. It was freezing in those metal tubes and they were very thankful to have heated flying suits. They plugged them in and were quite toasty while they checked their stations.

Nothing was forthcoming from Group. The word on the grapevine was that the snow of the last few days had moved east and covered Europe in a large fluffy blanket. While the mainland was socked in, the coasts were clear so the usual mining sorties went out but none of the Manchester's were called upon to fill in.

Frustrated at the lack of activity, Carter cast around for a new way to keep his crew occupied and keep them sharp. They could have gone on another flight to the bombing ranges at Wainfleet, but familiarity bred boredom.

When the crew truck was taking them back to the equipment hut, he had the WAAF drop them off at the hangars. Inside hangar three was a Manchester looking very worse for wear. One of the new crews had wrecked the undercarriage on landing the previous week and no one had come for it yet to take it to the depot. Carter had them all go inside and told them to adopt crash positions. He went up to the cockpit as did White. Everyone else took up position sitting behind the main spar. Todd produced a pack of cards and he started laying out a game of patience. Vos tugged a pulp novel out from a leg pocket and opened it where he'd marked a page by folding over the corner.

Once they were settled, Carter went through the checklist with White. Flaps to fifteen degrees, jettison fuel, check their Sutton harness. Jettison bombs? Jettison bombs. Lower the flaps to twenty five degrees, close the fuel jettison cocks.

"I think we're done," said Carter. White nodded his agreement. Carter looked back over his shoulder and shouted, "prepare to ditch!"

In the dim of the fuselage, Murphy put his hands up either side of his head and started making plane noises. He swooped left and right; Todd pushed him away in good humour.

"Neeeeeooooowwwww, plonk!" said Murphy, slapping his left hand against his legs.

"And we're down!" White shouted. Woods stood up and reached up to the escape hatch on top of the fuselage. They clambered out which was not so easy in bulky flying gear. They were laughing and joking about it but they all knew, doing this at night, in the dark with water pouring in, it would be no laughing matter.

Blinking as they emerged from the gloom, Carter stood on the canopy and watched as they gathered on top of the fuselage. Murphy and Todd straddled it, and pantomimed digging spurs into a horse. White had walked back and dropped down onto the starboard wing. Together with Woods they released the panel at the trailing edge of the wing and dumped it on the hangar floor. If they had actually ditched for real, the dinghy was designed to automatically inflate and deploy once the aircraft was in the water.

White and Woods pulled the rubber dinghy out and made a meal of it. They got vocal encouragement from the other three above them on the fuselage. Woods bit his tongue. It was not so easy pulling on the heavy rubberised dinghy, but he dug in and hauled it out and threw it over the side. A cord attached to the bay pulled on the dinghy and it inflated with a sudden hiss of air. It popped into shape on the concrete floor of the hangar.

They all slithered down onto the wing and then dropped into the dinghy. Carter had them check the contents, making sure they knew where the hand pump was and two of them broke out some crude oars and motioned rowing from the back of the dinghy. Woods went to the other end, put one foot on the top of the dinghy and aped tucking one hand into his flying suit, George Washington style.

"Row, row, row your boat, gently down the stream," sang Todd, with the line taken up by Murphy. Carter quietened them down as their laughter echoed around the hangar. It was just some play, but it was better than nothing and who knew, perhaps one day they might have to do it for real.

9 - One of those months

November was a bad month for 363 with a succession of accidents and mechanical problems. Around tea time on a windy Wednesday, the entire squadrons complement of aircrew were summoned by tannoy. They filed in and took their seats, curious. There were no ops on that evening so it was either a rush job or an announcement of some kind.

They found Asher pacing the stage in agitated circles when they came into the briefing hut. The gossip doing the rounds was that in the morning, Asher, the Adj and Church had disappeared in a rush so most people were leaning towards an announcement of some kind. Group Captain Etheridge stood at the back, grim faced with his arms folded. Saunderson was intently examining his nails, looking distinctly uncomfortable.

Asher waited until the doors were closed and then he strode forward to the edge of the stage. He planted his feet, bunched his hands on his hips and fixed the crowd with a hard stare.

"Certain events today make it necessary for me to bring you all together and make something *painfully* clear. In the next few days there will be the funerals of Flight Sergeant Edwards and Pilot Officer Altring and their crews."

A rustle of disquiet filled the room. Funerals on operational squadrons were rare. Funerals for whole crews were almost unheard of. It was an accepted fact of life that crews got the chop, but it was normally over foreign skies, blown into little pieces. Occasionally, a plane would make it back with wounded or casualties and medical orderlies would carry the dead away on stretchers.

Only the week before, Archer had lost yet another tail gunner. A JU88 had mauled the Manchester's rear before Archer dived for the ground. It was Archer who had scraped the bits of his gunner out of the turret; no one else had the nerve to do it. When they hosed down the turret afterwards; red spilled out of the holes as if the aircraft itself was bleeding.

Asher continued speaking.

"We know that every time we go up, we run a risk, it's the chance we all take. Edwards was lost on a training flight, those things happen. The other loss was avoidable and an absolute bloody waste."

Asher paused for a moment as fatigue washed over him. It had been a busy day. The first phone call had been from the Lancashire Constabulary. A policeman had been cycling round his beat when a Manchester had dived out of low lying cloud and caused a big hole on the moor. No chutes were seen and it had gone in almost vertical. The squadrons codes were still visible amongst the burning wreckage and a few checks soon had the phone call routed to Amber Hill.

It was soon established it was Edwards aircraft. A new crew with only two ops under their belt, they had been sent out to get some much needed practice on a navigation exercise.

The second phone call he received was an entirely different story. A Manchester had crashed next to the village of Fellholme after performing a series of low passes. On one of these low passes, witnesses reported that it had flown parallel to a row of terraced houses while it waggled its wings. The Manchester had clipped the trees as it climbed away. The wingtip and a few feet of wing parted company and took the aileron with it.

The bomber nosed in from thirty feet, cartwheeling across the fields and turning a perfectly serviceable aircraft to scrap and killing everyone on board. Further enquiries had revealed that a certain lady friend of Pilot Officer Altring lived in the end terrace.

By the time, Asher had got to the village, the fire brigade had put out the flames and all that was left were jagged bits of metal scattered over a field. Asher had spent some time staring at the six blanket shrouded mounds that were waiting to be taken away in ambulances. Saunderson had waited by the car with Church, talking to the Police officer who had been first on the scene.

"I don't much care about a man's personal life. What you get up to outside this station is a matter of supreme indifference to me; *but*," he paused, letting the word hang in the silence, looming over all of them. "When good men die, because one fool uses his aircraft to impress a bit of skirt then I have no choice but to become involved." He looked around the room, going from one face to another. His eyes were blazing in anger. "If you want to kill yourselves, you have my permission to go down to the armoury; hand over a shilling to pay for a bullet, draw a revolver from stores and go off beyond the butts. It's nice and quiet down there, you can blow your brains out with a bit of peace and quiet."

He was warming to his theme now and his voice was hard and flat, cracking like a whip on each syllable as he barely held his simmering temper in check. He had the rooms attention, each man absorbing every word like a sponge.

"If he'd not done such a good job of killing himself, then I would've had no hesitation in breaking, Mr Altring. There is no place for stunts and low flying on *this* squadron. Get yourself transferred to a Spitfire squadron or something, then you're only killing yourself.

Instead; Altring was a selfish *bastard*." Asher placed great inflection on bastard and everyone in the room flinched. "Yes, a selfish *bastard*. He took five other people with him and wasted a perfectly good airplane."

Asher had seen his fair share of accidents during his service life. Flying was a dangerous enterprise, but despite every admonition from instructors, when a pilot was given a powerful aircraft they got drunk on power. Roaring around the skies, they were tempted to make that turn just that little bit tighter, to dive that bit steeper. When there was a woman involved, that just drove them to take an even bigger chance.

Truth be told, Carter was no virgin himself. He'd thrown his Hampden around the sky as much as anyone else. He wanted to know the limits of the aircraft and there was really only one way to do that, but he'd never done it to show off for a girl. Corkscrewing at eight thousand feet was fine. Chucking it around at nought feet you might as well pencil yourself in for an appointment with Saint Peter and a pair of wings.

"NO. MORE. STUNTS!" Asher shouted. "NO. MORE. LOW. FLYING! If you get caught out, don't bother coming back because god help you when you land, because I won't." Asher looked over to the Group Captain. "Anything you'd like to add, sir?"

Etheridge just shook his head and did his best to look disappointed.

"No, I think you've covered just about everything I was going to say."

At that, Asher stalked from the stage, down the central aisle for the doors. The others trailed behind him. Chairs scraped as everyone came to attention.

Two days later the squadron filed down to the chapel, packed the pews and listened attentively while the Padre waxed lyrical about man having but a short time to live. It was grey outside which was appropriate to the mood of the day. They huddled against the cold in their best blue as they looked at the flag draped coffins while Asher read aloud the names of the twelve dead men. Carter flinched as the funeral party fired twelve shots into the leaden skies.

In the afternoon, Dickinson sent Carter up on a long navigational exercise, much as Edwards had done. North to the Tyne, turn left and then back down the west coast, a large box route. It was simple enough, but they would be lucky if they got home before it got dark. Carter skipped along to the cookhouse and asked for some sandwiches to take with them.

There was some good natured chat as they set off. Considering the mood of the last few days, Carter let them get it out of their system. Once they set a course north, they settled down and focused on the task at hand. Murphy called out landmarks from the nose as they sailed along. Woods marked out their track on his map, correcting for the wind.

Murphy silently grumbled to himself. Up front in the nose turret the meagre sun was shining through the perspex and giving him a headache. He was also cold. Frigid air rushed into the turret through the elevation slits and tickled his neck. He fiddled around, prodding and poking a silk scarf around to close the gaps. Since their first few trips, the 'who flew in what turret' arrangement with Todd had been modified. Now they took turns. Every trip they alternated who was in the tail, and a trip counted for the test flights in between as well.

The routine they had fallen into was that on outward bound trips, the one in the nose would throw out bundles of propaganda leaflets down the flare chute. Shoving a wad of paper down the chute twenty or thirty times with a broom handle was fun and helped kill some time.

Murphy's problem was that the flare chute was in the tail. To get there, he had to wiggle out of his turret, go up to the cockpit, squeeze past White and then clamber over the main spar. That was awkward enough on the ground. Throw in a pitch black fuselage, a vibrating airframe, bulky flying gear and numbed limbs and it left him sweaty, tired and grumpy. More often than not he banged his shins on something and once he was done chucking the bumf out, he had to retrace his route to get back to the turret. He couldn't wait until they got a different Manchester with a mid upper turret. Then he could just wriggle out of the turret and go about five steps to the flare chute instead.

He'd looked at one of the leaflets once. Kent had translated the German for him. It was pretty basic stuff, *Throw off your shackles, seize back your freedom. Do not suffer under the heel of National Socialism.* Garbage. All they were doing was giving the Jerrys some free toilet paper. Today he was in the nose, which meant it would be his turn to bugger about going back and forth to chuck out the leaflets the next time they went on an op.

While Murphy ruminated on the point of traversing the fuselage, things were not going so well in the cockpit. Both Carter and White had noticed a rise in temperature in the starboard engine. The port was rock solid for once but the starboard was behaving like an energetic puppy. Carter could physically feel it surging, the vibrations running through the controls in his hands, his seat and up and down his spine.

It would go up and down with little consistency. There would be a wave of sudden power before it faded away before picking up again. They made constant corrections, juggling the throttles, trying to find a sweet spot where it was happy but the instrument needles were going up and down like a fairground ride.

"Could be a blockage in the fuel pipe, or a fuel pumps buggered," suggested White. "That would explain why the throttle setting makes no apparent difference."

Carter frowned. His eyes scrunched up behind his goggles while he thought about that. White shrugged and gave the throttles another nudge. Flying Manchester's was certainly never boring. Engines could go bang at a moments notice; the hydraulics might break and that was just for starters.

At Blyth they turned left towards Dumfries. Carter went up to fifteen thousand feet but came back to ten after a strange vibration built up in the controls. They headed south. The vibration continued and Carter and White decided to call it quits although home was a good hour or more away. Woods gave them a steer and they cut the corner at Whitehaven, following the coast and crossing over Morecambe Bay. Fiften minutes later, the engine temperatures shot up alarmingly and this time they kept on climbing.

"We're not going to make home, Woody. I need something closer." He shared a look with White. "Better make that a *lot* closer."

Woods was already poring over his maps. He only had large scale maps for this side of England. He peered at the cramped symbols, figuring out their options.

"Make it one eight zero, skipper. Ringway, just south of Manchester."

Carter throttled back to spare the engines and traded height for speed, threading his way around the towns of Lancashire. Barrage balloons dotted these northern towns and they floated over the cramped back to back terraces and factories. Chimneys spewed smoke into the sky, casting a grey pall over the houses. A southern wind pushed the smog before it.

Murphy wrinkled his nose in distaste as a sulphurous tang stung his nostrils and he glowered at the chimneys of Wigan off to his right. An industrial centre, mills and factories surrounded the town which was a primary route on the canal between Liverpool and Leeds.

The large sprawl of Manchester was on the horizon and Ringway was on the far side of the city. The engine temperature was still creeping higher and Carter kept glancing at the altimeter, it was going to be close.

"What do you think?" he asked. White hunched his shoulders.

"Might hold. Then again we might explode or burst into flames."

"Oh, you're full of cheery thoughts."

The vibrations increased. The yoke juddered in his hands and even the instruments were starting to jump. Down in the tail, Todd was getting a headache from the shaking.

"Can we lay off the tap dance, boss? My fillings are starting to rattle."

"Ha," said Murphy with some relish. "Come up front, it's worse.

I'll trade you."

"No deal," cracked Todd. "You're up front, that's what we agreed."

The vibrations were not affecting how the bomber flew but it was a distinctly uncomfortable experience. Carter glanced at the port engine out of his window. Everything seemed fine, but the Vulture was like that. They could seduce you like a lover, make everything seem normal right up to the moment when they blew up on you.

They were down to fifteen hundred feet when they made it to Ringway. Carter could have brained Woods. One glance told him that the place was not an operational station. A menagerie or aircraft were parked all over the place. There were Whitleys, Ansons, Oxfords, Beaufighters, Halifaxes and even some single engined aircraft in Coastal Command colours. A runway ran roughly south west to north east and there were hangars both north and south of it.

Vos tried raising the tower but finding the right frequency was like finding a needle in the proverbial haystack. They made a few circuits while Carter got the lay of the land. He dropped the undercarriage to signal his intentions. Someone fired off a green flare from the tower. Carter looked around but saw nothing else in the sky so assumed it was for him. He continued to descend as they circled and had one last look around to size up his approach. The windsock by the tower was stiff and pointing straight south. Carter grimaced, that would make it a crosswind landing, just one more thing to cope with.

He had White drop the flaps and he came in from the south west. It was empty fields that side of the station, that way if anything happened and the engines did quit, they wouldn't have to worry about crashing into houses when they tried to put her down.

The vibration in the yoke was making his fingers tingle but he maintained control all the way. The wheels screeched as he thumped her down. It wasn't his best landing but he didn't care. They were down, style points cost nothing when you were nursing a sick aircraft. They turned off the runway and the bomber rocked as it rumbled over the grass. White pointed out two Manchester's by a north side hangar and Carter taxied over to them. He killed the engines and hit the brakes when they got within one hundred yards.

An assorted group of people came out of the hangars to look at this unexpected arrival. Some wore RAF blue; some wore brown factory workmen coats or other civilian clothing.

"Everyone all right?" he asked as his crew assembled under their bombers nose.

"Can I have a cushion to sit on?" asked Todd. "My bums gone numb."

"I'll settle for a bath," said White. He yawned and windmilled his arms. They watched as some of the men in brown coats walked towards them. One of them carried a clipboard and had that universally recognisable shop steward air.

"Can we help you?" he asked. His voice was clipped, daring them to try and be amusing. Carter hooked a thumb over his shoulder.

"Sick kite. Had to put down somewhere and this was the first place we came across."

The man sucked on his teeth as he flicked a glance to their aircraft. Carter had seen this look before. His father had taken the family car to a garage before the war and the mechanic had taken one look and sucked on his teeth like that. Then he'd rubbed his chin, tipped his cap from the back of his head to the front and then whistled tonelessly. You could almost see the pounds and shillings sign rolling behind his eyes when he told his father how much it was going to cost.

"Highly irregular," the man said. He looked at them like they had come from the moon.

Carter was starting to bristle. Bureaucratic little ticks like this wound him up. He was expecting him to say, *don't you know there's a war on,* next. A calming voice stopped any unpleasantness in its tracks.

"All right, Stevens. Let's get our guests a cup of tea and sort this out."

The officious older man nodded stiffly and spun on his heel, stalking off towards the hangar. That left them with the new arrival. Carter reckoned he was thirty odd. Dark hair was slicked back and a colourful silk scarf was wrapped around his throat. He walked towards them wearing a white shirt and Khaki officers' pants. A battered pair of flying boots completed his look.

"Welcome to Ringway. I'm, Andrews."

Carter made the introductions as Andrews looked up at their Manchester.

"What's wrong with her?" Andrews asked, looking at the Manchester with a critical eye. He spent his time flying factory fresh aircraft, it made a change to see an operational bird, even if it was broken.

"Starboard engines running hot," Carter told him. "Something else is up though. She was shaking fit to bust before we set down."

Andrews nodded, clearly interested.

"Not to worry. Follow me, we'll let your people know where you are and get this all sorted out." He led them back to the nearest hangar.

As they got closer, Carter saw the winged, triangular AVRO logo on the hangar above the doors. That explained the civilians in brown work coats but that was not what drew his eye. He looked at the second Manchester they had seen from the air. The fuselage was right, but it had a bigger wing and had four engines in streamlined nacelles instead of two Vultures. The underside was painted yellow and a yellow P in a circle was on the side of the fuselage. Carter had heard rumours a new version of the Manchester was on the way but this was the first time he had seen it. Andrews saw where Carter was looking and smiled. He was rather proud of her.

"Ah, I might have to ask you all to sign a bit of paper about that; loose lips and all that."

They crossed the hangar and were shown in to an office. The older man held out a phone. Carter took it and asked to be put through to Amber Hill. He perched on the edge of the desk and swung his left leg back and forth while he waited. Andrews brought him a cup of tea and a sandwich and Carter nodded his thanks.

The crew left him to deal with the call and went back outside. Undoing their bulky flying gear, they leaned back against the side of the hangar. Todd wadded up his jacket and lay down, his forage cap covering his eyes.

Ringway was a busy airfield. Since 1940, it had been the home of the No.1 Parachute Training School. No.14 Ferry Pool of the ATA also operated from there to deliver the hundreds of aircraft built by Fairey who were based on the north side of the airfield. They were awarding some returning Whitley's marks out of ten for their landing when Carter returned from his phone call.

Slurping on a fresh cup of tea he slumped down next to Woods and White who were playing chess on a small travel game set. Woods always carried one with him in his navigator's' bag, just in case.

"What's the news, skip?" he asked absently as he studied the board. He rubbed the pad of his thumb against his lips.

"Bloody shambles. It'll be tomorrow before they get some mechanics out to us to take a look."

"I might be able to help there," Andrews interjected. "You're here. It would be churlish to sit back and do nothing when you've brought an Avro kite to an Avro workshop." He let the hint trail away.

"You really mean it?" Carter was thinking the browncoats would be less than pleased.

"Of course I mean it. It's the least we can do. I should have *some* pull around here."

"Thanks awfully," said Carter.

"Think nothing of it," replied Andrews.

The crew watched with professional interest as some platforms were wheeled out of the hangar and placed around their Manchester. The cowlings came off the engines and the mechanics had a rummage. It was a matter of minutes before there were exclamations of surprise and Andrews was called over to take a look.

There was some pointing and gesticulation and a crowd gathered on the right side of the starboard engine. Chewing on a sandwich, Carter picked himself up and sauntered over to see what all the fuss was about.

"Now what?" Woods asked.

"No idea," said White. "You know how civvies flap. Check by the way." Woods turned his attention back to the chess board and frowned. "Check," repeated White. "I moved my horsey." He pointed to the knight.

"What's the problem?" asked Carter, talking around a mouthful of bread and bully beef. He peered up at the knot of men who were stood on the platform, staring at the engine.

"You're a very lucky boy," said Andrews. He got down next to Carter and pointed upwards, circling an area. The engine mount on the outside of the engine was completely burned through. He glanced at the cowling leaning against the scaffold and saw the scorch marks on the paintwork. Carter whistled between his teeth.

"Strewth."

"An understatement," said Andrews, deadpan. "You said the controls were vibrating?" he asked. Carter nodded; his eyes riveted to the engine.

"Yes, for a good hour."

"And the engine temperatures were high?"

"Yes, but not always. Power had been surging and the instruments had been going up and down like billyo."

Andrews nodded soberly, filing those things away. As a test pilot for Avro he was intimately familiar with the Vulture and all its little ways. He had worked for months with the engineers from Rolls Royce to address the issues reported by the operational squadrons. What was rare was to actually have an aircraft survive a catastrophic failure like this so it could be inspected. A few Manchester's had landed safely or force landed after a failure, but often, an aircraft lost on training or operations didn't leave enough evidence to identify the cause.

Carter saw just how close they had come to disaster today. With the mount burned through, there was not much to keep the engine in place. He had little doubt the vibrations he'd felt through the controls was the engine bouncing around inside the nacelle. Any sudden movement and the engine could have torn loose and doomed all of them. It was a lucky escape indeed.

Andrews and Carter went back to the office in the hangar to make some phone calls. Plans changed. Avro engineers at Ringway would inspect L-London and Rolls Royce would fly up to have a look at the engine. Andrews interviewed Carter and White about the flight and he made notes so he would have something to give the Rolls Royce boys when they turned up. The crew was driven to a nice hotel in Manchester, guests of Avro. They enjoyed the plush beds, turned the heating up, soaked in the bath and then took advantage of the tab Andrews put behind the bar for them. They were flown back to Amber

Hill the following morning by a delightful brunette from the ATA pool.

They made it back in time for lunch and Carter discovered he was not the only one to have suffered a mishap. Walsh was surrounded by a crowd of amazed onlookers. He was just telling the tale again when Carter and Woods sauntered into the Mess.

Woods and Carter came over and had drinks pressed into their hands. Walsh's complexion was a ruddy red and he rubbed his face again on a towel. He made exaggerated tasting motions with his mouth as he downed most of a pint.

"Go on," one of the throng urged.

"Again?" He scratched a patch of sore and irritated skin behind his left ear. "Really?" He yawned and stretched. They howled in protest at the delay. He grinned, playing to the crowd. "Well, I'll tell you," said Walsh, warming to his theme.

His was a short cautionary tale. The total flying time had been a mere eight minutes and it took nearly that long to tell the story. While the squadron was abuzz with the news of Carters adventures, Walsh had taken off that morning for a short air test. The erks had been tinkering with the engines and they'd asked him to make sure everything was operating normally.

Climbing away from the airfield there had been a sudden bang inside the cockpit. The hydraulic system had failed in spectacular style. Under 400lbs of pressure, the air was instantly filled with fine drops of oily hydraulic fluid, coating the controls, the instruments, the canopy and everyone in the cockpit.

At such low altitude, no one was on oxygen yet so Walsh got a mouthful of it. He had to hang on flying straight and level with his eyes screwed tight shut, tears streaming down his face. He choked as it caught at the back of his throat. Everything was coated in a film of hydraulic fluid, including his clothes, so when he rubbed his face with the sleeve of his flying jacket, that only made it worse.

Eyes burning, everything was a watery blur but he could see just enough to know where the horizon was. He kept his Manchester level and shouted for help.

"Someone get up here with a rag to get this crap off my face," he shouted.

His navigator, similarly affected, blindly scrabbled his way up and handed over a handkerchief. Walsh rubbed it across his eyes doing his best to get the worst of the fluid off. He kept blinking and opened the cockpit side window. As he cracked it an inch, there was a huge howl of suction and the oil laden air was sucked out of the cockpit. The noise, already loud was now unbearable but it was a small price to pay to get clean air to breathe. He spat to clear his throat and was still doing it two hours later when Carter came into the Mess.

Once he could see again, it was a simple matter to do a fast circuit, blow the wheels down with the emergency bottle and land as quickly as possible. Walsh had bathed to wash off the oil but his eyes still stung and were an angry manic red. His nostrils burned, his throat was sore and he could still taste the stuff on his tongue. Someone gave him another pint to wash the taste it away but it made little difference to his taste buds.

Carter knew Walsh had a very lucky escape. One spark in such an oil impregnated air mix could have turned the entire aircraft into a raging inferno, with Walsh and his crew the Roman candles.

The final highlight of the week was a moment of horror mixed with pure dumb luck and Carter had a grandstand seat. While L-London was still at Ringway, he'd had a late breakfast and went for a walk along the perimeter track. He'd gotten bored of being asked about the engine failure as had Walsh about his hydraulics adventure and the pair of them had gone for a stroll to the far side of the airfield.

Carter sat down on a frost covered mound of frozen earth. He fished a hip flask out of the pocket of his greatcoat and offered it to Walsh. His room mate unscrewed the lid and took a quick nip. The alcohol burned on the way down but he still couldn't really taste it.

"How long do you think it'll be before we get our girls back?"

"End of the week?" suggested Carter. "It can't take them too long to change an engine out surely? Yours just needs a wipe down."

"Funny man," said Walsh, his thick Liverpudlian accent mangling it.

He glanced up as the sound of engines starting thundered across the airfield. Carter and Walsh watched as the bomber trundled down the runway. The tail came up in good time and the pilot held it there, letting the speed increase before lifting off.

Despite the love/hate relationship, Carter never tired of watching the Manchester in the air. He loved the sleek lines, the rounded nose and the roar of the engines. It passed almost overhead and he saw the ID letter, N-Nan, Andrews aircraft; one of his rookie crews from OTU. The wheels came up and the Manchester climbed away, clawing for height.

Carter stood up and brushed the frost off his backside. They'd just turned to start walking back when they heard a loud bang above them. They looked up, transfixed as they saw a long banner of flame trail back from the Manchester's port engine.

Already, Andrews had dropped the nose and was looking for somewhere to land. Carter watched with a professional eye. Engine failures on takeoff were not unheard of. When it happened, you got it down as quickly and as fast as you could. At low speed and low altitude, there was little margin to get creative.

"Oh my god!" exclaimed Walsh. "What the hell is he doing?"

They stood, rooted to the spot in morbid fascination as Andrews came around, trying to make the field. Hovering just above stalling speed, he rolled left and leaned on the rudder.

"I have no idea," replied Carter. He'd drummed into Andrews time and time again, if your engine failed, you never, ever turned back and you never, ever turned into a dead engine.

Andrews carried on through the turn. The angle steepened. The wings canted over and the nose slid past the horizontal. Any second Carter expected the Manchester to fall out of the sky. Then, a miracle happened. Andrews levelled off, dropped the undercarriage and came straight in.

"I don't believe it," said Carter, his voice almost a whisper.

"He's had the angels watching him today," observed Walsh, shocked by what he had just seen. By every known aviation law Andrews should have been wrapped in a smoking pile of wreckage on the grass. The man must be blessed. At the very least it called for a few virgin WAAF's to be sacrificed to appease the gods.

"Well don't just stand there," he shouted at Carter as he ran towards the Manchester which had just touched down further up the field.

After so many mechanical problems so close together, Group acted fast. 363 were grounded pending further investigation. The ground staff felt this keenly, feeling the finger for these problems was pointing in their direction. With an intact example of another engine failure, Rolls Royce sent their experts to Amber Hill to take a look. N-Nan was wheeled into the hangar for inspection and relieved of her port engine. Particular attention was paid to the newly changed oil pump and filter but Carter thought they were just guessing and dressing it up as being thorough. Until Group had some answers that either indicated a fundamental design problem or poor work practices, 363 were on the ground.

Over gossip in the Mess, Carter discovered this was not the first time this had happened. The squadron had been grounded shortly after it was formed, again due to engine problems. The enforced inactivity made him twitchy. He was used to an operational tempo of at least one op a week, sometimes two, sometimes three. Even allowing for winter weather, he wasn't used to being parked on his duff, doing nothing.

L-London was returned from Ringway by Andrews. He explained what had happened over lunch, while the erks fussed over what had been done to her.

Stripping the engine down, they'd found the front bearings had become starved of oil. Normally, when Vultures overheated, they either burst into flames or threw a con rod when the bolts failed. In this instance, the engine casing had become so hot it had actually melted and burnt through the engine mounting arm. The whole time

Carter had felt vibration through the controls, was in fact the engine rocking from side to side in its mounting.

Carter thought about what a week it had been. Six aircraft down, three crews gone and only one of them lost to enemy action. Carter always knew ops could be dangerous, but this week had highlighted just how deadly the Manchester's could be. With an aircraft like that, who needed enemies?

10 - Tremors

The corridors of power in the Air Ministry echoed to the sound of feet striding down the polished halls. Tugging on his sleeves, Sir Richard Peirse fumed as he was shown to the meeting room. Only the week before, as the head of Bomber Command, he had been carpeted by the Prime Minister at Chequers after a dreadful night raid to Berlin.

The press headlines had been upbeat, squawking the propaganda line about smashing the Hun. In fact, it had been a near disaster. The main force had lost over twelve percent that night. Even though the experts were predicting storms, thick cloud, hail and probable icing he had sent them to bomb the big city. It had been a bad mistake, a costly one too, with thirty seven aircraft lost on that raid and others that had gone out that night.

Churchill had lashed him with figures, the gruff voice that was so familiar over the radio berated him for taking too many risks with his squadrons. In four months, Bomber Command had lost five hundred twenty six aircraft and crews, the equivalent of their entire front line strength.

Peirse knew where the figures had come from, Churchill's pet attack dog Baron Cherwell; Baron Berlin he was called behind his back. He was Churchill's leading scientific advisor, and never a day went by when he did not write a missive to the Prime Minister on subjects as diverse as redistributing shipping to the Atlantic or maximising egg production.

Born to German parents, he had that haughty German manner one sees in the Prussians and strong ideas on science and the advancement of society. A loyal friend to Churchill he had accompanied him on a trip to Germany in 1932 and been one of the few to see the growing shadows of war, even when everyone else did not.

Cherwell's personal brainchild was the statistical department, S-Branch, that collated millions of pieces of information to produce detailed analysis on a variety of subjects. Churchill did everything at a fast pace, he liked to have information at his fingertips and Cherwell and his statisticians provided it.

Peirse said nothing while fact after fact was trotted out to question the entire bombing effort. He knew the source of those figures too. Cherwell's secretary, David Bensusan-Butt had written a report that had crossed Peirse's desk in the middle of August. Peirse knew Bomber Command was under scrutiny. It was a behemoth that sucked up supplies, men and vital war material. Avaricious eyes would have been very happy to appropriate those resources for their own area of war.

Each four engined Short Stirling bomber drank over two thousand gallons of petrol and carried 14,000lb of bombs on a single raid. It had a crew of seven trained men who more often than not had spent the best part of the last eighteen months being trained in their trade. Times that by twenty or so for a squadron, times the number of squadrons by twenty, thirty, forty. That was an expensive night's work. The thing was, Bomber Command were just about the only ones taking the fight to the enemy and Peirse had said so, standing his ground and fighting his corner.

When Britain found itself alone after the miracle of Dunkirk, the three services discovered that the usual pecking order had been upset. The RN was doing what it had always done, keeping the sea lanes open and shepherding vital supplies to England, running the gauntlet of the U-Boat packs to do it. Unable to challenge the might of the German army on its own, the army had been relegated to the fringes of the action in North Africa against Rommel. That had left the RAF leading the offensive.

That fact had not gone unnoticed. The propaganda machine was hard at work, painting a picture of fighting men standing up to the Hun, even when the newspaper headlines were bleak elsewhere. During the summer, cinemas had been filled while people watched the plucky crew of F for Freddie going in at low level to duff up Jerry and give him a thrashing in *Target For Tonight*. It was good stuff and something that raised public awareness of what the RAF was doing. The RAF was fighting a battle every few days. Crews were going out into the dark night after night, reporting they had pranged the target and given Jerry another bloody nose, six of the best.

The thing was, this glittering vision of success came entirely from crew interrogations. Asking questions of men after they landed, hopped up on coffee and adrenalin, ears buzzing after hours in the air was perhaps not the best way of getting an accurate assessment of damage done. Aware of these limitations, earlier in the year, Bomber Command had fitted certain aircraft with cameras that went off when the bombs were dropped so the aiming point could be assessed. Reconnaissance aircraft also flew over in daylight to photograph targets and provide updates. That information was combined from what was known of the effects of the Germans blitz on England's own cities to estimate the affects on German industry.

When Butt's report landed it had gone off like a proverbial

bomb. Contrary to the prevailing view, Butt's analysis contended that only about one third of all aircraft actually reached their target and even that was only defined as getting within five miles of the aiming point in the first place. A third of all aircraft dispatched had not even managed that and when Butt analysed target information for the Ruhr those figures got worse.

Peirse knew there were new aircraft and navigational aids on the horizon, but that didn't help when the Prime Minister was flaying him with neat little charts that spelled out in stark terms the cost of waging war on Germany. Some people argued the cost was too high.

Coastal Command would have no hesitation in taking as many bomber squadrons as they could lay their hands on to patrol the convoy routes. Providing an airborne shield over the convoys might just deter a few more U-boats and let a few more convoys through. Putting more food on tables was an influential argument to divert resources from Bomber Command.

Peirse had called a meeting of his senior commanders and they had walked through Butt's report backwards and forwards. There were some hard truths in its pages. They all knew that bad weather played merry hell with navigation. New moon periods increased accuracy but also made things easier for the German nightfighters. Butt's report didn't have to make the choices these men made. Cold facts didn't take into account the compromises any commander had to face when sending his troops off to war.

Professional pride was stung. Butt was wrong, his statistics were faulty it was claimed. More simply, Butt was a statistician, what did he know about analysing photographs? He was twisting things to suit his conclusion went another argument.

The RAF fought back, their way. The Directorate of Bombing Operations delivered their response in September, concluding that a force of bombers could flatten German towns. How many bombers would that take they were asked? Four thousand was the response. Sir Charles Portal, Chief of the Air Staff went to bat and argued such a force of bombers could win the war in six months.

This was an old argument that had been heard before. During the inter war years, the phrase, 'the bomber shall always get through' had been used a number of times to keep the RAF funded. No one had ever considered the possibility that a bomber might get through but miss when it got there; now they were being told exactly that in Butt's report. The casualty figures showed not everyone got through either. Now Portal was arguing that with more aircraft they would be able to deliver the killer blow. Not everyone was convinced.

When he had returned to Bomber Command from Chequers, Peirse had half expected to find his posting on his desk. Churchill hated failure and he could be ruthless when the mood took him. In

North Africa he had swiftly replaced Wavell with Auchinlek. Peirse had no doubts he could suffer a similar fate in an instant if things did not improve.

He sent his bombers out two nights later, but he kept it small, one hundred aircraft. Hamburg was an easier target and only one Wellington was lost, but the damage to Bomber Commands prestige had been done. The seeds of doubt had been planted.

Summoned back to the Air Ministry on the 13th November, he had been pensive during the drive over. The summons had been suitably vague which was never a good sign. Civil servants could be quite cruel, a symptom Peirse was convinced was a result of that bastion of English gentility, the public school system. Ritual humiliation, fagging for your betters and being filled with lashings of Kipling and affirmations of colonial superiority could warp a fellow.

It was therefore with some apprehension that he was shown into the room to find Air Chief Marshall Portal stood by the marble fireplace. He was in mufti, dressed in a dark blue three piece suit, the twinkle of a watch chain visible across the waistcoat. Two of his secretaries were off to one side and Cherwell was sitting behind a heavy dark table topped in dark green leather. It was not lost on Peirse that a single chair was on one side of the table and everyone else's was on the other.

He was served tea but apart from one sip, he didn't touch it. The cup and saucer remained untouched on the table, slowly cooling. There was the usual small talk, but the tone was stilted, everyone aware of an as yet unnamed elephant in the room with them. Portal gestured to the chair and Peirse girded himself for the grilling to come.

"My dear, Richard, so good of you to come," said Portal, his voice friendly, as if this was how he talked every day when someone was about to get the chop. "I hope the drive wasn't too tiresome for you."

Peirse fumed on the way back to Bomber Command. Civil servants had intruded on the lawn and stuck their noses where they didn't belong and he was now going to have to pick up the pieces. His staff officer refrained from asking what had happened, one look told him the chief wanted some time to himself.

The Chief of the Air Staff was not unsympathetic to the situation. Portal himself had been AOC of Bomber Command in 1940 before being made Air Chief Marshall. He knew how difficult the job was, but despite his sympathies for his successor, the political landscape was very different now. There was also the personal connection. Peirse had been at the RAF Staff College with Portal in 1922 but even that was not enough to spare him from the full weight of political disapproval.

Politics was a matter of brinkmanship, balancing competing interests towards a common goal and at the critical moment, the Butt report had shown that Bomber Command was not measuring up. Butt and Cherwell had done their work well. Bomber Command itself had been the chicken on the chopping block, with the blade only an inch away from the neck.

The Air Staff had been able to argue that even if heavy bombing on its own did not win the war, it couldn't be questioned that a sustained bombing campaign would weaken their resolve. Even the Prime Minister couldn't argue with the logic of that. He knew that if you asked anyone on the street what they wanted to see done to the Germans, they would say they deserved a blitz of their own, in return for what had been done to Coventry, Liverpool and a host of other places. It had been a close call. Peirse took what few crumbs of comfort he could. Bomber Command would continue and he had his head.

Two days later, Group Captain Etheridge, was stood at the window to his office when Asher answered his summons. Located in the main admin building, Etheridge's office was on the upper floor. He had chosen a corner office with windows that allowed him to see the wide expanse of the airfield. The other side looked out over a sea of Nissen huts and low brick buildings that made up the layout of any wartime airfield. Despite the cold, he had the window cracked an inch so he could hear what was going on outside.

In the week since the squadron had been grounded, the usual sounds were missing and he was agitated at the inactivity. Airfields were places where planes flew and the air was filled with the sound of aero engines. At the moment, all he had was the sound of the wind in the trees and vehicles moving around. Occasionally he heard the tramp of feet as defaulters were marched to and from their allotted tasks.

He thought about the meeting at Group the previous evening. With no knowledge of what had happened further up the chain of command, when Etheridge had been called to Group, he was expecting trouble. Amber Hill was his station, a failure reflected on him. Like the erks, he had felt the grounding order as a personal slight on his competency. He had a feeling his career was about to crash for the final time.

Etheridge had known AOC 5 Group, Jack Slessor a long time. He had been his Flight Commander on the North West Frontier in 1922. Where Slessors career had seen a steady rise, Etheridge's own career had been far more pedestrian. A flying accident had stalled his promotion and when he emerged from hospital a year later in 1928, he found his contemporaries had skipped ahead of him. It was not until the pre-war expansion that he got his chance to rise up the ranks to Group Captain.

He was relieved when he found the other station commanders were also in attendance. Last to arrive, he had just taken a seat at one end of the table when Slessor came in from the door at the other end, his staff officer flanking him.

There was a knock at the door and Etheridge came back from his introspection as he called for them to come in. Asher entered and stood in front of Etheridge's desk, coming to attention and snapping off a salute. The Group Captain acknowledged his presence with a hint of a nod and continued staring out of the window. The sky was a hard iron grey, the clouds mere streaks as the brisk wind shoved them around. There was rain there, he thought, lurking just over the horizon ready to come down.

He closed the window, thumping the latch home before sitting down at his desk. He fussily straightened some folders that offended his sense of symmetry and order and then looked at Asher. His squadron commander waited patiently, composed. Etheridge had known Asher six months, since the squadron had been formed and come to Amber Hill. He had watched him take a bunch of men and mould them into a unit. It had been a hard struggle. Few of the original crews had much experience to stiffen the ranks and provide some seasoning.

Asher had to do things the hard way, leading from the front and encouraging his flight commanders to do the same. Gradually, they had come together but Etheridge knew that Asher felt there was something lacking. They had discussed it more than once in this very office but it had been hard to define. They both knew that their aircraft played no small part in this malaise. Crews had to have confidence in their tools and at the moment, they didn't have it. The recent spate of mishaps had unnerved the men and the only thing that was going to cure that was a good few operations under their belt.

"I hope the Rolls Royce men are being given every facility?" he asked Asher.

"Of course, sir. My instructions have been clear, but it's not the first time they've been. Our lads know what to do."

Etheridge nodded and grunted in response. Rolls Royce had been here twice already. It had felt odd, allowing a bunch of civilians onto the station, but they were there to make things better after all.

"Good. Is there any estimate on how much longer they'll be?"

"Two more weeks I would imagine, sir. There's a lot left to check. Pullen is giving me updates but progress is slow."

While everyone else had it relatively easy, as the squadrons Engineering Officer, Pullen had been rushing around trying to fulfill every demand. The first task after the grounding had been to pull the Form 700's for each aircraft and start acquainting himself with each aircrafts history before the Rolls Royce bods turned up. Since then he had been hovering in the background while they came up with snag lists and dictated what work needed to be done. After that it was a matter of coordinating the ground crews and making sure the right spares were available. Rolls Royce and Avro were ferrying in what they were short of.

"What are you doing about the crews in the meantime?"

"The usual, sir. Ground lectures, a bit of PT. Montgomery had the gunners out at the butts earlier in the week." Etheridge nodded; he had heard the racket as the men had blazed off an indecent amount of rounds at paper targets.

Asher had toyed with some kind of escape and evasion exercise but decided not to. The last time they had done something like that, two men had ended up in hospital after being 'captured' by the local territorials and trying to escape by jumping out of the moving truck. One had landed badly and broken an ankle and the other one had bounced off a fallen tree trunk and given himself concussion.

"I think in the circumstances we could hand out a few passes," Etheridge suggested. He didn't like the thought of mass leave, but there was little else for the crews to do. He had seen the building pressure cooker atmosphere amongst the men. If there were many more ground lectures or drills there would be rebellion. Bored aircrew made for trouble.

These men had been living on pure adrenalin and fear for the last few months, living each day as if it might be their last. This sudden halt to the normal proceedings had produced an ugly mix of pent up feelings. Two men had already been arrested for trying to get back on the airfield via the fence rather than the main gate. Only this morning a few men had been retrieved from the cells in Lincoln after overstaying their welcome in town. Asher had smoothed things over with the local Inspector but that would not always work. With so many airfields around Lincoln, the Police were robust in dealing with transgressions.

"I'll sort something out. Considering what's going on I'll make most of them seventy twos. The married men and those with further to go can have seven days."

Unmarried himself, Asher was not so churlish that he was going to make things difficult for others. There was little enough pleasure in this life and they could all be dead tomorrow.

"As soon as we're operational, I want us to hit the ground running," Asher said with some conviction.

"You might find the pace of things slowing down," Etheridge cautioned, his voice noncommittal. Asher's brow pinched in interest. The old man was not normally so circumspect. Everybody knew that operations were always curtailed over the winter months due to the bad weather but they would persevere as they always did.

"There's been a change of direction," Etheridge told him,

unburdening himself finally. Asher blinked rapidly, waiting for the punch line. "Air Ministry take the view that we need to conserve our forces for the good weather in the spring."

So that was what had happened at Group, Asher told himself. He had seen Etheridge going out the door like a scalded cat at the time, but there had been no sign that anything was particularly wrong when he returned. Asher thought about the raids of recent weeks.

Casualties had made things difficult to be sure. While 363's chop rate was no worse than anyone else's, everyone knew the Berlin job had been a balls up from start to finish. It had been a stroke of good fortune that 5 Group had gone to Cologne and avoided the bad weather. Asher thought it would have been cheaper if Bomber Command had just taken a few hundred of their men round the back of a shed and shot them.

Etheridge drummed his fingers on the desk top.

"The Butt report's stirred things up a bit," he said in clipped tones.

Asher nodded, keeping his face neutral. He'd not read it himself but he had heard the highlights from a friend at Group. Frankly he thought it was a load of old cods, but he was also aware of the stink it had caused in the higher echelons.

"It's felt in some circles that if it was to ever see the light of day in the press there would be hell to pay."

"*If*, this boffins right," Asher commented pointedly.

"I know, Peter," Etheridge soothed, "I know. But when have the members of the press ever let facts get in the way of a good story? Personally, I don't think these academic types can tell their arse from their elbow. They've never been on a raid, what on earth do they know about what's going on?" He shrugged, "But there it is. For the time being, Bomber Command will be limiting its offensive operations until we get better weather in the Spring. Once we're declared operational again, we have a real chance to use the lull to build the squadron back up, increase the tempo of training so we can be ready for whatever lies ahead."

11 - The Big City

Saunderson had a heart attack when Asher casually shoved his head around the door of his office and announced the whole squadron would be going on leave. As it was unknown exactly how long it would be before the squadron would be declared operational, Asher hedged his bets and sent them off in two batches. Robinson beat Church two out of three at paper, scissors, stone so 'B' Flight got to go first.

Those with further to go got seven days leave regardless of whether they were married or not. That may have sounded generous but Saunderson and the CO both knew that with intermittent trains and missed connections, a chap might spend half of their leave going back and forth in rickety carriages. Regardless, leave was leave and transport was laid on to get them to Lincoln train station.

Carter packed light. He had one medium sized suitcase and his gas mask bag. He wore his greatcoat, it saved him from having to carry it. Besides, it was a dull day and a train platform could be icy cold. He gathered his crew under the Ionic portico of the St Marks station before they went their separate ways.

"Two of us are on for Sheffield, skipper," said Murphy.

"Watch out for the Police," Carter warned. "I don't want to get a phone call from some magistrate asking me to be a character reference."

"We'll be good," Todd assured him.

"See that you do," Carter told them sternly. He fished in the pockets of his greatcoat for his gloves.

"No fear," said White. "Home for me." He was already thinking of some good home cooking and sitting in the parlour with his feet up, being warmed by the range.

"What about you two?" Carter asked Vos and Woods. Woods shrugged and spoke for both of them.

"Not sure." Strangers in a strange land, they were stuck. Vancouver was thousands of miles away and Vos couldn't go home even if he wanted to.

"We could go to London," Carter suggested.

"That sounds good," said Woods. "I haven't seen much of England since I came over from Canada."

"Agreed," said Vos. The Belgian Government in Exile was in

London and he wanted to make some enquiries about his family.

They got their tickets and waited on the platform. Todd and Murphy got away first on the Sheffield train. Walsh went with them to get the connecting train to Liverpool. Vos, Woods and Carter caught the later Cleethorpes train to King's Cross.

They got a compartment to themselves and Woods slept on the way down. Vos taught Carter a card game, Klaberjass. It was a strange game involving a thirty two card deck, tricks or trumps and bidding for points. Carter had trouble following the instructions but it helped pass the time.

Carter avoided asking about how Vos got out of Belgium and listened to him talk about his family instead. He was quite animated as he talked about his father, a baker. He had no siblings and only a small extended family, all he had was one Uncle, an Aunt and two cousins. All of them lived in a small village just outside of Ghent.

"Not long now and the canals would freeze over," he mused, staring out the window of the carriage as the countryside whipped by. He thought about the flat land around the mill, the network of canals at the back of his house. When it was really cold, he would skate up and down on the ice.

They got in to King's Cross at seven. There was a sea of uniforms of every colour, milling around in different directions on the platform. Some where running to catch a train, others were heading for the exit. There were few taxi's so Carter led the way and down from St Pancras they hopped on a bus.

They got rooms in a small Knightsbridge Hotel, *The Avalon*. The lobby was like stepping back in time. Wood panelled walls had faded prints in dusty frames and the carpet had a thin threadbare appearance. The concierge gave them two rooms at the back of the hotel on the top floor that were basic but clean.

Carter had a small window that provided a view of chimney stacks of various architectural styles and a slate covered roof. Barrage balloons in the background completed the look. The wallpaper was peeling on one wall by the wardrobe. Woods and Vos were in the larger room next door with their own bathroom and a bath. They dumped their gear and headed straight out. It was getting towards nine o'clock but they wanted to make the most of their time.

Over drinks in a pub they thrashed out a general plan for the next few days. Woods wanted to see Big Ben and Trafalgar Square, Buckingham Palace and Hyde Park. Vos wanted to go to the Belgian government building and then a few art galleries. Carter was easy. He knew London quite well so he had no problem being the tour guide.

They bought a newspaper and looked over the theater and cinema listings for the following night while they sipped their pints. There were quite a few variety shows on and they settled on ones where the primary feature was dancing girls. For the cinema, they picked out a few titles that intrigued them, avoiding the more obvious propaganda films. They had enough war back at Amber Hill, they didn't need to see it on the silver screen as well.

They moved on from the first pub, their tunic pockets filled with beer bottles. The streets were dark in the blackout and there was little moon light to show them the way. Walking the streets, they popped out at Hyde Park and Carter took them left until they got to the Royal Albert Hall.

They crossed over to the Albert Memorial. The grass around it had been turned over to cultivation and there were rows of turnips and cabbages along the tree lined avenue. An old man was sitting in a small wooden hut, guarding the vegetables from being pinched. He gave the three of them a suspicious look as they sat down on the steps leading up to the memorial. The Gothic canopy of the memorial covered an altar and a seated statue of the dead Prince. In the dark, gold highlights glinted, hinting at the intricate decorations.

They listened to the night time sounds of a city putting itself to bed. Even with petrol rationing, there were still vehicles on the roads. Red buses travelled their routes and a few taxis plied their trade. Behind them were the natural sounds of Hyde Park. The trees rustled, the bare branches swaying while squirrels scampered around in the grass.

Contrary to their expectations, they were in bed by eleven. Months of being geared for war finally caught up with them and they were asleep as soon as their heads hit their pillows

They slept late. They were less than impressed when they tumbled downstairs to find the that the dining room was no longer serving breakfast. They migrated down the road to Harvey Nichols and had toast and cups of tea in the restaurant. Carter winced when the bill came. They paid up and left without leaving a tip. Delivering a pot of tea and toast didn't warrant one.

They split up but arranged to meet up later at Trafalgar Square. That would give Vos time to do what the wanted and leave room for dinner before the evening's entertainment. Woods and Carter took the short walk back to Hyde Park.

An army Corporal threw them a salute as he strolled past with his girl hanging off his arm. They passed an old gentleman sitting on a bench, reading a book, his flask and sandwiches next to him. Every so often he threw a tidbit which was snatched up by a waiting red squirrel.

They went round the north side of the Serpentine following the path by the bank. The water was dark and still, thick with cold. Both of them were amazed to see people swimming by the lido on the south bank.

"Freeze the brass balls off a monkey," muttered Carter, shuddering at the thought of willingly getting into the water at this time of year.

They walked through the columned arch at Hyde Park corner and down the tree lined avenue of Constitution Hill towards Buckingham Palace. There was scaffolding up around the north wing where the palace had been damaged by German bombs the year before.

Woods was disappointed to find the palace was a lot smaller than he'd been expecting. He'd thought it would be this massive sprawling building with liveried footmen wandering around. What he got was guardsmen at the gate in standard army khaki. It was a bit of a let down after seeing all those pictures in school books of men in ceremonial red jackets and big black bearskins.

They went through St James's Park over to Big Ben. They waited to hear it chime at two and then sauntered down to Westminster Bridge. There was a man there with a stall selling chestnuts. Carter bought two bags and they watched the river traffic while they ate. Barges went up and down the Thames, shoving loads of coal. On the horizon were the cranes around Docklands in the East End.

When they got to Trafalgar Square, Carter relaxed on a bench while Woods walked all the way round the towering monument to Nelson. He straddled one of the great bronze lions and looked around. He liked the energy of the place. The square was busy with a constant stream of people hurrying to and fro.

Pigeons fluttered around him, disturbed by his presence. Wings beating, they looked for somewhere to perch. A big fat one settled on the head of the lion and looked at him disdainfully, head bobbing to observe him from a multitude of angles. He flicked a hand at it and it deigned to hop six inches out of the way.

He slid off the lion and flopped onto the bench next to Carter who was working his way through the last of the Chestnuts. Crossing his arms, Woods appraised the local female wildlife. His keen eye spotted more than one pretty girl in a dress who was on their way home.

"What do you think of it so far?" Carter asked his navigator.

"It's big," Woods replied. Carter smiled thinly, the scar on his cheek rippling. "My old man was right; the whole world goes through Trafalgar Square."

"How did he know?" asked Carter.

"He was here in the last show. He didn't say much about France, but he told me a lot about London."

Growing up on a ranch north of Vancouver, Woods was used to wide open spaces. The bustle of London was something new. Even going to Vancouver itself for initial aircrew selection was nothing like this. Watching everyone rushing about, he felt like an ant among many ants.

His father had gone to France as part of the 2nd Canadian Mounted Rifles in 1915 and been invalided out in 1917 after a whiff of gas. At weekends, his father would go out with a rifle and range across the countryside, enjoying the solitude and the fresh air. When he was old enough, Woods would go with him and this was when his father came alive to him.

The thrill of the hunt was in both of them and they would lie in wait for hours for a moose or deer. While they waited, his father talked a little about the war, but it was always funny stories about his training, or his time in London on leave; never about the trenches itself or what he had seen or done. Carter was fascinated by Woods descriptions of life on the Canadian frontier. It was a long way from his comfortable existence in Harrogate.

Both of them had trained in Canada and they swapped stories of their experiences. They were hip deep in conversation when Vos appeared. He looked like he was carrying the weight of ages. His head was down, shoulders slumped, chin tucked into his chest.

"Pull up a pew," said Carter, concerned.

Vos collapsed onto the bench like a leaky air bed.

"I need a drink," he muttered, his accented English flat and without colour.

They went in the first pub they found. Carter got the first round in. They drank in silence while they waited for Vos to say something. The Beglian sat bolt upright, his left hand on the top of his leg. A vein throbbed in his forehead and his blue eyes were overly bright.

After leaving Woods and Carter to explore, he'd gone along to the Belgian Government building on Belgrade Square. He'd spent half the day sitting in a corridor waiting to be seen. At one, he had been shown into a small office where a sharply dressed clerk listened to him, making notes in a book.

Vos wanted to know if he could find out anything about his family. The clerk was noncommittal. News from occupied Belgium was intermittent. They had contacts in the civil administration where discreet enquiries could be made, but messages passed could put people at risk. The clerk took down the details of his family and they parted on a handshake with assurances that any news would be passed along.

Vos had meandered around in Green Park for a while after that, oblivious to the pigeons cooing around his feet. He had gone with the expectation of answers. To be met with vague assurances had been dispiriting.

Dinner was a quiet affair. They found a quaint restaurant where the food was basic but hearty. Woods cleared his plates in short order.

His big frame needed fuel and he had walked a lot that day. He attacked his sponge with gusto and then finished off Vos' portion after that.

From there, they debated the evening's entertainment. Vos replied in monosyllables. Woods and Carter argued the merits of a show or the cinema. Neither of them felt like something noisy and loud music would do for another day.

They got tickets for the front of the upper circle at the cinema. Vos bought a packet of Woodbines in the foyer and lit up as the lights dipped. Pungent smoke wreathed around him, making him a murky shadowy figure in the dark.

The first feature was a short comedy. Carter had seen it before up in Scotland but it was funny and he found his mood lightening as he laughed along with it. The newsreel covered the recent action from the North Africa campaign. Tobruk was still holding out and a succession of clips showed the Australian garrison hanging on against shelling and air attack. It finished with an upbeat note that the Eighth Army would soon launch a counteroffensive to push Rommel back.

An usherette appeared during the interval and he bought some salted nuts. Vos declined, seemingly able to exist on Woodbines as he worked his way through the pack. The lights dipped again and the main feature kept them entranced.

The streets of San Fransisco were a million miles away from war torn England. Carter loved the story of greed and the obsession of finding a jewel encrusted figurine. He bounced out of the cinema in a good mood; it was exactly what he needed to lift his spirits after the weeks of stress.

They went to a pub afterwards and dissected the film. Woods and Carter argued over the history, wondering if there ever was such a thing.

"My word, it would be amazing if there was, wouldn't it?" Carter asked with some wonder, his imagination filled with the image of a golden bird, just waiting to be found.

Neither of them noticed that Vos was drinking fast. It was only at closing time that Carter realised just how far gone the Belgian was. When they got up to go, Vos couldn't stand. Carter and Woods took an arm each and manhandled him out of the door. His head hung down from his shoulders, his toes dragging along the road.

"Bloody hell, he's smashed," commented Carter.

"Stating the bleeding obvious, skipper. God, he may be skinny but he's bloody heavy." Woods staggered as he adjusted his hold. Vos was almost unconscious, all his limbs limp and his whole body weight hanging off their shoulders.

Halfway back to Knightsbridge, Vos started raving. Words streamed out of him. They had no idea what he was saying but it showed he was starting to sober up slightly. At least, Carter hoped he was.

They leaned him against a shop front to give their back a rest. Vos was warm, his skin slick with sweat. His eyes were wide, seeing straight through him.

"Come on, you dozy bugger," said Carter. He kept Vos vertical, letting the fresh air get to him.

"Kill them all," Vos looked almost wild. "The boche, they bomb my home."

"Yes, yes, old chap," Carter soothed. He guessed it was eighteen months of repressed frustration spilling out. All this time, Vos had to control himself, get to England and get through the training to get onto an operational unit. He had wound himself up as tight as a spring and now it was all uncoiling. Maybe that was a blessing, he thought, he had to let it out some time.

The ranting continued all the way up to Green Park. A Police Constable looked at them with some interest at one point but let them move on without interference. When they got to the hotel, Vos walked in under his own steam and they managed to get him up to the room without crashing into too many things. Thankfully there was no ranting or raving to disturb the other guests or cause any other problems. They dumped him onto the bed and looked at him. He curled up into a ball on the mattress and rambled to himself.

"Will you be okay?" Carter asked Woods.

"I'll watch him. As long as he doesn't snore, I'll let him live till morning," replied the big Canadian.

Carter went back to his own room and got into bed. He didn't bother pulling the curtains, he liked watching the night sky through the window as he fell asleep.

The following morning, the light streaming through the window woke him up. He stretched, felt his neck go crack and then rolled over. He peered at his watch on the nightstand and nodded. It was ten o'clock, there was plenty of day left over to do things. He went next door and knocked. There was no response and he pushed the door open. He sneaked his head round to see both of them were spark out. He threw a pillow at Vos and kicked Woods bed.

"Up, bed slugs." There were groans of protest. "Up. I'm going for breakfast."

He left them to it and went downstairs. He took his time over his powdered eggs and toast while he perused a two day old newspaper and sipped his tea. He checked his watch. Thirty minutes was long enough. He traipsed back upstairs to see what kind of shape they were in.

Woods was up. He was busy looking at himself in a wall

mounted mirror while he sorted his tie out. The other bed was empty. Woods nodded towards the bathroom. Carter found Vos kneeling over the toilet bowl. He looked up as the door opened. He was green around the gills and there were massive bags under his eyes.

"Morning!" Carter said, brimming with good cheer. Vos groaned and put his head back over the bowl. "Come on, old son. Let's get out and embrace the day."

"G'way," Vos choked. "I drank too much."

"Yes, you did," Carter agreed. "Come on. A quick wash will sort you out. You've got ten minutes." He put the plug in the sink and span the taps. He chucked a towel over Vos and retreated to the bedroom. He lay down on Woods bed and whistled to himself while the Canadian finished getting ready.

"That was a bit harsh," Woods said.

"Nonsense, he needed a boot up the arse to get moving, otherwise we'd never leave here till this afternoon. Besides, I don't want to give him time to wallow in self pity. Whatever happened yesterday upset the apple cart. We've got today to sort him out."

Vos emerged from the bathroom, looking a little better. His eyes were still red rimmed but he was up and walking which was something. Shaking fingers fastened the buttons on his shirt.

"I need a drink," he said, running his tongue over dry lips. His head was thumping. Most of the evening was a mild blur. He remembered going to the cinema but he had little recollection after that. Jamming his peaked cap on his head he followed Woods and Carter out of the door. His stomach rebelled when he caught a whiff of food from the dining room. He quickened his pace to get outside and was thankful when he got to fresh air. He sucked down big lungfuls of it and it helped his headache. Woods clapped him on the back.

"Feeling better?"

"A bit." Vos wiped a sleeve across his mouth. "I'm hungry."

Woods laughed. That was a good sign. Any man who could contemplate food after what he had put away last night was on the road to recovery. They asked a pedestrian if there was somewhere decent for a late breakfast. They were pointed towards a tea room near the Albert Hall that opened early. Carter stuck with a pot of tea while Woods and Vos demolished a rack of toast and a bowl of porridge each.

"What shall we do today?" he asked them, his tone upbeat. Woods ruminated on that while he spread butter on his last slice.

"Wide open spaces," he said.

"Something with a view," Vos demanded. Carter bent some thought on that. Greenwich was the wrong side of the river so that was out. Richmond Park, Hampton Court and Kew were all quite attractive but again a bit on the far side. Hampstead Heath wasn't far, neither was

Regent's Park.

"I think we can accommodate that," he told them.

They took a bus to Regent's Park. No one was interested in going to the zoo. Seeing a bunch of animals in cages held little attraction and they cut across the road to Primrose Hill. It was a gentle climb to the top and they relaxed on the benches while they got their breath back. Vos lit up his last Woodbine.

"How on earth can you like those?" Woods asked, his nose wrinkling in distaste. Vos looked at the cigarette and regarded the glowing tip. "Can't get Gaulois, this is the next best thing."

They enjoyed the view of the city spread across their line of sight to the south. They could just make out St Paul's Cathedral on the horizon. The breeze coming up the hill was nice and fresh and it helped clear their heads from the previous nights booze.

Woods dearly wanted to ask Carter about his first tour but it felt gauche to talk shop. Instead, he asked Vos about Holland, probing around the edges of his escape and how he came to England.

Vos cleared his throat and told his tale. He told them about the day the Luftwaffe came over and wiped out his airfield. When Belgium had surrendered at the end of May 1940, he had gathered a few like minded colleagues and commandeered a military truck. Taking the coast road, they beat it as quick as they could. Amongst all the chaos and confusion in France, no one was particularly interested in a few Belgian strays, so they took the next available ferry to England.

Vos smiled when he remembered the little piece of comedy at the RAF recruitment office in Dover. The Sergeant thought they were yanking his chain when they marched in wearing their Belgian Air Force uniforms demanding to join up. Vos could laugh about it now, but at the time it had gotten quite heated, until an officer came out of an inner office to find out what all the shouting was about.

When they found out he was a radio instructor he nearly found himself permanently grounded. He had fought tooth and nail to be made operational. He had come to England to fight, to play a part in defeating the Nazi's so he could go back home, not waste his time teaching trainees to bash out Morse in a classroom.

He thought back to the day before. He had been a fool to think he could find out about his family. He just had to accept that they would be a dream in his mind until the day he got back home again.

They rode the underground back to Piccadilly Circus. Even in wartime conditions, it was a riot of colour, advertising boards attached to buildings and the road stiff with traffic, the path choked with pedestrians.

They found a serviceman's club and got a mid afternoon snifter. Vos had recovered his vigour by then, but he took it easy, restricting himself to a half of bitter. They got a steer to a restaurant a few streets away from all the bustle.

It seemed dubious as they followed the directions. The route took them down a narrow sidestreet away from the bustle. A few ladies of the night emerged out of the gathering gloom. They spotted the officer rings on their shoulders and moved in for the kill. A ripe brunette tried her luck. Vos pleaded ignorance and sputtered a load of French at her as they retreated to the other side of the street. That bounced them into range of a trio of girls. Vos was about to shout at them when one of them spoke to him in French. She was a skinny little thing with dark hair, red cheeks and a thin summer coat wrapped over her slim frame.

"Qui es-tu?" he asked, *'who are you?'*.

"Denise," she told him, her voice nervous. Grateful to hear French, Vos stopped walking and she approached him. She flowed across the pavement, her lithe legs shown to advantage by a high heel and a skirt cut just above the knee. She stared up at him and shivered as she rubbed her hands up and down her arms.

Carter called to Vos to hurry up. The Belgian stared at her, almost transfixed. Carter called again and Vos shook his head, walking after his pilot and navigator. As he got to the corner, he looked back to see the girl standing in the middle of the street watching him.

The restaurant was one of those hidden gems that survived on word of mouth. There was little in the way of signs on the outside, just a green door that led to some stairs and a waiting area. The place was heaving. Small tables were everywhere and patrons had been shoehorned in to maximise the floorspace. They squeezed their way through the crush and were shown to a table by a window that overlooked the street at the back of the Apollo Theater. While they perused the menu, Carter asked if there were any shows the waiter could recommend.

"Depends what you want, sir," was the reply wrapped in a thick London accent.

"Music and something easy on the eye," Woods told him. The answer was quick.

"The Palais has a musical. The Palladium's got a cabaret show, *London Review*," he rattled off the cast list. "Dusty Miller, Mercy Daniels, The Jersey Dolls."

"That's for us," said Carter. The waiter sucked on his teeth, playing his part well.

"Difficult to get in that one," he said, beginning his pitch. "Popular show."

"How much?" asked Carter, cutting him off, not fazed by the patter.

"Ten bob, plus the ticket price on top," the waiter informed him, not missing a beat as he gave him his best smile.

"Done," said Carter without hesitation.

The waiter beamed. A nice easy transaction for tickets he already had burning a hole in his back pocket.

"I'll have the tickets in half an hour. Now what can I get you gents? We've got some nice things *off* menu, if you catch my drift?"

For three men fresh off an airbase where the food was passable but limited, he'd just said the magic words.

"Give us something resembling a steak and you can have my first born and a nice tip, you catch my drift?," said Woods.

"Perfectly, sir. Rapidly."

They watched him weave his way through the press of bodies to the kitchen.

Dinner was a treat. There was no starter but they got a plate with a thick bit of meat, mushrooms, a selection of vegetables and some chips. Vos asked for some Dijon mustard and got a funny look from the waiter. A pot and small spoon was produced that had English mustard in it. Vos made a face.

"What's that?" he asked the waiter.

"All we've got, sir. There *is* a war on."

"We noticed," said Carter tartly. The waiter diplomatically withdrew from the field.

It wasn't a real steak, but the chef had worked some magic and it certainly tasted okay going down. Considering the food being served, Carter couldn't believe the place was still operating. He was half expecting the Police to bust down the door any moment and arrest all the staff for being black marketeers.

The theater tickets arrived with dessert. Money changed hands and they found they had three seats from the upper circle near the front off to the right. Good enough. The bill when it came was suitably indecent. Carter got a raised eyebrow in return when he asked if a cheque was okay.

"Oh well, it was worth a try," he sighed as they fished in their pockets and dumped coins and notes on the small tray.

They headed off to the London Palladium and got there with ten minutes to spare. Vos paid sixpence for the program and was looking through the pages when the lights went down. It was a good show. Dusty Miller was the headline comic, there were some good singers like Mercy Daniels and June Fields and there were French girls doing the Can Can. Mercy Daniels had everyone singing along with her. There wasn't a dry eye in the house when she had finished her turn. There was lots of noise, laughs and attractive girls to catch the eye.

Miller got three slots, one of them a skit with him as a member of the Home Guard, a spy and a good looking girl. His jokes ranged from tame to the outrageous while he asked the audience which they preferred. The audience would shout out their choice and it was almost always something risque.

The show finished up with the entire cast on the stage doing a final musical number and then taking their bow. Somewhere in the middle of all that, Vos had slid out unnoticed. Carter and Woods only realised he was missing when the lights went up. They waited ten minutes thinking he had gone to the little boy's room. Woods offered his opinion of Mercy Daniels while they waited.

"She's a dream."

Carter looked at him and smiled that lopsided smile of his, the scar on his cheek making him appear cruel.

"She's got a good pair of lungs on her," Carter agreed. He blew a cloud of smoke to the ceiling. Woods eyebrows went up. "No I mean it. She's got a strong voice. What did you think I meant?" He smiled more warmly, his tone teasing. "I thought she was a bit plain."

"Come off it, skipper, the gals a doll."

When Vos failed to show, Woods just shrugged. They had no idea where he had gone and no idea when he'd left. He was a big boy, he knew where the hotel was, they'd just have to see him later.

12 - Lost Souls

Vos had left during Dusty Miller's second turn on stage. Everyone had been laughing with tears running down their faces but Vos couldn't get into it. Miller's style was to talk fast, a constant patter with words flying like a machine gun. Vos could speak English quite well but this rapid fire delivery was all too much for him. He suddenly felt a very long way from home.

He slid out unnoticed and just started walking. The cold air was a shock to his system after the stifling heat in the theater and he huddled inside his greatcoat as he followed the crowds.

He hated London. The crush of the buildings bore down on him. Everyone was on top of each other and he felt hemmed in. He needed someone to talk to. A stray thought made a connection and he retraced his steps from earlier in the day. He found her near the corner he had first seen her. She saw him approach, not recognising him in the dark. She stepped out from the doorway, her arms crossed across her chest, her breath frosting in the cold air.

"Denise," he said. She stiffened at being called by name. Six feet separated them. She looked back over her shoulder to see other women looking at her. Vos became very conscious that he had an audience. He stuck to French.

"Voulez-vous un verre?" *Do you want a drink?* he asked her. She nodded, her eyes wide, like a rabbit caught in the headlights.

"D'accord."

He grunted acceptance and he walked away, half turning and motioning for her to follow him. She fell into step next to him, matching his longer stride, her heels clicking on the pavement. There were mutters of disgust from the other toms as they missed out on some business.

Vos steered towards a pub he could see at the end of the road. He walked in and the girl followed him. The barman took one look at her and was about to voice a protest when Vos produced a ten shilling note. As the barman reached for it, Vos grabbed his hand and looked him in the eye.

"Two glasses and a bottle of something strong; no questions."

The barman snatched back his hand and rubbed it before taking the note and shoving it in his pocket.

"Back of the room," he muttered.

Vos motioned for the girl to go ahead and he caught a whiff of perfume as she went past him. She took the seat next to the radiator and huddled close to it, trying to absorb the heat. She was shivering and flinched when Vos reached across the table towards her. He withdrew his hand and sat back when the barman brought two glasses and a small bottle of gin. He was robbing him but Vos didn't want to cause a scene. He cracked the seal on the bottle and poured for both of them.

She didn't touch hers. He knocked his back and poured another. The gin burned on the way down and was like petrol to his tastebuds. He would have preferred to drink Jenever but hadn't seen a bottle of that since leaving Belgium.

"Francais?" he asked her and she nodded dumbly, her hands worrying the front of her skirt.

"Qui, Saint Omer," she bit out, her voice quiet. In the dim light of the pub he could see she was young, her small elfin features set off by deep green eyes. She had a long face and round chin. Whatever puppy fat she may have had had been starved away and her cheekbones stood out on her face. She had added too much rouge to her cheeks to give herself some colour. He couldn't decide if she was naturally pale or just frozen from being outside.

He asked her where she lived. She told him it was none of his business. He asked her again more firmly and she told him she lived in a small bedsit in the East End but did not elaborate further. She was a long way from home in this part of London late at night. Vos asked her how she was going to get back. She said she would walk whenever he was finished with her. That last she said with slight venom.

She hitched her chair round and grabbed his hand, pulling it over so it rested on her knee. She forced his hand down and moved it along her leg, making him touch her. He snatched his hand back.

"Non, non. I just want to talk," he said. Her eyes flared and her lips pulled thin. He was playing with her. She pulled away and began to stand up, but he grabbed her wrist to stop her getting any further. She was about to swear at him to let her go when she saw his face and she paused. His eyes were pleading for her to stay. She hesitantly resumed her seat, unsure.

She had been doing this for a while, but this was the first time someone had not gone straight to the main event. When their lips brushed her skin, she would think of something else. When they used her, she would think of other things, making noises in the appropriate places by rote. When they were done, she would get a few more coins to maintain her meagre existence. She had sunk a long way since coming to England out of necessity and circumstance.

Fleeing the chaos of France, a family in London's East End had found space for her while their son was away at war. The Blitz made her homeless when the family was bombed out. She was left with the clothes on her back and a few salvaged valuables with nowhere to stay. A volunteer society helped for a while and found her a secretarial job at a company that made belt buckles for the army.

It paid very little, barely enough to rent a room and buy essentials, but it was a start. Then one day the senior manager had forced himself on her in his office. It had been lunchtime and the office was empty. He had run his hands over her body and told her not to worry, he would help her out if she got into trouble afterwards. When she had fled in tears, he called her a French tart who was leading him on. When she returned to her lodgings, she found her suitcase in the alley and the landlady demanding more rent than she could afford to pay.

She went back to the society for help but the man had gotten there first and told his lies. He told them he had found her stealing. That door closed and she found herself adrift with no help and little hope.

One day, an older woman had taken talked to her while she was sheltering from the rain in a shop door. She brought her back to her flat. To start with, Denise was just happy to have a roof over her head and food. Then she was told what she needed to do to carry on enjoying the privilege.

Her mind had rebelled at doing; *that*, but desperate people do desperate things. She had lived on the street once; winter was coming and she couldn't face that again. Despair was suppressed by the human need to survive so she forced herself to it out of necessity.

The first time was just a blur she had done her best to blank out. She had cried the entire time. It had been a sailor, she remembered that. His beard had scratched her face while he spent himself over her. He had given her double, out of guilt or some thrill of power she had no idea. Since then, the myriad faces had blurred into a homogeneous whole with time. Some were rough, some as young as her with a uniform and a puffed up sense of pride. She remembered the occasional boy who was going off to war with no idea of what war was and soothed him as he fumbled with her in the dark.

Denise had seen war. She had watched as units of men had marched to the sound of the guns, never to return. She had seen what war did to people, but she had told herself she would survive. Now she had a man asking her to stay and looking at her with sad eyes.

"I miss home," he said simply, making this up as he went along.

"So do I," she replied, her voice glum.

While they talked, Vos looked at her more closely. Her hands were fine and smooth, a contrast to his rough millers' skin. Her green dress was of good material but was not as clean as it could be and the hem at the bottom was slightly frayed. Her coat was in similar condition, showing signs of being skillfully repaired where there had been a tear in the fabric.

He hitched his chair closer to her. She did not object when he took her hand and held it. Her eyes were wide like saucers as she looked at him, exploring his face. There was sorrow there, hardship, almost a haunted look behind his blue eyes. He had a strong jaw and a husky voice she found attractive.

She spotted the 'Belgium' flash on his shoulder and asked him about Antwerp. She had always wanted to go there but her parents hadn't allowed it. He told her about life as a miller in the country, the early starts, the long hours to make your own flour before creating something. Bread was basic, the stuff of subsistence but he spoke with passion about creating it and she enjoyed his enthusiasm.

It felt good to actually talk to someone again. The recent months had seen her taste bitter hardship and mean spirited people. Piccadilly Circus was a battleground of sorts, with women staking their claim to parts of it. God help youbif you strayed off your patch because the retributions could be vicious. Life had become one big catfight and she had to use what passion and fire she had left to fight her corner and speak up for herself. It had left little room for niceties.

He prevailed on her to have some gin. She gasped, hating the stuff but drank it anyway. By the time they'd finished the bottle, the barman was throwing filthy looks in their direction and Vos saw they had outstayed their welcome.

On impulse he asked her to come back to the hotel with him. She was about to say no but she paused. The thought of a warm hotel room with clean sheets was far more appealing than being pressed up against a cold brick wall in a dark alley.

Denise was nervous going back with him. She was breaking a lot of the rules she normally set herself, but at least if something happened, she could leave. It was just one night she told herself and besides, it would take her hours to get home anyway.

He flagged down a taxi and they sat together, the slim girl and the tall man. Despite her objections he had put his greatcoat over her shoulders in an effort to keep her warm. He held her hands while he thought about what to do.

He paid off the taxi at the top of the street and they walked the short distance to the hotel. Vos put his finger to her lips and bid her wait just next to the hotels entrance. The heavy door was open but a double set of blackout curtains were across the opening to stop any light leaking out.

She peaked from behind the curtains as Vos went over to reception where the night porter was hunched over reading a newspaper. She had no idea how Vos was going to sneak her past him without being noticed. The porter saw Vos coming and put the newspaper to one side. He grudgingly got to his feet and plastered a smile on his face that went nowhere near his eyes.

"Good evening, sir."

"Good evening," Vos replied, his voice very formal. "Could I trouble you for some extra blankets? It was cold last night."

"It'll take a few minutes, sir. Do you want to wait or I could bring them up to you?"

"I'll take them now. It saves you a walk upstairs."

"Thank you, sir. If you'll wait a moment, I'll just get them." The porter disappeared through a service door and as soon as his back was turned, Vos motioned towards the entrance. Denise rushed in with long strides and went for the stairs. Vos had told her the room number so he could meet her there.

Vos was casually leaning against the reception desk when the porter returned with two blankets for him. He took them and went up the stairs. Denise was waiting for him and he let her into his room. He pulled the door to, dumped the blankets by the other door and then went back downstairs. He coughed into his hand and disturbed the porter again from his paper.

"My apologies," he said, looking sheepish. "My colleagues aren't back and one of them had the key to the room, could you…?"

Sighing in irritation, the porter got back to his feet and they trailed up the five flights to the top floor. The porter let him into Carter's room with a master key attached to a chain.

He gave it a good forty seconds so the man was well down the stairs before he knocked once on his door. Denise peeked out from behind it and slinked into the other room with him. The curtains were open so Vos left the light off. Denise tripped over Carter's suitcase on the floor and rubbed her shin.

He popped next door and gathered up his stuff, shoving it into his suitcase. Denise was in the middle of getting undressed when he came back in. She was in her slip, bending down to take off her shoes.

"Sorry," he muttered. She was nervous and it made her angry. She thought she was past that. He went over to the chair and became very focused on taking off his shoes, undoing the laces slowly. He only looked up when he heard her slide into the bed.

She was in shadow, a dark shape. He picked up her slip and dress and laid them across the back of the chair, playing for time. She turned back the blanket and hitched across the bed slightly, patting the mattress.

Vos got in next to her, very self conscious as he lay down. Nothing had been said between them, the evening had just led to this. Now the moment was here he froze up. He found himself holding his breath, tense as a board. As his eyes adjusted to the dark, he could see her looking at him, her head propped up by her hand. Her lips glistened as she ran her tongue over them, then she leaned in.

She led the way, kissing him, moving slowly around his face, his neck. He gathered her into his arms and held her close. She cried out as he entered her and then they were moving together in sync, her hips meeting his, her fingers clawing at his back. The end came quickly and stars exploded behind his eyes.

She moulded herself to him, feeling the muscles of his lean frame. She draped one leg over his as she ran her hand up and down his chest. She snuggled, letting his warmth envelope her, driving the chill away.

The minutes dragged by and he lay there in the dark, holding her close. His arm circled her side and he could feel her ribs. She was so thin. He planted a kiss on the crown of her head and she tightened her grip on him.

Once he recovered his breath he reached over and fished his cigarette case out of his jacket and a book of matches. He lit a cigarette and they shared it, passing it between them. He asked her where her family were now.

"No questions," she told him. "What about yours?" she asked him back, her tone teasing.

"No questions," he said, smiling.

She slid on top, legs straddling him. This time was slower and she moved to a rhythm, back and forth. She leaned forwards, her hands either side of his head as she increased the tempo. Her breath came in short gasps. He held her sides and then his hands cupped her breasts, his thumbs teasing her nipples, causing them to stiffen. She groaned as she felt her stomach tighten, the muscles clamping down on him. The climax crashed over him like a wave and she went over the edge as well, shuddering as she ground her hips against him. He gasped and she chuckled, a deep throaty laugh. That didn't happen very often for her.

They lay in bed for a few more minutes and then the moment passed. Her breathing returned to normal and her brain became practical. It was late, she had to leave. Duty done, she got out of bed and started gathering her things together. Cool air chilled the sweat on her skin and she shivered.

Vos levered himself up, leaning on one elbow. He watched her, lit up by the moonlight coming in from the window. Her skin was pale, almost milky white, her long tresses dark. She was seated on the chair, starting to get dressed. She pulled the pink slip over her head and worked it down her lean body. She brushed it down over her hips.

"Stay," he asked. Her fingers stopped as she was buckling one of her shoes.

"Why should I?" she asked him. "I don't even know your name."

Abashed, Vos bit his lip.

"It's Christophe, Christophe Vos."

He held his breath. Her fingers remained still. She glanced up at him, chewing on her lip, the look between them electric. She straightened and crossed her legs, the toes on her left foot against the heel of her right shoe. She took it off again and closed the distance back to the bed. She hugged him close, kissing his face, her nails digging into his arms.

"All right, I'll stay; till the morning."

She got in beside him and he rearranged the blanket around them.

"Stay with me, Denise. Stay."

"Till the morning," she told him. "Then what? You go back to your war."

He came to a sudden to a decision. He dragged his trousers over and rummaged in the pockets. He took a wad of notes from his wallet and offered them to her.

"Take them."

Her eyes blazed. She snatched the notes from him and threw them across the room.

"I don't need charity," she snapped at him.

"Don't be a fool," he told her and instantly regretted it.

"Fool! Damn you!" She beat her fists against him.

"Denise, stop it. Stop it." He held her close, trapping her arms while she thumped him over and over.

"Stop it," he told her again, his voice soft and soothing.

"I never wanted any of *this*." She collapsed into him, her voice breaking, her resistance spent. He kissed her and could taste the salt of the tears rolling down her cheeks.

"None of us did, Denise. None of us did."

"And when you go..." she sniffed; her voice full of sorrow.

"We've got all the time in the world," he told her.

Woods and Carter walked up the stairs of the hotel to their rooms. After Vos had disappeared on them, they had gone on to a pub and then a clutch of aircrew invited them to a private bash at a hotel. Who were they to say no? They could have stayed longer but left at two in the morning.

"I don't know where he is. Dozy buggers probably got himself lost," said Carter. He fished in his pocket for the room key.

"You don't think he's gone AWOL do you?" wondered Woods, a sudden thought occurring to him. Carter groaned.

"Christ, I don't even want to go there. Could he?" he asked, concerned.

"You saw him last night," Woods reminded him. "What do you

think?"

If Vos had gone AWOL they would be facing some hard questions when they got back to Amber Hill.

"I need a bath," Carter muttered. "It was hot in the theater, too hot really."

"I'll get it started for you," Woods told him.

Carter opened the door to his room. A black Oxford shoe clattered off the door frame and missed him by inches.

"Get out of it," a voice shouted at him from the dark.

"Who's that?" Carter asked.

"Who do you think?" Vos said in his accented English.

"We thought you'd got lost."

"Well I didn't."

Carter tried to come in the room again and the other shoe hit the door.

"Hey," Carter protested. "You're in the wrong room."

"No, I'm not."

A girl's voice laughed in the darkness. Carter shoved his head round the door and caught a glimpse of two people in the bed.

"Ah," he said, suddenly realising what was going on.

"Exactly," said Vos with a smug tone. Carter went next door.

"Who was that?" Denise asked Vos.

"My pilot."

Woods heard the laughter and looked over his book at Carter as he came in the room.

"And you were worried he'd got lost," he said sotto voce, with a sly smile.

"I stand corrected," Carter admitted. "He's had more success than us."

"Ah, but we weren't really trying," Woods reminded him. There had been some women at the party. They had even danced with a few of them but nothing serious. He yawned and stretched. "I'm ready for bed."

"Bath first. I need the soak," Carter reminded him. He went into the bathroom and closed the door.

13 - The Stuff That Dreams Are Made Of

Carter waited until a reasonable time of the morning before going next door. He was loath to disturb the lovers but his fresh gear was in the room. He knocked lightly and cocked his head, straining to hear an answer. He knocked again and then tried the door handle. It opened and he went inside to find the place was empty. The bed was made and everything was neat and tidy. It was as if Vos and his girl had never been there.

There was a note on the bed. It was one sheet of folded paper with his name written on it. He picked it up, hesitant. He remembered the throwaway remark of the previous night about Vos going AWOL. He came back into the other room where Woods was shaving in the bathroom.

He weighed the note in his hand and opened it and breathed a sigh of relief as he scanned the lines of handwriting. Vos said he had things to do and would meet them at the train station at three. Woods came out of the bathroom dabbing his face on a towel.

"Problem?" he asked. Carter handed him the note. Woods grunted as he read it. "As long as he's at the platform for the ride home." He rubbed the towel in his ear, then he tried the other side, wiping away the last of the shaving soap. He got dressed, putting on a fresh shirt. "So, what's the plan for today?"

"I thought some shopping was in order. We can't go to London and not get presents with Christmas round the corner."

"Okay," agreed Woods, "I'm game."

They packed up, checked out and got a bus. Carter looked out the windows as they rode along. He saw a London, bowed but not broken. Every so often they passed a bombed out building. It was either a hole in the ground or an empty shell with no roof. Boards covered the burned out remains.

Everywhere, shops had blast tape on the windows. Propaganda posters urged people on to victory. On a street corner he saw a newspaper seller hawking his wares. The hoarding said they had the latest news from North Africa. People threw their pennies into his cap and picked up the paper reading the headlines as they walked.

They went to a big department store. Carter got some nice scarves for his mother and sister. Woods bought a set of illustrated

Beatrix Potter books for his mother. When they were finished, they went to a gentleman outfitters. Carter had got the address from the back of the theater program.

The tailors was a small family run establishment. It had plush maroon carpets and wood panelled walls covered in antique photographs and daguerreotypes in frames. They were served cups of tea, scones and cucumber sandwiches while they were being seen to. Woods had to hand it to the English, they turned clothes shopping into an experience. He would have just gone into a shop, tried something on and bought it off the peg.

They spent the final few hours of their leave being measured. Carter got three shirts and a pair of trousers. Woods bought himself a new greatcoat. His issue one had never fitted well and was always very tight under the arms and across the chest. When he had complained about that back in Canada, he'd gotten little sympathy, one size fitted all. He drew a disapproving glance when he demonstrated the fit to the shop assistant in the dressing room mirror. Carter persuaded him to push the boat out and paid for everything with a cheque, waving away Wood's objections.

"Call it an early Christmas present," Carter told his navigator.

"Thanks, skipper, I appreciate it."

They were assured their order would be delivered to Amber Hill the end of the following week. Job done, they moved on to a late and leisurely lunch.

In the restaurant, Carter caught a glimpse of a tall blonde being ushered to her seat and for a moment he felt a twinge of panic. It had been his fear that he would bump into Mary while they were in London but thankfully that hadn't happened. Mary hated the theater and they hadn't gone to any society parties. The chances of it happening were slim, but even so, it had been a worry that had played on his mind somewhat.

Over lunch they speculated on what their wireless operator was up to.

"Sowing his wild oats," suggested Woods with a grin.

Vos had risen early. He was careful not to disturb Denise which was no mean feat for two people sleeping in a single bed together. He watched her while she continued to sleep. He had lain awake for a long time last night, thinking. For a while he could not even order his thoughts as he pondered possibilities. Now that he had made his mind up, he hated waking her, but they had a lot to do that morning before he returned to Amber Hill.

He hitched forwards on the chair and lightly traced his finger down her cheek. She stirred slightly. Her brow wrinkled as her mouth twitched. She opened her eyes and for a moment she forgot where she was. Then she saw him sitting there and she relaxed. She yawned and stretched, a long luxurious stretch, like a cat.

"I have to go," she said. She swivelled on the bed, her feet dropping to the floor. She padded naked across the room and reached for her clothes draped over the back of the chair. Vos thrilled at the sight of her, remembering the feel of her skin under his touch.

She dressed quickly, suddenly feeling that she had lingered too long. She checked her bag, fastened her shoes and put her coat on. Vos stewed in silence, delaying the moment that he knew must come. She reached for the notes on top of the chest of drawers. Vos had picked them up from the floor where they had lain all night and stacked them neatly.

"It's time," she whispered.

He reached out and put his hand over hers.

"It doesn't have to be," he said quietly.

A thin laugh escaped her lips. It was almost a sneer, a sob.

"It was a dream last night."

"This dream doesn't have to end," he said.

"How?" the word was torn from her, a thin screech of despair.

"Come with me," he said simply. "Come to Lincoln."

She smiled and withdrew her hand.

"We know nothing about each other," she protested. She moved two steps to the right, putting the chair between them, her hands resting on top of it.

He couldn't argue with her logic but he harboured some hope. He could see the conflict in her eyes. The tug of being wanted, of being with someone.

"We had last night. It's a start. All things have a beginning, Denise."

She wrapped her arms around herself, suddenly shivering. She looked out of the window, watching the barrage balloons swaying on the breeze. It was a bright day; the dark clouds of the last few days having been blown away.

"Christophe. I live here, in London." She span on her heel to face him. "How can I go to Lincoln?"

"That's easily changed. Take a chance. On me." He got to his feet. He reached out towards her. "On us."

"Because of one night together?"

She avoided his hand and walked past him. She got to within a few paces of the door and then stopped as he spoke again.

"Yes, because of one night. And think about this. If things don't work out, it's a new start, somewhere else," he waved his hand around. "Away from *all* of this."

"I'm not strong enough, not again," she told him, still facing the door. Her head was bowed, her voice quiet, hesitant. A surge of strength rushed through him. He closed the distance between them and placed his hands gently on her shoulders. He could feel her trembling through her thin coat.

"You didn't have me before."

This was the critical moment. He couldn't force her to come. She only had to reach out her hand and open the door and walk away and he wouldn't stop her. Time slowed down, seconds stretched and then her shoulders sagged ever so slightly.

"All right."

He took that last half step and she leaned back into his chest, her head and shoulders resting against him. His arms wrapped around her and he planted a kiss on her shoulder.

"Let's go, there's a lot to do."

He wrote the note for Carter and pulled the door to. They walked out of the hotel together and made their way over to the nearest underground station.

It took them nearly two hours to get across London. As they rode the bus to the East End, Vos saw the prosperous centre of London change to densely packed residential streets. The theaters and galleries and government buildings and parks and grand buildings of marble and stone gave way to grubby brick. It was grim. Vos had never seen anything like this before.

There was row upon of narrow terraced houses and squalid lanes. Very occasionally there was a small square of green where children played, chasing hoops and balls around. Often, children were playing in the street, dodging in and out of traffic. Shops were surrounded on all sides by humanity.

They went to the heart of Whitechapel. It was here that Jack the Ripper had plied his trade fifty years before. Vos peered out the windows of the bus as it rumbled over cobbled roads. He looked down narrow dark alleys that led to courtyards or other streets. North of the Thames, the area was an overcrowded mix of migrant poor and working class labour.

He saw large areas of rubble and craters, the leftover work of the Luftwaffe during the Blitz the year before. The East End had borne the worst of it throughout 1940. Surrounding the important Port of London area, filled with warehouses and shipping docks, the East End had endured fifty seven successive nights of bombing. Large areas around these targets had been laid waste with thousands of people displaced. Those that remained were as tough as old boots, working and living amongst the squalor, hanging on, waiting for a better day.

Denise rang the bell and they got off at the next stop. Picking her way round some puddles of fetid water, she turned a corner and went down an anonymous terraced street. Vos followed behind, his eyes darting left and right as he looked around.

The bricks were soot blackened and the view was unchanged from the turn of the century. There was an air of world weary decrepitude about the place. On the street corner was a small mean looking shop. Farm Dairy was painted on the sign board above the door but the paint was cracked and fading. The window was stocked with tinned produce and a few wooden crates of limp vegetables were stacked on the pavement.

A woman nearly soaked him as she threw a pail of dirty water out of her front door straight onto the street. He avoided the splash and people gawked at the sight of an officer walking down the road. Others gave Denise reproachful glances as she passed them by.

She went down a narrow alley between two houses and stopped in front of a battered wooden door. It had been green once, but the paint had peeled badly and someone had slapped blue paint over the top so it was a lurid mish-mash of colour. She turned the key in the door and went in.

The doorway opened onto a small area at the foot of a steep flight of stairs. No more than three foot square, it was just large enough for the door to open. Vos closed it behind him to find doors to his right and left. Both of them had locks. Looking up the stairwell, he could see the wallpaper was peeling in places and showed signs of damp. The air was musty. He followed Denise, the stairs creaking under his weight.

The landing was another small space with three doors. Her room was at the top on the right. Directly ahead was the bathroom. To the left was another door with a lock on it. This one had a plank of wood nailed across one of the panels, covering some recent damage.

"Come on," she said. Her room was no better than the hall. It was dull, the only light provided by a dim bulb and a small dirty window that looked out over a small yard. He could see the backs of the row of terraces on the other side.

There was no carpet on the floor, just a threadbare rug one side of the bed. A wooden chair was in the corner with some things stacked on it. A wardrobe was in the other corner. A shelf contained some personal items.

Denise pulled the rug back and lifted a short piece of loose floorboard. She took out a small metal tin box and emptied the money from it into her clutch bag. She got a suitcase down from the wardrobe and put it on the bed. Opening the lid, she started throwing things in it. She was nearly done when there was the sound of a key scratching on metal and the door opened.

A woman was stood in the doorway. Round shouldered, she had lank and greasy dark hair put up in rollers. There were slippers on her feet and she wore a grubby floral patterned dress. An apron was tied around the waist.

"What's this? Where you been all night. Who's this?" she asked, her voice shrill, all indignation and outraged authority.

"Mrs Perkins," said Denise, her voice suddenly fearful.

"Mrs Perkins," the intruder nodded. "You *know* the rules." She gestured at Vos. "No guests; no men in 'ere. You get this room *cheap* enough without trying to sneak someone in," she said, her voice cracking like a whip with not a hint of kindness or soft edges.

Denise had shrunk into herself. Vos looked at the things in the suitcase. He looked around the room, totally ignoring the creature at the door. He quickly bent down on one knee, checking there was nothing forgotten under the bed. He opened the wardrobe door to make sure it was empty.

"Is that it?" he asked. Denise nodded, almost struck dumb. He flicked the lid of the suitcase shut and made sure the clasps were fastened. He gestured to the door. As Denise walked past him, he swept the route clear, shoving Mrs Perkins out of the way.

Not ready for that, the older woman staggered to her right. In the time it took her to regain her balance, Denise was down the stairs and Vos was following her.

"Ere, what's going on!" she demanded to know. The whole encounter had been a matter of seconds, but that was enough to make Vos' skin crawl. She charged down the stairs to follow them but they were already outside in the alley. Vos took the keys from Denise and waited for Mrs Perkins to get down after them.

She gained momentum down the steep stairs, her slippers slapping with each step. It was even money that she would fall and break her neck, but here, Vos was to be disappointed. She stood at the door, hands on hips, her face a picture of mounting anger. Without saying anything, he handed her the two keys and then walked towards the street.

"Come on," he told her, his tone crisp and authoritative. Denise followed him, heading back down the terrace. They crossed over the road halfway down and then turned right. Vos wanted to get away from this place and then they could catch a bus back to central London and the train stations. He heard Mrs Perkins outraged screech out on the street as they turned the corner and away.

Denise got the shakes on the bus ride back. That woman had ruled her for the last six months and more. Mean and grasping, she existed off the money of her girls and lodgers. She lived comfortably in a downstairs flat that comprised the rear first floor of the house. While everyone else had one room, she had three, with carpet, good windows and plenty of coal for the fire.

She had dreaded the confrontation she knew was to come and then it had all been over so fast. She was sitting sideways on one of the middle seats in the bus, her suitcase on her lap. She opened the lid and double checked what was in there. She knew she had everything. There was so little to bring but even so, it had all happened so fast, her brain hadn't caught up yet. She glanced at Vos and he gave her an encouraging smile, holding her hand for support.

They got off the bus and walked to Carnaby Street and went to a thrift store he'd seen yesterday. The clothes were second hand but in good condition. More importantly, their purchase didn't require any clothing coupons. He found a corner in the shop and waited while she tried on various things. They emerged with a dark blue winter coat, scarf, some dresses and a pair of shoes. The coat she had been wearing went into the suitcase. She gave him a little twirl when they got outside, pirouetting on one heel.

They caught the underground to Kings Cross. As they walked along, she transferred her case to the other side and slid her hand into his, their fingers meshing. It was the first time she had done that and he smiled.

Woods spotted them first as they hurried along the platform. Carter was looking at his watch muttering to himself about the time. Woods nudged his shoulder and pointed. Carter turned in the indicated direction and his eyes widened.

"What the-"

"Close your mouth, skipper, it's embarrassing," Woods muttered under his breath. Vos slowed his pace as they drew near.

"Did I miss much?" he asked. "Sorry I'm late."

"No worry," said Woods. "There's time yet. We were just going to have a last cuppa." He gestured to the cafe behind them on the platform. They occupied a table in the corner and Carter shouted an order for four teas.

"Denise, these are my friends, Alex Carter and Paul Woods."

"Denise Bonet," she said, holding out her hand.

"Miss Bonet," Woods and Carter said, holding her hand momentarily. They missed Vos turning pink. He might have known her first name but he had never asked what her surname was. He felt a fool once more.

It was a timely reminder that they still knew so little about each other. Carter collected the drinks and plonked a tray on the table. He handed round four cups of tea before sitting back down opposite Vos. He mopped up spilled tea with a paper napkin.

Vos' earlier resolve faltered slightly, his embarrassment denting his conviction that he was right to do this. Perhaps sensing his uncertainty, Denise stilled her own fears and reached for his hand under the table and gave it a gentle squeeze. He glanced at her and smiled, drawing some strength from her touch.

They had twenty minutes until the train left. They drank their tea in relative quiet, each gauging their thoughts. Vos half expected her to suddenly change her mind and leave at the last moment. She wondered if she was making the right decision. Woods and Carter exchanged glances, uncomfortable at the idea of seeing a tearful goodbye at the platform.

Carter used the time to study Vos' girl. She was a pretty little thing, but her face was thin, it made her seem even younger than she appeared. Her long dark hair was brushed, tied back with a red ribbon.

They finished their tea and returned to the platform as the porter went up and down announcing the train for Cleethorpes. They made an awkward tableau, stood there as Carter waited for Vos to say his goodbyes. The silence dragged on his nerves.

"Say goodbye to your girl then and we'll push off," he told his wireless operator. Vos fidgeted.

"Actually, she's coming with me."

Carters lips pulled thin.

"I see."

Saying nothing further, he picked up his suitcase and went down the platform until he found a carriage he liked. Opening the door, he went inside and stowed his suitcase on the overhead rack. They followed him and got aboard. Baggage was squared away and Carter opened a newspaper that someone had left in the compartment.

The train pulled out of the station on time and left London behind. Carter read his paper. Woods engaged Denise in conversation, telling her about Canada and the wide open countryside on the Pacific Coast. When she left the compartment to go to the ladies room, Woods took the chance to ask Vos what was going on.

"You've just met this girl. It's awfully fast. Is dragging her up to Lincoln such a good idea?

"There's nothing to keep her here. She's lost everything, she's just got me now."

Vos told them about the bedsit in Whitechapel but neglected to mention the exact circumstances of how they had met.

"So, you've rescued her?" Carter said, stating the position as he saw it. Vos recoiled in offence at having it put so bluntly.

"I wouldn't say that," he replied sniffily.

"I would." Carter saw he had caused upset and he softened. "Okay, fine. What are you going do to when we get there?"

"Find a place to stay I suppose," Vos said moodily, not happy at being put on the spot like this. He didn't like being reminded that his nascent plan had only extended as far as getting Denise to the train station. Woods lapsed into French.

"You're sure about this?" he asked.

"Yes. Could you-" Vos broke off for a moment, steeling his

nerve. "Could you lend me some money?" He asked, his voice appealing. He misinterpreted Woods hesitation. "Just till payday, so I can get Denise settled."

What the hell, thought Woods, if they couldn't look after each other, who else would? Besides, Vos would either repay him or they would be dead together. He dug into his pockets and produced a few pounds in notes. He kept one and some loose change and handed the rest to Vos.

"Here, take it." His head bobbing gratefully, Vos took the money from Woods outstretched hand and shoved it into his pocket.

"What on earth?" said Carter.

"I owed him some money," said Woods simply.

Before Carter could object to the blatant fib, the door of the compartment opened and Denise came back in. The men sprang apart like scalded cats. She raised an eyebrow in query but no one deigned to enlighten her.

She sat down next to Vos and tucked her feet up underneath her on the seat. She leaned against him and his hand found hers.

After a while, Vos and Denise fell asleep. The thrum of the carriage wheels on rails, the heat of the compartment, the lack of rest the previous night and the mornings events finally catching up with them. In sleep, she seemed a fragile little thing, a porcelain doll almost.

Not wishing to disturb them, Carter left the compartment to have a cigarette in the corridor. He opened one of the small upper windows and blew the smoke outside as he watched the gathering dusk. The light was fading and the sky was chased with purples and pinks, the clouds a kaleidoscope of colour. He turned as Woods joined him. He lit Woods cigarette from the end of his own and handed it back.

"What are we going to do with him?" Carter asked, nodding back towards the compartment.

"Nothing," said Woods. He picked a flake of tobacco from between his teeth and rubbed his finger on his trousers. "He's a big boy. He makes his own decisions."

"When we get back, go with him," Carter told him. "Help get things sorted. I'll beg, borrow or steal some transport and come back and pick you up later."

"How?" asked Woods.

"I'll square it," said Carter curtly, he blew a final stream of smoke out the window and flicked the stub of cigarette outside. He took a bundle of notes and shoved them into Woods pocket.

"Here, give the silly sod this. I spent money on you, I suppose I have to spend some on him too."

Carter went back to his seat. Woods shook his head and smiled, pleased that Carter was willing to go to bat for his crew, regardless of what happened. For the remainder of the journey they talked about their leave, rehashing the plot of the film. Carter had enjoyed it very much and he thought about how some women held power over men and got them to do things. He settled his eyes on Denise with those thoughts burrowing away.

They split up when the train got in, Carter told Woods he would meet them at the station in two hours and left to return to Amber Hill. Woods, Vos and Denise walked into town. Some discreet enquiries were made in a few pubs and they came to a respectable looking boarding house a few streets away.
The landlady showed them the room. It was clean, modestly sized and warm. A single bed was in one corner and it had a view of the street outside. They came to terms and Vos paid for two weeks. Woods accompanied the landlady downstairs and waited in the hall while Vos said his goodbyes.
"His girl, is she?" asked Mrs Peck, although she had already guessed as much, seeing the look that passed between the two of them.
Denise tried the bed, delighting in the feel of a thick mattress under her. The room was a vast improvement over her previous lodgings. Vos was pleased to see her happy. She had perked up immeasurably when they walked around Lincoln.
She flung her arms around his neck and stood on tiptoe as she planted a kiss on his cheeks and then a long lingering kiss on the lips.
"Thank you," she said.
"You'll be all right?" he asked her. She nodded, smiling, her eyes dancing.
"When will I see you?" she asked.
"Soon," he promised. "I'll send word when I can." He had explained to her on the train that when ops were on they wouldn't be able to get away or even communicate with anyone outside the station. Being away for a few days, he had no idea what would be waiting for them when they returned.
He kissed her again and left her then. He came downstairs at a fair clip, past Woods and out the door, his face set. Woods muttered a hurried goodbye to the landlady and then skipped along to catch him up.

When he got back to Amber Hill, Carter made straight for the Mess. The bar was heaving with the men back from leave. Buoyed by rest and time at home, they gossiped in good humour and with great animation. Carter scanned the crowd but the man he wanted was nowhere to be seen. He went along to the Admin buildings and found Saunderson hunched over his desk.
"Burning the midnight oil?" he asked, leaning against the

doorjamb. Saunderson started in his seat at the interruption.

"Good lord, Carter." He turned his attention from the returns he had been labouring over, glad of the distraction. "Good leave?"

Carter twirled his peaked cap around his finger and strolled casually into the office.

"Good enough. Cinema, booze, dancing girls, you know how it is. Yes, good enough."

Saunderson stuck his tongue out. While everyone else had been here, there and everywhere, he had been the architect of their adventures.

"I need a favour," said Carter. He perched on the edge of Saunderson's desk and pulled out his packet of cigarettes. He offered one to the Adjutant who shook his head. Carter lit one for himself. Saunderson narrowed his eyes, waiting for the request. "I need a car, Uncle, or a truck" Carter said, his voice muffled round the cigarette.

Saunderson's eyebrows shot up.

"My god, you could ask for the moon. What on earth for?"

Carter circled the area in front of Saunderson's desk, forming his thoughts. He had rehearsed what he was going to say on the bus ride and walk from Lincoln. He laid out the tale step by step and his concerns. Saunderson nodded in agreement, Carter got his car. Saunderson called for a driver and they waited. A Humber pulled up outside and a WAAF driver knocked on the door. Saunderson waited until he heard the car pull away, then he reached for the telephone on his desk.

"Put me through to Intel please, Flight Lieutenant Kent," he told the operator.

14 - Chance Meetings

While Carter, Woods and Vos had enjoyed the bright lights of the big city, Murphy had taken Todd to his home in Barnsley. A Yorkshire mining town in the Dearne Valley, there were nearly seventy collieries within a fifteen mile radius of the town centre. Vital to the war effort, the coal dug out of the ground fed the hungry furnaces of the steel foundries in Sheffield. Rough and tumble, the town never slept as the shifts worked flat out.

They went down the hill from the train station and cut over Old Mill Lane, coming to a row of terraced houses at the back of the gas works. That metallic tang of gas was on the air and they could smell it long before they turned onto the street.

The gas tanks loomed large out the back, big metal domes that would rise and fall as the gas was used and replenished. Murphy used to gauge the passing of the year by watching them. They always went back up to their full height at the end of October to mark the coming of winter.

As their row of houses backed onto the gasworks, they had a long narrow garden. His fathers prized lawn had been turned over to vegetables to supplement the ration. An Anderson shelter had been built at the end of the garden, a large mound of earth with corrugated sheeting at both ends replacing the rickety shed that had been there for donkeys' years.

Murphy's father was on shift at the gas works but his mother was in when they arrived. Todd was made welcome and they were shown to the box room above the stairs. It was cramped but it would do for a few days.

Murphy's younger cousins went mad when he gave them bars of chocolate he had sneaked out of his survival kit. Todd produced a tin of pears and half a bag of sugar from his kit bag that he had appropriated from the kitchens. The cousins were fascinated by his Australian accent.

They accompanied his father to the Working Mens Club that first night. Murphy saw some old school friends who now worked in the gasworks or the mine. In a reserved occupation, they were safe from the threat of conscription. Some eyed Murphy as a bit of a celebrity, looking at his RAF uniform and wondering about joining up themselves. Others were quite happy as they were, safe in the mines. A very few thought him a fool to volunteer for something so dangerous.

A native of Deer Park just outside Melbourne, Todd felt right at home amongst this robust night life. He turned on his Aussie charm to the local girls and nearly got clocked for his trouble. Some of the men objected to him looking at their dates and Murphy had to do some fast talking to stop him from getting his face filled in.

The following day, they spent a few hours down the allotments with Murphy's grandfather. He had them digging the ground over, doing some preparation work for the new year. Winter winds whipped down the hill and across the allotments and it made them feel like they were back at Amber Hill shoveling snow again. After cleaning the tools, they headed home to warm up and found Murphy's mother had put the sugar and pears to good use. She had made a big upside down sponge cake and lashings of custard. Home cooking like that was very welcome.

They were well sated by the time they met their dates and retired to the cinema for the evening. Sitting on the back row they saw little of the film. Murphy lost himself in the voluptuous figure of a cute blonde. Todd tried his best with her brunette friend but didn't manage much beyond a kiss, her legs stayed clamped shut. When the lights went up, they went to the pub round the corner. Todd had a Guinness and his date had a half of bitter while they made cursory conversation in the Tap room. She was a pretty girl, pleasant enough but there was no electricity there.

All too soon, their leave was over. Murphy's mother saw them off at the station with some sandwiches and they rode the train back to Lincoln.

White stayed with his parents in Essex. There was no direct route to Saffron Walden from Lincoln and it took him three trains and quite a bit of waiting on cold platforms to get back. He walked from the station with his kitbag slung over his shoulder.

Home was a modest cottage with small detached garage on the left. His mother had left his room untouched and it felt odd being surrounded by childhood things. It was so far in his past it was like stepping back in time. Balsa models of aircraft hung from the ceiling and RAF posters were pinned to the walls.

The first morning, White went up and down with the mower while his father watched from the living room, sipping his cup of tea. He went to Cambridge the next day and wandered around, just enjoying the opportunity to do things at his own pace. He visited the old haunts and did the same when he got back to Saffron Walden on the afternoon bus.

His father had been hauled out of retirement when the younger teachers had been called up. He taught at the local school and ruled over a pack of children as he tried to encourage an interest in Latin. White found himself the centre of attention when his father persuaded him to put in an appearance. His father wheeled him in after lunch and the boys bombarded him with questions, asking him what it was like to fly a Spitfire and how many kills he had. He didn't have the heart to tell them he was a bomber pilot. He told them some funny stories instead, and they had gone out to the yard where they ran around with their arms outstretched making engine noises and machine gun sounds. All too soon, his visit was over but his father shot up in his pupils' estimation after being able to produce a genuine war hero for them to see.

His father also saw his son in a new light that afternoon. White had left for the RAF a mere boy but his intermittent letters home had only given them a small insight into the man he had become. His father watched him quietly as he talked to the boys, answering their questions, telling a joke, giving them a sense of wonder at flying. His son was now part of a world far beyond this sleepy little town.

In the evening's his mother had the good sense to keep things low key, giving him the chance to relax. A few old family friends popped round but there was no big party or gathering. They listened to the radio and little was said about his own part in the war. His parents told him bits and pieces of what they knew concerning other people in the town and how their children had fared in the services. When the lights went out, he retired to his bed with a candle and reacquainted himself with his collection of pulp crime novels. On the final day his mother prevailed on him to pay a call on Elaine Bartholomew.

"She's been very good to us," his mother told him, almost shooing him out of the door.

The Bartholomew's were the local money and had been on the board of Governor's at Friend's School where White's father had once been a house master. One summer a long time ago she had stayed at their house while her parents were away.

Moody at having to play nursemaid to a girl, they had wandered the fields around Saffron Walden, flown kites and explored places on their bikes together. He delved into his memory for details and he had vague recollections of a gangly girl with lots of freckles and red hair.

He dressed casually, glad to get out of his uniform and walked up the gravel drive in tan slacks and a heavy winter coat. A large oak tree was on the front lawn, its branches bare. A groundsman putting a pile of leaves to the torch pointed him in the direction of the ornamental pond.

He walked round to the back of the big house to find her kneeling down, throwing bits of bread on the water. She stood up when she heard him walking towards her. White's pace faltered for a moment when he saw her.

The gangly girl of memory had been replaced by a tall woman; the red hair now strawberry blonde cut in a short bob. The freckles were still there though, a light dusting across her nose and cheeks. She had dressed simply, pairing brown brogues with a plain brown knee length skirt and a grey cardigan over a cream blouse. She tucked a stray strand of hair behind her ear and then clasped her hands together in front of her.

"Hello, Paul," she said.

"Hello, Elaine," he replied. There was an awkward moment when White fluffed his introduction. He started to stick his hand out to shake hers as she leaned in to lightly kiss his cheek. Then she started to put her hand forwards as he changed and leaned in.

"Sorry," he said. She was good enough to smile and he skimmed her cheek, catching a faint trace of perfume. She went back to the pond and picked up the brown paper bag which had the bread in. She handed him a crust and they stood close together as they threw crumbs at the fish. Large orange and white goldfish swam around, hoovering up the bread from the surface of the water

"How long has it been?" she asked him. He thought about that. He had been twelve, thirteen that summer?

"Ten years," he breathed.

"A lifetime. I do remember that summer fondly," she said, her voice wistful.

When all the bread was gone, Elaine up ended the bag and gave it a shake, letting the remaining flakes fall onto the water. They watched silently as the goldfish attacked, gobbling up each little morsel. The fish circled waiting for some more, but when it was apparent there would be no more, they sank to the bottom where the water was warmer.

She gestured towards the house and he followed her. They went into a modest sized drawing room that looked out over the pond and the garden behind. He imagined it must be a pleasant view in the summer. The room was nice and warm, with a good blaze going in the fireplace to the left. To the right was a glass topped sideboard covered with a rectangular lace doily. Various framed pictures stood on top. A low table was in front of the fire, flanked by two delicate armchairs covered in patterned lemon silk. A matching two seat settee was between the low table and the sideboard behind it.

She closed the doors and they seated themselves in the armchairs by the fire. Heat penetrated his bones and he relaxed. A servant brought in a silver tray with a tea pot, cups and some homemade biscuits. She waited until they withdrew, then Elaine poured as they sat in silence. He looked at her while he waited, trying to reconcile his memories of her from that long summer with the woman in front of him now. She put one lump of sugar in his tea and gave it a stir.

"Your mother told me how you like it," she explained, smiling as she handed him the cup on a saucer.

"What else did she tell you?" he asked. Her left cheek dimpled as she smiled.

"A few things," she replied, her eyes dancing in good humour. "Although I'm sure she told me more than she should have." He laughed at that.

"Oh, I'm sure she did."

She asked him what Lincoln was like, keeping the subject relatively neutral. White responded in the positive, a little stuck for something to say. He felt a little shy in front of this person who he knew but did not know. He felt at a disadvantage, wondering what else his mother had told her about him.

"When's your leave over?"

"Today. I'm getting the afternoon train."

"Oh, well I don't want to keep you." She put her teacup down and made to stand. "I'm sure you have lots to do before you have to go back."

"No, it's all right, I've got time." She frowned; sure he was just being polite.

Conversation stalled. He filled the gap first and asked her how she was and what she had been up to. He knew a few snippets of detail from his mother, but it had been so long since they had seen each other, he wanted to hear it from her.

She started hesitantly, but the more she talked, the more she relaxed. When her parents had returned at the end of that summer, they had sent her to a ladies finishing school near Gloucester. After that, she had lived with an Aunt in London for a few years, spending her summers in Brighton or on the continent, sometimes France, sometimes Italy. White was rather jealous, he had only been to the continent in his Manchester, that wasn't the same thing at all. Elaine went on to tell him she had given up her London job at one of the Ministries because her mother had been quite ill.

"I'm sorry to hear that," he said, meaning it.

"Oh, it's all right," she told him, downplaying the seriousness of it all, "Mother does like to make a fuss."

"Mine's the same. You should see her with my father, clucking around him like a mother hen, telling him off for not wrapping up in the cold."

"I remember," Elaine said, clapping her hands together in excitement. "Do you remember when you fell into the river? I reached out to pull you up and you ended up pulling me in as well." She laughed with the memory. White's face lit up as he remembered. They had gone down to the creek where the river was very narrow. The grassy banks were so close together you could almost jump across without getting your feet wet. In fact, that was how he had fallen in. He had announced he could jump the gap and she had dared him to do it. He missed by a country mile, landed short and fell backwards into the water.

"Of course, gosh, I'd forgotten all about that. She went mad when we got home, covered in weed."

"And she wouldn't let us in the house until we had stripped down to our briefs on the back door step," Elaine finished.

They laughed together. She saw the years fall from his eyes as he enjoyed the memory of happier times.

He coughed and then stood up and went over to a sideboard covered with framed pictures. Elaine swivelled in her chair to look at him in contemplation as he sorted through the pictures. He picked up a silver frame and scrutinised the photograph.

"You?"

"Me," she said, smiling. She rose from the chair in one lithe move and took the frame from him, their hands touching for a moment. It was a photograph of her in flying clothing, hand on the cockpit of a Tiger Moth, one foot on the wing's walkway. She stared at it wistfully before putting it back on the sideboard. She straightened it, putting in line with the other pictures. "The summer of '39. Then they closed the flying club when the war started."

"Did you get your licence?"

"Nearly. I needed a few more hours. I did solo though."

That broke the ice and they slotted back into the more easy manner they had shared when they were younger. He seated himself on the sofa and watched the flames as they danced in the grate. She poured him some more tea and joined him rather than staying on the armchair. They talked about flying for a while. She frowned when he told her he was a second pilot.

"When do you get your own plane then?" she asked.

"Five, six trips or so? There's not really a hard and fast rule about it. The idea is I fly a few trips to get some experience and then get moved up to a kite of my own."

"You don't sound very enthusiastic about the prospect," she asked. He paused as he drank his tea, the cup halfway to his mouth.

"It's not quite so simple, Elaine. I wish it was." He drank his tea while he marshaled his thoughts. "I *do* want my own kite, but we're a good crew, we work well together. Then just as we get used to each other," he clicked his fingers, "I'll be off."

"But you'd be getting a crew of your own," she objected. "Surely that's a good thing.?" White scratched his cheek.

"I know, but the skippers a great pilot."

"You'll be fine," she told him with genuine confidence.

Time time slipped away from them after that and White realised he would have to say his goodbyes if he was ever going to make his train on time. He had to get home, pick up his gear and then head off to the station. He could change once he was on the train. She walked him to the door.

"You'll tell me how you get on, won't you?" she asked him.

"If you want," he said, a little surprised. She nodded.

"I'd like that." He held her hand as they kissed lightly on the cheek. She lingered, resting her forehead against his cheek and he held her, one hand resting on her hip.

"Please be careful," she said. He promised her he would and she watched him all the way down the drive until he was out of sight, leaving her alone on the doorstep.

15 - Back In The Saddle

White was late but that was entirely down to the trains. He'd made his connection and then waited in the station for an hour due to a signaling fault. Todd and Murphy had timed their arrival to perfection, making it back to Amber Hill for dinner at the Sergeants Mess. 'A' Flight went off on leave and returned without incident in their turn a few days later.

Carter took his crew to the local pub their first night back to get everyone together. The mood was buoyant but they didn't push the boat out. Everyone was pretty much skint until payday and they pooled their pennies to pay for drinks.

Todd told a tale involving twins but he missed Murphy slightly shaking his head next to him. They laughed and ragged on him for shooting a line, but it was still a good story. White talked about Saffron Walden but said nothing about Elaine.

Woods and Carter told them about London, regaling them with descriptions of the show at the Palladium, the dancing girls and Mercy Daniels. Everyone loved the retelling of Dusty Miller's jokes, but it was nothing like hearing it from the man himself. Neither of them mentioned Vos' adventures until the Belgian slid out to go to Lincoln and see Denise. Todd was suitably impressed that Vos was able to get himself a girl so quickly.

"That's fast work, even for me," he said as he asked Woods what she looked like and where he might get one of his own.

Vos found Denise sitting up in bed, reading a book. She had turned in early. She had a hot water bottle warming her feet and a flask of tea on the night stand. The landlady had a daughter in the WRENS not much older than Denise and she was making a fuss of her. He stayed longer than he should have and got back to Amber Hill late that night.

Still banned from operations, the squadron continued to twiddle their thumbs and did nothing more dangerous than air tests of their overhauled Manchester's. In the meantime, the rest of 5 Group went on three ops, one of which was a milk run to the French coastal port of Lorient. There was some resentment at that. Easy ops were a godsend, a chance to get one more job scratched off the tally with little risk. The other two jobs were raids on Dusseldorf and Hamburg. By no means the easiest of raids, they were seen as missed opportunities.

In the end, it was nearly three weeks before 363 were declared operational once more. After the experts at Avro and Rolls Royce had pored over the aircraft and checked paperwork, it was decided a combination of factors were to blame for the recent problems.

As the squadrons Manchester's were in the main, hand me downs from other units, 363 had an unfortunate mix of aircraft which had different mods applied in line with the directions from Avro and Rolls Royce. The catalogue of errors was long. Some aircraft didn't have the increased oil capacity for the engines. Some lacked the modified pumps and filter systems that had largely cured the oil starvation problems. Some still had the intake lips on the wings which had been found to interfere with climb performance above ten thousand feet. Those should have been removed months previously.

Inspection of the engines themselves revealed other problems. Some Vultures had the latest mod44 update and some didn't. There was even the bizarre example of two aircraft having one engine that did, and one that didn't have the mod44 applied. Consulting the aircrafts form 700's showed that both of them had been returned to the depot with one faulty engine. That engine had been overhauled, but no one had ever bothered to check the other *healthy* engine at the time; an oversight that could have had serious consequences.

To cap things off, a few of the older aircraft, Walsh's included, still had the flawed Ermeto hydraulic coupling system fitted. Ermeto fittings didn't require wire locking which had sped up production, but under operational conditions, the vibrations in the fuselage led to the joints fracturing as had happened to Walsh. These aircraft were sent back to the depot to have their hydraulic system ripped out. New aircraft replaced them.

With this collection of niggles ironed out, the squadrons aircraft had finally been brought up to standard. There was still no cast iron guarantee that things wouldn't happen, but a lot of important issues were finally put to bed. Group received the report and 363 were declared operational again without much fanfare.

The men had been very subdued at briefing, with everyone pondering how reliable the Manchester's would be in their first real test since being grounded. After three weeks off it was a little odd to be flying at night. They took off early, taking advantage of the long winter nights as they slid into the dark.

Over the North Sea, L-London was labouring to get above ten thousand feet and was making a meal of it. Instruments were tapped, boost readings checked, throttles were juggled but it made little difference.

Carter tried an old trick. He would dive a few hundred feet and then pull up, converting the speed into a climb, bouncing her higher each time, eking out a bit more altitude at the top of each bounce. That got them up to eleven thousand feet and then she obstinately refused to go any higher and was almost hanging off the props.

Carter gave the engines a rest and then tried bouncing her again to no avail. They might have been burning fuel and getting lighter with every minute that passed but the gods weren't with them tonight.

He knew why. Bad weather had doggged them since take off. Thick cold clouds had wrapped around them and made it heavy going from the get go. Looking left and right he could see the sheen of ice glistening on the wings. There was a constant racket as slithers of ice flicked off the ends of the propellers and struck the canopy. Carter fought the controls. They felt mushy as more ice built up and it was proving difficult to keep her going, she was wallowing all over the sky.

The forecast had been for a cold front across the water and strong headwinds all the way there and for once it was accurate. They had hundreds of miles to go to get to Aachen. They just had to get above the clouds before the ice robbed them of too much lift. If they lost height, they would never get it back and they needed all the altitude they could get if they were going to stand any chance over the flak belts.

"How long to the coast, Woody?" asked Carter.

"Ten minutes give or take."

Carter drummed his fingers on the yoke. He really hated doing this but he saw no other way to get some height.

"Woody, get up front and drop one. We've got to give this bitch a kick in the pants."

White got out of the way as Woods barrelled through to the nose. He made sure the bombs were fused then opened the bomb doors. Carter felt the tug on the controls as the doors went down and disrupted the airflow. He used the trim wheel to give him a little more elevator authority. The Manchester gave a little leap as Woods dropped one of the 1,000 lb bombs. Woods closed the bomb doors and then resumed his seat.

Carter eased back slightly on the yoke and L-London responded. Lightened of some weight, she began to climb and Carter squeezed an extra two thousand feet out of her before she started to struggle again. It wasn't much, but it was enough to get above the clag into the clear air.

They turned south as they crossed the coast. It wasn't full moon but not far off. The worst kind of night for ops. A bright moon made it easier for the nightfighters to range amongst the bomber stream.

A patchy bank of cloud ahead of them was three or four thousand feet below which was fine by Carter. That would hide them from the ground but it would make things harder for Woods. Carter looked up, the sky was crystal clear and the stars twinkled brightly.

"Bomber going down to starboard, no flak." reported Todd, his voice high and scratchy over the R/T.

"Keep your eyes open everyone," Carter cautioned.

Todd saw a shower of sparks intermittently behind. Only one aircraft chucked out sparks light that, the Manchester, but he kept coming back to that shadow, watching it. If it got closer for no good reason, he would take no chances.

He thought back to his one and only kill. It had been a sitter handed to him on a plate. The next one would not be so easy. The only warning he might have might be bright balls of tracer exploding from the black.

Murphy shifted in his seat while he froze and carried on quartering the sky, slowly traversing his turret from right to left. Minutes began to drag as his senses went into overdrive. Eyes strained in the dark, looking to pick up the slightest sign there was another aircraft out there.

"Searchlights on the horizon. Forty, fifty miles ahead?" Murphy reported.

Woods checked his chart, plotting the estimated course. They had belts of flak coming up as they pressed on south. They had to thread a delicate course to avoid Essen and Dusseldorf. "Over the Meuse and on to Aachen," he murmured, tapping his pencil along the track.

He did some calculations and got a different answer for the third time. Rubbing his eyes, he picked up the chart and squeezed past White to go down to the nose. He patted Murphy's backside to let him know he was there. The tall man moved his feet to the side to try and keep them out of the way.

The fluffy bank of cloud Carter had seen earlier had been torn into pieces by the winds. Woods got glimpses of the ground amongst fluffy puff balls. Water twinkled under the moonlight and he could pick out rivers and canals quite easily in the dark.

They had turned south at the Wadden Islands off the Dutch coast. After skirting Deventer he had laid off a course, allowing for the westerly wind. The land should have been wooded around the river but through the blister he could see clear countryside with only a few patches of trees. Something wasn't right. He asked Todd what he could see out of the tail turret.

"There's a bunch of small lakes behind us, north of the river," said Todd.

"Can't be," responded Woods automatically.

"I'm looking right at it," said Todd, slightly offended at being doubted. Woods looked at his map again, peering as he followed the charted course with his gloved finger. There should only have been one lake next to the river on the south side, a bit of a horseshoe shape. He started looking further afield until he found something that looked about right but it was well to the east.

"Jesus, that puts us about forty miles off track," he said in exasperation, disgusted that he could be so wrong. "You're sure?" he asked Todd in some concern as the worm of doubt burrowed away.

"Look, if you don't believe me, come back and look for yourself. Small lakes, behind us, north of the river. I can see about ten of them, the surface of the water is glittering under the moonlight."

Woods came back up to the cockpit. White got up to let him through and then resumed his seat as Woods showed them the map.

"The predicted winds are all wrong," he said. "The forecast was for westerly winds so we've had to head a little more east to counteract for drift. Only its bloody veered one hundred eighty degrees and its blowing east."

"So, the correction has just compounded the error and pushed us off course," said Carter, following the explanation.

"If Todd's right," Woods began. "That puts us here," he said, tapping the map, "somewhere over the Rhine maybe."

They looked ahead over the nose. The searchlights on the horizon were going left and right. The clouds were lit orange from flames and there were sparks of light as bursts of flak exploded in the sky.

"Everyone's bombing over Essen and Duisberg."

"Christ, no wonder the flaks going mental."

Instead of a relatively soft target like Aachen, the main force was right over one of the hot spots they were supposed to avoid. The thick cloud had stopped them getting some good pinpoints on the southern track, so when the wind veered, they'd missed it. The Muese and the Rhine both wound in a leisurely south eastern course, it was an easy mistake to make, but Woods was still annoyed.

"Gimme a course, Woody."

"Steer two three five to get us clear of the city."

Carter turned onto the new course, a simple flat turn that kept them at the same height. He was well aware they could easily collide with someone by changing course so drastically.

"Eyes open lads, we're going to be on our own from the looks of it. Todd, we're cutting across the main route. Keep an eye out for anyone coming up from behind."

"No problem, skipper."

"Vos, get up in the astrodome. I want an extra pair of eyes looking around out there."

The Belgian left his set and went up to the astrodome at the rear of the canopy. He peered into the darkness, watching every shadow and seeing a fighter hiding behind them.

Todd rubbed his eyes and renewed his vigil, moving his turret from side to side. A shower of sparks went past his turret and Todd muttered to himself. When you were trying to disappear into the dark that was the last thing you needed.

"You know, this might work," said White. "If everyone's going to the wrong place, we'll have a clear run in." Carter shook his head at White's wishful thinking. Every flak gun they had would be aimed at them.

"Did I say it's my birthday?" said Murphy. "Well in a few hours anyway."

"I wasn't counting on that kind of surprise," said White.

"Are we having a blowout when we get back?"

"*If*, we get back," Carter responded sharply. "Settle down, we've got a long way to go yet."

Todd saw something below them, scudding over the tops of the clouds. At this range it was just a dark shape and too far for him to identify.

Their Manchester staggered as flak exploded close aboard. Accurate with the first burst, the aircraft bodily lifted from the force of the explosion and then plummeted two hundred feet, as if being shaken up and down by a giant hand.

Carter kept the yoke shoved forward, picking up some speed. The next burst went off above them which made him suspicious. For predicted flak to be so accurate, so quickly, firing blind through the clouds was not luck. The Germans must have someone in the bomber stream reporting back heights to night fighter command. The guns carried on firing for a few more minutes but got no closer than that first burst.

"That was exciting," commented Murphy. Bits of shrapnel had pinged off his turret like heavy rain on a flat roof.

"You ain't seen nothing yet," said Carter, suppressing memories of the flak over Berlin.

Todd traversed his turret slightly to his left. Their shadow was back, threading through the clouds as they did, weaving around the bigger wisps but always drawing nearer. As they got closer, details started to resolve themselves. Whatever it was had two engines and a single tail. That ruled out Hampden's or Me110's but not much else. It could just have easily been a Wellington or a Ju88. The aircraft suddenly banked hard to port and that convinced Todd. No Wellington would move like that.

"FIGHTER! Corkscrew Starboard! GO!"

Carter didn't hesitate, he shoved the yoke forward hard and turned it right. At the same time, he stamped on the right rudder pedal. Laden with bombs, the Manchester dropped like a rock while anything not tied down rolled around.

Vos was knocked off his feet. Momentarily weightless, he bounced off the ceiling before hitting the floor hard when Carter reversed his move. White helped Carter haul the yoke back, holding it against their stomachs and reversing the roll. L-London burst out of the clouds, nose high, left wing dropping.

Todd got off a burst as he saw the nighfighter cross to port. His tracers went wide, falling behind the fast moving fighter. L-London dived again and then Carter corrected the roll, leveling off inside the gloom of the clouds.

"Report," Carter got out between gritted teeth as he took stock.

"Lost him in the dark, skip," reported Todd. "He buggered off to port."

"Call in," Carter told them and they responded in their own way, calling him skipper, skip, boss, sir. Vos was slow to respond. He scrabbled back to his desk and plugged back into the intercom. He'd been thrown around the inside of the Manchester like a rag doll. His head was ringing where he had banged it on the ceiling.

Slowly, Carter pulled back on the yoke and emerged from the gloom of the clouds back into clear sky. They seemed to be on their own so he climbed hard for the next few minutes, wanting to regain the height they had lost. Nothing more was seen of the fighter but no one relaxed. Where there was one, there may be others and another fighter could have seen the tracer and been drawn like a moth to the flame.

Vos shakily unscrewed the lid of his flask and poured himself a hot chocolate. He had a bump on his forehead and a cracker of a headache. Looking out of the wireless operator's window on the port side there was a sudden flash and then a thin line of fire streaked to the ground. Ours or theirs, he wondered to himself.

The last of the clouds cleared ten miles short of the city. Two solitary searchlights swung across the sky probing for them. Flak guns started their symphony, the ground flashing as the heavy stuff started reaching upwards. They'd not been the only aircraft to bomb and there were isolated fires scattered all over the city.

Aachen itself held little strategic value, but it had psychological significance. The city had been the home of Charlemagne, leader of the first Reich as far as Nazi ideology was concerned. From 792AD the Emperor spent most of his winters there and the city became the focus of his court and the political centre of the Holy Roman Empire. The great man was buried in the cathedral.

Their target was the Nazi headquarters building. Woods picked up the IP but he had trouble seeing the actual target. One building in the middle of an urban area was rather difficult to discern, particularly with all the flashing of shell bursts, searchlights and jolting around in turbulent air. There was no way he was asking Carter to go round again. He knew it was near the railway station so he picked a spot, peered down the sight one last time and let the bombs go. As he closed the bomb doors, he felt distinctly unsatisfied.

While they made it back, three other crews of 363 squadron did not. That helped Carter hammer home his message of just how lucky they had been. Like thieves in the night, the nightfighters had been in their neighbourhood, they just hadn't knocked on their particular door.

One of the casualties had been Andrews, Carter's pupil from OTU. They had bought it coming off the target. Three managed to get out before their bomber rolled in, a flaming comet, chased all the way by flak and searchlights. Andrews had managed three ops. Bishop, his companion from OTU was still around but the loss of Andrews changed him. He had lost a friend, someone close to him. Up till then, losses on the squadron had just been other people.

Walsh had been the last one back. Long after many others had faded away, Carter had stood and waited at the control tower, head cocked, ears straining to hear Walsh's plane come in. They had been all set to rub his name off the ops board when he landed.

Carter cadged a lift in a Tilly over to the dispersal to watch Walsh taxi up. F-Freddie was a mess. There was a gaping hole in the bomb aimers dome up front and the wings were peppered with holes.

Carter got the full story back at their billet as they turned in.

"One minute we were flying along, the next, a gale was blowing in through the nose," Walsh told him. "A piece of shrapnel, this big," he held up his fist, "nearly took, Blake's head off. Gave him a nasty shock though." Walsh giggled inanely as the adrenalin was beginning to wear off. He giggled some more when he remembered that Blake had asked for permission before jettisoning their bombs.

While Carter's flight back had been relatively uneventful, Walsh's had been a nightmare. The icy gale blowing in from the nose had numbed every part of his body and shaved a good twenty knots off their speed. Coming down to five thousand feet and warmer air had made little difference. His hands and feet became blocks of ice and his handling of the controls became increasingly jerky and hamfisted.

It had taken him a good few hours of soaking in the bath to get any real feeling back in his body. They slept like the dead and didn't wake up until one. Punchy from the previous night's efforts, they gradually became human over toast and tea in the Mess. Walsh found his fingers still tingled slightly and he wondered if he'd gotten frostbite.

There was a buzz when the first word came through of the Japanese attack on Pearl Harbour in Hawaii. There had also been attacks on the Philippines and Malaya. Even more startling was the news that Churchill had declared war on Japan in support of the Americans. Suddenly the intelligence officer, Kent was incredibly popular as they pumped him for information. He fended off most enquiries with a polite smile or a shrug.

"Look chaps, there's not a lot I can tell you. The Japs have bitten the Yanks on the arse and they've attacked other places in the Pacific. Beyond that..." His voice trailed off.

They were glued to the radio for the evening news but the situation was very confused. There was even a report that a British gunboat had been sunk in Shanghai. Carter and Walsh picked and pawed at the newspapers and then retreated back to their billet for another snooze before tea time.

The Mess was jumping when they came back. Everyone else had surfaced and the bar was buzzing with conversation, swapping stories from the previous nights raid and speculating about the Far East. After three weeks of inactivity, their tails were back up. Asher listened as he circulated round the room, talking to each man in turn.

Only one Manchester had aborted due to mechanical difficulties and it had been a hydraulic issue rather than an engine problem. Three crews gone was a bit of a blow but considering most of the squadron had ended up over Essen, it wasn't a surprise. Scattered due to the winds, the main force had gone over piecemeal, giving the flak gunners a chance to concentrate their firepower.

He'd spent the afternoon at Group dissecting what had gone wrong and what could be learned for next time. He also had the word that ops were off for a few days. The cold front that hung over Europe was likely to last until the end of the week. Bomber Command would wait for better weather. Asher didn't mind, a pause would give him time to replace his losses and then they would be in at the start of a new dark moon period, which made for much better operating conditions.

There was no official announcement concerning a party, it just sort of happened. Drinks after dinner turned into a proper session and they were off and away. Walsh was paraded around the room on a chair for being the last one back. They managed one full circuit with him carried at shoulder height before he lost his balance and they all collapsed in a heap. Pulled out of the tangle of bodies, he stood on one of the sofas and held up a pint of beer.

"Gentlemen, I am touched." He gave a mock bow to the room. "It takes a special kind of skill to bring up the rear but I will endeavour to be equal to the task."

There were cheers and boos as he upended his pint, downing it in one. A bread roll fizzed past his ear. He batted the next one away, spotting it zipping towards him out of the corner of his eye; then he was inundated with a barrage of crumbs. He got down from the top of the sofa, empty pint glass held high, bits of bread in his hair.

Someone thrust another full pint glass in his hand and he polished most of that off as well. When he came up for air his nose was glowing and his cheeks were flushed. He retreated to the bar where Woods, Carter, Vos and Nicol were deep in conversation. Woods turned round at his approach and leaned against the bar surveying the crowd.

"Well done, sir."

Walsh parked next to him.

"Well done to both of us after that mess."

16 - On Their Way

In their billet, the Poker school was in full swing. Run out of Todd's hut, you could get a game most nights, ops depending. This particular evening, a Canadian Flight Sergeant, Donovan was doing quite well. He was six shillings up for the night but it was a volatile game with new players coming in and out all the time as their funds fluctuated.

Donovan was dealing. He expertly shuffled the pack and then started going round the players, cards flicking out onto a blanket spread on the floor. A freshly minted Flight Sergeant with a gunner's brevet frowned as he looked at his cards. He was Archer's latest gunner. Blonde, blue eyed and rather cherubic of face, his name was Winsor but he got called Queenie a lot. Another replacement, Tucker was sitting next to him. They had been on the same gunnery course together.

Todd watched the action from one of the other beds. He had a piece of grease proof paper on his lap with a block of cheese and some cream crackers and a bottle of beer to wash it all down with.

Conversation ebbed and flowed like the game. Topics ranged from across the board but they kept coming back to Pearl Harbour and the goings on in the Pacific. It had electrified their interest in life outside of Amber Hill. No matter how the sanitised news articles were phrased, it was pretty clear the American fleet had been given a drubbing.

Lord Haw Haw had announced that the British Battleships, *Prince of Wales* and *Repulse* had been sunk after a Japanese air attack. Everyone had dismissed this as the usual German lies but the BBC confirmed it the following day.

The biggest news was that Germany had declared war on America. There was an almost collective sigh of relief at this announcement. With America coming into the war in Europe and not just the Pacific, they would no longer be on their own.

"With the yanks coming in, we might not even finish a tour," said Winsor with some enthusiasm. "The war could be over by next summer."

There was a lot of laughter at that comment. Todd didn't bother saying that there were plenty of other ways that you might not finish a tour. He cut a piece of cheese with his knife and stuck it on a cracker.

"Look what happened in the last show," he cautioned. "It took them ages to get troops across the Atlantic to the Western Front. You watch, it'll be this time next year before we see any change. A *lot* can happen in a year," he said with meaning.

In North Africa, the fighting around Tobruk was still going on with nothing certain either way. Malta was getting hammered. There was not much to cheer about at the moment. If things carried on like this, there would be nothing for the Americans to rescue.

Donovan started another hand. Tucker folded. Winsor was about to throw tuppence into the middle to call the ante when he showed his cards to Tucker to elicit an opinion. Tucker shook his head and the young lad mucked the hand, tossing the cards onto the pile of coins.

"No good there, pet," Tucker advised, his Yorkshire accent strong. "Wait for something better to turn up."

The mood in the room was buoyant. A couple of days of mild activity, a chance for sleep and some runs to the pubs in Lincoln was always good. With Christmas coming up, thoughts were turning to happier things in this time of war.

The rumour doing the rounds was there was going to be a station dance. Those with girls talked about having some fun and a dance. Those without tried to think about how they would manage to get a girl between now and Christmas.

Winsor asked if there would be any leave. Considering they had just been given some, no one thought that a likely prospect. One or two of the married men might be allowed to go but it was odds on they'd be flying ops anyway.

Tucker pondered aloud when that next op might be and Todd tutted and coughed into his hand as the conversation stalled. Like the Sergeants Mess, talking shop was generally frowned upon but he was feeling generous, Tucker was new so he may not be fully aware of the rules just yet. He had yet to fly an op so his eagerness could be understood.

"One step at a time," Todd cautioned. He moodily chewed on his cracker and cut off another bit of cheese. He took a swig from his bottle of beer and then put it back under the bed so no one could knock it over.

The hand ended and there was another deal. Money flew into the pot and the Canadian scooped another hand. He grinned as he stacked the coins in front of him on the blanket.

"I don't know what to do with you guys," he said. "It's like taking money from children."

"Belt," said Tucker. He fiddled with the pile of pennies and shillings in front of him. "I've been watching you. You can't be lucky forever."

"Who said it was luck." Donovan shrugged in good humour, not in the least offended. He was ahead and money talked. He split the pack in two and riffled the cards back into a single pile. He neatened it up and started dealing. "Poker, my friend, is a game of skill and math." Donovan had helped fund his college education with poker. To him, it was almost a science. He span a card to land in front of Tucker.

"Maybe that's it. Gunners don't have a head for figures." He made a pistol of his hand, forefinger stretched out, thumb back like the hammer of a pistol and then pulled the trigger, blowing on the end of his finger.

Todd shook his head. Cribbage was more his thing. He polished off the cheese and munched on a cracker as he brushed the crumbs off his lap. He went over to the stove in the corner to find it had burned low. He was about to add some more coal when he found the tub almost empty. In the bottom there were three sorry looking lumps of coal and some coal dust.

"What happened to all the coal?" he asked aloud. Conversation around the game came to an abrupt halt and faces looked in his direction. "That was supposed to last us till the end of next week," he said sharply, extremely annoyed to find there was none left.

He fixed each of them with a hard stare, focusing particularly on the guests and newcomers. Murphy and Walsh's lads who also lived in the hut knew the state of play. A burly Yorkshire wireless op called Martin chest stood up.

"I think that might be us," he said, apologetically. He nodded to Tucker and Winsor. "It was cold when we got here earlier so we got the stove going."

There was an uncomfortable silence. Murphy was unimpressed. New lads they may have been but everyone knew when you got somewhere new, the last thing you did was just avail yourself of the facilities.

The station Quartermaster was notoriously tight with supplies and he guarded his stocks with an iron will. If word got around that he let one hut have some more, everyone else would want the same thing.

"Right, dead simple," said Todd. He picked up one of the pieces of leftover coal from the tub and tossed it to the Yorkshireman. "You used it, go get some more."

"I will," came the response. Martin tossed the coal back to Todd and the Australian caught it in one hand. "You'll have to show us."

There was a challenge there. Todd didn't back down from any challenge.

"Fine, but you're carrying it. If the MP's turn up, I'll deny all knowledge we've ever met."

With coal in short supply, there were a limited number of

choices at Amber Hill to get extra fuel for the billet stoves. Being in the countryside, they could go foraging in the woods, either cutting down some branches, or if you were really lazy, you could pick up twigs. It might not have been seasoned wood but it was better than nothing.

On this occasion, Todd didn't fancy wielding an axe in the dark, he might chop something important off. Besides, it was a bit late to be signing out at the main gate. That left the more risky option of snaffling it from another hut or store.

They slid out in the dark. Todd led the way, threading his way round the Nissen huts. With it being late, there was no chance of busting into one of the other huts and not being noticed. Everyone was indoors keeping warm, so Todd headed for the station's admin buildings. The SP's did the rounds occasionally, but provided you timed it right there was little risk.

As they walked along, Winsor was telling Tucker about a girl he'd met in Lincoln.

"Her hands were all over me. She kept kissing me on the neck, I didn't like that," the youngster complained.

"Well where did you want her to kiss you?" Tucker asked. Todd looked at Winsor in amusement as the lad just shrugged and threw his hands up.

"I dunno, she tried putting her tongue in my mouth as well. 'Orrible it was."

"What happened after that?" Tucker asked.

"She took me outside and was all over me like a python." Winsor shuddered at the memory. "She kept putting my hands on her chest and rubbing up against me."

"Sounds to me like you were doing pretty well," Todd commented.

Winsor blew a raspberry, suddenly embarrassed at mentioning something so personal.

They stopped at a junction in the road and had a cigarette break. Todd was wreathed in smoke as he lit up. He leaned against a sign board that pointed left for Ops, right for Supply and the Motor Transport Section. He asked the new boys what they'd do if they saw a nightfighter in the dark. The response was reflexive and entirely expected.

"Shoot at it, naturally," said Winsor as Tucker nodded in agreement.

"Wrong," replied Todd. "Unless he goes for you of course. Otherwise you should leave him well alone."

"That doesn't seem right to me," muttered Tucker. "What if he goes for someone else? Surely we should do something about that?"

"Luck of the game mate," Todd replied flatly.

Winsor and Tucker shared a look, shocked at Todd's attitude. In the weak moonlight he could just glimpse the mix of disgust and revulsion on their faces.

"Look chum, he's got cannon, we ain't. You open up with your popguns and all you're doing is letting him know where you are. You leave him to it and pray he passes you by."

There was a long pause while this distilled wisdom was digested.

"Well I won't," said Winsor stubbornly. The thought of leaving another plane to the mercy of a nightfighter didn't sit well with him.

"What can I say?" Todd's voice dripped sarcasm. "You got all the answers." He carried on walking.

"It's not the decent thing," Winsor announced suddenly. Todd snorted in derision.

"Decent is a peacetime word. It's every man for himself sunshine and the quicker you realise that, the longer you'll live."

That finished the conversation, the mood had soured. Todd's cut throat attitude had shocked them more than they cared to admit. He got a few steps before he realised they'd stopped following him. He looked over his shoulder.

"Come on. We getting this stuff or what?"

They avoided the main admin buildings and went for some of the ancillary stores. When there were no Ops on, guard patrols tended to concentrate where intel and the squadron operational staff were based which left other places relatively unguarded.

They stopped at the back of the laundry building. It was a low, single storey brick house with a flat roof and it had its own boiler and its own store. Todd produced an iron bar from his jacket and handed it to Tucker.

"You watch this corner, Queenie; Martin the other," Tucker whispered. His companions nodded and split up, going to either end of the building, peering into the dark. "You could help," he hissed at Todd.

"No chance. I'm just a friendly observer."

"You're good at just watching then?" Tucker sulked, still stung by Todd's earlier comment. He bent his weight on the bar and the padlock gave easily. He swung the door open, wincing as the hinges shrieked. In the quiet, it sounded like the wailing of banshees.

Tucker slid into the store. He was so smooth, Todd was convinced he was wasted in RAF life, he should have been a cat burglar. Tucker picked up one of the hessian sacks filled with wood and handed it to Todd. He tossed another bag over his shoulder and they headed back to the Nissen hut. Todd led the way, Martin and Tucker carried the bags, Winsor brought up the rear, watching behind.

They were almost back to their billet when there was a shout from behind. Picking up the pace, they legged it and melted into the dark, carrying the bags between them for extra speed. Just when they thought they had ditched their tail, they collided with another foraging party running in the opposite direction.

"Redcaps!" someone shouted in the ruck and they all scattered in different directions. Todd carried a bag with Winsor and they took the long way round to get back to their hut. Todd hammered on the door and it opened quickly. They almost fell inside.

"Quick, close the door!" he shouted. "The blackout."

"What happened?" asked Murphy.

"I dunno," said Winsor. "Someone shouted cops so I just ran."

"Be thankful we got back with some wood," said Todd. He kicked the sack. Murphy picked it up and emptied the wood into the tub next to the stove. He shoved some kindling in the grate and got to work getting it lit.

Tucker turned up ten minutes later sans sack, hot, bothered and very out of breath. He had been chased by the MP's and he had led them a merry dance around the huts. He flopped on the floor, leaning against a bed.

"Where's, Martin?" asked Donovan.

"I've got no idea." They looked at him. "No, seriously," he told them. "He went left, I went right, god knows where he is."

17 - Pushing Your Luck

"So we'll be going in daylight. Take off time is 0945 hours." The briefing room was as silent as the tomb. Normally when a target was announced there would be moments when a murmur went around the gathered crews as they weighed their chances. Men would look left or right and pass a few comments with a colleague. This time, no one moved an inch as the enormity of what Asher had just said sunk in.

The squadron had already been to Brest five nights previously to lay some mines in the approaches to the port. As operations went it had been relatively easy. A diversionary raid had been mounted on the harbour itself at the same time as they had gone in to lay their mines. It had been perfect, all the defences had been looking the other way while they had bumbled along at low level just off the coast.

During the Napoleonic Wars, the Royal Navy had blockaded the French and Spanish Navies to keep them in port and keep control of the sea. Fast forward a hundred years and things had changed. Minelaying had become the new way to blockade. With U-Boats roaming far and wide from the French ports, the Royal Navy was finding itself hard pressed to escort the convoys in the Atlantic and keep the casualties down.

In addition, the German Battleships, *Scharnhorst* and *Gneisenau* had put in at Brest earlier in the year after carving up some Atlantic convoys and there they had remained ever since. *Prinz Eugen* had joined them after the breakout into the Atlantic with the *Bismarck*.

For whatever reason, the big ships had stayed in port and not ventured forth again. Woods had joked in the Mess that Hitler was too chicken to send them out after what had happened to the *Bismarck*. Carter wondered if there was some truth to that. Whatever the reason, *Tirpitz* lurked in the Baltic while *Scharnhorst* and *Gneisenau* and *Prinz Eugen* were at Brest, always threatening to sortie and cause mayhem.

Bomber Command was doing its best to make sure they didn't leave again. A few squadrons had hit Brest last night, returning only a few hours before. Now the rest of them were being sent back to keep the pressure on.

"Command feels that going in once in broad daylight can finish the job," the CO explained, doing his best to whip up some enthusiasm and failing miserably. He looked at his crews with a long appraising gaze and he could see it was like water falling off a ducks back. He changed tack slightly. "Now look here chaps, we've been pecking away at these ships for months. You know it, I know it." He sighed and relaxed his stern demeanour slightly, leaning back against the table, hands gripping its edge. "There have been eight raids of varying size in the last few weeks. Some hits have been reported but its not been enough to really put them out of action. This is going to be a precision raid to deliver a knock out punch."

The silence became oppressive. Asher strode to the front of the platform and stood there, hands on hips. He imposed himself on all of them, looking around, waiting for someone to raise an objection. No one spoke.

The briefing continued but Carter found he wasn't really listening. He was still rocked by the thought of flying in broad daylight. All of his operational flying had been at night, he'd never flown a daylight raid before and he found his mouth had gone dry.

Linkletter told them the weather would be lovely and the predicted winds would be light. He got his usual applause when he told them the airfields would be clear upon their return. Black Jack went through the approach to the target, highlighting the aiming point.

Carter only started paying any real attention when Billy Kent took the stage and went over the likely fighter opposition. He pointed out that the nearest Luftwaffe fighter field was miles away at the other end of the Brittany peninsula. They were cheered somewhat when they were told there would be fighters escorting the raid in. The flak in the city was moderate but he told them they could expect the Battleships to put up their own barrage as well. Regardless, 363 would be bringing up the rear again so the defences would be well warmed up by then.

"The barrage from the ships might give you chaps an extra aiming point," he suggested with some enthusiasm, trying to gee them up. No one rose to the humour.

Etheridge came forward and took his turn. Normally, the crews liked his pep talks, that final bit of encouragement to send them on their way. This time it was different, he was almost apologetic.

"I realise that sometimes orders don't seem to make sense. We obey them anyway. That's what we do. There is a chain of command and we do what we are told, from the lowliest airman to the aircraft captain, to the flight leader and so on. You have your orders. So, let's get out there and do this right so we don't have to go back and do it again. Good luck to you all."

He gave them his best encouraging smile. He would have given a lot to be going with them for this one. When the orders had arrived in the early hours no one could quite believe it to start with. There had been a flurry of signals back and forth to Group until it was confirmed as being correct.

The aircrew had a similar reaction when they had been stirred from their pits at six am. They were never woken up so early. Theirs was a night time war with night time hours. Getting early wake ups was something the bods in 2 Group got to do. The men had slowly stirred themselves over porridge and then nearly choked on it when the tannoy called them to briefing at 0645 hours.

Carter felt ill while he was getting dressed in the equipment room. He had survived a tour of thirty ops but he had never experienced anything like this.

When he'd got to twenty five ops, he'd been twitchy. You weren't normal if you didn't. Men without imagination didn't last, they just slowly cracked up until one day they could no longer take it. You had to knuckle down and conquer your fear just long enough to get through it all. So he had buckled down and summoned the courage to finish his tour. This feeling of dread was far worse.

When they were driven out to the aircraft at dispersal there was none of the usual banter and joking. Each man had withdrawn into himself, lost in his thoughts. Even the erks were quiet, picking up on the mood of the crew. They kept a respectful distance while the men made ready. Carter walked round L-London and signed the Form 700. He looked at the armour piercing bombs in the bay. They would be heavy taking off and he reminded himself to take a long run before hauling back on the yoke.

Vos went through his radio checks but his thoughts turned to Denise and what would happen to her if he didn't come back. White thought about the letter he had written to Elaine. He should have dashed off an extra few lines before sealing the envelope and leaving it on his sideboard. It was too late now.

Carter went through the start up like a robot, his voice flat and lacking any of the usual emotion or conviction White had come to expect.

"Master engine cocks? THEY ARE OFF!"

"Throttles? SET TO HALF-INCH OPEN!" White nudged them to the starting position and gave Carter an additional thumbs up.

"Prop controls? UP!"

"Cut-out switches? SET TO IDLE CUT-OFF!"

"Supercharger controls? SET M RATIO!"

"Warning light? NO LIGHT!"

"Air intake heat? READS COLD!"

"Radiator shutters auto? RAD SHUTTERS AUTO!"

"Tank selector? NUMBER TWO TANK."

"Master cock?" ON, BOOSTER, ON."

Carter leaned out of the cockpit window and twirled a finger above his head. The erk raised a hand and pointed at the port engine.

The engine whined and the prop started turning. It caught

almost straight away with a loud throaty roar. Carter advanced the throttle to the idle position and watched the needles settle down. The starboard engine started up and Carter slid the side window closed.

He pulled on his soft Kidd leather gloves and gripped the yoke. He had a final go at moving the controls. White looked out of the canopy across the wide slab of wing, watching the ailerons move their full range of travel and nodded to Carter.

White advanced the throttles and they taxied out, slotting in with the other aircraft of the squadron as they went along the perimeter track. Asher was up front, then Church. A real maximum effort. A green flare went off from the tower and Asher started rolling.

Watching from the tower, Group Captain Etheridge leaned over the railing on the upper balcony. Dickinson stood next to him. They watched the first Manchester go into its run, engines blaring. The tail picked up and it hung on its mainwheels. Etheridge followed it as it slowly left the earth. Almost immediately the undercarriage retracted and it climbed away, turning to port to clear the runway.

There was a bang behind him and the smell of cordite irritated his nostrils as another flare was fired off. The second Manchester started its roll. A WAAF from the Ops room stood next to him. She was clutching a clipboard to her chest and her eyes glistened as she watched the squadron go to war.

"I've never seen this in daylight," she whispered. She had always waved them off in the dark before now. The Manchester's were creatures of the night, they blended into the background, heard as much as seen. You would hear the great roar of the engines, the orange stab of the exhausts, the deep bass throb of the Vultures and the glint of the canopies as they went off into the moonlight.

Etheridge could only nod. He was pensive as more Manchester's took off. The last time the RAF had tried daylight raids with heavy bombers had been at the beginning of the war. The theory of tight formation flying and defensive firepower had been put to the test and been found wanting. The Wellingtons had been cut to pieces attacking a coastal target not unlike this one. The Me109's had torn into them and picked them apart like foxes sniping at a bunch of chickens. If half the squadron came back from this, he would be very surprised.

Woods had to work hard on the outbound route. Rather than head east as they normally would, they went over the south west of England. They passed near Torquay and picked up a final pinpoint before heading out over the channel, keeping well to the west of Jersey.

Carter found things easier. Normally you had to strain and concentrate all the way there and back. You had to rely on the little things to tell you what was going on around you. There might be a short spark of orange flame from an exhaust, or you might feel the turbulence in the controls as you crossed in someones wake. In daylight, there was none of that. You could see the aircraft around you and the only danger was running into someone as you climbed through cloud.

They got up to fourteen thousand feet comfortably and then the Manchester made them work hard for another fifteen hundred feet. They ended up five hundred short of the briefed height but Carter could feel that they had reached their limit. The controls were soft and he was having to input more aileron on the yoke to keep level.

All the way across the channel the aircraft began to bunch up. No one flew formation as such, but the great gaggle of bombers clung to each other in the bright light, relying on safety in numbers and depth of formation to get them through. Any second, they expected the sky to be filled with 109's and Carter was convinced they were hiding behind each fluffy cloud.

The sky mercifully remained clear and they flew parallel to the west coast about four or five miles out before turning east for the bomb run. One of the last to bomb, Woods had a fantastic view of the show. In contrast, Todd hated it. It was his turn up front in the nose turret and he flinched as blasts went off ahead of them.

At night, flak was almost invisible, there was just the occasional bright flash which was there and gone, a mere flicker. In the harsh noon light, they were dark brooding puffs of smoke with an evil orange centre. In the tail he saw none of this sort of thing when he was in his turret, alone in the dark. His stomach dropped as L-London shook and a flak burst exploded below, bodily lifting the bomber.

Carter wrestled with the Manchester, doing his best to keep them straight and level. White rode the controls, ready to take over in case Carter was hit.

Woods peered through the bomb sight. For once he didn't have to do paint by numbers. There was no problem picking up the target today. Smoke from the previous night's raids lingered over the city and clung to the ground, but he had a perfect view of the harbour.

On the southern coast of the Brittany peninsular, Brests harbour ran roughly south west to north east. *Prinz Eugen* was tied up to the harbour wall and then there were the two large dry docks occupied by the other two Battleships.

South west of Brest was the La Phare Du Petit Minou, a spit of land that stuck out and had a small bay and a beach. The coast ran from there in a straight line to the harbour, a perfect starting point to make the final run in.

Beyond the harbour was the Rue Jean Jaures, a long straight road that led to the Place de Strasbourg. Other roads radiated out from here like the spokes of a wheel. Personally, Woods would have preferred coming in from the other direction. The Rue Jean Jaures was a wonderful line to follow in the run up to the target and it would be a good visual cue for Carter to fly. Also, if they had approached the target from this direction, any bombs that went long would still explode in the harbour. Woods was conscious that if he made a muck of this, his bombs could end up going into houses and killing a lot of innocent Frenchmen.

The flak was ferocious. With their undersides painted black, the bombers stood out against the sky like cockroaches racing across a white rug. The warships also added to the conflagration, their own flak guns firing into the sky.

Woods gave Carter a few corrections and watched as the targets crept into his sight. He had been briefed to bomb *Gneisenau*. She was the nearest Battleship of the two in drydock. He set his sight on a commercial building just before *Gneisenau*. If he went long, whatever missed would go on to hit *Scharnhorst* in the next dry dock over but not in the houses beyond. He dropped the bombs in pairs in quick succession, with a half second delay between each pair. He counted to three.

"They're off!" he shouted as he flicked the switch to close the bomb doors. Carter counted to ten, holding it straight and level for the camera to go off and photograph their aiming point, then he turned left to clear the city and head for home along with everyone else.

Two Stirling's went down over the target. Flying lower than the Halifax's and Manchester's they bore the brunt of the flak gunner's attention. One minute they were there, the next they were gone. 363 lost one of their own over the harbour. Flying ahead of Carter, they were off to the right and slightly below when a flak burst caught them close on the starboard side. The canopy shattered and glittering pieces of perspex flew in the air like wedding confetti. The starboard engine shed its prop and a bright streak of flame trailed back from the nacelle. Almost immediately, a small shape dropped from the nose, then another. One more dropped from the rear turret.

"They're bailing!" Todd cried out.

Two parachutes opened. The third man continued to fall, tumbling end over end. No one saw if his parachute opened or not before he was lost from view.

Before anyone else could jump, the Manchester rolled onto its back and dived vertically. Part of the tailplane broke away, then the third fin shed its canvas during its death dive.

Carter felt ill. He had never seen that in such detail before. He'd seen bombers attacked over the target get bracketed by flak and blown to pieces. He'd seen a nightfighter stitch a Whitley from nose to tail once, but never in daylight. It was too raw, too clinical. The dark hid many things.

"How many?" asked Carter over the R/T.

"I saw three," said Murphy from the back.

"Who was it?" asked Vos.

"I saw an H," reported Todd. His keen eyes had seen the letter on the side of the bomber. "Anyone?"

No one knew who it was. They would have to wait when they got back. A black pall of smoke hung over the city behind them as the remaining bombers made their runs on the targets. Despite everyones worst fears, the Luftwaffe did not put in an appearance and they got a free run home as fast as their engines could carry them.

Halfway home, they passed over a Halifax that had ditched in the channel. The yellow dinghy bobbed alongside the wreck waiting for pickup. Woods made a note of the coordinates in his log book to hand over at interrogation.

The station personnel were out in strength to see them in. They stood around the control tower waving as each Manchester touched down. They got back just as the light was beginning to fade, casting long shadows on the ground. They'd only lost the one Manchester and Archer had put down at an airfield in the south. The men were buoyant in interrogation, the room buzzing with chatter as they talked about the raid.

When he got back to his quarters, White retrieved the letter and read it again. He pulled out a fresh sheet of paper and began writing. Woods relaxed with a book. It was nice to delve into some detective fiction after the mayhem of the day.

With an early finish, Vos caught the first transport to Lincoln to surprise Denise. He caught her doing her hair. He watched, fascinated while she sat cross legged with her long hair over a basin of hot water, letting the steam do its work. Every so often she rubbed her hair in a towel to dry it and get the dirt out. Once she had cleaned it, she brushed it from crown to end till it was glossy and then pinned it in rollers. As she worked, he asked her how her day had been and listened attentively.

She talked about her new job. After a few days of hanging around the hotel and exploring Lincoln, she had gotten fidgety. She needed something to keep her busy when Vos was away during the day and he had encouraged her to find a job. She found one in the supply department of a factory that supplied diesel engines to the army. It wasn't highly paid but it was a start.

When she asked him about his day, he just said they had been training. She had heard the drone of bombers earlier in the day but she had no idea they had been on a raid.

He distracted her by talking about the coming holiday and festivities. He went through the newspaper, looking at the adverts for what was coming at the theater and cinemas. It would be good for them to go out and do something, ops depending.

Carter hovered around the Mess for a bit and then turned in early. He lay on his bed as he stared up at the ceiling, thinking about the day's events. The Manchester they had seen go down had been Bishops. This meant both of the crews Carter had passed through OTU back in October had gone for a burton within five ops. It was hard to write it off to the luck of the game even though he knew that was exactly what it was. His sleep was troubled that night while Walsh snored from across the room.

Archer flew in the following afternoon light one crew member. Carter heard the story in the Mess. Bracketed by flak over the target, Archers port engine had been knocked out. They'd also had a small fire in the fuselage and there was an anxious few minutes until the wireless operator got it under control, patting the flames out with his bare hands.

Unable to maintain height, they had thrown out everything that wasn't nailed down. The gunners left a few tails of ammo for the guns and dumped the rest. Even the Elsan chemical toilet had been unbolted and thrown out the door to avoid ditching in the Channel.

They'd made it back with a thousand feet to spare, the temperature gauge jammed in the red with Archer expecting the engine to burst into flames any minute. They thumped it down at the first available airfield, glad to be back.

18 - Bah, Humbug

The dance was in full swing. The gods of war had smiled kindly and there was a lull in operatons. High winds and bad icing conditions mixed with heavy cloud over central Europe had killed off the chance of ops for a few days. There was the usual minelaying along the coast, but 363 hadn't been called on to participate. They still went up flying and training but their war had taken a break for a short while.

Bunting had been strung across the rafters in the hall. Paraffin heaters had been used in the afternoon to banish the biting cold. A table was covered in glasses and two large punch bowls. Another bowl held the egg nog.

Carter's nose wrinkled in distaste and he moved away from the table towards a makeshift bar at the other side of the hall. He shouldered through the throng and held up one finger and flashed a shilling. He was handed a bottle and change and took a long pull at it before navigating the crowd back out.

He joined Walsh and his second dicky, Nicol by a table and stood with one foot on the rung of a stool. The general noise in the hall ebbed and flowed as more people arrived. He caught a glimpse of his crew as they came in as a group. He waved a hand and they steered towards him. Murphy took off his forage cap and slotted it underneath his epaulette.

"What kept you?"

"Laughing boy here," Murphy gestured towards White. "You were making yourself presentable, weren't you, sir?"

Murphy playfully cuffed White across the shoulders. White smoothed his hair back down and assumed a superior air. He brushed some imaginary dust off his chest.

"I'm not going to be rushed."

"Yeah, yeah, spare me," said Todd, rolling his eyes. White blew a raspberry at him.

"Where's Vos?" Carter asked, noticing he was missing.

"Sorting his popsy out," said White, with a wink at Woods. It was the first time the rest of the crew had seen her but they were curious to see the siren that had managed to charm their wireless op.

"No offense fellas," said Nicols. He stood up from his chair and shouldered his way through to the front of the group. "You lot have got nothing on me. It needs class to pull a lady." He pulled down his short battledress jacket and straightened his tie.

"You're going to need every ounce of luck you possess to pull that off; sir," Todd told him tartly. There was a chorus of agreement.

"We'll see about that," said Nicol, full of confidence.

He swept the crowd with his eyes. Amongst the RAF blue were splashes of colour of women in their finest, the crush of rationing and austerity thrown off for an evening. He started his target selection, his eyes fixing on a tall vision in a maroon dress stood in a group of four girls near the stage.

"Brother, that's for me," he murmured, like a thirsty man who had suddenly found a barrel of water. He shoved off from the crowd to move in. He clamped a hand around Murphy's upper arm.

"Come on," he said peremptorily, "I need a witness. And if you're really good, I'll introduce you."

Murphy managed a resigned, "But I don't even-" before giving up and trailing along in Nicol's wake.

Carter grunted in amusement as he watched the two of them wend their way across the hall. Talk about chalk and cheese, the officer and the Flight Sergeant, the Oxford man and the lad from Barnsley. The women spotted them crossing the dance floor and shifted position slightly. The tall blonde angled right so she could still talk to her friends but then turn to look at Nicol with minimal effort if she chose to do so.

They watched with an air of anticipation as Nicol made his final approach. Vague interest was thrown in his direction as he made an observation and gestured towards the girls in their dresses. Murphy was introduced and he took a reluctant step forward. There were smiles and then the group opened up to allow the two of them in. Conversation flowed. Nicol said something and the women laughed. The blonde gave him all of her attention and stood closer to him as he span a yarn.

"I don't believe it," said Todd.

"Beginners luck," commented White.

"He doesn't look glamorous," said Woods and in truth he was right. Nicol looked barely old enough to shave.

"It's the wings," Todd said with mock jealousy. "Have a pair of wings on your chest and they'll drop their knickers quicker'n winking."

At that, all gazes turned towards Carter and Walsh. Carter paused as he drank from his pint to see four pairs of eyes staring at him.

"Don't look at me," he told them. He licked off his beer moustache. "I'm not chasing any skirt tonight. No chance." He hooked a thumb left towards Walsh. "Try him."

145

Vos arrived with Denise. She walked a little behind him, clutching his hand tightly. When he'd mentioned the dance to her the week before she had been enthusiastic. Now it was here she found herself quite shy.

She wore a green dress with more pleats than she knew what to do with. As her daughter was away in the WRENS, her landlady had loaned it to Denise. Her dark hair was gathered up so it was curled into waves on top and rolled under into a chigon on the bottom. Gold studs shone at her ears and she had applied a little bit of eyeshadow and lipstick.

"Blimey," Todd whispered to Woods as he saw her.

"Bloody hell," said Walsh, coolly impressed. She was like a little china doll with her trim waist and long neck. She nodded to Woods and Carter, recognising them from London.

"Hello to all of you," she said nervously. "Christophe has told me so much about all of you."

"None of it's true," said Walsh deadpan, taking the initiative and stepping forward, embracing her by the shoulders and kissing her on each cheek, continental style. "Enchante," he said as he did so. Vos bristled at the familiarity. He introduced each of them and she said hello more personally although none of the others dared kiss her as Walsh had done.

Vos disappeared to get them both a drink and she stood next to Carter. He asked her how she was settling down in Lincoln and she told him she was all right, keeping her answers short. She looked around the hall. She'd not expected so many people to be here. Vos returned a few minutes later carrying two drinks, gin for her and a beer for himself.

"They didn't have any wine," he apologised. "Is gin okay?"

She nodded and took the drink from him, glad of some added courage.

Once the band started up the party really got going. After weeks of ops, the crews were quick to let their hair down. People paired up with feminine company and hit the dance floor. Others clung to the walls in clusters, fists clutching bottles and pints as they smoked and drank. The air was tinged with a hazy blue from the smoke. Nicol's blonde stayed glued to his side all evening. Murphy found a sympathetic brunette who listened with puppy dog eyes while he bared his soul.

Nicol was dragged onto the dance floor and struggled to keep up. He may have been be a deft touch in the air but his dance style was limited. His dance partner ran rings around him until they finally went outside for some fresh air and more besides.

Denise persuaded Vos to take a turn and they danced. The girl moulded herself to him, moving in slow time regardless of the music, oblivious of everything else around them. Woods watched them for a while, pleased to see that all had turned out well.

Carter and Walsh found a good spot near the bar and began working their way through pints of beer. Walsh told the story of his hydraulics blowout again. Carter had heard it more than once but it had improved with the telling. Walsh pantomimed rubbing his tongue on his sleeve and tasting the air, his lips flapping.

"Yuk, I can still taste it, nasty stuff."

"Have another beer and take the taste away," Carter told him as he handed him another pint.

Some late arrivals came into the hall. Asher drifted over to welcome them in and he guided the Air Commodore and his officers to a table. There were introductions all round as they took their seats.

"It's good of you to join us, sir," said Asher. The Air Commodore waved away the fuss.

"Nonsense, Asher. I'm not one to miss a party. A few drinks here and then we'll move on, more parties to go to," he said, smiling at his staff officer, who nodded agreement. "You're not my only stop tonight."

His staff officer disappeared to get some drinks. While he waited for service he looked around and blinked, certain his eyes were playing tricks on him. He crossed the distance and grabbed Carter's hand, shaking it off at the elbow.

With a few drinks behind him, it took Carter a few seconds to focus on his assailant. When his brain caught up, he let out a yell and they embraced each other.

"What on earth?"

"I didn't know you were back on ops!"

Carter gestured to the new arrival.

"Billy, this is Freddie Wilkinson. He was my second Dicky for a while on my first tour."

"And I saved your miserable life if I recall correctly," said Wilkinson, grinning broadly. Carter laughed and Walsh watched with interest, seeing his room mate come alive, the rigid control sliding away as the years rolled off him.

Walsh stuck out his hand and Wilkinson shook it, his grip firm and strong. The same height as Carter, he had thick dark hair and deep brown eyes. He had Squadron Leader rings on his shoulders and cuffs and a DFC ribbon on his chest below his wings.

"What are you doing here?" asked Wilkinson.

"They kicked me out of Scotland," Carter said simply. "They had enough of me. What about you?"

"I'm here with the old man." Carter and Walsh strained their necks to look around Wilkinson and saw the brass sitting with Asher and Robinson. "I'm at Group now. Look, pop in to Grantham when you can and we'll have a catch up and sort something out. Helen would be over the moon to see you."

Carter grinned; his mood buoyed up by seeing his friend.

"She hasn't left you then?"

"No, she hasn't you sarcastic sod."

"You better watch it then," Carter said, deadpan. "No dancing with anyone or Helen will get to hear about it." Wilkinson laughed; a good throaty laugh free from strain.

"No fear. I'm strictly a one woman man and I've got mine." Wilkinson looked around the sea of bodies. "In fact, where's, Mary?" Carter's face pinched.

"I'm afraid that boat sailed."

"Ah, genuinely sorry old man," Wilkinson said with real feeling. Carter shrugged.

"Wasn't your fault," Carter muttered, "her loss anyway." He knocked back the rest of his drink. There was a whole conversation there, but it would have to be one for another day. Wilkinson's time was not his own at that moment.

"Look, duty calls, but I'll see you soon?"

"Certainly." They shook hands again and Wilkinson collected drinks from the bar. He made his way back to the table and found the the Air Commodore making small talk with 363's CO.

His mood lifted from the brief encounter, Carter turned back to Walsh and launched into a story of one of his and Wilkinson's runs into Lincoln. It had ended with a foot chase involving the local constabulary. Escape and Evasion technique practice, Wilkinson had called it.

Carter realised that had been just about a year ago, New Years Eve 1940. Another time, another age, a million years ago. His face tightened slightly when he remembered who else had been with them that night. Bunny Barker, EDY, Flash Gordon, Stretch Jones, Taffy Morgan and the rest. All gone now.

Some had been lost in accidents. EDY and Flash were cooling their heels in a prisoner of war camp somewhere in Germany by all accounts. The rest were six feet under.

Coming back from an op, Bunny Barker had flown into the balloon barrage over Felixstowe in the fog. A cable had snicked off his starboard wing and he had nosed into a factory. Stretch Jones had been shot up by a nightfighter over Cologne. He had held the dying bomber steady long enough for his crew to bail out, then the control cables parted and he rode her all the way down. His mother had received his DFC in its box on his birthday.

Walsh saw the shutters coming back down and he shoved another pint into Carter's hand quick and the pair of them commiserated and bitched about the Manchester and its vices.

On the other side of the hall, two girls were talking in shouted conference over the noise of the band. They had come together to the dance but the brunette felt like a spare part. She had come because her friend Laura had asked her to, but when she got here, her friend had been swept away by her chap. Periodically, she would circle back for a quick chat before being whisked off her feet again.

Georgette Waters sighed in resignation as her friend's pilot zoomed in to take her away once more. They pirouetted onto the dance floor, him smiling, her mesmerised.

Miffed at being neglected, she smoothed down her blue dress. Feeling a little flushed, she extracted her compact from her clutch bag and flipped the lid. She looked at herself in the mirror, moving her head around to see herself from different angles. She refreshed her lipstick and ran a hand through her bob of black hair.

A drunken Pilot Officer lurched towards her.

"I say, wha...wha...what's a pretty-" he stammered, getting no further as she shot him a withering look and stood up, squaring her shoulders.

"I'm awfully sorry," she said her voice all sweetness and light, "my dates waiting for me," and she moved around the perimeter of the dance floor to put some distance between them.

She noticed two men near the bar and changed her line slightly to head towards them. They seemed to be having a serious conversation and this intrigued her, everyone else just seemed to be interested in drinking as much as possible or dancing or shouting. She looked back to see Laura in a world of her own, wrapped in her man's arms. Georgette felt like having some fun herself.

Keeping her eye on the two men, she looked at them more closely. One of them was quite short with a tousled appearance, his hair just that bit too long, his shirt collar open and showing a hint of red scarf underneath. The other was taller, slight in build with short dark hair and crystal clear blue eyes. The scar on his cheek moved when he talked, giving his lopsided smile a cruel edge.

She slid into the press of people next to the two men, close enough to hear them discussing the film *Target For Tonight*. They were picking it apart, scene by scene with black humour and biting sarcasm.

The taller one had the DFC on his chest but the ribbon was faded. His eyes told the story though. Eyes like that never belonged to someone on their first tour. He was someone who had been plucked from training and sent back out to do it all again.

"Does everyone have to be a film critic to be a pilot these days?" she asked them, inserting herself into the conversation. Their eyes swivelled in her direction noticing her for the first time.

"No, but it helps," said the shorter of the two, his voice slurring, his Liverpudlian accent a shifting mix of high notes and guttural catches. He looked beyond her. "On your own are you love?"

She shook her head and pointed towards the dance floor.

"No, but I might as well be. I'm the spare part. My friend insisted I come to keep her company. She's with that big blonde chap over there."

Walsh and Carter knew who she was talking about right away. Archer stood above the crowd and was holding onto a blonde as he gyrated around. He danced like he flew, bags of energy but not the most elegant display.

"So what's a girl to do?" She addressed the question to both of them but she looked at Carter. He shifted uncomfortably under her gaze and scratched at his left cheek, feeling the line of the scar tissue. He had managed to avoid female attention so far this evening but it appeared his luck had run out.

She was a pretty girl. She was slim, dark haired and had a lovely smile. Her accent was like silk, all smooth contralto and caramel tones. Her dark hair was swept back to show a long neck and bare shoulders. Her blue dress was cinched in at the waist and the sleeves ended at the elbow.

He could feel his nerves scraping, kicking and screaming as thoughts of Mary stirred from the depths. He could see the hint, it was there in her eyes, the waiting for him to ask, 'do you want to dance?'

Part of him wanted to. She seemed nice but he hesitated and the moment dragged. Seconds piled on top of one another. She shifted impatiently and chewed on her lower lip, feeling foolish for coming over and saying anything at all.

"Surely, you've something better to do?" he bit out; his voice flat. Her eyes widened. Walsh coughed into his hand, surprised at Carters bluntness.

"Maybe," she shot back, hurt. "I was only trying to talk to you."

"Whatever for?" He gestured left and right, indicating there were plenty of other people around for her to engage with. She didn't need telling twice, she turned on her heel. Walsh shot Carter a pitying look.

"Bad form, Alex. Bad form." He shook his head and dashed after her. Here was a pretty girl wanting to dance, it was just common decency to do so, even if you weren't interested in anything else. He caught up to her and got her to stop.

"Apologies for my friend," he said quickly. "He's had a bad day. Come for a dance?" He crooked his arm and she took it, letting herself be steered to the dance floor. While Walsh did a competent job of avoiding her feet, she calmed herself down.

"How's a pretty girl like you get in a place like this?" he asked her.

"Connections," she told him. "Actually, I'm a Section Officer. It's just nice not to wear that uniform for once." Walsh laughed and span her round in his arms.

"I'm, Billy." He held her close, his right arm around her waist as he shimmied through the crush on the dance floor.

"Georgette," she replied.

"How wonderful," he laughed. "I'll call you, George then. You look like a, George." She laughed with him, feeling the tension ebb away.

Carter watched her spin around, angry with himself. He'd handled that badly but there was little he could do about it now. Every time Walsh and the girl went round the room, she looked at him, her expression unreadable. He couldn't tell if she was trying to make him jealous or shame him into doing something. He removed himself from the equation and went outside.

It was cold and his cheeks tingled at the change in temperature. Frost covered the ground. It was dark, a quarter moon hidden by broken cloud. There was a group of aircrew off to the right and he sauntered over, nodding hello as he recognised Fish Salmon amongst them. He tugged out a cigarette and stuck it between his lips as one of them offered him their lighter.

The smoke warmed him as they huddled like penguins. He shuddered when a light breeze sneaked around the hall and carved through them. He glanced at his watch and had another cigarette as his teeth began to chatter. His fingers were starting to go numb as he worked his way through a third. Once he was happy sufficient time had passed by, he ground the cigarette under his heel and went back inside.

The hot air hit him like a wall. He paused at the door for a few moments, letting his eyes get used to the gloom and then hunted out Walsh. He saw no sign of a blue dress but then she could so easily be lost in the crowd. He found Walsh chatting freely with his crew who were getting down to some serious drinking with Carters own men. Nicol was missing, still otherwise engaged with his blonde.

Murphy was glassy eyed and being held up by Todd. His brunette had lost interest after a few dances and moved on. Put out, Murphy had polished off a few pints to console himself. The mistake had been mixing his drinks and having a nip of whisky from a hip flask Todd had sneaked in.

"Come on, old son," Todd said, keeping Murphy's face upright to stop him from dribbling down his uniform. "Will someone help me get him outside?" he asked aloud. White came over to give him a hand and together they manoeuvred the tall man towards the doors. When they got outside, they parked him on a wall and let him get some fresh air, which was a mistake as he threw up all down the front of Todd's uniform jacket.

Reacting too late to avoid it, Todd jumped back and without his support holding him up, Murphy fell back over the wall onto the grass.

"You dozy sod," said White.

"Look at me!" shouted Todd. "All down my best uniform." He was foaming. They got Murphy back up and took an arm each. "Right, I'm not buggering about, let's walk him around a bit and get him back to the billet."

Vos shook his head as he saw them half carry, half drag the drunken Murphy away.

"And you're paying for this to be cleaned!" was the last he heard as they rounded a corner out of sight.

"Will he be all right?" asked Denise in some concern.

"Probably," said Vos, offhand. "They know what they're doing," he reassured her.

He opened his greatcoat and she snuggled into him to keep warm. Her dress was lovely but it hadn't been made for cold winter nights. Even with her thick coat on, she was still cold. He walked with her, heading towards the bus stop.

Back in the hall, Woods was matching Walsh pint for pint across the table. Carter couldn't believe Walsh was even vertical. He'd drunk at least six pints and bottles when he was with Carter, let alone however many he'd now drunk at the table. His crew were egging him on and he upended another pint glass on the table after he emptied it.

Walsh saw him come back into their social circle. He had one more drink and then chucked a ten bob note on the table.

"I surrender," he said, he belched and tried to control his churning stomach. One more drink would have finished him off, it was time to quit. The big Canadian pocketed the note and then finished off his own pint just to prove he could do it.

Walsh took Carter by the arm and steered him over to the table with the punch and egg nog. He asked for two glasses and handed one to Carter. His room mate gagged as he saw it was egg nog.

"I can't drink this stuff," Carter wheedled.

"Tough," Walsh told him. "Consider it your penance for the evening. You snubbed a positively delightful girl earlier, you clumsy clot."

No matter how drunk he was, Carter could see that Walsh was serious and wouldn't let him go until he had drunk the ghastly stuff. He grimaced and then swallowed it in one go. He gagged but controlled himself and held it down.

"God that was awful."

"Too bad," said Walsh with little sympathy. "It happens you deserve it." Carter found he had to agree, flaying his soul with guilt for being such a churl. He needed to realise that not every girl who talked to him wanted to have a relationship with him.

19 - Under A Wandering Star

New Years celebrations had a nasty habit of going badly for Carter. While he liked a drink as much as the next man, he hated drinking to complete excess. The first sign it was time to quit was a tightening of the skin on his forehead, like someone had grabbed his hair and pulled back hard. If he was stupid enough to ignore that, the next thing would be a feeling that his vision was telescoping, that he was looking at things from a distance, down a tube. If he ignored that, then he would be heaving his guts up not long afterward.

Going to bed when he felt like this was always difficult. If he lay on his side, the room would start to sway and it would feel like the whole world would come crashing down onto him. If he could lay flat on his back and keep still, he could just about cope. He'd still feel like death in the morning, but getting to sleep without being sick was half the battle. This particular year, a number of circumstances fortuitously conspired together to spare him this fate.

The evening had started sedately enough. The CO had laid on transport and the trucks dropped them and some other crews in the centre of Lincoln. They were told quite clearly, pick up would be at 1am, no later. Anyone who missed the bus would have to make their own way back to Amber Hill.

Carter and Walsh's crew hit the pubs hard. They started at *The Tarleton* and went on from there, never lingering long before moving on to the next one. Along the way their numbers dwindled as Todd and Murphy split off after bumping into a bunch of gunners from some other crews. Carter had vague recollections of Nicol peeling off with the blonde girl he had met at the Christmas dance a week or two earlier.

Carter's forehead started tightening in a pub called, *The General*. The tunnel vision came on like an express train after White pressed him to have another under the counter brandy. It burned his throat on the way down and started a war on his already turbulent stomach.

Going outside for some fresh air he was joined by Walsh, Woods, White and Vos. Walsh offered him a bottle of beer but he shook his head and waved him off. Walsh shrugged and drank it instead. He belched as he finished it and chucked it towards the gutter.

Holding onto each other for support, they staggered back to the designated pick up point to find the street empty. There was no crowd of waiting airmen and no trucks. Leaving White leaning against a lamp post, Carter looked up and down the connecting streets but saw nothing vaguely like a truck.

"S'not here," slurred White. He blinked fast and then screwed up his face, letting the three versions of Walsh settle down into a single figure in front of him. Walsh tapped his watch and then flapped his arm around.

"Bloody watch has stopped." He shook his arm some more. He peered at the watch face, holding his wrist close so he could see the luminous dial glowing in the dark.

Stuck in the middle of Lincoln they had a loud conference about what to do next. No taxis were in sight and the buses had stopped hours ago. Stealing a car was suggested but quickly dismissed. Walsh could barely stand and Carter wasn't willing to drive in his current state. While they were talking, a couple of healthy looking young men in civilian clothes walked by. There were the usual nods of acknowledgement as total strangers pass one another, then one of them was stupid enough; or just drunk enough to make a remark.

"Can't take it RAFF?" he said with a sneer, delighting in seeing some flyers worse for wear. He managed half a step before Woods grabbed him by the scruff of the neck and had him in a head lock. The civvy grunted and flailed his arms as Woods patted him on the head.

"Hush now, hush," Woods told him, his voice a quiet whisper, smooth and reassuring.

The man's friend was about to intervene when Vos shoved him firmly in the chest and wagged a finger at them. They squared up to each other but one look at Vos drained the man's courage away. Drunk as he was, the Belgian was rock steady, his hands half open, poised on the balls of his feet, ready to act.

"Now then my little friend," Woods said, emphasising the word 'little'. Piglet like squeals emanated from the man's throat. He thrashed around a bit but Woods held him firmly, tightening his grip. "You got something to say about the Royal Air Force?"

"Leave him alone," said his friend, his voice thin and reedy. He wanted to do something but his heart wasn't in it. Woods looked up and fixed the new player with a piercing stare.

"He's a big boy. He can speak for himself." Woods looked down and gave his victim a shake. "Can't you?" He rapped his victim on the head with his knuckles. "I asked you a question."

"N-n-nothing, no problem at all," the man half shrieked, half whimpered in response.

"I didn't think so," Woods voice dripped with contempt. He gave him a final squeeze and then let go. The man collapsed on the ground, gasping for air. He scrambled to his feet, his face mottled, tears in his eyes.

"I'm in a reserved occupation see," he said quickly. "I'm up at the factory." The silence was deafening as he shifted from one foot to another and rubbed his throat. "I work the machines, keep 'em going. Besides, I've got flat arches."

Woods clicked his tongue, distinctly unimpressed.

"My heart bleeds. I've lost mates who wouldn't even wipe their shoes on you." He hooked his thumb over his shoulder. "Piss off."

They shuffled off, grumbling but not inclined to take matters further. Woods spat on the road behind them.

"Bastards," he muttered under his breath as they disappeared around a corner.

"Hey, forget it," said Carter, pulling on Woods arm, surprised at the sudden flare of anger. Woods shook him off and stood glaring at the empty street. "Come on," Carter said again, his tone more gentle, coaxing. This time Woods went with him.

"S'wat we gonna do?" asked White as they walked off.

"Hotel?" suggested Woods. "It's cold, I want to be tucked up in a nice warm bed with a cup of tea."

"Cor, I'd like to be tucked up in bed with something warmer than a cup of tea," said Walsh, thinking about the redheaded barmaid at *The Tarleton*.

"C'mere darling," White slurred, wrapping his arms around Walsh and hugging him close.

"Gerroff," said Walsh, struggling to get free from his grip.

They went looking for a hotel but Carter lost interest. The way he felt now, he would either spend hours staring at the ceiling waiting for morning to come or he'd be violently sick. He rubbed his forehead, massaging the tightness he could feel in the skin. Amber Hill was not that far he decided. He looked up. It was a full moon and the sky was crystal clear. If he was lucky, he might be able to hitch a lift on the way back. He announced his intention to walk back to the station. Amazed faces stared back at him.

"Don't be daft, skipper," said Woods, "It's freezing."

"I'll be fine," he assured them, "It's only a few miles."

Carter shooed them off and they parted ways reluctantly. Vos, the most sober of the group, promised Carter he would see the rest of them safely tucked up in bed. Leaving them to it, he walked down the High Street and headed south out of town. The pubs had closed their doors and the streets were nearly empty with just a few isolated groups of people walking home.

As he walked, Carters cheeks started to tingle from the cold and he quickened his pace to keep warm. The tips of his ears went numb and he hunkered down in his great coat, flicking up the collar. After two miles, he discovered that Oxfords weren't the best type of shoes to walk long distances in. His heels were starting to rub and his feet were like blocks of ice. The good thing was that he sobered up quickly. The cold chased away the the headache and the dull throbbing behind his eyes had gone away.

The route home was fairly simple, it was a straight walk out of town and then turn off after passing through Bracebridge Heath. Sitting on top of Lincoln cliff, it overlooked the city to the north and the valley of the river Whitham. The hard part was the uphill walk. Carter dug in as the incline got steeper, the smooth soles of his Oxfords, slipping on the frosty ground.

Halfway up he heard a voice cursing in the dark. He looked around but he was surrounded by fields in every direction and it was hard to see anything. A cow mooed somewhere in the distance. He listened but he couldn't place where the voice came from. He carried on walking and was grateful when the ground levelled off slightly. He rested for a few minutes, sitting on the dry stone wall to give his feet a break. The road widened here and ahead on the left was a car with a woman stood next to it.

"I say?"

She spun round, surprised at the voice from nowhere.

"Hello?" she asked.

He walked forwards and she relaxed as he emerged out of the dark.

"Could I trouble you for a lift?"

"You can if you can make it go," she said, gesturing to the car. He drew closer and recognised her the same time she recognised him.

"Oh," she said, her voice dropping.

"Oh indeed," he replied, his lips pulling thin. It was the girl from the Christmas dance. She was wearing a grey woollen coat. An emerald green scarf was wrapped around her neck. What were the odds? he asked himself. That was then, this was now. There was no reason why they couldn't be civil, he thought.

"What seems to be the trouble?"

"I'm not sure." She stood back from him, hands behind her back. "It just stopped."

He walked over to the car and lifted one of the bonnets side panels. The light of the moon was just enough to see what he was doing. She moved around behind him and peered over his shoulder. He could feel her stood there, her coat brushing against his legs. A hint of perfume wafted around him while he had a further rummage around.

He paused and half turned towards her. He held out a glove hand. "We were never actually introduced before. I'm Alex Carter."

She paused for a moment before smiling slightly at the absurdity of it all and shook his hand in return.

"Georgette Waters."

Now the pleasantries were out of the way, he went back to rooting around in the engine. He found the throttle cable and followed it to the engine. That was connected so no problem there. He checked the dipstick. There was oil in so that was fine. Lacking tools, there wasn't much he could do. He stood up and scratched his head.

"Give it a try," he told her. She got into the car and pulled out the choke. Saying a silent prayer, she turned the key. The engine turned over. Carter twirled his hand, telling her to keep going. It kept on turning but didn't catch. She stopped.

"You have got petrol in here?" his asked, his tone sceptical. She almost shot out of the car to stand in front of him, her chin jutting forward, hands on her hips, as she unleashed the frustrations of the last hour.

"I'm not a total idiot you know," she flared. "The engine stopped. There's plenty of petrol in the tank, I made sure I had enough before I left, *and* there's a can in the boot." She folded her arms. He held up his hands to ward off her anger.

"Okay, okay, it was only a question." He carried on poking. He found one of the ignition leads were disconnected and the others were loose, so he pushed them home on the spark plugs. "Try it again," he suggested.

She stared down her nose at him, a haughty look that made his stomach flip flop. Her eyes were blazing and her skin was pale under the moonlight, her dark hair framing her face.

She got in and turned the key again. The engine turned once, coughed, turned and then caught. The sudden roar shattered the silence of the night. She eased off on the throttle as the engine settled down to a steady hum. When she closed the choke, the engine note dipped but she caught it deftly and gave it a bit more on the pedal.

Carter stood staring at the engine but it was more for show than anything else. It sounded like everything was working, beyond that he had no clue. He fastened the bonnet panels and got in the car.

"Where do you need to go?" she asked.

"RAF Amber Hill please, or as close to it as you can."

"I can manage that," she told him.

"Do you know where it is?"

"I do," she said primly as she put the car in gear and pulled away.

Carter remembered then that Walsh had told him she was a WAAF but where she was stationed escaped his memory.

"Where were you going?" he asked her, fishing for more information. She hesitated for a moment before answering him.

"Group," she said, half distracted as she concentrated on driving in the dark. With the headlamps rigged for blackout, only a small slither of light illuminated the way ahead. She was grateful it was a full moon, that helped a little.

"Grantham," she elaborated.

They nearly went into a ditch when the road suddenly kinked right with little warning. She wrenched on the wheel and kept them going.

"Sorry," she muttered, concentrating on the road ahead. "How come you were out walking?" she asked him. "It's a bit far for a midnight stroll."

"We were in town for New Year's. I missed the last bus home so I thought I'd walk back." She looked askance at him; sure he was joking.

"You're serious?"

"I am. It's not *that* far."

"If you're so keen on walking, I could drop you here if you want," she said, teasing. He laughed then and the ice broke a little.

"No, it's all right. This is fine," he assured her. His feet reminded him they had done quite enough walking for one night. "What about you? What have you been up to?"

"I was seeing my friend off. The one I was at the dance with," she reminded him. Carter nodded, gripping his seat as they jolted over a few potholes. He remembered the girl who had danced the night away with Archer. Georgette elaborated. "She goes back home tomorrow so it was my last chance to see her before she left."

She'd wangled a forty eight hour leave and spent it at Laura's hotel, availing herself of the facilities. There may have been a war on but one thing that wasn't rationed was hot water. She'd enjoyed a long and lazy hot bath and a big bed with feather pillows, a marked change from her digs in Grantham. The hotel had put on a good spread in the afternoon for New Years Eve and then they had gone out for some drinks, a final goodbye before Georgette headed back to Grantham.

"Nice night," she said, making small talk, filling the silence, very conscious that he was sitting right next to her. "I suppose you love it."

"Sometimes. Flying at night is a challenge even before you add flak and everything else." He scratched his cheek, the scar tingling from the cold as some feeling came back into his face. "And all I ask is a tall ship and a star to steer by," he murmured.

"What?"

"Poetry; Masefield," he explained, smiling. The moon glittered brightly, a glowing disc of white. "Of course, I'm just a poor pilot. I suppose you types at Group know more than I do," he said, trying to ferret some information out of her.

"Oh, we just throw darts at a map and use divining rods," she told him offhand, her voice teasing. Carter grinned, the tension easing away.

"I'd ask what you do, but I know you can't tell me."

"Nothing very glamorous I assure you," she told him. She took another sharp corner and increased the speed a bit.

"You're not going to suddenly appear at the squadron one day to deliver a target analysis briefing, are you?"

"Good lord, I hope not." She laughed, glancing quickly at him. His mind did jump about.

"Just checking," he replied, his teeth showing in the dark as he smiled.

"How long have you been at Amber Hill?" she asked, trying a different topic.

"Only a couple of months. It's okay to tell you that I suppose. One squadrons very much like another."

She made the last turn onto the road that led to the airfield and pulled up outside the guardhouse. They sat for a moment in the car. Neither of them quite knew what to say.

He turned to face her and she smiled, her eyes hidden in the dark. The rest of her was wrapped under the thick grey coat but he remembered how she had looked in the dance hall. The dress had been a dark blue and she had worn matching shoes. He remembered seeing them while he watched her dancing with Walsh.

"Here we are," she said, breaking the spell.

"Thank you, you're a lifesaver."

"So are you. You got the car running. I was just about to break out the blankets and settle down for the night."

He got out of the car and went round to her side. She wound the window down and looked up at him, her eyes dark unfathomable pools.

"Goodnight, Miss Waters."

She inclined her head in a slight nod.

"Mister Carter."

He stepped back as she let in the clutch and pulled away. She turned around smartly and gave him a wave as she drove past, back up the road they had come. He watched the brake lights recede into the distance before going into the guardhouse.

20 - Milk Runs

Apart from the op to Dusseldorf on the 27th December, the Christmas period remained relatively quiet for 363. The officers served the non commissioned men their dinner in their Mess on Christmas Day and a light dusting of snow on Boxing Day provided the only excitement.

None of his crew came a cropper after Carter left them in town on New Years Eve. For the right price, they had prevailed on a B&B to let them have two rooms and some extra blankets. When they returned, White spent the rest of the day in bed nursing a monumental hangover, swearing off booze for the rest of his life.

Carter received a letter from home. He wrote back telling his mother what he could about life at Amber Hill and about his crew. He glossed over the mechanical problems and instead he wrote about Woods coming all the way from Canada to join the fight and what it had been like going back on operations. His mother knew the drill, she could read between the lines with the best of them.

Bomber Command stirred itself on the 5th of January and 1942's roll of operations finally got under way. They were to begin the year the same way they had ended it, with another run to to Brest and another chance to hit the three German warships. While Bomber Commands future was being debated by the Air Ministry, they made themselves useful. *Gneisenau*, *Prinz Eugen* and *Scharnhorst* were priority targets, so that was where they went.

Half bombed the ships; half went for the naval installations along the waterfront. It wasn't a full moon but Woods had been able to pick out the docks easily enough. As they went into their run, smoke pots were set off. Woods lost his aiming point as a thick grey cloud began to blanket the harbour. The warehouses, cranes, docks and ships all dissolved into the grey murk.

He thought he saw flashes from the ship's flak guns amongst the smoke so he tried to keep the sight on them but it was difficult. The flak intensified and their Manchester rocked from the blasts as they got closer. Woods let the bombs go but no one saw where they went. There were some dull explosions amongst the smoke but what that signified was anyones guess.

The squadron suffered no losses and were sent back on the 8th to do it all again. There was almost a groan when Dickinson announced the target at the afternoon briefing. Brest had been attacked all week. Wellingtons had gone in on the 6th and 7th for little discernible result so the heavies were being sent back in to see what they could do.

The airfield rocked to the sound of the engines at startup time. It was like the place came alive from a deep slumber. Nesting birds shot into the sky, rudely awakened. Asher watched from the control tower along with the rest of the ground staff as the squadron went to war again. The air thundered as the Manchester's taxied round the peri track to the end of the runway.

"Do you think they'll do all right, sir?" Kent asked the CO as they watched Dickinson lead off.

"Mr Kent, I would think they could probably get there and do it blindfolded," Asher told him curtly, his frustration coming out and the Intelligence Officer slid back along the rail to watch them go up to give the CO some space.

Asher hated being on the ground. He wanted to be out there, leading his squadron but he knew he couldn't fly every mission. He led from the front as much as he could, but he had to be choosy, as did the Flight Commanders. He leaned on the rail and wrung his hands while he thought about what was waiting for them. This was the fourth raid in four nights. The Germans would be tired, but they would also be ready for them. Their defences had been tested and they had those blasted smoke pots to make things difficult.

Those bloody Battleships seemed to lead a charmed life. Reports said *Prinz Eugen* had suffered some damage below the waterline but that was unconfirmed. Tons of bombs had been dropped on them and they were still there, lurking on the fringe, threatening great and terrible things if ever they put to sea again.

Dickinson started his takeoff roll and the staff cheered. The big bomber lumbered along the runway, the tail went up as it barrelled along, then it lifted into the dark. Before he even took off, the next bomber swung onto the runway. It paused only a moment while the ground controller made sure there were no obstructions and then he gave them the green. They started their roll.

Outward bound over the Channel, Carter let White fly. This was their fifth op together and he had been happy with his performance so far. The whole point of his stint as second dicky was to gain experience to progress and get a crew of his own. Only that morning, Dickinson had asked Carter how White was doing so he took the hint. It was time he gave him a real test. Brest was a short hop, but a raid was a raid. Getting them there and back and making the decisions under his supervision would go a long way to seeing if he was ready.

He watched in silence, adopting his OTU instructors pose as

White flew. Carter's feet rode the rudder pedals but he kept his hands off the yoke and folded his arms in front of him so White could see he was doing it without interference.

White did his job well. He had Vos keep watch from the astrodome. He threw in some gentle weaving, banking from side to side to give the gunners a chance to see underneath. Woods brought them in to the target on time. It was all very hum drum but there of course was the danger. They might go back to Brest twenty more times but it was when you let your guard down that things went wrong. A fighter might catch you napping, a navigator might miss a pinpoint. White did the rounds of the crew on intercom and told Todd off for being slow to respond.

They ran in to the target, and this time they came in from the city side which made Woods very happy indeed. They came in at nine thousand, dropped their load and came home without a scratch. No fighters put in an appearance; they didn't even see anyone go down.

Carter was content to let him take them home. They got back at 3am and taxied in. White shut down and pulled his helmet off his head. His ears were ringing but his face was shining. His first op, on his own.

"How was that?" asked Carter, smiling broadly.

"That was grand, sir." White did nothing to hide the excitement in his voice. That was it, everything he had been training for.

Carter laughed. White floated his way out to the three tonner and all the way through interrogation. Kent asked his usual questions and noted down the answers on his clipboard. Todd was enthusiastic when he described seeing the bombs go in.

Kent bit his tongue. This was the fourth crew he'd heard say they'd plastered the target. If he had a shilling for every time, he'd been told that he'd be a very rich man indeed. Todd went into vivid detail about seeing fires on the dock. Kent asked a few supplementary questions around the target, the flak and their flight home. He scribbled some extra notes in the margin but fully expected the ships to still be there come the morning reconnaissance photos despite what anybody said.

"Thank you, gentlemen. That'll be all. Get yourselves off so you can get your egg." He gestured to Everett and his crew who were waiting. Everett slumped onto the seat, the ever present cigarette hanging from his lips.

"Bang on target," he drawled, almost horizontal as he lounged on his chair. "Buckets of smoke, no fighters, didn't see anyone go down." He plucked the cigarette from his mouth and tapped off a bit of ash from the end.

Kent covered his smile with his hand. Next to Fish Salmon, Everett was the most senior man on the. His laconic exterior hid a steely determination that surprised many when they got on the wrong side of his temper.

"I, ah, have a few questions if it's not too much trouble," said Kent, trying to keep his voice neutral.

"Oh, all right, old man. I was just trying to save you the trouble that's all." Everett levered himself up and started going into more detail.

As Carter left interrogation, Dickinson caught his eye. One eyebrow went up. Carter gave him a slight nod and Dickinson smiled.

After a good sleep Carter went prowling for something to do. The problem with not knowing what you were doing a few days in advance was that people tended to default to the easy things. They went to the Mess, had drinks, went to sleep, had an air test, repeat. That was fine as far as things went, but Carter had run out of funny stories and he was sick of hearing the same old ones from everyone else.

The Padre played at least three films a week but he got the cast offs from cinemas in town. The newsreels were sometimes weeks out of date and the films tended to be the B-grade movies that played for a week and then got shunted off to make way for something else. Occasionally he was able to do a trade with some of the other stations but it was poor fare. Carter checked the notice board but nothing grabbed his attention.

Carter would have gone to the theater in Lincoln but it was sold out so he took Woods and White to *The Duck and Drake* instead. They had a leisurely game of darts and a few pints to while away the hours.

Todd and Murphy skipped the invitation and went to town with Vos instead. Vos went to see Denise the same as he always did any night they weren't flying. Todd and Murphy peeled off and went to *The Crown* on Clasketgate. Murphy had an easy approach with a pretty blonde behind the bar and was doing his best to turn that into an evening out.

"Why don't you chuck the towel in?" Todd asked him.

"Because she's coming round," said Murphy, smooth as you like, his face brimming with confidence. "She's warming up to me."

Todd snorted. Murphy had been trying since before Christmas with this one.

As was usual, when ops were off, the place was busy, stuffed full of aircrew. According to rumour, the secret police practically lived here. A story did the rounds that on one occasion, a Flight Sergeant had been propping up the bar when the barmaid asked him what he was doing there as there was a flap on back at his station and the target was so and so. Murphy didn't believe it himself. If that had really happened, the place would have been shut down.

Regardless, Muriel was working so that was his evening taken care of. He slithered through the crowd and shouldered himself a space at the bar. He waited patiently while she served someone else which was fine as it gave him the perfect opportunity to watch her.

As tall as him, she had legs that went on for miles and he got a nice view of her stockinged calves below a floral print dress. She was very thin, broad shouldered, with an athlete's figure and she had a dazzling wide smile that made her chocolate brown eyes dance in good humour.

He caught her eye as she pulled a pint for Tucker. She topped off the pint and then sashayed down the bar. She ignored two wireless ops that waved ten bob notes at her and went straight to him.

"And what can I do for *you*?" she said, her voice neutral although the corners of her mouth twitched in a smile.

"Two pints to start with and a pork pie would be nice." She glanced over her shoulder back towards the door that led to the kitchen.

"I'll have to see if there are any left."

"Oh come on, Muriel my love," he wheedled, batting his eyes at her and simpering across the bar.

"Don't you, my love me," she told him tartly.

She pulled his pints for him and then went off to the kitchen to shout at chef. Todd reached over and picked up one of the pints.

"You're lucky she doesn't brain you. How many times have you asked her out now?"

"Only three," replied Murphy, a little offended that he was being scrutinised so closely.

"Four," interrupted Muriel. She handed over a plate with one small pork pie cut in half and a portion of dark chutney.

"On the slate?" asked Murphy hopefully. She cocked her head to one side, her smile lopsided.

"What do you think?"

Grumbling, Murphy dug into his pocket and put the coins on the bar top. Muriel scooped them up with the flat of her hand. Before she moved on to the next eager customer, Murphy chanced his arm again.

"What are you doing tomorrow night?"

"Working I expect," she said, offhand, her voice distracted as others clamoured for her attention.

"What about the night after?" Murphy persisted.

"Working."

Murphy tried one more time.

"There's some new films on at The Ritz. Some comedy thing with George Formby or a thriller called *The Tower*."

Muriel made a show of thinking about it for a few seconds before giving him a firm no. Murphy's shoulders slumped slightly but he took it well. He picked up the plate and stumped over to where

Todd had snagged two stools at a small table. Todd reached over and had his half of pie off the plate. He dipped it into the dark chutney and shovelled it into his mouth, crumbs of pastry dropping onto his chest.

"Glutton for punishment," he told his friend, speaking round the lump of pie in his mouth. More crumbs spilled out of his mouth onto his uniform jacket. "Anyone else would have given up by now. I would have."

"You're not me."

Todd nodded. He dipped a finger into the chutney and chased a lump of carrot around the plate.

"Get yourself a nice girl like, Vos did."

Murphy grunted and moodily bit into his half of pie. He ruminated in silence while he munched on the pastry.

"Can't. She's gorgeous, there's only one of them lying around."

They stayed near to closing time. Todd flirted with the idea of a lock in and getting some more drinks, but they had to get back. The transport laid on finished at eleven and he had no intentions of walking back like the skipper had at New Year.

As they stood up to go, Muriel came round from the bar to collect their empties. As she scooped up their pint glasses she leaned in close to Murphy.

"Outside the Ritz, Sunday night, six o'clock. I shan't wait," she said briskly.

Murphy practically choked as she said it. He had to replay it in his head to make sure it had happened and he hadn't just imagined it.

"Turning on one," Carter shouted. The erk manning the trolley-acc waved their arm. The port propeller started turning. The engine coughed once, twice and then span into a blur. Flames and sparks shot out of the four banks of exhausts; the air stank with the tang of petrol.

"Cut out!" Carter shouted.

"To running position!" replied White.

The erk pointed to starboard. Carter twirled his left hand, nodded and White jabbed the starter button. They watched the starboard prop kick once, twice, three times. It carried on turning and then just as it looked like it would catch it juddered to a halt. White jabbed the starter again but nothing happened. Carter shot a look out of the window. Latimer was giving him a cut throat signal.

They shut down the port engine. Even running such a short time, the noise had been deafening. There was a babble of voices as the crew asked what was going on.

"Quiet down," Carter shouted over the R/T. Up front, the erks opened the nose hatch and fitted the ladder. Chiefy Latimer appeared and White got up from his seat to give him room.

"What's up, Chief?"

"Dunno, sir. The lads are looking now."

Ladders went up around the starboard engine and the panels came off. Shaded torches waving around as they hurriedly pored over the engine.

Carter leaned back in his seat; arms folded while his blood slowly boiled. Walsh's Manchester across from them moved off and turned left onto the peri-track. He watched it disappear into the dark. He glanced at his watch; the luminous hands glowing. He clicked his tongue in irritation as the minutes ticked by. He could hear the erks shouting back and forth outside. Latimer appeared again, clearly upset.

"Sorry, sir. The starter motors gone. Looks like the teeth have stripped. She's not going anywhere tonight."

Carter cursed, venting his frustration.

"Dammit." He hit the yoke with a bunched fist. "You cow, you rotten bloody cow." He pinched the bridge of his nose and closed his eyes, his face screwed up in anger. He decided fast.

"Right. Broken kite, chaps. Everyone out." He looked at Latimer. "Chief?"

"Sir?"

He pointed to the three tonner waiting on the apron. It had dropped them all off earlier and then remained so it could run the groundcrew back to their billets once the kites were away.

"Transport, I want transport now!"

"Rapidly." Latimer disappeared and clattered down the ladder. He ran over to the three tonner, waving his arms to get the drivers attention.

"Come on," Carter shouted down the fuselage. "The spare kites by the hangars. Let's just hope no one else has already snagged it."

They They hustled in double quick time over to the truck, threw their bags in and then clambered aboard. Latimer and some of the other erks got on as well. Carter pounded his fist on the back of the cab. The truck shot off with a crash of gears as it went barreling around the peri track.

During a break between take offs, they dashed across the runway and careered over to the main hangars. The spare was still there and the truck screeched to a halt. They pelted over and got in.

"Bloody hell," Carter complained. "The seats all wrong." He messed about, adjusting it to the height he wanted. The rudder pedals were set a mite too close but he was just going to have to lump it.

Vos grumbled as he waited for the radio set to warm up. Although it had been airtested earlier in the day, someone had obviously played funny buggers because it was not tuned in to the tower frequency. He twirled the knobs and waited for it to come on.

Woods spread his gear over the navigation table. He unfolded his charts, dumped a pile of pencils into the pot and opened his log to the right page. He fished around in his navigator's' bag for his stop watch and other paraphernalia. He hated rushing like this, you always forgot something when you rushed.

In the tail, Murphy settled himself in the turret while Todd got comfortable in the mid upper. The fuselage rattled as the port engine started. Almost immediately the starboard engine came to life as White and Carter flashed through the startup sequence as fast as they ever had before. Vos checked in.

"Q-Queen to Rabbit control, radio check, Q-Queen ready to go."

There was a long pause.

"*Uh, say again?*"

The engine note deepened as the Manchester moved off.

"Q-Queen taxying. Reading you strength five."

"*Rabbit control, received.*"

"Okay chaps, settle down. Take off positions please."

Woods looked at his watch and noted the time in his log. They were thirty five minutes late.

"We'll be one of the last over the target, skipper."

"Can't be helped, Woody."

Carter gunned the throttles, chancing it a bit to get round to the end of the runway as quickly as possible. The rest of the squadron had already gone. They were going to have to hustle to stand any chance of catching up.

Latimer and his erks watched Q-Queen go. They were coming down from their adrenalin high. The last thirty minutes had been a madhouse as they had all raced to get Carter and his crew in the air. It was only when they got back in the three tonner that they found the last surprise of the evening, a parachute pack in the back of the truck.

Todd only realised he'd forgotten his parachute when he went to pitch out the leaflets. Getting down from the mid upper, he used his torch to move around in the dark. One thing he always did when moving around was check for where his parachute was in case he needed it. He couldn't see it. He tried to recall where he'd dumped it when they got on board and found he couldn't remember doing it. He went very still as it hit him. His mouth went dry. There were no spares on board. There was absolutely nothing he could do about it. If they went down, his goose would be well and truly cooked.

He took it out on the leaflets. He shoved bundles of them down the flare chute and smacked them around with the broom handle, jabbing until they dropped free. He opened the lid of the chute for the next bundle and a blizzard of paper flew into his face. Todd raged as the air was filled with bits of paper. He grabbed another bundle and threw it across the fuselage. The rubber band snapped and more paper flew around.

They got back, six and a half hours later, well after everyone else. Their groundcrew had been anxiously waiting for their return. Dickinson and Kent waited with them.

They did the debrief on the way back in. There was lots of back slapping all around. Dickinson pondered putting Carter in for an award of some kind. Not everyone would have had such a press on attitude.

Carter just wondered how they had made it back with only a few holes. They never did make up the lost time. On the outward leg, they had pushed hard but the engines wouldn't take it. Q-Queen was a dog. She had been slow to climb and they'd never got anywhere near the briefed height. They'd crossed the coast at ten thousand feet and had an interesting few minutes with some coastal flak batteries that tried their hand.

Over the target, it had seemed like they had the sky to themselves. Searchlights had waved around trying to latch onto them while the flak over Wilhelmshaven went bananas. Every gun seemed to be pointing at them. The flak had been so thick you could have walked on it. Somehow, they had managed to thread their way through the barrage so Woods could drop their bombs. After their recent frustrations, he was happy that they dropped them on the money this time.

As they headed out over the water, fires raged behind them. Warehouses were gutted shells and the ground was a roiling sea of orange flame. Murphy had watched the glow on the horizon a long time on the way home. It was like the glow of the sun, rising in the east.

The truck dropped them at the equipment room and they got changed. That was when Carter made the announcement. That had been White's last trip as their second dicky. He'd be getting his own crew. They were cheered by that, but it was bittersweet news. It was well deserved, but they would be losing White for some unknown rookie. Regardless, it was an excuse for a party.

21 - Silver Screen

Murphy double checked his tie in the reflection of a picture frame in the lobby. He brushed his hands down his pants and then straightened up. He was nervous and he paced up and down, checking his watch every thirty seconds. He saw her across the street and waved.

She waved back at him and looked up and down the road before crossing over. She was wearing a maroon skirt and paired it with a cream blouse and a grey overcoat with a fox wrap around her shoulders. A small red pillbox hat was pinned on her blonde hair. The effect was striking. She offered him her left cheek and he lightly kissed her.

"You came."

"Of course, I came. I said I would. I knew you weren't flying today."

Murphy's eyebrows shot up but he could see she was being serious. He scratched his cheek and looked at her askance.

"You'll have to explain that trick to me one of these days."

She gave a little laugh and tapped her nose.

"State secret."

The mantra of 'Loose Lips, Sink Ships' hammered at the back of his head. Murphy left it at that, not sure he wanted to have a row on the first date. He gestured to the film posters on the wall out front.

"What shall we see?"

Muriel ignored the posters and looked at him, gauging him, looking at him properly for the first time outside of the pub. He looked very dapper in his uniform. The short battledress jacket gave him a slim waist and broad shoulders. He had a nice smile, she thought.

"You choose," she told him.

Murphy suppressed a shudder at the choices. He wasn't a big fan of George Formby; his high voice gave him a headache. The other film was billed as a spy thriller and in the dark, he might just get a cuddle out of it. He got tickets for the thriller.

Two hours later they came out almost shell shocked. Nothing could have prepared them for what they saw. Someone had decided it was a good idea to mix a wartime thriller with a psychological drama. What they had got was a mess of a film that even by B-movie standards was an implausible melodrama.

They stood off to one side as the rest of the house emptied. People walked off into the night, wrapping up from the cold as they transitioned from warm cinema to freezing streets. Murphy broke the silence.

"That was awful."

"It was, wasn't it?" she agreed, giggling. They laughed, amused at how bad it had been. "Drink?" she asked him. He nodded and she led the way to a quiet little pub she knew off the beaten track. It had just turned eight.

"Why did you finally say yes?" he asked her as they walked along. He crooked his left arm for her and she looped her arm through his.

"Because you kept asking. Someone that gives up at the first turn isn't worth it."

Murphy walked along, absorbing that.

"It sounds like there's a story there," he said hesitantly.

"It's.....complicated," she replied. He stayed silent, waiting for her to fill in the blanks. "I was involved with someone." He nodded and waited for her to continue. She glanced at him, reading nothing in his face. Her voice carried on, staccato fashion. "Well more than one just someone. I was engaged. You know? He-died."

Murphy felt like a fink for forcing it out of her. He gave her hand an encouraging squeeze.

"I'm sorry."

She looked at him, her eyebrows raised in irritation. Why was it the first thing people said when they heard someone died was, 'I'm sorry.'

"Why should you be sorry?" she asked him, her tone challenging.

"Well-" Murphy paused. "Well..." he stalled. He had no response to that.

"But it was nice of you to say so," she said, softening her tone, not meaning to be so sharp with him. "Then I was seeing someone else for a while," her voice trailed off while she thought about George. He was a blur now and it was difficult to remember what he'd looked like.

"What happened? Did he break it off with you?"

"In a manner of speaking. He's a POW now in some camp in Germany." She shrugged her shoulders, her cheeks puffing as she blew out. "So here I am, being chased by airmen," she giggled at the thought of it. "Lots of airmen, but I'm still waiting for the right one."

She took her arm back and drifted left slightly, putting a small distance between them.

"Makes me stupid I guess."

"No, just human."

He closed the distance to her until their shoulders were bumping along and took hold of her hand in his. Her fingers were cold.

They went into the pub and found it half full. People glanced at them as they came in and then turned back to their own business. Two soldiers, a Private and a Corporal stood at one end of the bar, playing skittles. A fire burned in the grate off to the right. Murphy asked her what she wanted and he went to the bar. He held up two fingers and pointed to a pump. The girl behind the bar drew two pints and he carried them over to where Muriel had secured some space on the bench seat along the far wall.

She sat close; her right leg pressed up against him. She cradled the drink in her lap, occasionally sipping at it as she talked about a wide range of subjects. She told him about life at the pub, coming to Lincoln from Mansfield and her typical day. Murphy watched her, seeing how animated she was, very different from her sterner persona from the pub. She carried on until she suddenly stopped and put a hand to her mouth.

"Oh, but you must think I'm terrible, wittering on like this. I've not asked you anything."

"It's fine. You know that's the most I've heard you say at one time."

She nudged him on the shoulder at that remark.

"Beast."

He laughed. She asked him about where he was from to give him a break from her and he told her a bit about growing up in a rough mining town, his whole life practically mapped out in front of him. His grandfather had worked in the mine, his father had bucked tradition and got a job at the gas works and he would have been expected to follow in their footsteps. Then the war had come along and he'd escaped just in time.

"Drink?"

She pointed to his empty pint glass. He flicked a quick glance at his watch and saw it was gone nine. She saw his hesitation and got cross.

"Somewhere you'd rather be?" she asked, irritation creeping into her voice. Murphy looked pained. "No…yes, no." He could have spun an elaborate lie but he told the truth. "My second dicky's getting his own crew. Its our send off tonight."

"I see." She nodded understanding. Men and their rituals.

"Sorry," he apologised, his face showing the conflict.

"No, I quite understand. You better get going then." She made shooing motions with her free hand. "Off you go."

"I can walk you home," he offered.

"It's all right, I'm a big girl. I'm only round the corner from here." She pointed to the street corner ahead. "You run along, deary. Find your crew before you miss the party."

Murphy was about to argue with her but it was just one of those things that this had all fallen on the same night. It felt like the whole evening had been a bust. Here he was with a pretty girl, she was giving him his whole attention and he was sloping off and leaving her alone. Some date he was. She stood on tiptoe and pecked him on the cheek.

"Tomorrow's my day off. If you're not flying, come and find me."

She turned on her heel and walked away from the pub. She looked left and right before crossing the road. Murphy's voice stopped her.

"Wait, how will....?" his voice trailed off.

"You figure it out," she said, her tone a challenge and left him standing there.

Glasses were raised up in tribute.

"To the best second dicky a man could have," said Carter. "May you always fly true."

There were cheers from the assembled men. Walsh's crew had come out with them and after crawling from pub to pub, they had ended up at *The Tarleton* again.

"Pilot Officer White," they chorused. Speeches done, they resumed their seats and carried on talking and drinking.

"When do you get your new crew?" Walsh asked him, genuinely interested.

"I'm not sure," replied White. "Squadron Leader Dickinson wants to see me in the morning."

"Well be careful," warned Walsh. "Look what I ended up with." He gestured in a wide sweep of his arm, encompassing the men in front of them.

"Hey!" said Nicol in mock outrage.

"Seriously, don't just settle," advised Carter. "You saw how we all came together. Take a few days, feel some people out if you have to."

"Just make sure you get a good navigator," said Woods, rooting for his profession.

"And radio operator," said Vos.

"I know," said White, nodding sagely.

"And gunner," said Todd, belching over his pint.

"*Gunners,*" corrected Murphy, who had just come in the door of the pub. His cheeks were red from the walk between where Muriel had left him and *The Tarleton*. He picked up one of the spare pints from the table. He downed it in one go and then offered his hand to White.

"Congratulations, sir. Sorry I'm late."

"It's all right, Murphy. Glad you made it."

Todd handed Murphy another pint as his friend seated himself next to him.

"Drink up lover boy. You're way behind."

Murphy sipped from the pint and made a face. It was bitter, not his taste but he was stuck with it now.

White stood up and motioned for quiet. There was exaggerated shushing from the assembled throng. Eleven pairs of eyes stared at him. He blinked; his mind suddenly blank. He licked his lips.

"I'll miss you chaps." There was a pause. "But now I know what the standard is, I've got something to measure against for my own crew. You'll be a hard act to follow."

He dried up. When they realised that was it they cheered and applauded, beer sloshing over their glasses as they did so.

"Aw, thanks, sir. I guess we'll miss you too," Todd told him. He rooted amongst the empties on the table, finding there were no more spare pints ready for drinking.

"Beer!" shouted Todd, his right hand slapping the table top. He turned to his navigator and nudged him in the ribs.

"Come on, *sir*," he said, his Australian accent laying emphasis on the, sir, a word he rarely used. "You know she likes you. Get us a nip of something, it's a special occasion."

Woods sighed at being so arbitrarily nominated. He levered himself upright and went over to the bar. Wiping her hands on a small hand towel she walked over to Woods, her face lighting up as she recognised him. She gave him her best smile. He shifted, a little uncomfortable at having to ask.

"We're having a bit of a celebration tonight, is there any chance...?" he folded his arms and rested his elbows on the bar and nodded downwards. She cocked her head to one side, looking at him for a moment. Her eyes narrowed and then she nodded, her green eyes dancing in amusement.

"I shouldn't really." She leaned forward and pitched her voice just for him, her tone husky, inviting. "but as it's you asking."

She knelt down and disappeared behind the bar. Woods leaned forwards and saw her rummage on the middle shelf. He heard glass chinking against glass. She produced some bottles of Burton's and a tumbler with a generous measure of something dark in. He sniffed the tumbler and coughed, the sting of Whisky tickling the back of his throat.

She put the bottles and tumbler on a tray and then pulled him some more pints of beer. As she put the pints on the tray, she covered his hand with hers. He glanced up, his cheeks pink.

"Thanks, Ruth."

He slid the tray on the top of the table as the empties were stacked and moved out of the way. He handed a Burtons to Carter, the tumbler he put in White's hand.

"Here we are, don't waste it," he said with meaning. White swirled the Whisky around the glass and then knocked it back fast. His face screwed up and tears sprang from his eyes as the vapours tickled his nose and the alcohol burned on the way down.

"Put hairs on your chest that will," Todd commented, laughing at White's reaction. He wiped a finger around the inside of the tumbler and licked it. He coughed. "Strewth, that must be pre-war. Wonderful stuff. Why can't we get more of that?" he asked aloud.

"There is a war on you know," muttered Murphy at his side.

"Gosh, really?" Todd said in mock surprise.

They laughed.

22 - Take A Chance On Me

War is unforgiving. Mistakes were punished swiftly. For the crews that usually meant being shot down and either taken prisoner or killed, it was that simple. In the rarefied atmosphere of command, it was a little different.

When you got a rocket for not measuring up, improvement in performance was expected. Air Chief Marshall Portals rockets were legendary. As Chief Flying Instructor at Cranwell just after the Great War, they may have been rare, but you never forgot them. When he issued orders, he expected things to be done and he expected there to be demonstrable improvement within a short space of time. Anyone who consistently failed to deliver was on notice. Accordingly, when Peirse had been carpeted in November, he was then let loose to make what changes he could and produce some results.

Winter was not a good time to achieve that. The bad weather interfered with operations. Wind and cloud over the continent made accurate navigation and good bombing difficult if not impossible. When you threw in flak, nightfighters, spoof targets, bombs that sometimes failed to go bang when they should and conflicting target priorities, the odds were stacked against him.

Peirse did his best with the tools available. Despite the attendant problems he had inherited, the failings of the last year summed up so succinctly in the Butt Report had fallen on his shoulders. The reserve of patience at the Air Ministry had evaporated, results needed to be delivered to ensure the continued survival of Bomber Command and it was felt his time had run out. Fresh blood was needed to turn things around and he now paid the personal price.

Portal sacrificed Peirse on the altar of expediency and packed him off to the Far East as Commander of allied air forces in South East Asia. His task would be to stem the continuing onslaught of the Japanese Empire.

To most, Peirse was a remote figure. They had never met him and he was nothing more than a name at the bottom of an operational order or some directive. When the boss was changed, another would take his place soon enough, brass hats had a habit of looking and sounding alike anyway. The squadrons knuckled down to the task at hand as they always did.

A few days later, a memo was posted on the notice board in the Mess. The language was stark but the words drew a veil over one mans career. It was short but to the point.

Air Marshall Peirse relieved of command, effective 9th January. Air Vice Marshall J E A Baldwin, AOC 3 Group, appointed acting commander, Bomber Command till further notice.

Carter saw the notice when he went into the Mess for lunch. He scanned the brief lines of text, shrugged and then looked at what else was new.

There was a notice asking for volunteers for special operations which he quickly ignored and next to that was a list of people who were to report to Saunderson to help with a concert party. He breathed a sigh of relief when he saw his name was not on *that* list. Carter's skin crawled at the thought of being put into a dress and wig and having to prance around a stage.

After tying one on the night before to send White on his way, he was in no hurry to move around much. He had a leisurely lunch and then grazed on a newspaper while he pondered what to do with the rest of his day. He suddenly remembered the open invite from the Christmas dance and acted on an impulse. He tracked Archer down talked him into loaning him his car.

When Carter pulled up at the gate to St Vincent's Hall, he produced his ID card to the SP's. They asked him what he was doing there and Carter fibbed a bit, telling them he'd been ordered to see Squadron Leader Wilkinson. They kept him waiting while someone rang through to check. After a few minutes, the barrier went up and he was allowed to drive on to the grounds.

The hall was a lavish Gothic revival mansion just to the east of Grantham. Before the war, the extensive grounds were immaculately groomed fields of green. Now, they were covered with a growing number of Nissen huts and duckboards. He found Wilkinson waiting for him as he drove up to the front of the hall. His friend stood on the steps; hands shoved in his pockets as he slowly shook his head.

"I know I said drop in any time but you do pick your moments, old man."

"I had the day off," replied Carter smiling broadly.

"I know." Wilkinson pointed to a cluster of Nissen huts off to the right. "Park over there and then we'll have a talk."

A Corporal brought them two cups of tea on a tray. Once the door closed, Wilkinson put his feet up on the corner of his desk and leaned back in his chair.

"Welcome to my world," he said, gesturing around the small office. His desk was covered in a stack of files. A telephone occupied a

177

corner and on the opposite side there was a green banker's lamp. A photograph of his wife Helen was on the window shelf behind him.

An adjoining door led to a larger office where his staff of four fussed around with target files. After life on ops, Wilkinson was finding it hard to adjust to flying a desk but it was better than the risk of trainees killing you at an OTU.

Wilkinson asked how things were going and Carter told him about the mishap with the starter motor and having to use the spare. His friend winced in the appropriate places. Flying a strange aircraft with all of its little ways was not a pleasant experience. After a misfortune like that, Carter had been lucky indeed.

Every time orders came through from Bomber Command Wilkinson was making a lot of phone calls to the squadrons wanting to know how many they could put up. The Vulture engines general lack of reliability was proving to be a constant headache even with the improvements Rolls Royce had brought in. Things had been better recently but there were never any guarantees.

"How's your new crew working out?" he asked as he slowly stirred his tea. Carter shrugged as he nibbled on a biscuit.

"Okay. My second dicky has just gone to get his own crew. I'm waiting for the new one to arrive. They're not a bad bunch really. How's, Helen?" he asked, changing the subject. Wilkinson became more animated, brimming with good humour.

"Wonderful. Blossoming, I think the word is. She keeps asking me why you haven't settled down yet."

Carter almost choked on his tea.

"What did you tell her?"

"I told her you'd been busy."

"Good answer."

A thought suddenly occurred to Wilkinson.

"Hey, we're having dinner tonight. Helen's over from Lincoln at a hotel on the other side of town. Why don't you join us?"

"I've not got anything planned. Unless there's something you know that I don't?" Carter arched an eyebrow in good humour. Wilkinson laughed.

"You're fine." He glanced at his watch. "Now I'm sorry if this sounds rude, old chap, but I've got a meeting with SASO in ten minutes. I'm sure you can amuse yourself for a few hours until dinner."

Carter stood up and straightened his tie and tunic.

"Where do you want me to meet you?"

"The hotels called *The Madison*. It's on the other side of Grantham not far from the Great North Road. Say seven o'clock?"

That gave Carter a few hours to kill but he wasn't too bothered. He had nowhere else to be and he'd never been to Grantham before. He'd find something to do.

"I'll see you there."

Wilkinson led him back to the entrance. Carter was nosey on the way out, looking in open doors on his way past. He caught a glimpse of a familiar face working at their desk before the door to their office closed. Wilkinson left him at the entrance and hurried back to get the things he needed for his meeting. Carter paused until his friend was out of sight and then doubled back inside. He retraced his steps until he stood in front of the door he'd noted before, geeing himself up. He made a final check of himself to make sure he was presentable before knocking on the door.

There was a crisp, "come in," so he committed himself and turned the handle. He was dismayed to find the door opened onto a large room and not the small office he was expecting. Two WAAFs and a Corporal were sitting at their respective desks ploughing through piles of reports. The air was filled with the chatter of typewriters. To the left was another door leading to an adjoining room. She was sitting next to the door behind her own desk. Her face dropped when she saw him come in.

"Oh," she said.

"Oh indeed," he replied, suddenly very aware that they had an audience. Her lips pulled into a prim line. She looked at her staff. All activity had stopped at his entrance and she glared at them. Work continued but all eyes were sneaking looks over the tops of their typewriters. Her cheeks coloured and Carter shifted uneasily on his feet. He thought quickly.

"Squadron Leader, Wilkinson has a meeting with SASO shortly. He asked if you had that report he requested?"

Following his cue, she nodded slowly, picking up a folder from her desk.

"Of course," she replied crisply. "I was just going to bring it for him."

She strode round her desk and made for the door. As she passed him, she grabbed his arm with her free hand, gripped it tight and pulled him after her.

"Come on idiot," she hissed once they were in the corridor. She turned left down the corridor, going back towards the halls entrance. Carter thought she was going to chuck him out. Her shoes clicked a rapid staccato pattern on the parquet floor as she went at a brisk pace. Carter skipped to keep up and just about drew level with her when she abruptly turned left and entered an empty office. He followed her in and she slammed the door behind him. She turned on him, eyes blazing.

"Of all the-"

"I know, I'm sorry." He held his hands up defensively. "Look, I was here seeing my friend but truth be told, coming to see Freddie was only part of the reason I came over. I wanted to see you too."

That stumped her. She clutched the folder to her chest, armour between herself and him. Her chin jutted out defiantly.

"But whatever for?" she asked innocently in theatrical fashion. Her eyes widened and she lifted her eyebrows. "Surely, you've something better to do?" she asked, mimicking his own words from the Christmas dance.

"I deserved that didn't I?" he said, abashed. "I'm sorry. I was rude at the dance and I wasn't in the best frame of mind when you came over to talk to me."

"The thought had occurred to me," she said, her tone softening slightly, but she wasn't going to make it easy for him.

"I'll be the first to admit I was being a bit of a prig." He apologised again. "I'm sorry."

She unwound a little and stopped clutching the file so tightly.

"So, what's changed now?" she asked.

"Life goes on," he responded, blurting out the first thing that entered his head. Her brow pinched in annoyance at his flippancy, so he carried on talking. "Look, can't we start again? Sometimes a fellow realises he's made a stupid mistake; it would be a shame to punish me for it."

The silence was deafening. Carter clenched his teeth and flinched at the gulf between them. She looked uncertain at first but then nodded to herself.

"All right," she said reluctantly. "Forgiven."

"Good." He visibly brightened, some of the tension ebbing away. "Now, what time does your watch end?" he rushed on, not wanting to give her time to think.

"Five. Unless there's a flap on," she warned him.

She found the remainder of the afternoon excruciating. No one asked her anything but she saw them exchanging looks across their desks. She let them all get a flyer just to get rid of them, then spent fifteen minutes finishing off before leaving herself at ten past five. She was going out the lobby when a figure sprang up from a low sofa under the main stairs.

"Taxi?" he asked her. She looked at him with some surprise.

"I thought you were joking."

"Me?" he asked innocently. "Never. Come on, the meters running." He led the way outside and round the corner of the hall where the Frazer Nash was waiting for him. He sped into Grantham and parked the car outside a pub she directed him to. They got a table in the tap room and Carter got the drinks in, bitter for her, half a beer for him.

"Thanks for coming," he repeated for about the tenth time since he'd picked her up.

"I told you, it was fine," she assured him. She put her gas mask bag, cap and coat on a stool next to her and crossed her legs, right over left. She cradled the half pint glass, hands resting in her lap. "I'm just glad you didn't come back into the office."

Carter grunted and cleared his throat. He did a little dance on his seat and he felt his cheeks colour slightly. He coughed to clear his throat.

"Yes, well, I'm sorry about that. Not exactly my finest moment." He took a long pull on his beer to stop himself saying anything else stupid. She asked him how he'd been since the New Year. That was a safe topic, he was okay with that. He kept things light, avoiding talking shop too much if he could help it.

She cleared her throat and looked off to one side, her hand playing with a loose curl of hair that hung down by her ear. The conversation between them was very stilted and he knew it. She sipped her drink and fidgeted and he could feel the opportunity slipping away.

His coming to Group had caught her off guard and she felt very self conscious being the sole focus of his attention.

"So, Georgette? Unconventional?" he blurted out, but she was good enough to smile.

"I know, call me, George, please. Everyone else does." He dipped his chin, indicating agreement with her wishes. "I think father wanted a boy. He already had a house full of daughters when I came along. I imagine he must have been quite disappointed when I turned up."

"How many sisters have you got?"

"Five," she told him. "Three are married and the other two are in the services like me." He whistled tonelessly. He thought things had been hectic having one older brother and sister when he was growing up. "It gets very noisy at Christmas," she commented.

"I can imagine. What about you?" he asked her.

"Me?" she shrugged. "Not much to tell really. Married, widowed, joined up." She drunk quickly; eyes downcast.

"I'm sorry."

"It's all right." She looked off to the left and played with her hair again. "It was a while ago now. He was in France."

Georgette neglected to mention the hammer shock of receiving the telegram. That moment was ingrained on her mind forever, etched on her heart. She had never felt such pain, but when it all kicked off for real in France, she had a premonition something would happen.

Charles had been one of those freewheeling daredevil pilots. The war was a jape to him. His letters were never serious and painted a jolly picture of life on the line. She knew in her heart, if he hadn't fallen in France, he would have bought it later in the summer over the southern skies of England.

She'd joined up not long after that. The flat in London had suddenly seemed very big and cold and lonely once she was on her own. Ever practical, rather than sit sobbing in the parlour and feeling sorry for herself, she had picked herself up and enlisted in the WAAFs. After six months in northern Scotland, she'd wangled a posting to 5 Group and remained at Grantham ever since. She had thrown herself into her work, doing her bit, as her mother would say. The pain went away with time and she began living again.

She found life at Group interesting. A veritable hive of activity, the place never rested. Ops days were busy and the teletypes would clatter like crazy as a blizzard of orders flew out of St Vincents Hall to the squadrons spread around Lincolnshire.

At night, the skies were filled with the drone of bombers and in the days following, she and her staff would collate the intelligence reports as they came in, summarising the interrogation forms and target photographs. On the face of it, it was dull stuff, but she found it fascinating. Each report was a crew, a single plane going to Germany and back. Even a bare report had flickers of life, a description of an explosion, or an attack by a night fighter. She also read accounts of men killed, men wounded on bombers that struggled home in the dark. It turned dry bold facts into something else.

She wasn't a nun, there had been men since, but nothing serious. She had promised herself after Charles, no more operational Johnnies. Now here she was, having a drink with another pilot. So much for promises. It was only a drink she kept telling herself, justifying the lie.

She looked again at the man seated across from her. He was just like she remembered, the steady clear blue eyes and the pale freckled face. She had been thinking about him off and on since Christmas and that drive in the dark at New Year. He seemed very different from Charles. Carter was more reserved but not in a boring, plodding way.

Once she got back to work, she had easily found out what squadron was based at Amber Hill and since then she had kept an eye out for his interrogation report and target photo. She had looked at them, hearing the phrases of the report in his voice. It made him more real somehow.

A fellow WAAF from Group came into the pub. She looked at Georgette and raised an eyebrow before glancing at Carter, expecting to be introduced. Georgette ignored her and suggested a walk. Carter had no objection and he shrugged his greatcoat on before holding hers up so she could put it on.

"Thank you," she said, as their fingers touched. Carter made a strangled coughing sound and headed for the door. He held it open and they stepped onto the street. It was cold after the warm of the pub and she set a brisk pace heading wherever her feet decided. Her mind was elsewhere, thinking. Carter filled the silence.

"I'm meeting, Freddie for dinner in a bit. Is, *The Madison* far?"

"Not very. It's a short drive from here. You just have to make sure you don't miss the turning. There are high hedges that mask the lane on the right."

"Good. I'm having diner there with him and, Helen, his wife."

Georgette cocked her head, her interest peaked. His voice had come alive then, full of genuine enthusiasm, the mask of reserve slipping away. She remembered him saying earlier he'd come to see a friend. She steered them down a lane that led downhill.

"Is that who you came to see?" Carter nodded. "Have you known Squadron Leader, Wilkinson long?"

"We went through our first tour together. Then he was my flight commander. I introduced him to his wife many moons ago."

She nodded quietly. So few words to cover so much. They must have gone through a lot she mused. He asked her how her she had been since New Year.

"Fine," she replied. "Busy. You know how it is." He glanced at her as they walked. He could see her smile, the line of her teeth in the growing gloom. That exchange took them to the end of the lane. They stood close together on the corner.

"This is me," she gestured to the left. The cobbled street fell away down a gentle slope with residential houses on either side. "Your cars that way," she told him, pointing to the right. Carter saw the pub they had been to in the distance, they had virtually gone around the block. He was about to go when he screwed up some nerve.

"Come with me to dinner," he asked.

"But your friend," she demurred. "I'd be intruding."

"Not at all," he assured her.

"You mean it?"

"Well, of course I mean it." He took that half step that closed the distance between them and took her hands in his. "Helen will be over the moon at having some company. Come with me," he urged her again.

She looked down for a moment, suddenly hesitant. His thumbs stroked across the top of her fingers. She chewed on her lower lip and then looked up into his eyes. A smile dimpled her left cheek as she decided.

"All right." She let go of his hands and did a small pirouette, bending her right leg at the knee. "Does a girl get time to change?" The scar on his cheek danced as he laughed. She smiled again, liking the way the years fell of his face. He checked his watch.

"I don't suppose it matters if we're a little late. Will fifteen minutes be enough?"

"I'll manage it in ten," she assured him. Pulling on his hand, she led the way back to where he had parked the car.

It actually took her twelve minutes but Carter was not so churlish to begrudge a girl a few minutes. He'd waited in the car while she had flown inside the boarding house, she shared with some other WAAF officers. He spotted a few female faces peering at him from the front bay window. He gave them a wave while he waited.

She came dashing out, clutching a bag in one hand, coat draped over her arm while her other hand kept her hat on her head. The unflattering uniform had been replaced by an emerald green dress, pre-war judging by the number of pleats. A cream cardigan with green and brown decorative stitching was draped across her shoulders. An enamel brooch of a hummingbird was on her left breast. A red brimmed hat with pheasant feather was pinned at an angle to her dark hair. Her feet were sleeved in a pair of green sling back heels, her toes peaking out at the front. She finished her make up on the way, applying a swipe of lipstick while looking in a small compact.

Carter snatched glimpses of her as he drove and she gave him directions. He muttered in annoyance when the windscreen started to steam up. The heater in Archer's car was pretty poor so he rummaged around with his free hand for a rag.

They missed the turning for the hotel and the car skidded to a halt on the damp road. Georgette was sitting quietly, an amused expression on her face as Carter reversed and then went up the drive.

The hotel had been a sprawling country pile until the first war. The army had requisitioned it as some obscure headquarters in 1915 for the duration. By wars end, there was no lord of the manor left to retake possession. Two heirs had fallen in the Fields of France while a distant cousin had been shot by a sniper at Gallipoli. A rich industrialist bought the house but his own social pretensions came to an abrupt halt during the Great Depression. The hall was auctioned off to settle his debts and turned into a hotel. Just outside Grantham, it was neatly placed to take advantage of business from weary travellers on The Great North Road and the train station in town.

Carter parked the car under a huge oak tree out front. He held the door open for Georgette and their shoes crunched on gravel as they covered the short distance to the entrance. The entrance hall had a fire blazing in the grate and was decorated in warming shades. Carter followed his nose to the dining room. Originally two reception rooms, it had been knocked through into one large room that ran the length of the house. The parquet floor shone, tables were laid with white cloths while fox and deer heads looked down from the walls.

Helen Wilkinson waved to him and Carter leaned in and kissed her on the cheek.

"You'll forgive me not getting up," she said.

Carter noticed her large belly; she was clearly a few months gone.

"Helen, you look wonderful," he assured her.

"Alex, you're such a dear, it's lovely to see you but you're a terrible liar. I'm a whale." She rubbed her rounded tummy with both hands and patted the top of her stomach.

"You're positively glowing," he told her again.

Newly married, pregnant and her husband was safe on the ground. Helen Wilkinson was content; the stars had aligned in her world.

She had first met Carter and Freddie at a squadron dance late in 1940. Nineteen, she'd clutched her handbag tightly to herself while looking around the hall, a wallflower that needed saving from the more predatory types on the squadron. Carter had seen her first and drifted over to introduce himself. They were dancing when Wilkinson cut in and that was it. Cupid's arrow struck home and she monopolised him for the rest of the evening. It was a whirlwind after that. They had married a month later, when Wilkinson and Carter were both only halfway through their tours.

Carter had thought them insane at the time but it was an incredibly happy marriage. Their home had been a haven for him during his tour until Mary came north.

"Where's, Freddie?" he asked, looking around the dining room.

"Little boys room," she told him. "You're late by the way," she said in good humour.

"Dearest, Helen, forgive me," he pleaded. "Helen, may I introduce Section Officer, Georgette Waters."

The two women looked at each other in that critical appraising way that women do so well, a quick up and down, shrewd eyes missing nothing. Freddie had brought Helen up to date where Carter and Mary were concerned so she was interested to see what this new person was like. Carter held the chair for her while Georgette took the place across from Helen.

"So, you didn't get lost then?" Helen asked him, smiling sweetly, her tone teasing.

"I don't need a navigator for *everything*. I just had a slight course correction."

"I see," said Wilkinson, coming up to them unnoticed. "Good evening, Miss Waters," he said, looking down at Georgette as he stood to her left.

"Sir."

"Good grief, Freddie, don't be such a bore," his wife admonished him. "You're not at work now." Georgette smiled, liking her already.

"I..er, asked Miss Waters if she would like to join us," said Carter, a little sheepish. Wilkinson scowled for a half second and then grinned.

"I think we can manage that," he replied in good humour. He

185

caught the eye of the waiter and indicated it would be one extra for dinner. The man reacted quickly and laid an extra place setting in front of Georgette. Drinks were ordered as they perused the menu.

"What shall we have?" Helen asked Georgette. Although rationing was firmly in effect, the hotel was able to provide a varied menu of fare. The hotel grew its own vegetables and rabbit was abundant locally so it feature strongly in various guises. The chef was a French evacuee who had been classically trained in Paris. Their loss was the hotels gain and the waiter assured them there was a wonderful sauce to accompany the roasted rabbit.

After the drab offerings at her digs and at Groups canteen, Georgette's mouth was watering and she saw the printed words having the same effect on Carter. She settled on Lapin a la Cootie, *rabbit stew,* and tore into a crusty roll while she waited.

Carter was careful to avoid talking shop while they waited for their food to arrive. They were in a public space after all but there was little harm in talking about his time up north and Helen loved hearing about Scotland. Georgette chipped in with some of her own stories about life in the Highlands. Helen told Carter off for not writing in the intervening months.

"Sorry," he said, abashed. "Been busy." His hands played with the stem of his wine glass.

"As long as it doesn't happen again," she told him. Wilkinson sipped his glass of red wine slowly, appreciating the flavour. How the other half live, Carter reflected, not that he begrudged his friend his promotion or position, he had earned it.

Carter took in the ambiance of the dining room. It was half full. One or two uniforms were evident but the rest were strictly civilians. His attention snapped back when Helen asked how his family was. He filled in the details in broad strokes. Wilkinson asked Georgette how long she had been at Group, his face all attention, the mark of a good listener.

It turned out Georgette grew up not far from Wilkinson on the Sussex Downs although her family had moved to Kingston when she was seven. Small talk kept them going until dinner arrived.

The rabbit stew was excellent. There were big chunks of tender meat in a puddle of sauce laced with garlic and herbs. Carter forced himself to take his time. Good food should be savoured; especially when he had no idea if he'd be coming here again.

"This place is a gem," he commented, licking sauce off his fork.

"Rather," rumbled Wilkinson in agreement. "A Wing Commander told me about it when I said I was looking for somewhere for, Helen to stay."

He reached over and gave his wifes hand a reassuring squeeze. Helen hadn't been keen on the idea at first, but once she saw the hotel she'd felt at home. It was nice to have company in the evening's when Freddie was busy. Once the baby was born, she would go back to her parents in Lincoln.

Wilkinson recommended the souffle for dessert and Georgette and Carter weren't disappointed. Sated, Carter leaned back in his chair and half listened to the dance music filtering in from the radio in the room next door. The ladies excused themselves and Wilkinson ordered tea and cigars. Carter grimaced slightly at the extravagance. Flight Lieutenants pockets were not exactly flush with gold. Wilkinson must have caught his look because he waved away his worries.

"Special treat old man. Some things are beyond price."

Carter nodded a thank you. There were a lot of things to say but between himself and Wilkinson there was that unspoken language. A look here, a nod, a lift of the head that said more about all those yesterdays than words ever could.

Wilkinson looked around to make sure there was no one else in earshot. Satisfied they could talk; he hitched his chair round so it was closer to Carter. They leaned in. Wilkinson fished in the breast pocket on his uniform jacket.

"By the way, I've got something here for you." He held up a folded piece of paper between two fingers. "I forgot to mention it earlier." He handed over the note.

Carter frowned as he took it, wondering what it was. He glanced at Wilkinson before he read it.

"Report on your man and his girl," Wilkinson told him. He leaned back and sipped his tea, while Carter scanned the tightly typed words. "I was going to ring but you've saved me the call."

The report of concern had crossed his desk the week before. As it involved a member of Carters crew, Wilkinson had taken a personal interest. As a refugee from an occupied nation, Denise had been compelled to register her address when she came to England so it had not been hard to find out some details about her. A few discreet enquiries had been made.

"Nothing to worry about," Wilkinson emphasised. There had been a few eyebrows raised over her suspected profession in London but nothing that would compromise security here. Carter grunted when he read the conclusion. Past was past. She seemed a lovely girl and if Vos was looking after her, who cared? She wasn't a spy or something else nefarious so that was his worry taken care of.

In the ladies room, Helen looked in the mirror and checked her hair was in place. Georgette refreshed her make up, tutting at the state of herself. Twelve minutes hadn't been nearly enough time to get ready.

"You've struck lucky with, Alex," Helen told her.

"So have you," Georgette replied.

"Is, Freddie a good boss?" Helen asked, her voice hesitant, wondering if it was indiscreet to ask.

"He's not directly in my section but I've heard he is."

Helen nodded, relieved to hear it.

"It's good to see, Alex happy," she observed as she peered in the mirror. "I was concerned when, Freddie told me, Mary had thrown him over."

"We've not known each other long," Georgette replied. "He hasn't made it easy for me to get to know him," she said, thinking about their two previous encounters as she walked with Helen down a wide corridor back to the dining room. Helen snorted.

"I didn't think so. He needs a good prod sometimes. He doesn't see what's in front of him sometimes."

Georgette frowned while she considered that.

"Has he always been so serious?" she asked, keen to hear from someone who knew him before. Helen thought for a moment before answering. She stopped at a bay window half way down the corridor to have a rest. The bay had a low padded bench seat built into it and she gratefully took the opportunity to sit down and rub her back. In days past it had afforded a splendid view of the ornamental gardens. Now the window looked out over rows of broad beans and onions.

"Sometimes he's serious." She nibbled on her lower lip while she thought about how to phrase an answer. "He's deep that one, thinks a bit too much maybe; dwells on the past. But no matter what, I'd do anything for that man." Georgette nodded slowly but Helen wasn't finished. She laid a friendly hand on the older woman's wrist. "Forgive him his flaws. He looked after me when, Freddie went missing. He came to see me to break the news. He wouldn't let anyone else do it. He'll never let you down."

She remembered that night as if it was yesterday. She'd been frantic with worry after the squadron got back and Freddie was amongst the missing. When Carter had walked up the path, his face set she had almost fainted dead away. Married two weeks and already possibly a widow, Carter's stoic calm had steadied her ship all through that day.

"It was all a false alarm of course. Freddie had landed somewhere else and couldn't send word immediately." She tugged a hanky from her sleeve and dabbed her eyes.

They walked back to the dining room to find Carter and Wilkinson slumped in their chairs, finishing off their cigars.

"Like I was telling you," Helen said in an overly loud voice to announce their presence. "Thicker than thieves these two when they get together." The men straightened up and fiddled with their ties. They half rose out of their chairs as the ladies resumed their seats.

Georgette glanced across the table at Carter with new eyes. She knew her promise to herself had gone out of the window.

They left the hotel close to ten. Helen was tired and Wilkinson took her up to their room to relax. Georgette promised to give Helen a ring and confirm their shopping trip when she next had a free day.

The drive back to Grantham was quiet, both of them lost in their thoughts when Georgette suddenly asked him to pull over. In the dim circles of the blacked out headlamps a layby suddenly appeared out of the gloom and Carter dabbed the brakes and turned off smartly, the car bouncing over the rough surface. He switched off the engine and was surprised at the sudden silence.

"Anything wrong?" he asked in the quiet.

"No, I'm fine, it's all fine."

The seconds ticked by, then she put her hand on his knee and hitched over in her seat until she was leaning against him. Her right arm went around his shoulders. It was dark in the car. He couldn't see very much but he could feel her, her body pressed up against his. She rested her chin on his shoulder, her breath huffing on his cheeks. Perfume filled his nostrils.

"Georgette-," he began. She put her finger over his lips.

"-Shh, they call me that at work. I told you, it's George. Goodgie to my friends. The only time someone says Georgette, I'm usually in trouble." He grinned behind her finger.

She kissed him then and he wrapped his arms around her, holding her close as they lingered in the moment, making it last. They came up for air and sat like that for a while, his arms around her, his chin resting on her head. His brain shorted out like a faulty radio and he was lost for something to say. She could hear his heart beating, its rapid beat slowing to a relaxed rhythm as Carter came down off his cloud.

"Goodgie," he murmured softly, testing the sound of it, the sound of his voice rumbling through his chest.

"Mmmm," she purred. "Yes, Alex?"

"I could stay like this forever, but we've got to move some time."

He hated saying it, but Wilkinson had dropped enough hints during the evening that Ops could be back on again tomorrow. The clock was ticking.

Reluctantly, she hauled herself to an upright sitting position and fussed her hair back into place. She straightened his tie, her hand lingering on his chest. Everything was back in its proper place.

He placed his hand over hers before she could withdraw it and she looked at him, his face all harsh shadows and angles for a moment as a car drove past in the opposite direction. The inside of the car plunged into darkness again.

She leaned in, tilting her head towards him, her lips parted. They kissed once more and then Carter dragged himself back to reality and turned the key in the ignition. The engine roared into life.

When they got to her digs, she had him park around the corner and they stood for a few minutes in the dark.

"Don't walk me to the door," she told him, "tongues will wag."

"Let them," he told her with a sudden flare of defiance. She was good enough to smile.

"I've had enough adventure for one evening. You've got my number?" she asked. He patted the pocket of his coat to reassure her.

"I'll get over when I can," he told her with conviction. "I'll miss you."

"Take care, Alex."

She gave him a quick peck on the cheek and hurried down the street. Her mind was whirring at the speed of the evening's events. She looked back once up the hill to see him standing on the corner, a silhouette back lit by the scant moonlight. The key turned in the lock and she went inside.

23 - Again, Again and Again

Carter rang Georgette's lodgings the following evening. A Scottish woman with a sharp tone answered the telephone and scolded him that she wasn't a messenger service and hung up. Carter flirted with calling Group but talked himself out of it. He called again at eight and this time a girl answered. He waited while they got Georgette.

He looked left and right in the lobby of the Mess, conscious that he was in full view of everyone walking past. He brightened immeasurably as soon as he heard her voice. He could picture her smiling at the other end of the line.

"Darling," she breathed. "You're lucky, I've just drawn a bath before the hot water goes off. I got back late."

Carter could hear giggling in the background and he could imagine there were a few of her housemates earwigging.

"I got the landlady earlier."

"Oh dear," she said. That explained the frosty look Mrs Lloyd had given her when she came in. "We'll figure something out for next time," she told him.

"When do you get some time off?"

"It's a bit up in the air at the moment," she demurred, both of them well aware this wasn't a secure line. She wracked her brain, thinking about how they were going to organise this. Amber Hill was not a five minute walk away and both of them had borrowed someone else's car previously, which was not something they could always rely upon.

"I'll tell you what," she said, inspiration suddenly striking. "I'll let, Helen Wilkinson know. Then you can let her know at the hotel. You've got more chance of catching her in and she can pass the message."

It wasn't exactly ideal but Carter couldn't come up with a viable alternative. It reminded him of passing notes in school but it was better than nothing. They talked for a few more minutes and then he reluctantly let her go, conscious that her bath water was cooling.

The next day, Carter took L-London up. The ground crew had replaced the broken starter motor and fiddled with the starboard engine and she was good to go again. She started first time and Carter did a few circuits of the station before coming in for a touch and go. As the wheels kissed the tarmac, he put the throttles through the gate and hauled her back into the sky and stayed up for another hour, giving the engines a good workout at different altitudes. After the laboured flight of Q-Queen, it was good to be back in their own aircraft again.

Their new second dicky, Flight Sergeant Jensen went with them. From Newcastle, he was confident, his voice assured and his handling of the Manchester was on the money. Despite his confident air, they found it hard to take him too seriously as he looked about twelve. His flying kit swamped him and they quickly called him 'Kid' Jensen over the R/T.

They saw little of White. He spent the next few days gathering a crew together and getting used to his new Manchester K-Kilo. Another hand me down, she was a little different to the other Manchester's on the squadron. The elevators were bigger, there was no third fin and the vertical stabilisers were much bigger in surface area as well.

White thought she handled much better. Throwing her around the sky in a corkscrew she was more responsive and he had much more positive control in a sudden dive or climb, particularly when trying to recover back to level flight.

On the morning of the 14th, the gate was locked and all outside communication was stopped. No one was allowed out. Ops were back on. Brest was no longer the only thing on the menu and there was a ripple of interest when they were told the target was Hamburg. Located almost directly east of Wilhelmshaven at the mouth of the Elbe, it was a large city with a variety of juicy targets.

The briefing was crisp and efficient. Black Jack went into some detail on their track to and from the target. With the estuary on the coast leading right to it, there would be few excuses for missing the target this time. They were briefed to bomb the shipyard. The centre of Hamburg was a mass of docks, slipways and warehouses, a blind man should be able to hit this.

They would come in over the North Sea, pick up a fix from Heligoland and Cuxhaven and then go in. Coming out was more interesting. They would turn south and then do a wide circle around Bremen, avoiding Emden before heading out over the Ijsselmeer.

Kent took them through the potential defences, pointing out the areas of flak around Bremen, Bremerhaven and Lübeck that were ready and waiting to catch the unwary. The good news was that it was a no moon period giving them plenty of dark to hide in. There was every chance they could be in and out before the nightfighters found them.

Linkletter told the usual tale. Mild weather, watch out for icing conditions and the predicted winds were thirty knots easterly over central Europe. The last to step forward was Church. He was leading this one and he addressed them from the stage.

"This is it, chaps. We've had an easy time of things lately but now it's back to business. All the kites have been serviced, all the little niggles have been ironed out, the weather is with us and there's even no moon. Everything is in our favour; so let's get out there and show what we can do. I'll see you all when we get back."

They came back in dribs and drabs six hours later. The mood at interrogation was mixed. The weather had been lousy. Halfway across the North Sea they'd run into a bank of heavy cloud that turned a simple navigational problem into a nightmare. The predicted winds had also been way off, pushing them all over the place.

Some of them claimed to have bombed on the target. Some had just let them go on dead reckoning with no real idea where their load went. Three diverted to the secondary and failed to even find that.

Most of them were jolted around by flak both to and from the target. Following the set route proved to be almost impossible and they blundered over other cities all over the shop. Two went down over Bremerhaven. Another popped out of the clouds over Bremen and got turned into a Roman candle for their trouble.

Carter had battled on through the clouds. There was no way he was letting down to see the ground. They had no idea how low the cloud base was and he wasn't about to sacrifice the advantage of height and serve them up on a plate for some flak gunners.

When they hit their dead reckoning ETA they circled. They couldn't even divert to the secondary target until they knew where they were. After ten minutes, they spotted the glow of some fires to the north and the flash of flak. The beams of some searchlights waved around.

With nothing better to go on they drifted north towards it. Woods lined up on the brightest glow and let the bombs go. It was distinctly unsatisfying all round.

They fought the headwind all the way back. The only consolation was that the strong winds blew the clouds away as they got close to the English coast. Shore batteries opened up on them and carried on even after they fired off the colours of the day. It rounded off a perfectly dreadful demonstration of strategic bombing.

They moaned about the waste of it all over their bacon and eggs. Carter slid into bed, ears still ringing from the howl of the engines and looked forwards to a lie in. He was rudely dragged from his slumber a few hours later. A Corporal knocked on the door to his room. When he got no answer, he shoved his head round the door and flicked the light switch on. He gave Walsh's bedframe a kick. That got a grunt in response.

"Wakey, wakey, sir. Ops again tonight. Briefings at four."

"Time is it?" Carter muttered from under his pillow.

"Eleven, sir," came the response. The Corporal moved on to the next room and left them to it.

Carter flailed around. He pressed his face into the mattress and tried to will himself back to sleep. Walsh threw his pillow at him.

"Up, bed slug," he told him. Carter grunted. Walsh opened the blackout curtains and light streamed into the room.

They shambled to the ablutions and peered bleary eyed into the mirrors as they shaved. Carter was still half dead while he had his porridge. He glanced at the newspaper, not absorbing the words on the page at all.

"Where do you think we're going tonight?" he asked around the table.

"After yesterday, I'll take Brest again," commented Walsh. "What's not to like?" He lit a cigarette from the end of his last one. Walsh never had breakfast. He seemed to exist purely on a diet of tea and cigarettes. "Short route, cushy target."

They got in a quick air test. Carter let Jensen fly. He watched him take L-London through her paces. When they shut down, Vos stayed behind to tinker with the radio. He wasn't entirely happy with the reception and they left him deep in conference with the erks, arguing over what might be wrong.

At briefing, White was sitting next to them with his new crew. This was to be their first operation and White's navigator glued himself to Woods side throughout, taking copious notes as he tried to absorb the details of the briefing.

It was Hamburg again. As the night before had been such a mess, Command was sending them back to do the job properly this time. There was little change from the previous days briefing. The route was the same and there was little variation in the details.

Linkletter amended his weather report. The heavy cloud remained over much of mainland Europe but was moving east which meant a lot of the coast should now be clear. Extrapolating from the previous night's information, he predicted a tail wind of forty knots or more to push them along. That was fine outbound, but it would make the return journey a bugger, flying into a stiff headwind.

The first surprise of the night for Carter and his crew came as they crossed the coast north of Mabelthorpe. Todd and Murphy tested their guns and the next moment the sky lit up with flashes of light. L-London jolted as they were bracketed by flak.

"What the blazes!" Without being told, Jensen shoved the throttles through the gate and the Vultures howled as they accelerated. Carter hauled back on the yoke to get some more height. Todd and Murphy started frantically scanning the sky, wondering what the hell was going on. In the tail, Murphy saw some flashes far below on the water.

"It's a bloody convoy!" he reported. "The dozy bastards." He was half tempted to send a squirt in their direction.

Todd went barreling down the fuselage, bumping into everything going while their Manchester jolted up and down amongst the barrage. He was thinking evil thoughts when he fired off the days colours down the flare chute. The coloured dots of light fell behind them and the flak came to an abrupt halt. Todd rubbed his shins as he made his way back to his turret.

"Bloody Navy," said Woods. He checked his map. The convoy was in the wrong place. They were supposed to be well south of here.

The rest of the outbound trip was uneventful, but the clouds blotted out the sea when they were still forty miles short of their landfall. Woods managed to get a fix on the small Heligoland Archipelago in the German Bight before he lost sight of the ground. That fix confirmed the predicted winds were wrong again, but he was able to make the correction. From there it was a simple compass course south east, allowing for drift to put them over Hamburg.

The clouds were thinner over the city, with gaps giving glimpses of the ground below. Hamburg was three sides of a square, north, east and south around the Elbe. On the north bank, there were fires blazing merrily away. Flames flickered on the surface of the water. Their target, the harbour area in the centre was hidden from view.

There was a hurried conference over the R/T. They could go lower until they saw the target or they could circle for a while and wait for a break in the clouds. Neither option was particularly palatable.

On his first tour, Carter would have done this without thinking twice. He remembered one occasion when he had been second dicky and they had criss crossed over Mannheim six times at ten thousand feet until the bombs had been dropped. The game had changed a lot in a year. Going lower now would make you a sitting duck.

Circling, waiting for a break in the clouds carried its own risks. The weather might have been lousy, but a nightfighter could find them in this clag and spoil their night. Flak could still get lucky, firing blind through the clouds. Hanging around a target area was asking for trouble, like a matador trailing their cape in front of a mean bull. Finally, there were one hundred other bombers out there, collisions were not unheard of.

He decided to go in and they'd drop on whatever presented itself. Woods lined up on the fires and he recognised it as the Altona train station, the main station on the north side of the city. As he peered through the sight, a stick of bombs from another aircraft hit the ground, cutting across the tight bunch of rail tracks heading north out of the station. They went off, one after another like firecrackers, blossoms of orange light. Woods lined up on the ridged roof of the main building and selected simultaneous drop for everything.

He passed the corrections to Carter as they got nearer. Jensen rode the controls, feeling the small movements that Carter made. He glanced at his pilot, looking at his hands. Jensen had seen some pilots that gripped the controls like they were clinging on for grim death, over correcting, forcing the plane to behave. Carter held the yoke firmly, but lightly, feeding in small movements and the Manchester responded in kind, gliding along, threading her way through the flak, riding the waves of rough air.

More guns joined the party. L-London was buffeted by the blast waves of explosions. A shell detonated under the port wing and Carter caught it smartly before it flicked them over. Shrapnel peppered the fuselage and punched holes in the skin. One jagged piece went through Vos' logbook and he batted at the pages with his gloved hand to stop it burning. Woods gave one more correction and then released their load.

"They're off!" he shouted. The incendiary containers fell away and Carter counted to ten as he held her level, waiting for the camera to take its target photograph. He turned south, easing away from the city. Woods came up from the nose to get back to his navigator's' station.

"Right on the money, skipper," he announced when he plugged back in to the R/T. He looked at the compass and keyed his R/T again. "Slight correction, skipper. Go starboard and steer one, nine, five."

Carter took up the new heading but the controls felt strange. He had to make more input to keep the wings level.

"Somethings up," he told Jensen. The yoke was stiff as he tried to move it through its full range of movement.

"The ailerons?" Jensen said.

"Must have been that last hit," Carter agreed.

It was nothing that would stop them getting home, it just meant more work for them to keep her pointing in the right direction. After rounding Bremen, they headed straight west.

Carter did a check of the crew to keep everyone on their toes. He had Vos keep watch in the astrodome. The Belgian was less than thrilled about this. The last time they'd been bounced by a night fighter he'd been flung around like a rag doll.

Murphy yawned and rolled his head around. He blinked twice and then rubbed his gloved hand up and down his face. His eyes were heavy and he was tired. He'd not gotten much sleep the night before and he found his thoughts drifting towards Muriel. He smiled at the thought of smooth thighs and her warm mouth on his. He shook his head, berating himself for getting distracted.

"Idiot," he muttered. He quartered the sky again, panning his turret right as he resumed his vigil.

The Messerschmitt Bf110 was a sleek, twin engined killer. In 1940 they'd mauled the Polish air force and cut a swath across Holland, Belgium and France. In the Battle of Britain, they'd met their match as a fighter but at night, the 110 and the Junkers 88 were the top predator. Armed with heavy cannons and directed to the target by ground controlled radar they were lethal in the right hands.

Northern Holland had a number of airfields and the Germans had built a string of radar stations set inland. Each station controlled a box of airspace and the searchlights and nightfighters within it. The nightfighter prowled around and was directed to attack whatever came through the box. On a filthy night like this with heavy cloud and virtually no moon, the odds were good at getting through, but the nightfighters could reap a heavy harvest when the situation favoured them.

Flying out of Bergen, this 110 had been circling their ground controlled box for the last hour when the first reports of enemy bombers had come in. The pickings had been light tonight. The main raid was further north and only one bomber, a Halifax had fallen to their guns. They were reaching the end of their stint when ground control directed them to the north of their box. There was a contact passing their area of coverage.

They went north east over the Ijsselmeer. A great inland sea, it was often traversed by bombers going to and from the Fatherland, choosing this route as a way to stay clear of flak for a time. It had become the graveyard of more than one bomber crew who thought it was a chance to relax.

A flare of sparks caught his eye off to port. It happened again and he caught a glint of light off perspex. They were below him, just above a bank of clouds a few miles distant. The 110 banked to intercept and descended slowly, ducking in and out of the fluffy tops. Every few minutes he went into the clouds and then popped up, stalking his target like a U-boat captain following a convoy, putting the periscope up occasionally.

He stayed low, playing the cloud cover for all it was worth and accelerated, edging in to the bomber from the port side. He banked hard to make his attack and lined up his gunsight on the fuselage roundel behind the wing. Murphy saw it late. There was no time to shout a warning.

They opened fire at the same time and tracers flew back and forth. The 110's pilot was startled to find bullets flying in his direction. He thought he had made the perfect unobserved approach. He tightened his turn, pulling away to starboard.

The 110 flashed across Murphy's line of sight, passing right to left. Murphy traversed the turret to follow, keeping his thumbs jammed on the triggers as he struggled to keep a good lead on the target. The four browning .303's rattled as they stripped round after round of ammo from the belts.

Before he got the chance to see if he hit anything, Carter dived into the muck and Murphy's world was reduced to a grey wall.

Carter had reacted instinctively as soon as the first rounds started to lash into L-London's skin behind him. He shoved the yoke forwards and rolled left. Woods stuck out an arm and Vos grabbed on for dear life as he had his feet taken out from under him. Everything not nailed down, got tossed around. L-London shook fit to bust. The airframe creaked and groaned in protest at the rough handling.

Carter watched the altimeter unwind fast, counted to five and then hauled back on the yoke. As they levelled off, Carter stuck to the clouds that wrapped around them like cotton wool.

"Crew, report!" he shouted over the R/T. Jensen gave him a thumbs up, Woods called that both he and Vos were okay. Todd was next and then Murphy shouted up. His heart was racing, his pulse hammering in his ears from the excitement of the last thirty seconds.

"It was a 110, skipper. The sneaky bugger came in from underneath. Last I saw he broke away to starboard with a bunch of tracer up his backside."

"Vos, Woody, get back there and tell me what kind of shape we're in."

Woods hooked up to a walkaround bottle and both he and Vos clambered over the main spar. Grabbing a torch, they explored the rear of the kite.

Air screamed and whistled through various holes down the port side. One hole was as big as Woods fist. Woods waved the torch around, assessing the damage while Vos went aft, squeezed over the elevator bar in the tail and knocked on the doors to the tail turret. Murphy opened one and Vos stuck his head over his shoulder.

"All right?" he shouted in Murphy's ear.

The Yorkshireman nodded; his eyes as big as saucers above his oxygen mask. Vos clapped him on the shoulder and then went back. Murphy buttoned the turret back up and carried on looking in the murk, his eyes trying to be everywhere at once. Woods got back down at his navigator table and plugged in to the intercom.

"It's a bit draughty, skipper but it looks like we're okay. The cable runs are all right and none of the ammo trays have been hit. There are some nasty holes but the frames are intact."

Carter flicked a glance at Jensen and the pair of them shared a look. They had just burned one of their lives. Woods retrieved his chart from the floor and scrabbled around, trying to find a pencil. He ended up using the reserve he kept tucked into the top of his flying boot.

"Steer three, one, oh. That'll get us out of here quick and then we'll head west for home," He chewed on the end of the pencil, hoping he was right.

On the way back, the engines protested at the abuse and they had to back off on the throttles making them one of the last to get back. When they set foot on terra firma they spent a good ten minutes staring at their ravaged bomber. The port side of the rear fuselage had been peppered.
"Lumme, the mice have been at it," commented Murphy.
"Good grouping," said Todd, making light of the damage. There were a few holes in the left rudder too.
Carter stood under the port wing with Chiefy Latimer. They looked up at the hole. Just in from the port wingtip was a jagged rent about twelve inches wide. A rash of smaller holes surrounded it and bare metal was shining where the black paint had been scorched away.
"It might look bad but its really cosmetic sir." Latimer reassured him. "We can replace the wingtip easily enough. The holes in the fuselage will take a little more time but it's nothing that'll keep her grounded. We'll have her right as rain by the weekend," he predicted, although he knew Mr Pullen would be breathing down his neck to get it done faster.

At Saint Vincent's Hall, the place was buzzing with activity. The staff were burning the midnight oil. Any night their squadrons were operating, then the Group staff stayed up as well, monitoring what was going on. The boards in the Ops room were updated as each squadron reported their current status. On some nights the AOC or SASO were there. Some nights both of them did if it was a particularly important target.
They would hang around until the squadrons were on their way, then they would retire to their offices for a while. Paperwork would sit on their desk, they would make some calls, doing the circuit of the stations, finding out for themselves what was going on. Eventually, the pull of the Ops room would draw them back, like tugging on the end of a piece of string.
They had seen action themselves once upon a time. They had flown in rickety biplanes on the Western Front and then weathered the long lean years on the far flung frontiers, protecting the Empire. The Ops room was as close as they got to the action now. Occasionally, they would drop in on a station to see the troops off. Once in a blue moon they would hang around on the fringe of an interrogation, the stench of smoke and cordite and petrol permeating the air, listening to the crews make their report.
Georgette came in on the days shift as the ops staff went for

some shut eye. One of her Corporal typists came out as she came in.

"Morning Ma'am," he said, all bright and breezy. He made her feel one hundred years when he said Ma'am. "I've gone through most of the target folders from the 14th. Some of last nights have started coming in but the target photos haven't landed yet."

"Thank you, Edwards."

He left her to it and headed for his bed. She hung her gasmask bag and hat on her peg and parked herself behind her desk. Edwards had been his usual efficient self and arranged the buff coloured folders in squadron order and by date. The clock on the row of filing cabinets ticked in the silence. Her fingers drummed the desk while she chewed on her bottom lip, glancing at the folders.

She'd thought of Carter often the last few days. A thrill shot through her at the thought of his touch, his holding her and his blue eyes looking at her. Something had stirred in her that had lain dormant for a while.

She wanted to call him, to hear his voice, but with ops on there was no way he could call out from Amber Hill. She had flirted with the idea of putting a call through from her desk. A call from Group would be put through straight away but she couldn't bring herself to do it, that would be going one step too far.

Her left hand reached out for the pile from the 14th but snapped back as another one of her staff turned in. She said good morning and turned to her In-tray. More reports came in from the squadrons and her staff began collating the data. The AOC wanted concise summaries backed up with facts and figures. Damage estimates would come later once the reconnaissance flights were made. Then they could start comparing what was claimed against what was evidenced.

She managed to keep herself occupied for an hour before her eye was drawn back to the folders. She could farm them out to her staff to look at, she knew that, but she needed to see for herself. She dragged one pile in front of her. She sorted through them, 44, 49, 50, 61, 83 squadron and so on until she got to fourth folder from the bottom and it was there, 363.

Her hands opened the folder but it felt like it was someone else doing it. She felt light headed and her fingers trembled as she looked at each sheet until she came to the one she was looking for. L-London, pilot, Flight Lieutenant Carter. The language was brief as most interrogation forms were. It noted the take off and return time, the bad weather and the difficulty in reaching the target with some other comments scrawled at the bottom.

The target photograph was clipped to the back of the report. She lifted the page and looked at the photo. There was not much to see. You could just make out the silhouette of another bomber below heading in the same general directions. A blanket of grey filled the frame and there was little ground detail visible. There were a few brights spots where the glow of flames lit up the clouds from below.

She put the reports back in the folder and closed it, shoving it back into the pile of squadron papers. She did the same with the reports from the previous night. She did well to hide her reaction when she read the account of the night fighter attack and the flight back. He'd made it back alive, that was all that mattered to her.

Carter slept badly. He found it hard to relax and let go from the night's events. That stab of fear he felt when the rounds thumped home had chilled him. It had been that close. He lay in bed, drifting in and out of sleep. It was odd not hearing Walsh snore in the bed across from him but the Liverpudlian had put down at Dalton Bride in south Lincolnshire. He would be back later.

He listened to the sounds of the airfield coming to life. Engines coughed as they were run up, the day shift starting to tend to the kites. As sleep remained elusive, he eventually rolled out of bed and went on the prowl.

He found the erks hard at work on L-London in the hangar. The port wingtip was off and he looked at it again in the daylight. You could put your arm through the hole. Carter was amazed to find Chiefy Latimer still up and awake and directing the work. The man was a machine. Carter left them to it and headed to the Mess. He found White in the bar and handed his ex-second dicky a cup of tea and asked how he was.

"Tired, elated," said White, his eyes shining as he tried to describe how he was feeling. "It's like when you've drunk too much lemonade, sir. My stomach hasn't quite settled down yet." Carter grinned. He'd felt exactly the same when he flew his first op in charge. While other things had blurred with time, he would never forget that first operation.

Amber Hill remained locked down and the crews were summoned to briefing once more in the early afternoon. It was a tired bunch of men that shambled in to the briefing room for the third day in a row. Carters thoughts about the op were dark and malevolent. Bomber Command had them going in via the northern track across the North Sea once again. It was the same route they had flown the last two nights.

Although L-London wasn't ready, Carter and his crew were on the duty list assigned to fly the spare, Q-Queen. The afternoon air test showed she was still a dog and Carter promised himself he'd have Woods ditch some of the load as soon as they were over water to give them a fighting chance to get up to height.

He was tempted to break Q-Queen or get stuck on the grass

when taxying round to take off to avoid having to fly her. It had been bad enough flying her the first time, he didn't really want to repeat the experience if he could help it, particularly when they were going back to a target that was bound to be waiting for them.

After all the work and preparation, they were scrubbed at 8pm. The winds were still high and the previous nights raid had shown the havoc a headwind could create. The main force had been scattered and the bombing results had been been poor. In addition, returning bombers had landed all over the place and none of the squadrons tasked for the night's operation had a full complement of aircraft to send up. A late decision was made to cancel the nights efforts.

The groundcrews trailed out to the aircraft to remove the bombs and return them to the bomb dumps. The men got changed out of their flying kit. Carter had been in the middle of pulling on his long johns and extra socks when the cancellation was announced. Carter found himself feeling conflicted at the news and his experience was not unique. After summoning the courage to fly and brave the flak and the fighters and the weather, it was an anticlimax to suddenly find the rug pulled out from under your feet.

Once you had steeled the nerve, it was better to just go. You had to mentally reset your clock to the next time. You had stolen another night of life and payment would be demanded in full at some point. Many found solace in alcohol, drifting out to the local pubs. A few hardier souls went to Lincoln but most stayed close to home.

Carter and Walsh retired to their billet. Wrung out from the last two days of flying they lay on their beds talking for a while. Walsh nursed a bottle of Whisky he dipped into for special occasions. Carter wrote a few letters and penned a note for Georgette. Carter finally fell asleep, propped up by pillows with paper and pencil in his lap.

Their relief at being spared the wrath of the reaper was short lived. They were called to briefing the following afternoon and it was with some trepidation that Carter took his seat in the briefing room. When jobs were cancelled, you just knew you would be going back sooner rather than later. Hamburg seemed to be the current focus so they were pleasantly surprised when they were briefed for Bremen. It was a harder target than Hamburg but it was not quite as far to go.

A large industrial town, Bremen had a lot of anti aircraft guns around it but it was near the coast and didn't suffer from the persistent haze you would expect over cities in the Ruhr. Carter had flown some of the early raids over the Ruhr on his first tour. The whole area was usually wrapped in a pungent smog from the factories and foundries and very often, you couldn't distinguish where the boundaries of one town ended and another began. You always knew you were over the Ruhr from the smell. You could almost navigate your way there if the wind was blowing in the right direction.

L-London was still not ready so once more they mounted Q-Queen. Walsh flew the other spare with a new wireless op. In the morning he'd been told that Bellamy would be away for some time after the doctors had picked bits of shrapnel out of him and rebuilt his arm. Whether he would ever fly again was not certain.

The whole ground staff were out to see the crews off. Etheridge and Dickinson watched from the rail as Asher led the squadron to war. It was not his turn in the rotation. By rights, it should have been Dickinson's turn but Asher was not oblivious to the prevailing mood and grumbling that had done the rounds the last few days. The men were tired and their patience had been tested so he invoked Squadron Commanders privilege and went instead.

Georgette was at her desk when the Interrogation reports and target photos were delivered from Amber Hill. She closed her eyes and said a silent prayer before thumbing through the stack. Her heart froze when she got to the end of the pile and there was no sheet or photograph for L-London. Her hands tightened and crinkled the paper. She had to school herself not to panic or make any outward show of feeling.

She went through the reports a second time. She looked at each one more carefully, checking the name of the pilot and the names of the crew. She found his name on the very last sheet. Alex Carter, Q-Queen. She read the report, making careful note that they had bombed the target late due to strong headwinds.

She frowned as she looked at the photo. There were fires on the ground but a lot of the detail was hidden by thick globs of cloud. A streak of tracer went across the frame, great balls of light. What she could see of the ground didn't have very many buildings visible. There was a cluster of large industrial type buildings in the top corner, but she had a sinking feeling that they had dropped on open countryside to the south of the city.

She had heard about the Butt report. Working at Group, there were few things that didn't filter down eventually. She'd heard the claim that most bombs hit nothing or blew up a lot of cows and sheep. She'd not believed it before, but it was hard to argue with what she could see in front of her.

Her team worked their way through the reports from 363 and all the other squadrons, but it didn't take a genius to see it had been another bad night. 5 Group had put up just over forty aircraft. Half had claimed to have attacked the target. Of those, only two thirds seemed to have gotten near anything of value. The rest had dropped on the countryside or other places. Of the remainder, some seemed to have drawn been away by a decoy fire near Oldenburg. In return, 5 Group had lost two aircraft. One over the target, another presumably to a night fighter somewhere on the way home. Two more had force landed upon return. Overall, not a stellar night in the annals of Bomber Command.

She was drafting an initial summary of the figures around lunchtime when the telegram came. She signed for it and then read the ticker tape pasted onto the card.

HELLO DARLING. DONE 3 IN 4 NIGHTS. AM OKAY BUT VERY TIRED. MISS YOU. A

She asked Wilkinson to take a note to Helen as they were going out the door of Group that evening. He gave her an encouraging smile as he took the note from her. She was very pale.

Carter received a message over dinner. One of the Mess Stewards brought him the note on a silver tray while he was tucking into his pudding. Never had sponge and custard tasted so good.

The nights op had been another struggle to get to and from the target. The winds had shifted and the heavy cloud still clung to the ground in thick clumps making it difficult to get a good fix. It had been a dark night and with Germany blacked out, Woods had a devil of a job finding the way.

They had been drawn towards the glow of flames on the horizon but even in the pitch black, Woods could see it wasn't Bremen. None of the salient features were there and there was no river visible wending its way north as there should be. They pressed on until they got to Bremen and dropped their bombs after ploughing through a ferocious flak barrage, the worst Woods had ever seen. Poor old Q-Queen had been tossed around like a cork on the ocean. They picked up a few new holes and then beat it home.

Carter rang Georgette's digs after dinner. He moved a chair from the lounge into the hall and parked himself by the phone, one hand clapped over his ear while he waited for the switchboard to put him through. He heard voices on the other end of the line.

"Georgette?"

"I'm here."

It was a bad connection and her voice sounded flat and without colour.

"I got your message."

She laughed. Two of her house mates came down the stairs, their voices chattering away.

"I got your telegram."

"I'm sorry I've not been able to call the last few days."

"I know." She knew full well why he couldn't call. That had never been a problem with Charles, but bomber squadrons were different to fighter units. "I've been following you from here."

"I miss you," he said, meaning it. Time had telescoped for Carter these last few days. It had only been five days since he had seen her and it felt like a month. He could sleep for a week. His earlier energy was flagging fast. "A lots happened. I'm not sure if I'm coming or going." He stopped himself as his attention wandered.

She heard the fatigue in his voice.

"I miss you too."

"I need you," he said. He wanted to see her, needed to. He needed to get away from Amber Hill, even if it was only for a few hours. "Can you get away?"

"I'm not sure. I'll know in the morning."

Monday was her normal work day on the roster. If there was an Op Order in from Bomber Command Headquarters then it would be busy, if not, then she might be able to organise something. He understood what she meant but it was frustrating having to wait.

He shot an evil look down the hall as a noisy group of men came out of the bar and headed for the exit. Archer and a few others were heading out.

"Get your number dry," Archer said, his voice dripping with sarcasm. The hangers on laughed like drains, liking the joke.

"Sorry," Carter said. "I missed what you said."

"I said, if there's nothing on, I'll get over somehow."

"I hope so. I'll wait to hear from you."

"You sound dead on your feet," she said with some concern.

"Nothing a good night's sleep won't cure." He tried to sound offhand but his voice failed him.

"Then look after yourself," she told him with feeling. "Tomorrow will come soon enough. Goodnight darling."

"Goodnight darling."

24 - Love And War

Saint Vincent's Hall was set in large wooded grounds. Ever since the war began, the staff at Saint Vincent's Hall had increased and the manicured grounds had gradually disappeared. Nissen huts surrounded the tennis court and more huts had been put up under the trees. The last vestiges of the hall's former glory were a small ornamental garden and some long Victorian greenhouses at the rear of the house.

The tall Flight Lieutenant and the petite WAAF walked next to each other, very conscious that there were people around them. They needed to find somewhere out of view if that was even remotely possible.

Georgette suggested walking beyond the greenhouses and keep going into the trees. Before Christmas she had found a path that led to a bench seat set in a small clearing surrounded by clumps of thick bushes. Judging from the cigarette butts on the ground, the sentries sheltered here when the weather was lousy. She hoped it would be empty when they got there. Carter had turned up out of the blue and they had slid out to the canteen while she got over the shock.

"You could have let a girl know you were coming," she gently chided him as she reached across the table and took his hand in hers.

"Sorry, it was a spur of the moment thing," he said again. "My Flight Commander was coming across and I cadged a lift."

She blushed under his gaze, fizzing inside. Both of them wanted to say a lot but they were very aware that an Air Commodore was a few tables away. A few WAAF's were at the other end of the canteen, chattering away and Georgette saw them looking in her direction, wondering who he was.

"You are naughty," she told him.

"I'm using my initiative," he corrected her, "I *needed* to see you," he said with feeling. She blushed again, pleased he had come and smiled behind her cup of tea. When a clump of Wing Commanders and Squadron Leaders came into the canteen, they decided it was time to move. Still on duty, Georgette couldn't go far so she took him for a walk around the grounds.

It had been pure chance that he was here. Walking back from the hangar to see his plane, Dickinson had pulled up alongside him in a

Tilly and asked how he was doing. After a good night's sleep, Carter felt remarkably refreshed. They chatted for a few minutes about his Manchester and when she would be ready and then Carter asked his Flight Commander where he was going. When he found out he was going to Group, he'd talked Dickinson into letting him come along.

"I'll be there a few hours," the New Zealander warned him.

"That'll be fine, there's someone I need to see." Carter replied, offhand. Even a few hours was better than nothing and he wanted to see Georgette. Besides, he didn't know when he would have another opportunity to get back over.

It took Dickinson forty minutes to cover the twenty odd miles. The New Zealander was a cautious driver and Carter occupied the passenger seat with a briefcase and a bundle of papers in his lap. A conference of squadron commanders had been called to Group to discuss upcoming changes to operations. Asher had gone on leave that morning and made Dickinson acting CO in his absence.

Dickinson's fingers drummed on the steering wheel while he drove in silence. He was sure Asher had known about this conference ahead of time and strategically taken some leave to avoid it. Dickinson hated these meetings. Being in a conference room, the low man on the totem pole, surrounded by braid was not how he wanted to spend his afternoons.

During the drive, Carter blandly asked when he could have some leave. Dickinson's grunt was non committal while he concentrated on the drive. He fudged a gear change and banged the stick. Generally, crews got a few days off every few weeks so by the usual rule of thumb, Carter and his crew were due, but the mass leave when the squadron was grounded had messed up the schedule to some degree. Dickinson wanted to know what Group had planned before he could properly answer that question.

They had gone their separate ways in the lobby. After a Flight Lieutenant took Dickinson to the conference, Carter scuttled along to Georgette's office. He wished he had a camera when she looked up from her desk and saw him standing there. He remembered the last time he'd come into her office and the look she had given him then. This time was totally different. She was still shocked, but the warmth in her eyes was worth the trip.

They found the bench and sat together. It was a good spot, sheltered from the wind and out of sight of the huts. It was as private as it was going to get for them. Georgette linked arms with him and they held hands under the shade of the trees. Carter had thought about seeing her for days, now he was with her his mind had gone blank.

"I didn't know when I'd see you again," she said quietly and leaned in to him. He sneaked his hand round her shoulder and gave her a reassuring squeeze.

"I would have come sooner if I could."

"I know. I've had to watch and wait each night. I didn't think it would be so hard watching those reports come in," she said glumly. When Charles had been on his squadron, she'd not been a WAAF then. She only ever heard snippets from him of what went on so she had no idea what really happened. Her eyes got shiny when she thought back to reading Carters reports, the bare language that glossed over the details but said so much.

"I might be due a few days leave soon," he said to cheer her up a bit and she brightened at that. It had been hard the last few days not being able to just talk to him and see him whenever she wanted. There was no bus to Amber Hill and she wouldn't be able to borrow her friend's car again any time soon.

"I'm owed a few days as well."

"Now we just to have to figure out where." The only hotel he knew near by was *The Madison* and he didn't particularly want to take Georgette to somewhere in Lincoln. He wanted somewhere they could be together and be themselves for a few days and really get to know each other. Something on the coast perhaps.

"Goodgie?" he whispered. She smiled when he called her that and gripped his arm. "We'll sort leave, but let's go for dinner this weekend, make a proper evening of it. How about that?"

"If we're free?" she cautioned, keeping her tone light and teasing, knowing how hard it was to look too far ahead.

"If we're free," he agreed, knowing she was being sensible for a reason, but he was finding it hard to stay grounded when he was with her. He glanced at his watch, knowing the minutes were slipping away. She stiffened as she heard feet on the grass on the treeline behind them. A sentry must be doing the rounds and while they were doing nothing wrong, she didn't want to be caught like lovers in a clinch. Gossip could be poison around this place.

They walked slowly back down the path towards the greenhouses, joined at the shoulder, hands welded to each other, talking to each other in hushed tones. Just before they emerged, he took a chance and they kissed for a moment. They were strictly regulation when they came into the open, a good twelve inches between them as they walked along the duckboards past the tennis courts.

She went round the back of the building and he went round the front. Just before he rounded the corner, he looked back over his shoulder and saw her staring at him, her face drawn with strain. He gave her his best encouraging smile as she walked out of sight.

Dickinson's conference was still going on, so Carter cooled his heels in the lobby for an hour. He read the newspaper, did the crossword and then moved onto a well thumbed technical manual.

Bored, he asked the Corporal at reception for some paper and he fished his fountain pen out of his pocket.

He wrote a few short lines and asked the Corporal to take it to Georgette in her office when he had a minute. A door opened with a bang and footsteps thundered down the corridor. The Corporal scooped the note into the top drawer of his desk in one well practised move and resumed his seated position, shoulders back, rigid in his seat by the time the officer went past them and up the stairs. Carter smiled; it was not often you saw a Wing Commander rushing around like a scalded cat. Another door on the first floor slammed shut. The note reappeared back on the desk.

"I'll deliver it now, sir."

"Thank you."

The conference ended a few minutes later. They were buzzing as they walked out clutching their briefcases and folders. Dickinson caught Carter's eye and pointed towards the exit. He got up to follow his Flight Commander out of the door when he saw Freddie bringing up the rear, escorting everyone out.

"Good lord, Alex." Carter came to attention and flicked off a casual salute. "I'm afraid it's a wasted trip old man, I'm going to be busy for a while."

"Just checking to see if you'd be free on Friday, sir?"

Wilkinson laughed.

"Don't you, sir me, you reprobate," he glanced across and addressed Dickinson. "We did out first tour together," he explained. Dickinson gave a knowing nod. "Yes, I think Friday should be okay. What did you have in mind?"

"I thought *The Madison* again, it would make things a bit easier for, Helen?"

"All right," Wilkinson agreed. He patted Carter on the shoulder. "We'll get it sorted, but about six or seven makes sense to me."

"Make it seven," suggested Carter. "*We'll* see you and Helen there," Carter said pointedly as he shook Wilkinson's hand.

Dickinson was waiting for him by the Tilly. Most of the other staff had already left, the sound of their vehicles receding up the drive. Dickinson shoved the bumf he'd been given into a briefcase and then chucked his peaked cap behind his seat. He looked back at Carter, one foot in the car, hand on the top of the door.

"Now that we've sorted your social life, are you coming?"

"Coming, sir," Carter replied, getting in the other side. The drive back was more spirited as Dickinson's mind whirled with details. Big things were coming and the possibilities they opened up sounded impressive. Asher was going to love this when he got back.

As they sped along the country lanes, Dickinson dropped down a gear and swept round the corner, exhaust roaring which was no mean feat in a Tilly, it was hardly built for speed. Carter braced himself against the passenger door as the car leaned into the turn. The spring leaf suspension creaked in protest and then they were down a long bit of straight road. As they careered towards the next corner, Dickinson spoke.

"Now, Mr Carter. About that leave, I think we might be able to do something there."

When the tannoy announced that the squadron was stood down, there was an exodus of personnel from the station. After four days of being cooped up at Amber Hill, the men were keen to see a little bit of life and recharge their batteries. The pubs in Lincoln did a roaring trade and the Police were kept busy keeping things under control while life was experienced with gusto and intensity.

Vos had to cool his heels for a while. As it was a Monday, Denise was at work until teatime. She found him nursing a bottle of beer, sitting on the steps of her B&B when she got home. They fell into each others arms, then they fell into bed and came up for air a few hours later.

Since leaving London, life had settled down into a pattern for both of them. She had her job to keep her busy and he came when he was able, telling her what he could, making it funny, avoiding the tragic bits as much as possible but four nights on the trot had tested her nerve.

Night after night, she had heard the bombers go out, the air thrumming with the sound of the engines as the squadrons of Lincolnshire went to war. Each night she heard them come back in. Before going to sleep she had knelt at the side of her bed, hands clenched in silent prayer, willing him to make it back and return to her. She had to force herself to slow down and time seemed to stand still while she waited for any news.

Todd and Murphy went to *The Crown*. The place was jammed and there was a fuss when some soldiers blundered into the bar. They were just drunk enough to think they should stick around. One of them made a comment and the atmosphere turned very frosty. They were bundled from the pub and dumped outside, the only injury being to their pride when they were divested of their trousers. After five minutes their pants were thrown to them from an upstairs window and they disappeared before anything else happened.

Todd consumed beer at a prodigious rate and talked shooting with some fellow gunners from Waddington. One of them also hailed from Melbourne and they were like kindred spirits until the subject turned to Australian Rules Football and the relative merits of Essendon and St Kilda were discussed. Loyalty to a particular team was almost tribal and something that was fiercely defended. No blows were exchanged but the parties had to be separated and plied with more beer before things settled down again.

Murphy watched this little byplay of Aussie camaraderie perched on the end of the bar. He shared what time Muriel could spare him inbetween serving thirsty airmen. When the pub closed for a few hours in accordance with the licensing laws they went back to her place, a small one room flat above a grocer. She did him an egg on toast with a pot of tea but food was soon forgotten in a frenzy of lovemaking. He told her about the nightfighter attack while the sweat dried on their skin in between sessions. He had stoked the fire back up in the grate and added a few lumps of coal before getting back into bed with her.

She lay on her side, watching the flames leap and dance in the darkened room. He lay behind her and moulded his body to hers, their legs wrapped around each other. He nuzzled her hair and she closed her eyes, almost purring as he traced his fingers up and down her ribcage. She rolled onto her back and looked up at him. He thrilled at the sight of her laid on the bed. Under the glow of the fire and the dim light from the curtained window, her pale skin almost glowed.

He ran his left hand over her thigh and then moved up, over her stomach, around her belly button and then down to the glistening thatch between her legs. She looked at him through hooded eyes, her thoughts unreadable as his finger got closer to its target. Just as he teased her blonde hair, she shoved his hand out of the way and laughed. She pushed him back onto the bed and got on top, sliding down onto him to start it all again.

White went out with his new crew. It was their first chance to go for a drink since getting together and they had a lot to celebrate. They'd completed three ops without a scratch, not bad for a rookie crew just getting to know each other.

Later, he was sitting at his desk in his billet and wrote to his parents, giving them the news of his getting a crew of his own. Then he lay back on his bed and almost devoured the two letters Elaine had sent him.

Both had been dated the week before. They were chatty letters, full of details of her daily life. He liked her loopy handwriting, the big bold strokes of the pen, it seemed to suit her somehow. Her mother's health had improved significantly but she would remain at home for some time to come. She talked with yearning about going back to London and going back to her job. She felt a bit like a spare part back home.

He wrote her a long letter in response, trying to put into words what it felt like being the man in charge and what life was like on the station. He read it again and made some changes. Lots of it would never get past the censor, he was sure.

As soon as Carter got back to Amber Hill he headed to the Mess and made a beeline for the phone. The operator put him through and someone answered it on the second ring. Carter could hear Mrs Lloyd's voice ringing out in the background, announcing tea being served. He asked for Georgette and the voice on the other end of the line called her. She came to the phone in a rush.

"Darling, Mrs Lloyd's just serving dinner."

"I'll make it quick. Are you free Friday evening?"

"I should be," she said, her voice teasing. She was smiling and Carter could hear that down the phone, her voice bright.

"Good, we've got a dinner date with Freddie and Helen again."

"Do I get more than ten minutes to get ready this time?" she asked him. He laughed.

"Dinner's at seven. And I've got some leave coming. The boss told me it's soon, maybe another week."

"I'll find out and get organised," she promised him. They said goodbye and she went back in to dinner. She was floating along, not even hearing Mrs Lloyd's reproach for the interruption. The next seven days could not go fast enough, she just crossed her fingers that nothing would happen to upset their plans.

After a period of intense activity, the erks swarmed over the Manchester's. All of them needed some kind of work doing, ranging from the patching of holes all the way up to an engine change. Morale was good, after being grounded in Novembers the aircraft were now behaving themselves. Pullen scurried around making sure the men had what they needed. As engineering officer, he keenly felt any problems and he spent a lot of the day chasing down a delivery of spares that hadn't arrived from the depot.

For all their best behaviour, that was not to say that things couldn't happen. The next day, Everett's Manchester petulantly refused to feather the port engine when it overheated on a cross country flight and he had an interesting few minutes bringing it back to Amber Hill.

Carter air tested L-London, fresh from the repairs in the hangar. Everything handled okay, the engines operated within the acceptable range and the controls were nice and solid. He thought the ailerons were still a little stiff but Latimer assured him they had changed the cables for new ones.

"It'll just take a bit of time to bed in, sir," he promised Carter. "They'll soon have that little bit of give, you'll see."

Carter left it that. When it came to the aircraft, he trusted Latimer implicitly. If he said it had been checked, then it had been.

That evening 363 had a party and there was good reason to

celebrate. Archer had been awarded the DFC with immediate effect after his amazing efforts getting back from Brest. His radio operator was awarded the DFM for dealing with the fire. After the extinguishers had been exhausted, he had patted out the flames with his bare hands. He was in hospital recovering. Walsh got a mention in dispatches for bringing his Manchester back after getting shot up on the Brest run. Dickinson had been given the citations when he was at Group the previous afternoon, it had cheered him up no end during the meeting.

Archer was the centre of attention that night and he basked in the glow of congratulations, pint after pint being pressed into his hand. Drink flowed and the piano was liberally watered to make it sound better. They sang the Eton Boating song with gusto before transititioning into a stirring rendition of Bless 'Em All, with a few changes to the lyrics to suit Bomber Command.

Amongst the chaos, Everett boasted he could get round the Mess without touching the floor. Walsh bet him a pound he couldn't which was quickly accepted. Everett started at the fireplace, which was a large brick chimney breast with a polished mahogany mantelpiece. He took off his shoes and his tunic and rolled up his shirt sleeves before clambering onto it, using one of the Chesterfield sofa's as a stool. He shinnied round the corner, hand flailing for the picture hanging rail he knew was there. He gripped it firmly with his fingers and swung a leg round, feeling for the wooden chair rail about three feet up from the floor.

It was impressive stuff, he clung to the wall like some monkey and shuffled around the corner of the chimney breast. He would edge his foot along, then his right hand. He got to the bookcase halfway along the wall and took a breather. His navigator handed him a pint and Everett drank from it before getting ready for the next stage. There was a solid ceiling height bookcase on the next wall and he would be able to use that to cover some ground. He had no idea how he was going to deal with the door but it had a big frame around it, He might be able to swing onto the small round table next to it.

Everett was making this look too easy. The squadron spiced it up a bit. Pillows started flying. One thumped the wall in front of his face and he turned the air blue, telling them what they could do with their pillows. The barrage increased. His foot missed a step and he clung on for dear life, his fingers gripping the rail. He got his balance back and clung on, breathing hard.

"You rotten sods," he bellowed. More pillows flew. One of them hit him in the face and he dropped to the floor. His eyes fixed on Nicol who was stood there pillow in hand. He came up out of his crouch with a roar. Nicol threw the pillow at him which bought him vital seconds before he pelted for the nearest door. There was a spirited chase before someone grabbed Everett and pressed him to accept another pint which mollified him somewhat.

Two broom handles magically appeared and they decided to have a game of spinning. They split into flights. Furniture was moved out of the way to clear a space the length of the room. Two stewards were shanghaied into standing at the far end, holding the broom handles vertical. Asher stood on a stool, raising his hand for hush.

"Gentlemen. Dead easy, up to the end, drink a pint, spin round the broom five times and then run back to tag your team mate to go next. On three, two, one." He dropped the bar towel like Caesar starting gladiatorial games.

Dickinson and Church went first, they were the flight commanders so that was only fair. Church got off to a flyer and reached the brooms first but he was not as hardened a drinker as Dickinson. The New Zealander necked his pint in seconds and then put his forehead to the broom, going round and round. He lost count and actually went round it six times but he was still in front when he started running back down the hall. It was a picture. Seeing two Squadron Leaders staggering along, their heads canted one way while their bodies wanted to go the other. Dickinson crashed into a bar stool, picked himself up and lunged forwards to tap the next man in line as Church caught up to him.

Walsh was off, neck and neck with Archer. They went round the brooms in different directions and collided on the way back. Walsh dug himself out of the tangle of legs first and got back to the start line.

So it went on. As each man finished, they stood off to one side, on and around the Chesterfields. "Flak," someone shouted and pillows were utilised to spice up proceedings. White veered wildly off course, his balance thrown out of whack and clatttered into the crowd. Willing hands shoved him back onto the field of play and he fell over again, head reeling from spinning round the pole.

Carter managed to get up and down the run with the minimum of fuss, unlike Archer's navigator, Turner. His stomach revolted at the spinning and he threw up, narrowly missing the steward who deftly dodged out of the way. 'A' Flight were awarded victory by default and the men lined the bar while Turner was handed a mop and bucket to clean up his mess.

Carter ducked out when two bicycles magically appeared. Limbs tended to get broken when bicycles appeared. At his last squadron one navigator broke his leg in two places after bicycle racing in the Mess. Walsh joined him on the steps and they shared a cigarette.

"You too, huh?"

"Where fools and angels fear to tread," Walsh replied, blowing smoke to the sky. He shuddered when the sound of broken glass came from inside. He handed the cigarette back to Carter and clapped him on the shoulder. "Once more unto the breach."

"Act III, scene I, Cry God for Harry, England, and Saint George," Carter finished for him.

"I'm going to regret this, aren't I?" Walsh asked as he walked back in.

25 - Hoodoo Boy

Three days later they were called to briefing. Walsh was still hobbling after a heavy fall cycling round the Mess. He shifted gingerly in his seat, trying to find a comfortable position.

"I *warned* you," said Carter.

"I know, I know. I'm an idiot. God that hurts."

With Bomber Command still doing what they could to conserve their force over the winter months, only fifty odd aircraft would be going on this one. Asher unveiled the route on the board. The target for tonight was Munster. A big city, east and a little north of the Ruhr it was a huge military district and home to the sixth and twenty third Infantry Corps amongst other units. As it was an old city, they would be carrying mainly incendiary loads. Old Cities burned well with their narrow streets and wooden buildings.

After briefing, Carter went out to L-London. Fully repaired, this would be the first op he had flown in her for a week, but it felt like an age. The repaired panel on the fuselage stood out, the fresh paint on the roundel a sharp contrast to the grey fuselage lettering which was dirty and worn. He did his walk around more thoroughly than usual, paying attention to the control surfaces, the bomb door and, the undercarriage. He stood staring up at the engines, willing them to behave this time. Chiefy Latimer watched closely, patiently standing off to one side with the Form 700 ready for signature.

After the air test Carter retreated back to his billet. For the first time in his operational career he seated at his desk and pulled out some notepaper. He spent an hour writing two letters. After he was finished, he wrote names on the envelopes and sealed them. He leaned them against a bottle of aftershave and stared at them until Walsh came in. Carter quickly got up and pushed his chair back, clearing his throat as he stood up.

"You ready?" Walsh asked, not looking as he chucked his flying helmet onto his bed and shucked off his boots.

"As I'll ever be," Carter replied reluctantly.

"You should have heard, Archer earlier," Walsh continued. "The arrogant little shit was saying he was looking forwards to this."

Carter shrugged, for once not bothered to hear about the ongoing feud, other things on his mind. Walsh got into bed, set the alarm on the small travel clock and got his head down, still grousing about Archer without pausing for breath. Carter picked up the two envelopes and left Walsh to it.

He went to the admin blocks and found Saunderson behind his desk censoring mail. He knocked on the door jamb and Saunderson motioned at one of the spare chairs. Carter flopped down and put his feet up on the other chair. Saunderson carried on reading. He'd seen the moody face on Carter as soon as he came in, so he waited, sure that he would speak when he wanted to.

He chuckled to himself as he read the letters, impressed at Flight Sergeant Baxter's tales of sexual prowess. He got out the big brush, dipped it in the pot of indian ink and wiped out a few lines of text. He tutted as Baxter made mention of operations and wiped out some more words. Carter watched silently as Saunderson put the letter back in the envelope and moved on to the next one.

"Don't you ever get bored of that?" Carter asked, pointing at the letters.

"All the time," replied Saunderson without looking up from the next page. "I've seen it all, sex, war, medical problems, relationship problems, home sickness, you name it." Saunderson was about to make a crack about it being a dirty job but thought better of it. "Have you come to volunteer your services?" he asked instead.

"God no," Carter choked, suddenly remembering that Saunderson was still hunting for people to help out with his concert party.

"You sure? I see you doing a bit of Shakespeare."

"No," Carter told him, his voice flat.

"Oh well, it was worth a try. Think about it, won't you? What about the rest of your crew? Surely there's a budding thespian amongst them?" Saunderson persisted. If Carter wanted to invade his office, then the price was someone for his party. Carter locked gazes and then gave in, suddenly not bothered.

"Jensen's young and keen. I'm sure he'll be what you need."

Saunderson leaned back and picked up a clipboard hanging on a hook. He wrote Jensen's name down on the list and put the clipboard back. Carter stayed in the office, watching quietly as Saunderson worked through the daily business of the squadron, all the background stuff that kept the machine oiled and moving along. He took another hour to plough through letters of complaint from local councils and landowners. Mail from Group went into a tray to go to Asher.

Eventually, Carter cleared his throat. Saunderson didn't look up from the Air Ministry circular he was reading. Carter leaned forward in his seat and produced the two envelopes from his tunic pocket.

"I wanted to ask a favour."

Saunderson stopped reading and looked up. He'd seen many

sides to Carter the last few months, but he'd never seen him so serious before, not even when he was voicing his concern over Vos's girl. Carter slid the two envelopes across the desk. Saunderson picked them up and weighed them in his hands.

"If I don't come back, you'll make sure those get to the right people?"

"Of course, old chap. No problem." He opened the top drawer on the left side of his desk and put the envelopes inside. He slid the drawer slowly closed. "Consider it done."

Carter nodded a silent thanks and then glanced at his watch. Time had crept round to four thirty, it was time to start getting himself ready. He swung by his billet, woke up Walsh who was spark out and they went to the Mess together.

It seemed like time slowed down as he ate lightly and without much appetite. Around him, everyone talked like it was just another op, the banter running along well worn lines. A sense of foreboding grew inside of him and there was little he could do to stop it taking hold.

The feeling continued as he got ready in the crew room. Carter tried to blank out the clamour of noise as he sat on the bench, pulling on his fur lined boots. His legs felt like lead and it was difficult to do anything quickly. Today was his thirteenth trip on this tour and he'd been twitchy like this on his first tour as well. Everyone had their little quirks and superstitions and he was no different. He just felt uneasy and it was a hard feeling to shake off. He knew he'd only be able to relax once they got back to Amber Hill safe and sound.

His thoughts strayed to Georgette but he put her away in her compartment and focused on the task at hand. He promised himself he'd think about her when he got home. He made sure he thought about it in terms of *when*, not *if*.

He rode in silence in the truck out to dispersal. The crews joked amongst themselves but he withdrew into himself. Walsh gave him a thumbs up before he jumped down from the truck, Carter gave him a weak smile in return, devoid of his usual confidence.

His crew gathered by the entry hatch to L-London and looked at him. He suddenly felt tired of it all, tired of being the leader who had to bottle his feelings inside and paint a smile on his face.

"Time to go, lads," he told them. "I've been to Munster once before. Piece of cake. This is no different to any other trip." He mentally kept repeating this to himself, convincing himself that if he did it enough, then maybe it would be fine.

They got in and went about their tasks, checking things were in the right place, doing what they always did. Todd came back out of his turret in the nose and double checked where he had stowed his parachute pack. He hated being up front but a deal was a deal.

In the cockpit, Carter was happy to be back home again. Flying Q-Queen the last two ops had been uncomfortable so he was glad L-London had been ready for tonight. He went through the checklist with Jensen and then tried to relax, waiting for the start up time. While they waited, he broke the news to Jensen that he had volunteered his services to perform on stage. Jensen thought he was joking, that it was just a wind up to divert him from thinking about the trip, then the penny dropped that he was serious.

"Skipper, you can't do that to me; I get stage fright. I froze at a reading at school."

Carter laughed for the first time that day.

"Well you know what they say," he said to his hapless co-pilot, "practice makes perfect."

He leaned out of his window and twirled his finger above his head. Chiefy Latimer pointed at the port engine.

"Contact!" Jensen flicked the cover off the starter button and jabbed it hard. There was a huge belch of smoke and flame from the exhausts as the prop span into a blur. The airframe vibrated from the power.

"Cut out!" he called.

"RUNNING POSITION!" Jensen shouted and gave him a thumbs up.

Latimer pointed to starboard.

"Contact" he shouted; his voice snatched away by the roar of the port engine. The starboard engine came to life and Carter slid the cockpit window shut, settling himself in his seat. He made sure he had the brakes on and then ran up the engines. He could feel the power as L-London edged forwards and pushed against her chocks. The engines warmed quickly and the temperatures settled down. Across from them Walsh's Manchester was also running, the props, yellow tipped discs in the dark.

"Crew check in please."
"Nav, here."
"Radio."
"Second pilot, present."
"Nose gunner, skipper."
"Tail ready."
"Assume take off positions."

Todd squirmed up from the nose and went back down the fuselage. He leaned back agains the main spar facing forwards, his legs stretched out on the floor. Vos was next to him. The engine note deepened as Jensen brought in the power and they taxied out.

Todd hated this part. The engines blaring like banshees as they shot down the runway, tail up, balanced on the mainwheels, before climbing away into the sky. All he could do was sit and wait for it to

219

happen. He had complete faith in the skipper, but it was still twenty tons of metal convincing gravity that it could actually fly. He gritted his teeth as they jolted and moved along, waiting for their turn to take off. His stomach clenched when he felt them do one big last turn and then come to an abrupt halt as Carter dabbed the brakes, lined up at the end of the runway.

"Final checks, please," he instructed Jensen. "Compass!"

"NORMAL."

"Pitot heater!"

"ON."

"Trim!" Jensen double checked the trim settings. Carter had specified what he expected for take off. The pilot notes said slightly forwards for elevator but Carter preferred a few notches more. He found the Manchester heavy on the elevators and he preferred to make it easier to get the tail up on the take off run.

"ELEVATOR SET FORWARD, RUDDER AND AILERONS, NEUTRAL."

"Prop!"

"FULLY UP AND SET."

"Fuel!"

"MASTER COCKS ARE ON, CROSS FEED OFF, BOOSTERS ONE AND TWO ARE SET."

And so it continued. Each system checked and ready. Jensen dropped the flaps for take off and then put his left hand behind the throttles. They both looked towards the control hut at the left side of the runway. The glow of an Aldis lamp appeared in the small perspex dome. They were cleared to go.

Carter pushed hard on the throttles, driving them forwards with the heel of his hand. As they started moving, Jensen took over, his fingers threaded between them as he pushed. Carter gripped the yoke with both hands, feeling all the bumps as L-London started to roll. Jensen called out the speed as they accelerated down the runway. Carter kept the nose lined up, using the rudder to keep them straight.

"Max!" he called. Jensen shoved the throttles to the stops.

"MAX POWER!"

The engines howled as they were taken to the limit. The nose came up and now came the tricky part, keeping twenty tons of bomber balanced on her mainwheels without burying the nose into the concrete. Carter could feel the air over the control surfaces as the speed built up.

"Passing one hundred," Jensen called. "One ten."

Carter kept her glued to the ground. He had enough experience with Manchester's to know that you didn't yank them off the ground. You treated them with kid gloves and you gently coaxed them into lifting off.

"One twenty, and five."

Now was the time. He eased back the yoke. Not much, just enough to let the air get under the wings. He wanted to tease her into the air. He waited a few more moments and slowly pulled back. L-London left the ground and they were on their way.

"You look beautiful," he told her, meaning it as they got into Archers car. Once again, Carter had prevailed on Archer to loan it to him. Archers girl was away and he was going into Lincoln with his crew so he had no need of it tonight anyway.

The drive to Grantham had been pleasant enough. He bumbled along at a fair clip, not paying much attention, the car almost driving itself. He got to the street of Georgette's digs and parked a few doors away. Then a bolshy streak took hold and he let the car creep downhill until it was parked outside the house. He got out and almost skipped up the three steps that led to the front door. He knocked twice and waited.

After an appreciable wait, the door was opened by a tall silver haired woman, her blue eyes slitted and measuring as she looked him up and down in an instant. A pinafore was tied around her waist but she was meticulously turned out all the same, with not a hair out of place.

"Can I help you?" she asked in clipped tones, her Scottish brogue much more noticeable in person than it had been on the telephone. Clearly this was the formidable, Mrs Lloyd.

"I'm here to escort, Miss Waters to dinner."

There was a moments pause as she decided what to do. Her house had rules. They were her girls and she was charged with looking after them. Admitting a gentleman caller was unheard of. But Miss Waters had told her a few days ago she would be missing dinner that evening because she had another engagement. Mrs Lloyd liked that, it showed respect and consideration. She eyed Carter again with some suspicion and then stepped back as she opened the door.

"Come in," she said stiffly, gesturing down the hall with her right hand. Carter stepped in to a spartan hallway. Spacious, it was about eight feet wide with a patterned terracotta tiled floor. Flower print wallpaper adorned the walls and a number of decorative plates hung from the picture rail on thin chains. A coat rack to the right was full of ladies coats of all colours and greatcoats in RAF blue.

"May I take your coat...?" she paused, waiting for him to introduce himself.

"My name's, Alexander Carter."

"Arabella Lloyd; Mrs," she almost sniffed her title at the end, hinting that she was a respectable woman who should not be crossed.

"A lovely house, Mrs Lloyd," he said, trying to break the ice, She took his coat and hung it on a hook, but he kept hold of his battered peaked cap. Mollified somewhat by his comment about her home, she led the way to the front parlour on the left.

The room was about ten feet square with a large bay window at the front. Heavy blackout curtains were drawn across the windows. A bevelled mirror hung above the fireplace. The alcoves either side of the chimney breast had been fitted with shelfs filled with books. Two armchairs faced the fire, their arms draped in white lace covers. Carter imagined it could be quite a cosy room if it felt like it, but there was no fire in the grate and it was chilly.

Entry to the house did not include an invitation to sit and he stood by the mantelpiece. Mrs Lloyd left him there while she went up to inform Georgette her gentleman caller had arrived. He craned his head to look at the titles of books on the shelf to the left of the fireplace. Mrs Lloyd's tastes appeared to run to the conventional. He saw a bible, a set of Encyclopedia Britannica and a treatise on British birds.

Carter did his best not to gape when Georgette came downstairs ten minutes later. She was wearing a dark green dress she had borrowed from one of the other girls. Off the shoulder, it pinched her a little bit at the waist but it would do. A black fur wrap was across her shoulders. Some slide clips pinned her hair back from her face.

"Hu-hullo," he stuttered, taken aback. She smiled, pleased to have made such an impression on him.

"I'm not late, am I?" she asked.

"Not at all. A lady can never be late anyway," he said with arch gallantry, coming over to her from the fireplace and taking her hand. He would have hugged her but Mrs Lloyd was stood at the door, her face a rigid mask of marginal disapproval, her hands clasped in front of her. He gestured to the door. "Shall we?"

"Be careful dear," cautioned Mrs Lloyd as they made for the door. She knew what these flyer types were like, all flash and talk, no substance. She hated to see her girl's heads being turned by a smart uniform and a pair of wings.

"I will, Mrs Lloyd," Georgette replied, suitably abashed and demure. The door closed with a bang as they went out to the car. Carter didn't look back but he would have bet money that he was being watched through a slit in the blackout curtains. He opened the passenger side door for Georgette and took her hand as she got in the car. He let in the clutch and they pulled away smartly.

"So that's the dragon," he commented, concentrating as the front window steamed up slightly. He wiped it with a rag.

"Oh darling, you mustn't. She's not too bad really."

"I can tell. Do you have to be back by a certain time or does she raise the drawbridge for the night and leave you to the mercies of the ravening hordes?"

"No, she doesn't. She's just looking after us."

"That's one thing to call it," he observed, his tone more acid than he intended.

"Well, she is a little strict sometimes," Georgette grudgingly admitted.

"Sometimes!" exclaimed Carter. "My God, a smile would kill her."

"Cheer up grumpy. We're not having dinner there."

He mellowed at that. He drove out of Grantham and a short time later he went up the drive of *The Madison*. Carter parked near the entrance and they walked through the front door. He took her coat and handed it to the porter who gave him a ticket for it. It was a little before seven so he escorted her to the lounge and left a message at reception so Wilkinson would know where to find them.

The decor themes of the dining room had been carried through to the lounge. The heads of stags and deer looked down on a room painted in pale yellow shades. Oriental rugs adorned the polished woodblock floor. An old military type was sitting by the fire, basking in the warmth while he read his newspaper. Two old ladies were in their finest having aperitifs before dinner.

Carter picked a table farthest from everyone else and held the chair for Georgette. She settled and he hitched his chair round so there was no space between them. The waiter asked what they wanted and Carter ordered drinks without really paying attention, mesmerised by her.

He'd been thinking about this since seeing her earlier in the week. Now the moment had come he found himself tongue tied. She looked at him, seeing his nerves and she smiled, her cheek dimpling with her lopsided smile. She reached across the desk and placed her hand over his.

"Worth waiting for?" she asked. He nodded.

"I'm just glad to be here," he managed to get out.

He yawned, fighting it. His body clock was still racing to adjust after the previous nights op. He stared into the distance, distracted a little by the leftover feelings of foreboding he had suffered the day before. Even now it was hard to shake off that sense of doom that had fallen over him.

"Alex?"

"I'm sorry; it's just." He breathed out hard, his cheeks ballooning. He pinched the bridge of his nose. Georgette detected the edge to his voice and was dismayed.

"If you're tired, we can do this another time."

"No, NO," he said firmly. "It was just hard last night."

The worst part had been when they had flown over the

Ijsselmeer. Sucking down oxygen, Carter found himself breathing faster than normal, his eyes raw from staring into the dark. The patchy clouds were stacked up above them, the weak moonlight making them glow like ethereal ghosts. This was where they had been attacked the last time so he had been on edge all the way until they had left it behind them. He put that and other thoughts away and turned his attention back to her.

"I've been thinking about this all week."

"I have as well. It seems a long time since we were here last."

"Two weeks," he murmured.

"Too long."

He tapped his glass off hers.

"Here's to us."

She lifted her glass in salute and then sipped.

"To us."

They talked about their coming leave, throwing suggestions into the hat. Georgette suggested Skegness. It was not far away and some good seaside air could be quite refreshing. Carter wrinkled his nose in disapproval. He'd gone there with Mary on his first tour and he didn't relish the idea of revisiting old haunts.

One thing they did agree on was to avoid Lincoln. That really was too close to home. On the other hand, Carter didn't want to go too far. On a short forty eight, he wanted to spend as much quality time with Georgette as possible, not just cooped up in a train carriage going back and forth. Eventually they settled on York. They were still discussing details when Freddie Wilkinson and Helen were being directed to their seats by the waiter.

"Here you are," his friend said breezily, full of bonhomie as he saw them sitting there clearly lost in one another.

Helen was all smiles as usual, pleased to see him and pleased to see the new romance blossoming so well. She liked Georgette very much and they had talked a few times on the telephone in the last two weeks.

They went through to dinner. Chef outdid himself again, turning rabbit into a delight and the accompanying sauce was magical.

"This was a good idea," said Wilkinson as he attacked his apple pie with gusto. He caught the waiter's eye and asked for more cream. Carter grunted agreement; his mouth full of confectionery.

Helen commented that she had spent the afternoon choosing baby names. Wilkinson choked on his drink at that announcement.

"But I thought we'd agreed. Edward if it was a boy, Eloise if it was a girl. After my father and your mother."

"Freddie that is sweet of you, dear, but it's not carved in stone. I just wanted to see how some others sounded before making up my mind."

"Just don't forget, Alex is a good name for a boy," said Carter, smiling wide like the Cheshire Cat. Helen playfully swiped at his hand.

"You're a perfect rotter."

The plates were cleared away and soon after, Helen announced she was tired and everyone fussed around to make sure she was okay.

"I'm fine," she assured them as she levered herself up from her chair. "Just tired."

In the hall, Helen hugged Georgette with genuine warmth.

"It was lovely to see you again. You promised me a shopping trip."

"I know. How about tomorrow?" Georgette suggested. "If you feel up to it, that is."

Helen's face lit up with enthusiasm.

"That would be wonderful. A good night's rest will see me right. It would be nice to get out of this place and go shopping." She hugged Carter close. "Goodnight, Alex." She turned to the stairs and called her husband to heel, "Freddie."

Wilkinson said his goodbyes.

"Goodnight, old man. Georgette."

"Come on, darling," Helen insisted.

He caught her halfway up the stairs to find her moving at a fair clip.

"I thought you were tired," he protested. She lightly slapped him on the arm.

"Oh, Freddie you can be dim sometimes." She paused on the landing and looked back down into the hall as Georgette and Carter walked arm in arm back through to the lounge. "Look at them," she cooed. "They want to be alone and not hanging around with an old married couple like us."

Wilkinson laughed, a sharp bark.

"Old man. I'll show you an old man." He made a lecherous grab for her behind and she squealed and did her best to get up the stairs to their room. Wilkinson chased after her, his eyes twinkling in mischief.

The lounge was empty on their return so they sat by the large fireplace. A three seat settee was in front of it and an armchair either side. The Colonel had left his newspaper behind on one of them. Carter chose the settee and Georgette settled herself next to him on his left, her feet tucked underneath her. She rested her chin on his shoulder, pleased at last to have him all to herself. She'd not felt like this for a long time.

"I suppose it sounds selfish, but I'm glad they went to bed," she murmured.

"So am I," he replied. The scar on his cheek rippled as he smiled broadly. They giggled like teenagers. Carter quickly looked around and then kissed her.

"Alex!" she scolded, but she was thrilled he had done it. "Someone might see."

"I don't care. I wanted to do that in the woods at Group," he said earnestly. It had been maddening, having to restrain himself, half expecting a sentry to appear at any second.

His heart soared at how lucky he was, but then the black mood of the previous day washed over him. Georgette sensed the change, seeing his eyes darken, feeling his arm tighten.

"What's wrong?" she asked him, concerned. He shook his head.

"I'm sorry. It was just hard yesterday." He tried to explain as best he could the feeling that had come over him. It was difficult putting into words that itch at the back of your head that this was *IT*; that today could be *THE* day. "Thirteen's the magic number, the bogey man."

He shuddered as he said it. Georgette relaxed slightly. She had feared something far worse.

"You shouldn't let things get you down. It's just a number," she said simply, trying to demystify it all.

"I know. No; really, I do. It's just hard to shake off these feelings sometimes."

"My husband used to be like this." She avoided finishing the sentence by saying, *towards the end*. Carter guessed anyway. He'd heard her voice trail off and it pained him to upset her. "Charles used to say, when your numbers up, it's up."

He thought that was very dour. He was a believer in skill, experience and being alert. It was careless people that were begging to get the chop.

"I can't say I subscribe to that."

"It was strange really," said Georgette quietly, her fingers playing with the hem of her dress. "Charles was never one for fate, or pre-determination."

"Neither am I. Never have been. I've always thought a chap makes his own luck. War's no game."

She thought about that summer, when the skies were full of German aircraft and everyone was waiting for the German invasion. If Charles had not gone up that day, he would have fallen another time; she was sure of that. He had lived life at full throttle and whisked her along on his coat tails and it *had* been fun; while it lasted. Time had just caught up to him, that was all.

Alex was different. He was much more controlled and she was sure he flew the same way. Nothing would be left to chance, but maybe that was the difference, she mused. Charles had flown by the seat of his pants and went thundering into combat, guns blazing.

Carter stared at the fire, seeing the flames that had consumed

Munster. The city had burned well. Their target had been the railway station and the mixed load of high explosive and incendiaries had rained down on the surrounding area. The relief he felt when he landed had been almost tangible.

He didn't discover the price the boatman had demanded for his safe passage until they got to interrogation. The squadron had lost two planes that night. One had belly landed after the wheels stubbornly refused to come down but the crew got out okay. The other casualty had been White and his new crew. What made it worse was it hadn't even been the Germans. White had made it back to England, only to be shot up by a northbound convoy hugging the coast.

With the starboard wing on fire and flames consuming the fuselage, he had forced the crippled aircraft to stay up while he crossed the coast and given his crew a chance at life. At dangerously low level he had bailed out and landed hard only a few hundred yards from the wreckage of his Manchester. Worried locals found him lying there, with his face and hands badly burned.

Carter told Georgette what had happened. She watched him as he talked, his voice brittle, his hands clenched in his lap. She could see he felt this loss quite badly. She remembered White's name from the Christmas dance. That prompted another memory as she tried to change the subject.

"How's your friend?" she asked him. "The dancer?"

"Walsh?" Carter brightened a little. "He's still cutting a dash." He sprang to his feet and pulled her up, his mood changing again. He twirled her round and drew her close, his right arm around her waist, his left hand extended. They did a quick waltz, a circuit around the sofa and finished with another twirl, her dress flaring around her legs.

"You're not a bad dancer yourself," he told her.

"Why thank you, sir."

She giggled and looked up at him. She smoothed down the lapels of his uniform jacket, her fingers lingering over his wings and DFC ribbon. She blushed as a uniformed member of hotel staff poked their head around the door to the lounge, curious at the squeal of noise.

Helen's advice came back to her then. She stepped back out of his encircling arms and held out one hand. He took it and she pulled him towards the door with an impish smile on her face.

"Come on," she told him. "I want to show you something."

She took him outside and they walked round the side of the house. They went past the vegetable patches, skirted past the fountain and struck off across the grounds.

Carter let himself get pulled along, curious where they were going. It was pitch black and it took a few minutes for his eyes to adjust to the darkness. Soon he could see the subtle difference between the sky and the ground. The trees were a darker band of black. The stars were beautiful, a blanket of bright dots. Carter stopped walking and craned his neck to gaze up at them. When he was on ops, he was too busy to admire the view.

He found Orion's belt to the south, the three stars together. He circled round and found the great bear, then he followed that to Polaris, the north star. Georgette stood there quietly, holding on to his hand, patient. It was peaceful out here. In the black, in the middle of nowhere he found himself in the moment and his worries washed away. He blinked as he came back to himself then.

"Where are we going?"

"Somewhere," she said coquettishly, her voice full of promise. She pulled him onwards. "Come on."

She took him to a hexagonal shaped summer house with a sloping roof and a sorry looking rooster weather vane on top. Georgette bent down and moved a plant pot out of the way.

"Success," she held up the key and tried it in the door. It gave with a squeal of hinges and opened outward. Carter poked his head inside.

"Nice, get some net curtains, some carpet, it'll be great."

It was quite large inside, about eight to ten feet wide. There were two stools and a side table stacked up to the right. An armchair had a sheet over it. He parked himself on it and bounced up and down a few times.

"Cosy."

"Ass." She stepped around him and dug around in a pile of things in the dark. "Perfect." She pulled out some blankets and laid them on the floor. Carter closed the door. "Helen said it used to be used by an artist. Apparently, the light's very good in the summer."

She moved a box of oil paints out of the way and lay down on the blankets, legs stretched out in front of her. She toed off her shoes and leaned back on her elbows, looking up at him from the floor.

He didn't need telling twice. He moved off the armchair in one smooth move. They locked lips. Georgette wrapped her arms around him and sank to the floor, nestling in amongst the thick blankets. Carter shifted so he wasn't laying fully on her. His left leg overlapped with hers and she pulled him down on to her.

Carried along with the moment, they kissed again, a long lingering kiss that set off stars at the back of his head. The final strands of worry and doom left him then as her perfume enfolded him.

"You planned this all along?" he asked her.

"Yes. No. Maybe," she teased. She relaxed into the blankets and he lay down next to her. His hand found hers in the dark and their fingers danced together, his thumb stroking her palm.

He listened to the night time sounds outside. The trees rustled in the breeze and some branches pattered off the glass. He felt a tickle of draught from somewhere inside the hut. He reached over and pulled the last blanket over them, flicking the corner to make sure her feet were covered.

She rolled to face him and undid the buttons on his tunic, running her hand over his chest, following the line of his muscles, her nails teasing him through the fabric of his shirt.

"Alex, try not to think about last night too much," she soothed. She kissed him again, willing her strength into him.

"I know. This second tour is just harder than I thought it would be." She listened quietly, letting him get it out in his own time. "I didn't know much the first time. Maybe it's better that way. Coming back and doing it all again when you know what's waiting for you." He looked down at her. "You know, it's true what they say, ignorance really *is* bliss."

"You're nearly halfway-"

"-With a long way to go," he finished for her, his voice quiet. In the dark, here, he could admit things to himself he had never faced before.

He levered himself up and hugged his knees, his chin balanced on them, his nose resting on his arms. He stared through the wall of the hut, thinking about how much had changed in the six months he'd been away.

Ops had evolved and become far more deadly. The days of swanning around the target looking to pick your spot were coming to an end. The flak was waiting to reach up into the sky and claim you and the nightfighters were more lethal than they ever were before. It was all part of the great game, the pendulum swinging back and forth almost like a metronome. They would have the advantage for a while, then the Germans would steal it back again, a never ending cycle of move and counter move.

"It's a long, long way to Tipperary…" she intoned, her voice quiet, her eyes misting. She rubbed his back and shoulders, tracing patterns with her fingers until she could feel the tension slowly easing. She waited patiently until he turned and gathered her in his arms.

His left hand moved down her body, following the line of her leg to her feet. Then his finger traced back up until he got to her knee and moved her dress up. She shifted, bending her leg over his as he skimmed over her stockings to the top and then around her thigh. She giggled as she kissed him. She tugged on the lapels of his jacket and pulled him down on top of her. She smiled against his teeth and laughed. She *needed* this. It had been too long since Charles and she wanted to be held, to be reminded that she was still alive.

Carter came up for air and looked down at her. Her hair had come loose and was a dark fan around her head. He was intoxicated with the feel of her, her perfume, her smile, the throaty laugh as she chuckled in the dark. His thoughts strayed to Mary for a moment. She would never have done something like this.

She kissed him; hard. Her tongue traced around his mouth, mapping his teeth, slick, warm. She arched her back as he leaned in to her. A moan escaped her lips as she kissed his cheek, moving round to his ear, moving back along the line of his jaw, down his neck. She unbuttoned his shirt, her nails dragging down his chest.

It would be so easy to yield as his body responded to her, drunk on her. He propped his head up with his right hand as he stared down at her. She met his gaze, her eyes glinting in the moonlight as she tried to read his thoughts. He couldn't stop grinning with excitement. His blood stirred, hammering in his ears, his heart roared in his chest but the reality of his surroundings intruded.

They were in a musty wooden hut, fumbling in the dark like some lovestruck teenagers. It suddenly felt very grubby and cheap and she was worth more than that. He passion cooled rapidly as his controlling head kicked in. It was not that he didn't want to, he did, but not here, not like this. His thoughts turned to leave and York. That would be perfect. In an instant, a shadow reared up in the background, *if you last that long.* He stamped down on it hard, crushing it under his heel squealing and wailing. He would *make* the time, he promised himself. He broke the spell as he pushed off the floor and got to his knees.

"I think it's time I get you home," he breathed. "I wouldn't want to disappoint, Mrs Lloyd."

Georgette rolled her eyes and was good enough to laugh.

"Heaven forbid," she said as she ruffled her hair. She giggled at the thought of Mrs Lloyd's disapproving scowl at her current predicament. It was most improper behaving this way with a man she had just been introduced to. She gathered the loose strands of hair into a bun and felt around on the mattress for some pins to keep it in place. He rummaged around and found her shoes. She pointed her feet and he put them on for her. She took his hand as he helped her stand.

"Thank you," she said, brushing dust from her dress. They bumped together in the dark. She lifted her chin to see him looking down at her. She could see the desire in his eyes, the ardour. He took her hand, his skin warm.

"Goodgie, don't think I didn't want to." She was glad the gloom hid her blush. "It's been a while for me."

"Me too," she said, her voice husky. He kissed her again, the fires stoking up once more.

"Believe me, I do-" he murmured.

"-I'm a big girl, Alex," she told him. "You don't have to explain."

"But I do. I just want it to be…" words failed him.

She put a finger up to his lips and said, "Shhhhh. I understand."

The car started first time and he drove her back to her digs. He stopped up the street, out of view of the house.

"Time to face the music," he said ruefully. She put a hand on the steering wheel and leaned over. He met her halfway, their lips colliding with force as they sought each other.

"Goodgie, about earlier-"

"No need to explain darling, I understand." She traced the line of the scar on his cheek and then wiped her finger across his lips. She could not say she wasn't a little disappointed that he had stopped when he did. The heat had stoked high in her as well but she knew what he was thinking. He wanted to be gallant. *Men*, sometimes they were such babies.

The curtains twitched as they pulled up outside. Carter was certain Mrs Lloyd would be watching to make sure there was no hanky panky. He escorted her to the front door. They embraced again and she kissed him demurely on the cheek as the lock went click and the door opened. Mrs Lloyd was stood there in a powder blue dressing gown, arms crossed, a scowl of disapproval painted across her face.

"Goodnight, Alex," Georgette said, her eyes saying far more than words ever could.

"Goodnight, Georgette."

Mrs Lloyd hustled Georgette over the threshold and slammed the door without so much as a good evening. Shaking his head, Carter abused the clutch and gearbox as he shifted the car into gear and pulled away. The entire drive back to Amber Hill he berated himself as an idiot. He had turned her down, what on earth must she think of him?

In her room, Georgette was sitting on the end of her bed while she brushed her hair. Her room was in the loft and moonlight streamed in the window, giving her more than enough light. She looked up at the stars, thinking about the evening. She sighed as she got into bed, leave could not come soon enough.

26 - All The Fun Of The Fair

Todd strolled into his billet after eating in the Sergeants Mess. He felt like a relax and then maybe a bit of poker later if the game was on. Being the weekend, a few bods had passes so it depended who was still on the station.

He found Murphy looking into a broken square of mirror he kept on a shelf above his bed. His tie was straight, his hair was slicked back and his uniform was nice and neat.

"You coming out tonight?" he asked the Australian as he rubbed his face, feeling for stray hairs he might have missed when he'd shaved.

"I might," Todd replied, his tone non-committal. He flopped onto his bed, his hands hanging over the sides.

"It's a dance tonight," Murphy prompted him although Todd already knew that. Every Saturday, there was a dance in Lincoln. If there were no Ops on, the place was always jammed, awash with RAF blue and girls. There was the occasional brown job, but they never got a look in. A wing on the chest was what got attention, everything else was just second best.

"You meeting, Muriel?" he asked.

"No," said Murphy curtly. He tied the laces on one shoe. "I'm meeting a nice little dark number."

"What about, Muriel?"

"What about her?" Murphy shot back; his tone combative.

"You've been seeing her, that's what," Todd said shortly.

Murphy scowled as he stood up. He looked at his shoes, tilting them back and forth to see the toe caps shine.

"When did you become my dad?" Murphy challenged. "She's not my keeper, it's not like we're married or anything."

"Clearly," replied Todd. He got off the bed and went over to his locker. He tugged his best blue off its hangar.

They rode one of the trucks into town. All the way, Murphy had stewed in silence, arms crossed. It was ridiculous, he was an adult and he was being made to feel like the boy who got caught scrumping apples.

"Are you going to say anything?" he asked Todd as he got down from the truck.

"Nope, mate. I'm not. It's your bed."

"We're not married you know," Murphy said again as they stumped up the hill to the hall where the dance was.

"I know." Todd fished out his cigarette case and extracted a Churchman's medium. He snapped the case shut and looked at it, turning it in his hands before putting it back in his pocket.

He had picked it up in an antique shop in London when he first came to England. It was a silver art deco case with a deep blue sunburst guilloche enamel design on the lid. It had cost him a tidy sum, but it was worth it. He hated crushing his fags in their cardboard packets and it was a nice thing to have. Murphy held up his lighter and Todd lit it, nodding gratefully as he drew down a lungful of smoke.

Todd had not really felt like coming but he thought he needed to keep an eye on Murphy and see what was going on. He shook his head. It was supposed to be the Aussies that had the reputation of being a bit too fancy free with their favours. Clearly that was not a hard rule.

"Rough about, White," said Murphy, trying to change the subject. Todd grunted agreement. He had gone through this before when his first crew had copped a packet. It was a shame; White had been a decent lad and the rest of his crew had been all right as well.

He used his cigarette hard while he thought about the fickle hand of fate, pondering just what exactly decided who bought it and who didn't. Take Archer for example. He had built his reputation as the press on type and he did, despite everything he kept going and kept coming back. But not all of his crew did. His wireless op had yet to return after getting his hands turned into burnt stumps and he'd lost god knows how many gunners. A memory of Winsor flashed into Todd's head for a moment. Blonde hair and blue eyes, as he had been, before a 110 had mangled his pretty face. Once regarded as lucky, things had changed lately and suddenly not everyone was so keen to be a part of Archer's crew.

Murphy paid them both in and they strode into the hall. The band was already playing a warm up number and quite a few couples were on the dance floor, slowly circling round. The evening was just starting to warm up.

"I'll get the drinks, Spud. What's your poison?"

"Just a bitter," said Murphy, his eyes searching the crowd. He saw who he was looking for and waved. Todd shot a look across the hall and saw a thin brunette threading her way past the dancers towards them. Murphy kissed her quickly and put an arm around her waist.

"Joan, this is, George." Todd shook her hand with little enthusiasm.

"Pleasure to meet you," she said, her voice giggly. Up close she was short and perky, her dark eyes dancing in good humour. Her hair framed a heart shaped face and pointed chin. She was thin as a rake and straight up and down. She hung off Murphy's side like a limpet.

"He's not staying," Murphy said pointedly. He nodded towards the door. Todd's eyebrows shot up at the casual dismissal. He moved to the other side of the hall but didn't leave right away. He parked at the end of the bar and nursed a pint. When he finished it, he left and went back to Amber Hill. Murphy was a big boy, he would just have to deal with this himself.

The following morning, a missive was issued from Air Ministry, which in turn landed at Bomber Command before being moved on to 5 Group and thence on to Amber Hill. The signal was short and to the point. Squadron to be made ready, inspection of personnel and aircraft by persons from the Air Ministry on the Sunday. All courtesies to be extended etc, etc.

It was quite surprising what could happen in two days. Parties of defaulters swarmed the station, whitewashing kerbs, trimming grass, pruning weeds and tidying the place up. The erks did the same around dispersal. The concrete handstandings were swept and sand was put down to cover the oil leaks.

Some of the more rickety crew sheds were either tarted up or taken apart. The aircraft were left alone. Etheridge was all in favour of a bit of spit and polish, but the Manchester's were off limits. They were marked by war and he was going to have them display their wounds proudly.

The men were a different story. They needed to be presentable and there was a frenzy as shirts were ironed and trousers were pressed. What passed as good enough for day to day operations and nights in town was not the same as a full inspection. In their billets they were bulling their Oxfords.

Todd wiped his rag across the tin of polish and rubbed it over the toecap. He made sure he covered everywhere and did the same for the other shoe, giving it a good going over. He put them on the bed in front of him and put the rag to one side. His forefinger had gone black where polish had soaked through the rag. He sniffed his fingers and wrinkled his nose in disgust. There was a distinct aroma of sweaty feet and the thick petroleum stink of polish. Wiping his fingers down his trousers he used a toothpick under his nails, digging out black. He wiggled his toes, watching his socks move.

"Bloody waste of time," he muttered. "All this guff and for what? So we can stand in pretty little lines while some bigwig gets to act all god like."

"Nothing wrong with a bit of spit and polish," said Murphy deadpan. He was rather enjoying this. He'd not done any square bashing since basic training. Todd looked at him like he was crazy. He needed to march up and down and stand on parade like a tailor's dummy like he needed a hole in the head.

"You're remarkably cheery."

"And why shouldn't I be?" Murphy was still fizzing after his night with Joan. She was dynamite in bed and there had not been much sleep, she kept him too busy for that. Todd scowled but refrained from commenting further. Things like this could tear a crew apart and he was not about to Mess things up over a bit of skirt. He knew what he should do, but said nothing.

Murphy finished buffing his buttons and put his tunic on. He brushed it down, pulling the material taut across his shoulders.

"Very smart," said Todd. "You'll fit right in with all the other little soldiers."

Murphy stuck his tongue out and picked up his forage cap.

"Ten minutes," he said as he went outside.

The crews assembled outside one of the hangars. Some of them with aircraft nearest to the main part of the airfield were sent to stand by their kites. The rest would parade in front of three Manchester's which had been drawn up by the hangars. Each crew were to stand in a line, their pilot to the right and the rest formated off him. There would be ten paces between each crew.

Carter checked his men out before the dignitaries arrived. He gave them a quick once over but he wasn't particularly bothered if their shoes weren't glossy mirrors. As long as there were no missing buttons and the trousers had something approaching a crease, he was happy.

They huddled like penguins by the hangar until it was time to move. Cigarettes came out and they were wreathed in smoke while they waited.

"Anyone know when they're turning up?" asked Walsh. He shivered inside his greatcoat with the collar turned up. He stamped his feet to keep the blood pumping.

"Doesn't matter, they'll be late anyway, they always are," said Everett with his usual bored tone. Conversation drifted from topic to topic, girls, flying, war news, tonights dinner. After ten minutes they ran out of things to talk about. After twenty minutes they were bored. After half an hour they were starting to feel the cold.

Everett glanced at his watch and scowled. He'd asked if they could wait inside the hangar but Dickinson had said no, he wanted everyone outside ready for parade. He lit one cigarette from the end of another and blew a cloud of smoke towards the sky. He looked up as a Corporal waved from the control tower. He glanced across the field and saw a parade of cars heading in their direction. "Looks like we're on, chaps," he announced. He stubbed the new cigarette in his glove and pocketed it to finish off later.

They lined up and waited. The motorcade pulled up in front of them and a crowd of dignitaries piled out and shook themselves into order. Group Captain Etheridge was the guide with Asher alongside him. A Squadron Leader from Group brought up the rear. Two suits from the Air Ministry fussed around the VIP, an Under Secretary of State for War. He wore a dark grey trenchcoat and fedora. He set off at a brisk pace and went to the end of the line.

He worked his way down, taking his time to talk to one or two people in each crew. Hands were shaken, the pose occasionally being held while an official photographer took a few shots. War Correspondents hovered in the background, taking notes.

The VIP got to Carter's crew and noticed the darker blue of Todd's uniform. He walked over to Todd and used his best smile, the kind you saw on the campaign trail during an election.

"An Australian. And what brought you all the way across the ocean?" Todd's answer was prompt.

"Me mum was English, sir. It seemed like the thing to do, help the old country like."

"And it's appreciated. Where was your mother from?"

"Cheltenham. She liked horses, sir." The VIP smiled sympathetically.

"Well, she'd have seen lots of them there. A nice part of the country."

He looked at the crew as a whole. Three officers, three enlisted men. Short, tall, all types. He saw the shoulder flashes on their greatcoats. Men who had come from all places to fight for freedom.

"I say, this is a very multi-national crew."

"Flight Lieutenant, Carter is on his second tour, sir." Etheridge said.

"Is he by jove." He shook Carter's hand warmly. "Well done, well done."

They moved on. At the end, they went back to their cars and were off for a drive around the perimeter to see the kites. As the cars pulled away the men gathered together. All that work for ten minutes of being shown off like prize bulls at a fair.

"I thought he'd be taller," commented Walsh. Carter laughed. The men started to disperse. Murphy clapped Todd on the shoulder.

"I didn't know your mum was English."

"She's not."

"You fibber."

"First rule on parade mate, tell 'em something they want to hear," Todd told him as he pulled out his cigarette case. He extracted a cigarette and tapped the end against the lid. "It avoids those awkward silences you get; like on first dates," he said, with a pointed look at

Murphy. He lit the cigarette.

Saunderson came over before they left.

"I say, chaps. No one going anywhere tonight? I've managed to secure a few ENSA acts to beef up the concert party."

Jensen breathed a sigh of relief. He had been dreading getting up to perform.

"So, you won't need me then, sir?" he asked hopefully.

"No fear, Jensen." Saunderson beamed as he used to when he was selling insurance. Selling was all about making the client relax and trust you. You had to butter them up to get them on side. "I need *you* for the first act after the interval." Jensen grimaced.

"Oh, God."

"Any girls?" asked Murphy smoothly. He was rather enamoured of the idea of a few professional acts. There was bound to be some dancers or something.

"A few," Saunderson told him. "And too good for the likes of you." He wagged an admonishing finger at Todd and Murphy.

"Aw, you're no fun...*sir*."

"No. No, I've got a duty to them. I can't let any of you types get near to them." He turned his attention back to Jensen. "Have you decided what you're going to do for me?"

"Boy stood on the burning deck?" suggested Woods with a grin plastered on his face.

"No," said Jensen. "I'm sticking to me roots, sir."

Carter had been to a few concert parties in his time in the RAF. He had even performed in one at training school when he was still wet behind the ears. The shows were usually rather stale affairs with everyone on reasonably good behaviour. The CO and Station Commander would sit at the front and people would clap appropriately. If an act was particularly bad, there would be a lot of cat calling to put them off some more. Time would drag. You would look at your watch every five minutes, praying for it all to end while some spotty erk in the instrument section blew his trumpet.

The large briefing room had been turned over for the use of the performance. Blankets had been strung across the back of the room to provide an area for the performer's backstage. The huge map board had been covered with a red backdrop Saunderson had loaned from one of the local theaters. Two Corporals were working the lights. Some staff who accompanied the ENSA performers had brought microphones and speakers and other equipment.

The show went down as one of the better ones Carter had attended. The ENSA acts helped enormously. Normally, the first one to go on stage got a frosty reception from the crowd but no one was going to cat call Ella Redfearn.

She appeared in a floor length red satin dress that hugged her figure in all the right places and the men caught a glimpse of ankle as she moved up and down the stage. She charmed them with some music hall numbers, belting out old favourites and leading them in a stirring rendition of *Wish me luck as you wave me goodbye*.

There was a comic who was okay. Nothing flashy but he got a few good ones in. Three fitters did a charming bit of Elgar, then Flight Sergeant Martin took to the stage and delivered an impassioned delivery of the St Crispin's Day speech from Henry V. The room had been hushed, rapt with attention as he spoke of the happy few, they liked that. He left to thunderous applause.

The next ENSA act was a dance troupe which drove the temperature of the room up. They came on to a roar of voices and nearly took the roof off when they danced to a variety of Andrews Sisters numbers. One was dressed as a WAAF, one a WRNS, and the other an ATS girl. They finished in a line, facing the crowd and throwing a salute.

It was the interval after that. The lights went on and there was tea and donuts. Those with foresight had sneaked in a few bottles in their pockets. Etheridge bowed out at this point. He'd made the required appearance and Asher and Saunderson saw him to the door.

"Good show, Saunderson. Very commendable effort."

"Thank you, sir." Saunderson beamed, pleased to be commended. He went backstage to get things ready for the second half. He found Jensen retching over a bucket. One of the ENSA dancers was rubbing his back and holding a hanky for him.

"Good god, are you all right?" Saunderson exclaimed.

"I'm okay," Jensen muttered, before retching again.

"There, there luvvy," the dancer said in a thick London accent.

Jensen was sitting ont the floor with the bucket between his legs. He was green around the gills and his skin had taken on a waxy sheen.

"Are you going to be able to perform like this?" Saunderson asked. "You're on first you know."

"Gimme five minutes, sir. I told you I get nervous at this sort of thing."

"Righto." Saunderson gave him an encouraging thump on the shoulder and then hustled around checking everyone else was ready. One of the armourers played a few experimental notes on his French Horn.

"I can't wait to go on, sir," he said. "Me mum'll be dead proud when I tell her."

"That's the spirit, Jones," Saunderson told him.

The dancer eyed Saunderson in some suspicion.

"He's a brute making you go up like this."

Jensen looked at her like she was an angel.

"You know, it's canny of you to look after me like this," he said with a lisp, his tongue thick in his mouth. She was a lovely girl. She had gorgeous green eyes that mesmerised him. He didn't even notice her skimpy costume that showed off acres of leg and shoulders.

"Nonsense." She handed him another hanky and he wiped the sweat off his face. "I hate seeing someone in distress." This was true. She had a flat back in London that she shared with three cats and two dogs. All of them had been rescued from one situation or another during her travels. The girl in the flat across from hers fed them while she was on tour doing shows. "Do you need the bucket again?" she asked with genuine concern.

"I don't think so. I could do with a cup of tea though," he replied, his voice distracted as his head flopped around like a puppet on a string.

"I'll see what I can do," she told him. He was just far enough gone to totally miss the hint of interest in her voice.

Saunderson reappeared from behind the curtain like some apparition, all business, all bustle.

"You ready, old chap? You're up."

Jensen turned green again and fought back the queasy feeling in his stomach. He got to his feet and tugged down his short battledress.

"I'm ready, if you are," he said, voice quavering. He swayed forwards, the floor moving around, his head swimming.

"That's the spirit, break a leg," Saunderson encouraged him.

The following night they went to Hannover. It was one of those raids you would rather forget. Things got off to a bad start when one of the new boys strayed off the peri track and got stuck in the soft ground. There was a delay while it was pulled clear. Carter and Walsh took off an hour late battling headwinds and bad visibility.

The weather was atrocious and everyone got spread from hell to breakfast out and back. A tailwind shoved them along and Carter dreaded the return journey, flying into the teeth of a strong headwind. The bombers were so scattered, the Germans thought it was a general raid with no specific target in mind.

Woods bombed somewhere. His dead reckoning was way off. He hadn't had a fix since crossing the coast and he had no idea where they were. They steered for the glow of fires and the bursts of flak on the horizon. When they got there, cloud covered the ground and blotted out any chance of figuring out their exact location, but the flak gunners were going bananas so there must have been something down there.

On the trip back, Jensen watched the instruments while Carter flew. There was little conversation between the crew, they all knew that this was one of those times that Carter wanted them concentrating on their jobs. The Manchester went up and down like a yo-yo in the turbulent winds and Jensen knew enough pilots that would have fought them with brute force, trying to bend the aircraft to his will. He watched as Carter played the controls like a concert pianist, feeling the vibrations through his seat, the tug on the yoke as the air washed over the elevators and ailerons, the kick as his feet rode the rudder pedals.

Jensen's world shrank to the few dials in front of him and the throttle levers. While he focused on the vibrating needles, he kept thinking about the ENSA girl who'd looked after him the previous night. He smiled as he remembered her lovely eyes and smile.

He had marched onto the stage in a fog and did his bit, a halting rendition of *When the boat comes in*. As soon as he got off stage he threw up in the bucket and had a pounding headache. He'd felt like a fool singing it but it was the only song he knew by heart without nerves getting the better of him.

She had stayed with him until it was her turn to go back on stage and he never got the chance to thank her for looking after him. He never even knew her name.

Thinking about it afterwards, he felt a right idiot for not asking her out for a drink but he was hardly in his normal frame of mind to think about such things at the time. He brooded on his ineptitude as they jolted their way home. Maybe Saunderson would know how he could go about getting in touch with her.

When they got back to Amber Hill, the final thrill of the evening was the discovery that they had no hydraulic pressure. Somewhere on the way back some flak had nicked the hydraulics and by the time they returned all of the fluid had leaked out. Carter blew down the undercarriage with the emergency bottle and made a delicate landing with no flaps and no brakes.

They got back long after everyone else, did interrogation, had their egg and turned in. The whole trip was a washout. Hardly anyone had claimed to bomb the target and quite a few of the squadron had landed elsewhere. While Woods had been hopelessly lost for most of the flight, he felt some pride that he had actually managed to get them back to base; it was the sole crumb of comfort he could take from the evening.

27 - London's Burning

Just after lunch, Todd ducked out of the poker action and went for a walk. He wanted some peace and quiet and there was no chance of that in his hut. The same old faces still came to play, the only change is that they now paid tribute.

After the last debacle when the huts coal supply had been used up, anyone coming to play had to bring either wood, coal or some other commodity with them. As a result, they had a nice stock of coal and wood for the stove and other things like tea bags, chocolate and biscuits. Their hut had become one of the places to be. It was always toasty warm and there were hot drinks available.

Todd borrowed one of the bicycles propped against the wall and struck out for the perimeter fence. He wasn't a confident rider and he took his time, sticking to the road while he worked up a bit of speed. He tried the rear brake and was rewarded with a high pitched squeal that set his teeth on edge. He cycled past the hangars and kept well away from the front gate. The SP's liked to bugger about when they saw someone on a bicycle.

Bicycles were actually issued to individuals but the crews had evolved a more fluid idea of ownership when it came to bikes. They treated them more as a collective pool from which you could use one if they happened to be lying around. This was particularly useful if someone actually assigned a bicycle caught a packet. It seemed daft to return it to stores to be reissued, so over time who actually owned what bike had become quite blurred.

That might have worked in practical terms, but in the rigid world of the SP's, such fluid notions were anathema. By and large, the crews were left alone, but occasionally, Service Police liked to flex their muscle and cause some issues. Todd took a dim view of that. The only people actually doing any work on the station were the erks and the flight crews so any interference in that irritated him. Add in his general dislike of stuffy officialdom and he tended to hate SP's on sight. He regarded them as a redundant waste of oxygen and uniform and he wasn't in the mood to tangle with them today.

He lifted his backside off the saddle and leaned into the handlebars, building up a head of steam. The spokes creaked as the frame wavered from side to side, his feet working the pedals. He got the fright of his life when a Corporal driving a Bedford leaned on his horn behind him and then swung out wide to overtake. Todd shook his fist as the truck breezed by leaving him in a cloud of exhaust smoke.

Turning onto the peri track, Todd passed a few Manchester's and then cut onto the grass. The bicycle bobbled across the uneven ground, the tyres leaving a trail behind him in the frosty grass. He pushed hard, feeling the grass tugging on the wheels.

Soon enough he came up to the perimeter, an eight feet high chain link fence with coils of barbed wire on top. Running parallel to the fence he kept going until he came to the familiar mounds of grass beyond the bomb dump. On the eastern side of the field there were eight of these long, cigar shaped mounds. The biggest was fiften feet high and about forty feet long and covered in rough long grass. White had told him once they were barrows. He steered between two of the larger ones and stashed the bicycle behind a big gorse bush.

What few people knew was that behind the gorse bushes there was a gap in the fence that got you off the station without having to sign out at the main gate. The other side of the fence was a thick copse of trees which hid you from sight. Todd looked around to make sure the bike was hidden from view and then went down on his hands and knees. The bottom two feet of the chain link fence was not attached to the mounting post and he squeezed through the gap.

He waited in the trees until there was no traffic and then crossed the road and struck out across the lane that ran parallel to the field. Setting a brisk pace, he got to the farm house within ten minutes.

The blue tractor was in the yard and Todd sauntered up to the back door with the ease of familiarity. He had come across this farm within his first few weeks of coming to Amber Hill but kept it a closely guarded secret. Aside from growing vegetables, it was also a chicken farm and next to the machinery barn were long sheds full of squawking birds. In exchange for chocolate and other items, Todd had a ready supply of eggs. He knocked on the door and a dog went beserk on the other side of it. He waited until he heard the familiar tread come to the door.

"That you, digger?"

"Aye, it's me."

"Hold on," came the gruff reply. There was some strong language and the dog quietened down. A latch clicked and the door opened to reveal the farmer, a big slab of man in corduroys and shirt sleeves, one meaty hand with a firm grip on the Alsatian's collar. The big dog tugged and barked, tongue lolling.

"Hey, Shadow," Todd said, cuffing the dog on the head and rubbing his hands up and down the animal's lean sides. The farmer let go of the collar and the animal sniffed Todd before padding back into the kitchen. It settled itself on its blanket in front of the range.

"Come in for a warm," said the farmer.

"Bonzer," replied Todd. He bent his head, going through the low door and walked into the kitchen. The floor was great flags of grey stone and the walls were white plaster, stained with the marks of everyday life on a farm. A walking stick and two pairs of mucky boots were by the door.

Todd pulled up a chair and parked himself to the left of the range. The Alsatian eyed him suspiciously and then lay back down again, muzzle resting on his front paws.

The farmer leaned back in his chair and eyed Todd through slitted eyes. He puffed on his pipe and blew the smoke out of the corner of his mouth. Forty five years old, Bill Edwards was twice Todd's age but the pair of them had become firm friends over the last few months.

Edwards was a widower and he'd led a relatively solitary life the last few years until the RAF had built a new airfield on his doorstep. The roar of the airplanes disturbed the hens but he hadn't written angsty letters to the Air Ministry complaining about it like some people did. He'd been a soldier in the first war, his big hide carried the scars of shrapnel he had picked up at third Ypres. He knew all too well that life in the forces was measured in weeks so he was not about to create a fuss.

Todd relaxed. Time seemed to slow down here on the farm. He liked that. He enjoyed the heat seeping through his bones. The one thing he hated about England was the bloody weather. The persistent cold never went away and he thought about home. Right now, he would be simmering in the summer heat back in Melbourne.

"You came at the right time," Edwards said. "I was just getting a brew going."

"Fine." Todd leaned forwards and ruffled the dog's ears.

"The usual?" Edwards asked.

In reply, Todd dug into the pockets of his greatcoat and pulled out two big slabs of ration chocolate and some bacon. The crews regularly raided their escape kits for the chocolate bars and Todd's hut had a few spare after the poker players had brought them. There was no point in leaving them lying around. Chocolate had more value than just being randomly eaten as a snack. Edwards put the bars of chocolate in the top drawer of the Welsh dresser. He picked up the chunk of bacon and brought a long knife out of the cutlery drawer.

"Bacon butty do?" he asked as he began cutting slices from it.

"You read my mind," Todd replied with enthusiasm.

Edwards pointed to the frying pan hanging to the left of the range. Todd got it down and put it on to warm up. Edwards took over, slapping the bacon onto the pan, turning it occasionally as it cooked.

When it was ready, the crispy bacon was transferred to wedges of bread on two plates. Edwards took a bite and smiled.

"Here's to you, Digger."

Todd stayed there an hour before retracing his steps back to the fence around the airfield. He shuffled through the tightly packed trees, squeezed through the hole in the fence and then cycled back to his billet. His cheeks were tingling with the cold when he came into the warm hut. The game was going strong with the usual diehards dealing the cards round the circle. Murphy and Jensen were not in the hut.

"Anyone seen my mob?" he asked as he chucked his forage cap onto his bed.

"Went out ten minutes ago," Tucker said, distracted by the three tens he was holding.

Todd shrugged and stashed the box of eggs underneath in a cardboard box with some of his personal items in. He would share them later with the hut once the poker crew had gone. The run out on the bike had been enough exercise for one day and he needed a lie down after a big mug of tea and the bacon sandwich. He got five minutes respite before Murphy came running into the hut.

"Where have you been?" he asked sharply. "Come on, move it. The skipper wants to do an air test."

Todd groaned. He was nice and warm. He would have to get up now, get dressed and get very cold. It was not how he wanted to round out his day.

Part of him wanted to rebel but he knew there was no getting out of this. He looked up when he realised conversation in the hut had come to a stop. The poker players were all looking in his direction.

"Run along," said Tucker with a big grin on his face.

"It's my bloody hut!" said Todd, outraged. He threw a pillow across the hut at Tucker who deflected it easily. "Right," he muttered. He got up and went out with Murphy.

Carter was not amused when Todd and Murphy finally arrived. The erks were stood around waiting for them and the rest of the crew had made ready for takeoff. Carter was sitting on the blue trolley acc in his flying gear, his hands shoved into his pockets while he waited.

"Good of you to join us gentlemen," he said sarcastically, getting to his feet as they approached on their bicycles. "I'd like to get this done before we lose the light."

Carter hated landing at dusk. There was always an hour or so as the sun was going down where he had trouble looking into the sky and then the ground. His eyes had trouble adjusting from the bright sky and the dark terrain below, particularly on final approach.

Todd just got on board without saying anything. How was he to know there was going to be an airtest before he went to the farm? He settled down against the mainspar and waited for the engines to start. It was freezing inside the fuselage and the sooner this was over, the better.

Carter settled himself in his seat and fastened the straps, leaving them loose so he could lean forwards if he wanted.

"You all right, skipper?" asked Jensen.

"Fine," Carter replied shortly. "Why?"

"Oh, you just seemed a bit off."

"I'm fine, it's just been one of those days. You ready?" he asked his co-pilot. Jensen grinned, theatrically cracked his knuckles and then pulled his gloves on.

"As ever."

There was the usual chatter as they checked in over the intercom. Carter knew they would be all business when they got under way. Vos contacted the tower and got permission to taxi.

"Anyone know what's for dinner tonight?" asked Jensen. The food in the Sergeants Mess was a bit hit and miss and man could not live off chocolate bars alone.

"A little fishy on a dishy?" offered Murphy.

"When the boat comes in, mind," Woods quickly finished, mangling the Geordie accent. That cracked them all up.

"Why you…" Jensen stopped himself, what could he say to that.

"Nothing like a little joke to brighten the day," said Carter, smiling behind his oxygen mask. "Turning on one."

The engines started with the usual roar and Carter took reassurance from the familiar. The plane vibrated as the engines were throttled up and tested, then there was the jolting as they taxied to the runway. On the way round the peri-track, Carter saw he line of mud on the grass where the rookies had strayed off the concrete and gotten stuck the previous night.

Todd hugged his knees to his chest and squeezed his eyes shut as they swung onto the runway. There was a moments pause, the bomber shuddered as Carter dabbed the brakes, then there was a massive roar as the throttles were shoved forwards. Carter held her on the brakes for a second, feeling the revs build up, then he released her and they shot down the runway. Todd endured every bump, then his stomach lurched as the tail lifted and they were airborne.

There was the familiar thump as the wheels nestled into their bays and the flaps came up. Once they got up to one thousand feet, Carter relinquished control and he watched as Jensen flew. His eyes caught every move and he smiled as he saw Jensen holding the yoke as he did, emulating him. They climbed easily into the afternoon sky; a blue bowl chased with wisps of cotton. To the west it was more purple as day was giving way to the approach of night.

Today's flight was just a short hop to test the hydraulic system so L-London would be operational again. It had been a simple fix but a mucky job. A chunk of flak had nicked a pipe near the main hydraulic pump and needed to be replaced. Then it had been a simple matter of recharging the system and bleeding out the air. On the ground it tested okay, but Latimer knew that this meant little where the Manchester was concerned.

"Simple box route please, Woody. Say forty miles a side and get us back inside an hour if you please."

Woods duly obliged and passed him a course as they flew the first leg north. Jensen took it up to two thousand feet and Lincoln quickly slid underneath them, the Cathedral on the hill pointing to the sky like a spear.

On the second leg, Todd and Murphy tested their turrets. Carter knew when the tail turret moved, he could feel it in the controls. Whenever the Fraser Nash turret traversed left and right he could feel the tug on the rudders and he made small corrections to keep the nose straight. The same thing happened when the nose turret moved either side.

On the third leg they slowed down and Carter trimmed slightly nose up while they dropped the flaps and the wheels. Everything worked as it should have done. Latimer had done his work well but Carter had come to expect nothing less. Latimer took genuine pride in his work and he looked after L-London like it was some vintage car.

Five minutes later L-London proved them all wrong. The starboard engine coughed twice, backfired in a huge shower of sparks and then packed up. The Manchester immediately lurched to the right at the loss of power and Carter and Jensen had to work hard to keep her level. Jensen feathered the prop, but the mechanism seized up before the blades had fully turned into the airflow and the engine began to windmill creating even more drag.

They advanced the throttle on the remaining engine but even lightly laden, L-London was not playing ball today. They had difficulty staying level and Carter knew there was no way they were getting back to Amber Hill.

He glanced at the altimeter. They were at three thousand feet and with a dead engine there wasn't much margin to trade for airspeed. The good thing was he knew the terrain hereabouts like the back of his hand. Lincoln was surrounded by airfields. Ahead of them was Woodhall Spa and Conningsby. It would be close but they should be able to make one of them if they went straight in.

He had barely altered course to head towards them when the port engine packed up in sympathy. There was a massive bang and it came to a shuddering halt as it threw a con rod straight through the cowling in a gout of oil and a burst of flame. Carter was startled by the sudden quiet and he glanced at Jensen. There was no way they were making an airfield now. They were too low to bail out so it was a matter of putting her down straight ahead before they ran out of height and airspeed.

"Jensen, start looking for a big field. Fellas, get ready, we're going in."

Up front, Murphy scrambled out of the nose turret and sat on the step at Jensen's feet. Woods abandoned his navigator's table, brushed past Vos to sit on the floor of the fuselage with his back to the mainspar. The Belgian sent out a mayday and got an answer from Amber Hill. He gave their approximate position and then joined Woods, linking arms.

Todd scrambled out of the rear turret and leaned against the spar behind Woods and Vos. In the dark, he suddenly found the power of prayer. Not a particularly religious man, Todd had not been to church in years, but now seemed an appropriate time to offer up a few words to the divine powers to spare his miserable life.

In the cockpit, Jensen and Carter had their work cut out for them. With so little height to play with there was no time to get creative. Carter had already decided to go in wheels up. There was no guarantee they would find a nice big level field and with the undercarriage down they could ground loop or worse on touchdown. Carter and Jensen craned their necks, hunting for somewhere to put down. The land ahead was mercifully flat but it was dotted with trees, walls and other obstructions. Dropping steeply at eight hundred feet a minute, Carter spotted a large flat area surrounded with a thin tree line dead ahead. If they could just make it over those trees, he could set her down there.

He dropped the nose to keep up their airspeed and set up for the final approach. As they got closer, he could see they weren't going to make it, they simply lacked the height to be able to stretch the glide that far. He sideslipped to the left, aiming the nose at a gap in the trees. At fifty feet, Carter and Jensen hauled back on the stick, flaring off the remaining airspeed but they were still doing over one hundred knots when the tailwheel touched down.

The nose dropped with a thud and smashed into the ground so hard it made their teeth rattle. L-London slithered along the field on her belly. The propellors were bent back like pipecleaners as twenty tons of aircraft barrelled along towards the tree line.

Along for the ride, Carter and Jensen clung on to the yoke. In the back, Todd howled in pain as he'd jolted his back when they touched down. There was a loud tearing sound around him, like paper ripping and then the tail parted company with the rest of the fuselage. The rudder, elevators and his turret started to tumble end over end and smashed into an Elm tree. The outer section of the port wing was ripped off beyond the engine and the starboard wingtip was left behind, peeled away like the lid of a tin can.

What was left of the bomber tore through the tree line into the field beyond. The problem was it wasn't a field but a large lake. The Manchester skipped off the surface of the water like a flat stone and then came to a juddering halt as it touched down for the second time. The nose dug in and water cascaded over the canopy as she began to settle down. Murphy appeared from the nose like a scalded cat and scrambled over Jensen. The bomb aimers perspex blister had been smashed in and Murphy had been half drowned as a wall of water flooded in.

The Manchester sank quickly, going down at a steepening angle as water filled her up. Vos and Woods scrambled out of the escape hatch in the roof. Todd bit down the pain as he crawled up the fuselage and jumped out the hole in the back. He howled from the shock of the freezing water and started doggy paddling to shore, his Mae West only half inflated.

Jensen unfastened his straps and scrambled back up the fuselage with Murphy hot on his heels. The water was freezing and already around his knees. He gripped the sides of the escape hatch and hauled himself outside, adrenalin giving him the strength to do it.

Vos and Woods were sitting astride the top of the fuselage and they clung on to each other, trying to maintain their balance on the wet metal. Jensen pulled the toggles on his Mae West and was reassured when the lifejacket inflated with a sudden rush of air. They slid into the ice cold water as the bomber sank deeper.

"Ye gods, it's freezing," gasped Jensen between clenched teeth.

"Over here," shouted Todd from the bank. He had managed to haul himself up and he was stood, hands tucked under his armpits, stamping his feet to get feeling back into them as water dripped off his sodden clothes. They started swimming towards him, the cold seeping into their bones, dulling their muscles and making every movement slow. It was only then that they realised Carter was still inside the bomber.

They turned, treading water as the Manchester took the final plunge, going down at a forty five degree angle, nose heavy with the inrush of water. The canopy was underwater and rear of the wings were just breaking the surface of the lake.

"Skipper!" Woods shouted. "SKIPPER!"

When L-London had plunged into the water, Carter had been flung forward in his seat. For once, he had been lax and only loosely fastened his straps and he paid the price when he bashed his face on the yoke and the instrument panel. He woke up when the chill of the water stabbed through his clothes. He tasted blood and his chin and neck were killing him.

Bleary eyed, he looked around the cockpit to find he was up to his chest in freezing water. Loose items bobbed around on the surface and his nostrils stung from the stench of petrol and oil. The Manchester was sinking fast, slicing into the lake and she was taking him down with her. He grappled with the release for the harness but when his stiffening fingers failed him, he squirmed out of the seat, the loose straps giving him the room to do it.

His legs flailed, looking for purchase so he could start hauling himself up the steep floor to the world above him. He just managed to grab hold of something when the Manchester lurched and went down for the final time. The cockpit was plunged into darkness as it slid below the surface of the lake.

Fear gripped him and gave him new strength as he pulled upwards. His head disappeared underneath the rising water and he spat to clear his mouth. He was losing the race. He kicked again with his legs and pushed off from the back of the pilot's seat. He kept his eyes fixed on the square of light that was the upper escape hatch behind the cockpit canopy. Water was already beginning to pour through it from the lower edge. His voice echoed of the walls, all whimpers and whines, like an animal fighting to get out of a sack thrown into a river.

His fingers scrabbled with the edges of the hatch, desperately trying to pull himself through. As he got his face out of the hatch, he was met by a wall of water that rushed in. Choking, he went under again. He fought back the panic that was beginning to take hold of him, half remembered terrors playing with him, laughing at his feeble efforts to cling to life.

When then doctor asked him later, he had no idea how he got out. He remembered his Mae West caught on something and he kicked and kicked as he felt himself being dragged down. The world went dark and then he found himself bobbing on the surface, Woods and Vos swimming towards him. He floated amongst the debris, staring up at the sky as he sucked down great lungfuls of air. They dragged him to shore and helping hands pulled him out of the water.

They lay on the bank, wet through as they stared at the bit of the fuselage that stuck up in the middle of the lake. They giggled inanely when the dinghy suddenly appeared. It popped up, like a cork in a bath and stayed there on the surface, still tethered to the wreck.

Woods took the roll call. They were all cold, shocked at how rapidly things had gone wrong but no one had broken anything which was a small mercy. Vos had a hanky pressed to the back of his head where he had caught his scalp going out the hatch. The back of his neck was red were the blood had flowed.

Todd lay on the ground, complaining that his back hurt. He was finding it hard to bend or move. Woods sucked his thumb where he had torn a nail. Murphy sported a gorgeous bump on the back of his head where he had banged it when they plunged into the lake. Only Jensen had got away with a few scrapes.

Carter felt around his jaw and wiggled his teeth. His neck hurt and he worked his jaw open and closed. He ran a finger around inside of his mouth between his lips and gums. It felt like he had gone six rounds in the ring. He stood up; his balance shaky. Water sloshed inside his left flying boot. He had no idea where the other one was.

He looked at what was left of his plane sticking out of the water. That was L-London done. Even if they managed to pull her out of the lake, she was going to be a write off.

After ten minutes, a dog barked and came bounding through the trees. A large energetic Red Setter, it fussed around them and went charging back out of sight. It was joined by a rather portly figure clad in a thick winter coat and tweed pants. He pointed the end of his walking stick towards them.

"I say, are you chaps okay?" he asked in a plumby accent.

"We're alive," Woods replied.

"You've made a mess of my field," the man complained, his tone plaintive. He gestured behind him, indicating the line that L-London had taken across the ground.

"Sorry, no choice," said Carter, his voice shaky, detached, almost robotic. "Spot of engine trouble."

The man grumbled and walked round the lake, gesturing to the wreck in the water, the rainbow sheen of the oil and petrol on the surface.

Ambulances magically appeared half an hour later and they were whisked off to Coningsby and taken straight to bed. All the way back, Murphy had gabbled away, talking a million miles an hour. The orderlies watched him closely, shock did odd things to a chap.

Todd was carried out on a stretcher, finding it hard to move. All of them were dunked in warm baths and then put to bed with a hot water bottle and a stiff drink. They wouldn't be going anywhere for at least twenty four hours while the doctors kept an eye on them.

Dickinson and Asher came to see them that evening. After the obligatory pleasantries, they assured Carter there was no need to hurry back. Carter did his best to smile at the weak joke. He was lucky to be alive and knew it. He winced as his neck twinged and reminded him not to move too quickly. A purple bruise was coming up nicely on his chin.

On the drive over from Amber Hill, Asher and Dickinson had already agreed that once the hospital released them, they would be sent on leave. They were due a forty eight anyway so it made sense to send them on their way after a close shave like that.

"You can take that girl of yours away for a few days," Dickinson teased him and Carter had blushed to the tips of his ears.

After leaving them in the hospital, Asher and Dickinson went to the lake. In the gathering dark there wasn't much to see. Work parties had already cleared away the bits of wing and a long trailer was loading what was left of the tail section. A guard of three men had been put on the lake until daylight when a recovery team would see how they were going to drag the remains of L-London out of the water. The landowner reappeared with his dog and buttonholed them.

"Disgraceful," the man complained. "The lake's ruined. I shall be expecting compensation of course."

Dickinson glanced at Asher and could see his anger building. Asher was sorely tempted to kick the Red Setter as it sniffed around their trousers. He made sympathetic noises and the landowner took this as an invitation to continue.

"Yes, mark my words, compensation. It'll cost a pretty penny for all this. Trees damaged and as for the stupid aeroplane in my lake; well." He shrugged theatrically. "What about my fish? Eh? I expect them to be replaced."

That threw Asher, "Fish?" he asked.

"Fish, sir. FISH!" The man grabbed Asher by the right bicep and pulled him towards the bank of the lake. He used his stick for emphasis and pointed to the white oblongs that bobbed all over the surface of the lake. "There, sir. There." The stick pointed again and again. "And there. Trout, dead because of the petrol you've spilled into my lovely lake."

"It *was* an accident, sir," Dickinson soothed, his tone conciliatory. The man snorted, his nose twitching.

"That as may be. But this was a lake of prize fish. I expect to be paid in full." He sniffed in indignation, outraged that his word should be questioned.

"You will be," Asher said with supreme calm. "You will be."

28 - On The Fence

The crew went their separate ways for their short leave. Carter took Georgette to York. Woods returned to London and took Jensen with him. His second dicky had never been to the big city so Woods took it upon himself to begin the lad's education. Murphy stayed at Amber Hill and made a few phone calls. He spoke to Muriel and arranged to see her that evening and then spoke to Joan and made his plans for the following day.

Todd cleared out and checked into a guest house on the other side of Lincoln near Scampton. He wanted somewhere with a bit of scenery and a few walks. There was no chance of that at Amber Hill and if he went to a hotel in Lincoln it would cost an arm and a leg. Going to the other side of Lincoln got him away from the squadron which was the main thing.

The guest house when he got there, and that is what it was really, was a small row of three houses with thatched roof that had been knocked together to make one building. The roof space had been turned into extra bedrooms and he had to duck when he was shown to his room. The bed was soft, the room warm and it was quiet. Even the sound of aero engines from the airfields was far enough away he could ignore them. It was perfect. No one else was in so the landlady heated him up some hot water special and ran him a bath. Todd sank gratefully into it and let the heat penetrate his aching bones.

Vos couldn't get out of the main gate fast enough and went straight round to see Denise. She was at work but he let himself in with the spare key the landlady had given him. Denise came back to find him stretched out in the armchair, a blanket covering his legs and his head covered in bandages.

She showered him in loving kisses and bid him sit on the floor while she sat on the end of the bed and massaged his shoulders and neck. He dozed under her touch and woke refreshed. She gave him a cup of tea and he drank deeply, relaxing for the first time since the accident.

He told her a little bit about what happened, not wanting to worry her too much. He saw her jaw tense when he airily dismissed the risks and he thought there might be an argument but the moment passed without further incident.

She traded her shift at work for the following day and they went to the coast on the train. There wasn't much to see, but the sea air was fresh and blew away the cobwebs. Vos watched her on the train, as she stared out the window at the countryside rushing by. She had changed in many ways in the three months since she had journeyed up with him from London.

She had put on weight; the harsh angles of her face had softened. Her hair was longer, glossier now that she had more time to look after herself, not wondering where the next meal was coming from. There were times when he would be reminded just how young she was, but others, she looked at him with adult eyes, the girl wiped away. She looked at him then in the train, catching him staring at her and those same eyes softened and looked at him with such need and affection. He put his arm out and she snuggled next to him and sighed in contentment.

The tide was in so they walked along the length of the prom. They got to the end and paused in one of the wooden shelters that were spaced periodically along the seafront. They huddled together in their heavy winter coats as the breeze rushed past them, not touching them.

She stretched out a shapely leg and angled her foot left and right, admiring her new red square heeled shoe. She turned and put her arms around his shoulders, settling herself in his lap. His arms circled her waist. She was still tiny, a china doll in his embrace. They said little, content to be in each others company. They didn't discuss the future much. Vos measured his life out in small chunks, from op to op; to do otherwise was foolish, the war had taught him that. The next milestone on the horizon was their long leave but that would not be for a few weeks yet.

They talked a bit about where they might go but made no definite plans. Lunch was in a tea room by the train station before they went back to Lincoln. It had been a simple day but neither of them would have changed it for the world. On the way back, he saw a few windmills in the fields, their sails turning in the evening breeze and that reminded him a little of home.

Carter stood leaning on the old stone of the city walls next to Monk Bar. He turned and faced into the wind, his eyes slitted as the remains of the setting sun dipped below the horizon. To his left loomed the large bulk of the Minster and he glanced once again at the big building. He had bombed churches like this in Germany and he wondered if they were still standing. It all seemed wrong somehow to think that he could have destroyed something like this which had seen so much history across the centuries.

Georgette tucked in next to him and he put an arm around her shoulders, keeping her close. She had been mad keen to get straight out when they arrived in York and they had already done the walk around the wall. Carter was tired and his legs were protesting at having to do so much walking, particularly after the accident. He moved his head around and grimaced as stabbing pains shot up the side of his neck.

Carter had packed a suitcase and met Georgette at Lincoln train Station. A quick phone call had Freddie square everything and she was granted leave at short notice. She made a fuss of him and he let her, as long as he was not expected to move too quickly. The Doctor had told him he had whiplash but it was nothing rest and a soak in a bath couldn't cure. He was given some painkillers and waved on his way.

Carter let all thoughts of his crew and flying drift away on the breeze and focused back on the woman beside him. She had listened attentively to his account of the crash on the train asking the occasional question to prompt his memory. He omitted how hard it had been to get out. That would have only worried her and he didn't particularly care to think about that bit again.

Her face had lit up as they discussed what to do in York. They had modified their plans slightly to accommodate his injuries but she had insisted they still do the walk first to work up an appetite.

It was a good few miles around the limit of the city walls but they took their time, they were in no hurry after all. To start with he had been a bit stiff but the walk did him good and by the end his muscles had loosened up. They had started at one of the great medieval gates that granted entrance to the city and walked round the southern walls till they ran out at Cliffords Tower. Then they had walked back along the river and did the northern bit of wall that ran from the western entrance and round the back of the great cathedral ending at Monk Bar.

He was glad they had picked York. He loved the city, the wonderful mix of new and old, the feeling of history that surrounded the place. Everyone had been through York, the Romans, Vikings and he had loved having an explore when he was younger on day trips from Harrogate.

Georgette moved off again and pulled on his arm as she led the way down some steps back to street level. They walked into town until they found a pub they liked. *The Royal Oak* was an old fashioned building that breathed history from every pore. Built in the 14th Century, it had low ceilings, small windows and a cosy feel about the place when they went inside.

Carter commandeered a small table near the front so he could look out the windows and watch the world go by. Getting round to tea time, there were a lot of people on the street and uniforms were everywhere. As much as Lincoln was 5 Group's preserve, York was the destination for 1 and 4 Group. The surrounding countryside was dotted with airfields where their Wellingtons and Halifaxes operated from.

He felt odd wearing a suit. He'd even had to borrow a fedora from Saunderson to go with his brown three piece suit and brown shoes. It had been the first time in a year he had worn anything other than his uniform and he felt quite self conscious when everyone else was wandering around in RAF blue. Georgette had no such qualms and had willingly ditched her uniform as soon as she had left Group HQ and got back to her digs. She had met him in a white and blue knee length floral print dress and tan coat. Her dark hair was curled up and a blue hat was pinned in place.

They had one drink each and then moved on to the next place, another small pub before turning their thoughts to dinner. After the walk, Carters stomach was grumbling and not finding a restaurant to their liking they went back to their hotel by the train station. Spoiled by the food at *The Madison*, it was a bit of a letdown. The chicken pie was actually pretty good but the potatoes and cabbage were just bland, boiled to within an inch of their life and the thin gravy was like dishwater.

Georgette talked throughout dinner and Carter was content to listen, loving the sound of her voice. After months of living with men, it made a pleasant change to devote his attention to one woman. She told him about going shopping with Helen Wilkinson around Grantham. They had grown close in the intervening weeks and Georgette almost regarded the younger woman as another sister.

Helen bought a few things for the baby but wasn't in the mood to buy a dress for herself. So close to her due date, she felt like a beached whale and there was no point buying something now when she was only going to lose the baby weight later. She still harboured hopes she would be able to fit into her old things given enough time.

After three shops they retired to a tea room and gossiped like they had known each other for years. Carter was pleased Georgette had given up one of her valuable days off to take Helen out.

They retired after dinner to the lounge with a pot of tea and a pack of cards. They took up residence at a card table and started playing Gin Rummy. Carter was amused to find Georgette took it quite seriously and she had a killer instinct at finishing him off. She took the first three games before he won one back. They tried draughts but got bored so went back to Rummy where she thrashed him again. He watched as she deftly shuffled the cards, riffling the pack, tongue clamped between her teeth in concentration.

"We used to play this all the time," she told him. Every year their father took them to the Lake District for a week in the country and it always rained. She remembered the family holidays when they played

Hearts and Gin Rummy in the evening's while the rain hammered off the windows outside. Why her father favoured the Lake District was a mystery, but she and her sisters had to occupy themselves for hours when the weather stopped them going outside.

She dealt another round. Carter nearly beat her, but Georgette got the ten she was waiting for first and called 'Gin', laying her hand on the green felt. Carter sighed. He'd needed one more nine.

"I surrender," he said. He sipped his tea and watched as she gathered the cards in and shoved them back into their box. She leaned back in her chair and looked at him with hooded eyes.

"Now what?" she asked him.

Carter wasn't sure. Well, this wasn't strictly true, he knew what he *wanted* to do, but now the moment was close, he was growing shy like some virgin teenager that had no idea what went where.

He made enquiries at the front desk but discovered there were no dances that evening that the receptionist was aware of. The cinema would have started already and he didn't want to go back out to a pub. Kneeling down at the radio, he was just about to turn it on when Georgette suggested they retire to their room. There was that awkward silence that seemed to last forever. Carter's brain was stuck in neutral. She smiled, her cheeks dimpling as she got up.

"I'm going to change," she announced, hand resting on the door handle, her cheek resting against the door. "I've been wearing this all day and I want to relax."

Carter didn't even get to a count of five before he followed after her.

Built as a flagship for the North Eastern Railway Company the hotel interior was quite grand with over one hundred rooms spread over five floors. The corridors were wide and the ceilings were high. This extended to the rooms and they had been given a generous sized suite on the corner of the third floor. Georgette giggled as she turned the key in the door. Carter had signed them in as Mr and Mrs.

A bay window looked out over the the grounds and showed the traffic that went past the busy train station. In the distance they could hear the sound of shunting trains. A large double bed had a low backed sofa at the end of it. To the right of the door was a writing table and chair. On the other side of the bed was a door that led through to an adjoining room. Carter made sure the corresponding door on the other side was shut before closing theirs and locking it.

He shrugged off his suit jacket and waistcoat and draped them over the chair. With the blackout curtains drawn, it was gloomy and Georgette turned on a standard lamp in the corner. The room was warm and cosy, decorated in dark creams. The bed had a dark red blanket across it as a splash of colour.

Georgette flopped onto the sofa at the end of the bed and flung out her arms. She took off her shoes and stretched her legs out in front of her, wiggling her toes.

"Phew, that's better."

She leaned her head back and stared up at the ceiling before closing her eyes. She remained like that for a few moments before bringing her head back up. She peeped through one eye and smiled. Carter was sitting opposite her and she patted the open space on the sofa by her side. "I don't bite."

That broke the spell. Carter laughed and crossed the distance between them. He leaned in and kissed her, remembering the summer house in the grounds of the hotel. Her hands came up to his face before moving down to his neck and shoulders, touching, stroking. Her perfume filled his nostrils and he encircled her in his arms, holding her close.

She pulled at his tie, working it left and right, loosening the knot until she could pull it off. She started undoing the buttons of his shirt.

"God, I've wanted this for so long," he murmured, eyes closed.

She laughed, grinning against his teeth. Her tongue darted out, tracing around the inside of his lips. She grabbed one of his hands and guided it down over her breast. Her breath came in short huffs as his hand worked back and forth, rubbing rhythmically.

His other hand walked up her leg, pushing the dress up past her knee. He ran along her thigh, thrilling to the feel of the stocking and her smooth leg. His fingers played with the top of her stocking, searching for the suspender catch. He found it and tried to release it but it wouldn't give and he pulled at it, trying to tease it.

Georgette chuckled; a deep throaty laugh full of promises. She moved his hand out of the way and he watched for a moment as she gripped the catch between thumb and forefinger and released it with a deft flick. She made it seem all so easy. She stood up and lifted her dress, feeling round to the back of her leg and releasing the other catch. She did the same to the other leg before sitting down next to him. She stuck out her left leg and rolled the stocking down over her knee, towards her ankle. She took her time and Carter watched silently, his pulse pounding in his ears.

He reached for her and she twisted out of his grasp, laughing. She tossed the stocking at him and it lazily fell to the floor, forgotten as he chased after her. She got to the bay window before he caught her in his arms. She stood on tip toe and kissed him again, working her way down from his chin, his neck to his chest. She sighed and rested her face against him, her hair tickling his skin.

She hummed softly to herself, a few bars of something Carter didn't recognise. He held her close and they slowly rocked left and right, circling round in a slow dance.

She went over to the bed and shrugged out of her dress, letting it fall to the floor. Carter stood transfixed, his blood stirring at the sight of her. Her skin was pale, unblemished and she wore blue silk underwear trimmed in black. Even the ribbon in her hair matched. She slid under the covers, her dark hair a fan of black on the white pillowcases.

He shed his own clothes, kicking off his shoes and dropping his shirt and trousers as he advanced on the bed. He got under the covers and she came up fighting, kissing him, her hands pressing on his shoulders, pushing him back onto the bed. She got on top of him, her legs straddling either side of his waist. She groaned as she ground her hips down against him, back and forth, rubbing.

He gasped as she took the lead. His hands moved up her sides, feeling the line of her ribs and slid round her back, undoing the catch to her bra. It fell loose and she moved her arms to get clear of the straps and threw it across the room. Neither of them noticed where it ended up. Her breasts pressed against him, her skin warm and soft and smooth.

Her right hand worked down, nails teasing as she felt for the top of his underwear. She worked her hand inside and he gasped as she found what she was looking for and stroked, rubbing up and down. He groaned, finding it difficult to contain himself as she guided him in.

Their lovemaking was frantic that first time. Months of pent up need and desire was spent in a rush of passion. They had a rest for ten minutes and then began again, slower this time, exploring each other. Carter was going to get up to turn the lamp off in the corner but she put a hand on his arm and stopped him.

"No," she whispered, "I want to see you."

His lips found hers and they lay next to each other, legs entwined, sweat cooling on their skin.

"This is much better than that summer house," he murmured. She laughed.

"Maybe, but it was murder having to wait."

"I know." His face pinched in concentration. "I just wanted the first time to be;" he paused as he hunted for the right word.

"Perfect?" she finished for him.

"No, not perfect, just…" words failed him. His fingers made wide circles over her stomach, down to the curve of her pelvis and back up to her breasts. He teased one nipple, rubbing the areola gently. "I just didn't want it to be some clinch in the dark." He frowned, knowing he was making a terrible job of expressing himself.

"Are you trying to protect me?" she asked in mock horror.

"No. Goodgie, I just-" she put her finger to his lips.

"I know. You don't need to explain Alex. I know."

She giggled and lay across him, resting her face on his chest, listening to the regular metronome of his heartbeat. He kissed the top of her head and felt foolish. She smiled and closed her eyes and sighed. At that exact moment, all was right in the world. Nothing existed beyond the four walls of their room, no war, no loss, no heartache or pain.

She stroked up the left side of his ribcage and felt some rough skin. She stroked some more and could feel patches of smooth skin with ridges of scar tissue. She hitched over slightly and peered at it up close. His left side and the inside of his arm were similarly marked, dotted with patches of pink right down to his thigh.

"Flak," he told her. "I picked up these souvenirs on my European vacation a year ago."

He'd been half way through his first tour at the time. A flak burst had gone off close on the port side. Shrapnel had bounced off the canopy like rain and torn into the skin of the fuselage. He'd fought to keep the Hampden straight and level and then the pain had hit him. It had felt like someone had repeatedly stabbed him in the side with a red hot poker. The doctors had picked out twenty pieces of rubbish when he got home and sown him back up again. She hunted them out, kissing each mark gently. Insistent hands made him roll on to his side and she traced them with her fingers.

"Is that where you got that?" She asked, pointing at the scar on his cheek.

He scratched at it and nodded. She placed little kisses up and down his face.

"Steady on, old girl."

"Old?" she said in mock protest.

"You've been married," he told her, his face the model of innocence. She playfully slapped his arm.

"So, I'm an old maid am I?" She picked up one of the pillows and swiped him with it. He held up his hands in defence.

"Ow, the chin, the neck," he warned her between laughs and gasps for mercy. She dropped the pillow and hugged him, kissing his chin.

"Oh darling, I'm so sorry."

"Got you," he grinned. His eyes glinted as he grabbed her and tickled her sides. She doubled up, clutching her stomach and rolled into a ball, laughing, begging him to stop. He rocked back on his heels and wiped the tears from his eyes. "I got you," he said.

She almost growled as she unwound and lay on her back and they swapped places, with him on top. She could feel him stiffening again and wrapped her legs around him, drawing him in.

Later, they lay together in the dark. She was welded to his side, her leg draped over his, one arm flung across his chest. His left arm was folded behind his head, propping him up. He listened to her steady breathing and the noises outside coming from the train station. There was a shrill whistle and then the steady, huff, huff as another train pulled away from the platform. He was wide awake, his brain firing on all cylinders.

The intensity of their love making had surprised him. Her touch, the feel of her skin, her perfume, the way she moved under him, responding to him, the movement of her hips. Every sensation and movement had been burned into his brain. It had never been like this with Mary.

She stirred, and he shushed her, kissing the top of her head, his thumb stroking her neck. She shifted position slightly and then awoke, her eyes blinking as she took in her surroundings.

"Hey," she whispered. She rolled off him and lay next to him on the bed. She waited as her eyes adjusted to the dark. "What time is it?" He moved his hand from behind his head and looked at the glowing dial of his watch.

"Nearly eleven. It's still early."

"Huh, early for you," she breathed, her voice sleepy. She was in that fuzzy drowsy place where your brain was wrapped in cotton wool and everything was slow and you were not quite awake.

"True," he agreed. "It's a good thing I'm a night owl with the job I have."

"Well it's late for me." She rolled over and he moved up behind her. She backed into him, a perfect fit, his legs tucking underneath hers and his arm cuddling her around the waist.

They woke naturally around nine. Neither of them had set an alarm or asked for a wake up call from reception. Georgette woke up first shivering. She was cold and found that at some time during the night Carter had rolled over and dragged the covers with him. She dug him in the ribs. He grunted and waved a hand in the air. She dug him in the side again and then pulled on the blanket until she had enough to cover her.

"Greedy boy," she said, her tone light and teasing. He opened one eye and glanced to his right. He moved quickly, his hands reaching out, tickling her. She squealed in surprise and shot out of bed like a rabbit darting out of the bushes. She threw a hair brush at him and scrabbled amongst her open suitcase, looking for something to put on. Carter admired the view from the bed and could feel his blood stirring at the sight of her.

She twirled a finger at him and told him to turn around. He sighed theatrically and did as he was told and as soon as he did so, she leapt on him, hands racing to find his sensitive spot. She found it and he laughed; big deep belly laughs as her hair tickled around his neck.

Leaving him gasping for air she slid off the bed and put on the robe hanging off the back of the door. Laughing, she flopped onto one of the armchairs.

"Good morning."

"Morning, darling." He rubbed his neck. It still hurt but wasn't as stiff as it had been yesterday. He had one of the painkillers the doctor had given him and drank from the glass of water by the bed. He lay back down and sighed, willing the throbbing pain to die down.

"Breakfast in bed, or shall we get dressed and go downstairs?" she asked him.

"Whichever you prefer," he told her as he yawned and stretched. She pondered the choices.

"I think downstairs. If we have breakfast up here, we'll never do anything today and I'd like to get out and about before this afternoon."

"And what's wrong with that?" he protested, dropping his voice to a husky undertone.

"Tempting." She threw a shirt from his case at him. "Come on. You can treat me to lunch."

They went for a walk along the river. Barges ferrying coal chugged up and down and they watched them for a while. Some of the local wildlife came over to inspect them and Carter fed them bits of bread roll he'd bought from the tea room at the train station.

They went into the city and spent an hour poking around some of the shops. Georgette bought some brown leather gloves. The ones she had been issued with were too big and she had been on the lookout for another pair that suited her for quite a while.

The rest of the day passed slowly which was how Carter liked it. They had a leisurely lunch and after a look inside the Minster they explored some shops on The Shambles, a narrow street with old timber framed buildings that dated back to the middle ages. A sudden rain shower drove them indoors and they had afternoon tea at a tea room off St Helen's Square. It was all very genteel and it was a pleasant change to have dainty sandwiches and scones.

The rain started to come down in sheets. Even walking fast, they were wet through when they got back to the hotel. She took a robe and some towels and went down the corridor to take a bath. Carter dried himself off and stretched out on the bed. Georgette found him spark out when she came back. All the strain of the last few weeks had finally caught up with him and his body insisted on being heard.

She hated doing it, but she sat down next to him and nudged him. He stirred slowly and opened his eyes.

"Good morning," he said, bleary eyed.

She draped a shirt over his chest.

"Good evening in civilisation. Get dressed so we can have

dinner."

He propped himself on his elbows and lifted up the shirt.
"Yes Ma'am."
Before she could move, he reached up and grabbed the front of her towel. She squealed as it pulled loose.

After dinner they went back to their room, talked for a while and then fell asleep in each others arms. She slept lightly until a sound woke her up. It was Carter. He was twitching, muttering under his breath. His legs kicked, his hands making small scrabbling motions. She stroked his arm and made shushing sounds, trying to soothe him when he suddenly screamed out. His eyes were wide open but he saw right through her. His hands clawed at empty air, then the moment passed. Alarmed, Georgette shook him until he woke up. He looked at her blankly for a moment and then he recognised her.

"Are you all right?" he asked her, his eyes wide, his skin damp and clammy.

"I should be asking you that question. What's wrong?"

"Nothing," he muttered. He ran a hand over his face and she noticed his fingers were shaking.

"Alex. You *can* tell me, you know."

She waited patiently but when he didn't reply straight away, she felt hurt that he didn't trust her. It was not that, it was anything but that.

He was embarrassed that Georgette had seen him like this. She must have thought he was crazy. Strands of terror still clung to him as he marshaled his thoughts. He found his senses heightened; his skin sensitive to the touch. He could hear the slightest movements, the creak of the bed as she shifted her weight, the sound of his breathing.

He told her again about his crash landing, the proper story this time. The story came out in fragments as he described each moment. The whistle of air over the wings as they glided down, the creak of the airframe, the shouts of the crew as they got into crash positions.

His voice cracked as he got to the part about going under, the water surging over his head, choking on the spilled fuel and oil as he struggled to get out. Georgette leaned against the headboard with his head in her lap, hearing the distress in his voice. Then he came to the source of his fear. He couldn't swim, never had. When L-London went down he was convinced he was going to die and when the water pushed him back from the escape hatch, for a moment he really thought that was it.

He'd never told his crew, never thought it was important until then and by then it was too late. When they had practiced ditching drills in the hangar, he knew he could never do it for real. Even doing it in a pool would have been too much for him. Ditching in the ocean deeps, treading water with nothing underneath him scared him beyond measure. When they pulled him from the lake he had been almost paralysed with fear. If he'd not been wearing his Mae West he would have drowned, for sure.

She soothed him back to sleep, but she stayed awake for a long time after that. She fluffed up the pillows and read some poetry as she always did when her thoughts troubled her. The book was a slim volume of poetry she had won as a prize at school. Her name was written neatly on the fly leaf. She idly flicked through the pages, stopping as a title or a line caught her eye. Poetry didn't flow naturally for her, but she preferred to give her brain something to do as a distraction in moments like this.

She sorted through the myriad of thoughts rolling around her head as she read in the dim light. She felt alive, more alive than she had for a long time. After Charles had died, she had shut down and it had taken her a long time for her to become herself again. Now, a spark had reignited inside. It was not just the sex. Sex was easy. The physical act was one thing, her connection to Carter was something else. She stroked his arm, feeling the strength in him and the vulnerability too. It's what drew her to him, the way he held himself in check, conquered his fears but found the strength to carry on.

In the dark she could be honest with herself. It scared her, the thought that he could be taken from her. She thought about bombing operations and him finishing his second tour. She knew the odds better than most, but she also knew that there was no going back now. She loved him beyond measure.

29 - Two Down, One To Go

Carter held out his hand and helped Georgette down to the platform. They headed to the exit, holding hands, shoulders bumping as they walked, trying to stretch out these final moments. The time had passed quickly in the end as it always did. They had risen early and no mention was made of his dream from the night before. He'd ordered breakfast in bed and the porter brought them mackerel and powdered eggs, buttered toast and marmalade on a silver tray.

They made love one last time. He gazed into her eyes and she poured all of herself into him, trying to let him draw whatever strength he needed from her. Afterwards; they dozed the morning away and she clung to him, reluctant to let go.

He rang the station and Saunderson sent a car to pick him up. He changed in the station toilet and was in his uniform when it arrived. Stood by the kerb, he was just another officer with pilot's wings and a DFC ribbon on his chest. Georgette knew different and she knew what made him special to her.

The Austin pulled up at the kerb and the WAAF driver got out and opened the back door.

"She comes too," Carter told her.

"That's what Mr Saunderson told me, sir."

The suitcases were put in the boot and they got in. On the drive to the station, Carter and Georgette held hands, gripping each other tight and saying little. At the gate they said goodbye and she did her best not to cry. She had promised herself she wouldn't cry but it was hard. He leaned into the car.

"I'll ring you later,"

She nodded, not trusting her voice. He kissed her and then closed the door. He took his case from the boot and the car turned around to head to Grantham. He waved her on her way until the Austin was out of sight and then went up to the main gate. The SP saluted.

"Are the rest of my crew back?" he asked. "Mr Woods, Vos, Sergeants Jensen, Todd and Murphy?"

"I'm afraid I don't know, sir," said the SP, his voice vague and noncommittal. He asked for Carters ID card and scrutinised it. Satisfied he was the right man, the SP let him through and Carter signed in.

He dumped his bag in his billet and headed for the Mess, feeling refreshed after two days away from Amber Hill. The tensions had ebbed away as the CO hoped it would. The only thing waiting for him in the mail slot was a Mess bill so he left that alone. He nodded to some familiar faces and had just settled down with a pint and a newspaper when an orderly asked him to report to the CO. Carter nodded, took a final sip of his pint and headed over. When the Wingco asked you to attend the presence, that meant *now*, no ifs, no buts.

He was shocked to his boots when he went in and found Squadron Leader Dickinson ensconced behind the desk. Carter had to correct himself when he saw Dickinson now sported Wing Commander rings on the sleeves of his jacket. The New Zealander gestured to a seat and Carter settled himself.

"How was your leave?" Dickinson asked briskly, all business.

"Good, sir. Two days makes a lot of difference."

"Yes. Yes, it does." Dickinson cleared his throat and nodded to himself, brooding on the last forty eight hours. While Carter had been off enjoying himself, a lot had been going on.

Dickinson canted his head to one side and regarded Carter. The younger man returned the gaze without flinching.

"How's the neck?"

"All right." Carter moved his head around for show. He stopped himself from grimacing but Dickinson caught the involuntary flinch in his neck as he tilted his head back and looked at the ceiling. "It still hurts a bit but I'm okay to fly."

The fact that Carter was keen to get back in the saddle was a good sign. Dickinson needed men to be the press on types, who would carry on even when things went wrong. He gave Carter the official answer.

"We'll let the Doctor make the final decision on that one. The same goes for the rest of your crew. Get a clean bill of health and you're back out there."

Carter nodded, that was fair enough.

"What about an aircraft?"

"There's one waiting for you. Another L-London, so you won't be breaking your luck getting something else," Dickinson assured him. "Now get out of here and meet your new Flight Commander."

Carter rose from his seat, came to attention and saluted.

He closed the door behind him, nodding to the clerk in the outer office. He went down the corridor and rapped on the door of 'B' Flights commander. The voice that called him was gruff.

"Come."

Carter poked his head around the door to find Fish Salmon behind Dickinson's old desk. The squadron photos were gone from the back wall and had been replaced with a family photo of Salmon, a woman and two children. There was another photo of him posing in swimming trunks by the pool. Some swimming medals hung from a nail. He looked at Carter down his thin nose, the blue eyes hooded with fatigue.

"Ah, Carter. Take a seat. How's the neck?"

Carter got the story later in the Mess from Walsh. The day he had gone on leave, most of the squadron had been sent to Munster. It was a relatively small raid, not even one hundred aircraft. The weather had been dismal and most of them had bombed blind on dead reckoning. They had taken off at eight and straggled back in the early morning two short.

One of the casualties had bought it on the return trip, making it back to England miles off track and blundering into the balloon barrage over Great Yarmouth. Asher had been the other one. His last call had been a standard morse signal, 'enemy coast ahead' and that was the last anyone had heard from him. He was posted as missing but everyone knew what that meant.

Losing Asher had been a bit of a shock and Etheridge had acted swiftly to stabilise the squadron. Bringing in an outside man after having the same CO for nearly eight months would have been too disruptive. Dickinson had been due a squadron of his own anyway, he just happened to inherit 363. Group had made him up to Wing Commander and told him this would be officially confirmed in due course. Fish Salmon got bumped to acting Squadron Leader.

Carter found the squadrons mood was subdued and there was none of the usual banter or horseplay. The biggest bit of news floating round was that some pilfering had been discovered from the officer's Mess supplies. Exactly when it happened, no one knew but it had clearly been going on for a while. Chocolate, some alcohol and a quantity of eggs were missing. There was the usual speculation but Carter assumed the kitchen staff had done it. Someone could make themselves a pretty penny on the black market with that sort of stuff and they had the most access to the stores. Since the theft the SP's had been prowling around with more vigour than usual. Suspected parties had been asked questions and their personal affects searched but nothing had been found so far.

Carter spoke to Georgette briefly on the telephone, confirmed she got home okay then turned in for an early night. Walsh put in an appearance later, crashing into the billet after midnight and making a nuisance of himself. He flopped onto his bed, fully clothed, clutching an empty bottle of Guinness.

Carter gathered up his navigator and popped round to Todd's hut after breakfast, curious to see if his non commissioned men had turned up. He found the poker school in full swing. Todd had been persuaded to play for once to make up the numbers and was two shillings ahead. Murphy froze when Carter and Woods came in, a bowl in one hand, spoon in the other, halfway to his mouth with a bit poached egg on it. He stood there tongue out, waiting for the food to be delivered.

"So," said Carter, his tone stern. Theft, and his own bloody crew was in on it.

"J'Accuse," said Woods, half joking, pointing at their gunner. "Well done, Holmes, case solved," he quipped. He clapped his hands together. "Oh well, that didn't take long."

"No' ee," muttered Murphy, his mouth full of egg. Carter twisted his face in distaste, he didn't really fancy seeing masticated egg in Murphy's mouth. He pinched the bridge of his nose and shook his head.

"Some trick, guys."

"Hey it wasn't us, Skipper" said Todd, protesting their innocence.

Carter wasn't buying.

"Oh, come on," he said in exasperation. He nosed around the hut and went over to the two shelves by the stove. There were tins of spam, god knows how many bars of chocolate and packs of cigarettes. He picked up a tin of condensed milk and peered at the label. "If the SP's found this little lot you'll be up the creek without a paddle, the whole bloody lot of you. They won't be bothered about figuring out who did what, you'll all be stuffed."

"Put up against a wall and shot," Woods finished for him. "Well, maybe not shot, but you'll be on yankers for the rest of the war."

"No, really," Todd said again, his tone insistent. "It *wasn't* us. I get the eggs from a local farm not far from dispersal. You can come with me tomorrow if you want, I'll show you."

Carter eyed his rear gunner with some suspicion. It all sounded convincing enough and he seemed earnest. He shook his head. Problems like this he could do without.

"Okay, so that's the eggs accounted for, what about the rest?" he gestured at the shelves. "You don't get this stuff from a farm."

"The lads bring it," explained Murphy, weakly. It had sounded better in his head.

"Well it's going to have to stop," Carter said, genuinely cross. "Jesus, it's like you're preparing for the next flood or something. There must be a fortune in stuff here."

"We'll get rid of it," Murphy assured him. Carter rounded on all of them, not confining the rollicking to his own crew.

"You'd better, because if I come again and find this little lot, you're all for the high jump."

He stamped from the hut, his temper up.

"Strewth," muttered Todd. He had seen the skipper get annoyed before but nothing like this.

"Don't look at me, chum," said Woods. "Self inflicted I call it." He appropriated a bar of chocolate, tipped them a casual two fingered salute to the temple and left the hut to catch up with his pilot.

"And move your head for me."

Carter swung his head right and left, back and forth like a pendulum. The doctor pressed on his neck with two stiff fingers, feeling the muscles move.

"How's that?"

"Fine."

The doctor uncapped his fountain pen and made a note on his clipboard. He looked up and down his observations, tapping the pen off his teeth.

"How have the painkiller's been?"

"All right," Carter said warily, keeping his answers short.

"Not making you drowsy?"

Cater shook his head. The doctors voice was a dull monotone as he went through his list of things to check. It was his way; he was a cold fish who pronounced on whether they were fit to fly but he kept himself to himself. Even in the Mess he was this aloof figure who kept his own counsel and said little.

"Relax, Mr Carter. I'm not trying to trap you into an answer."

Carter was sitting on a padded examination table, his legs dangling over the side as he looked around the room. A ten foot square box, the lino was grey and the walls were painted in a chalky white colour, a perfect accompaniment to the tang of antiseptic in his nose. A yellowed skeleton grinned at him from one corner. A garish poster on the wall extolled the virtues of abstinence ands saying no to prostitutes to avoid spills and gonorrhoea; charming.

Carter kicked his legs back and forth while his hands gripped the padded bed. He glanced at the clock on the table. He had been in here for nearly an hour and was starting to get browned off.

The doctor had done his bet to poke and prod all over the place. He'd hit knees with a hammer, scraped soles with a thin wooden stick and peered down his throat and ears.

"Sleeping okay?" Carter shrugged. What could he say to that? *Oh yes, I get nightmares. Do you know what? Funny story. I woke up screaming next to my girlfriend a few days ago, scared the living daylights out of her.*

"I suppose so. Sleeping in the daytimes always a bit rough with all the noise going on. I'm always chasing the clock on days off to get back to normal."

He lied of course. He'd lied about his neck as well. Of course, it had bloody hurt when the bloody man had pressed on it with his bloody fingers but he kept his mouth shut and controlled himself. If he was a fighter pilot it would have mattered, but he was a bomber pilot, he had gunners to do his looking for him.

"Hmmmm." The doctor nodded. He did that often, a nasal hum as he listened to what you said and wrote on his clipboard. He rarely made eye contact, masking his thoughts behind an almost blank visage.

"Your reactions seem to be normal." He gestured vaguely towards Carter with his pen. "Your muscle tone etc. Your bodyweights a bit low, you need feeding up a bit."

He glanced up from his clipboard, suddenly fixing Carter with a stern look.

"Movement on your neck all right?" He moved his face left and right, regarding him from different angles. It was eerily similar to what Dickinson had done the day before in his office. Carter nodded in response.

The doctor looked at the little chicken scratch marks of ink on the paper. It was all just words. He knew Carter had lied like a trooper. Just like Todd had lied about his back earlier. They were all mad, the whole bloody lot of them.

He watched new men arrive on a regular basis and passed them fit to fly. They were all meat for the grinder, but they willingly went to their fates wrapped in the cloak of duty and patriotism. It was all a little much for him.

He occupied himself with his work and didn't think about the rest. At Amber Hill he was surrounded by hundreds of healthy young men and women in the prime of life. Aside from the odd muscle pull or cold or accident, there was little to do. Few men returned wounded from ops, so getting six aircrew to evaluate for fitness to fly constituted a sudden rush. He'd not been so busy since the chickenpox outbreak last year. He signed the bottom of the form in a flourish.

"You know best. There's nothing wrong with you as such, there's no reason why you can't fly."

Carter let out a sigh of relief.

"Thank you, doctor."

Cleared to fly, the crew stood looking up at their new Manchester in one of the hangars. The paint was fresh and unblemished. The squadron codes had already been painted on the side and an enterprising soul had marked up the bomb symbols of missions flown under the cockpit.

This was the latest version of the Manchester and incorporated all the design improvements which had come from operational experience. The biggest visual difference was the tail. There was no third fin on the fuselage and the two vertical stabilisers were much bigger than they had been before. Carter liked that; bigger control surfaces should make things easier.

The other big change was this particular aircraft had a mid upper turret. Murphy couldn't wait to get in there. There would be no more cramming himself into the front turret and buggering about trying to keep his feet out of the way of Woods on the bomb run.

They took her up for a flip that afternoon, their spirits high. It was good to get back in the air again and wash out the bad taste of the crash.

At lunchtime the following day, Carter knew there was something up when he saw a Naval Lieutenant sitting at Dickinson's table. He smelt a rat when Kent took a chair next to them and they huddled, deep in conversation. The nautics lived on the coast. They had their toy boats to play with and you never saw one up in Lincolnshire unless they wanted something. When they did, that was always bad news for everyone else.

Carter noticed the wavy golden rank rings on the man's sleeves. Wavy navy, a hostilities only officer, a hobbyist almost. He was a blonde young man with piercing blue eyes and a full beard and moustache. Amongst all the RAF blue he looked quite dapper in his dark jacket and bright buttons and white shirt. The WAAFs would be eating out of his hand.

Carter absently scratched his right ankle while he ate. The skin was sore and giving him some grief. He'd lost one boot in the lake after the crash and the new pair he'd bought were giving him some trouble. His other boots had been lovely and soft and it had taken ages to break them in. These new ones were still stiff and they had been playing him up the entire time during the air test.

After lunch he went back to his room. He peeled back the sock and hissed. The skin on his right heel was red and there was a gorgeous blister coming up. He lanced it with a sewing needle and squeezed, watching the thick liquid leak out onto a tissue. He stuck a plaster over it and bit on his lip as it stung like blazes.

He lay back on his bed, notepad in his lap while he tried writing a letter to Georgette. He found it difficult trying to put his thoughts down on paper. He smiled to himself as he thought about their time together in York, how she'd felt under him, yielding to him, pushing back at him, how she'd looked at him with such intensity, like she was burning every moment into her mind.

The tannoy sounded and called the crews to briefing. Carter locked the pages in his drawer and shuffled off to the briefing room, favouring his right leg.

His earlier guess was proven correct when the squadron

assembled in the briefing room and he saw the naval officer on the stage with the command staff. The room settled down and almost immediately, Dickinson yielded the floor to the visitor.

The naval officer stepped forwards to the edge of the stage, gripping the long pointer in both hands in front of him. All eyes were trained on this navy Lieutenant in hushed anticipation. Someone coughed and it was loud in the room. Carters mouth was dry, there was only one target which merited a personal visit, the Battleship *Tirpitz*, skulking in the German ports. It was a long way to the Baltic for a Manchester but he could almost hear the navy screaming for it to be sunk before it got into the Atlantic like the *Bismarck* had done.

"I'm not one for long flowery speeches gentlemen," he said in the most cut glass accent Carter had ever heard. "I respect you chaps too much to blow a lot of sunshine about something that is so serious. Your target for tonight; is Brest."

The room got even quieter if that was humanly possible. A pin dropping would have sounded like a hand grenade going off.

"For some time, I know you've been raiding enemy held ports and going for his shipping. Capital ships can scythe through any convoy they come against and destroy the escort without ever letting them get into gun range. After that the transports are easy pickings."

He walked over to the big map on the back wall and pointed out the German ports and some on the French coast.

"We managed to stop *Bismarck* but there's no guarantee we can do that every time. Look at the mayhem, *Graf Spee* managed in the south Atlantic before she was brought to heel. *Scharnhorst* and *Gneisenau* sank over 100,000 tons the last time they broke out." There was a murmur of disquiet when he quoted the tonnage figure. "I know you chaps have gone to Brest god knows how many times. I'm sure you've been told god knows how many times that it's important. It must feel like you're tilting at windmills, having to keep going back but we can't afford to let them put to sea again."

He rocked back on his heels as he considered what to say next. He turned around and walked to the back of the stage towards the map, speaking over his shoulder.

"I'm sure you're wondering what makes this time so important that I'm here?" He span round and faced them. His knuckles gripped the pointer. "What's different, is that we've had word that *Scharnhorst, Gneisenau* and *Prinz Eugen* have been making ready for sea." That caught their attention.

"Intelligence indicates they're going to move soon but we don't know where they're heading." He gestured with the stick, sweeping down towards Gilbraltar. "If they get into the Mediterranean, we might lose Malta." The stick swept towards the wide expanse of the Atlantic. "If it's the Atlantic, well I think I've painted the picture in enough detail for you already."

He came back to the front of the stage and let the stick thump on the floor, the point digging into the palm of his left hand.

"We're not going to get many more chances to get in there and stop them before they can start. Sinking them or damaging them enough so that they can't move won't shorten the war, but it *will* stop it lasting longer."

He handed the pointer to Dickinson who took his place on the stage.

"There it is gentlemen. I don't think there's anything else I can add that can emphasise how important this is. We're putting up every aircraft we can. Maximum effort tonight. I know the last few days have brought a lot of change, but this raid is no different to any of the others we've flown. Concentrate, do your jobs, and get home and we'll have the beers waiting for you."

That produced a good humoured laugh and the mood lightened.

Carter kept bending down to scratch at his ankle. Walsh leaned over and whispered out of the corner of his mouth, "constipated mate?"

"It's my bloody boots," he hissed back. He wiggled a finger down the boot and grimaced as it brushed against the plaster.

"I told you to piss on 'em," Walsh reminded him. Carter shot him a cross look as he carried on rubbing. He wasn't looking forward to flying tonight.

Dickinson handed over to Black Jack and the big man took centre stage, oozing confidence and command presence.

"I'll not repeat the obvious. We've been there enough times I'm sure you could sketch it on a sheet of paper with your eyes closed. When this briefing concludes, individual bombs aimers see me and I will give you your target assignments. Tonight of all nights, I need you to drop when you're sure you're on target." He punched his left fist into his right palm. "If you have to go around again, you go around again. If those bloody searchlights get in your eyes and you lose your aiming point, you go around again. If smoke blots out your view, you go around again!"

They went through the usual suspects. It was a full moon tonight so Linkletter told them to expect fantastic weather and clear visibility over the target.

Kent put up the same target photos they had seen god knows how many times already. The only difference was there were more bomb craters around the ships but they were still there in the middle of it all, the same brooding hulking shapes that defied all attempts to sink them.

"Eeny, meeny, miny, mo," said Woods as they got on board.

They had been given *Scharnhorst*. He would have preferred *Gneisenau*. Covered by camouflage nets and moored against the quay, he would have the line of the harbour wall to follow and aim for. *Scharnhorst* on the other hand was towed out every night to a mooring point in the middle of the harbour. Woods would have to hit her bang on. A miss would go into the water and just make a very big splash.

He started unpacking his things from his new navigator's bag. Everything had gone down in the lake in the crash. He sharpened a pencil and opened the navigator's logbook to a new page. He wrote the date and checked the time on his watch as he thought about his leave to London.

He'd taken Jensen to the same hotel they had stayed in before Christmas. It was still the same drab grey city. Full of bustle, rubble and odd glimmers of beauty amongst the destruction. They caught a show, ate well and relaxed.

He unfolded the map and glanced at the track he had sketched out. He twirled the pencil between his fingers as he pondered the timings. They were going to be one of the last off, bringing up the rear of the raid. Woods grimaced. Tail end charley again. The engines started with a roar and Carter taxied out.

No one went off the peri track this time and the squadron got off on schedule. Their new L-London flew like a dream. She rode the night time air like an eagle and easily got up to 15,000ft. Navigation was a doddle. The sky was bright and it was a virtually cloudless night.

They picked up the pinpoint on the peninsula, the snow dusted countryside contrasting sharply with the dark water around it. They had no trouble locating Brest. The skyline was lit up with the flashes of bombs and flak, the glare of flames and searchlights weaving back and forth.

There was a sudden blossom of light in the sky and then a streak of flame rushed to the ground. Jensen called out the sighting and Woods made a note in his log. That was the fourth one he had noted tonight. He closed the log and went up to the cockpit.

"I'm going to get ready, skipper," he shouted in Carters ear. Carter nodded and gave him a thumbs up. Jensen folded up his seat and let Woods go down into the nose.

Carter came in from the west to cross the length of the harbour like they had once before. The searchlights were late picking them up and Woods could see *Scharnhorst* in the middle of the harbour. Her guns flickered as they fired into the night sky. He started passing corrections to Carter as the sight drifted.

The searchlights caught them in the final run up. Woods held up a hand to shield his eyes. He felt naked, like a deer caught in a cars headlights as the interior of the dark fuselage was illuminated by thousands of watts of candle power. In the final seconds, Woods lost it. The Battleship disappeared in the glare and he had no idea if he was sighted on empty water or the *Scharnhorst*.

"I've lost her!" he shouted.

Carter cursed. They bounced around as the flak boxed them in. A burst went off in front of them and the Manchester surged through the smoke, the stench of sulphur filling the cockpit. He climbed as they peeled off to the right, circling round to the south, away from the city. Carter wanted more height before going back in.

On the other side of the city, Dickinson was finding things equally difficult. He had already made two runs and each time the searchlights had blinded him. He made his third run from the east. This time he closed the throttles, gliding down from 12,000ft to 6,000ft. The flak nailed him as he let the bombs go.

Bracketed by two bursts, the fuselage was perforated. His mid upper gunner was killed outright and his tail gunner was trapped in his turret as the hydraulics let go. Oil leaked out of the port engine in a steady stream, covering the rear fin. The undercarriage dropped and Dickinson fought the controls as the wheels added extra drag.

Jensen shrank into himself as they made two more runs. Each time, the searchlights coned them and the flak bounced them around and he found it difficult to concentrate on his job. He jumped as the windscreen starred in front of him with a loud crack.

"This is getting tired, Woody," Carter said through clenched teeth. He gripped the yoke hard, fighting to keep the nose on course. The Manchester fought him as she bucked through the turbulent air.

"Nothing!" shouted Woods. "I can't see a bloody thing."

Carter snarled and broke off to port. He let the nose dip below the horizon and watched the altimeter unwind. Passing ten thousand he flattened out and headed inland. Coming in from the south had failed; perhaps they might have better luck attacking from the north.

The flak batteries were still going mad when they came back in. Carter took a wide circle, keeping his eyes on the harbour. The searchlights weaved around, probing for a new victim. They found it. A luckless Hampden was fixed in their glare and the flak began walking upwards. Carter rammed the throttles forward, the engines screaming full belt as they turned in.

"Get ready, Woody. I really don't want to have to do this again."

It was all on Woods this time. If he didn't drop the bombs on this run, it would be even money the crew would lynch him when they got back; *if* they got back, he contemplated for the first time.

They passed over the harbour at eight thousand. Carter felt naked as a searchlight washed over them. He steeled himself for the flak but it never came.

Woods got lined up, passed a correction and Carter kicked on the rudder pedal to snap the nose back around. Woods waited one more second for the sight to settle and hit the release.

Carter stuffed the nose down, peeling off to the right as he called round the crew. They checked in briskly and breathed a sigh of relief as Brest disappeared behind them.

Woods felt like an old man when he sagged back into his navigator's chair. He rubbed a gloved hand over his face and wiped the sweat away. He glanced at his chart and asked Murphy and Todd to get him a pinpoint. He picked his log off the floor and paused. He tugged a glove off and poked a finger in the hole that went right through it. Cold air tickled his face and found a ragged hole to his left in the skin of the fuselage.

Jensen eased off on the throttles and they slowly climbed into the night. His nerves were jangling and it took him a while to settle back down. None of the previous raids had been anything like this.

"Did anyone see the bombs go off?" he asked. No one had. Todd was blinded by a searchlight that had chased them out of the harbour. They would have to wait for the target photograph when they got back.

Carter was never so relieved when they touched down back at Amber Hill. His arms were like lead. He'd not felt so exhausted even by the end of his first tour. He'd let Jensen fly them back and only took the controls again to land. He felt like he could sleep for a week. Those five runs had really taken it out of him even with Jensen's help.

That had been his fifteenth op. He was halfway through his tour and if the rest of them were like that, he wondered if he was going to make it. He tempered that gloomy thought with the knowledge that at least they were among the lucky ones who had made it back. The price of their clear run in to the *Scharnhorst* had been the Hampden they saw coned by the searchlights. It had twisted like a minnow, diving and swooping trying to shake them off, but the guns got them in the end, as they always did.

The erks scowled as they looked at the damage. The fuselage and wings were peppered with holes and Latimer shook his head as he counted the holes on the underside of the fuselage. The new L-London was not so new any more.

Kent was waiting in interrogation with his staff, hovering like a pack of vultures.

"Describe the target?"

"Where there any particular differences in the defences to what you had seen before?"

"Did you hit the target?"

"What were the defences like?"

275

And so on. Pick, pick, pick questions that grated on the soul. It was quite easy to become flippant in your responses back, even if it was a girl asking the questions. For some of the intel staff it had almost become a game, being able to extract blood from stones was probably easier than getting the little details from tired men with red raw eyes and nerves on edge.

There would always be a wall between the ground types and the crews. They hadn't seen what they had, how could they? How could you really describe the bittersweet horror of seeing a Hampden, or a Manchester or a Stirling or a Halifax go down, fuel tanks blazing like a Roman candle. Bitter because men were dying, sweet because it was not you and you had been spared once more.

Group Captain Etheridge and the naval Lieutenant floated around the room, listening to the crews as they made their reports. Dickinson had yet to return and Etheridge waited anxiously for the New Zealander to breeze through the door, his face split with that familiar gap toothed smile.

The naval officer was a bundle of energy despite being up all night. He had wanted to fly on the raid and nearly got his way until Bomber Command HQ said a firm no. He had to content himself with waiting in the Ops Room and listening to the occasional snatch of radio communication or morse like everyone else.

Carter took a seat in front of Kent. He slumped in the wooden folding seat, his body as limp and disinterested in the process as he was. Carter and his crew automatically munched on sandwiches and drank the cups of hot tea, letting their first food in hours do its work. Cigarettes were being used hard and the air was tinged blue with smoke.

Kent was not inured to the mood of the men; he had seen the way the other crews were. Clearly the raid had been no picnic. He kept it mercifully short while Carter described their bombing runs.

"Did the smoke screen cause any problems?" he asked.

"Not this time," Woods interjected. "It was the bloody searchlights. I could pick things out fine until they caught us."

Kent kept a count down the side of his sheet. About half the squadron reckoned they had bombed the targets for sure. Three others were maybes, Not bad.

When all the crews had been seen, Kent and the naval officer retired to his hut to tally the results. A blonde WAAF volunteered to assist, to no avail. This was secret work and he was all business. A preliminary report was rung through to the Admiralty but they would have to wait for the PRU Spits to get back later in the day. By sunrise the naval Lieutenant was on his way back to London in a staff car.

The Squadron lost two. There were the usual phone calls around the stations but no one had any stray Manchesters belonging to 363.

Past the point their fuel would have run out, Dickinson and Slattery's names were wiped from the Ops board.

Ailing, with the wheels down and a sick engine, Dickinson had given up any hope of making it back home. Over the channel at perilously low altitude, he had run east and ditched not far from the Channel Islands. In the morning a partially inflated, bright yellow RAF dinghy washed up in a Guernsey cove but Dickinson and his crew were never seen again.

Slattery and his crew had been another of the old hands who had been on the squadron since the beginning. A rowing blue from Oxford, Slattery was also a good miler and could often be seen having a run around the airfield. His end was less ambiguous than Dickinson's. After making two runs over the harbour, the exhortations from Dickinson and Black Jack ringing in his ears, he made a third run to press home his attack when a chain of light flak guns had nailed him.

The port engine was smashed and his Manchester dropped like a stone. Slattery had shouted at them to bail out but only the Navigator managed to slither out of the nose hatch before they went in.

30 - Best Laid Plans And All That

The squadron had a party that night, part wake, part celebration. A remembrance for Asher and Dickinson and Slattery and all the others who were gone and a joyous salute to life. Etheridge bumped Church to acting CO until Group decided what to do and the laconic Everett was made 'A' Flight Commander to fill in the gap.

Carter slid out of the officers Mess and made a call from the telephone in the hall. It was answered on the third ring with a peremptory snap. Right at that moment there was a huge cheer from the main bar that echoed down the corridor into the hall and Carter winced. He could almost hear the disapproving silence oozing down the phone. Georgette came to the phone, her voice light and cheery.

"Darling, where are you?" she asked him. "It sounds like a zoo."

"I'm in the Mess. We're having a thrash. We earned it after last night."

"I know," she said quietly.

That remark sobered him for a moment. He forgot that Georgette saw the interrogation reports up at Group.

"I just wanted to hear your voice," he told her honestly.

"Did you?" she asked, genuinely pleased. He could hear her smiling, the way her voice lifted along with the curl of her lips, the way her eyes crinkled in good humour.

There was another roar from the bar and some bodies crashed through the double doors behind him, pillows flying after them. Carter scowled and jammed a finger in his other ear, struggling to hear what else she was saying.

"Sorry, darling, what was that?"

"I said I got a letter from my sister."

"Wonderful. Which one?"

She laughed.

"Julie."

Carter's mind whirled with the list of names of Georgette's sisters. He had difficulty keeping them straight in his head.

"Which one's that?"

"She's a WAAF like me, but she's down south."

He was about to ask her what the news was, when the pillow fight came barreling down the corridor. Archer was running full tilt to get away from Woods who was pounding him with a pillow. Not looking where they were going, they crashed into Carter and took his legs out from under him.

Life at Amber Hill continued. Aircraft went up for air tests. Every few days, some of them went out to do a bit of gardening. Occasionally, one might not make it back. That was the luck of the game. The one truism with service life was that nobody was irreplaceable. People came and went and that included commanding officers but losing two in three days was a bit unusual.

Squadrons dealt with loss in their own way. When casualties were heavy, the survivors would drink to remember, drink to forget and drink to thank their lucky stars that they had survived. When a leader went and got the chop that was different. A CO set the tone and guided everyone else along.

Asher had led 363 since the beginning. Church and Dickinson had led the flights, moulding each of them to their own character but it had been Asher's hand on the tiller.

Now that Church was CO things changed perceptibly. The strong silent type, Church led from the front but he was not one to make inspiring speeches or tell the men to pull their socks up. They were adults, they had to deal with it as far as he was concerned, there was no need to wrap them in cotton wool.

The weather worsened and some people got sent on leave. Archer left with a crash of gears and a spray of gravel, his yellow car rocketing through the gates.

Cold flurries and gusts descended on Amber Hill. A cold penetrating wind hunted out every nook and cranny and the crews huddled in their billets. The skies went as dark as lead and threatened snow as the temperature dropped further. Walsh shuddered, remembering the last time it had snowed.

Church laid on some lectures to keep the men busy. He brought a gen type from Group to talk about escape and evasion. They were told about double frontiers and fake border crossings. They got lectures on how to live off the land, what berries were safe to east and whatnot. They got told about pneumonia and hypothermia and what they could do about it.

Some made notes. Some took the chance to have a snooze in a warm darkened room. A few let it run in one ear and out the other. It was all informative stuff, but the veterans knew it was of little use. Falling out of the sky, in the dark, fighting g-forces as you tried to jump out of a dying aircraft, it was an even money chance for most of them to even bail out let alone worry about what to do once you got on the ground.

Murphy brooded on that very point in the dark of the lecture room as another slide of red berries was put up. He had started thinking about Joan, the feel of her lean body, her breasts pressed against his chest while her hips rocked back and forth against his pelvis. The image morphed into a vision of Muriel, her eyes flashing at him from under her blonde curls as she smiled at him. He imagined her arms holding him close, wrapping tightly around him and not letting him go and he found his thoughts inextricably staying to his new turret.

He'd been over the moon when he found their new Manchester had a mid upper turret. That fascination had lasted one op. The FN7 Botha turret might have seemed roomy on the outside but it was a different story once you got in it. A strange elongated teardrop design, it was tall but not very roomy inside. There was plenty of room for his legs to dangle in the fuselage which was good, but there wasn't a lot of room for his shoulders. He found he had to hunch up over the guns to give himself space but it was still uncomfortable.

The lecture mercifully finished and the lights came up. Murphy blinked the spots from his eyes and yawned as he stretched. Some rubbed their faces to wake up. They adjourned for dinner. Murphy bent his thoughts towards the evening's activities. He perked up when he realised Muriel was working tonight, so he could glide over, see her for a bit at the pub and then see Joan afterwards for some fun.

Walsh rushed into his room and closed the door as cold air whooshed in behind him. He stamped his feet and then began unbuttoning his greatcoat. He started as he turned round and saw Carter in bed, under a pile of clothes, his own coat draped over everything.

"Jesus, you gave me a shock."

He put his pyjamas over some long johns and left his socks on, it was too cold to go without socks. He got under the covers and copied Carter, pulling his greatcoat over everything.

"How come you missed the show?" he asked his room mate. Carter shrugged.

"It's no secret. I was out at dispersal talking repairs on my kite."

He watched as Walsh riffled through the limited selection of records for the gramophone and make his choice. He pulled a record from the sleeve and put it on the turntable. He wound up the player and the room was filled with Vera Lynn's voice.

They listened for a while, Carter reading a letter from White as the music played in the background. He looked at the envelope and saw it had come from Norwich.

The writing was big and loopy and very feminine. Carter discovered the reason why when he read down the first page. White's hands were still bandaged so he had sweet talked a nurse into writing for him. White asked how the boys were and said little about his crash, or being burned. He mentioned that Elaine had come to see him. She had taken the train to Norwich and stayed overnight, spending as much time with him on the ward as she was allowed.

He moaned about the hospital but said the food was reasonable and the nurses were pretty. Carter tried to conjure up a smile but it was difficult. White would be a good sport in hospital, the staff would like him, but he grimaced at the thought of having your day reduced to considerations about food and being prodded by doctors while they stared at you like some specimen. The tone was upbeat but Carter could read between the lines easily enough. It had taken White a lot of guts to write a letter so soon when the future was bleak and unknown.

Carter put the letter back in its envelope when he finished and shoved it in the top drawer of his bedside cabinet. He pulled out a half bottle of whisky and two glasses. He clinked the glasses together and Walsh brightened.

"That'll help take the cold off," he said.

Carter poured.

They fluffed up their pillows and tried to relax as the music played.

"How many runs did you make?" Carter asked, his voice a murmur, his eyes closed, the glass cradled on his chest.

"Too bloody many," Walsh replied. "Five? Six? I lost count."

He shuddered again at the memory of going back and forth across the harbour, the flak guns filling the sky with lead. What stuck in his mind the most was the dull thud of shells that went off near him. He couldn't see them, but he could feel them, hear them, that bass shiver through his seat as his bomber rode the maelstrom.

"Do you think we got them?"

"We bloody should have," muttered Carter, sitting up. Some whisky slopped over the edge of the glass and he sucked his hand, tasting the bite at the back of his throat. "We've thrown enough bombs at the beasts. It's a coconut shy," he announced, trying to make light of it all. "Roll up, roll up, every one's a winner."

"I didn't get a teddy bear," Walsh complained.

Todd used his knife to cut a piece of cardboard to shape. It looked about right so he offered it up to the window. It was a snug fit so he shoved it into place, wedging it into the frame. Cold air still got around it but it was better than nothing. He turned back to the room and relaxed on his bed, letting the heat from the stove wash over him. He didn't have much energy to go anywhere this evening. The cold had sucked the motivation out of him and he was content to sit in the warm.

He stared at the fire flickering in the grate of the stove as he cast his mind back to the raid on Brest. Sitting at the back had been murder while they went around again and again. Sparks flurried past his turret and all he could do was sit and take what was thrown at them, jolting up and down as they ploughed through turbulence and the fury of the defences.

A piece of shrapnel had gone through his turret, left to right and out the other side. One moment they had been flying along, then a wicked piece of steel had whizzed in front of his eyes. The suddenness of it had shocked him.

He joined the poker game. Money seemed less important for once. He played carelessly, bet big and came out ahead. Some would have said it was beginners luck but he knew the real reason why he won. When nothing scared you any more, you took the chances you might normally hesitate over.

On the 4th February, Carter was briefed to lay mines off the Frisian islands. The weather was foul and they took off into leaden skies. They kept low over the water while Woods prayed to the navigation gods and hoped the forecast winds were right.

They got recalled halfway there and Carter was grateful that sanity prevailed. The weather had worsened over the North Sea, the cloud base dropping with every mile so that they had ended up at a mere two hundred feet. The tips of their props had been teasing the undersides of the clouds and Carter had his hands full, working the controls in the roiled air to stay level. They were so low; they were getting turbulence from the undulating waves. Their canopy had been hosed with spray as the wind snatched drops from the tops of the waves and threw them at them as they pressed on.

They turned for home and dumped the mines at the designated spot off The Wash and then stooged around for a while to burn off enough fuel so they could land. They defrosted during interrogation, their hands like claws as they gripped hot mugs of tea. The final kick in the pants was being told that the trip wouldn't count. They'd never made the enemy coast so there was no credit for it.

Of course, Group were never ones to let a perfectly good bit of operational planning go to waste. On the 6th, Carter and two other crews were sent back to the Frisians to give it another go. The catch was they would be going in daylight.

It was with some trepidation that Carter drew his parachute from stores and got ready to fly. He did his walkaround with his usual thoroughness, having a deep conversation with Latimer about the engines. They had a quick flight test in the morning and then they were ready to go.

The weather had marginally improved over the last two days but it was still bumpy and cold. Carter was very aware there was a good chance of icing in such cold weather which would rob him of positive control and airspeed. They went up to ten thousand but the clouds were a solid mass of fluffy grey, very uninviting and very dangerous.

He discussed the forecast with Woods. They had been briefed for clear skies above five thousand with light winds carrying them along. That was clearly wrong as they were fighting a stiff headwind and the clouds kept on going up as far as the eye could see. Carter wanted sharp navigation to get them bang on target with no faffing around. Spooning around off the enemy coast like some moron would attract attention. He wanted to deal with fighters like he wanted a hole in the head and in daylight, even in such bad weather, that was a very real possibility.

"Balls to that," Carter announced. He throttled back slightly and dipped the nose, taking L-London down. He watched the altimeter unwind and bottomed out at three thousand feet, a clear thousand or more below the clouds.

He was on edge the entire time there and back. When it came time to drop the mines, he found himself straining in his seat, leaning forwards against the straps wanting to be away from there. Every second on the run felt like an age. He was relieved when they left Terschelling behind and headed for home.

Wilkinson got the phone call at four. All aircraft dispatched returned. He had been against gardening in daylight but Bomber Command HQ had insisted upon it. He glanced out of his office window and saw a figure he recognised walking across the grounds towards the greenhouses. Grabbing his cap and coat from their stand, he went out.

He found her sitting on a bench at the far end of the grounds. She was a forlorn little figure, hands in her lap, head down. His feet crunched on the ground and she looked up sharply when she heard him approach. She quickly got to her feet and was halfway through a salute before he could stop her.

"No need for that Georgette. No one else around."

He motioned for her to sit and then plonked down next to her. He looked around the clearing.

"Do you know, in all the months I've been at Group I never knew this existed."

She did her best to smile but it never reached her eyes. Her hands tied a hanky into knots. Wilkinson did his best to studiously ignore her obvious anxiety.

"I've never thanked you for looking after Helen," he told her.

"It was nothing, sir. I was glad to spend time with her."

"Even so, you have my thanks. It's not easy for her being stuck at that hotel when her family are miles away in Lincoln. I know she goes back when she can but even so." His voice trailed off. He shrugged. "Anyway, there it is."

Georgette nodded, not saying a word.

The bare trees rustled with the stiff breeze. Wilkinson clapped his hands together, regretting not bringing his gloves with him.

"Lovely day. Bit crisp, but I suppose we take what we can get at the moment."

"There is a war on you know," she said with a laugh.

Wilkinson was impressed that she could make a joke even when she was upset. He knew what was bothering her.

"He got back okay if that's what you're worried about," he told her, his tone light. Her hands froze and she became very still. He looked sideways at her. She was almost frozen, eyes wide. She had gone very pale. He leaned close to her shoulder and dropped his voice. "No need to worry now. He's back."

She nodded woodenly.

"Alex told me how much he dreaded daylight raids," she whispered.

Wilkinson let slip a snort of humour.

"He's not the only one," said Wilkinson. "*I* hate daylight raids. Fighters, no night to hide in. Horrible." He clapped his hands on his legs. "Well, I could sit here chatting all day but the war waits for no man. Besides, won't you have some interrogation reports to collate soon?"

He gave her an encouraging smile as he walked back to the hall.

31 - Elan And Greek Myth

The weather clamped down that night. The wind picked up, the clouds dropped and damp coated everything. Sentries huddled in their coats. Their noses dripped as the cold penetrated their bones while they waited for their stint to finish.

The crews got back from their leave. Archer breezed into the Mess full of energy as ever with tales of London and female conquests. Carter looked at him askance, knowing full well he was seeing one of Georgette's friends.

He got the other half of the story a few days later when he saw Georgette. Archer had thrown over his girl the first day of his leave; just like that. He had walked into her flat and just finished her there and then and walked out the door leaving her high and dry. Georgette had spent hours on the telephone, listening to the tears and trying to piece her back together.

It was a side to Archer no one saw at Amber Hill. Walsh had hinted at such a ruthless streak all that time ago in the pub in Lincoln. Carter had seen glimmers of it himself in the way Archer went through replacement crew members with seeming indifference. To everyone else, he was the life and soul of the party, the press on type that oozed dash and elan that personified bomber crews in the propaganda reels.

The weather cleared slightly. In other words, the strong winds blew the clouds away but the cold and the damp persisted. Three crews were briefed for minelaying but they were scrubbed before they even took off.

The squadron did nothing more than air tests and navigation exercises for the next few days. Even bombing practice was suspended when coastal fog covered the bombing ranges at Wainfleet. The tail end of winter was having a bite, to remind you it was still there. The temperature dropped and a strong wind blew in from the east, clamping everything down. Snow fell and blanketed the field in white.

The quiet was broken one morning when the crews were called to the briefing room. Intrigued, confused, they shambled in. Obviously, it was something important, all of the command staff were stood on the stage looking very serious. Group Captain Etheridge spoke first.

"Gentlemen. Word has been received that *Prinz Eugen*, *Scharnhorst* and *Gneisenau* have put to sea." The room mumbled in excitement. Etheridge continued. "Sightings put them in the channel, hugging the French coast heading past Dover." The room rumbled again. Heading past Dover, they weren't *in* the channel, they were almost through it; halfway home. "Aircraft are being made ready now. Your task is to knock them to blazes before they get back to Germany."

The CO glanced at the clock on the wall and nodded as Etheridge looked at him.

"We're going to drop sea mines off the Frisian coast on the route they'll have to sail through." One or two voices raised in protest and Church held up a hand for quiet. "I know, there are fighter fields just inland. If the Germans get one whiff of what we're up to we're in for it, so strict radio silence is to be observed. If they don't know we're coming, we'll be fine."

For once, the natural order of the briefing was different. Linkletter came to the fore. He was more excited than usual, geed up by the suddenness of it all.

"You know, the Germans have been jolly sneaky," he said, diverging for once from his narrow field of expertise. "It's the most perfect weather to do something like this."

His hands moved in animated fashion as he detailed the weather front over the coast of Europe. He warned of low cloud base, driving rain, strong winds and the possibility of icing with the kind of enthusiasm normal people reserved for wooing their beloved.

They got changed and went out to the kites. The rain was almost horizontal and swirled around as the wind made its mind up which way to blow. They scurried aboard to get in from the cold and took off.

Linkletter's forecast was spot on. The weather was appalling. Turbulence threw them around and rain ran off the canopy in sheets. Jensen had his work cut out rubbing the perspex with a cloth as it misted up.

Carter felt a certain amount of deja vu, mine laying in daylight off the Frisians again. Woods dug out his navigational log and dredged up the route from the last time. As the enemy ships would be coming up from the west, they would fly further east and then loop back to lay their mines in the channel before heading for home.

Woods made careful note of the marks on his chart which showed where some flak ships had last been seen. In briefing, Kent could offer nothing new but Woods thought it unlikely they were still in the same place.

Near the coast, he came up from his cubbyhole back in the fuselage and stood by Carters shoulder for a while, discussing their options. He went down to the nose but saw little to aid navigation. The water looked cold and uninviting. Wind whipped spray off the wave tops, driving it in flurries across the surface. They dropped down to five hundred feet but it was no better. Roiled air off the waves made it a bumpy ride and surface mist cut visibility almost to nothing.

When the Frisians came into view, Woods came back up to the cockpit and looked around. The islands were low dark slithers of land that were barely above the water. Surf broke over rocks on the coastlines to make them visible. He looked at his chart, back out to starboard and then down at his chart again. He glanced to his left, about ten o'clock.

"That's it. Bang on." He pointed in that direction. "See the gap between those two islands, skipper?" Carter nodded. "Head for them, take a line towards the shore of the one of the left."

Jensen was impressed. Hitting their landfall after two hours in lousy visibility with nothing but dead reckoning, very well done indeed. Carter turned on the indicated course and dropped down to two hundred feet.

"Pilot to gunners, are we clear?"

Todd and Murphy span their turrets left and right. Nothing was in view but the cloud base was so low, a Jerry fighter could come diving out of nowhere.

"Good to go, boss," said Murphy from the mid upper turret.

"All clear," said Todd, his tone clipped. Down in the nose, Woods got ready. As they made the final run, he opened the bomb doors and activated the bomb release panel.

"Bomb doors open."

"One thirty, skipper," Jensen said to remind Carter. He checked the IAS and edged the throttles back slightly while Carter flew the plane. The engine note changed as they slowed down.

"One twenty," he called. Carter nodded; his attention focused on keeping them out of the water. L-London was skittering around and he was working hard to keep them pointed in the right direction.

"One gone." L-London gave a slight jump as 2,000lbs of sea mine fell away from the bomb bay. Ten seconds and the next one went, then the third, the fourth and then the fifth. The Dutch coast got nearer. Carter banked to port in a climbing turn to put the enemy coast behind them. Jensen started getting nervous, this was the time he imagined the fighters would come screaming down on them from out of the clouds. Rain lashed them all the way home.

They got back to Amber Hill damp and cold. Walsh arrived ten minutes after them. Carter and the rest of his crew waited as they taxied up to dispersal. Walsh gave him a relieved wave as they shut down. The ground crew shoved chocks in front of the main wheels as the big propellers span to a stop.

A truck took them to interrogation but there wasn't much to tell. They hadn't seen anything going out or back. Considering all the excitement it was all very boring. They hung around once they had been spoken to, waiting to see the rest of the boys come in.

Everett showed up twenty minutes later. He'd gone further east than them and had some fun dodging a flight of 110's out on the prowl. Salmon had gone back and forth for half an hour before getting a fix to drop his mines. Visibility off the Dutch coast was dreadful when he arrived and it had taken some effort to find their target area. It got worse on the way home and he had flown at two hundred feet all the way back to stay out of the clag.

Walsh and Carter went for food after Everett hinted they might be going out again later in the day. No one got changed, it was cold and Carter couldn't be bothered to put his uniform on. The prospect of going out again in these conditions filled him with dread.

32 - Left Hand, Right Hand

Taking advantage of the horrendous weather, the Germans had timed their breakout well. The conditions hampered the efforts to find and attack the Battleships as they swept up The Channel, past the Frisian Islands to reach friendly ports. It was frustrating for the bomber crews. Big juicy targets were at sea and the weather was conspiring to make them hard to find.

News filtered through from some of the other squadrons. While 363 had been out laying mines, a lot of 5 Group had been sent to try and find the Battleships and bomb them. In the rotten weather, most of them had hared around like blind mice in the dark. Few aircraft found the ships. Those that did were mauled by flak and escorting fighters as they attacked piecemeal and paid the price. Suddenly laying mines didn't sound so bad.

There was a lot of grumbling about the navy. The Channel was supposed to be their backyard. Hadn't a navy officer had even come to their briefing and told them they were expecting these Battleships to be moving soon? Quite how three German Battleships and their escorting Destroyers had managed to sneak through The Channel without getting spotted until they go to Dover was the big mystery. They avidly read the news headlines the next few days but there was scant detail.

The escape of the Battleships caused a monumental stink in the press. Old Adolf had cocked a snook at England in their own playground and it smarted. Kent was pumped for information but he had nothing new to add. Intelligence had the ships in the German ports, tucked up for bed.

Church and the flight commanders were whisked to Group for a conference. Everyone knew where there'd be going next. They'd missed them at Brest, they'd got through The Channel, it would be natural to go after them again.

The next two nights were frustrating. 363 were briefed to go back out both nights. The first time to lay more mines off the Frisians, the second was a trip to Aachen. Both operations were scrubbed late. The crews had been driven out to the aircraft and had started up before they were cancelled. It was a lot of pissed off people that traipsed back to the crew room to get changed. The ground crews were just as unimpressed. Late scrubs caused a lot of extra work for them. The aircraft had to be debombed, guns had to be taken out of the turrets and ammunition shoved back into boxes.

Amber Hill remained blanketed in white and the erks worked like mad to keep the aircraft operational. Working in the open, they froze as chilled hands fiddled with the engines. Even inside the fuselage, it was icy, the only difference was that you were out of the wind.

On the 16th February, Carter was tasked to go gardening again off the Frisians. Three of them had been picked to go while the rest of the squadron stayed home, Carter didn't know if he should feel special or note. They were briefed to take off at one hour intervals with Carter going second.

Again, they were scrubbed, but this time it was really late. They were taxying out to the runway when an Austin staff car came barreling along after them. Carter thought Todd was kidding when he told him they were being followed by a car flashing its lights. He hit the brakes and Kent went running round in front of them. He looked ridiculous standing there on the grass, giving a cut throat motion with his hand. It was an irritating twenty minutes to taxy back to dispersal and shut down.

The Manchester that had taken off the hour before them was recalled by radio. Either they didn't get the signal or the transmission was garbled. Whatever happened, they were never heard from again. A few days later a trawler picked up four bodies floating in the water.

Air Vice Marshal Baldwin was sitting in his office at Bomber Command HQ when a missive from the Air Ministry landed. He had been holding the reins for a little over a month since Pierse had been shuffled off to oblivion in the Far East. He eyed the directive on his desk with mixed feelings.

In November 1941, the axe had been poised over Bomber Commands neck. All though the winter the men had slogged through rotten weather conditions to attack their targets in small numbers to conserve the bomber force. Now they were finally being given permission to take the other arm from behind their back. The new directive gave him carte blanche to attack the targets specified therein with everything he had with no more restrictions. That was pleasing but it was small consolation after the activity of the last few days.

Questions had been asked in Parliament. Bomber Commands response, the lack of coordination with Coastal Command and other issues had been laid bare. Armchair generals who had never been closer to an aircraft than the pre-war pageants at Hendon picked over these questions like Hyenas ripping into an animal carcass.

Acting on the intelligence information, Baldwin had placed a number of squadrons on two hour standby in case of a breakout. In line with his orders they had been loaded with armour piercing bombs. The only problem was you needed at least 7,000ft or more of altitude for them to penetrate armour. With heavy cloud and poor visibility down to 500ft there was little chance of that. Vital time had been lost while these aircraft had been reloaded with standard HE bombs.

The fault of course lay with Coastal Command. He'd been assured of four or more hours notice of the ships sailing. Lack of reconnaissance had fouled up all the careful planning and turned it into a free for all while everyone ran around like headless chickens. His bombers had been sent out piecemeal and a good many of them had been hacked from the sky while they blundered about trying to find their targets. It was all rather embarrassing and in his view not a fair reflection on the service. When Bomber Command was already being scrutinised because of the Butt Report, it was the last thing he needed to deal with.

Despite all this, it had appeared Portal had worked his magic once again. Baldwin had no idea how much Portal was responsible for the reprieve, nor did he care. The directive was proof that they were being given a second chance.

L-London went north. Carter took them up the North Sea and then turned left when Woods had them west of Newcastle. At ten thousand feet they spotted the barrage balloons above the dockyards. The wide mouth of the Tyne was dead ahead. Two large breakwaters, one on the north bank, one on the south covered the approach to the river. On the northern headland was the remains of an old fortress. A long stretch of beach was visible north and south of the river. A few miles north off to the right was a white lighthouse on some rocks.

He went between them, firing off the colours of the day as they flew over Whitley Bay and headed inland. He waited until Woods had them turn south before he shouted out a fighter attack and took L-London through a series of gut wrenching corkscrews.

Vos hung on for grim death as his stomach lurched. He grunted as the big bomber bottomed out of its dive. He let his head rest on the little table as his weight trebled, quadrupled. He could hear his breath rasping through his nostrils as he sucked down oxygen. He went light in his seat as they went up again and Carter levelled off at the top of the climb.

"That wasn't too bad," Carter said to himself. He handed over control to Jensen and watched as the younger man kept them on course, correcting for drift, barely moving the controls. Carter was impressed. Jensen was an instinctive pilot and he was not sure what much else he needed to learn. He leaned over and whispered in Jensen's ear. Jensen nodded his eyes crinkling in good humour behind his flying goggles. Carter tightened his straps, kept his feet and hands clear of the controls and switched his intercom on.

"Fighters! Fighters! Corkscrew port. GO!"

Todd was soaked when his mug of tea went flying. His hands flailed but he lost his grip on his flask and its contents were sprayed over the inside of the turret. Woods banged his head on the corner of the navigation table as he was reaching for his log book and pencils. He rubbed his temple and turned the air blue as the engines howled at full throttle.

Carter let them go through two more gyrations before giving Jensen the thumbs up and taking back control. Before anyone could gather their wits, he took L-London down in a steep dive. Leveling off at two thousand feet he let the bomber run, using the speed built up in the dive to fly along the valley, following the route of the South Tyne river. They flew the length of the valley to Barnard Castle and then Carter stood the Manchester on its starboard wingtip and headed south east towards Lincoln.

"Bloody hell, skipper," said Murphy, thumbing the mike. "You should be charging for this. It's like being at a fairground."

Carter laughed like a drain.

The big joke was when they got home. Just as they shut down, there was a tinkling sound from the port engine as the prop windmilled to a stop. It jerked to a sudden halt and there was a final crunch. Latimer felt it as much as heard it and he was scrambling up a ladder even before they got out.

The exhausts pinged as they cooled. Latimer had a cowling off in double quick time and passed it down. The engine radiated heat as he shone a torch inside letting the light play up towards the front end of the block. Bits of metal came tumbling down onto the concrete from the reduction gear.

After more days of late scrubs and confusion and with the weather worsening, Church called Group. Europe was blanketed in a cloud bank and the Battleships were back in their kennels so there was nothing doing. 363 was stood down and Church released the men for the day.

The crews couldn't get off the station fast enough. After days of hanging around Amber Hill, they had run out of magazines and newspapers to read and seeing the same four walls was getting boring. They hopped on the trucks and buses and headed to Lincoln en masse.

Carter rang Wilkinson at Group to ask about Helen but there was no answer. He resisted the urge to call Georgette. Ringing her in her office would be unfair and might embarrass her. He had a snooze in his room then went to the Mess for lunch, retiring to the smoking room to let his food settle. He pawed at the magazines but nothing tickled his fancy. The newspapers were days old and he had no energy to read about the continuing advance of the Japanese. He had a wander and found Walsh in the lounge reading a book.

"I'd have thought you'd have gone to town?"

"Skint," replied Walsh, his voice monotone while he focused on his book. Carter settled himself in the armchair across from him. He caught a steward's eye and asked for a beer. Carter heard snatches of someone playing the piano in the bar as the lounge doors opened and closed. The clock ticked loudly.

Carter twisted his mouth and drummed his fingers on the sofa. He levered himself up and walked over to the sideboard. He opened one of the cabinet doors and dug out a chess board and a box of pieces. He walked back over to Walsh. He held up two pawns, one white, one black.

"Fancy a game?"

Walsh looked over the top of his novel. There was an obvious pause while he thought about it, then he closed the book with a snap and put it on the side table next to him.

"Why not?"

They began laying the board. Carter pointed at the side table.

"What were you reading?"

"Detective novel." Walsh glanced back at the spine to remind himself of the title. "*The Case of the Screaming Man.*" Carter grunted.

"Never heard of it."

"Neither had I."

"Any good?"

Walsh shrugged. He had been reading without really absorbing anything. He would have been pushed to name the main characters if Carter asked him.

With the board set, Walsh moved first as white, advancing a pawn two spaces. Both of them played without really concentrating. They were like two house cats. Bored, but too lazy to expend any energy doing anything else. Even walking from their billet to the Mess had been an effort. The wind cut through you and it reminded Carter sharply of his little stroll in the countryside on New Years Eve.

They won two games each. The hands wound round the clock. A few people turned up, said hello and went through to the bar. It got dark outside. As they were setting up for another game, Saunderson came rushing into the lounge like scalded cats, buzzing with energy as he looked this way and that.

"Drop the game, chaps. Bit of a flap on," he said in a rush.

That got their attention. Kent's head appeared round the double doors. He hooked a thumb over his shoulder.

"Come on, Harold. I've got them from the bar."

"Follow me," Saunderson told them. "There's a rush job on."

Without waiting for a reply, he was already heading for the door. Carter and Walsh were hot on his heels. In the time it took them to get their coats and caps, Saunderson was well ahead, waiting for no one. They skipped to catch up as the tannoy crackled into life calling all available aircrew to report to the briefing room immediately.

Church and Everett were waiting for them. Group Captain Etheridge arrived in his staff car the same time Carter and Walsh got down from their truck. They quickly snapped to attention and fired off a salute as Etheridge went straight past them in the gathering gloom, his face set, his attention focused elsewhere.

Saunderson disappeared in the trucks in a cloud of blue exhaust smoke. Fish Salmon rounded the corner leading a pack of Flight Sergeants. A few more bodies trailed across in the distance. Some jogged, one or two rode bicycles across the snow encrusted grass, the wheels leaving a dark trail behind them, like slugs on a patio. They settled themselves down, the atmosphere in the room electric as Etheridge took the stage.

"Gentlemen. It would appear that Jerry has been getting a bit cocky. Not content with trailing their coat tails under our noses a few days ago, it would seem that *Prinz Eugen* has been gadding about again. The only difference is that this time, a submarine has slammed some torpedoes into her fat behind and she is now sheltering in a Norwegian fjord near Trondheim." There was a rustle of interest. "The Royal Navy are going in for the kill and will strike using aircraft from a carrier." The buzz of excitement ratcheted up a few more notches. "We are going to clear a path for the Fleet Air Arm and make diversionary raids on Luftwaffe airfields." The excitement became consternation. He looked at the assembled throng and nodded to Church. "Carry on."

The room came to attention as Etheridge left the stage and strode down the central aisle. Church stepped up, looking at the men. There was not one complete crew in front of him with most of the squadron off the station doing god knows what. He thought someone had been kidding when he answered the telephone in his office. Rounding up the men was going to be difficult; they had a few hours head start and could have scattered all over the place with money burning a hole in their pockets. He'd had to move fast. The groundcrews were getting the aircraft ready while Saunderson had been tasked to round up whoever he could lay his hands on as quickly as possible.

"Listen. We're going to attack the fighter airfield at Stavanger." His voice dropped into a pit of silence.

After Etheridge had said *Prinz Eugen* was in Norway, the navigator's in the room had done some maths in their head and the sums didn't come out too well. It was a long way, not far off the limits for the Manchester. What was worse was the long run over water there and back. If anyone had engine trouble they'd be ending up in the drink and they all knew the odds of surviving in the frigid waters of the North Sea at this time of year.

Kent saved the final touch while they were getting ready. They had to attack Stavanger before first light, shortly before the fish heads were due to launch their raid. Under no circumstances were they to attempt a daylight attack over a fighter airfield. He made his instructions very clear. If they couldn't make it in time, they were to dump their bombs and come home.

Woods thought about that as he went through his locker, making sure he had everything. Although Carter flew the plane, it was his job as navigator to get them there and back; a lot would depend on him. The thing was, there wasn't much he could do this time. There was no big dogleg they could cut short; it was straight out and straight back. A lot would depend on the predicted winds, particularly on the way out.

He shoved a few spare pencils into his navigator's bag and two more down the side of his left flying boot. He emptied his pockets of personal items and chucked the bits and pieces into the locker before closing the door. He clumped down the aisle and went outside. The cool air was refreshing and he unzipped his jacket slightly, letting the cold get in.

Carter looked around the crew room as he dressed. No one had a complete crew and everyone was talking over each other wondering what they were supposed to do. Kent and Church walked into the middle of the babble and shouted for quiet.

"We need to hustle on this chaps. No point waiting around to make up your regular crew. Get your heads together, sort yourselves out and get down to the kites as soon as you can."

The noise started again as they tried to organise. It was like being back at OTU, when they had stood in hangars and got together. People shouted, "need a nav here. Gunners, we need gunners!"

Order came out of the chaos and Carter picked up two gunners from the room. He went out the door with Jensen and Vos to stand by Woods. Vos had his jacket under one arm and his parachute harness over his shoulder. He dumped them on the ground and checked the pockets on his short battledress, hunting for a packet of cigarettes. Woods gave him one and the Belgian cupped his hand to shield the match from the breeze.

A truck took them out to dispersal and Carter looked across at his two new additions. One of them, Anderson was casually smoking a cigarette, completely calm. A ten op man, he had flown with three crews already so this was nothing new for him. He was a journeyman who bounced around from one crew to another.

The other, Paulson, had been Dickinson's tail gunner. This was his first time going back out on an op and he was quiet with mixed feelings of guilt and relief that he was still here. When the Flight Commander had gone down over Brest, Paulson had been in a warm hospital bed with a bad cold and swollen glands.

Vos stared back at him with his usual laconic expression, passive blue eyes hooded, guarded. Woods looked fed up. Carter arched an eyebrow at him but the big Canadian just shrugged and moodily stared at the floor of the truck, shuffling his feet. Jensen was the only one who seemed eager to go. Carter marked that up to his inexperience.

L-London was still being bombed up as they arrived. Latimer and the erks were rushing around, doing the final checks. Snow had been brushed off the wings and fuselage and the canopy was being polished as they got down from the trucks. Carter turned as Walsh called over to him.

"Hey, Alex."

"You ready?" Carter asked his room mate. Walsh's mouth twisted and he looked genuinely worried. He only had Nicol with him, the rest of his crew had gone to town so he had a real pick and mix. His gunners were two first timers fresh out of OTU and the navigator had only done two trips. Walsh looked around to see who was in earshot but everyone else was too busy.

"Look, no blame on the lad but a rush job like this with no prep is not the way I want to find out if my man is any cop as a navigator. Can I tag along after you?"

"Sure. Just follow me in."

Walsh looked visibly relieved and they shook hands before going to their respective aircraft. Latimer was waiting for Carter under the nose. Fresh snow was starting to fall and the wind was beginning to rise again. Latimer blew into a handkerchief.

"Sorry, sir." He wiped his nose. "She's all ready for you." He held out the form 700 on a clipboard. Carter took it and began his walk around. He peered into the long bomb bay while the armourers were still in the process of winching up the last bomb. He left them to it and walked towards the tail.

They took off ten minutes later. Latimer blew into his handkerchief again as he watched them go. The snow was getting heavier.

They took off into the night. It was just under five hundred miles to Stavanger in a straight run which left very little in reserve in case of problems. The crew was silent as they flew on. Murphy and Todd scanned the inky black sky, occasionally seeing a shower of exhaust sparks from another aircraft heading in the same direction as them. Some elected to go high but Carter kept them at 4,000ft. Linkletter had told them there could be heavy clouds on the way over and the last thing he wanted was to ice up the wings and props.

Heading east as they crossed the coast, Carter looked left over his shoulder. Walsh was still there, a few hundred yards away keeping loose formation on him. The atmosphere on board was grim. Everyone was unsettled at the rushed nature of the raid. Being given a point on a map to go to and told to figure out the rest yourself didn't fill a chap with much confidence.

They picked up a headwind and were surrounded by flurries of snow. Woods started tapping a pencil off his teeth as he did some sums on a scratch pad. He had Jensen get the readings off the fuel gauges so he could figure out their consumption. Jensen was wary as he watched the engine temperatures slowly climb. They could keep the engines going full belt for a while but sooner or later they would have to back off and give them a break.

They flew on in the dark, the thick clouds stacked up ahead of them as the headwind increased. Carter peered through the gloom and could see the dark sky starting to lighten. The deep blues and blacks were tinged with purple as the first rays of day were creeping over the horizon. It got slowly lighter as each minute passed. Carter glanced at his watch.

"Talk to me, Woody."

The silence was agonising. Woods checked his sums, crossed one set of figures out and added them up again.

"Can I flip a coin?" he asked, his voice tinged with strain. "It's going to start getting light at 0540 hours. If the headwind doesn't get any worse, we can *just* make it, but it's going to be close."

"Five to one," Paulson muttered, voicing what everyone else was thinking.

"Cute, but keep the R/T clear please," Carter admonished.

They carried on while Carter considered what to do. Ultimately it was his decision. He never held with polling opinions on this sort of thing. He was the aircraft commander; it was up to him.

It wasn't just the attack he was concerned with. He wanted to drop his bombs in the dark and be on his way home before the lightening sky left them standing out like a pair of Bulldogs bollocks. Going in late, the defences would be stirred up, and if fighters managed to get airborne, they were dead. He hated turning back but there was pressing on and there was pushing your luck. He waggled his wings to let Walsh know what he was doing as he gently guided L-London round the turn.

As they were briefing at Amber Hill, Todd and Murphy were playing darts in *The Crown*. Near to closing time, the pub was heaving. It felt like all of 5 Group had descended on the place. Murphy kept looking over to the bar, seeing Muriel moving back and forth, serving drinks. Every so often she looked over to him when she had a moment. He checked his watch. Another half hour or so and he could have some fun.

Todd stubbed out a cigarette and lit another one. He took a long drag on it and then threw his three darts. Fifty five, pathetic. Murphy marked it up on the blackboard to the left of the dart board. They changed places. Murphy fired off his three darts in quick succession, one after another. Two double tops and a twenty. Todd grimaced and added one hundred to Murphy's score.

"You going to tell her?" he asked Murphy.

"Nope. No plans to change anything." He gave Muriel a little wave while he stood leaning against the wall, his left hand on top of the dart board.

Todd's mouth twisted in disapproval. He shot a look towards the bar, caught Muriel's eye and tried to give her an encouraging smile. She scowled at him in return.

Todd sighed and fired off a dart which hit the board well above the scoring area, a mere inch or so from Murphy's hand. Murphy tugged his hand back in reaction.

"Hey," he warned.

"Sorry," muttered Todd. "My judgement must be a bit off." He threw another one well wide to the left, not far from where Murphy was standing. His third one went into the bullseye. Murphy glared at him. Before he could make a cutting reply there was some shouting at the bar.

Flanked by some SP's, Kent was stood on the bar shouting for attention. When he got a modicum of quiet, he called for any 363 squadron aircrew to come forward. Todd and Murphy pushed through the press of bodies to make themselves known.

"Here, sir."

"Outside," Kent said brusquely. "Trucks are waiting." This was his fourth stop so far and he was in no mood to explain himself again and again. Murphy leaned over the bar and planted a quick kiss on Muriel's lips.

"Save me a drink, love, I'll be back later."

"Hey, lover boy," said Kent. "Move your arse."

As soon as they got back to Amber Hill, they were taken straight to the crew room to get ready. Fish Salmon was waiting to tell them what was going on. They sorted themselves out as they got ready. Murphy ended up with Tudor's crew. Todd got lucky and was going out with Salmon.

Carter watched from the interrogation room as big fat flakes of white settled on the ground and started to pile up. The iron grey clouds moved in, driven by heavy winds and visibility dropped even further.

He didn't completely relax until Todd and Murphy appeared. Murphy got back with Tudor just after 8am. They had got within twenty miles of the coast before deciding to turn back.

Fish Salmon got in not long after. He made a nice three point landing, flaring on final approach and putting his Manchester down with finesse even in the lousy weather.

The atmosphere at Amber Hill was odd, not at all like normal operations. Everyone was hanging around waiting for people to get back. Everything had been so rushed and so piecemeal, no check had been kept of who was flying with who. As each aircraft came in, they waited to see who got down from the trucks to get changed.

Saunderson rang round to see if anyone put down elsewhere. No one had. By the end of the day only Archers aircraft was missing. The press on man had perhaps pressed on once too often. Walsh felt the loss keenly, but not because Archer was gone. He couldn't care less about Archer, but his wireless op and tail gunner had been flying with him. Walsh stayed up well past time in the Ops room waiting for a phone call that never came.

33 - New Broom

Prinz Eugen had gotten away with it again. In the Channel she had been shelled by coastal batteries at Dover but they had just caused a bunch of big splashes in the water. Some MTB's had a go but the escorts had driven them off. Five British Destroyers were next but had missed with their torpedoes.

Getting torpedoed by a British submarine had been a bit of bad luck, but the navy had been hampered by the same bad weather as 363 and the Fleet Air Arm strike sent to finish her off was an abject failure. *Prinz Eugen* waited in her fjord, blowing raspberries at them, daring them to have another go.

After such a panicked mess, Bomber Command had a halfhearted stab at Wilhelmshaven that same night. There was a floating dock there the Germans might use to repair *Prinz Eugen* when she got back to home territory. The clouds got in the way again and most aircraft bombed blind, dropping their loads all over the place.

363 had no part of that so Church used the lull of the next few days to consolidate his squadron. After the chaos of the run to Norway, he had the crews up on training flights to settle themselves back down and return to the normality of routine.

After a suitable pause, Archers parents received the standard letter from the Air Ministry. Church sent a more personal missive, extolling Archers virtues of pressing on, his cool courage under fire and how well he was regarded on the squadron. It was a nice letter but it did little to dry a mother's tears.

Saunderson was in for a surprise when he packed up Archer's stuff. There was a neat pile of letters waiting for him on the bedside cabinet and his clothes were all tidy in the cupboard. There was a cheque to settle the outstanding Mess bill and five pounds for the ground crew as a thank you for looking after him. His Swiss watch was in an envelope with a note asking it to be returned to his father. The keys for his yellow car lay on top of a scribbled note with a question mark and the line, *'give it to someone who can use it, Uncle.'*

Saunderson gathered everything up and took it back to his office to check carefully. This was the part of his job he hated the most. Having to do this three or four times a week wore a man down. Crews came and went, but the administrative staff like him had to count the names and do all the work. It had reached the point where he couldn't picture them anymore, they had just blended into a homogeneous, anonymous mass. It was not that Saunderson didn't care, he did, but it was the only way he could get through the day. While the men were on the squadron, he did his best to make sure their needs were met, but once they were gone, they just faded away.

Going through the personal effects, he shook his head at how men seemed to know when they needed to get their affairs in order. He glanced through Archers journal but there was nothing secret written down and no smut that would embarrass his family. He tossed it onto the acceptable pile. He noted the letter to a girl in London. It was full of the usual platitudes, *'you're a great girl, I'm sorry I won't be there, embrace life, don't wait around expecting me to come back through that door.'* He read it and then sealed the envelope.

The newspaper clippings about the DFC he put with the medal in its box. He glanced at it when he opened the lid, the silver wings of the cross glinting under the light. He ran his fingers over the white and purple ribbon and then snapped the lid shut.

In the end there were no surprises. It looked like Archer had tidied up after himself quite well. Saunderson put his flying log, journal and other bits and pieces into a box so it could be sent to his family in the next few days. He twirled the car keys around his finger while he pondered what to do about them.

At Bomber Command there was a change as well. Baldwin was gone, shuffled off and away. He didn't even go back to 3 Group to resume his old job. Portal wanted a new broom to start fresh and he found it in Arthur Harris.

In the early part of the war, Harris had commanded 5 Group before spending some time as Deputy Chief of the Air Staff. A veteran of the first war, Harris had stayed in the RAF during the lean years and served in Mesopotamia, Persia and India. During the almost annual tribal uprisings he had chopped holes in the noses of his Vickers Vernon transport aircraft and fitted them with bomb racks. To those who didn't know him, he could appear bullish, almost arrogant. To those that did, he was firecracker of energy who tolerated fools not at all and was driven with a single minded purpose in achieving his objectives.

For Harris that meant proving that strategic bombing alone could win the war. In the American Civil War, General Sherman had been one of the first proponents of the concept of total war. He had posited that dislocating the civilian population from being able to support the war effort was as important as the destruction of purely military targets. Harris had fully embraced this theory of war.

In the modern era, what that meant was the pummelling of

German industry, the Ruhr and other big targets to cripple their ability to wage war. Attacks on Coventry had shown what affect heavy bombing could have on cities and on the morale of its citizens and Harris wanted to do the same to the Nazi war machine.

Harris knew how difficult it was to navigate at night. Commanding the first heavy bomber squadron he had trained his crews hard for night operations. Despite all the advances in aviation since the First World War, navigation still came down to a man's individual talent and their ability to grope their way over a darkened continent. Even the most skilled navigators found it difficult and for some, it was no better than randomly sticking pins in a map and hoping you jabbed the right bit.

While serving on the Air Staff, he knew there was technology coming that would change that, but during his first few days at Bomber Command HQ he took stock of his stable. He had inherited a force that on paper totaled nearly five hundred aircraft, but bare numbers as always only told half the story.

Eighty percent of his bombers were still the aircraft that Bomber Command had started the war with, Whitley's, Hampdens and Wellingtons. Medium bombers, they lacked the ability to carry really heavy loads which is what it was going to take to get the job done. Harris found that frustrating.

In 1935 he had been one of those pushing for a four engined heavy bomber when such ideas were out of fashion. Now he was being given the tools to prove his theory right as the new Halifaxes, Stirlings and Manchesters were starting to come out of the factories in increasing numbers. The directives from Portal and the Air Ministry gave him the room to get the job done.

The bigger danger was his strength being hived off to satisfy the demands of Coastal Command and the Middle Eastern theater. Now the Japanese were in the war, the Far East was also making demands on the strained resources at his disposal.

He needed time to bring his command up to strength, introduce the new navigational aids and get everything working the way he wanted. Whatever he thought of the Butt Report personally, it had shown that raids needed to be concentrated to saturate the defences.

Harris knew he would no longer allow his crews to be easy pickings to the German flak and fighters. He also knew he needed to increase the tempo of operations to put the Germans under pressure, to give them no chance to recover or adjust and above all, not scatter his strength all over the place.

He called his Group Commanders to HQ for a conference and started to lay out what he wanted to do and what he expected from them in the months to come.

34 - When Luck Finally Runs Out

The appointment of Harris as their new Chief attracted little comment. As men came and went on the squadron, so did commanders. They would wait and see. He didn't keep them waiting long. It was no great secret that Harris was not a fan of the Royal Navy. He had once commented that of three things that shouldn't be allowed on a yacht, one of them was a naval officer. As much as he wanted to get stuck into German industrial targets, he recognised that Bomber Command had unfinished business that needed taking care of first.

Prinz Eugen was out of the way in Norway. Intelligence reported she had heavy damage to her stern and wouldn't be going anywhere for a while so that left *Scharnhorst* and *Gneisenau* in Kiel. Both of them had been damaged during that headlong dash up The Channel but they were still as big a threat as they had been at Brest.

Photo reconnaissance showed both of them were in docks. While the weather forecast was bad, it was a good moon period and a coastal target would make it an easy navigational problem for the crews to find their way there and back. The orders went out to go for Kiel.

Walsh said little in the two hours between briefing and takeoff. Normally he either slept or he talked like there was no tomorrow. This time, he remained silent and brooding while he lay on his bed. Carter asked what was wrong but got a noncommittal grunt in return.

Figuring he would speak when he was ready Carter went back to his writing. He finished a letter for White, telling him about the mess of the last few days, putting in as much as he dared. He wrote a longer more heartfelt letter for Georgette. They had seen little of each other the last week or so and only spoken twice on the telephone. Even those calls had been brief, but when he got back, he wrote, he promised her they would see more of each other. He eyed the car keys on the bedside cabinet and considered himself very fortunate indeed.

Two days ago, Saunderson had knocked on his door. Casting an eye over Walsh's unmade bed, he had swept his flying boots off the mattress and sat down. Carter was sitting across from him, intrigued by the reason for the visit. Saunderson had never called before now and he was not his usual smiling self so Carter knew something was up. Saunderson had danced around the subject at first, talking about opportunities and how funny it was how certain things turned out. Finally, he produced the keys to Archer's car.

"He told me to give them to someone who could use it," he said as he handed them over.

"Why me?" asked Carter. "I wasn't a particular friend. What about his family?"

"Because I reckon he would prefer it was kept at the squadron. If his family have it, it'll only end up sitting on bricks getting dusty in some garage. They can't get 100 octane fuel like you lot can." Saunderson saw Carters eyebrows rise in surprise. "Oh yes, I know about the fiddles you lot pull. The old man turns a blind eye to it so I do as well. Archer let you drive it before, so I reckon he trusted you, certainly enough to drive his car anyway."

Carter weighed the keys in his hand and Saunderson read that as a refusal.

"If you don't want-," Carter clenched his hand around the keys, the points digging into his palm.

"No, it's not that. I was just surprised that's all."

"Your welcome."

Duty done, Saunderson made for the door. Carter's voice stopped him.

"If anything happens to me-" his voice trailed off. Saunderson caught the meaning.

"I'll pass it on, old boy. Never fear."

Saunderson walked off back to his office, shaking his head at the strange way grown men could talk about their own death in such an abstract way. They were all loonies the lot of them.

Carter glanced at his watch and got up. He'd gotten cold last time out on the run to Norway and he rummaged in his drawers, looking for a fresh pair of long johns. He got changed while Walsh continued to stew on his bed. He put on a thicker pair of socks and then tried them with his flying boots, wiggling his toes. Happier, he put his trousers back on, then his shirt and a white turtleneck sweater his mother had sent him.

"You look like you're going to sea," murmured Walsh. "You just need the beard to complete the look."

"No chance," Carter made a face. "I get sick as a dog on boats. Horrible things. They rock, they go up and down, you get wet." He shuddered. "No, not for me."

That seemed to break the mood and Walsh got up smiling. He talked about the penny ferry he had ridden growing up as a boy in Liverpool. His father had been one of the masters and many was the time his father let him at the wheel as a treat. The old man was crushed when he'd joined the RAF, he'd set his heart on his son becoming a sailor.

They walked to the crew room to get ready. This was the first time Walsh would be flying an op with his new gunner and radio op. He'd kept Paulson which pleased all parties after the Norway debacle. Paulson had lost one crew and was happy that he was going to an experienced bunch of blokes. The radio op, Taylor was just as happy to get a crew after bouncing around as a temporary replacement for so long. After a few days they had been accepted into the fold like long lost brothers.

Carters crew gathered round the small table at interrogation. The WAAF started filling out the details on her clipboard, the serial number of the aircraft, it's squadron code letter, pilot etc. Carter relaxed while he munched on a sandwich and sipped from a cup of tea. His cheeks were frozen but the rest of him was toasty. Murphy lit up and drew the smoke of the cigarette in deep, feeling it warm him, before releasing it in a long stream through his nostrils.

He glanced at the WAAF, a pretty little thing she was, with a cute button nose and curly red hair. Not a patch on Muriel of course, but still, she was pretty. He shot a look at Todd who caught his eye. The Australian was still on his case about Joan and it rankled that he was being judged like that. Carter did the talking, not that there was much to tell. If Harris had been wanting revenge, his hopes were to be dashed.

"Awful weather, never found the target, bombed something, came home. Anything else?" Carter asked tartly. The WAAF clicked her tongue in annoyance as she wrote notes on the form. Her green eyes flashed as she fixed Carter with a stern gaze.

"You know there is," she said sharply. Carter slurped his tea while he thought about how to put it.

"Cock up. You can tell whoever the bright spark is at Group or HQ that said the weather would be clear over the target that they need to read their maps again. We had clumps of thick cloud all the way and it was bloody cold."

Linkletter had briefed them for heavy cloud on the way over. It had actually been better than that, with no low lying clouds at all, but there had been squalls of rain and a persistent ground haze that made navigating difficult. Woods had managed to get a good fix as they passed north of Heligoland but after that it had been pure guesswork.

"The winds weren't as forecast either," put in Woods. "It kept trying to push us south of track. Quite a few must have been put off course because there was a lot of flak and rubbish in the sky near Wilhelmshaven." He glanced at his log. "At least one aircraft, maybe two went down south of us by about ten or fifteen miles." Murphy had reported a flash and a streak of flame zooming to the ground at the time. The WAAF kept on writing.

"Any fighters?" she asked him. Woods grunted and leaned back, looking over at his pilot. Todd and Murphy glanced at each other and then looked at their navigator. The WAAF looked to each of them, waiting for someone to fill the silence. She had nice hands, Woods noticed, pale and smooth, with long fingers. She lifted one eyebrow, her eyes boring right into him. Carter gestured towards him.

"It's your show, Woody."

Woods cleared his throat as he started the tale. Close to the target, he had gone down to the nose. There was nothing to see, just an unending wave of gray cloud, the fluffy tops limned by moonlight. He was mesmerised for a while, watching their shadow undulating up and down over the cloud tops, like a horse taking a succession of jumps. The hairs on the back of his arm had stood on end when he had seen a smaller shadow running parallel to them to port.

He'd called out a fighter over the R/T and Carter had taken immediate evasive action. L-London responded like a thoroughbred and twisted and turned, climbing and diving to throw off their pursuer. No one shot at them. No one else saw a thing but the shadow never reappeared.

Telling the story hours later Woods felt a fool. He wondered if his imagination had played tricks on him. On the way back, Todd and Murphy had some fun, promising to buy him a sack load of carrots to help him see in the dark.

The actual attack had been a farce. The target had been blanketed in a thick ground haze and flurries of snow had made getting a fix nigh on impossible. After the second time around, Carter had come in from the north east, heading in from over the sea where it was clear. It was a timed run; all they could manage with the city covered by cloud. Woods counted them down off his navigator's watch and let the bombs go on the biggest patch of flashes that lit up the clouds from below. For all they knew they could just as easily be dropping on a flak battery as the Battleships. Some raids were like that, moments of blind terror punctuating the boredom.

"Happy now?" Carter asked. He rolled the piece of greaseproof paper the sandwich had been wrapped in into a ball and threw it towards the bin in the corner. It missed by a country mile and skittered across the floor.

"I think I've got everything," the WAAF said primly.

Woods lingered as they left, he wanted to stay something to her but the next crew shouldered him out of the way to give their report. She glanced once in his direction before turning her attention to the next crew.

Harris sent them back the next night. Carter got the feeling if they didn't get the Battleships tonight, they would keep going back until they did. He was concerned when he saw the route marked on the map in the briefing room was the same one they'd used the previous night. He wasn't his usual relaxed self when the crew got together before take off. Normally there would be a few words of encouragement from him but not tonight. He bumped heads with Woods and discussed altering their track slightly to take them wide of the main route, just enough to put a bit of distance between them and the run in.

There was little change from the previous night. After soldiering through the heavy clouds over the North Sea, mainland Europe was relatively clear. There were broken clouds in layers up to about ten thousand feet with persistent haze clinging to the ground. The moon was brighter tonight. That made the difference for Woods to get a fix and they sailed into the attack with Kiel laid out below them like a photograph. Everything was where it should be. *Scharnhorst* was tied up alongside the quay and *Gneisenau* was in a dry dock.

He got a good sight on the approach and some fires started by earlier bombing let him see what the wind was doing. He guided Carter with small adjustments to correct for drift.

"Left. Left a bit, skipper."

The bomb doors opened and Carter flinched as a flak burst exploded to their left. The cockpit lit up with a bright flash and the big bomber rocked in the shockwave of the explosion. Vos jumped as a bit of shrapnel landed on his desk in front of him.

In the tail, Todd was concentrating, his eyes scanning the sky. He felt every jolt as the aircraft dipped and bobbed on the roiling air over the target. The nearest he could equate it to was being in the rear car on a rollercoaster, so you got all the jolts and lurches after everyone else. He listened to the R/T, willing Woods to get on with it.

"Left, left, skipper. More left, there's a breeze shoving us over."

Carter used more rudder. He could feel the wind pushing on them and L-London was almost crabbing sideways.

"Steady, steady." They were nearly there when his thought process was broken by a massive flash. The dry dock suddenly lit up in stark relief. It looked like the whole front of the ship had disintegrated as a huge explosion reached skywards. Spots danced in front of his eyes and he shook his head to clear them. He sighted on the rush of flames, waited two more seconds and then hit the release.

"BOMBS GONE!" he shouted in the excitement of the moment.

Carter dived away to port after the camera took its picture, heading north, out over the water. Woods came up from the nose, jubilant, his eyes shining. He leaned in close to Carter and shouted.

"Bloody marvellous, skip. You should have seen it! Someone got right on the money tonight." He gave an excited thumbs up and almost floated back to his seat. He'd never seen anything like that. Normally, he saw bombs exploding amongst factories and buildings. Some ammo or something must have gone up to produce a huge explosion like that. As they headed home, a huge plume of smoke went billowing into the air, hanging over Kiel as the flak guns continued to send up their barrage.

They were in buoyant mood when they got back. After the recent weeks of minelaying and duff weather it felt like they had actually earned their pay for once. This was what it was all about, hitting the target and getting home to tell the tale.

The recce photos showed the full story later in the day. The whole front of the *Gneisenau*, forward of the bridge structure was blackened and smoking. Fire crews could be seen still spraying water on the hull. By all reports, *Scharnhorst* had hit at least one mine during that headlong dash up The Channel and would have to be repaired before she could put to sea. *Gneisenau* was clearly out of commission and *Prinz Eugen* was stuck in Norway. That was that. After more than one thousand sorties, the three bogeymen had finally been laid low. *Tirpitz* was still lurking up in Norway but they could worry about her later. Harris was pleased. The Royal Navy was more pleased. Too many ships had been kept in reserve in case these monsters ever put to sea. Those ships could now be freed up for convoy duty and other action.

35 - Without, Which, Not

Carter papped the horn. After talking to Georgette the night before, he had been counting the hours until he could see her. The gossip round the station was that ops were off but it wasn't until after breakfast that Group stood them down. He covered the short distance to Grantham and parked outside her digs. Mrs Lloyd stared balefully at him through the net curtains. Georgette came down the steps and got in the car. She kissed him quickly and yelped as he let in the clutch and they were off.

He drove into the countryside, weaving along the narrow lanes. Georgette gripped the door handle tightly with one hand while the other clung on to her seat.

"Careful darling, I would like to get there in one piece." Carter grinned and let his foot off the accelerator. The lithe sports car slowed down a fraction. "Incidentally, where are we going?" she asked him.

"A little place in the country someone told me about," he said, distracted as he spotted a truck ahead of them coming in the opposite direction. He slowed down and pulled over to give it room to get by on the narrow road.

Saunderson had told him about this place a week or so ago when Carter had been pondering where to take Georgette. Carter was getting sick of Lincoln and he wanted to get away from having eyes on him.

The Fairfax coaching inn straddled the road between Grantham and Skegness. It was a lovely old fashioned building, built as a square around a central courtyard. Two sides were the inn, another the old stables, some of which had also been converted into rooms. The front of it was two storeys high, covered in white stucco and an archway gave entrance to the inner courtyard. The quaint old fashioned look was completed by a big thatched roof. The whole building had a feeling of being big and solid. Carter wondered how on earth Saunderson knew about the place.

Georgette was pleased to find Carter in buoyant mood. After his funk at *The Madison* she had been worried for a time, but their time in York had done wonders to settle her worries. It was good to see he'd put it all behind him.

As it was a weekend, the inn was quite busy. The locals had gathered after the morning church service and the landlord was doing brisk business. Seeing the place so crowded, Carter was expecting at least one person to collar him and expound their views about the war but they were good enough to leave him and Georgette alone.

They ordered drinks and sandwiches and waited while they were made. Carter felt like he was floating. It had been a week since he had last seen Georgette, and a month since their leave in York, it felt like forever. He watched her and she him, the unspoken connection between them strong.

Of course, she worried, he knew she did, despite what she said to reassure him but he felt closer to her than he ever had with Mary. Physically and in temperament, Mary and Georgette weren't alike at all, but it was more than that. With Mary there had always been a brittle edge to things, particularly when she moved up to Lincoln during his tour. With Georgette, he actually believed there would be a tomorrow and that perhaps was the difference.

Georgette reached across the table and held his hand, her eyes smiling. They sat like that in silence until the barmaid came with their sandwiches and drinks on a tray. Carter ate like a starving man, his appetite stimulated by the drive.

They made reservations for dinner and then went for a drive. Carter parked the car at the edge of the Fens. The wide expanse of The Wash was in front of them, mile upon mile of salt marshes and farm land. Some sheep grazed among the tough grasses. They set off along a well worn path and walked until they got to a low lying hill where the earth had been piled up to provide a break from the wind for two bench seats. One of them had a brass plate on it, but it was so worn, Carter couldn't read the inscription.

Sitting here, overlooking The Fens, it was like being in the middle of nowhere. There was not another soul in sight. A pair of Harriers swooped on the afternoon breeze, combing the ground below with their keen eyesight. Carter shaded his eyes and watched as suddenly, one of them braked in flight, its wings spread wide and then it stooped, going down like a rocket. It flared at the last moment, talons extended and landed on something.

Georgette snuggled up to him, holding him close. He chuckled and she asked what he was laughing about.

"You," he told her. "Clinging on to me." He put his arm around her shoulders and tilted his head so their foreheads were touching. "I'm not going anywhere you know; not without you."

That pleased her and she sighed.

"I worry you know," she said quietly.

"I know."

"No, you don't," she told him. "I don't mean ops. I'll always worry about them until your tours over, but that's part of who you are." She traced a hand down his cheek and followed the line of his scar. He moved his head so he could kiss her fingers. "I mean, I worry about *us*. I didn't think I would be happy again after, Charles."

He shivered a little at her words. Her voice was so bleak at the end. He tightened his arm around her and kissed her forehead. She burrowed into him; her face pressed against his chest. Her shoulders shook slightly and he leaned back. Georgette turned her face away, reaching for a hanky she had stuffed up her sleeve. He wiped a tear off her cheek, his thumb stroking. Her eyes glittered, sparkling with tears.

"Goodgie," she laugh-hiccuped at his use of her nickname. "Darling, I love you." He kissed her as her eyes went wide. "I love you so much," he said again as the words registered and she half sobbed as she kissed him back, wrapping her arms around his neck.

Similar platitudes were being expressed elsewhere. In Lincoln, Vos had gone for a walk with Denise. He'd grown a little tired of their room and wanted some fresh air. They went up Steep Hill towards the castle and Cathedral. They had to stop halfway because Denise was tired and felt a little ill. Vos offered to go back, but Denise insisted on carrying on to the top. She wasn't about to let a steep hill get the better of her. At the top, the narrow road opened out into a large square. To the right was the Cathedral, the left, Lincoln Castle.

Denise pulled Vos to he right. She wanted to see the Cathedral. He fell into step beside her and she gripped his hand tightly. They had arrived not long before the afternoon service. They walked around the Cathedral slowly. Denise marvelled at the stained glass windows but also found the church too plain for her tastes. Even the small church in Saint Omer she had gone to with her family was more decorated than this grand structure. There were no statues of the Virgin or murals on the walls; nothing.

The Priest appeared from somewhere and started the service. Denise felt caught. She'd not intended to stay for the service. She hadn't been to church for a long time. Conscious that it would be rude to stay standing, she seated herself in one of the pews near the back. Vos took position next to her, remembering going to church with his family on Sundays while the priest solemnly gabbled away in a dead language.

The service was unlike anything he'd seen before. It was all in English and neither of them knew the hymns. Vos said plenty of prayers to be spared more dangers and brought safely home. Denise prayed for the same.

She was terrified that one day he would just never come back. She had no idea what she would do if that happened. In the months since he had brought her from London, she had come to love this man who was sitting next to her. He was quiet and withdrawn sometimes but so was she. They needed each other very much. He was kind and gentle and he had done everything for her, she felt very humbled by that.

Vos pleaded god for forgiveness as he knelt in the pew. Every day they went out dropping bombs that must have killed hundreds, perhaps thousands of people. He felt torn inside. Part of him wanted to wield a huge sword and cut a swathe through the Nazis, revenge for all the ills and hurts they had inflicted on the world. In the same instant he was squirming for absolution for killing civilians, families, children. He felt awful. His head started pounding. It became too much. He was overcome by a feeling of doom, like he was about to die and the ground would open and swallow him up. He rose suddenly and fled from the Cathedral.

Outside, he gasped for air, his head was reeling and he came close to being sick. His stomach clenched as he leaned forwards, hands on his knees. Denise ran out to find him sitting on the steps, his head between his knees, sucking down big gasps of air. His skin was clammy, his back wet with sweat.

"Mon cher," she said. "Qu'est ce qui ne va pas?"

He retched again and she fumbled in her bag for a tissue or a handkerchief. She rubbed his shoulders. He was shaking. An old woman took in this little scene as she walked past and scowled and tutted. Denise shot her a venomous look in return.

Gradually, Vos took command of himself again. He coughed to clear his throat and sat up properly. He eyes were red rimmed, wide. He got unsteadily to his feet, leaning on the wall for support.

"Are you okay?" she asked him. "What's wrong?"

He cleared his throat again and straightened.

"Nothing, it's nothing."

"Cheri, it's not nothing, you can tell me."

"I'm fine," he bit out, embarrassed at such a display. He lit a cigarette and drew into himself. His world narrowing to the cigarette in his fingers as he focused on the glowing tip, seeing burning cities in the embers.

Denise busied herself with her make up. She extracted a small compact from her bag and flicked open the lid, looking at herself in the mirror. She tilted her head from different angles, seeing the glow of her cheeks. Her stomach churned again and she suddenly felt very tired. She pulled out a lipstick and applied some, pursing her lips as she looked in the mirror.

Vos finished his cigarette and the mood passed and he was his normal self again. He gave her his best smile as he offered his arm. Smiling, she took it and they walked towards the castle. They walked the grounds and saw the outside of the old prison. To the east was the Crown Court building which was still in use. They abandoned the idea of walking the walls after Denise said she didn't feel well again.

Concerned, Vos shepherded her back to the square and they found a tea room. They stayed there for a while, lingering over a cup of tea and saying little to each other. She didn't ask him what had happened in the service and he volunteered nothing about his thoughts of doom. Vos left payment on the table as they went to catch a bus back to their room.

Mrs Peck had a vegetable casserole ready when they got in. She pressed Vos to stay and he sat in the parlour while she brought him a small bowl along with a buttered roll. He polished it off quickly, his appetite stimulated from the walk and the fresh air.

Afterwards, he suddenly felt very tired and Denise took him upstairs. He dozed on her bed and he woke in the middle of the afternoon to find the room stifling, Denise had a good fire going in the hearth and she was sitting with her feet up, darning his socks. He felt drained. He yawned and stretched.

"Hello," she said quietly. She snipped the thread with a small pair of scissors and tied off the loose end. She bunched the socks into a ball and threw them at him. He caught them and put them back on.

He rubbed a hand over his face and went to the basin in the corner. He wet a flannel and rubbed his face, patting with a towel afterwards.

"Sorry about earlier," he said sheepishly. He settled himself by the fire and crossed his legs as he stared into the embers. He chewed on the pad of his thumb.

"God forgives all things," she said.

"How are you feeling?" he asked her. She shrugged and put away her sewing things. The queasy feelings had passed and she felt much better now.

"How am I feeling?" she arched an eyebrow. "How are *you* feeling?"

He couldn't bring himself to say it. He attributed it to something he ate. Denise had seen some subtle changes in him the last few months, the way he buried his fears deep inside. He told her very little about ops but she could read newspapers. She heard snippets from people at work who had family in the services. It had to come out some time, why not in a church?

"Christophe, don't be scared to tell me things. I won't break." He grunted in response. She decided then. "Shall I tell you something?" she asked him.

He tore himself away from looking into the fire and stared sideways at her. A worm of concern gnawed at him, wondering what she was going to say. Since they had been together, he had studiously ignored asking anything about her time in London. He didn't want to know about such things.

"I once said that this was all a dream, do you remember?" He nodded slowly. "This is more than a dream now, you helped make it so." She got down from her armchair and joined him on the floor. "This is real." She kissed his fingers and then moved to his right shoulder, his neck. She looked at him. "I love you. Je t'aime."

He covered her mouth with his and she pushed him back onto the floor, straddling him with her legs.

36 - Send In The Heavies

With the Battleships taken care of, Harris wanted to open his bombing campaign with a real maximum effort, something that would make a statement and set the tone of operations to come. Every morning he would come into the operations room at High Wycombe to be told the casualty rate from the previous nights ops. Target photographs showing damage would be ready for his inspection. More detailed briefs were prepared and ready for him if he wanted some specific piece of information.

After that, there would be discussion of that day's business and what options there would be for operations that evening. The meteorologists would be consulted and possible targets would be looked at in more detail. Eventually, Harris would make his choice and that would be the days morning prayers concluded.

On this occasion, the Air Ministry had asked Bomber Command to attempt a raid on one of the French factories that was known to be supplying the German war machine with materials. A target was selected but Harris was well aware of the political dimensions to such an attack.

France may have been occupied by the Germans but it wasn't the same as bombing Germany itself. With the row over the Butt report and the recent mess over the German Battleships, there was a real need to avoid providing Bomber Commands enemies with even more ammunition to damage the service. Civilian casualties had to be avoided at all costs.

The weather forecast for that night was good so he was comfortable selecting a target that had such political significance attached to it, but he was conscious that there would be no second chance at this. If he was going to send in his bombers, they would have to smash this target in one go. The orders went out later that morning and the wheels began turning at Group and then at squadron level.

At Amber Hill, the station swung into action; gates were closed, the phones were turned off and aircraft were tested; the sense of anticipation palpable as it always was when ops were on. While the crews were called to briefing at 5pm, the erks got to work checking the kites, filling the fuel tanks, loading the ammunition and bombing up.

Carter slumped into his chair at briefing with a horrible headache. It had been building all day and his forehead was throbbing. He forced himself to pay attention while Everett got things started. He would be leading this one and Church was up on the stage, listening as his Flight Commander went through the route and the target. Everett gave them both barrels to grab their attention.

"Tonight, we will be taking part in the biggest raid Bomber Command has yet staged in the war." That focused the mind and Carter blinked as the room erupted in murmurs of surprise. Everett let them confer for a few moments before continuing. "Up until now, there has been an embargo on bombing of French industrial targets to avoid the possibility of civilian casualties. That ends tonight."

He strode over to the back of the stage and picked up the stick leaning against the map board. He slapped the pointer at Paris.

"Over two hundred fifty aircraft are going to attack the Renault works at Billancourt in the western suburb of Paris." The murmurs from the assembled crews went up again but he spoke over them this time, raising his voice, pitching it to carry without having to shout. "We are going to go over the target in two hours."

Voices got louder. Some shouted an objection to packing so many aircraft into such a small amount of airspace in so short a time. Everett held up a hand for quiet and came back to the front of the stage.

"Now I know what you're thinking. One hundred twenty aircraft an hour over the target area means there's a good chance of a collision, but the risks have been considered." Someone snorted at the back and Everett shot them a steely look, his usual casual demeanor absent. "It's nearly a full moon tonight, so you'll have bags of opportunity to see whats going on around you."

He cocked his head, seeing the doubt on some of their faces.

"Maybe this will help," he told them. "The attack will be staged in three waves. We will be going in as part of the second wave." He let that sink in; then unleashed the final surprise. "And we'll be going in at four thousand feet."

The room erupted in consternation again while Carters mouth went dry. He was appalled. Even on his first tour, he had never bombed lower than seven or eight thousand.

"Yes, that's not a mistake, four thousand feet. Like I said, casualties is a concern. Going in low, means getting a good sight on the target. To help things along the first wave is going to be preceded by aircraft dropping flares to improve visibility even further."

That quietened them down a bit. Flares had not been used before, but it made sense. Air dropping a bunch of flares to illuminate the target should make this easier.

"I cannot impress upon you enough, that if you *cannot* get a good fix on a target. Do NOT drop your bombs. That is a direct order from Bomber Command HQ. Am I clear?" He was clear and no one said anything.

Everett handed off to Kent and the intelligence officer took them through the plan in more detail. 363 would start taking off at 9.30pm at one minute intervals. Church reminded them to watch where they were going, he didn't want the schedule getting screwed up by someone straying off the peri track and getting stuck.

Kent showed them enlarged photographs of the factory complex, the equipment sheds and the main factory buildings. Carter could see why there was a concern over casualties, the place was surrounded by residential buildings. A few stray bombs would cause havoc.

"The factory makes trucks, thousands of trucks for the Wermacht and Luftwaffe. If we can go in and knock it flat, we'll put a massive dent in their war production. There are very few flak batteries in the area so there shouldn't be much to worry you. Defences should be light." For once that failed to attract the usual chuckles of good humour from amongst the crowd. The mood was brittle and a joke about flak was no laughing matter when you were going in at four thousand.

"I bloody hope so," Walsh half hissed, half whispered to Carter. "At four thousand they'll be able to pick us off like bloody pigeons."

"Coconut shy," murmured Carter, echoing their previous conversation.

"Har bloody har," said Walsh, genuinely worried. Over Brest, the flak had been stiff, but at ten thousand feet, a bomber weaving back and forth was hard to hit. At four thousand feet, coming over in a more compact group, there would be little point in jinking. The mood lightened slightly when someone at the back asked what the Michelin guide rated the canteen at the factory.

Linkletter did his usual skit. He showed them the weather charts. To everyone but him they were just a bunch of lines and he got the usual applause when he said the station would be open on their return as long as they were back by midnight.

Church came up last. He was stern and serious. This was a big thing tonight, the biggest raid yet but there was a lot of risk attached. The chatter was loud when he walked from the room; a staff car outside was waiting to take him to Group.

Conversation on the truck out to dispersal was spirited.

"I always wanted to see Paris," said Murphy.

"You'll certainly be doing that this time," replied Jensen. Flying over the big city at four thousand feet, yes they would be seeing a lot of Paris. "We just might be seeing more of it than you thought," he cautioned. "We won't have much time to bail out if anything goes wrong so make sure you have your chutes close to hand."

That killed the conversation for a moment while they thought about that one.

"You're full of good news, boss." complained Todd. "It's alright for you. I'm stuck in my turret."

Jensen clapped him on the shoulder, exuding bonhomie.

"You'll be fine digger. Knowing your luck, you'll jump out, crash through someones skylight and land in a brothel."

"They'd keep you there for the duration and you could breed lots of kangaroos," said Murphy.

There was much hilarity at that, they liked that. Even Todd smiled, cheered by the thought of lots of plump French pigeons wrapping their thighs around him.

"That would be nice," he said dreamily.

Only Carter kept himself apart. He couldn't bring himself to participate in the bravado. He felt sick to his stomach at the thought of going in at four thousand feet. If ever there was a night for L-London to behave, this was it. There would be no buffer of altitude to get them home.

The truck dumped them off at dispersal and they got aboard. Jensen christened the rear wheel and then fastened himself up. He had started to do it since that run over Brest and this was his little tradition now before the engines were started up.

Carter couldn't believe it. The sky was devoid of explosions as the bomber force droned over the city. He was tense on the controls, straining forwards in his seat, expecting the guns to open up at them at any moment. L-London bobbed around as he over corrected the controls.

Ahead of them, the factory was burning. They came in from the north, following the line of the Seine, the water glittering silver in the moonlight. All around them were other aircraft and Carter felt hemmed in. He'd never flown with so many bombers in such close proximity before.

He stayed above four thousand feet. With so many bombers in the air, the last thing he wanted was someone dropping their load from overhead and a stray bomb smashing into them.

Up in the nose, Woods was enjoying the view. He hadn't bombed from this low since training school in Canada and England. One searchlight waved back and forth but all it did was help guide them in. The factory was easy to find anyway. The first wave had done their work well and the centre of it was burning quite nicely by the time they turned up. He opened the bomb doors and fused the bombs.

He called out the corrections, sighting on a big triangular area filled with long sheds to the left of the main fire. They passed over the racecourse and he picked up his sighting, a long boulevard that led right to the factory.

L-London rocked in the turbulence of someone ahead. Carter caught it and smoothed out the ride, his hands working the yoke back and forth, softening the undulations. Woods voice was a dull monotone as he called out the corrections.

"Steady, steady. Almost there."

L-London droned on. The crosshairs passed over the sheds and he hit the release.

"It's away!"

Carter peeled off, circling east to go round Paris and then head north before handing control over to Jensen.

"You take her," he said through clenched teeth, his head pounding fit to burst.

It was straightforward after that. They went north, passing over the places that were famous from the first world war, Arras, Bethune, Saint Omer. They crossed the coast between Dunkirk and Calais and stayed over the water until Norfolk was behind them. Their first flak of the evening was off the coast of Lowestoft when a Destroyer opened up at them. Rocking in the shockwave, Murphy ducked down from his turret and fired off the colours of the day. He had to do it twice before the idiot sailors stopped.

They followed the coastline, crossed The Wash and passed north of Skegness before turning left. Jensen was surprised when Carter let him land. He brought the Manchester in over the fence, flared to perfection and put L-London down with hardly a screech of rubber. He taxied to dispersal and shut down.

At debriefing, the squadron was jubilant. More raids like that would make them very happy indeed. The only casualty was a tail gunner who'd caught a piece of shrapnel from the Lowestoft guns in a very embarrassing place. He was whisked off to hospital but he wouldn't be sitting down for a while.

During interrogation, Woods tried to catch the eye of the red headed WAAF but she was busy with another crew. He hung around afterwards but couldn't summon up the nerve to say anything to her. Feeling like an idiot he went back to his billet to get some sleep.

Still feeling rotten, Carter went sick for the first time in his RAF career and went to see the MO. The doctor shone a light in his eyes, looked at his tongue, asked him to balance on one foot and then told him to sit down. Taking the top off his fountain pen he made a few notes.

"How long have you felt like this?" he asked, his voice abstract, almost disinterested.

"A day or two. It was just a headache at first."

He winced when the doctor shone his little torch in his eyes again. His nose stung and his eyes were sore.

"Been anywhere cold?"

"You mean apart from the billets?" Carter asked sarcastically.

"Yes, apart from the billets." The doctor waited patiently for him to answer.

"I went to the coast a few days ago."

The doctor tapped the pen off his teeth. He cocked his head to one side and looked at Carter again with an appraising eye. Pressing gently with his fingers he touched either side of his patients' nose. Carter flinched and pulled his head back.

"That might do it. Did you get cold?"

"Not that I'm aware of. I was well wrapped up but I was out for a few hours."

"Hmmm." The pen scratched on paper. The doctor reached for a shelf above his desk and handed over a small glass bottle of pills. "Take these. You've got very swollen sinuses, Mr Carter. Painful?"

Carter hesitated, his natural contrariness coming out. He nodded.

"A bit."

The doctor grinned. In aircrew parlance, a bit equaled, a lot; probably very much. Typical air crew, toughing it out. He'd heard from an MO at another station that one pilot had flown three ops in a week while suffering from pleurisy. Stupid, but brave. He nodded in sympathy.

"Well you were flying pretty low, weren't you? I assure you it'll be a lot more painful up at twelve thousand feet, or fifteen thousand even. You'd be screaming your head off then. You've managed to get a sinus infection, maybe picked up a cold at the same time, so you're grounded for a few days." He finished writing in Carter's notes. "Come back in three days time and we'll see how you are."

37 - Fingernails

Being grounded on an active station was hell. Carter spent two days in bed, his head aching fit to burst. It hurt to sneeze, his throat was dry and he had no energy at all. He managed to beg a few lemons from the cookhouse so he could sit up in bed, sipping on hot water with slices of lemon in.

He spoke to Georgette on the telephone and she was full of concern but he talked her out of coming over. For one, it was no easy trip for her coming over from Grantham, secondly there was not much she could do. Besides, he didn't really want her seeing him like this. It was stupid, but he had an awful bedside manner and he knew he'd be no fun.

His crew came to see him. No one brought grapes, Murphy brought a packet of salt and vinegar crisps. Carter let Walsh eat them later. With his throat feeling like it did, it would be like eating razorblades.

Walsh regaled him with tales of the Mess party the night after the raid on Paris. Everyone coming back in one piece was a good enough reason to celebrate, not that they needed much of a reason for a party. Lord Haw-Haw decried the bombing, claiming hundreds of French civilians had been killed but they dismissed the broadcast as blatant propaganda. Church had read out a letter of congratulations from Bomber Command HQ passing on the thanks of the French government in exile.

On the third day, he went back to see the MO. The examination was cursory, the doctor could see he was no better. His nose was an angry red, his eyes were mere slits and he was running a slight temperature. The doctor gave him some more pills and told him to come back again in three days.

He spent the morning in the bath. He ran the water until it was just under his chin and he let the steam work its magic. His headache eased and he lay back, eyes closed. Walsh came looking for him to make sure he was all right.

"Bloody hell, you alive in here?" he asked, wafting his arms at the clouds of steam that cascaded through the door.

"Oi!" Carter objected as the draught rushed into the room. "Yes, I'm alive." Walsh left him to it, telling him he was going to Lincoln for some liquid relaxation.

After soaking for an hour, he felt slightly more human. All pruney and wrinkled, he got dressed and went off to see Georgette. There were no ops on and with it being a Saturday, she had the day off. The drive over was hell. He took his time with the window wide open, his eyes streaming.

Mrs Lloyd let him into the parlour and Georgette almost flew down the stairs to see him. She was full of concern as soon as she saw him. He looked grotty. His eyes were puffy and there were dark circles underneath them. She went to kiss him and he turned his head so she ended up kissing his cheek.

"Darling, I was worried about you."

"I'm okay," he sniffed and tried not to wince at the pain. "The doc says it'll be a few more days." He shivered at the cold in the parlour. Georgette would have taken him up to her room, but Mrs Lloyd had very strict rules on that. There was no chance of sneaking him up there without getting caught.

They went out in the car to the pub a few streets away. They could have walked but Georgette didn't want him getting any colder than he had to. She almost dragged him into the back room and parked him nearest to the fire. She came back from the bar with a horlicks for him, a cup of tea for her.

The drive over might have been hell, but Carter was pleased he had made the trip. It was good to see her, especially since their walk along the Fens the previous weekend. She held his hands and was amused to see him feeling so sorry for himself. He had slumped in his seat and there was something almost endearing at how pathetic he looked.

They discussed their upcoming leave. Carter asked if she minded his changing where they went. Rather than go north, he wanted to see White which meant going south of London. Georgette wasn't bothered where they went, she was just happy to spend some time with him. Besides, if they went to London, they could stay a few days with her family. She was looking forward to her sister's reaction when she introduced him.

He dropped her off at her digs and returned to Lincoln. Worn out by the excursion he went straight to bed and was asleep as soon as his head hit the pillow.

The following day, he felt marginally better. His nose still hurt, but the sore throat was on its way out. Feeling vaguely human he took his time over breakfast and then retired to the lounge in the Mess. He sank into an armchair, his eyes shaded with sunglasses while he consumed cups of tea.

He surfaced after lunch and went for a walk. It was mild outside, the cold of the last few weeks banished by a warm front moving in.

The sun feebly poked through some clouds, perfect weather for ops. Carter's suspicions were confirmed when the crews were called to briefing. He shuffled in with them to find it was a run to Essen.

Like the raid on the Renault factory, over two hundred aircraft would be going and Carter got a feeling that this was how operations were going to be from now on. Gone were the days of them going here there and everywhere in small penny packets. This was the big leagues now, with massed raids to big targets. The main target was to be the Krupps factory with lead aircraft going in to mark the way for everyone else to follow.

Still grounded, Carter was concerned when he saw his crew were listed to fly. He went to see Fish Salmon who informed him that Jensen would pilot L-London and a new second dicky, fresh from training would fly the right seat. Carter was about to object when Salmon reminded him that he himself had recommended that Jensen was ready for his own crew now.

"Look on this as a dry run," his flight commander had told him evenly.

Time dragged. Normally he would be busy, geeing himself up for the coming op, getting some rest, sorting his stuff out before that final walk out to the aircraft. Grounded, there was none of that, just a looming pit of time that needed to be filled. When it was time, he caught the flight truck out to dispersal with them and watched them get on board. Jensen did a thorough walk around and got on last. He seemed very young all of a sudden. Carter shook his hand warmly.

"See you when we get back, sir?"

"See you do," Carter told him.

He stepped back and joined Latimer at the edge of the hard standing. Jensen gave him a thumbs up out of the side window of the cockpit. Latimer pointed at the port engine. Jensen shouted, "CONTACT!" and the engine coughed and spluttered as the prop started turning. It caught and blurred into life with a roar. L-London taxied out and never did Carter feel more bereft than at that moment. That was his crew going off to war and he wasn't going with them.

Walsh followed them out and he stood watching as the two Manchester's disappeared into the dark, the blue stab of their exhaust flame the only thing visible. As the noise of the engines receded, a Tilly drew up alongside him. Church wound the window down on the driver's side.

"I thought I would find you here. Come on, no point moping, get in."

Carter opened the passenger door and got in. Church pulled away before he even shut the door and drove to the control tower. Church went straight up to the second floor and went out onto the balcony with Carter following silently behind. Group Captain

Etheridge was already there as was Everett.

Fish Salmon was leading the squadron tonight. Kent and Linkletter hung off the rail at the far end. The senior WAAF and a few others lurked at the back. Carter had never thought about this much. When he was taking up position on the runway, he always saw people in the tower and he saw them waving, but he was too busy to think much beyond that.

Jensen was second last to go. Carter watched with a keen eye as L-London swung on to the centre line. He could see movement in the cockpit and he could picture Jensen as he went through his final checks. It was his first time flying in the left seat and he could imagine how the lad must be feeling. There was no more training, this was it. No matter how much time went by, Carter would always remember his first op in a Hampden. You were going off into the night and the lives of everyone in that aircraft were in your hands.

L-London started rolling. Everyone on the balcony started waving. The tail came up and Jensen held her there, letting the speed build up. Walsh was the last to go and Carter sent his friend on his way with a prayer.

Kent and Linkletter went indoors to get warm as soon as the last bomber was away. Etheridge and Church stayed for a smoke and Carter moved over to join them, hovering a few feet away in case they were discussing something particularly sensitive

"How did that feel, Carter?" asked Church.

"I know where I'd rather be, sir."

Etheridge nodded in understanding.

"I know what you mean. It never gets any easier," he said.

Church produced a cigarette and his face was all harsh angles from the flame of the match. He was wreathed in foul smelling smoke.

"Christ, Church, what is that?" asked the Group Captain.

"Turkish. Strong stuff."

"That's one way to describe it," Etheridge replied deadpan, his teeth showing as he grinned. Church offered him one, but Carter shook his head, he liked his cigarettes mild. He got one of his own out and offered the pack to Etheridge. They lit up and hung on the rail, listening to the rumble of engines as they receded in the distance.

When it had finally gone quiet, they went downstairs and sauntered over to Etheridge's staff car. The WAAF driver got out and held the back door open for him. Etheridge got in but wound the window down as the car was about to pull away.

"I'm off to Group but I should be back before the boys come home. I'll see you chaps later."

The car moved off and they watched it go, the blacked out tail lights little dots in the distance. Now it was just Church and Carter. Church lit another cigarette and Carters nose wrinkled at the smell.

Whoever made those things should have been shot but Carter supposed it was commanders' privilege. They started walking.

At a loose end, Carter debated what to do next. Church was heading to Ops, so he followed the CO. Ops was an anonymous two storey brick building, next to the admin blocks, there being nothing to distinguish it from any of the others in the row.

An SP checked Carter's ID before allowing him into the hallowed room, a big windowless square. The Ops Room was somewhere Carter had never been, not even on his first tour. To his right the wall was covered in a large blackboard. Every crew was listed, their names chalked next to the letter and serial number of an aircraft. The long wall to his left had doors that opened to a number of small offices. Each office had a big window that gave their occupants a view of the main room when the blinds weren't down.

A large map board table occupied the middle of the room. On the wall opposite the blackboard was a stage with three tables covered in a number of telephones and ledgers. Two WAAF officers and a Flight Lieutenant were sitting there, filling out paperwork. Behind them was a large scale map showing England from the south coast as far north as Newcastle. Various coloured pins were stabbed into it, presumably to mark the locations of airfields and other things of interest.

With the squadron up, Ops was understandably busy. Kent hovered around the large map table deep in conference with the intel WAAF who had caught Woods eye. There was lots of noise with people talking over one another and telephones ringing. Church scrutinised the blackboard then disappeared into the nearest small office. He kicked the door shut as he picked up the telephone on the desk.

Carter found a quiet corner feeling like a spare part. He tugged out his handkerchief and wiped his nose. Coming into the warm from the cold outside, it was starting to run. His throat tickled and he tried to snort without drawing too much attention to himself. He fancied a fag, but daren't aggravate his throat any more. A WAAF handed him a cup of tea and he stood there, holding the saucer in one hand while he moodily sipped from the cup.

Church emerged from the office and beckoned him over. The WAAF handed Church a cup of tea as well. "Thank you m'dear," he said warmly. He gestured round the room with the cup.

"What do you think, Carter?"

"Impressive, sir," Carter replied neutrally. Church smiled behind his cup.

"I'm off to Group," the CO said conversationally. Carter's ears pricked up at that. His mind raced as he tried to think of a way to hitch a ride, he might be able to see Georgette for a few moments, she was bound to be working tonight. Church dipped his voice and leaned in.

325

"Something's brewing that I need to find out about."

Church parked his cup on the corner of the map table. A WAAF Corporal appeared and deftly spirited it away before it marked the surface. Carter made to follow but Church stopped him.

"Best stay here, old man. It's cold out there, don't want your sniffle getting any worse, do we?" He looked past Carters shoulder around the room. "Make yourself useful here. See the lay of the land." He clapped Carter on the shoulder. "I'll see you when I get back."

Before Carter could say anything, Church was gone. Carter froze, it felt like every eye was looking at him. He drifted over to the map table and looked at the European coastline. He mentally judged distances, say two hours to get to the coast and head inland. He glanced up at the clock mounted on the wall above him.

This was the first op he had ever had to sit out due to illness. Getting wounded on his last tour didn't count, there was not much you could do to stop flak tearing whacking great lumps out of you.

Kent was stood near by muttering about German nightfighter airfields in Holland. He kept glancing at a sheaf of papers in his hand and then jabbed his finger into the map.

"There," he said. His finger moved and jabbed another point on the map. "There too. Well, that's something to bear in mind next time." He straightened as he realised Carter was close to him. "Not for your ears, Mister Carter." He handed the papers to the WAAF who put them back into a buff coloured folder. "At least, not yet anyway."

Kent withdrew to his office and left Carter staring at the map. A Scottish brogue brought him out of his reverie.

"Over here," they said. Carter blinked and turned round to see the Flight Lieutenant on the stage looking at him. He had a telephone handset glued to one ear and he was all contorted as he used his shoulder to keep it there. He scribbled on a bit of paper as some voice bawled down the telephone.

He had wings on his chest and DFC and AFC ribbons. His face was a shiny angry pink down one side and that extended down his neck, out of sight below his shirt collar. A patchwork square of raw skin covered his forehead. The left eye was almost milky, unfocused. He gestured to the empty chair next to him on the stage.

"Pull up a pew."

Carter walked round to the end of the stage and parked himself in the chair. The officer ended the call and shoved the handset into its cradle. He handed the piece of paper over to the WAAF to his right.

"Marjorie, be a dear and ask the Observer Corps to keep an eye out for one of ours on the northern coast of Norfolk, sounds like there's a problem." She nodded and picked up a telephone, asking the switchboard to get the Observer Corps. He turned back to Carter and held out his hand. "Welcome to the heart of the machine. I'm, John

326

Wheeler."

"Alex Carter." He noticed Wheelers left hand was scarred like his face, the flesh puckered and taut in a lurid ridge, the knuckles shiny. Carters gaze lingered a moment too long and Wheeler snatched his hand back.

Carter had seen him in the Mess once or twice, but the man never hung around long and was never around on the Mess party nights. Carter had heard on the grapevine that he had flown Battle's in France before being wounded. The wings, the medals, his appearance told their own story.

"I hope you're not tired," he joked. "It's going to be a long night." He pointed to the blackboard. "Every aircraft sent out has the relevant information recorded, time off etc."

Carter glanced at the board. A Corporal was clambering up a short ladder to add information to the various columns. He saw the entry for L-London. It showed Jensen as the pilot, the serial number and the time of departure.

Wheeler explained his job, trying to make it sound more interesting than it really was. The Squadron books were open in front of him and he was in the middle of writing out the entry for tonights op, specifying the target and other salient details. It was all so routine, reducing hours of flying down to a few lines on a page, a mere glimmer of what was involved to make it all happen.

As reports were received, they would update the board, the books and Group as necessary. Group would contact them if there was information regarding enemy movements. Depending on jamming and other vagaries of wireless transmission, occasionally they would hear reports as their aircraft tapped out their morse messages as they bombed the target and turned for home.

Wheeler mentioned that Saunderson always appeared later on to find out what was happening and of course the CO and Groupie would turn up before the boys got back.

Carter had never thought about this. All of this was an extension to the one thing he was bothered about; flying. He'd never seen what went on in the background. He jumped as a telephone rang, breaking the quiet. The WAAF to Wheelers right answered it on the second ring.

"Ops," she answered crisply. There was a moments silence while she listened to a crackly line. "Understood, thank you." She put the handset down. "Confirmed, sir. K-King down near the coast. Home Guard report some survivors. Apparently, it just avoided a village."

Wheelers lips pulled into a grim line and he gave a mere hint of a nod.

"Dodds!" he called sharply. The Corporal up the ladder turned, wobbling as he did so.

"Sir?"

"Mark off K-King. Crashed in Norfolk." He glanced at the wall clock, "make it twenty two hundred."

"Yessir."

The Corporal turned back to the board, went down three rungs on the ladder and leaned across, marking up the time next to K-King's row. Carter winced as the chalk squeaked across the surface of the board setting his teeth on edge. K-King was Whites replacement. He sighed; another rookie crew gone for a burton.

Time dragged. Carter had two cups of tea. Wheeler offered him some biscuits. Carter had one and chewed rhythmically while he went through the squadron's operations book. He randomly turned pages. He noticed the dates. 8th January, their run at Brest, then the raid on Wilhelmshaven on the 10th. That one had been White's last trip as second dicky. Then there was that raid on Munster on the 22nd, unlucky number thirteen. His mouth twitched at the mental anguish he had gone through on that one. He closed the book.

There was one other early casualty. I-India lost an engine over The North Sea and turned back after dumping their bomb load. They ditched short of the coast. Carter made himself useful and spent half an hour passing information to Group so the rescue launches knew roughly where to look. He didn't give much for their chances. The black water would be like ice. Even bobbing in a life raft, lashed by cold wind, it would only be a matter of time.

Everything was slow time in Ops. Now the squadron was on its way, there was a lull. Linkletter put in an appearance, his face creased in concern as fog started drifting across the field. He disappeared into one of the offices and communed with his brethren around Group to see how they were fixed.

It wasn't much better north of Lincoln. Patches of fog were clinging to the ground moving slowly and 1 Group had it even worse with visibility down to a few hundred yards. If it was still around in a few hours time they would have to start diverting them to other stations down south.

It was a side of Linkletter Carter had never seen before, the care, the seriousness, the worry that the weather coming home would be bad. At briefing his predictions for the winds were often wrong. That was about par for the course. Forecasting the weather over central Europe was problematic at the best of times. As much as the crews made a joke of it, often applauding when he told them the target would be clear, his forecast for the weather over the drome on their return was almost always right. Now it looked like Linkletter's perfect record was spoiled. He left ops a worried man, his face creased in concern.

A report from Group had the lead elements of the raid approaching the target. Halfway there. Carters mouth went dry and he felt himself sweating as he thought about the flak. He could almost feel the jolting and the bouncing as you were thrown around. His nostrils burned and he had a sneezing fit. His eyes watered when he was finished and his throat stung.

"Sorry," he muttered, shoving his hanky back up his sleeve. He wiped his nose across the back of his hand. Wheeler grunted. He had been watching Carter, the struggle within him as his mind ranged over the map, on the raid in spirit. He'd been like that himself for quite a while after France. It took a while to lose the itch when everyone else went off to war and you were left behind.

Time dragged. It was agony for Carter sitting here. His world was a cockpit, ears being battered by the drone of the engines while he shivered in the dark, every sense of his body finely tuned while he ran on the adrenalin that raced through him. Here, on the ground nursing a pulsing headache, every minute dragged. He looked at the clock god knows how many times but the hands stubbornly refused to spin round at high speed. He gnawed through one set of nails and was doing a good job at working through a second set while he waited.

By one Carter was starting to fade. Ops was hot. The radiators were going full belt and the room was stuffy. He felt his eyelids drooping and he shook himself awake, angry that he could even contemplate sleep at a moment like this. He went for a walk outside and Wheeler joined him.

They found a stiff breeze had blown the fog away to leave a clear dark sky. Stars winked and the moon was bright in shadowed profile. A few stubborn patches of fog clung to the grass and swirled around his feet as he walked silently in a wide circuit. Loud banging came from one of the hangars where the nights duty crew worked.

"Linkletter'll be pleased," Carter murmured.

"Yes," agreed Wheeler. "He takes his responsibilities quite seriously, poor man." The Scot lit a cigarette and studied the glowing end. "His son was killed you know." Carter's eyes went wide. "A training accident. He joined up after that. Felt he had to do his bit." Wheeler flicked the cigarette onto the grass. "Time to get back to it," he muttered.

Church had come back from Group with Etheridge while they'd been outside. The Group Captain was in one of the side offices shouting down the phone. The CO was studying the board.

Wheeler scanned two messages that were waiting for him. The fog had moved east and was covering the coast. He started calling round the Grouops to find out if they were clear. The fog might have gone for now but it paid dividends to guard against every eventuality.

Etheridge emerged from the office looking peeved. The CO looked as annoyed as the Group Captain as they talked in hushed whispers. When he saw Carter watching him, Church nodded and forced a smile onto his face that stopped at his eyes.

329

The clock wound round to two and the room started to come alive again. Saunderson appeared, as did Kent. Everyone stood looking at the map. The squadron would be coming home soon, straggling in one by one. As they crossed the coast, individual aircraft transmitted and the signals were relayed to the ops room. Dodds started updating the board, the chalk squealing as he wrote.

Soon enough, they had word that the first aircraft was in the circuit and they gravitated outside. Wheeler stayed inside at his desk, his fingers gripping a pencil so tight his knuckles went white. He never watched landings; it was too much of a reminder. The phone rang and he answered it briskly. He nodded grimly and thanked the caller.

To the right of the take off and return times was a long box for other comments to be put. So far there were two entries there, I-India and K-King. Dodds made his third entry of the night. P-Popsie, crashed on landing in Norfolk. Three out of sixteen aircraft dispatched tonight had failed to return so far. Wheeler wondered how many more there were to come.

On the top floor of the control tower, Carter squeezed through the gathering crowd to get himself a spot on the rail. The wind was brisk and blew into his face. He sneezed hard and his eyes watered. Blowing across the field the wind was at a straight right angle to the main runway. Carter glanced at the wind sock, watching it bobbing up and down as the gusts fluctuated.

"Won't be long now," Church muttered as he slid in next to him. The first fingers of light were streaking the dark but it would be two hours or more yet before the sun crept over the horizon. Higher up, the crews would be racing the light home.

After seven hours and more in the air, Carter knew this was also one of the most dangerous times. All it would take was one lax moment and an intruder could catch you napping, exactly what had happened to Lambert. Carter studied his palms and found his hands were shaking. He knew he wouldn't be able to relax until L-London returned and shut down.

They heard them before they saw them, the drone of the engines building slowly. It rumbled from the east, growing louder. They waited patiently. There were quite a few airfields close by; Coningsby was east of them and Waddington was to the west. Just because they could hear engines, it might not be for them. Then the first call came over the radio, Y-York requesting permission to pancake.

For once, Walsh was one of the first back. He sailed in and the ground staff cheered before he taxied smartly towards dispersal. Fish Salmon was the next to return. He had a nasty hole in his port wing and he landed gingerly, bouncing twice before getting it on the ground. Three more straggled in over the next ten minutes, then there was a sudden rush, like last orders at the pub. Five Manchester's arrived one after the other. Some had to circle and wait their turn.

Carter looked for the ID letter on each one as they went past the tower but there had been no L-London yet. He found the waiting agony. Nothing was under his control; he just had to stand there and wait. Church could see how keyed up he was but there was little he could do about it.

Finally, L-London arrived. The tyres squealed as they kissed the runway, the big bomber bounced, once, twice and then stayed down. There was a shower of sparks out of the starboard engine as Jensen closed the throttles.

"My god!" someone exclaimed. There was a huge hole in the port rudder and as it trundled past the tower, Carter could see the tail turret had been damaged. Some of the perspex was missing and his heart was in his mouth as he imagined Todd mangled inside. Even as L-London was turning off onto the peri track, he was pelting down the stairs, chasing after her.

There was the roar of a car engine behind him and Carter waved his arms at the ambulance. It obligingly slowed down and he jumped onto the running board on the passenger side.

"Follow that kite," he shouted, pointing after his disappearing aircraft. The ambulance caught L-London up and kept pace alongside her as she went back to her dispersal. Someone waved to Carter from the mid upper turret but he couldn't see who it was.

Jensen dabbed the brakes, gunned the port engine and L-London swung one hundred eighty degrees to face back the way she had come. Latimer appeared out front with his arms held high and he watched as erks dashed in from under the wing and jammed big wooden chocks in front of the main tyres. Once they were in place, Latimer dropped his arms and Jensen cut the switches. The deafening racket from the engines died away as the props windmilled to a stop.

Even before the engines stopped, Carter was off and running, the medic from the ambulance hot on his heels. An erk was putting the ladder in place at the rear entry hatch as it opened. Murphy jumped down and shouted at them to hurry up. Blood was splashed across his face and his eyes were wild. The medic bounded up the ladder into the dark fuselage. Vos was crouched over Todd up by the main spar.

"I'm bloody fine," roared Todd. "It's just a headache!" He tried getting up and winced as the pain washed over him. His flying jacket had a ragged red hole in it around the stomach area. Carter wanted to know the trick because the Australian shouldn't have been alive with a wound that big.

Todd had no idea just how big a mess he looked until they got him out of the Manchester and into the ambulance. A bullet had creased across the top of his head and ploughed a furrow. Dried blood covered his face, his neck and had run down his chest. The medics slapped a fresh dressing on the wound and whipped him off to the hospital.

Carter went round to the nose as Jensen climbed down. His second dicky looked wrung out, he blinked back fatigue as he dumped his parachute pack on the ground.

"Hey, skipper."

"Welcome back."

"Rough ride," said Jensen. His hands were shaking while he tried to fish a cigarette out of its pack. Giving it up as a bad job, he stretched, digging his hands into his back. He rolled his neck and worked his jaw, trying to make his ears go pop. He turned to look at L-London but it took him a few seconds to take it all in.

"Bloody hell."

"Shaky do, sir?" asked Latimer. Jensen nodded.

"When can you have her ready?" Carter enquired.

"Don't know yet, sir." Latimer disappeared to answer a query.

"Bloody 88 nailed us over the target," Jensen said bitterly. "Spud got him I think, scared him off anyway. He gave us a hell of slap on the backside."

Everything had been going fine until they reached the target when searchlights had coned them on the final run in. Half blind, Jensen had dived and thrown the Manchester around the sky to escape the grip of the light. Flak had battered them and just as they were sorting themselves out, the nightfighter had pounced.

Carter tugged on his arm, trying to get him into the truck but Jensen pulled away and walked towards the tail. Carter didn't stop him; he had seen that look before. Jensen was riding high on adrenalin right now, every sense finely tuned.

The left rudder had a huge lump out of it and the elevator hung down drunkenly. Latimer appeared from underneath and hooked a thumb back at it.

"Cables are sheared on that side, sir."

Carter was impressed. To get back with that kind of damage took an outstanding feat of airmanship.

"Come on," said Carter, tugging his second pilot towards the waiting truck, "you can tell me all about it."

It helped to talk and get it out of your system. Jensen did most of the talking at interrogation but the rest chipped in where they could. Kent struggled to keep up taking his notes.

Six hours later they visited Todd in the small station infirmary. A Nissen hut had been turned into a ward for minor injuries. A nurse's station was at one end and there were ten beds, five down each side of the hut with a central aisle. The nurse balked at being descended on en masse. Carter sweet talked her round and got them fifteen minutes.

"No more mind," she told them, her tone stern. "We mustn't tire him out."

Todd was in bed, noisily discussing the nights raid with the bomb aimer. His head was swathed in bandages. He was very pale and there were dark circles under his eyes. He perked up considerably when his crew flooded in and surrounded his bed. Murphy handed over a bar of chocolate which was quickly stashed under the sheets. "Typical digger," chided Murphy, "Anything to get out of ops."

Todd objected rudely, blowing a raspberry and flicking the 'V's at Murphy.

"Anyone got anything strong?" he asked hopefully. Woods hitched his chair closer to the bed and cleared his throat. He looked around shiftily before producing a small hip flask from his tunic pocket.

"The good stuff," he said, holding the flask out. Todd unscrewed the cap and upended it. "Puts hairs on your chest," Woods told him.

Todd coughed and some Whisky spilled down his chin. He winced as pain shot through his head, a stabbing flare that went from front to back across his scalp.

"Jesus, that was good," he breathed. His eyes were watering but he was smiling. The nurse stood up from their table at the end of the hut but Todd ignored her. "They're all bitches in this place," he muttered. "They woke me at eight this morning and gave me a bloody sponge bath, like I was an invalid."

"You *are* an invalid," Murphy reminded him. Todd gingerly fingered the dressing.

"This is just a scratch," he said bullishly. He had asked for a mirror when they changed his dressings and saw the channel the cannon shell had gouged across the top of his scalp. He counted himself lucky. Another inch or two lower and it would have taken his head off.

The 88 had just appeared out of nowhere. Swooping on them from above, it had opened fire at close range, raking their backside. All Todd remembered was a bright flash and a massive thump across the head and a slap in his stomach before the world went dark. One round even passed through his trouser leg missing the skin by inches.

The controls had jerked out of Jensen's grip and the damaged Manchester had plunged towards the ground, probably the only thing that saved them. The searchlights lost them and the fighter broke off. Woods dumped the bombs while he clung on for dear life in the nose as they went down.

It took every scrap of strength Jensen and their terrified temporary second dicky could muster to pull them out of that dive. This was no surprise now, considering they only had one elevator, but

333

they didn't know that at the time. They had pulled out over the burning city at three thousand feet, rocked by flak and the roiled heated air from the fires. It had been a long flight back. Jensen had to have the yoke pulled right back into his stomach just to keep it level. They undulated up and down, taking it in turns as their arms got tired.

The rear turret doors had been jammed solid and it took them twenty minutes hacking away with the fire axe to get them open. When they first saw Todd slumped over his guns, they thought he was a goner. Air shrieked past the gashes in the turret, howling like a banshee. They dragged him back to the main spar and propped him up.

His face had been covered in blood and his stomach and legs were wet with red. Vos shot him up with some morphine expecting the worst. When Woods opened his jacket, he'd expected to find his guts hanging out, instead he found a damaged thermos flask tucked inside his clothes. A 20mm round had hit the flask and doused the Australian in tomato soup, lucky boy indeed.

They talked for a few more minutes and then the nurse looked pointedly at the clock on the wall. They took the hint and shuffled out. Carter split off from them and went to see the MO about his cold.

He opened his mouth, got prodded and poked and was told to get dressed again. The doctor wrote on his notes.

"Excellent progress," he said, putting the lid on the fountain pen. "A few more days like that and you'll be fit to fly. "

Carter groaned, realising there were no short cuts round this one. The doctor sent him on his way and Carter poked his head round the CO's door. Church was surrounded by paperwork and Saunderson was shoving various bits of paper under his nose for signature. Church waved him in and pointed to a chair in front of his desk.

"What can I do for you, Mister Carter?" he asked as he peered at an Air Ministry directive. "The doctors already told me your prognosis."

"Isn't that a breach of some rule?" Carter asked.

"Of course not, old chap," Church soothed. "Make it quick, we're on again tonight." Carter nodded; he'd heard the tannoy announcing briefing at four. The air was already alive with the sound of aircraft being air tested.

"I wanted to recommend, Jensen for the DFM."

Church put his pen down and propped his chin on his hands. He nodded and reached for a bit of paper.

"I thought you might," he waved a copy of Kent's interrogation form. "Write me something up and I'll sign it, I think he deserves it too after last night." He glanced at his watch. "Now you better get some sleep, I want you in Ops again tonight."

Carter controlled himself enough not to groan. He wanted another night in ops like he wanted a gammy leg. The only consolation was he wouldn't be sweating the wait until his crew got back this time. Due to the losses last night, there were more crews than kites so Church was giving his mob the night off.

Before he turned in, Carter strolled over to the hangars to find Latimer and his crew slaving away on L-London. They had been working hard. The rear turret had already been taken off and was mounted on a trolley. Sand had been scattered underneath to soak up a puddle of leaking hydraulic fluid. The damaged rudder had been removed and they were in the middle of clearing the runs of debris to rig new elevator cables on both sides.

He peered at the turret. Everywhere was smeared in red although exactly which was blood and which was tomato soup wasn't clear. The port side was torn up. The perspex was starred and panels were missing. A 20mm shell had exploded at the back of the turret and made a right mess of the feeds for the ammo trays.

Latimer came over wiping his hands on some cotton waste. He looked exhausted and Carter doubted he had been to bed.

"She looks a lot worse than she is, sir," Latimer assured him.

"I'll take your word for it."

"A few days and we'll have her ready for you, sir."

"Just don't kill yourself doing it," Carter responded.

Latimer grunted and went back to work. Dog tired, Carter went back to his billet to find Walsh buried under a mound of blankets, snoring away as always.

38 - Paraskevi

Carter glared at the offending aircraft above him. For once, it wasn't the engines that had let them down. Latimer and his erks had worked their usual miracle and four days after being shot up, L-London was ready to be airtested. Carter had taken her up only for the hydraulics to fail. The rear of the fuselage was awash with hydraulic fluid and a steady trickle was spilling out of a previously unpatched bullet hole. It looked like the stricken bomber was having a piss on the tarmac.

Murphy got out and squelched his way over to the crew truck, his pants soaked with hydraulic fluid. Todd followed, quiet and a little more subdued than usual. Jensen was bickering with Vos and Woods over a Lord Haw Haw broadcast they'd heard on the radio the night before.

Carter noted the bomb symbols painted under his cockpit window on the port side. There were nineteen little bombs. One more and he had a weeks leave coming, seven days away from the madness with Georgette. He mentally heaped abuse on the MO. If the cold hadn't grounded him, he would already be on leave. The squadron had flown three nights on the trot to Essen. 363 got lucky and only lost one more aircraft on the 9th and 10th, making it five crews and six aircraft for the three nights of operations.

The closest Carter had got to the action was flying a desk next to Wheeler in ops each night. He'd had to endure another night of agony on the 10th when the CO borrowed Woods after his own navigator had been wounded the night before. Woods had been phlegmatic about the experience on his return, "he's okay, skipper, but he isn't you." Carter rather liked that compliment.

Sitting and watching on the sidelines while his own crew were up was hard and he'd told Georgette as much when he saw her yesterday. She'd silently sipped her drink while she listened to him. She could see new lines of strain by his eyes and could tell he wasn't sleeping even if he neglected to mention it.

He threw a glare at his broken bomber one last time and went over to the truck. He just knew something was going to happen, it was Friday the 13th after all. The sense of doom he always had on this day had descended as soon as he woke up. Even as a child he'd never ventured far and always stayed inside if he could. As he got older he would never ride on public transport or even get on a bicycle, let alone drive a car. Dumb superstition it may have been but he was always overwhelmed with a terrible sense of foreboding and there was little anyone could do to convince him otherwise. When Latimer told him L-London was ready for an airtest he was less than thrilled.

In a black mood, he had rounded up his crew and trudged out to dispersal. Sitting in the cockpit he moved the yoke around. New elevator cables had been rigged and he was happy with the movement. Then the hydraulics had decided not to play along and spoiled everything. Latimer had been very apologetic, taking it personally that his aircraft had failed. Carter assured him it was fine but inside he was just relieved it hadn't been anything more serious like an engine fire.

The day took a further turn for the worse when the tannoy summoned them to briefing. This was it, something he had avoided all his life and now tonight of all nights, he was being asked to go out and fight. To round things off, with L-London U/S they would be going in the squadron spare, Q-Queen.

Briefing passed by him like a blur. The target was Cologne, but if anyone had asked him for any details, he'd have just given them a blank look. It took him an age to get ready and his limbs felt so heavy he needed a hand to pull him up into the back of the truck. He felt sick to his stomach as he tried to concentrate while doing his usual walk around.

He wasn't the only one battling personal demons. In the tail, Todd was steeling himself for the coming mission. It was his first time going up since he'd been wounded. In truth, he should probably have still been tucked up nice and warm in a hospital bed but he'd talked the MO into passing him fit. When he shut the turret doors behind him, it had felt like a coffin lid closing on top of him. He tried keeping himself busy. He checked the guns, the belt feeds and spent ten minutes polishing the perspex.

Once he'd done that, he stayed for a while, staring at the grass outside in the dark. They would run the tractor towed mower over it soon, then there would that wonderful smell of freshly cut grass, the smell of spring. He jumped out of his skin when Murphy knocked on the turret doors and opened them.

"Come on, we'll be starting up in a minute."

Todd nodded dumbly and got out of the turret, making his way up the fuselage to the back of the main spar. The engines started, the fuselage vibrated from the raw power and he bit down hard on his lip as they started moving.

They took off at nine and climbed into the night sky. Q-Queen needed virtually the entire runway to get off the ground. Carter took his time. He got the wheels up fast but held her low, just clearing the trees at the far end. He let the airspeed build up before climbing slowly away. Jensen looked sideways at him. He knew something was wrong because Carter wasn't his normal self. He was tense, almost leaning over the yoke and he barely blinked. Jensen put his hands lightly on the controls.

"I'll take her for a bit if you want, skipper?"

There was no verbal reply, but Carter nodded and released the controls. Jensen took over and nursed Q-Queen ever higher. He hadn't flown her before, but he'd heard Todd and Murphy moaning about their previous experience in her. Not much had changed. She was still the hack spare that was used and abused by everyone on the squadron.

Jensen got them up to twelve thousand feet as they crossed the coast, following the line of the Haringvliet, an estuary of the Rhine-Meuse delta. Carter took over as they skirted north of Eindhoven and ran east.

Ahead of them was the Ruhr, the industrial heartland of Germany. All the popular Bomber Command holiday destinations were found here and Carter knew them by heart, Essen, Duisberg, Hamm, Dortmund, Oberhausen and Gelsenkirchen. Even at altitude you could smell the poisonous fumes of the chimney smoke, the chemical tang stinging the nostrils.

With all the factories, coal mines and refineries down there, the area was covered in an almost perpetual fog, making it the bane of navigator's and bomb aimers alike. Even when you could see the ground, it was hard to tell which was which. The cities almost blended into one another, making it almost impossible to figure out where you were in the dark. The Germans complicated this further by building dummy targets, surrounding them with guns and starting fires in open countryside to lure RAF crews away from their destination.

Carter hated the place. He'd been over the Ruhr god knows how many times on his first tour when the RAF had ranged back and forth, dropping bombs for little discernible result. A lot of friends had fallen over the Ruhr; no doubt many more would fall before the war was over.

"How long to the turn, Woody?" Carter asked; his voice clipped and flat. Woods checked his chart and looked at the watch on his wrist. The thick cloud that had hung around over the Ruhr the last three nights was largely gone, blown south. That same wind would be pushing them along. He clicked the R/T switch in his oxygen mask.

"Twenty minutes to the turn, skipper. Turn onto course one, seven, zero magnetic. Time on target twenty three forty hours."

Carter smiled for the first time tonight, an almost crazy, manic smile. Over the target before midnight, it was the final card fate had to deal that day. He tensed up on the controls and Q-Queen; already wallowing at fourteen thousand feet, lurched to port. Jensen grabbed the yoke and could feel the tremors, the edge of the stall lurking there.

He wrestled with Carter getting the Manchester level again with brute force.

"Sorry," muttered Carter, abashed at the lapse. He shook his head to clear it and blinked rapidly. He schooled himself to settle down, immersing himself in routine. He did an R/T check and everyone responded promptly.

In the tail, Todd was fighting to keep himself going. His head was thumping and his eyes were two hot marbles rolling around his head. His scalp itched like crazy but his head was swathed in a dressing and he could do little about it. Frustrated, he ripped his new flying helmet off. He dumped it in his lap and tugged a woolly hat out of a pocket. That helped a little but he still had to last the run home.

They made the turn and Woods went down to the nose. Flak rocked the Manchester long before they got to the target. To get to Cologne, they had to go over Dusseldorf and Duisberg. All of them were targets themselves on any given night and they threw up a huge barrage, worse than the one they had endured over Essen a few nights before.

Searchlights wove back and forth, hunting for a target. Woods had heard there was something like two hundred AA guns around Dusseldorf. It certainly seemed like it. A kaleidoscope of flashes filled the nose as the guns fired. Carter did his best to weave, going left and right, either side of the main track.

There were one hundred fifty bombers up tonight. Normally, they would meander over the target back and forth in penny packets for two, sometimes three hours which gave the defences plenty of time to concentrate on one or two aircraft. This time they were going over in sixty minutes so there was plenty going on.

The raid was well under way when they got close to Cologne. Bright flares burned amongst large fires in the Nippes district of the city. 4,000lb cookies had blown off the roofs and the incendiaries had torched the rubber works and surrounding factories. Although there was no moon, Woods could still see the Rhine, the water a thin glittering ribbon that bisected the city down the middle, north to south. Woods tensed as a searchlight passed over them but it carried on, still hunting for a target.

Jensen was breathing hard, leaning forward in the straps, expecting a sharp thump or a hurried warning. His heart was hammering in his chest and his palms were clammy in his gloves. He swallowed hard and shot a look at Carter. His pilot seemed to have overcome his earlier ham fisted nerves and was flying smooth as silk. He was holding the yoke with a fine hand and guiding Q-Queen as if she was running on rails.

Woods peered through the sight at the destruction below. Whole streets were on fire, the houses gutted shells. He saw a big church at the edge of a large square surrounded by tenement blocks, it was illuminated by some flares that had dropped short. There was a big flash as a cookie went off and collapsed a block of flats on the southern corner. He blinked to clear the spots from his eyes as he held the crosshairs on some factories on the north of the old town. He could see a few tall chimneys next to them that were belching black smoke into the sky.

"Ten more seconds, skipper!" he called.

Ten seconds was an age for Carter, because it wasn't just ten more seconds. He had to hold it level after the drop for their aiming point photo. He dabbed the rudder one more time and then Woods hit the release.

Carter counted to ten and looked at Jensen, giving him the nod. Jensen rammed the throttles to the stops. The vulture engines screamed and Carter breathed out a huge sigh of relief as the cares of the world fell away. Then fate reminded him it was still there. A burst of flak exploded under the tail and sent the Manchester plunging for the ground.

Todd bashed his face on his gunsight as the bomber fell out of the sky. Shrapnel punctured the turret and stung his legs. Woods had just squeezed past Jensen when Q-Queen dived. He lunged forwards to grab something, missed, lost his footing and floated for a moment before crashing to the floor.

She was going down almost vertically and the altimeter unwound at an alarming rate. The controls stiffened as the airspeed built up. Jensen and Carter hauled back on the yoke with all their strength but nothing happened. The ground was looming up before them and Jensen squeezed his eyes shut, uttering a silent prayer.

For a few seconds Carter thought they weren't going to get her back. Everything was shaking around them as they approached terminal dive speed. Then gradually, inch by miserable inch, the nose started to come up. They levelled off at two thousand feet and it felt like they had just run a marathon, their arms were like lead.

"Everyone call in," Carter shouted over the R/T as he got his breath back. Vos responded immediately. Woods nodded as he got back to his feet behind them. Murphy's reply was shaky and faint, Todd's was a few more seconds coming. He turned the air blue until Carter cut him off and asked him if he was okay.

"No, I'm not bloody all right!" the Australian retorted as he wiped at the blood on his face. "I've hurt my bloody nose!"

Murphy slumped in his turret in shock. It had suddenly hit him that there really was no way out of these deathtraps. If he could have grabbed his parachute, he would have bailed out during that insane dive, but he had been stuck in his seat.

It was easy for Todd. He could wind his turret to one side and just fall out. Everyone up front was fine, they could open the hatch in the nose and go out that way, but he couldn't. He had to squirm out of his turret, grab his chute, clip it on, go back up the fuselage, open the exit hatch and then jump, praying to god he missed the tail on the way out. He was rooted to the spot, drained of energy while the import of that sunk in.

Woods crawled around, picking up his bits and pieces from the floor. His pencils were broken and the glass on his stopwatch was smashed. He muttered to himself as he refolded his chart and sharpened his pencils.

They headed home, but it wasn't going to be an easy run. They had to do a wide circuit to bypass the Ruhr and they began the long laborious climb to regain the height they had lost in that mad dive.

When they got back up to ten thousand, they levelled off but Carter found she wouldn't stay level, she naturally wanted to descend. The flak must have damaged something because the elevators felt soft and the yoke needed to be pulled back to keep the nose up. They tried to trim it out but that made no difference. For the second time in as many days, Jensen had to ride a stricken bomber back to base.

Three hours later they touched down at Amber Hill without further incident. The usual crowd was at the tower and for the first time, Carter waved back. There was a collective sigh of relief when they got down from Q-Queen. They gathered by the tail as Woods handed round his hip flask. Each of them took a sip to steady their nerves. Murphy coughed and wiped his sleeve across his mouth.

"My god, I thought that was it this time," he blurted out.

"For a moment, I did too," said Carter. "When we pulled out and I did an R/T check, I wouldn't have been surprised to find you'd all bailed out."

There was a nervous laugh from everyone in response to that comment.

"The thought did cross my mind," Todd said casually. He gingerly fingered his nose, convinced he had broken it this time. He ran his tongue around his mouth, his top teeth felt loose.

"You been in the wars again?" asked Murphy, nudging him on the shoulder. Todd made a rude face.

"Come on, let's get this over with," said Carter, heading towards the truck to complete the ritual of interrogation, breakfast, then bed. He walked along, riding out the last of his adrenalin as the feeling of doom washed away.

After shutting the engines down, he'd bent down to pick up a glove he had dropped on the cockpit floor. Sitting back up, he saw the clock on the instrument panel was broken. The glass on the dial was smashed and the hands had stopped; at 11.59; precisely.

39 - To Shelter For A While

Carter relaxed into the armchair and enjoyed the warmth of the fire. It had been a long drive from Lincoln to Surrey and he was tired. The plan was to spend a few days with Georgette's family, go to East Grinstead and see White and then finish with a few days just for them on the south coast somewhere. That was as far as his planning had gone.

He settled down, closed his eyes and listened, absorbing the feel of the house. Some houses were like the grave, morbid mausoleums to the past. Others were warm and lived in, a hive of life. Georgette's home positively hummed. There was a babble of voices from the kitchen and he could hear a herd of children charging up and down the stairs.

Georgette's mother, Harriet had been warm and welcoming. Her brown eyes twinkled in good humour as she introduced her family. Carter felt like he'd been paraded around like a prize petunia. To the children he was like some mythical figure. The two boys had stared up at him open mouthed, their eyes on his wings and medal ribbons. The girls just giggled, all shy when he got down on his haunches, shook their hand and said hello.

When they were finally shown upstairs, Carter was amused to find his things had been placed in a spare room and Georgette's suitcase was in her own bedroom. Harriet had given him a pointed look when he tested the mattress, giving it an experimental bounce. Georgette had blushed to the tips of her ears and he had to laugh when she retreated to her bedroom to, 'do her hair' and freshen up.

He opened the suitcase and started putting a few things in drawers but paused when he came across a brown paper parcel in the bottom drawer. Inside the parcel was an RAF battledress jacket with wings on the breast. He silently wrapped it back up again and left it undisturbed, restricting himself to the top two drawers and the wardrobe.

Supper had been full of vibrant chatter as Georgette caught up with her married sisters, Claire and Margaret and Julie who was on leave from the WRNS. The children had been on their best behaviour. He had offered to help wash up but he was parked in the lounge while the ladies retreated to the kitchen, chattering away.

He did a circuit of the room, having a good nose around while he was on his own. The bookshelf had an eclectic mix of titles. There were weighty tomes on the basics of British law and the judiciary, a slim treatise on fly fishing, books on embroidery, a full set of Britannica and some old leather bound copies of Dickens. One shelf had a number of P.G Wodehouse. He pulled out a battered copy of Piccadilly Jim. He had started this once at university but never finished it. He settled down in the armchair and flicked through the pages, diving back into the world of high society in New York.

The clock on the sideboard chimed seven and he glanced at his wristwatch to find it had stopped. He was winding it up when he realised a pair of eyes were watching him. He beckoned them over and Claire's son, David came in. He was a tall boy, all long gangling limbs. A shock of blonde hair was attached to his head. He looked at Carter, studying him in detail. Carter put his book to one side, well aware there were questions coming. David plonked down on the pouffee in front of the armchair.

"How many missions have you flown?" the boy asked.

"Too many," said Carter, trying to be offhand. He saw that answer didn't satisfy the boy so he told the truth. "Fifty one."

"Have you killed many, Germans?" Carter shifted in his seat, uncomfortable with that kind of topic.

"Probably, but I try not to think about it."

"But they're, Germans!" the boy protested.

"Well they're people too," Carter temporised. "I'd rather bomb factories than people if I can," he said truthfully. That answer seemed to satisfy the lad, then his brain lurched off onto a new tangent as young boys' brains were apt to do. He pointed at the ribbons on Carter's chest.

"How did you get those?"

"I won them in a raffle. They handed them out with the sweets back at the station."

"And what about that?" David pointed at Carter's scar. Carter scratched at it absently for a second. He smiled and the boy watched, fascinated as the scar rippled and changed shape.

"I walked into a door."

"Don't believe you," was the almost instant response.

"David!" admonished his mother from the door. The spell was broken. David shot to his feet like a startled rabbit..

"I'm so, so sorry," said Margaret. "He asks so many questions all the time. I hope he didn't offend you?"

Carter got to his feet and tugged down his battledress. David received a swift cuff to the backside and was propelled towards the door by his mother. Margaret turned back to face him and tucked a stray lock of dark hair behind her ear.

"I'm so sorry about that, he's so inquisitive."

"He's young," Carter agreed.

"I'll leave you to it," she said, gesturing to his book. "I need to get them ready to go home for bed."

Carter left the book on the armchair.

"I'll give you a hand," he offered.

It felt very strange for Carter, putting on a dead mans pyjamas. He would have put on his own but Harriet had already been through his luggage and extracted the things that needed a clean and he had nothing left for bed. Georgette knocked on the door and came in wearing a long powder blue nightgown with her hair loose.

"Duty done," she breathed, smiling. Her sisters and the children had left an hour before and everything had been cleared up downstairs. It was just them, her mother and Julie who was occupying her own room down the hall.

"Noisy," Carter grinned. "My family gatherings aren't quite like that."

"We'll have a nice relax tomorrow," she promised him. She stepped forward and smoothed down the lapels of the pyjama top. "They look good on you," she said. He wrapped his arms around her and buried his face in her hair.

"That sounds good." He laughed suddenly. "It's a good job your mother doesn't see us like this."

"I suppose, but I can't say I won't be tempted to sneak down the corridor tonight." She giggled as she broke out of his grasp and planted a kiss on his cheek. "Goodnight darling."

"Goodnight."

Unseen demons woke him screaming four hours later. They retreated from the edge of his vision as he suddenly sat up. He felt for his watch on the sideboard and peered at the glowing hands. He groaned when he saw the time. He got out of bed and paced up and down but he found he couldn't settle; he had the fidgets in his legs. His brain was awake and whirring at a million miles an hour.

He padded downstairs, wincing at every creek and groan as he went. He went into the kitchen and poured himself a glass of milk before taking up his seat in the lounge. The fire in the grate had burned low and he put some more coal on, watching as the flames burst back into life amongst the embers. Once it got going, he went back to Wodehouse.

The clock struck three when Julie came in. She had a blanket round her shoulders over a red night dress.

"I'm not disturbing you?" she asked.

"Not at all," he assured her. "It's your house." Julie chose the armchair across from him, folding her legs underneath herself.

"I'm often up at night with the late watch so I find it hard to sleep sometimes," she told him. Carter nodded quietly, dodging the obvious question.

"Georgette said you were on the south coast somewhere?"

Julie nodded, her face becoming very animated.

"MTB's. Exciting stuff, seeing them tearing around the high seas."

"Sounds fun," he said, enjoying her enthusiasm.

"Oh, it is," she replied, speaking from firsthand knowledge. She'd managed to wangle a few trips out when they were training and loved it. She loved the roar of the engines as they went full belt, the spray hitting your face as they raced over the waves was incredible.

Carter was amused to see her light up in excitement. He'd been like that once on his first solo. That fizzy nervous feeling in the pit of his stomach, the elation as he climbed into the sky, the slipstream tugging at his flying helmet.

He stared at the fire and lost himself in the flickering flames. There was a draught somewhere and the fire danced back and forth.

Julie watched him quietly, noting the rigid way he was holding himself, the set of his shoulders. In her months at HMS Wasp she had seen similar looks from mere boys who'd suddenly had the weight of command thrust upon them. Many was the time she had stood at the jetty with the Flottila's CO as the boats came back in. Sometimes a boat would be missing, others would be shot up, their hulls blackened and splintered. On some occasions she had seen blanket shrouded shapes carried ashore on stretchers. The survivors would talk loudly, their eyes wide, coiled like springs; just like Carter was now.

She knew a little bit about him. Georgette had painted broad strokes in a few letters over the last few months. She knew he was younger than her sister, but with the whole world on fire, what did that matter? After seeing a nineteen year old AB sobbing for his mother while nursing a stump covered in bloody bandages, age was just a number. The pace of life had accelerated and the normal conventions of peacetime just looked silly.

"Is it very bad?" she asked quietly.

Carter didn't answer her immediately, wondering how to answer such a question. He just nodded, not quite trusting his voice. In the dark, by the glow of the fire with the clock ticking in the background, it almost felt like a confessional. He cleared his throat and rubbed his hands together.

"Yes, yes it is," he said slowly.

He glanced at her for a moment and she nodded for him to continue. He turned his attention back to the fire and stared into the distance. The fire burned low, the light a faint glimmer playing over him. His face was in shadow, his eyes dark pits, his cheekbones highlighted.

"I'm surprised I've lasted as long as I have," he admitted, being honest with himself, allowing that guard to come down in this one moment. He sighed and leaned back, disappearing into the black. Julie heard the fatigue and strain there of someone who was hanging on by his fingernails, doing his best to cope with it all.

"I should have died so many times before," he breathed, his voice disembodied in the dark.

Carter regarded her in the gloom, wondering how much he should say. He told her about being a wallflower in the Ops Room for a few days and how difficult it had been, worrying about his men, especially as he had already lost one crew.

"How do you go on?" she asked.

He muttered to himself, suddenly tired of talking and delving inside. Then he thought about how strange things could be. On any given night, if you were given the choice between being in ops and sitting one out, or going on an op, he knew what the choice would be. The thing was, when it truly came to the crunch, no one wanted to be left behind, even if that gave you another day of life. He wondered how Wheeler could stand it, to fly no more ops and put yourself through that agony, of seeing other men go up night after night.

"You don't want to let everyone else down, I suppose."

She thought about that as she compared him to Georgette's husband Charles. He had been tall and dashing in his uniform with a killer smile. Charm personified; he was the glamour boy who carried everyone along with his bubbling enthusiasm.

Charles would never have bared his soul like this. He would have sneered at such thoughts and expression of feeling. His world had been all bluster and bravado even to the very end. Julie had always thought that Charles had lacked imagination. Maybe that wasn't such a good thing, she considered.

She knew you had to have belief in yourself and your abilities to get by. Getting the chop? Oh, that was something that happened to the other fellow. The MTB boys were like that. They were brash and loud, shooting a line while sipping their pink gins, not thinking about the close shaves out of their control.

She had seen how Charles' death had affected Georgette and it had been good to see her sister come alive again. They had gossiped earlier in the kitchen and she had seen her sister bright and animated for the first time in a long while. A lot of that was down to the man in front of her now.

They talked for a little while longer staying on safe topics such as school and family holidays. After a few more minutes, Julie took her leave and went back upstairs, leaving Carter dozing in the armchair, her blanket over his legs.

He woke shivering with the dawn. He stretched and winced at the pain in his neck. He got up, draped the blanket over his shoulders and went into the kitchen. He put the kettle on to make some tea. It had been a while since he had to make tea. At Amber Hill it was all done for you. He spent a few minutes rummaging around to hunt out the makings. He took two mugs upstairs, toed the door to Georgette's room open and went in.

Being the youngest, Georgette had drawn the short straw as a child and got the smallest room in the house. She was in a small box room, about nine feet by six. There was room for a single bed, a wardrobe and a small table and even that was a squeeze. The room was dark with the blackout curtains drawn. He edged into the room and perched on the side of her bed. She stirred and turned over.

"Good morning." He held out the mug of tea. She sat up and he kissed her.

"Good morning," she replied. "Sleep well?"

"Wonderful," he lied. He painted a smile on his face while he thought about his late night chat with Julie with some misgivings. If he had said things like that back at the squadron, they would have though he was going soft; cracking up. She shifted over on the bed to make space for him. He lifted his feet and leaned back against the headboard, bumping shoulders with her.

"So, what's happening today?" he asked.

"Go into town, have a browse around maybe," she suggested. "There's a nice walk along the river that goes to Teddington."

Carter liked the idea of seeing some nature and leaving modern life to one side for a while. Kew Gardens was not that far away either. He kissed her forehead and went back to his room to get changed. He came onto the landing and saw Georgette's mother standing there, arms crossed, her face a picture.

"Just delivering a cup of tea, Mrs Waters," he reassured her. She nodded with a thin lipped suspicious knowing look and watched him all the way to his room. He shook his head and smiled to himself while he put on his socks.

Julie walked into Kingston with them. The sisters walked arm in arm looking like peas from the same pod, all smiles and chatter. Carter trailed behind, hands jammed in his pockets, fedora slouched back on his head. It felt strange being out of uniform but he wanted to enjoy it while he could. Soon enough he would be back to the usual routine at Amber Hill.

He'd never been to Kingston before. It lacked the bustle of London but it had wide streets and big shops. The girls went into

Bentalls, a huge department store that ran the length of Wood Street. Inside were floors devoted to female fashion, makeup and other mysteries. Once Julie and Georgette started trying on hats and discussing in fine detail the cut of a coat he bailed out. He told them he would see them later in the cafe on the top floor.

He mooched around the rest of the store. He hovered in the sportswear section and took some experimental swipes with tennis rackets. A salesman tried to sell him a full set of cricket whites but Carter politely declined. He went down to the ground floor and stood in the centre of the store, staring up at the glass ceiling.

"Can I interest you in a pen, sir?"

He swivelled his head towards a tall brunette behind a counter. He blinked twice as he processed what she said. He focused on the glass cabinet and realised it was the pen counter. He drifted over. She held out a black barrelled fountain pen. He took it in his hand and hefted it. It was very light, not to his taste at all. He'd always wanted a decent pen and settled on a classic black fountain pen with a medium nib. He bought a bottle of black ink to go with it and pocketed the lot.

He sauntered up to the cafe and picked a seat by the window. A waitress came over and he asked for a pot of tea and scones. He tugged out Piccadilly Jim from a pocket and picked up where he'd left off.

Georgette found him like that thirty minutes later. Sitting across from him and had the last half of scone on his plate. She slurped his tea and gave him a beaming smile.

"You ready?" he asked without looking up from the novel. He had just got to the bit where the hero found out why his lady love hated his guts. It was the usual superlative bit of farce from Wodehouse that he found such good fun.

"Done," Georgette announced. "Julie's gone off to do some more shopping. Shall we go?"

"Provided you're done. I don't want to drag you away from your sister if you're not ready."

"Spent up," she told him. He closed the book and glanced at her hat. A dark blue creation it was angled to the right, like pilots wore their peaked caps. Two long pheasant tail feathers trailed out the back.

"Very nice," he told her.

He got up, left some coins on the table to cover the tea and scones. She took his hand and they walked out of the cafe together.

As they descended the stairs in the central atrium, Georgette told him about coming to the store as a little girl and rushing to the toy department to see the dolls. She remembered; they always came in the entrance to the store that led through the china department.

"Mother always kept a tight grip of my hand," she told him solemnly. "She always warned us, 'nobody touch anything', with a face like thunder and that if we broke anything we'd never get any more pocket money forever." She smiled at the memory. "Bentalls has a special place in our family. Mother went into labour twice in the lift here. Dad often teased her about that."

Carter laughed, amused at the stories. They got to the bottom of the stairs and walked past the perfume counters. Exotic smells wafted over him, a pleasant change from his usual diet of aviation fuel, rubber, cordite and smoke. Georgette looked around to get her bearings and then went left towards the main entrance.

Stepping outside the store they turned right on Clarence Street and went down to the river heading along the footpath on the east bank towards Teddington. Apart from a few dog walkers they had the path to themselves. They walked arm in arm, literally glued together, taking their time. As they walked, they talked about life before the war. Carter recounted tales of Cambridge, being in halls while he studied law. Georgette detected what she thought was a hint of reluctance on his part.

"Expectation," he said. "Dad was a barrister, so it seemed only natural for me to follow in his footsteps."

"And now?" she asked, encouraging him to talk about it. He scratched at his scar, caught her looking at him and shoved his hand in his pocket.

"I've never really thought that far ahead to be honest. Once the war started, I left all of that behind." He kicked at a pebble on the path and watch it skitter along before abruptly turning left and falling into the river. Ripples radiated across the water. "Then it was all the fuss of flying training and going solo, then getting on to ops, then getting through a tour."

"I always had a hankering to go off and do something," she told him. "Go to Greece and see the Parthenon, sit in the Colosseum; squash grapes at a vineyard. Being the youngest I saw my sisters go off and get married and have children, I just didn't want to do the same thing and follow them into domestic oblivion right away."

"It's a big world out there," he admitted.

Two heavily loaded barges went the other way downriver, the engines chug-chugging along. The man at the stern gave them a cheery wave as he went past.

They lunched at the pub by the lock gate. Cater enjoyed the activity as people came and went. The river was busy and it was an obvious stopping point for people to get a drink or a sandwich on their travels.

In the afternoon they took a bus to Richmond Park. Georgette wanted to take him to King's Mount in the grounds of Pembroke Lodge but they found it all fenced off with barbed wire. She had to settle for showing him the view from the approach slope which was not the same thing. Even so, it was still impressive.

Looking east he could see London on the horizon. St Paul's Cathedral was surrounded by a shoal of floating barrage balloons that bobbed and drifted on the breeze. Distance hid the scars of the Blitz he remembered seeing on leave before Christmas.

They carried on walking and went off the beaten track, through a patch of trees and found a wide area of tall grass on a gentle declining slope. Wading through it, they came to a glade surrounded by wooded slopes on all sides. A footpath ran alongside a thin stream and Carter saw a bench further up. Wind ruffled the trees, but the surrounding slopes acted as a wind break around them. He sank onto the bench; his legs grateful for the rest. Georgette snuggled up to him, her arm linked through his. He planted a kiss on her forehead and she stirred.

"I've waited all day for this," she murmured.

"So have I." He hummed to himself, starting with a few bars of Glenn Miller before blending into a bit of Vera Lynn. She could feel the rumble through his chest and closed her eyes, content. Her hand hunted for his and closed around it, holding it tight.

They heard the grass rustling and looked around. A red deer stared back at them. It licked its nose and then bent down again, sniffing their way towards them. Georgette made shooing motions with her hands. There was a moments pause and then it ran off to the left. Carter stood up to see the deer join a small herd of ten or twelve that had a big stag with antlers in the lead. Georgette appeared at his shoulder and made an 'oh' sound as she saw them.

"They're wonderful," she breathed.

Another group of deer which included some younger bucks followed the first group. A big female stopped ten yards away and stared at them and remained in place, on guard, until they had all crossed the glade. The doe shook her head, snorted at them and then followed up behind.

They got the bus back home, footsore and tired. Harriet had dinner waiting for them when they came in. They found Julie relaxing on the sofa in the living room, listening to the radio. She looked up when Georgette poked her head around the door.

"Hello you. Good day?" she enquired.

Julie sprang up from the sofa and smoothed down her skirt.

"Pretty good. I got a nice dress and a pair of shoes. How about you?" Julie arched an eyebrow and Georgette blushed.

"We had a nice time," she replied.

After dinner they settled down in the living room as the weather turned. A squall moved in and rain lashed the windows. Carter got a good blaze going in the hearth and they were nice and snug. Harriet knitted, Julie read a book and Georgette dug out a puzzle. Carter wrote a letter with his new pen. The radio was on low in the background as the conversation went back and forth, always coming back to the war before striking off on another tangent.

American forces were starting to arrive in the UK. Carter was buoyed by this, but it would be months before they actually started to do anything. The news from the Far East was still bad. Singapore had fallen causing shockwaves in government. Churchill had considered it his Gibraltar of the Far East. The Japanese seemed to be advancing on all fronts and had reached Java, Burma and the Solomon Islands. Curious, Carter picked up an atlas from the shelf and was shocked to see how far their reach had extended in such a few short months.

Gloomy, he took the seat next to Georgette and fiddled with the puzzle pieces. She playfully slapped his hand.

"If you're going to do it, don't mess up my piles. Edges there, inner bits there." Grumbling, he put them back and paid more attention.

Harriet asked them about their plans for tomorrow. Carter played a wait and see card. He fancied going to Kew Gardens but if the weather stayed the same, he would rather give it a miss. Julie demurred. She had a date for tomorrow night but she wasn't about to say that in front of her mother.

The bedrooms were cold and Carter was glad to have a hot water bottle to keep him company. He was out like a light within ten minutes.

It rained all night but cleared with the dawn. A night owl, it was past ten before Carter roused himself. Harriet had gone out and Julie was busy dressing in her room when he shambled into the kitchen.

Georgette was spreading margarine on some bread when he came in. She was wearing a knee length, short sleeve mint green dress paired with white and brown Oxfords. A dark green long sleeve cardigan was draped over the back of a chair. She pointed to a wicker basket with a knife.

"I thought we might have a picnic."

"Sounds good," Carter agreed, buffing an apple on his trousers.

They drove to Kew Gardens and spent the day wandering the grounds. After the rain, the day had a fragile quality. The moody sky threatened rain but a fresh breeze kept it at bay. Large parts of the lawns had been turned over to cultivation and there were rows of new potatoes and other vegetables waiting to be picked.

They finished early and headed for home, calling on her sisters, Mary, Claire and Margaret and to see the children again before they left the following day. David didn't ask any awkward questions this time and Carter had a kick around with him in the narrow garden at the back of the house. Georgette helped Claire and Margaret make tea while Mary played with the other children in the living room.

"He seems nice," Margaret said primly which Georgette knew was a resounding endorsement where her sister was concerned. Margaret had never approved of her marrying Charles so this grudging comment was welcome indeed. The next question was a surprise.

"Is he going to marry you?" she asked directly.

"If he wants to," said Georgette, stung by the question. "I'll not force him one way or another."

Margaret sniffed, that haughty, huffy sniff she always did when the answer didn't measure up to her expectations.

"Well, you know your own mind," she replied and Georgette left it at that.

In the evening, they relaxed. Georgette completed the puzzle. Carter wrote a long letter to his brother. Away from Amber Hill, he had a chance to say a few things without fear of Saunderson's critical eye.

Julie was floating from her date when she came in later on. She had gone to the cinema with her new man. That meant she'd seen the news reel and the opening and end credits of the main feature, being otherwise occupied inbetween.

When her mother asked her about the plot, she was able to give her a summary of the plot because she had seen Pimpernel Smith the week before in Dover. Her mother was suitably mollified, reasoning that such a good understanding of the film could only have occurred if there had been no monkey business on the back row. They turned in early, Carter again welcome for the hot water bottle, this time he kept his socks on as well.

They left early the following morning. Mother and sister saw them off.

"Don't do anything I wouldn't do," whispered Julie as she hugged her sister goodbye.

Harriet was a bit teary as Carter let in the clutch and pulled away. She had wished him luck and hugged him as they said their goodbyes, much to his surprise. To her daughter, she worried and did her best to hide it. She'd seen Georgette hurt badly once already and didn't want to see it happen again.

On the drive to East Grinstead, Carter found himself tensing up again. He disliked hospitals and wasn't looking forward to this visit at all, but he'd promised White he would come and he intended to keep his word.

The hospital was just outside the town on the north east side. Carter parked the car and looked around. The grounds were beautifully kept and there were paths that led to secluded groves. He could see men walking around, some of them accompanied by nurses.

The first indication this would be a testing time was when he walked over to a man in RAF blue sitting on a bench calmly smoking a cigarette. His back was towards them and when he turned to look in their direction, Carter felt ashamed that he visibly flinched.

There was no way to tell how old he was. His face was raw and shiny. One eye was wide and staring and the other was half closed, surrounded by swollen eyelids. A small tuft of dark hair stood up on top of his head. He ran a gnarled hand through it and got to his feet. Carter noticed the thin blue pilot officer ring on his sleeve and the DFC on his chest below a navigator's brevet.

"Can I help you?" he asked. His voice was pure cut glass, each vowel enunciated perfectly from a withered ruin. His good eye looked right at them.

"Uh, we're here to visit one of my crew. I'm, Carter." He stuck out his hand immediately. The man grasped it firm and strong.

"I'm, Butchart." He looked beyond Carter at Georgette who hovered behind him.

"Oh, I'm sorry," Carter half turned and held a hand out to Georgette who gripped it hard. "May I present Section Officer, Waters."

The man took a half step forward and then shook her hand.

"Charmed," he said, what was left of his lips pulling into a parody of a smile.

Georgette felt weak at the knees and found her mouth had gone dry. She just nodded. Butchart had seen the look before, he was used to it by now. He pointed towards the building behind them.

"Straight up those steps, old man. Through the doors to reception and they'll be able to tell you where your friend is."

Carter nodded a thank you and headed in the direction indicated, Georgette clinging to his arm.

40 - Humpty Dumpty

White got up very slowly. Days were like that at the moment. Everything happened slowly; very slowly. It hurt to move, breathing was an effort sometimes and when he did finally get comfortable, a nurse or doctor would come along and prod him or ask him to move.

As much as he hated the routine, it helped to regulate time in the wards. It was early days for White. He had been brought to East Grinstead after a few weeks in hospital in Norwich. Those days had been a blur of pain, morphine and fuzzy memories, shouting, cursing, tears and nightmares. One night, the nurses had found him on the floor, ripping at his dressings while he raved in delirium. His pain medication had been increased after that.

The night it happened would stay burned in his memory forever. He'd been sitting in the cockpit, lord of his domain, doing it the way Carter had taught him. There and back he had done regular R/T checks to make sure they were awake. They had dropped the bombs right on the money, at least, that's what he told himself. It was the only crumb of comfort he could take away from what happened afterwards.

They had been nearly home, just crossing the coast and thinking about bacon and eggs when the world came apart around them. There was no warning, no indication it was all about to go wrong. One moment they were bowling along, the next, they were in a flying ashcan as the Manchester was perforated end to end. White had kept the yoke pulled back with one hand while he used his other to keep what was left of his second dicky from slumping forward over the controls.

The bomber jolted as flak continued to explode around them, punching holes in the thin aluminium skin. He shouted for help but no one came. There was no point firing off the colours of the day, the damage had been done. His navigator hauled the body out of the way so he could get through to the nose. There was a howling gale as he bailed out through the hatch.

A wall of frozen air hammered down the fuselage and took White's breathe away, the cold stinging his cheeks. He somehow managed to haul the Manchester back to level to give the rest of them a chance to get out. Wallowing at the edge of a stall, he rammed the throttles forward to the stops. The engines howled, the air screamed past him, flak lit up the cockpit in a kaleidoscopic light show.

When the controls went soft on him, it was time to go. He hauled back on the yoke, undid his straps and got out of his seat, more in hope than with any real certainty he would actually make it.

Dragging himself through the escape hatch behind the astro dome, the slipstream almost hammered him flat. He kicked; he wriggled and fought, using the last of his strength to slither out into space. There was a lurch as the Manchester began to dive for the final time and White was thrown out. As he went over the side, the Manchester rolled to the left. Tumbling end over end, White could only stare in horror as the blazing wing rotated in his direction, the great banner of flame reaching for him.

After that, all he could remember was agonizing pain. His clothes caught fire. The oxygen mask melted, bits of it clinging to his face. Flames licked at his neck, burning through his silk scarf in seconds. His gloves had been tugged off by the slipstream and he batted at the flames with his bare hands.

He had no memory of pulling the ripcord, but he must have done because a search party of the Home Guard found him on his back in a field. He was easy to find. They heard him screaming every time the light breeze caught his chute and he was dragged another few yards along the ground.

Mercifully he passed out when they shoved him into the ambulance. At the hospital his burns were coated in tannic acid and then dressed to stop any infections. He lingered for a few days in a twilight world. There were faint memories of someone spooning food into his mouth, or giving him a drink. He could remember a pair of tear streaked brown eyes, looking down at him and a soft voice telling him it would be all right as the morphine sent him under again.

When Elaine came, he could barely bring himself to speak. What was left of the skin on his fingers had contracted into clenched claws and he hid them under the sheets. He felt embarrassed that he couldn't even hold a fork or feed himself.

His mother fainted dead away when she came to see him. His father walked her sobbing from the ward and then came back, assuring White it would all get better in time.

For weeks afterwards, his mood was very dark. Elaine visited a few times but it was difficult for her as her mother was still ill. It took some choice words from one of the nurses for him to stop moping and buck his ideas up but his mood went up and down.

A few weeks later he was visited by Dr McIndoe. White had no idea who he was at first, he was just another doctor in a white coat but the nurses, in particular matron, looked at him as if he was the second coming. McIndoe spent some time with him, talking about what he could do and if White would like to move to East Grinstead to get sorted out.

He fussed over White's hands, tutting to himself as he turned them over again and again, front and back. He asked White to move his fingers and he watched intently as the clenched fingers opened and closed a mere fraction.

It took a while for White to realise what was being offered. He had seen himself in a mirror once, there was no fixing that. McIndoe assured him it would take a lot of time, a lot of operations, but there was a very good chance he could make good a lot of the damage.

The journey over had been very tiring and White had slept for almost twenty four hours upon his arrival. He had been put into a ward with seven other men, all of them were fliers and all of them had been burned. Some had been there for months, a few had arrived not long before him. That had been ten days ago. Once he had settled in, McIndoe had come to see him.

He discussed the plan with White and did his best to emphasise that there was no quick fix. It would be baby steps and there would be setbacks along the way. Now White was awaiting his first round of surgery. The first thing he came to realise was that he was a damn sight better off than some of the other chaps on the ward. While the burns to his hands and neck and face were severe, that was nothing in comparison to some of the other lads.

In the bed across from him there was the Pole, Piotrwski; Peter for short, who had crashed on a training flight. He had been knocked unconscious and was in the flames for some time before they were able to cut him free. Next to him was the big Scot, MacAdam. He had crashed his Whitley coming back from Cologne. He had got out without a scratch but had gone back into the burning wreckage to pull out his trapped Navigator. He got badly burned and the other man died, despite his efforts. He got a DFC for that, small consolation for the personal cost.

He had been here for months being slowly rebuilt. He had a new forehead and nose already. Next week they were going to start work on his fingers. MacAdam had told White a lot about the comings and goings of the place. The man was irrepressible, the classic happy go lucky type that carried people along in their wake. He had a cheeky approach to the nurses who tolerated his advances with extreme patience.

On Whites second night in the ward, they had been sitting on the side of their respective beds, talking in hushed whispers when White had asked him how he could be so positive. MacAdam had fixed him with a hard stare before replying.

"Because it's a bloody horrible world out there and if I stop to think it'll all get too much for me lad. There are people in far worse shape even than me." He gestured at his face. "This is nothing."

He told White about a Flying Officer in another ward who had been burnt to a crisp flying a Gladiator. The petrol tank in the upper wing had split and drenched him before igniting. Wreathed in flame, he had bailed out before spending hours floating in the ocean waiting to be picked up.

"I'm cheery because I have to be. I make the best of things and hope that one day it'll all come right. Have a little faith," he suggested.

That was the big thing with this place. It was not like a normal hospital by a long chalk. Beer was allowed on the wards for one thing. The other nod to sanity was that there were no rigidly enforced visiting times here. Patients could also come and go as they pleased; within reason. The grounds were peaceful and there were some nice walks when the weather was good. The people of the town were supposed to be very nice and welcoming, but White had not yet summoned the nerve to go quite so far afield just yet.

The girl at reception directed them to White's ward. Carter peered into each open door as they went along, noting the tidy, brisk organised air about the place. The place was clean, quiet and very restful. When they got to White's ward, Carter paused outside for a moment. He steeled his nerve and walked in, a smile painted on his face as he entered the chamber of horrors.

Fire, and being burned was Carters greatest fear when he flew. In the Great War you stood no chance at all. With no parachute, if your plane caught fire, you either put a bullet in your brain or you jumped to spare yourself the pain. Things were better now, but even so, the evidence was all around him of what could happen if you were careless, or unlucky, or brave.

The ward was a modest sized room with double French doors at the end that opened out to the grounds. The walls were painted soft pastel shades and despite the vases of flowers, there was the usual antiseptic smell on the air, common to all hospitals. There were four beds on each side of a central aisle. Each bed had a side table, a lamp and two chairs for visitors. White was in the middle of the room to the left. The bed nearest the window was curtained off and groaning sounds came from behind it.

If the nurse hadn't told him where White's bed was, Carter would have been pushed to recognise him. The top half of his head was fine. He still had the mop of brown hair neatly combed with a side parting and the brown eyes were steady. Everything else below that was a mess. His cheeks were ragged strips of flesh, his neck was swathed in bandages and his hands were like something you would see on a mummy in a museum.

He visibly brightened when he saw Carter and more so when he saw Georgette. There were some appreciative whistles when she walked onto the ward. She blushed and kept her eyes fixed on Carters shoulder. Carter stopped in mid motion as he stuck out his hand to shake White's and realised he couldn't take it. Embarrassed at such an obvious mistake, Carter coughed and took his seat, glancing at the floor while he fiddled with his peaked cap.

"Here we are," he said blandly. White nodded.

"Here you are," he looked between Georgette and Carter. He remembered her from the Christmas dance. She was not as beautiful as Vos' girl, but super all the same. Where Denise had a fragile quality about her, Georgette seemed to radiate an inner strength. The girl bit her lip and looked around the room, everywhere but at White. He could tell she didn't want to be here, but here she was anyway even though she was shaking inside.

"They boys send their best," Carter told him. White nodded. It would have been good to see the lads. Carter took a photograph from his tunic pocket. "I brought you this."

It was a photo of their crew in front of their first L-London along with Latimer and a few of the other erks. It had been taken last October not long after coming together as a crew. Carter was in the middle with everyone around him. White stood smiling next to him, with his arms folded across his chest. Carter put it on the side table, leaning it against a framed photograph Elaine had brought with her the last time she had visited him in Norwich.

It was a posed studio shot with her in a blouse and skirt with a cardigan draped over her shoulders. She was looking straight at the camera, smiling, her cheeks dimpled in good humour.

White lingered looking at her photo before turning back to Carter. His pilot looked at him, almost transfixed, his eyes tracing over his face, noting the burns and the shrivelled skin. White was glad his neck was covered, he doubted Carter would be ready to see the raw puckered flesh. Georgette remained quiet, letting Carter lead the conversation, what little there was of it.

"What's the plan?" he asked, thinking it best to keep things focused on the future. One thing he didn't want to raise was the crash, he doubted White wanted reminding about that.

"The start of a long road," White said, noncommittal. "The doctor wants to do some skin grafts on my face first, my cheeks and chin."

McIndoe had explained the procedure to him. He would take a flap of skin from White's thigh or ribcage and attach it to his arm, rolling it into a tube so it could draw the blood supply from there. Once that had healed, it would be grafted to his face so they could start to rebuild his features.

"Once he's happy with them, then he'll tackle my mouth and my neck." Carter was pleased to hear White speak so matter of factly about it all. He took that as a good sign. "It makes a chap feel like a jigsaw puzzle."

Carter grinned, playing to the humour, keeping the tone of things light.

"You'll have some line to shoot for the girls," he suggested. "You could pass them off as duelling scars."

White laughed. Perhaps he would go into town a little sooner than he planned. Take his scars for a spin and see what kind of attention he got. A shirt collar would cover most of the damage and he could always wear brown gloves, it was just cold enough to get away with that.

"Maybe I will," he replied, feeling better about himself. "I'm not so sure, Elaine would approve though." He smiled, at least he thought he did.

"Your fiancee?" Georgette asked.

"No," replied White, his voice a little distant. He glanced at Elaine's photograph again. That was not something he wanted to think about just yet. He wouldn't accept pity as a person's reason to stay. Maybe later, once McIndoe had done the best he could, only then would he let his mind turn to such things.

"What are you doing with the rest of your leave?" he asked Carter, changing the subject abruptly.

"Heading to the coast," Carter told him. "I need a few days away from everything." He looked across the bed and stared at Georgette and for just a moment, that mask of control slipped and his face softened.

White caught the look and nodded in understanding. There were questions he wanted to ask but he knew they would have to wait for another time.

"Why don't we try a walk?" he suggested. "Lunch isn't for a while and it seems to be a shame to waste such a marvellous day?"

Carter was about to ask, "if you feel up to it?" but he felt in this place, it would be the wrong thing to say. Instead, he said, "I'll get your coat," and stood up.

White leaned forward and gave a sharp intake of breath as hot knives shot up and down his back. Georgette held out a hand to steady him and he bit down hard on his lip as he fought the pain. It took him a moment to master himself, then he nodded and she released her hand.

He moved the blanket out of the way and swung his legs over the side of the bed, shoving his feet into the slippers that he knew were there. He paused a moment, tensed his stomach and stood up. Carter held out the dressing gown and White slid his arms into it. After he tied the belt with clumsy fingers, Georgette took his arm and steered him towards the door. Someone whispered, "get your number dry," and White laughed at the ribald humour as Georgette blushed to tips of

359

her ears.

It was bright outside and White took a moment to adjust from the dim lighting of the ward. He blinked and then pointed to the right. There was a big circular patch of soil in the middle of the lawn with a gravel path around it. It would be full of daffodils soon.

"Twice around," said White. "I don't want to wear myself out," he got out through gritted teeth. He leaned on Georgette for support as he put one foot in front of the other. Every step jolted up his back and turned his neck afire.

"How are the boys?" he asked.

"Oh, you know, the usual," said Carter. "Todd's his usual cheeky self, Vos is…well," he shrugged.

"Mysterious," White finished for him.

"He goes to Lincoln every chance he gets to see his girl."

"I don't blame him," murmured White, "I would too." For a moment, he let his thoughts drift beyond the next day to the weekend ahead. Elaine had said she would come down and he was looking forward to that. He wanted to put on a good show, talk, be everything he wasn't the last time she had seen him.

They carried on walking around under the midday sun. White rested on a bench as his strength faded. He talked about life at the hospital, how good the staff were and some of the characters on the ward. Carter let him talk, pleased to see him so animated, so positive despite what had happened. Now the doctors just needed to piece him back together again.

41 - It's So Bracing

Georgette woke up screaming. The sheets were damp and she was wet through. She scooched into his arms, shivering at the images that had flashed through her head. Carter did his best to soothe her. Shaking, she went to the dresser and poured a glass of water.

This was the second night in a row she'd had nightmares since going to East Grinstead. Carter knew why; his own sleep had been disturbed with images of burnt and ruined men. Now he had something extra to add to his list of demons that haunted his sleep. Not once this week had he gone an entire night without waking up with a feeling of dread reaching for him. Sometimes he thought he was at the bottom of a dark place, reaching for a patch of light that he knew would be his salvation. As he reached for it, water would come spilling over the sides into the gap, filling his mouth, his nose, making it difficult to breathe.

The most prevailing dream was riding the controls of his Manchester in a final dive. The engines would be on fire, the wind would be howling in through large rents in the fuselage. He always woke up when the wings ripped off.

Now Georgette was haunted as well and that pained him. He thought she had enough to worry about as it was wondering if he would ever come back. She got back into bed and they cuddled in the dark. He could feel her heart going like the clappers.

"How do they do it?" she asked. "How on earth do they go on? Those young boys. It's all too horrible to think about."

She wondered how White's girl did it. How she found the courage to go to that place. Georgette would have liked to meet her to find out.

They dozed off and on until the sun came up. Carter ordered breakfast and one of the hotel staff brought it up to their room. Tea for two, toast and jam were quickly consumed, their appetites ravenous and Carter put the tray back by the door. He fluffed up the pillows and leaned back against the headboard. He opened Piccadilly Jim up at the bookmark and carried on reading.

Georgette stood at the foot of the bed, looking at him. She thrilled at the sight of him laying there, the lean muscles on his legs and chest, naked apart from his briefs. She climbed onto the bed, straddling his legs, just above his knees. He made a show of ignoring her. She tugged the book out of his hand and held it up out of reach.

"Hey!" he protested. He came up fighting. Grabbing her around the waist, he reached for the book. She laughed and shifted it to her other hand. Putting one hand around her waist he heaved and rolled to the left. Georgette gave out a yelp and ended up on her back, Carter on top of her.

"I surrender," she said smiling. Carter leaned forwards and kissed her.

Vos paced up and down the hall waiting for Denise to join him. Bored, he parke himself in an armchair in the bay window of the B&B. Noisy seagulls wheeled back and forth in the sky, hovering over the fishing boats as they came back in. He drummed his fingers on the arm of the chair and glanced at his watch again. Denise's idea of ten minutes was fluid indeed. He debated going up to see where she was then thought better of it.

Vos hadn't travelled much in England. London held little attraction for either of them. Vos didn't like the big city and the capital held so many bad memories for Denise she had no wish to return.

The week before they went on leave, he'd floated down to Saunderson's office for a chat. He asked the adjutant if there had been any contact from the Belgian embassy. There had not. He danced around the subject some more and then asked where someone went with a woman on leave. Saunderson choked on his tea, particularly at how quaint the question had been put.

"Well, there's lots of places," Saunderson had said, while he bent some thought on it.

"Somewhere with a bit of fresh air would be nice. Not a big town, *not* London," Vos had said, rattling off his list of wants.

Saunderson leaned back in his seat, tapping his teeth with the end of his pencil. Vos was a country boy, so he could understand the Belgians dislike of built up towns. He made a few suggestions and the Belgian left to make a few phone calls. He asked around the Mess and in the end settled on Skegness. It wasn't hard to get to and he was assured that there were cliff side walks and beaches.

That was only partially correct as it turned out. There were nice walks along the cliffs and a long pier, but there the facts diverged. Most of the pier wasn't accessible. One hundred yards out there was a barrier and beyond that, soldiers patrolled and waited in makeshift pillboxes. The beach looked nice, but there were no donkey rides and the yellow sand was buried under a mountain of barbed wire and tank traps. The beach huts were all shut up and the fairground rides were closed for the duration.

The town was also crawling with sailors who went up and down the prom in their uniforms as the nearby holiday camp had been turned into a naval station. The town wasn't a fancy place but that was why Vos liked it. There was no veneer of pretension like there was around London.

He enjoyed fish and chips by the sea, it seemed to improve the flavour somehow, eating them out of newspaper. He was not so keen on pickled cockles or rollmops; those were not to his taste at all.

The days passed simply. They rose late, had walks, explored the Pleasure Gardens and meandered through the day. It had been a long time since Vos could do what he wanted without having to worry about a call to duty.

Denise tried talking about the future but Vos found that difficult. Up till now, he'd every faith that the skipper would see them through, but lately, Vos had begun to wonder. When Q-Queen had upended and gone on that death dive he'd thought that was it. What if it wasn't all skill but pure blind luck after all? Discussing the future suddenly seemed moot.

When he was training for aircrew all those lifetimes ago, he had a fantasy of life back home in Belgium when the war was over. He dreamed about returning to the mill and picking up the threads of life where he'd left them. More recently he had thought about Denise fitting into those dreams but those dreams had turned to smoke with that last op.

He heard the stairs creak and turned in the chair. Denise appeared at the door with a bright smile on her face. She wore a cream blouse and a tweed skirt and jacket. A red handbag hung from its strap on her shoulder.

"I'm ready. Sorry if it took a bit longer than I thought."

He smiled and crossed the room to be by her side.

"I was about to send out a search party," he grinned and kissed her. "Je t'aime. You look lovely." He took her hands in his and she stepped back, turning left and right slightly making her skirt swish around her knees. He laughed.

The landlady at the B&B had told them about some good walking around Gunby Hall on the edge of the Wolds. They had sandwiches on the bus and held hands, talking in hushed whispers. The hall was privately owned but allowed visitors to walk around the grounds. The mansion dated from the 1700's and was a modest red brick house with a stable block and walled Victorian garden. The gardens were not formally laid out, but followed the style of Capability Brown, rolling undulating lawns, clumps of trees and small lakes. Denise thought it was delightful.

They got the bus back to Skegness, worn out but happy with the day and got back in time for tea. While Denise went upstairs to freshen up, Vos went back to the armchair and grazed on the day's newspaper.

It was the usual war news and nothing particularly cheery at that.

In the bathroom on the second floor, Denise knelt over the toilet and used a tissue to wipe her mouth. She shakily got to her feet and braced herself off the sink. She looked in the mirror and saw a pale face that was decidedly green around the gills. She had been sick yesterday as well. Denise knew it wasn't the food, Vos had eaten the same as her, but something was obviously wrong. She would see the doctor when she got back to Lincoln she decided. Feeling better, she had a drink of water, adjusted her makeup, smiled at her reflection and went downstairs for tea.

Back at Amber Hill, Todd had relocated to Bill Edwards farm for his leave. He subjected himself to a week of physical labour, helping every day to feed the chickens and do other work in the fields. For two days he was up to his elbows in grease and oil, fixing the tractor.

Each day he started early, rising with the dawn. He washed in freezing cold water from the well in the yard, ate sparingly and went off to work. The evenings were spent in conversation by the fire in the kitchen, the big Alsatian at their feet.

Todd liked the change of pace. Bill Edwards led a solitary life, did little to court female company and the farm hands left to go to their own homes at tea time.

In the passing weeks, Todd was becoming more and more taken with the idea of having his own farm when he got back to Australia. He would leave the big cities behind and head to the outback. There was plenty of space out there, where a man could be master of himself and beholden to none. After the First War, the government had made farmland available to returning soldiers. Maybe they would do the same thing this time when it was all over.

If Todd's leave was restful, Murphy's was more tumultuous. He stayed at Muriel's flat for three days. As Muriel mainly worked the evening shift at the pub that suited Murphy just fine. The first day was devoted to bedroom gymnastics before they came up for air. They almost consumed each other, taking time out to eat before going back at it again.

They relocated to the pub that evening and Murphy took up his perch at the end of the bar, talking to Muriel while she worked. He watched as she deftly handled the glasses and pulled pints. He smiled as she nimbly avoided advances and cast glances in his direction loaded with promise. The pub locked up late and they returned to the flat to start all over again.

That second morning, he woke tired and spent to the smell of buttered toast. Muriel hovered over him with a pot of tea in one hand and a loaded plate in the other. He slurped his tea while Muriel sat at the end of the bed and watched him eat.

Trouble brewed that afternoon when they went for a walk in the park. Murphy knew something was up. He could see the internal struggle going on in her face, the furtive glances and the chewing of her bottom lip. He walked on in silence. As they rounded the bandstand in the Arboretum, she finally came out with it.

"What happens when your tours over?"

"Time off, hope I don't get killed by a pupil and then go back and do it all again, why?" he replied shortly.

"How long is that for?" She knew the answer but she wanted to hear it from him.

"Six months, give or take."

He flicked his cigarette stub onto the grass. She shuddered at his flat voice.

"Where will you go?"

"I don't know." He shrugged. "The skipper got posted up to Scotland for his rest. I can't say as I like that myself; too cold," he said, trying to inject a bit of humour back into the conversation. The joke fell flat. Her brown eyes pinched in annoyance and there were glimmers of tears lurking there.

"And what about us?" she asked at last.

He cocked his head, his antenna picking up the danger signals too late.

"I'll stay in touch, Muriel."

She stiffened at the casual way he replied to her question. *Us,* meant far more than staying in touch as far she was concerned. She had devoted herself to him and she felt it was poor compensation to be told that he would, *keep in touch*. Murphy backtracked fast.

"What I mean is, I'll come whenever I can get leave, letters, calls." He gave her hand a squeeze and kissed her cheek. "You know that." He looked her in the eye and said it again. "Anyway, I'm not going anywhere at the moment. There's still ten trips left to do. I'll be around for a while."

Suitably mollified, she clung to his arm as they walked along.

The second act came two days later. Murphy and Muriel were walking back from the high street when a female voice shouted his name. He cringed as soon as he heard it. He carried on walking, determined to bluff it out but of course, his luck wasn't good enough for that.

Hurried footsteps caught up to him and Joan came into view in front of him. One hand kept her hat from falling off and she was winded from having to run to catch up to him.

"I thought it was you," she said. Murphy grimaced. Joan took in the situation in a fast half second. She saw the way this woman hung off his arm, literally glued to his side. "Who's this?" she asked, nodding

365

towards Muriel.

"I might ask you the same question," Muriel shot back tartly. She straightened to her full height. Her nails dug into Murphy's arm. Joan looked from one to the other. Murphy just had a pained expression painted on his face.

"Martin?" Joan's voice went up a few strident notches.

Murphy coughed, cornered and he knew it.

"Right." Joan stepped back; her mouth pulled into a thin line. Her hands shook from gripping her handbag so tight. The slap came from out of nowhere. It caught him on the left side of his face with a resounding crack. Joan turned on her heel and stalked off down the street without a backwards glance.

Murphy rubbed his face and suddenly found staring at his shoes incredibly interesting. He dare not look up to see who was watching him.

"Well, that was unpleasant," he said, trying to brazen it out.

Muriel separated herself from him and held herself rigid.

"I see," she said. She couldn't trust herself to say anything more. Murphy reached out to her but she flinched and took a step back. "I see it all now."

Certain things clicked into place. The evening's when he was busy suddenly took on a whole new light. She thought about that conversation in the park two days before. "I'll stay in touch," he'd said. She gave him a knowing nod, turned on her heel and walked off at a fast clip.

"Mureil!" He raced to catch up with her. He got within arms reach when she turned on him, eyes blazing and caught him a corker with an opened handed slap. He didn't bother following her after that

When he returned to the flat an hour later, he found it locked and his bag on the threshold step. His clothes had been shoved into it willy nilly and his shaving kit dumped on top. He pushed his forage cap back on his head and scratched his forehead.

There was no way he was going back to Amber Hill with his tail between his legs. He found a boarding house, paid a weeks rent and unpacked his things into the rickety chest of drawers in the corner. Now he was free, he could stretch his legs a bit.

42 - To Fight Another Day

Carter pulled into Amber Hill at the main gate. The Corporal scrupulously checked his ID and nodded to the other SP to raise the gate. Carter let in the clutch, shoved it into gear and sped off to the mess. Woods was walking up the entrance steps as he parked outside. His navigator turned at the sound of the engine, saw who it was and waved, waiting for Carter to join him.

"Hi, Woody, good leave?" Carter asked, his tone breezy. The big man grinned.

"Good enough. Time for a drink?" he asked, making the universal sign of holding a glass.

"I should think so. Lead on." He opened the door and Woods went in first. Carter breezed past the message slots, the only thing waiting for him would be a Mess bill and that could wait. They got themselves a space at the bar and Carter ordered two beers. Once they were served, they turned, backs to the bar, hand clasping the pint pot.

"Be it ever so humble," said Carter.

"There's no place like home," Woods finished for him.

Considering how fast they wanted to get out of this place one week before, it felt good to be back. Batteries recharged; Woods was raring to go. The Mess was pretty empty and Carter asked the steward where everyone was.

"There's no ops on are there?"

"No, sir. I expect they're all up trying the new aircraft out," he replied matter of factly, polishing a beer glass before putting it back on the shelf.

"What new aircraft?" Carter asked.

The steward looked at him like he was stupid.

"They started arriving yesterday. The squadrons stood-" but he was talking to empty air, they had already scrambled out the door to Carter's car. They sped off to the hangars, ignoring the speed limits.

Carter stood, open mouthed as he saw three aircraft alongside each other outside the hangar. The one nearest to them lacked any squadron codes and only had the roundels on it. It was an Avro Lancaster. He wandered over and had a good look round. It was just like the prototype they'd seen all those months ago at Ringway.

They went back to the Mess, finished their beers and had

another one. Some other officers came in and said hello. Vos appeared around four, had one drink, mumbled something about having a good leave and then went to get changed for tea. Carter drove over to his billet and breezed into his room, wanting to talk about the new kites with Walsh.

He found Saunderson, packing up Walsh's stuff. That rooted Carter to the spot. He suddenly felt faint, his legs turned to rubber and he sank onto the corner of his bed. His mouth had gone dry and he looked at Saunderson with horror.

The Adjutant looked like a kid caught with his hand in the biscuit tin. He finished fastening the clasps on the suitcase and put it with the kitbag behind the door.

"Sorry about this," he said, his tone abjectly apologetic. "I thought I could get this done before you got back."

Carter was too shocked to respond at first. He licked his lips and found his voice wouldn't work. He tried again.

"How? When?"

"Two nights ago, minelaying off the Frisians. We got the code that they'd dropped, but they never did get back."

Carter nodded dumbly. He looked at the pile of stuff on the mattress. Saunderson followed his look.

"Spare kit. No need to send that back to his home. You might find it useful. If not, I'm sure you'll know someone who cam make use of it."

Saunderson held out an envelope. Carter took it, turning it over in his hand.

"He left that for you."

Job done, Saunderson picked up the case and kit bag and left Carter to himself. The room suddenly felt very empty.

After dinner, Fish Salmon asked to see him. Feeling a little bleak, Carter ambled along to his Flight Commander's office. Not standing on ceremony, Salmon pointed to the seat in front of his desk. Carter sat himself down and took the offered cigarette. He tucked it behind his ear to save it for later.

"Good leave?" asked Salmon briskly. Carter noticed he looked tired. Dark rings were under his eyes.

"Pretty good," Carter replied. "A week off was just the fillip I needed."

Salmon nodded grimly.

"Good, because we're right back in it. We've got to work up with the Lancs as quick as we can. A few bods have come over from 44 at Waddington to give us some tips, but we'll have to work it out as we go along. We're keeping some of our Manchester's for now in case Group want a job laid on but we're off ops for the time being." He handed over a book to Carter. "Pilot's notes. Get reading and you can see your new kite tomorrow. You can meet your new crew then as well. You're getting a Flight Engineer and a dedicated Bomb Aimer."

"So, we'll have a crew of eight?" Carter asked, making sure he did his arithmetic right.

"Seven," corrected Salmon. "The Lancs don't have a second pilot, but you needn't worry, Jensen's been awarded a commission. He'll be going off on a course tomorrow."

"Good for him," Carter said, genuinely pleased for him.

"I'm glad you agree. I think it's well deserved. Get weaving, it's good to have you back." He held out his hand and Carter shook it, surprised at Salmon's warmth.

That night they went into Lincoln to give Jensen a proper send off. Carter lost count of the number of pubs they went to. They spent some time at *The Tarleton* on Portland Street. It got a bit blurry after that. Carter had no idea how they got back to Amber Hill let alone get to bed.

They gathered under the nose of their new bomber the next day looking decidedly the worse for wear. This was the third time they had looked over a new aircraft, it was getting stale.

A pilot from 44 was waiting for them. To all outward appearances, the Lancaster was a Manchester with a few tweaks. The wingspan had been stretched to over one hundred feet. There was no third fin on the fuselage and four Merlin engines hung in pods under the wings. There would be no more Vultures to worry about.

They got aboard. As similar to a Manchester as you could get, there were still technical differences. There was not one station on the Lancaster that didn't have changes.

Both Murphy and Todd had new turrets. Happiest of all was Murphy, who had come to hate the cramped conditions of the Botha mid upper turret on the Manchester. In the tail, Todd had the FN20 turret and four .303 machine guns as per the FN5, but he had a bit more room to move around in.

In the cockpit, there were the extra throttles and starters and extinguishers for the four Merlin engines. Gone were the second set of flying controls. Instead, there was a new panel on the right for the Flight Engineer. Vos had a few new tweaks to his radio equipment. Woods was the only place untouched, but there were rumours some new navigational aids were coming.

When they got back, they gathered at the tail, well pleased with their new mount. Once again, she sported an L on the side behind the squadron codes.

"Could we have a name on this one, skipper?" asked Todd.

"London III?" Carter suggested after some thought.

"London's a bit of a dive," commented Murphy. "Can't it be something else?"

"Such as?" asked Carter.

"Something a bit livelier would be good," said Woods.

The two new men stayed out of this conversation. Carter twisted his face. As a rule, he didn't like painting nose art on his kites. He never had on his Hampden's throughout his first tour and he wasn't keen on the idea now.

"If we're going to have something, then the name needs to suit the letter," he said.

"I don't care, as long as its got curves in the right places," said Todd with a leer.

"Keep it relatively clean gents, no nudes," Carter corrected. As skipper, he was going to have the casting vote anyway, but even so, he didn't want to stifle them too much.

"How about L for Lady?" offered Vos.

That was perfect and they agreed. Two days later, she sported a rendition of a reclining female in a red chemise and stockings above flowing script on the left side of the nose. She was now 'The Lady'.

They buckled down to the conversion training with gusto. After the first flight, the crew's mood was sky high. Here was the aircraft that would get them through the rest of their tour. As much as L-London had been reasonably well behaved, Carter found he was far more relaxed in *The Lady*. He had four tried and tested Merlins, reserve power and no fear that an engine might burst into flames without warning.

The final proof came when he had Byron, their new Flight Engineer, cut both port engines on one of their flights. He advanced the throttles on the starboard engines and the Lancaster stayed up with not a hint of a problem.

When Carter threw her into a corkscrew, it was like flying a fighter in comparison to the Manchester. The controls were much lighter, particularly in the climb and the Lanc flew with poise and precision.

The new crew members settled in. Their Flight Engineer Byron was young, dark haired and serious. A failed pilot, he'd been desperate to stay on as aircrew, so he'd retrained to whatever he could get. Carter couldn't care less about that, the fact Byron had twenty hours of stick time was what mattered, it was some insurance in case of difficulties. He started giving Byron some instruction and he soon had confidence, that in the event he was ever hit, the Engineer could at least take the controls and hold it level long enough for the crew to bail out.

The Bomb Aimer, a Flight Sergeant called Colin Flynn, was tall, athletic and by his own account, a ladykiller. He insisted on being called Errol and clearly modelled himself on the movie star, right down to the pencil moustache. He and Murphy became firm friends. More importantly, he was also a pretty good bomb aimer. He proved that over the sands at Wainfleet, dumping practice bomb after practice bomb on the target from sixteen, seventeen and eighteen thousand feet.

During their conversation training, Woods moved in with Carter. He brought his stuff over and filled the gaping hole that had been left by Walsh's loss. The big Canadian also acquired a dog. One of the other navigator's had grown tired of going out for walks in the cold and wet so Woods took him on. A blonde Labrador called Merlin; it was a gorgeous dog if a little on the tubby side.

Carter balked at the idea of having an animal share their room. It was big and there was something about the smell of damp dog that his nose found objectionable, but once he saw the big eyes and trusting face, he couldn't bring himself to say no so Merlin stayed. Officially he slept in the corner, but most nights he ended up on Woods bed, a big yellow furry hot water bottle. Woods wished he'd thought of this during the winter when it was cold.

A week later, Carter encountered another problem. On a fighter familiarisation exercise, he had been throwing the Lancaster around with gusto to see how far he could push it. On one corkscrew he went through a really steep climbing turn to port, cutting across the diving fighters' approach. As it broke off the attack, Carter reversed the turn and dumped the nose, diving to starboard. He let the altimeter unwind. At five thousand feet, he hauled back on the yoke and there was an abrupt shudder through the airframe.

He levelled off immediately and got the crew to call in and check for any damage. Murphy told him to look at the wings. Carter looked left and saw a ragged edge of metal where the wingtip was missing but Murphy wasn't referring to that one, he was looking at the other one.

Byron looked out of the canopy to the right. The last few feet of the wingtip was vertical and fluttering in the slipstream. Carter glanced right and blanched. With the wingtip gone he might lose an aileron. With the tip bent, it might nip the aileron and jam it in position. Either way, they were in trouble.

Woods gave him a straight course for home. Gingerly, they made the turn with a combination of rudder and manipulating the throttles. A few miles from home, the starboard wingtip fluttered one last time and then finally tore away. Carter kept the movements small and made a beautiful landing to stop anything else from falling off.

To have a failure like that on a new aircraft drew attention. Pullen was good enough to doubt his word, the Group Engineering Officer went one step further than that and accused Carter of stunting and low flying and trying to talk his way out of it when it had all gone wrong. Such a brazen accusation pissed Carter off and he stuck to his guns.

Saunderson made a few phone calls to some local schools and passed the word that a bit of aircraft was missing. The first to find it could claim a reward of ten shillings. There the matter lay for a few days until one of the missing wingtips turned up. Two boys had found it inside a hedgerow and taken it to class.

Maps were consulted and the location jibed with Carters track back to Amber Hill. There had been no reports of low flying aircraft in the area that day so Carter was grudgingly taken at his word.

Of course, this then begged the question of what had actually happened. The Group Engineering Officer changed tack and accused Carter of deliberately over stressing the airframe. At this point, Church stepped in and backed his man. Stunting at low level was against the rules, everyone knew that, but he wasn't about to have his pilots accused of bad flying by a pencil pusher.

An Anson flew in with some Avro staff from Ringway. While they looked at *The Lady* in the hangar, the Anson's pilot went looking for Carter. He found him stewing in his billet.

"Can I come in?" he asked.

Carter brightened at the interruption. He recognised Andrews and gestured to Woods bed opposite. Merlin looked up for a moment, looking at the visitor before going back to snoozing in his basket.

"Hello again. I asked around where you might be."

"Better be careful," said Carter. "It might be difficult being seen with a line shooter."

Andrews cocked his head to one side and gave Carter a shrewd look.

"Is that what it is?"

"No, of course not!" Carter snapped back, temperature rising. It took a moment for him to reign himself back in. "Group just pisses me off." Andrews nodded knowingly. He knew how the service could be. He was ex RAF himself and during the 1930's, transgressions were jumped on with little mercy.

"Take a walk?" Andrews suggested. Carter nodded and made for the door.

"Why not? Nothing else to do at the moment."

They headed to the peri track, Merlin tagging along behind. The remaining Manchester's were at dispersal and Andrews took a stroll around. He kicked one of the mainwheels and then leaned against it, hands shoved in the pockets of his white flying suit. Merlin christened the tail wheel then went sniffing the grass, looking for rabbits.

"How are you finding the Lanc?" Andrews asked him.

"Marvellous. She flies beautifully," Carter said with enthusiasm.

"When bits aren't falling off that is," he finished, his tone sarcastic.

"You still stand by that?" enquired Andrews.

Carter felt insulted that his word was being questioned but he kept his temper under control. He stuck his chin out.

"I do."

Andrews nodded and folded his arms. He looked off to his left, staring at the horizon as he chewed on a blade of grass.

"I don't think I can stress to you just how much efforts gone into the Lanc." They watched a Lancaster drone overhead in the circuit. It came in, flaps down, floating along the glide path before touching down with a screech of rubber. "If this was just fun and games gone wrong," Andrews continued, "it goes no further after today. Production will press on. If you say it's right…" He left the out hanging there to be grabbed with both hands.

"It happened," Carter said with hard certainty.

Andrews gave him a very long, appraising stare. The silence dragged out. Finally, he pushed off from the big mainwheel and clapped Carter on the shoulder.

"Fair enough."

They walked back towards the main part of the airfield. They said their goodbyes when Andrews headed to the hangars. The Avro staff left that evening, taking the wingtip and the remains of the mountings with them. *The Lady* was fitted with new wingtips and a test flight was scheduled for the following morning. Nothing was said, but Carter knew they thought it was his fault.

The following day, word reached them that another Lanc lost its port wingtip over at Waddington. It was recovered and comparisons were made with that and the one recovered from Carter's Lancaster. A week later, it was decided it had been a faulty batch of mountings that attached the wingtips to the rest of the wing. Carter felt vindicated, but it had left a bad taste in his mouth.

43 - New Lease

Carter stamped into the hut and shrugged off his greatcoat. Woods was sitting at the table writing a letter home.

"Where you been?" he asked.

"Got snagged for something didn't I?" Carter answered, his irritation evident. Woods shrugged and turned back to his letter, wondering how he was going to tell his parents about Yvonne. While everyone else had shot off hither and tither on leave, Woods had stayed at Amber Hill and finally made his move.

He had caught her coming out of Intel when her hands were full with folders. Ever gallant, he offered to help carry them for her and she let him. They talked all the way to the briefing room and arranged to meet at the cinema that evening. He suddenly wondered what he had been so worried about all those weeks.

Since then they had been almost inseparable, spending their time off the station. The only person who knew was Carter and even he'd only found out the week before. He had seen them walking hand in hand late one night when Woods was walking her back to the WAAFery on the far side of the station.

Carter had buttonholed him when he got back to their room. At first, Woods had tried to bluff it out, but when Carter told him he had seen them, he folded and told him. Putting it down on paper just made it seem more real somehow. He also mentioned the coming squadron dance and the fuss over the squadron photograph that had been taken that lunchtime.

After nearly three weeks of work ups and training, the squadron was going back on ops, but before that, there was one last chance for a party. With no ops on, a definite date had been penciled in and Saunderson had spent the last week making arrangements. Invites had gone out and the men had spent the day making themselves presentable.

Seeing as they were sprucing themselves up for the evening's entertainment, Church took the opportunity to do a squadron photograph. He'd had them parade outside the main hangar in their best blue, with their trousers pressed, their shirts stiff and their shoes bulled. In front of the hangar a Lanc had been drawn up on the pan with a row of chairs in front of it. Aside from the station photographer, there was one from Group, a few people from the press and a Pathé news crew.

Everyone had suddenly felt like celebrities and put on their best faces. It took about twenty minutes to get the photos. They could have done it in half the time but there was the usual horseplay and pushing and shoving. It felt like posing for the school photograph.

The Pathé crew took some footage of the lineup, with Church, Everett, Salmon, Etheridge and the squadron ground staff sat on chairs in the middle. They shot some more film afterwards of the crews milling around, having a chat and a smoke until they were released.

Woods looked up from his letter when he saw Carter get out of his best blue, pull on his long johns and put on his beat up battledress and scruffy pants.

"Need a favour Woody," he asked shortly. Woods set his letter aside.

"Name it."

"Get your warm gear on, you'll love it."

Carter had been about to head off in his car when he was summoned to see the CO. He was going to pick up Georgette to bring her to the dance but he thought he'd go early to see Helen at *The Madison*. She was due any day so Carter was sure she might want some company after being cooped up at the hotel.

He'd smelt a rat when he saw there was a full house waiting for him in Church's office. Etheridge was sitting behind the CO's desk with Church hovering by his right shoulder like some metaphorical pirate's parrot. Salmon had stood in the corner, arms folded, his backside perched on the windowsill.

The Group Captain was all smiles in his best bib and tucker, his breast sporting the usual rows of medal ribbons below faded pilot wings. His hands were clasped on top of the desk, the four broad rings visible on each cuff.

"Come in, Carter, sit ye down, sit ye down."

Carter parked himself as directed. It was at this point he became aware there was another person in the room. In the corner behind him there was a man in a brown army type uniform. Tall and lean as he was, he didn't look like a soldier with wire rim glasses perched on his nose.

"I've got a job for you," Etheridge told him. "As the Lancs are so new, Group is rather keen to show people what we can now do. You know, newsreels, that sort of thing." Carter was already putting two and two together and wasn't liking the answer. Etheridge continued, indicating the man in the khaki. "So, Mister Cullen is here to do a piece on the life of a bomber squadron, follow a crew around etc. We thought you could assist with that." The Group Captain beamed at him.

Carter had frozen at the thought of being made into a poster boy for Bomber Command. He didn't particularly care for shooting a line. Even Archer, the press on type had been pretty discreet.

"Nothing flashy of course," Cullen reassured him. "I'd like to go up on a test flight, talk to your men if I may."

"I think that can be accommodated," Carter temporised, his voice neutral.

"There we are then. Settled," said Etheridge, pleased that Carter was proving so amenable. Obviously dismissed, Carter stood to attention, saluted and then left the office, Cullen followed after him. He caught up to Carter after some effort, the young pilot was walking fast.

"I've been around you know. I was in France with a Blenheim unit right up to Dunkirk," Cullen said to try and reassure him. "I was in the Western Desert last year." When Carter didn't reply he carried on, "I do know what I'm doing."

"I'll take your word for it," Carter said without humour. He jammed his hands into his pockets as they walked past the pyro store. "Have you ever been up?"

"A few times," Cullen told him. "I got the slow boat to Egypt, but I went up for a flip in a Martin Maryland and I went on two raids in a Wimpy," he said matter of factly. One raid had been on an Afrika Korps troop concentration along the coast near Tobruk. The other had been a five hour marathon hunting for shipping in the Mediterranean. Seeing the flak and tracer at night while they had played tag with the convoy escort had been a hair raising experience. "All unofficial of course."

Carter looked askance at him, trying to judge if he was pulling his leg. He looked up at the sky and then decided.

"All right then, lets take you to go and get kitted out."

He changed direction and headed to the equipment hut. He left Cullen in their capable hands to draw a parachute and some flying kit before heading back to his billet to get changed and get Woods. The rest of the crew had been rounded up and were waiting for him when they got out to dispersal. None of them looked impressed at having been summoned.

With the skies threatening rain, no one had felt like going far. Murphy, Todd, Byron and Flynn had been in the Sergeants Mess. The dance might have been that evening but that was no reason not to lubricate their pipes beforehand. Vos had been found in the Mess drafting another missive to the Belgian Embassy in London asking after his family.

Latimer helped Cullen get on board and showed him where to plug in for the R/T. The reporter stood at Carters shoulder behind the pilot's seat, his eyes darting everywhere trying to take in as much as he could.

An erk clambered up the starboard mainwheel and used the foot rests halfway up the oleo legs to plug in the trolley acc at the priming panel. That was dead easy in the daytime, not so easy at night. Latimer stood out front where Carter could see him and pointed at the starboard inner. This engine was always started first as it powered the pneumatic and hydraulic systems. The engines were started in sequence and then they were off. For a moment, Carter stared at the hard standing where Walsh's Manchester had been all throughout their tour. One of the new replacements occupied that spot now but Carter had no interest in knowing his name.

"Just a quick flip, Mister Cullen to give you a flavour of what things are like."

Cullen nodded. Going up in a military aircraft was always a treat for him, particularly when he could ask questions. Even on first impressions he liked the Lancaster. It felt solid and was like something out of Buck Rogers in comparison to the Wellington.

Etheridge had told him he was getting one of his best men and Cullen believed it. Carter handled her like a pro, flying comfortably. His eyes never rested as they moved in a constant circuit. He looked at the instruments in a particular order, he looked forwards over the nose, he glanced left and right out at that big wing. He took nothing for granted and he maintained his vigilance, even as he answered Cullen's questions. Cullen compared him with other RAF personnel he had known, in France and in the desert. He was a good man, he decided.

44 - Waltz The Light Fantastic

The dance was on a par with the one at Christmas. Some of the Avro staff had been invited and Carter saw Andrews amongst them when they came in. A few bods from other stations came as well as officers from Group. Church was not above using an evening like this as an opportunity to grease the wheels and keep the Group staff on side. The field was rounded out with some nurses from a nearby hospital as well as a few local dignitaries. Aircraft made lots of noise so it didn't hurt to keep councillors sweet.

After taking the reporter up, Carter had hustled to get changed and then hot foot it over to Grantham. He saw Helen for twenty minutes over a cup of tea and then took off to get Georgette.

Mrs Lloyd invited him into the parlour to wait and Carter cooled his heels again in the dour front room. The battleaxe was more friendly this time and she stayed in the room, making conversation with him. Carter wondered what he had done to earn such condescension.

Georgette brought an excruciating ten minutes to a close and Carter was grateful for the interruption. After two minutes, his cheeks were tired from smiling. After five, it had been getting painful.

He retreated out of the house, held open the passenger door of the car for Georgette and then they were off. He drove fast all the way and Georgette clung to the door as he rounded corners above what she considered a sensible speed in the rain.

Carter escorted her into the hall and relaxed once they were inside. He snagged a table and got a few extra chairs for when the rest of his crew arrived. Woods brought Yvonne over and introduced her to Georgette. Yvonne was tall, with a lithe figure, a knockout, even when wearing the less than flattering WAAF uniform. She was the same rank as Georgette and the two women hit it off straight away, deep in conversation almost immediately.

Woods disappeared to get some drinks and Carter relaxed, content to let someone else do the talking. He scanned the room, seeing the ebb and flow of people as they moved and talked and danced. It was the same hall where the Christmas dance had been held and a band were on the stage, banging out a mix of big band music. Various couples were on the floor, moving around with a great deal of energy.

No doubt he would be prevailed on to dance at some point. Carter did his best not to brood. The last time he had been in this hall was with Walsh and his crew, White, Archer and a host of others. Even Wilkinson had cried off tonight. To be fair, with a wife about to give birth, Carter would give him that one. He shook his head and took the pint that Woods handed him. Life went on. It was a dance, a chance to let his hair down.

He saw Flynn, Byron and Murphy at the bar. They nursed pints while they looked at girls. Todd was nowhere in sight but Carter just assumed he was lost in the crowd somewhere. Woods sat down next to Carter. They shared a look, nodding to absent friends.

Georgette turned to him and gave his hand an encouraging squeeze. He smiled and pushed the gloom to one side, pleased to have a night off with charming company.

"How long do you think it will be before we're back on ops?" Yvonne asked him. Carter thought about that. He didn't particularly want to talk shop, but he could understand Yvonne's curiosity; she was only asking what everyone else was wondering. Now that the squadron was operational again, it was only a matter of time before they were thrown back into it.

"I'm no wiser than everyone else," he demurred. "I'd have thought you'd have more of an idea than most of us." He could see her green eyes gauge that. Obviously, she assumed his being a senior man on the squadron meant he had an inside track to some information the rest of them didn't have. "No crystal ball, but I can't see Group hanging around for long, can you?" He batted the question back to her. Suddenly he noticed someone he had not expected to see.

"In fact, ask him." They all turned to see Wilkinson approaching their table. "Hi, Freddie. How did you get permission to be out tonight?"

Wilkinson smiled. He stood behind Carter, leaning on the back of his chair. He looked tired, with dark rings under his eyes.

"Flying visit. I'm here with the old man but I'll be heading back soon enough."

There was something in the way Wilkinson said that which peaked Carter's antenna.

"Flap on?" he enquired.

"No, nothing like that. I've just got to get back to, Helen."

"How is she?" asked Georgette.

"Climbing the walls," Wilkinson replied, laughing.

"You staying for a drink?" Carter motioned to a free chair.

"Can't," said Wilkinson. "I'm heading back shortly. I just wanted to take the opportunity to say hello." They shook hands. He nodded to Yvonne and Georgette. "Ladies."

379

He was gone as quickly as he had come, gliding over to the Air Commodore who was talking with Church and Etheridge.

As Wilkinson left, Vos arrived with Denise. Unlike Georgette and Yvonne who were in uniform tonight, Denise was in a dark green off the shoulder dress. Her hair was pinned up to show her neck to the best advantage.

"Good evening, mademoiselle."

Denise grasped him by the shoulders and kissed him French fashion on either cheek.

"Good evening, Monsieur Carter."

"You look lovely," he told her. Her cheeks coloured as she took the sea next to Vos.

"Would you like to dance?" Carter asked as he turned to Georgette.

She didn't need asking twice. They went to the floor as the band struck up with a pacy number that stretched Carters dancing skills. Georgette laughed when she saw how clumsy he was. Cool in the air, bit of a mess on the ground.

Across the room, Flynn saw Carter dancing and low whistled when he clapped eyes on Georgette.

"Brother, get me one of those and I'll be happy."

Murphy laughed like a drain.

"Fat chance, the skippers been seeing her for ages, aim a little lower."

They had already exchanged knowing looks when they clocked Woods with his red head. Flynn looked round the rest of the hall and saw a few girls that caught his eye. He discussed the finer points of a blonde sitting across from them on the other side of the dance floor and a pretty brunette near the bar. Byron held himself more reserved than his two companions. He'd been out a few times with these two and once they had a few pints in them, they were like two rutting stags, egging each other on.

He detached himself from them and went to get another pint. He couldn't wait to start ops. No doubt, Todd would tell him he was insane to be looking forward to something like that, but he didn't care. It had been over a year of hard work to get to this point, now he would get to put into practice everything he'd been learning. He was swinging away from the bar when he bumped straight into someone, spilling his glass.

"Oh god, I am so, so sorry," he apologised. He bent down to pick up her purse and as he came back up, he locked gaze with a pair of deep blue eyes. He straightened up, tugging a handkerchief out of his pocket and tried wiping beer off her arm. He stopped as she took the hanky from his hand, their fingers touching.

"I'm; George," he said, tongue tied.

"I'm, Louise."

He guided her away from the the bar towards the exit, neither realising they were still holding each others hand. Flynn saw Byron leaving with her.

"Bloody hell. We're stood in the wrong place," he muttered. Sick of waiting, he crossed the floor, smoothly moving round the dancing couples as he straightened his tie and approached the blonde who had been flirting with him.

The evening went well. It was a good way to round out three very intense weeks of learning to fly all over again. Carter drank more than usual and was quite tight come the end of the night. He went outside to get some fresh air and clear his head while Georgette went to freshen up in the ladies room. Denise was already in there when she came in. Her eyes were red rimmed while she tried to apply some liner. Georgette offered hers and Denise took it gratefully.

They stood next to each other, looking at their reflections. Georgette brushed her hair. It had flattened a little and she put a bit of bounce back into it, looking at herself from a few angles as she did so.

She glanced at Denise out of the corner of her eye, noticing how pale she was. She looked quite down, which was strange. She had danced as much as Georgette had, dragging a reluctant Vos onto the floor before also dancing with Carter and the big Canadian.

The band had finished with a few slow numbers for the couples and Georgette had enjoyed moulding herself to Carter as they went round in slow circles. She had rested her head on his chest, happy while his arms were around her. She had seen Vos and Denise doing the same, talking softly as they danced.

"You make that dress look wonderful," Georgette told the French girl. Denise brightened at the compliment and straightened, running her hands down the fabric.

"Thank you. It's a little tight," she patted her stomach, "but there's so little choice these days with the ration coupons. The landlady helped with a few alterations. I'm not so good with sewing."

"My compliments to the tailor," she said with a wry smile. She wasn't so good at needlework herself. The girls figure was lovely, although she had gained some weight the last few months. Georgette's reasoning came to a crashing halt with that thought. She looked at Denise again, seeing where the weight had gone.

"Does he know?" Georgette asked the French girl. Denise's hand froze as she applied some lipstick. She shook her head and leaned on the counter, her shoulders shaking.

"Non, I haven't told him."

"Don't you think you should?"

Denise looked at her in the mirror, her eyes wide, scared.

"How far along are you?"

"A few months I think." Her eyes welled up, big fat tears rolling down her cheeks. "It wasn't supposed to be like this," she said, her words halting.

She turned to Georgette and buried her face in her shoulder, finally overwhelmed by it all. Taken by surprise, all Georgette could do was put her arms around her, patting her shoulder as she tried to soothe her. Her mind raced as she tried to decide what to do. There wasn't much she could say here in the ladies room.

"I know it's scary. Listen, we need to talk about this, I mean *really* talk about this, but not now." Denise sniffed, nodding. "We'll take you home and I'll come and see you, and we can have a good chat about it, okay?"

Denise brightened at that. She blew her nose and once her eyes had calmed down, they spent a few minutes putting her makeup to rights. They came out as if nothing had happened to find Vos and Carter impatiently walking up and down outside. Carter glanced at his watch, looking a little surprised at how long it had taken.

"We were about to send out a search party," he said, his tone playful.

"She wasn't feeling well," Georgette replied. "She's been a bit sick."

Vos came over, his face creased in concern. Denise nodded, mute as he asked how she was. Georgette buttonholed Carter about taking them home.

"Darling, it's pretty late to try and get a bus and I hate the idea of Denise riding in one of those mouldy old trucks. Could we give them a lift?" She gave Carter her best smile. There was not much he could say after that.

They had to get creative to squeeze everyone in. The car wasn't really built for four. Vos was sitting in the front and Denise was on his lap, arms around his shoulders. Behind the front seats was a void which could take a few suitcases. It was tight, but Georgette squeezed herself in there. She could look over Carters shoulder while he drove. He had the window down to stay sharp, his brain was still a bit soft from the booze.

Somehow, they got to Lincoln without hitting anything and Carter pulled up outside Denise's digs. Denise and Vos went up. Georgette went with them, making a fuss of her and then talking with the landlady. Georgette could see Mrs Peck thought a lot of Denise, so it was easy enough to enlist her help and get a phone number.

"Thinks the world of her, he does," said Mrs Peck. "Always round to see her when he can, which must be quite hard being on them bombers."

Georgette nodded. Vos came down the stairs and stuck his head round the door to the parlour at the back of the house.

"She's sleeping now. She was sick again," he told the landlady.

"I'll look after her, don't you worry," Mrs Peck reassured him.

"I know you will."

On the drive back to Amber Hill Georgette sat on Vos's lap this time. Carter dropped his radio operator off at the gate and then went on to Grantham.

He yawned as they set off. He was flagging a bit after a few drinks and he still had to get back to Amber Hill after this. He took his time as the blacked out headlamps did little to light the way. He was concentrating on his driving, half listening to Georgette when something suddenly caught his attention. He hit the brakes when Georgette told him the secret.

"She's what!"

"Pregnant, darling," Georgette said it slowly so he could absorb that. "With child," she repeated. Carter digested that news for a second.

"What about, Vos?"

"He doesn't know yet. And don't you go telling him either," Georgette said sharply. "That's not our story to tell."

"I know." He put the car in gear and pulled away. He shifted up through the gears and went a bit faster. "Well this is a fine old situation," he muttered.

45 - With Great Power

Two days later, Group put them on the line. First time out, half the squadron was going and there was a crowd at the notice board outside the briefing room when the list went up. Carter was down to go. Cullen floated around in the background, picking up on the mood of the men, the elation at being chosen, the disappointment at missing out.

He watched as the squadron went to war. He went to the dump and saw the armourers getting the bombs ready, fitting the tails and fuses before loading them onto the trolleys. He rode one out to dispersal and watched the erks winch the bombs up into the cavernous bomb bay. Bowsers trundled round the peri track and each kite had its tanks topped up.

He attended the briefing. Rather than sit at the front, he picked a seat amongst the crowd so he could soak up the atmosphere. The mood was grim when they were told it was going to be another run at the Krupps Works at Essen. Flak city again. The Ruhr was something Cullen only read about in press releases or heard about in the news. Seeing the reactions of the crews made it seem more real.

He tried to think about how he could phrase what it was like. He thought about his own experiences on those raids in the desert and his time in France. That gave him some of the flavour to make the comparison. Briefings in the desert were very similar. The hushed quiet as you waited to hear what the target was going to be, then the details about bomb loads and take off times.

What struck him is that it was the scale that was different. Here, this squadron was just one of many that were going out this night. It was a long way from a single squadron of Blenheims and Wellingtons going out to bomb an encampment, or a vehicle park in North Africa.

Carter felt buoyant. He had every confidence in the Lancaster. They were going to be able to get a lot higher than they could in their Manchester so they'd be able to avoid a lot of the flak. He glanced across at Byron and Flynn. This would be their first time out. Flynn grinned back at him. In contrast, Byron looked sick to his stomach.

Cullen rode out with them to dispersal. Sitting next to Carter, he watched him, trying to gauge his mood. Carter said nothing. He was starting to think about the mission ahead of them, picturing the route. Flynn and Byron said little. Todd and Murphy on the other hand were very chatty, joking away, trying to get a reaction from Vos who was quietly chain smoking, lighting the next off the remains of the last.

Murphy was talking about a new conquest of his, a WAAF in the parachute section. He'd already had a secret assignation with her in the packing shed out of hours. It turned out silk parachute canopies made a wonderfully comfortable mattress.

"Of course, I told her she needed to be careful," said Murphy, drawing his story to a close.

"Is this the blonde?" Todd asked. Murphy nodded. "I know the one you mean," said Todd. "She's a magnet that girl."

Murphy's brow scrunched up while he thought about that.

"I don't get it," he replied, his face showing his confusion.

"A magnet mate," Todd prompted him. He paused for effect. "Attractive from behind, bloody repulsive from the front."

The truck erupted in laughter, they loved it.

"Yeah, yeah," moaned Murphy, trying to shake it off. He banged his head when the truck stopped with a sudden jerk.

"L-London!" shouted the driver.

They got out and Todd took it upon himself to correct the driver.

"That's L for Lady mate, and don't you forget it!"

The groundcrew were waiting for them. Todd nabbed some cotton waste and shoved it into the front of his leather flying suit. Byron took his position, the row of dials swimming in front of him. This was it. He felt a thump on his shoulder and he turned to see Woods smiling at him.

"You'll be fine," the big man told him. Byron nodded, not trusting his voice.

Carter climbed up the ladder into the nose and came into the cockpit. He stowed his parachute pack and settled himself in his seat, working the rudder pedals back and forth. He pulled back on the yoke and then plugged in the R/T.

"Crew check in." They were prompt as ever.

The engines started up. Todd was sitting next to Murphy, leaning against the rear spar. He closed his eyes and murmured a silent prayer to himself. Last time out they had a roller coaster ride for free. All he wanted tonight was a nice easy mission with no surprises.

Cullen stood next to Latimer and watched quietly as the Lancaster moved off. The four engines roared like banshees, the bass rumbling in his chest. The sounds battered his ears as the tang of the exhaust washed over him, the smell stinging his nostrils.

The truck dropped him off at the control tower. He went up to the second floor and joined Etheridge at the rail. Linkletter and Kent were there as well as Pullen. Tonight, was a big night. As only the third squadron to be operating Lancasters, a lot of eyes were turned in their direction. After the Manchester's had been such a disappointment, Group, Bomber Command HQ and the Air Ministry were anxious to see how this new bomber would perform.

Carter lined up at the end of the runway. He dabbed the brakes and brought the big bomber to a stop. He pulled the yoke back while Byron advanced the throttles, running up the engines, looking for mag drop. The airframe vibrated. Carter looked at him and Byron nodded, they were good to go. Carter released the brakes and advanced the throttles, Byron's hand riding behind, ready to take over.

The Lady ran straight, Carer putting in a bit of rudder to offset the torque from the engines. The tail came up and he held her poised on her mainwheels. Byron read off the airspeed. Fully loaded with fuel and bombs, Carter held her down, used to the Manchester and her little ways. He needn't have worried, the Lancaster almost leapt into the air as they climbed away into the night. Flaps up, wheels up, throttles set to climb, piece of cake.

No one got stuck on the peri track and there were no aborts. Etheridge went down to ops once they were all on their way. Wheeler was in his usual place, fielding phone calls from Group while the Corporal updated the blackboard with the takeoff times for each aircraft. In six hours time, Etheridge wanted to see that board full with everyone back home. He saw Cullen parked in the corner with a cup of tea, nibbling on a biscuit. He walked over to him.

"What did you think of that?" he asked. Cullen stood up, brushing crumbs off his front.

"Impressive, sir. It wasn't like that in the desert."

"I'm sure," said Etheridge smoothly, preening at the compliment.

"A lot less sandy too."

Etheridge was good enough to laugh. He sat down next to the correspondent.

"It's a game of patience. It's not like the fighters who dash around and are up and down in an hour and back to see their popsie. We play the long game here. You might find it's a bit boring for a while now the squadrons on the way."

Cullen patted the pocket of his battledress tunic. He tugged out a pad and a pencil.

"I've got some notes I can start writing up, sir."

"I think we can do better than that," Etheridge told him. He gestured towards a WAAF Sergeant. "Can we get Mister Cullen a typewriter and some paper please?" He pointed to a desk on the floor next to the big map table. "There okay?" he asked. Cullen nodded.

The WAAF went through the door in the corner down the

corridor to one of the empty admin offices. She came back a few minutes later lugging a typewriter.

Etheridge went over to the bank of tables on the stage. Wheeler was sharpening a pencil, putting a sharp point on it. He carried on updating entries in the squadron book.

"I'm off to Group," said Etheridge. "I'll be back in a few hours." Wheeler nodded.

Over the North Sea, *The Lady* was climbing like she was on rails. Carter thought about poor old L-London. At this point they would be straining for every foot. Now, it seemed effortless. He relaxed and rolled his neck. The only thing with the Lancaster having no second pilot was that he couldn't hand off to Jensen to take a break. With some trepidation, Carter turned on George, the autopilot. He could never quite bring himself to completely relax when a machine was running the plane. He watched the yoke as it moved on its own, twitching back and forth.

So far, the good weather Linkletter had predicted held. The sun had gone down two hours before but the western sky was still purple on the horizon, the rest a cloud streaked darkening blue. Stars twinkled in the gathering dark. Carter looked over the big expanse of wing, seeing a thin sheen of ice glistening in the weak moonlight. The Lancaster was purring along.

In the tail, Todd tugged the cotton waste out of the front of his heated suit. He polished the perspex on the inside of his turret but he wasn't happy with it. There was condensation starting to freeze on the perspex which could affect his view.

In the mid upper turret, Murphy span his turret slowly one way in a complete revolution and then the other, very happy indeed. It was a relief to no longer have to scrunch up his shoulders like he'd had to in the Botha turret.

They crossed the coast on track, it was when they turned inland that they ran into a headwind. Gusting between twenty and thirty knots, it was like pushing against a pack in the scrum.

"What's that going to do to us?" Carter asked his navigator.

Woods, did some quick calculations. He took a mean average and assumed that would remain constant on the outward legs. He clicked on his R/T.

"Puts us about fifteen minutes behind, skipper."

"Roger."

In the nose, Flynn was calling out landmarks for Woods. With a full time bomb aimer, they had an extra pair of eyes to help with the navigating for which Woods was eternally grateful.

He stood up from his navigating table and went to the astrodome to stretch his legs. He saw Vos twirling the dials, searching the frequencies for any snatches of German. Looking down the gloom of the fuselage he could just make out Murphy's legs dangling down where he was sitting in his turret.

Going back to his station he dug into his navigator's bag and pulled out a thermos flask. He poured a cup of tea and nudged Byron on the shoulder. The Flight Engineer looked at him and Woods nodded towards Carter. Byron understood and he held the steaming cup up for his pilot. Carter took it and cradled the mug in his lap, sipping from it slowly as they cruised along.

Murphy saw another bomber off to the right. It was a Lancaster and he edged in, careful in case the gunners took a sudden shot at them. He saw the letter M on the fuselage. It was Fish Salmon's aircraft and Carter advanced the throttles slightly until they drew level with him.

Salmon rocked his wings. Carter rocked his back and they flew like that for a few minutes, as if they were the only aircraft in the sky. Carter saw Salmon waving in the cockpit. He waggled his wings one last time and then closed the throttles, letting Salmons Lancaster slowly draw ahead.

They turned south at Borken. At least Woods hoped they were. The cloud cover Linkletter had predicted had moved in and played havoc with his dead reckoning. Carter climbed to take them over the clouds to avoid any icing conditions. Even with Flynn up front, he could only pass on sightings if he could actually see anything. There were occasional breaks in the clouds but that didn't help very much if there was nothing identifiable underneath.

As they got closer to their time on target, something had obviously been bombed, as the horizon was glowing with flames. The usual trick with the Ruhr valley was whether or not it was the right place. Aside from hitting the wrong town, there was always the possibility that decoy fires were drawing attention away from the actual target. Flashes on the horizon showed the flak had started.

In the cockpit next to Carter, Byron looked over the edge of the canopy, his eyes wide like saucers. Minelaying with a scratch crew in a tired Stirling at OTU was nothing like this. This was what it was all about, the big leagues.

Flak went off above them, bright sparkles in the darkness. Carter started weaving left and right, putting in gentle turns either side of their track. He told the gunners to keep an eye out for nightfighters.

Murphy and Todd acknowledged and redoubled their efforts to sweep the skies around them. Todd muttered and cursed under his breath. He wiped at the perspex again with the cotton waste, pissed off that he couldn't see properly. A 110 could get within fifty yards and he'd probably miss him. That wasn't how he wanted to go out.

Up front there was a three way debate between Carter, Flynn

and Woods. The Canadian had come up to the cockpit beside Carter and was looking outside, trying to pick up any landmark. Flynn peered below at a sea of white. They were close, but close wasn't good enough for Woods.

When they turned south, the headwind had become a crosswind. Woods had laid off a course allowing for that deviation, but without a fix, he had no idea if they had drifted west or east.

The clouds were lit up from underneath by the flashes of gunfire and the beams of searchlights. Whiteout. Up ahead there was a sudden flash and one big streak of flame was followed by three others. A bomber had blown up and the petrol tanks were consuming themselves during their rapid descent.

The flak intensified and *The Lady* rocked in the turbulence of another bomber ahead of them. Carter sideslipped left to find some clear air. In the next moment there was a massive flash a few hundred yards ahead and for a brief instant, Carter had a glimpse of a twin tailplane, silhouetted against the explosion as its bomb load cooked off. Carter climbed to get over the flying bits of wreckage.

"Jesus," muttered Flynn. "You could walk on this."

"You ain't seen nothing yet," replied Carter, "wait till we're over Berlin." Flynn held a hand in front of his face as they were suddenly lit up like a Christmas tree. A blue master light fixed them in its glare and two other searchlights began moving to cone them.

"Hang on everyone," Carter shouted over the R/T. He shoved the throttles through the gates and Byron appeared at his shoulder, ready to take over just in case. The Merlins screamed at full power and the Lanc bucked through the hailstorm of shrapnel as the flak guns zeroed in.

Carter banked right and the world went sideways. Byron sank almost to his knees as his weight increased rapidly, his feet glued to the floor. Carter reversed the turn, banked left and then used the speed gained in the dive to haul the nose up to claw back the altitude he'd lost. They left the searchlights behind, the sky filled with bursts of flak. For a moment, Carter thought this must be how U-Boat Captains felt when they were being depth charged by Destroyers.

"Everyone okay?" he asked. Flynn and Vos responded rapidly. Murphy replied next. Todd took a moment as he wiped vomit off his front. His head was spinning and his skin was clammy. He used the cotton waste to clear the crap from his oxygen mask.

Byron managed to make his voice sound normal while his stomach tried to tie itself in knots. Woods was the last to respond. He had fallen over during the evasive manouveurs and unknowingly tugged out his intercom connection.

"Make your mind up Woody. I don't want to stooge around here tonight."

Woods went back to his station. He picked the chart up off the floor and smoothed it out, peering at it under the small lamp.

They could be over Essen, Gelsenkirchen, Duisburg or even Dortmund. He couldn't believe they were further south than that, but if they were, they could be over Dusseldorf. He did some quick calculations and scratched his head as he pondered the possibilities. He erred more towards Dortmund or Gelsenkirchen himself. Both Duisburg and Dusseldorf were on the Rhine and even with the heavy cloud they should have been able to see the winding river.

His stomach lurched as a burst of flak went off underneath them. The Lancaster reared up and then dropped again as Carter fought the controls.

"Bollocks," he muttered to himself. There was no way they were going up and down tonight to find the right place. The Ruhr was filled with bloody factories. He was the captain; it was his decision. "Flynn, find something that looks like a factory and get cracking."

"Yes skipper." Flynn looked through the bomb sight. Find a factory the man had said. That was easier said than done. The clouds were thinner to port, they should have a look over there. "Come left twenty degrees," he ordered.

Carter duly obliged. He saw the gap in the clouds himself and realised what Flynn was doing.

Flynn settled himself. It was only a partial break, but at least he could see the ground. There was no water in sight, but apart from that there was little else of note. The wisps of cloud at least let him have a stab at guessing the wind strength and allowing for drift. He adjusted the sight and blinked, trying to pick up a feature.

Even at altitude he could see a row of large flat roofed buildings and some tall chimneys that belched dark smoke into the sky. There were a few fires down there and he sighted on the biggest clump.

"That'll do me," he murmured. He looked at the smoke, watching it move to adjust for drift. "Left a bit, left." The cross wind was pushing them right and he ordered more left to counter it. Flynn selected to drop everything with a half second delay so they could straddle the buildings. "Steady now. Keep on this. Steady." He jabbed the release.

"Bombs gone!" he shouted.

Carter waited for the camera to take its pretty picture.

"Course Woody?" he shouted.

"Steer one seven five!" said Woods. "Then in five minutes come to two six five magnetic."

"Roger, one, seven, five then two, six, five. Eyes peeled everyone, there might be fighters waiting for us on the run out."

A few random bursts of flak went off near by, but nothing came in their direction. Byron relaxed when they left it behind. He kept himself busy with his instruments, making sure the engines were behaving. After a few minutes they turned and headed west, pushed along now by the wind. The heavy cloud began to thin and Carter climbed back up to their starting height.

In the nose, Flynn did his best to steady his jangling nerves. That had been worse than he imagined. He couldn't imagine doing this another twenty nine times. He got into the nose turret and tracked left and right, scanning the sky ahead. It was colder in the turret, but right now he needed some fresh air to keep himself focused.

Coming up to midnight, the moon was high in the sky but it was only a thin sliver of light. Flynn continued to pass sightings of rivers and lakes and Woods got a decent fix at last. With the tailwind pushing them along they were ahead of schedule. Once clear of the known flak belts they turned north and headed home.

The rest of the trip was the usual monotony. Carter did regular checks to make sure everyone was awake and alert. Vos picked up some stations on the DF loop and passed fixes to Woods. Todd continued to fuss in his turret. The condensation on the perspex had turned to a thin sheen of ice and he was resigned to sorting it out once they got back.

They returned six hours after leaving Amber Hill. There were isolated clumps of ground mist but nothing to cause any issues in the circuit. They touched down and taxied to dispersal. Latimer was waiting to see them in and he directed them to their hard standing. Byron closed the throttles and shut the engines down once the chocks were wedged in place.

After being battered for the last six hours, Carter worked his jaw to clear his ears. They assembled under the bomber all smiles, that was another one chalked off. Carter patted the left mainwheel.

"Good girl," he said. "Mark it up," he said to Latimer. He signed the form 700 and they clambered wearily into the waiting truck to be taken to interrogation.

Cullen was waiting for them at interrogation. Sitting with Kent, he listened to the crews make their reports, writing furiously in his pad. He yawned as he took a moment to refill his pen. It had been a long night for him. He'd talked with Wheeler for hours in ops. He found the man's story fascinating; perhaps he would get to tell it another day.

Etheridge and Church circled the room slowly, listening to what the crews were saying. It was becoming clear that tonight had not been a good night. The heavy cloud and high winds had ballsed everything up. Aircraft had bombed all over the shop and they'd have to wait for the target photographs to get an idea of how the squadron had done. Back in ops, Wheeler was fielding reports of three Lancasters landing at other fields in the south.

Carter noticed her across the room when he picked up a tray of tea for the lads. He'd forgotten she'd be working tonight and he was amused to see Woods reaction. He looked very nervous and started hopping slightly from foot to foot, almost as if he needed to go the toilet. Yvonne was one of three WAAF's that were doing the interrogations with Kent so it was a coin toss that she would be free when it was their turn. Of course, fate being fate.

"Next," she said, without looking up from the table. She checked the form, made a correction and then signed the bottom of it. She put the sheet on the top of the pile. Carter and the rest of the boys slumped into the chairs in front of her. He had to admit she was good. She hid her surprise well, a mere widening of the eyes and a slight upwards pull to the sides of her mouth when she saw Woods.

"Crew?" she asked, her voice neutral.

"L7585, L-Lady," said Carter

"Lady? You mean London?" she corrected him.

"He means, L for Lady, L-A-D-Y," insisted Todd, watching carefully as she wrote down the serial number and letter, ready to pounce if she wrote London.

"Did you hit the target?" she asked and so the questions went on.

The biggest controversy was trying to pin down exactly where they bombed. Woods had been trying to figure that out on the return trip, backplotting once they'd got a fix. He gave up in the end. The Ruhr was too built up and places blended into one another. She wrote, 'Not Determined' on the form. Maybe the target photograph would provide the answer later on.

They passed the information of the aircraft they had seen going down, one over the target and two more on the return trip. She made a note of the approximate positions in a separate box. There were the usual questions after that regarding flak concentrations, enemy air attack and any other remarks. Woods said little, he just shifted in his seat, praying for it to end.

They went to the Mess for breakfast and Cullen went with them. It was his final step on the raid, the journey from beginning to end. He watched as tired meant ate, their reward after a long night full of danger. Woods wolfed down bacon and eggs. Vos had his hard boiled and was fastidiously cutting buttered toast into sticks so he could dip them into the yolk. Cullen asked how often weather interfered with operations.

"One in three? One in four maybe," Carter informed him while munched on some toast. "I remember on my fist tour we used to go out on some filthy nights."

"But if you go out on filthy nights, that makes bombing difficult right?"

Woods nodded.

"It's not like throwing practise bombs in Canada," he assured the reporter. "You've got to *see* something to bomb it."

"Then why-"

"Because nightfighters love bright moonlit nights." Carter cut him off, getting irritated by the questions. He was getting a little too tired to humour the man. "They roam up and down, hunting for targets. They can't shoot down what they can't see."

He nibbled on some toast. His stomach was playing up. He wanted to get to bed, get some sleep and then see Georgette.

While the crews trailed off to bed, Church sipped tea in Etheridge's office. He was slumped in a chair, his backside perched on the edge so he could stretch out, his legs extended in front of him, the cup balanced on his chest. He closed his eyes for a moment, fatigue washing over him. As he drifted off, he snapped awake. He twitched and the cup jumped in his hands. Tea slopped over the sides all over his hands and the top of his battledress. Church sat up, flicking tea off his hand.

"Goddammit," he cursed. He drank more tea and then pushed the half empty cup onto Groupies desk. He looked down at his top and wiped feebly at the damp with his hanky. He ran his hands up and down his face, rubbing away the tiredness, stubble rasping on his chin. He was tired after flying last night, he wanted a bath and he wanted to sleep but there were things to be done. He had eight letters to write.

Flak had slashed the throat of the rear gunner in F-Freddy. The crew got to him an hour later after they had bust open the jammed doors to the turret. It was like a slaughterhouse inside; blood had gone everywhere. It was surprising just how much mess a few pints could cause.

The other seven letters were for Salmon and his crew. It was long past the point of no return and there was no report of him landing anywhere else. The Home Guard had not reported any crashed aircraft and there had been no mayday received either. Salmon's letter was going to be the most difficult. Church had met his wife a few months before and she was a lovely woman. It was going to be hard, getting news like that with two children to look after. He reminded himself to organise a car so he could go and see her. He slumped back into the chair; his eyes heavy.

Families had it hard enough as it is. They would get the standard form telegram from the Air Ministry, with its cold, clipped and efficient language, *The Air Ministry regret to inform you that your husband is missing after operations on 10th April 1942. The Air Council express their sympathy, blah, blah, blah.* He thought Salmon and the others were worth more than a few sentences on a telegram.

The door opened and Etheridge came in, settling himself behind his desk, looking as fresh as ever. Church wondered how the old man

393

did it. He seemed to have boundless energy on ops nights, going to briefing, seeing the off, spinning over to Group and then putting the boys to bed. The routine never changed when ops were on. A Corporal came in with a cup of tea and Etheridge pointed to his desk. The Corporal put it down and left the office quietly.

"How much longer are we going to have the reporter?" Church enquired quietly.

"A few days. I would imagine he'll want to see another raid before he goes. In fact, after the results tonight, I'd rather he stayed to see a good one, go on another training flight maybe." Church was not over the moon about that prospect. Reporters asking questions made people nervous.

"And if he asks to go on an op?"

Etheridge thought about that.

"No," he said flatly. "Definitely not. Can you imagine what Group would say if we lost a reporter on a raid? No, he stays on the ground."

"I'll be sure to tell him the good news," said Church, feeling a little better.

"Bad luck about, Salmon," Etheridge said, changing the subject.

Church simply nodded, there wasn't much else to say. People came and went, that was the way things were on ops. He wondered if one day someone would be saying the same thing about him. The big question now of course was, what to do about it.

"The boys did well tonight," he said. Etheridge nodded. That was fair. First time out with a new aircraft on ops, things *had* gone well. The fact the bombing had been poor was no one's fault. Sometimes the weather got the better of you and that was that.

"I wanted your view before we looked at bringing in an outsider." Etheridge looked at Church as he slowly stirred his tea. "How do you think the boys would react?" He drank the tea. It was nice and strong, the way he liked it. Church pondered the question before answering.

"I'd rather promote internally if we could. Maintain some continuity." Etheridge considered that. 363 was still a young squadron. Its bank of senior men was getting a bit thin on the ground. Only Everett and Church were left of the original starting cadre.

"I don't object, but who did you have in mind?"

46 - Baby Steps

Carter sat in the office; his office now, feeling uncomfortable. He still felt a little surprised at the suddenness of it all. He knew he could call one of the clerks in the office outside, but he had no idea what he would ask them to do.

He cast his mind back to late yesterday morning when he had been having some toast in the Mess. He woke up five hours after the raid, stiff and sore. He'd thrown a pillow at Woods to wake him up and they had shambled to the Mess, the taste of rubber in their mouths from their oxygen mask.

He'd just settled himself at the table when a white jacketed steward came over and told him the Group Captain wanted to see him. Woods looked across the table at him with some concern. Carter stopped by the bathroom to splash some water on his face before he went over there. The summons had said immediately so he had no time to tidy himself up.

He had felt a certain measure of deja vu when he went into Etheridge's office. The Group Captain was behind his desk as before. Church was stood next to him. Carter half expected to see Cullen behind him in the corner.

"Sit down, Carter, sit down."

Carter settled himself.

"How was your evening?"

"I got back, sir."

"We've had to come to a decision, Wing Commander, Church and I." The hairs on Carters neck stood on end. That statement had an ominous air to it that set his nose twitching. "I'm afraid, Squadron Leader Salmon is overdue." Etheridge let that sink in for a few seconds.

"He's a good man," Carter said, filling the silence.

"Yes, he was. I'm sure his wife would say the same," Church chipped in, a little irked at the comment. He didn't care for Carter's talking in the present tense. "Saunderson's been ringing around all night but there's been no word. You know how it is," he said offhand.

"Wing Command Church feels that you're ready to make the step up." Etheridge said as he opened a buff coloured folder. Carter couldn't see what it was, but he could make a good guess. Etheridge glanced at the top sheet of the folder. "A two tour man, DFC. I think your record speaks for itself."

"Thank you, sir." Carter was suddenly nervous, seeing where this was going. Clearly the wingtip incident was forgiven.

"I just wanted to see you for myself first before I make the decision." Carter felt like a bug under a microscope. Etheridge was sitting there, his fingers steepled in front of him. Church lit up and was soon wreathed in smoke, the acrid smell of the Turkish tobacco filling the air. "Do you think you're ready? Ready to lead men, look after them?"

"I think so, sir," Carter replied with certainty. His time at training school had given him administrative experience, an appraising eye. It had taught him the cost of making decisions, deciding who was ready and who wasn't. A lot of his pupils were dead now, some were prisoners, he would have to live with that. Yes; he was ready.

Etheridge gave him a long appraising stare, looking at the little things. The hands in the boy's lap were steady, a good sign. Carter looked back at him, his blue eyes not flinching. Etheridge nodded. He liked to think he had the measure of a man. He stepped round from his desk and held out his hand. Carter shook it.

That was it, the decision was made and Carter was now acting Squadron Leader, commander 'B' Flight, 363 Squadron (Heavy). Georgette was over the moon when he told her the news over the telephone that evening. She couldn't give a fig about it only being an acting rank. it was the advancement that was key, the rank could come later. Even Mrs Lloyd was visibly impressed when Georgette imparted the news at dinner to the other girls in the boarding house.

He'd helped Saunderson pack up Salmons stuff from the office. All those swimming trophies and the framed photos went into a box. The walls looked depressingly empty so Carter had a big copy of the squadron photo put into a frame and hung it on the wall. It was more neutral and when he went west, there would be no need for his successor to redecorate. If he lasted long enough, he might add a few more knick knacks of his own.

The only personal item he did have was the clock from the cockpit of L-London. When Latimer had replaced it after the Cologne raid, Carter had asked for it. It was a reminder of just how close he had come to death, he needed something like that to keep him grounded. He thought it was better facing something than ignoring it.

He had the clerk move the desk. He hated having a desk in the middle of the room that was a barrier between him and anyone else. He moved it to the corner and rearranged the chairs so he could sit facing someone more informally.

He left everything behind with a flight test after lunch. His crew took the edge off when he turned up at the equipment hut. They were sitting on the benches getting changed when he came in. As soon as they saw him, they got to their feet, clicked their heels together in unison and gave him a jerky Teutonic bow.

"Ve are deeply honoured, mein Kapitan!" barked Todd with irreverence. He gave another mock bow and bent forward, reaching for his hand to kiss it like you did with a Catholic Priest. Carter managed to snatch it back in time.

"Congratulations, skipper," said Woods, crushing his hand as he shook it. Even Vos seemed pleased, his dour face smiling like he had won a teddy bear at the fair.

"Well, what are you waiting for?" he asked them, "let's go."

They rode out to *The Lady*, cock a hoop, buzzing at the promotion, genuinely happy at Carters good fortune.

"I'm not confirmed yet," he warned them, his tone cautioning. "The CO could wake up at any time and realise he's made a big mistake." They snorted at his scepticism. They got down from the truck to find Latimer and the erks were waiting for them outside their hut at dispersal.

"We just wanted to say congratulations, sir," said Latimer, pulling off a crisp salute. Feeling a little sheepish at all the attention, Carter returned the salute and then shook Latimer's hand. Beaming, Latimer walked him round the Lancaster to do the pre-flight check.

He was back in his office two hours later; reading. Aside from the flight crews, Carter had also acquired responsibility for some of the ground staff. Saunderson came to him after tea with some leave requests and other matters to discuss. Carter fastidiously went through each one, letting Saunderson fill in the blanks when he didn't know the person concerned. He needed a stiff drink at the bar later on in the evening to wind down.

A quick drink turned into a party when word came through from the Red Cross that Asher was a prisoner of war in Germany. There was no detail about how he'd been shot down, but it was confirmed that he was in good health. That really was something to celebrate and Carter sang with gusto with the best of them. The Mess games were a little more energetic that night, and the following morning Church had to authorise some squadron funds to make good the damage and replace the pillows.

Carter rolled his neck, his head still light from the evening's merry marking. The sun was getting warm and he reached over and opened the window. The usual airfield sounds leaked in from outside. He could hear a Lancaster in the circuit, the engine note fading away as it went down the runway. Nearby he could hear a tractor chugging down the road.

Dickinson had told him once that he could never wait to get out of his office and do an air test. Carter understood now what he'd meant when he glared at the piles of paperwork on the desk waiting for his attention. If Carter thought he was used to administration after being at Training School he was sadly mistaken. He had ten crews under him now. Seventy men to look after and get home if he could. He knew most wouldn't make it on his watch despite his efforts. The first thing he did was pull the records of each crew and he spent the remainder of the morning going through them.

His reading was interrupted when orders came through from Group ordering them to make ready for another raid that evening. As 'B" Flight commander, Carter now had a lot to do before the tannoy called the crews to briefing in the afternoon. He went to see Kent to discuss the target. It was the Krupps factory again and the route varied little from the last raid. For the first time, Carter saw references to Gee, a navigational aid. There were no specifics as to what it was, but the lead elements would be using it to mark the target with flares for the two hundred fifty bombers going out tonight.

In ops, he went over the route with Nancy, Church's navigator who was the squadrons navigation leader. They now had specific times on target as part of their navigation. Being part of a stream, they had to slot into place. If they were early, or late, things could get very crowded up there. After working himself up, he was disappointed when Church told him he wasn't going tonight.

"You're a Flight Commander now, Carter. We have to take it in turns, you know that."

"Yes, sir," said Carter, a little deflated. "I'd just forgotten about that."

"You've got the next one, I promise. Besides, you'll need some time to practice, you're giving the briefing tonight."

Church left him to carry on the mission planning. Lunch was a rushed sandwich as Carter called the bomb dump and gave them the loadouts. Half the Lancs would carry incendiaries, the other half bombs. A few of the incendiary aircraft would also be carrying the new 4,000lb light case bomb dubbed, the 'Cookie'.

At two he snagged a bicycle and went around dispersal, visiting each bomber and the ground crew, making sure they would be ready. He wanted to be able to tell Church they were on top line when he asked. He watched intently when he saw one of the big Cookies being winched up into the bomb bay. It was a long green dustbin with no pointed end or fins at the back. It made the incendiaries around it seem tiny.

He set off on his bicycle again and at the far end of the field came across four Manchesters drawn up facing each other. They looked rather sad parked there, discarded and forgotten until someone remembered to come and get them. Over the last three weeks, the rest of the squadrons Manchester's had been taken away in ones and twos.

These four were the last to go. He dumped the bicycle under the nearest one and went round to the tail, he started when he realised there was someone already there.

"Only me, skipper," came the strong Australian voice.

It was Todd. He was drawing heavily on a cigarette while he looked glumly at the bomber.

"What are you doing here?" asked Carter.

"Same thing you are I suppose," muttered the Australian. "Paying my respects to the dead so to speak." He walked forward and patted the perspex of the rear turret. "You might have been a cow sometimes but you got us home when it counted girl," he said to the wind. The Manchester made no response. "Just wanted to see them one last time before they disappeared."

L-London had been flown out when they were on leave so they didn't get to say goodbye to her. Since then they had been too busy getting up to speed on the Lancs to think about it, but now Todd had some time to kill, he thought he would disappear for a bit while everyone else was rushing around.

As he picked up his own bicycle, he asked Carter a question.

"Can I take the perspex off my turret, skip?"

Carter was surprised.

"Whatever for?"

"I iced up on the last trip and it was difficult to see things," Todd explained.

"It'll be bloody cold," Carter warned him.

"Huh, better cold than dead," replied Todd, deadpan. "I can handle a bit of draught. I'll throw on an extra scarf and I've got my heated suit."

Carter sucked on his teeth. He could just imagine Pullen's reaction to this, but then the engineering officer didn't have to fly and fight in these things. If Todd said he needed it, he was saying it for a good reason. What the hell, his authority had to count for something, he may as well use it.

"All right. If that's what you want to do. See Latimer and tell him I've given you permission."

Todd nodded and went off, leaving Carter alone to look around the abandoned plane. The rear hatch was open and he pulled himself up and went inside. It was deathly quiet, his footsteps echoing inside the metal tube. He went up to the cockpit, slithering over the main spar. He got in the pilot's seat for a moment and looked around. There was no voice, no strange communion, just an airplane, mute and immobile. He took one last look and then got back down. Cullen was waiting for him outside. The reporter hooked a thumb over his shoulder.

"I passed your gunner going the other way. He said I might find you here." Carter scowled.

"Why did you want to see me?"

"I've decided I'm doing a story on you," Cullen announced. Carter could see he was serious. His cheeks burned.

"I'm nothing special."

"I disagree." Carter got on his bike and Cullen came over to stand next to him, one hand touching the handlebars. "I've asked around. A lot of people say you're the best pilot on the squadron."

Carter snorted.

"Thats a long way from the truth," was his quick response.

Cullen did nothing to correct him. As a reporter, his basic rule of thumb when chasing a story was if you wanted to know about someone, ask around. You got the occasional blowhard, but most of them were modest about their own achievements, effusive about everyone else's.

"You're a hero. A two tour man, DFC," Carter found it strange hearing Cullen repeat Groupie almost word for word.

"I'm not the only one to have a DFC-"

"-but there's not many on their second tour." Cullen finished for him.

Carter pushed off on the bike, the wheels creaking over stones on the concrete. Cullen walked alongside him, almost jogging to keep up.

"Are you really sure that's something you want to write about?" he asked the reporter. "Look, Mister Cullen, I'm flattered." Cullen made to speak but Carter carried on talking. "No, really I am. But there are other heroes to do a story on." He pulled on the front brake and the bicycle came to a stop. He turned to face the reporter.

"Do you know where I went on my leave recently?" Cullen shook his head. "I went to a hospital in East Grinstead to see a friend. All the patients there are burn victims. All of them burned from flying. They're lying in beds with some horrendous wounds to their hands, their face, their legs." A sudden flash of memory flickered in Carters head and he struggled to contain his temper. "I saw more courage in one room than I'll ever have. Do a story on them," he said more harshly than he meant. "They deserve it."

Without waiting for an answer, he pushed off and pedaled fast while the tears ran from his eyes.

Cullen watched him go, a blue figure receding in the distance. He had seen the pain in the boy's blue eyes for a moment as he talked about the hospital. He thought that was a good measure of the man. How many would go to a place that was a terrible reminder of their own mortality just to see someone, not many he reckoned.

47 - Teething Troubles

Carter found the briefing torture. Sitting up front with everyone looking at you was not the same as being sat amongst a crowd. Church chucked him in at the deep end and had him do the opening delivery. Carter cheated and tried to remember what he could from the Essen briefing a few days before. The target was the same so that was easy, the route was similar and he could at least talk about that in general terms having helped prep the details earlier in the day. He just found it hard to relax so his delivery was stiff and disjointed.

When he was finished, his heart was pounding which was just ridiculous. He'd flown through flak barrages and not batted an eyelid and yet here he was, sweating over standing front and centre in a room talking to a bunch of people.

After that, it was the usual; met, navigation, armaments, target info and then the final pep talk from Etheridge. The crews went off to war and he saw them away from the tower. Seeing the Lancs in the dark was impressive. They almost leapt into the air, which was a big difference to the Manchesters which had always proven to be reluctant to unstick.

When they got back six hours later it was the same story as the last time. In interrogation, they had their mugs of tea and talked to the intel staff. Although most of them claimed to have bombed the target, Carter wasn't so sure. Thick cloud had made a mess of navigation and strong winds had scattered the bombers all over the Ruhr valley. The navigator's log books were filled with dead reckoning, calculations, corrections and guesswork. Even with Gee and flares guiding them in, not many of them could be certain they had actually hit where they were supposed to.

Cullen seemed to be everywhere, floating around at interrogation, lurking around the tower as the aircraft returned. He hung around for one more day and then got a lift to catch the afternoon train back to London. Carter saw him off at the gate.

"You still want to write about me?" he asked.

"Maybe. I haven't decided yet," Cullen replied. "I thought about what you said." He double checked his bag while they waited for the transport to the station, making sure he had everything. "The thing is, any story needs a framework, something to focus on, give the public someone to root for."

"Make it something else then. The squadron, all of us."

Cullen thought about that.

"I won't make any promises, but I'll consider it."

A Humber from the pool turned up and took him to the station. Carter watched it down drive off down the road.

Mid afternoon, a replacement crew arrived. Church gave them to 'B' Flight to replace Salmon. Carter had the pilot come to his office. The admin clerk wheeled him straight in. He was twenty two, tall, strawberry blonde with a dusting of freckles across his nose. He had that keen air about him that all the fresh ones had. Last week Carter wouldn't have been too bothered about learning his name right away. If he lasted four or five ops, then perhaps he might have noticed him. Now, as his Flight Commander he had to get to know him.

Once the usual military pleasantries were out of the way, he told Harding to take a seat. The young Pilot Officer sat down, perched on the edge of the seat, hands on his knees. Carter offered him an open box.

"Cigarette?"

Harding shook his head.

"Don't smoke, sir." Carter took one for himself and lit it. Harding wasn't the first person Carter had come across who said they didn't smoke. The thing was, within a few weeks, most of them were smoking ten or twenty a day just like everyone else. It was a wonderful way to calm the nerves.

"Why did you want to be a pilot?"

"My brother was a pilot, sir." Harding answered quickly.

Carter caught the 'was', the lilt of finality. He asked the obvious question.

"Was?"

Harding's eyes tightened for a moment as he thought about his brother, the older brother he had worshipped.

"He was killed on ops in 1940, flying Blenheims."

Carter left it there, what else was there to say? He changed the subject.

"Where did you go to School?"

"Perse School in Cambridge, sir." Carter wasn't familiar with that particular school, but judging by Harding's cultured tones he was sure it was expensive.

"Good school?"

"I thought so. I can't say I can compare it to anything else."

"And after that?"

"I managed a year studying French at university; before I joined up."

"I read law," Carter said. "Didn't finish, the war got in the way."

Harding smiled at the shared common ground.

"Tell me about your flying training." Carter knew he could read it in Harding's training file but he wanted to hear it for himself.

"I did most of it in Canada, sir. I started on Harvards. Did my multi engine training on Oxfords and Ansons and then did my OTU here in England."

"How many hours have you got on Lancs?"

"Something like forty hours."

"It's a start. The main thing to remember is that you can throw the Lanc around with confidence."

"I'll try to remember that, sir."

Carter thought about that. Forty hours was not a huge amount of time on a new type. He made a note to speak to the CO about the remaining Manchester's they had on strength. It might be an idea to keep them so new replacements could get in some extra practice on them. They were enough like a Lanc it would be a good way for the crews to learn without worrying about bending a new Lancaster. He lit another cigarette.

"We'll sort that out, Mister Harding. You'll start tomorrow. You know, you're pretty lucky. The squadrons only just converted onto Lanc's so you'll find plenty of people talking about it in the Mess. Pin your ears back, you'll learn a lot."

"Yes, sir."

"Off you go. Get settled in." As Harding got to the door, Carter said one more thing. "Oh, and Harding. The doors always open if you need anything."

Harding grinned, his eyes alive. It pained Carter to think that would change; if he lived long enough.

"I'll remember that, sir."

That evening, Todd and Murphy took Byron and Flynn to town for a proper lash up, all the NCO's together with no fools of officers around to complicate things. They started at *The Tarleton* and went from there. They'd all got on well the last few weeks. Flynn had become a natural foil to Murphy and the pair of them almost egged each other on when it came to women.

Byron was more reserved, but that wasn't to say he couldn't drink. He could stand toe to toe with any of them and he could also stand up for himself. He'd proved that one night in the Sergeants Mess when a remark was made and he squared up to a much bigger, heavier Navigator with no fear whatsoever. Todd didn't want to be scraping up what was left of him and had intervened, smoothing things over with some fast talking.

After two hours, Todd broke off from the gang as they headed to the *Gulliver Arms*. Pantomiming being caught short, he ducked down an alley and said he'd catch them up. As soon as they staggered out of sight, he slid round to Glossop Street.

He found the door he was looking for at the side of the grocers. There was no immediate answer and he was about to knock again when he heard feet on the stairs. The door opened a few inches and he saw her standing behind it, looking at him through the gap. Her eyes narrowed in displeasure.

"What do you want?" Muriel asked shortly.

"To talk to you."

She began to close the door and he stuck his foot over the jamb. He winced as his foot got squashed.

"I'll scream for the police," she warned him, her voice almost hissing.

"I'm not here for *him*," he snarled, his foot burning. She stopped pushing and the pressure relented slightly. "I just wanted to make sure you were all right."

"Why wouldn't I be?" she said in defiance, daring him to say otherwise.

"After what happened-" his voice trailed off.

Realisation struck her and she made to shut the door again. He put his hand against it and pushed. She resisted for a moment and then gave way. The door opened onto a narrow stair. She stepped back away from him and crossed her arms. Her hair was tousled and her eyes were red rimmed.

"So how long had you known?" she asked him directly. Todd looked sheepish and glanced down at the doormat. "I knew it," she snapped. "Thick as bloody thieves the whole bloody lot of you!" She moved forward to slam the door in his face.

"Would you have believed me if I'd told you?" he asked her. That stopped her.

"What do you care?" she challenged, tossing her chin at him. "You never approved of me anyway. Always staring at me with that dour face." She pointed at him. "You never even spoke to me when we were all together."

"Because I bloody fancy you all right," he almost shouted back at her, the answer dragged from him. "I fancy you; always have," he muttered. She put a hand up to her mouth and her eyes went wide.

"Well I never," she said finally. "I never thought-"

"I know you never," he said, cutting across her. "You were seeing my mate. What did you expect me to do? I have to live with the fella, fly with him; fight with him. We have to trust each other. I hated what he was doing, but..." he shrugged.

"I see," Muriel said more quietly.

"I hope so." He checked his watch; the boys would be starting to wonder where he was. "Look, I have to get back. Can I see you another time?" he asked, his tone humble, almost pleading.

She thought about it for a moment and then nodded slowly. "Maybe."

He grinned, winked and was on his way.

Church agreed with Carters suggestion and applied to Group to keep their remaining Manchester's for now. Harding started in the morning with some ground instruction. In the afternoon, he snagged Byron and took Harding and his crew for a flip in a Manchester.

Byron helped with the start up routine. Once they were in the air, he swapped places with Harding. Carter had Harding do some circuits and bumps to warm up and then took them up to eight thousand feet, wanting to see what he could do.

Bimbling along, Harding was fine. The Manchester behaved, the engines purred, it was a clear day, everything was good. After twenty minutes, Carter took back control.

"I've no doubt you're a good pilot, Mister Harding. You wouldn't have got through OTU and all the other flying training if you weren't. Did you go on any trips towards the end of your course?"

"Just the one, sir. A gardening trip to the Frisians."

"Did anything happen?"

"No, thankfully. There and back. The only excitement was getting shot at by our own guns on the way home." Harding leaned back and looked down the fuselage. "We strayed a bit off course didn't we, Oliver?" he said with emphasis over the R/T.

There was some good natured laughter and Carter waited for them to settle down. Better to make a mistake like that on something easy like a gardening trip. Do that over Germany and there might have been a different result.

"I hope you're a quick study, Harding, because you're going to have to pick stuff up fast."

Carter had pre-warned Byron, but even so, the sudden drop when he shoved the yoke forward took him by surprise. He clung on to the back of Carters seat as the Manchester plunged for the ground. Carter held her in a forty five degree dive and watched the altimeter unwind. He pulled up at three thousand, hauling the yoke back into his stomach. After flying the Lancaster for three weeks, he had forgotten how much heavier the Manchester was on the elevators. The nose came up and they were climbing.

"The thing to remember. These kites are tough. It might feel like you're going to pull the wings off, but you won't. When the bullets are flying, hesitation will get you killed. You've got to learn to react instinctively. Now you try."

Carter handed back control and talked Harding through the maneuver.

Vos sat on the corner of her bed, shocked to the core. She stood by the fire, head down, hands behind her back. He hair was loose and hung down in front of her face. The silence was heavy in the air. Vos didn't know what to say.

He looked at Denise as she chewed on her bottom lip, becoming more worried the longer the silence went on. Georgette had convinced her everything would be okay. She'd come on the Sunday as she promised and the two of them had talked for over an hour about what to do.

This was when Georgette saw how young Denise really was. The thought of being pregnant terrified her. With no family to support her, it weighed heavily on her. What worried her more was that Vos would leave her once he knew and that she'd be on her own.

Georgette did her best to soothe her fears but she was never able to answer the one key question; what would Vos' reaction be? In the end, logic prevailed. Georgette pointed out that there would come a time when Denise could no longer hide her condition from anyone. She would have to tell Vos eventually, so it would be better to tell him at a time of her choosing.

"Wouldn't it be better to know how you stand?" Georgette had asked her. Denise knew she was right but the prospect still terrified her.

He'd come round on Monday evening once she'd finished work. Thankfully she hadn't been sick but she'd eaten little all day. Mrs Peck had tried to tempt her with some stew, telling her she needed to keep her strength up.

Vos could tell she wasn't well as soon as he saw came into the room. She was pale and listless and he made a fuss of her to try and cheer her up to no avail. Later in the evening she sat in his lap, a blanket drawn up around them as he read to her from a book of French poetry.

One of the poems struck a chord with her and she leaned forwards away from him. She stared into the fire, consumed with thoughts of loss. Her parents, home, family, all gone. She steeled her nerve and turned to face him, searching his face, trying to see deep into his eyes. Her expression concerned him. She looked almost frantic, her eyes wide, the whites showing.

"Beloved, I, I have something to tell you." Fear gnawed at Vos, wondering what could worry her so much. "I know why I've been sick for the last few weeks." He looked up then, eyes fearful that it might be something terrible. "It's morning sickness," she blurted out in a rush. He had nodded, mute. "I'm going to have a baby."

"You..we." Words failed him. He blinked twice. Scared, she had read his hesitation as rejection and she got to her feet to stand by the fire. Vos paced around the room, struck by the enormity of what she had said, the boundaries of his world shifting around him. Before, he had been alone, a stranger far from home, fighting the enemy who had taken him away from everything he held dear. Then he'd come to love another and now this. It just took him a while for his brain to catch up.

He crossed the room to sit on the bed and look at her again. He sorted through the feelings crashing through his head. He was going to be a father.

"I'm going to be a father," he said aloud, his voice lost in wonder. He went to her then, a smile creasing his face, his eyes alive and dancing in good cheer. He covered her cheeks in kisses and brushed away the tears that glistened at the corner of her eyes.

"I love you, Denise. I love you. I'm not going anywhere without you."

She sobbed then, the weeks of pent up fear releasing itself in one moment.

48 - Picking Up The Pieces

Vos told his crew the news the following day. Carter acted suitably surprised and they went out that night to celebrate. They could have gone on all night, but prudence tempered their good cheer and they got back to Amber Hill before midnight nursing heavy heads. It was a good job too. The new day brought orders from Group.

The squadron was going back to the Ruhr but they were going to Dortmund this time for a bit of variety. Good as his word, Church sent him out on this one. Carter felt like he was floating as he walked around on his pre-flight. He hadn't felt like this since the first op on his first tour way back in the dark ages.

Being a Flight Commander came with one privilege, you got to go first. He lined up, got a green and was on his way. They sped past the tower and took off into the night, climbing away from Amber Hill and heading for the coast.

The trip out was routine. The crew had settled down in the intervening weeks and Byron and Flynn had settled down without any problems. Vos got a good fix and passed the position to Woods who marked the location on his chart.

In the tail, Todd debated how wise it had been to get Latimer to remove the middle perspex panel in his turret. He could see a treat. There were no reflections or misting to obscure his view, but by god it was cold. By the time they went on to oxygen, his teeth were chattering, his nose had gone numb and the whistling of the slipstream past his turret was getting annoying.

Before take off, he'd scrounged around for extra clothing to stay warm. Carter had given him a thin pair of silk gloves to wear under his gauntlets. At least his fingers were nice and toasty. He had pulled on an extra pair of socks to help keep his feet warm and that was working so far. He debated getting a hot water bottle for the next time.

Halfway over The North Sea, it all went wrong. It wasn't so obvious at first. The port inner began to lose power and Byron spent a good ten minutes tapping dials and juggling the throttles to try and figure it out.

"No dice skipper," he said in the end. "Either the plugs are fouled or there's some crap in the fuel tank. The other engines are running okay so we're still good to carry on."

Carter nodded while he considered his options. They were a hair under seventeen thousand feet and still a long way from the target. Their airspeed had reduced which would mean they would be late. Being late held little concern for him, they'd been late before.

"Skip it, it might clear on its own," he told Byron. "We'll press on."

Byron went back to his panel, fretting over the engines and trying to will the port inner to work. Twenty miles from the Dutch coast, the starboard inner packed up.

Carter felt the engine let go, there was a massive judder through the airframe and a gout of sparks out of the exhaust. The revs dropped off and the prop started to windmill.

With the sudden loss of power, the Lancaster slewed to the right and Carter had to work hard to get them back on an even keel. The R/T came alive as the crew asked what was going on and Carter shouted at them to keep quiet.

"Talk to me, Byron."

The Flight Engineer was not one to sugar coat it.

"Starboard inners buggered."

He looked over the canopy at the offending engine a few feet away as he feathered the prop. Smoke was spilling out from the exhaust stubs in a steady stream.

"Spud, can you see any flames?" he asked.

That focused everyones attention. In the tail, Todd went pale and he suddenly thought about grabbing his parachute just in case. Murphy span his turret so he could take a look. He peered into the gloom. He could see the stream of smoke, gray against the black, but there was no orange lick of flame visible.

"No fire that I can see."

"Watch it," said Carter.

They tried to bring up the power on the port inner but it wasn't playing along. They flew on for another few minutes but Carter knew he was fooling himself. No inner engines meant no hydraulic power for the bomb doors, the flaps or the undercarriage. They could drop the bomb doors by using a hand pump but it would take fifteen minutes to manage that and once they were down, they couldn't get them back up again. The inner engines also powered the electrical generators which meant no extinguishers and no power for the fuel booster pumps amongst a whole host of other things.

"Woody, course for home," he said in clipped tone, his anger building. It was the first time he had ever had to turn back in his operational career, but there was no way he was risking his and everyone else's life just to keep going. "I'm sorry lads, but its an early shower for us. Flynn, let the bombs go as soon as you can."

They were subdued on the way back. Coming home early left a

bad taste in their mouth. They all knew it was the right decision, but to actually come back without even making the coast, they felt awful. The final slap in the face was that the port inner picked up again when they were twenty minutes from home. It suddenly burst back into life and acted as if nothing had happened, mocking them. Carter felt sick to his stomach when he called up Amber Hill on the radio and asked for permission to land.

With the port inner playing along, Carter dropped the flaps and the undercart and came straight in. He literally thumped the Lancaster down and then used aggressive bursts of throttle to get back to dispersal. He dabbed the brakes and then kicked the throttle, giving one last savage burst of power to swing round. In the back, Todd felt like he was on a waltzer at the fairground.

No one was waiting for them when they disembarked. They had to wait a few minutes before a Bedford turned up to take them back to interrogation. While they waited, Murphy looked at the Lancaster, throwing daggers in its direction.

Interrogation was quick. The form was easily completed, ER, Early Return. They dumped their kit and split up. Woods and Carter went for a walk. Still running on adrenalin, it would be hours before they'd get to sleep. The air was damp and wisps of ground mist swirled around their feet as they walked. Moisture soaked the bottom of their uniform trousers and their shoes. Neither of them particularly cared about that, the mood they were in.

They got as far as the butts; a big mound of sand surrounded by high bricks walls. Carter sat down on a stack of wooden boxes. He suddenly deflated. He had never had to abort an op before. He knew these things happened, he just never imagined it would ever happen to him. He felt embarrassed more than anything, especially now that he was a Flight Commander.

"Come on," said Woods. He tugged on Carters sleeve. Carter stood up and they walked back towards civilisation. Carter lit up. He stopped and blew smoke up to the sky and let out a sigh. It was pitch black up there.

"Bombers moon," he whispered. He carried on walking and checked his watch. Right now, they should be on their way back from Dortmund, threading their way through the flak. They rounded the hangars and headed towards the ops room.

Woods went with him, curious for once to see what went on in the background. There were no other early returns and when the squadron got back in the wee small hours no one else was missing either. A good night overall.

Carter went to interrogation and circled the room, listening to the crews; *his crews* now, telling their stories to the Intel staff. Carter felt embarrassed to be in the same room as them. Etheridge tried to gee him up.

"Don't worry about it, Carter. You aren't the first person to abort; you won't be the last either."

Carters mouth twisted in a moue of disgust with himself. After interrogation, he went in search of Pullen. The Engineering Officer was in his office in the main hangar going over the snag list for the night. While no aircraft had been shot down, a number of the Lancs had sustained flak damage that would need to be put right before they went up again.

He assured Carter that he was top of his list. Merlin engines were proven and generally reliable and the fact he had suffered a double engine failure was cause for concern. If it was because of negligence, Pullen would have someones pelt on the mat, rest assured. In the morning, the Lancaster was towed to the hangar and Latimer and the erks removed the two inner engines. She looked rather sorry for herself with the firewalls exposed and puddles of oil and hydraulic fluid on the floor beneath her. Both engines were stripped down.

The starboard inner was easy. In the sump they found an interesting collection of metal particles and cracks in two of the cylinders. Some bearing bolts had sheared and the engine had literally torn itself to bits when it conked out.

The port inner proved more mysterious. The fact it had cut out and then picked up again pointed to something else. At Pullen's direction, Latimer had the fuel tank out, the pumps were checked, the fuel filter and the lines were examined but they found no blockages or contamination to explain it. The port inner was put back on while a new engine was fitted as the starboard inner.

She was ground run first and then Carter took her up for a short air test. Pullen rode along, standing behind Carters seat the entire time, listening intently to the engines in the air. Byron watched the gauges like a hawk, looking for any fluctuation in temperatures. She passed.

That evening the squadron was on again and with their Lanc laid up and Carter now on a rotation system, Woods had the evening off. With ops on, Yvonne was busy so he took Merlin for a walk. The Labrador sprang up, tongue lolling, face happy. Woods clipped the lead on his collar and they were off, the dog taking him past the hangars. Banging noises came from inside as the evening shift were hard at work. He waited while Merlin cocked a leg and relieved himself against the side of the hangar. Woods kept an eye out for any SP's on the prowl, they would just love to write him up for that.

They circled back to the admin blocks and Woods hung around, waiting for her to come out for some fresh air. He didn't have long to wait.

"Hello, darling." It was dark enough to risk a kiss. Yvonne bent down to the Labrador.

"Hello, Merlin. Who's a good boy? Has daddy been looking after you?" The dog barked in obvious pleasure and zoomed around her legs, tail wagging like mad. "He's lovely. I always wanted a dog. My mother couldn't stand animals."

Woods produced a ball from his pocket. Merlin got one look at it and barked loudly. Woods threw it and he was off like a blonde missile.

"You are clever," said Yvonne as she watched the dog overshoot the ball and then double back to collect it. He gathered it into his mouth and came flying back towards them.

"More like sneaky," Woods said. "I knew you had to come out some time. You're always telling me it gets too hot in there and you need a breather."

She looked sideways at him, a smile twitching her lips.

"I never think of you as sneaky."

"Start. Any way I can figure out to see you, I'll try."

She laughed, her voice echoing in the quiet. They sat down on the bench at the side of the building. Merlin bounded up tot them, dumped the ball in Woods lap and he sent it sailing off into the night again.

"Your tours almost up soon," she said aloud and Woods caught the note of concern in her voice. Worry for him, worry for her and what happened next.

"Nine to go, yesterdays debacle doesn't count," he told her. "Still a ways to go yet." She tucked her hands under her legs. "This isn't a casual thing for me, you know," he said.

"Me neither," she replied, looking at him.

They remained like that for a few minutes, Woods absently stroking the dogs head.

"Gosh, is that the time," Yvonne said suddenly. She got to her feet. "Some of us have to work for a living."

They said good night and arranged to go to town their next free evening. Woods left then, chasing after Merlin, trying to get the ball from him.

49 - Flogging A Dead Horse

Life settled into a new pattern for Carter. His mornings were usually spent in the office, seeing to personnel issues, training requirements, leave requests and other admin. Most afternoons he escaped to prowl around the station. He spent quite a few of them with Pullen, discussing the Lancs in his Flight and making sure the new aircraft were up to scratch.

The squadron went up again on the 17th to Hamburg and lost three. After a few weeks with no losses, it was a hard blow and a stark reminder that life was measured out a day at a time. Church spent the following day writing letters to family while Everett and Carter helped Saunderson sort through some of the mens more personal affects.

The BBC made little mention of the raid on Hamburg the following day, they were a mere footnote; 'some of our aircraft are missing'. The airwaves were full of a startling daylight raid on Augsburg by Lancasters from 44 and 97 Squadron. The crews gathered around the radios in the Mess and listened, rapt as the BBC communique trumpeted details of the raid led by Squadron Leader Nettleton, 44's CO. The attack had been pressed home at very low level. There had been some casualties, but the damage to the MAN U-boat factory was described as extensive and the operation was hailed as one of the bravest acts of the war.

Carter shuddered at the thought of flying a thousand miles over enemy occupied territory in daylight. The Wimpy's and Hampdens had tried it at the beginning of the war and the fighters had chopped their formations to pieces. It had been one of the reasons why Bomber Command had been switched over to night bombing. Now some madman at HQ was having another go at sending them out again in daylight.

As soon as the news of the Augsburg raid hit the airwaves, Church realised what all the complaints he'd been receiving had been about. For the last week the squadron had been getting inundated with complaints about four engined bombers flying low and causing mayhem. Only yesterday, Saunderson had come into his office with a raft of letters from farmers and the local constabulary. One vicar had complained his service had been disrupted by the drone of low flying aircraft. A local MP had complained about the noise upsetting his chickens.

Church had been ready to nail someones hide to the wall for this. The last thing he needed was some hothead flinging his Lancaster around causing trouble. Now it all made sense. 44 and 97 had been practising for the run on Augsburg. Church was just a bit miffed that 363 hadn't been invited to the party. Despite the risks, people would have killed to be part of this operation. Church knew he would have had a queue down the corridor and round the corner if he'd asked for volunteers.

He rang Group to have a moan but got little sympathy. The Augsburg raid had been one of Harris' pet projects to see if the Lancs could do a precision raid in daylight. He'd even picked the target and gone toe to toe with the air Air Ministry who had wanted other targets hit instead.

Replacement men and aircraft came in to make up the squadrons losses and Carter talked to the new arrivals assigned to his flight. Once again, he took them up in a Manchester to start with before letting them loose with a Lancaster. Amber Hill hummed to the sound of engines; the skies full of aircraft.

Pullen worked the erks hard. Some of the new Lancs had come straight from the factory missing certain equipment. He had to harass the local stores to provide what they were short of to bring them up to spec. When some proved reluctant, moaning about channels and correct paperwork, Church went to bat. He turned the air blue, delivering rockets down the telephone with ferocity and cutting vective. The walls shook and the WAAF's outside his office flinched when he slammed the phone down.

On the 19th, 363 sent five aircraft to go gardening off the Frisians. This was a nice easy one so Carter sent Harding to give him a chance to get his feet wet. He was on tenterhooks the whole evening until the lad came back. He did, eventually. His navigator got badly lost and they showed up over Amber Hill practically flying on fumes.

Carter had Harding in his office to find out why they hadn't just put down at some other airfield. Harding explained he felt it was important to get home. They couldn't just take the easy way out and he needed his navigator to improve.

"After all sir. If he can't cope with this, what chance will I have over Germany?"

"The one thing we're not short of is navigator's," Carter had advised him. "If your man's no good, I could get you another one assigned, no problem." Harding resisted. He'd brought his crew through OTU and he wanted them to keep together.

"You know best," Carter said with a sigh. "Just think about it."

One day, Church gathered up Everett and Carter and took them to a conference at Group. This was nothing unusual; every few weeks the AOC 5 Group liked to get his squadron commanders together for a bit of a chat to talk tactics and developments over tea and cake.

"If I'm going to be bored senseless, there's no reason why I should go alone," Church told them.

It was a dreary affair. As the meeting broke up for lunch, the deputy Group Commander asked Church and his Flight Commanders to stay. They waited patiently as everyone else left for sandwiches and mugs of tea. The deputy AOC waited until the room was clear before shoving some of the seats out of the way and sitting in front of them.

"Nothing to worry about gentlemen," he reassured them. "I'm not one to make a show about certain things." He addressed Carter. "I know such matters usually involve official dispatches and such like. I'm sure the paperwork will catch up eventually but from this moment, you are now promoted to Squadron Leader." He stuck out his hand, "my warmest congratulations."

"Thank you, sir," stammered Carter, quite overwhelmed.

"Go see that girl of yours," said Church as they went to catch up the rest to get some lunch. Carter almost floated along as he went to find Georgette. He found her in the archive, sorting through a target folder, a pencil between her teeth while she riffled through the papers.

"Jus a mi-ut," she got out around the pencil.

Carter stood leaning against the filing cabinet, an amused smile on his face. He took the moment to admire her legs and her figure as she crouched down by the bottom drawer.

"I should come round more often," he said. Georgette jumped up with a little squeal of surprise. Her pencil hit the floor unnoticed.

"Darling, what on earth are you doing here?" she asked, surprised at the interruption.

"Conference," he explained, hooking a thumb over his shoulder. "We're on a break so what could be better than going for a walk with my girl?"

She checked her watch.

"I really shouldn't" her mouth quirked as she let herself be rebellious for once, "but I don't suppose ten minutes will matter."

They walked briskly to their spot beyond the greenhouses. It was a lovely day, the early morning gloom blown away to be replaced with a bright, warm sky. They walked alongside each other, a good two feet apart to maintain decorum; at least until they were out of sight. He whistled to himself as he walked.

"You're very happy today," she commented.

"When you've been made a Squadron Leader maybe you will be too," he beamed.

"Oh darling, that's wonderful." Past the trees she hugged him tight, letting her enjoyment show. "I told you that it would come." She brushed down the lapels on his battledress, very proud of him.

They talked for a few minutes, making tentative plans for the next few days, ops depending of course. *The Lady* had been fixed so they were due whatever Church decided was good for them. All too soon, they went back to the hall and their day jobs.

After lunch, the meeting ran for another two hours. The AOC emphasised servicing rates and aircraft availability. He wanted to put up as many aircraft as possible whenever orders came through from Bomber Command HQ for a maximum effort.

The end of April marked a milestone for 363. They had their full complement of Lancasters at last and they participated in the next phase of Harris' bomber campaign, the attack on Rostock.

On the northern coast of Germany in the Baltic, it was a long way. Two hundred bombers would be going, another big raid as Harris marshaled his strength to hit key targets in massed attacks. Only the year before a big raid would have been one hundred aircraft passing over a target in a period of four hours. Now their efforts were becoming more concentrated, two hundred aircraft or more going over in two hours or less.

In response, the German flak belts were getting thicker, the intensity of the barrages more pronounced. According to popular rumour, there were now hundreds of guns around the port cities like Kiel and Hamburg.

They'd listened with rapt attention in briefing while Church had explained the target and its importance. There was a Heinkel factory on the southern outskirts and Harris wanted it dealing with. 363 would be part of the main force to hit the centre of Rostock. An old city with narrow streets, the place should burn easily. Gee and flares would again be used to guide them on to the target.

Later, Carter watched silently as they winched a cookie into *The Lady's* bomb bay. It hung there; a big green malevolent dustbin surrounded by incendiary canisters.

"Everything's ready, sir." Latimer said earnestly, holding out the clipboard and pen. Carter said nothing as he signed the Form 700. He knew Latimer had slaved over the Lancaster personally, double checking everything to make sure it was perfect.

It had been ten days since they had last been on an op so Carter took his time getting ready. He pulled on his gloves, settled himself in his seat and handled the yoke.

"Assume positions for take off!" he shouted down the fuselage.

Murphy and Todd sat behind the main spar. Flynn produced a paperback novel from a pocket and turned on a small torch so he could read. Vos smiled to himself in the dark, thinking about approaching fatherhood. He took it as a good sign for the future. Woods thought about Merlin. The poor animal had been quite upset at being locked in the billet. The whines of distress had cut him to the quick so much he'd brought the dopey dog to dispersal and Latimer had promised to look after him until they got back. His thoughts turned to Yvonne and he smiled.

The previous night they had gone into Lincoln. He'd found a quiet pub off the beaten track where they could have some time to themselves. Afterwards they went to the cinema and watched a re-run of *Pimpernel Smith*. He'd seen it before but Yvonne hadn't. Woods enjoyed the sharp dialogue and double play on words, Yvonne thrilled at the sight of Leslie Howard as the titular hero.

Afterward they'd ridden the last bus back to Amber Hill. Woods got them seats in the back and he unscrewed the lightbulb so they could have some privacy. Yvonne snuggled into him, her head resting against his shoulder.

He walked her part of the way back to the WAAFery. In the lee of some trees on the road, he had drawn her to him and kissed her long and hard. Yvonne responded by moulding herself to him. She left him then, her perfume lingering as she disappeared into the dark.

Carter went through the routine with Byron. The back and forth flowing with well drilled practice.

"Switches? ARE OFF!"

"Tanks? INNER TANKS SET!"

"Pumps?" ARE ON!"

"Seat? SECURE!"

"Brakes and pressure? BRAKES ARE ON...PRESSURE IS GOOD!"

It went on, a droning mantra that they all knew. They went through the list. Engine controls, throttle settings, props and superchargers and radiators. Finally, they were ready.

"Ready to start up, skipper."

Byron jammed down on the starter button for the starboard inner. The airframe rattled and shook while the engines warmed up. Carter held the brakes on and waited while erks came out front, holding the chocks in view. Satisfied everything was ready, he released the brakes and the Lancaster moved forwards, sluggishly at first.

They picked up speed around the peri track and Byron juggled the throttles and Carter used the rudders to keep them going. It would screw everything up now if they strayed onto the grass and got stuck, everyone was behind them.

At three thousand feet the crew took up their stations. In the tail, Todd settled down to another six or seven hours in the freezer. This time he had brought a hot water bottle and he put it in his flying suit between layers. He flexed his fingers and gripped the control sticks, panning the turret left and right and elevating the guns.

He thought about Muriel. He'd been to the pub to see her twice. She'd been civil to him but it had been stiff and awkward. He wondered what he could do about that as he slowly froze.

After crossing the coast, they tested their guns and settled down for the long run to Rostock. Carter nagged them all the way there to keep their eyes open and he had Flynn make himself useful and get in the nose turret. Vos kept watch out of the astro dome.

Woods fussed over his charts. A long run over water left him little chance to get a fix. They were far enough off the coast that he couldn't even get a sight of the Frisians. Of course, that was a double edged sword. Wander over the Frisians and a flak ship could nail you. Someone obviously got careless as Murphy spotted jewelled lines of light on the horizon to the south and an explosion immediately afterwards that was swallowed up by the dark.

Over the target, the flak was light. Carter almost enjoyed himself as it reminded him of the early days, weaving back and forth over Germany at eight thousand feet trying to find a juicy target to bomb. He lost his humour when Flynn asked him to go round again.

There was a stunned air of disbelief that Flynn wanted a second run at the target. The wind was light, the visibility was reasonable and there was very little flak that could cause a distraction. There were barely even any searchlights to cause problems either. It was like a training flight with knobs on.

"I lost it!" he shouted over the R/T.

He had sighted on a town square with tall tenement blocks around it. Suddenly he had lost it and for some perverse reason he wanted to hit that block specifically. Amongst all the damage, it looked untouched and that would not do at all.

"Well you better find it again, quick!" shouted Carter, not in the least bit amused.

The Lady jolted as a burst of flak exploded below, lifting them on the shockwave. Flynn searched frantically but there were fires on the ground confusing him. Ten more seconds went by. Carter drummed his fingers on the yoke. Byron peered over the edge of the canopy.

"Drop. The. Bombs!" Carter told him.

If Flynn was looking for pinpoint accuracy, he was dreaming. The cookie was a big, long dustbin with the ballistic properties of a brick. Once it left the bomb bay it could end up anywhere. The incendiaries were just as bad. Little 4lb bundles of flaming joy that fluttered on the breeze like the seeds off a dandelion.

"Drop them now!" he ordered.

Flynn cursed and pressed the release and the bomb load fell on the city below. Flynn closed the bomb doors and stayed down in the nose, looking at the fires.

That was the only excitement on an otherwise boring trip. The squadron suffered no losses and there was only one early return.

On the way back to interrogation, Carter tore a massive strip off Flynn in full view of the rest of the crew. For once, Carters normal contrariness of following the forms of behaviour slipped. He'd been steaming all the way back and it came flooding out in the back of the truck. Flynn's ears burned but he had the good sense to keep his trap shut.

Recce photos showed the Heinkel factory was virtually untouched even though bombs had rained down all over the city, getting a good blaze going. Harris sent them back to Rostock the next night. Tired erks prepped the kites to go again.

Carter sat this one out, it was Everett's turn to go. He cooled his heels in the Ops room, chatting with Wheeler and flicking through the squadron record book while he was plied with tea and biscuits. Before the squadron even got back, the word came from Group that they were on again that night, to the same target.

Church led the third trip but the men were tired, running on pure adrenalin. Two aircraft didn't go. Taxying round the peri track, one tired pilot lost focus for a second and went straight into the back of the one in front. The propellors shredded the rudders and had a good nibble on the elevators. Everyone else made it back.

When the op order came through for the same target for a fourth night in a row, even Etheridge thought command had taken leave of their senses. After he calmed Church down, he went back to his office and called Group himself and voiced his objections personally to the AOC. He was politely listened to but it made no difference; Maximum Effort, everyone goes.

In briefing, the mood amongst the men was almost mutinous and Carter had to agree with them. He may have thought it, but he didn't say it. Carter was a Flight Commander now, part of the machine, one of *them*. Even to his own crews grumbles he said, "let's just get it over with."

His own fears were confirmed when the flak was more intense than the first raid. The Germans had obviously brought up more guns over the last few days. It was nowhere near as bad as flying over Happy Valley, but even so, one gun in the right place could easily kill you, ten could just do it better.

Over Rostock, Carter was shocked by the scale of the devastation. The city was aglow, gutted by flame. The firemen must have given up in the end. What was the point of putting the fires out when the bombers kept coming back to start them again, night after night? This was what total war looked like. The systematic destruction of a town to dislocate the local population and disrupt war production.

Woods had found the way easily enough. It was a clear night and they saw the glow of the flames from miles away. Closer, the pall of smoke that hung over the city climbed thousands of feet into the sky.

When Flynn let the bombs go, Carter just felt it was a waste of time. The city was one massive conflagration, burning from end to end. Shells of gutted houses were silhouetted by the fires. Smoke billowed up and the Lancaster undulated over the roiled hot air.

It was very tired men that shambled into interrogation for the fourth time in four nights. Kent had instructed his staff to keep it mercifully short. Unless anyone had seen anything out of the ordinary, it was a matter of a few questions and done. A few hardy souls stayed up for their hard earned bacon and eggs but most went straight to bed, past caring.

If the aircrews were tired, the ground staff were exhausted. After such a concentrated effort, Group had the good sense to call it a day and the squadron was stood down for twenty four hours. Men and machines both needed time to recover their strength.

Still running on adrenalin, Carter went to his office and sat in the dark with the door closed and the curtains down. In the gloom, he thought about the raid. He found himself questioning why they had bothered going back for a fourth time. His eyes fell on the unopened envelope on his desk. He turned on the desk lamp and picked it up, turning it over in his hands. Gripped by a mood of despair he suddenly tore the envelope open and pulled out the folded letter inside. He smoothed out the paper on his desk and then started reading.

My dear Carter,

If you're reading this, then I didn't come back from this one. Running in low to drop those bloody mines is not what I signed up for, but somebody has to do it I suppose. I don't know what it is about minelaying, I just had a feeling this time, like someone was walking over my grave.

I've been troubled by the thought of bombing lately. Does that surprise you? I might present a tough face, but I do think about these things you know. I never told you but my parents were bombed out in the raids on Liverpool last year. One night they had a house, the next it was a stinking crater. My Aunt and Cousins were killed in one raid when a bomb hit their shelter. I suppose that gives me as much reason to hate the Germans as anyone, but I ask myself if two wrongs make a right?

I often think about German children who no longer have parents because of what I've done. I've come to the conclusion that there can't be a god. I wonder if god was so merciful, why he lets such things happen. I don't have an answer to that.

I'm sorry for snoring, but there's some things I just can't change about myself I'm afraid. I only hope my going doesn't put anyone else on the spot, I don't think I could bear that. Take any spare kit you want before anyone else manages to get their grubby fingers on it.

Take care, your friend,

Ambrose William Walsh.

It was too much. Carter leaned back in his chair and rubbed his eyes, suddenly very tired and worn out from the futility of it all.

There was a knock at the door and he looked up, wiping his eyes.

"Come," he croaked.

The door opened and Merlin rushed into the room. The dog barked and lunged at Carter, almost knocking him out of his chair.

"Merlin!" Woods said. The Labrador lay down, tail beating the floor. Woods lowered himself into the other chair. He fished a bottle of beer out of his coat pocket and handed it to Carter. Carter took it and cradled it in his lap.

"A bit early isn't it?"

"Never too early to have a drink," said his navigator. "Come on, skipper, tie one on with me. I don't feel like sleeping."

Carter drank from the bottle without really noticing. He stared off into the distance, oblivious to Woods being in the room. Woods gave Carter a searching glance, curious at his demeanour. It was more than being tired. In the seven months they had been together, he had never seen him appear so deflated. Picking up on his mood, the dog shuffled forwards and shoved his nose into Carters lap. Carter absently stroked the dogs head as he finished the beer. He picked up the letter and silently handed it to Woods. The big Canadians face turned grim as he read it.

"Dour stuff."

"Did you know any of that?" Carter asked.

"About his family?" Woods shook his head. "No. He kept his personal life pretty private."

Carter looked down at the Labrador. It looked back at him with big eyes, with unquestioning loyalty. Carter thought about that. He thought about loyalty and what made men kill other men. Real men looked their enemy in the eye when they did their killing. Carter just dropped bombs on towns and factories and train stations and scuttled away in the dark. He'd never thought about the people on the ground until last night. Rostock had been different.

"How do we keep going back to do this?" he asked, his voice

cracking. Merlin barked.

"It's the job we volunteered to do," Woods said simply, recognising the need for candour.

He wondered how long Carter had kept this pent up inside himself. They were all guilty of this on aircrew, suppressing fear and ignoring the close shaves; hoping to god the fear didn't show, dreading being labelled LMF or having the twitch. Every day you got up and went where they told you. It was natural to be scared, that was part of the job but you had to believe that you would come back to get the job done. If you started thinking too much, that was when the whole pack of cards so carefully constructed came crashing down around you.

Woods had been scared many times. At the beginning he'd stood behind Carter in the cockpit to see the outside world. As the tour had progressed, he'd stopped doing that. Sitting at his navigator's table with the light on he was oblivious to most things on an op, it was easier that way. The terror came when they were attacked by fighters and Carter flung the bomber around the sky. Each plunge could have been their last but every time, Carter had brought them home.

Woods believed that confidence was the key. You had to believe in yourself. That provided the core you needed to get through, mentally ticking off the ops until the tour was over.

"Look, skipper. We didn't start this war, but the Nazis made it our fight when they bombed London and Liverpool and Rotterdam and god knows how many other places. When we joined up, we did so for a reason, do you remember that?"

Carter glared at him and simmered, the anger lurking beneath the surface like the embers of a fire. Woods could see it there and he was pleased, he wanted to stir the fight in Carter, to pick him up by his bootstraps and shake him until he fought back.

"There are people counting on you," Woods told him. Carters eyes flashed, the scar on his cheek rippled as his mouth pulled into a sneer. That one had stung. "The crew, me, the Flight; Georgette-"

"You leave her out of this," Carter snapped back, his temper rising.

"No, I won't," Woods flared. "I saw how she looks at you. I saw how she cares for you, and you her. Surely that's worth something?" When Carter stayed quiet, Woods carried on, baring his soul. "You know, I've never told anyone this, but after the first few ops I thought I wouldn't live to see the end." Carter shot Woods a look of disbelief.

"Oh yes, I did. I made my peace with that, I thought it was worth it. Then one day after the trip to Bremen, we were all tired and you said we just had to keep going until the job was done, no matter how long it took. Do you remember that?"

Carter nodded slowly. Woods called the dog and Merlin padded over to him. He stroked down his back and ruffled his ears, Merlin liked that.

"Nothings changed, boss. There's still a job to be done, but you're not doing it alone. No man can get by on his own. We all need someone to get us through. You've got Georgette. I found, Yvonne."

That struck a chord in Carter. He'd said something similar up in Lossiemouth when he was training the crews at the OTU. More than once he had told them they needed to depend on each other as a crew if they were going to survive, no man could go it alone, he'd forgotten that.

The conflict within him suddenly receded like waves on a beach. He straightened, refreshed, as one does after facing a hard truth about yourself. There would always be doubts about what he was doing, but he recognised that it was such a broad problem it was beyond his ability to solve on his own. The simple truth was, he wanted to survive. The rest he would worry about another day; if he lived to think about it.

He went to the window and opened the curtains. The horizon was starting to get light, the sun would be up soon. His mood lifted and he turned to Woods. The Canadian saw the change come over him. His pilot was standing a fraction taller. His shoulders straightened and his eyes were bright and strong, just as they were the day he first saw him, telling them what he expected of them.

50 - Bull And Brass

On the 28th April, the London Gazette published the citation for the award of the Victoria Cross to Squadron Leader Nettleton. The Augsburg raid had already been a sensation in the press. Nettleton's VC gave the action renewed prominence. Whether by accident or design, Bomber Command was no longer a dirty word.

Suddenly, the press wanted to see Lancasters. The Propaganda Ministry sent them to Amber Hill. One squadron was like any other and besides, code letters on the aircraft could be blanked out by the censor.

The station was made presentable and the men tidied themselves up a bit. The weather held and the VIP's turned up right on time. A motorcade of staff cars came through the main gate and drove straight past the admin blocks to the hangars.

Four lancs had been drawn up to make three sides of a square. One on each of the sides and two in the middle. The men lined up. Heels crashed on concrete and they came to attention when the AOC 5 Group alighted from the lead vehicle. His staff and guests got out of the other cars.

The station photographer was on hand along with the war correspondents. Flash bulbs popped as the dignitaries walked up and down the lines of men, talking to a few here and there.

Eventually, the AOC came back to the middle of the square and stood on a dais. He made a speech full of the usual platitudes. They'd heard them all before. The greenhorns puffed up their chests with pride, the rest tuned out, waiting for it all to end so they could go for lunch. A few decorations got handed out. Everett got a DFC, a few DFM's were pinned on chests and two others got mentions in dispatches. Saunderson made a mental note to make sure the press got the right spellings. It wouldn't do for a chap's moment of glory to be spoiled by some grotty little reporter who couldn't spell.

Once the parade was dismissed the AOC and guests retired to the Officers Mess. The Deputy AOC went to the Sergeants Mess. As a Flight Commander, Carters presence was obligatory and he hung on the shoulder of some man from the Air Ministry who had come along. The man droned on about production and the difficulties of introducing new types without interrupting factory output. Carter put on a pained smile and nodded in the right places. Eventually, Wilkinson rescued him.

"If you'll excuse us, sir, I need to arrange some things with, Squadron Leader Carter."

"Oh, but of course," the man from the Ministry said in understanding. He floated left and attached himself to a small knot of pilots so he could ask them some questions.

Wilkinson pressed Carter to have a beer.

"Congratulations, old man. Well deserved and in my opinion, overdue."

Carter perked up. The last few days he had pottered about, doing admin, seeing to some niggles down at the hangar and doing the rounds of the men. He'd gone to the cinema with Georgette and they'd dined at *The Madison* as a celebration for his promotion.

She had almost preened with pride to be out with him. By the same token, he'd been floating to be with her. Mrs Lloyd spoke to him before Georgette had been ready. The woman had been almost warm. Clearly, one of her girls courting a newly promoted Flight Commander was a step up from seeing a mere pilot and now made him worthy of her attention. Carter made polite conversation for a few minutes in the glacial parlour.

After dinner, Georgette had guided him back to the summer house in the grounds. Here, her plans were to be frustrated as someone had padlocked the door and they couldn't get in. Carter burst out laughing at the absurdity of it all. Two grown adults and they were reduced to sneaking around like a couple of lovesick teenagers.

During the short drive back to Georgette's digs, the air in the car was electric, both of them almost drunk on each other. She kissed him goodnight and bit her lip with frustration before going inside. When she left him in the car, the blood was pounding in his ears. He had driven back at a million miles an hour with the windows down to clear his head.

"How's Helen?" Carter asked.

"Marvellous," said Wilkinson, almost buzzing with enthusiasm. "Sends you her love. They both do actually."

Carter grinned, pleased to see his friend so happy.

"How does it feel?"

"I'm still floating, old man. The miracle of life. It's quite remarkable."

A week ago, Helen had been wheeled into the maternity ward and Martha Louise Wilkinson had been born in the early hours of the morning.

Wilkinson had paced up and down in the corridor outside. Her father had been more stoic, he'd done this three times already. Sitting in an armchair, he smoked his pipe and read the paper, counselling patience. In contrast, Wilkinson had gone through at least two sets of nails and chain smoked like there was no tomorrow.

He didn't mention the sleepless nights. It was remarkable how well one could do on two or three naps. He just had to be careful not to nod off in the afternoon in his office; the mid afternoon fade he called it. A well timed cup of tea usually managed to ward it off.

"You must come round and see the baby. You and Georgette both."

"We will. There's just not been a lot of free time lately," Carter cracked. Wilkinson had to laugh at that. It had been just as manic at Group as it had been on the stations.

Wilkinson suddenly saw one of the bods from the press heading towards the AOC with purpose and their notepad and pen out. There was going to be a press conference back at Group later, but Wilkinson wasn't surprised one of the reporters would try to get a few minutes to themselves. He congratulated Carter again and then he was off.

"No rest for the wicked," said a voice at his shoulder and Carter jumped. He turned to see Cullen standing there, one hand gripping a pint pot.

"You're back," said Carter stupidly.

"Of course. I go where the stories are. Lancasters are big news."

Carters mouth twisted.

"And what's the story this time?"

"I'm not sure. I doubt Air Ministry will let me get within a million miles of, Squadron Leader Nettleton. They must have thousands of requests for an interview."

They looked across the room to see Wilkinson deftly divert the reporter away from the AOC.

"But all I want is a few words for my paper," the man protested.

"You'll have everything you'll need in the communique we issue later," Wilkinson told him firmly. One of the Americans for Associated Press, the man had tried to buttonhole him earlier that morning about the number of aircraft quoted as going on raids. He was questioning the figures.

"What I can tell you, old man? We send our returns to Air Ministry and they draft the official communiques. I can't possibly comment on what the other Groups are putting up. Not my area. Not my area at all."

"But what about your own Group?" the reporter had persisted.

"Each station reports how many aircraft are away, and it's just a matter of simple sums after that," Wilkinson said smoothly.

"But you can't say how many actually hit the target, can you?"

Wilkinson had sighed. He knew this sort of thing would come up. The whole issue of Bomber Command was still meat to the grist in some quarters, particularly as the first American bombers were coming over from the United States preaching the mantra of precision daylight bombing.

Wilkinson had his own view on that. Lobbing practise bombs in good weather on a bombing range was one thing. The Americans hadn't seen European weather yet, or the Luftwaffe come to that. He doubted they were going to find it as easy as their own newspapers were saying it would be.

Only a week or so ago, the AOC had asked for his opinion on another report doing the rounds in government circles which had come to be known as the Dehousing Paper. Wilkinson had read it. Since Lord Cherwells protege, Bensusan Butt had pointed out the flaws of the bombing campaign in all the grisly details; the Dehousing Paper expressed the view that Germany *could* be bombed into submission. It proposed building up the bomber force with the express view of breaking German morale by demolishing their towns and making the population homeless. At a time when the Japanese were carrying all before them and North Africa looked like it was going to drag on for another year; the Dehousing Paper made the point that bomber Command were the only force taking the fight directly to the enemy.

The paper had provoked fierce debate between the Ministries and Parliament. Once more, the argument over allocation of resources was in full swing and Bomber Commands fate hung on the decisions of those in the corridors of power. Rostock and Augsburg had helped divert attention from the unpleasantness the previous Autumn, but Wilkinson knew the debate about Bomber Commands future was far from settled. The Butt report had only been the start of it.

"My dear chap," he soothed. "Our target photos show we're hitting the enemy. If you don't believe me, I'm sure I could get permission for you to see some of them. You'll discover we're hitting Jerry right where it hurts. Take Rostock for example. A model German town. Now it's been blasted into matchwood after only a few raids. Marvellous effort from our chaps to take the fight to the enemy. I'm sure your Air Force will experience the same rousing success once they get going."

Ladbrook grumbled agreement as Wilkinson took a grip of his arm and steered him towards the bar.

Once the last of the VIP's were gone, Amber Hill let out a collective sigh of relief. Personnel rapidly left the station in search of booze and entertainment. After a week from hell, they needed to escape the confines of the airfield and see some life.

Vos, Woods and the others were on their way out the door when an orderly asked Todd to report to the CO. Todd thought he was pulling his leg. There was never an honest debt that couldn't wait for morning, but when the CO asked for your presence, it would be a brave man indeed who would just carry on walking. He looked at the rest of them, stood there with a mix of concern and confusion painted on their faces.

"You blokes go on ahead."

"We can wait," Flynn told him. Embarrassed at the concern, Todd brushed them off.

"Nah, I don't reckon this'll take long. I'll catch a later bus."

"If you're sure?" asked Woods.

"Of course, I'm bloody sure; *sir*." He gestured to the orderly. "Lead on mate, let's get this over with."

As they walked back to the admin block, Todd wondered what it was about. There'd been no recent thieving from kitchens and there was nothing else he could think of that would have brought him to the CO's attention. He knocked on the door and Church said, "come in," from inside.

Todd caught up with the rest of the crew an hour later. He took the lit cigarette Flynn handed him and sat down amongst the crowd squeezed around the small table in *The Tarleton*.

"I told you it wasn't anything to worry about," he reassured them. "They wanted to screen me and pack me off to training school." He giggled at the absurdity of it all. "Can you imagine; *me*, a teacher?" he asked them.

"Gawd save us," said Murphy.

Todd neglected to mention that his knees had been knocking when he went into Church's office. The CO had been behind his desk with Everett to the side of him. Todd had looked around but Carter wasn't in the room. When he saw that, Todd's anxiety had gone up another notch. Church had opened a file and commented that his tour was nearly up.

"Then they suggested sending me on a course," he told his attentive audience.

That produced a stir of interest. After the last week of four ops on the bounce, a few weeks at some station sitting in classrooms and learning some theory suddenly seemed quite attractive. Todd shook his head.

"I did a course once before and look what happened?" he asked them, gesturing around the table. "My mates got the chop and I ended up with you bums."

That produced a laugh.

"Yeah, we got the shit end of the stick," agreed Murphy.

"Charming," Todd said in mock outrage. "Anyway. I said no." He took a long pull on his pint and smacked his lips. They looked at him intently; they knew he hadn't finished his story yet. He dropped the surprise. "Then they offered me a commission."

Their faces were suitably shocked.

"I know right? Me, an officer?"

"You're too scruffy by half," quipped Flynn. He got to his feet and clicked his heels together, putting his hands on his hips. "Just look at you man," he said in a plummy voice, rolling his vowels. He gestured at Todd's tunic. "Your top buttons undone. There's no polish on your shoes. Disgraceful."

Todd ran a hand through his unkempt hair and shoved his forage cap back on his head.

"Exactly. I said I was happy as I was and I just wanted to do my job. The main thing is we get to finish our tour together; as a crew."

"You got that right anyway," commented Murphy. He raised his glass in salute and they all followed suit.

51 - Monkey And The Grinder

While most of the squadron went out to enjoy themselves, the squadron were called upon to send out four aircraft to attack the *Tirpitz* which was skulking in a Norwegian fjord. Always one to lead from the front, Church picked three other crews and took off heavily loaded with petrol and the big 2,000lb armour piercing bombs. All four aircraft returned after a marathon nine hours plus in the air.

It was another raid trumpeted in the press although the exact damage to the *Tirpitz* was subtly not alluded to. The rhetoric was strong and uncompromising. With more of the new four engine heavies coming into service, the RAF could range all over Germany. Nowhere would be safe from attack.

Carter saw the article in the Mess a few days later. He wasn't so keen about the range at will bit. The German nightfighters would certainly have something to say about that. The tone of the article sanitised the bombing, giving a heroic slant to something that was far more deadly and violent. The rest of the page had a large photograph of smoke billowing from a factory with the Eiffel Tower in the background. The inside pages boasted about a large raid by one hundred aircraft on the Gnome aero engine factory outside of Paris.

He took the front page off the paper, rolled it into a ball and lofted it at the bin in the corner. It missed and Woods stooped down to pick it up. He smoothed out the paper and saw the headline, a particular phrase caught his eye, "the sword and the shield," he murmured.

"Bumpf," muttered Carter darkly.

Woods rolled up the page and put it in the bin slowly. He hooked a thumb over his shoulder.

"The CO wants to see you. Looks like we're on for tonight."

Carters face twisted, lacking enthusiasm. He levered himself up out of his chair and stretched.

"Let's see what's going on, shall we?"

The gods were obviously not content. After giving 363 a few days off, Bomber Command HQ had decided that the Germans were having things too easy and ordered minelaying on a massive scale along the coast of occupied Europe. The skies would be crowded tonight. Aircraft from both 3 and 5 Group would be going out to range from Brittany all the way round to Germany. 363 were given a short stretch of coast off Cuxhaven covering the approach to the Elbe.

It wasn't the Frisians but not much further. Church asked Carter to pick five crews from his flight to go out. Carter picked four of the new boys including Harding and told Latimer to get his Lanc on the line. He was damned if he was going to send them out on their own. The other replacement crew could go and drop bundles of leaflets over the French countryside.

He found Vos and Woods in the Mess. Vos carried on drinking, oblivious, but Woods picked up on the glint in Carter's eye, the set of his shoulders and he just knew.

"We're on," Carter announced quietly. Woods nodded. He had a feeling something like this was going to happen. He started to steel himself for the night ahead.

At interrogation, Carter anxiously paced up and down waiting for the last crew to come in. They were late. Kent was sitting at his small table, the clipboard in front of him, his fingers drumming on the table. Etheridge tried to make himself inconspicuous and stood looking at an aircraft identification chart filled with silhouettes of German aircraft.

When it was past time, Wheeler updated the board in Ops for T-Tommy; FAILED TO RETURN. He rang Group to give them the report for the evening's operations; five aircraft dispatched, four returned. Carter would have gone back to his office to sulk, but Etheridge came alongside him and murmured, "let's take a walk, shall we?"

The Group Captain struck out in a random direction and Carter followed along behind. He kicked at the heads of some daffodils; his hands jammed into the pockets of his greatcoat as he went along.

"It's going to be a long war, Carter," Etheridge murmured. "Try not to spend so much of yourself at once," he cautioned.

"I just hoped they would have lasted more than one trip."

Etheridge nodded, hearing the ache behind the words. He'd heard Asher, Dickinson, Salmon and Church say similar things before.

"You know the odds as well as anyone."

"Yes, sir."

Etheridge looked sidelong after him, seeing the war going on in inside. Carter tried a grin, but it just ended up looking like a grimace.

Losing crews was nothing new. Life on a bomber squadron was like that, a constant merry go round of replacements, filling in the holes left by those who had gone before. During his first tour he'd seen a lot of crews go west. Others had died at his OTU in the Scottish Highlands flying clapped out aircraft but this had been the first loss on ops of men under his command. What unsettled Carter the most was that he couldn't picture Bartholomew's face.

"Chin up, Carter," Etheridge pointed off to the eastern side of the aerodrome. "It's a new day."

They turned in as the first streaks of dawn lit the sky.

There was the usual thrash in the Mess to celebrate the honoured dead and thank the gods for another day of life. Carter put in an appearance, had two drinks to be sociable and then returned to his office.

He dug out the personnel folders of Bartholomew and his crew and thumbed through them. When he was finished, he put them on the desk of one of the squadron clerks and vowed to never do it again. Ghoulishly looking through service records of the missing was tantamount to self flagellation.

He threw himself into his work with renewed determination and pushed his flight hard. He went over to Group and had Georgette pull the target photos of his aircraft and he spent the afternoon looking at aiming points. He went back to 363 and had his flight assemble in the briefing hut and laid down the rules.

He wanted them to get better at identifying their targets before dropping their bombs. Some of the photo's had shown some crews were dropping miles off the target. A few had dropped on completely open countryside. There was no point risking their necks to drag tons of bomb across occupied Europe if they were going to just drop them on nothing. From now on, he wanted his crews to press home the attack. He sent them to Wainfleet on some rotten days. Bombing in good weather was easy. He wanted them to be able to hit the target when there was a crosswind blowing and cloud cover made sighting difficult.

Never one to ask people do something he could not, Carter dragged his own crew up on a particularly miserable day. The rain was almost going sideways when they got down from the truck. Flying into the teeth of a headwind, Flynn moaned as they were jostled in the turbulent air.

"It'll be good practice for you," Carter told him. "Just imagine it's flak bouncing us around."

Results were mixed. Carter sent them all to do it again. He went up with each crew, not just the rookies, to see how the crews operated. Some of them treated the Lanc like a delicate flower. He repeated what he had told Harding, when it was your life on the line, you flew as far to the limit as you could go and take nothing for granted. There were the usual grumbles in the Mess, but they knew he was right.

In the air, he was his usual crisp self. On the ground, he withdrew into his shell. When the crew went to town, he didn't go as often and Woods became one of the few companions, he would have a drink with. He lived for the hours when he could get off the station to see Georgette. A quick call to find out when she was off duty and he was out the gate, making the drive to Grantham.

One evening, Vos was in the armchair by the fire in their room. The radio was playing some dance music in the background. Denise was on a cushion in front of him, leaning against his legs, her head tilted back as he brushed her hair.

Her stomach was bigger and she was talking about needing to go shopping for new clothes. Vos nodded absently as he looked around the room. It was a nice room. It had served them well all these months, but it suddenly occurred to him they were going to need some place bigger. Vos frowned as he thought about what to do. Mrs Peck had been good to them; very good to Denise. She had treated her almost as a daughter all this time; he didn't want to upset her. This would need some delicate handling and he bent some thought on what to do.

52 - Joyride

Carter was buried under a load of work in his office. The 'to do' pile was on the right, those completed on the left. Once a month, each flight commander had to sign up the crews log books for the hours flown, each page being initialled and at the conclusion of a month's entries, the page was stamped and signed by him. He'd just signed the bottoms of Todd's book with a flourish when his office door burst open and the formidable figure of the senior WAAF strode in.

"What the devil?" Carter asked. The WAAF Sergeant clerk scampered in wringing her hands.

"I'm awfully sorry, sir. I had said you were busy-"

"It's quite all right, Sergeant," Carter said, reassuring her. "Shut the door."

The terrified WAAF retreated, closing the door behind her. He swallowed hard and sipped his cold cup of tea as he gestured to the chair in front of his desk.

In the movies, WAAF's were pretty and dashing and went all starry eyed at the sight of a pair of wings on a chest of blue. In reality, many of them were plain and the uniform did them no favours whatsoever. The enlisted womens uniform was adapted from the mens pattern and unless you were very tall, it made a girl look like a sack of spuds. The hats were atrocious and known as the pie crust. Officers were luckier, they could afford to have their uniforms tailored.

Squadron Officer Mildred Hakes was the proverbial battleaxe. She was as wide as she was tall, a great barge of a woman and she went at a problem like a bull at a gate. God help anyone who crossed her and woe betide if someone transgressed against her girls; then the whole arsenal came out to play. She lowered herself onto the offered chair, steam coming out of her ears.

"What can I do for you, Squadron Officer?"

"I want something doing about your animal aircrew, Squadron Leader."

"I'm afraid you're going to have to be more specific."

"My girls are not whores!" she raged. Carter blinked, a little taken aback at the language.

"I never said they were."

"Of course, you didn't," she snapped at him. "I never said you did. What a ridiculous thing to say."

Carter clicked his tongue, then stopped as Hakes fixed him with what he could only imagine was her death stare. Her ice blue eyes slitted up and her mouth pulled into a thin line of disapproval. Georgette had looked at him like that once. He sighed as he rubbed the bridge of his nose and waited for Hakes to continue.

"Two of your men tried to break into the WAAFery last night. They scared the devil out of my girls when they saw one of them at the window."

Carter groaned. WAAF's and aircrew mixed, WAAF's and ground staff mixed; it was a fact of life. There were numerous rules about fraternisation but blind eyes were turned to most of them. The one line never crossed was going to the WAAFery. Anyone stupid enough to go over there was asking for trouble.

"I'll have the SP's make some enquiries although I'm not sure how easy it'll be for them to find out who it was."

"Those idiots," Hake sniffed dismissively. "They couldn't find a polar bear in a penguin enclosure."

"I'm not sure what else I can suggest, Squadron Officer. I'm not a private detective," he snapped his fingers. "I can't spirit up two guilty men and have them confess." A thought suddenly occurred to him. "With something so serious, shouldn't you be talking to, Wing Commander Church about this?"

"I did," she said shortly. "He said I should talk to you. I've already tried to talk to that little weasel, Saunderson. He's been giving me the run around for days." Carter groaned. Hakes misinterpreted that. "I am *serious*, Squadron Leader. I want something *done* about it."

"And it *will* be," he said firmly.

"Then get a pen," she told him.

She rattled off a list of transgressions. Two WAAFs had gotten pregnant and she provided the names of the alleged fathers, meticulously spelling the names and giving their rank and dates of birth. One girl had been caught in a compromising position with a Corporal in the armoury. Hakes had already posted the transgressor to Oban in Scotland. She wanted the Corporal hanging up by his thumbs. Failing that, she wanted him posting, preferably somewhere remote.

"Is that it?" Carter asked thinly, his tone glacial.

"Not quite."

Carter shot her a look. He could almost guess what was coming.

"Joyrides," she said. "I want them to stop."

It was not unknown for erks to get taken up for flips in the kites but never on ops. He himself had done it for Archers erk in return for borrowing his car. He personally knew Walsh had done it as well on at least two occasions. WAAF's being given joyrides was a much rarer event. On his last squadron he knew of just one instance when a navigator took up his WAAF girlfriend for a quick trip to the heavens.

It wasn't always fun of course. There had been an accident when an idiot had run his Hampden into a hill with two WAAF's on board. The fallout from that had been huge and the CO had absolutely banned the practice after that. It still went on, you just had to be discreet about it otherwise your flying career was over.

Carter was surprised that Hakes had mentioned this. There had been no hint about it happening on 363, not even whispers in the Mess.

"Is that just gossip or do you have anything specific to tell me?"

"Oh, I *know*," said Hakes, warming to her theme. She had Carters attention now and she was not going to stop until she had satisfaction that her complaints were going to be dealt with. "Sneaking around, flying, making a spectacle of themselves. Disgusting."

Hakes had ended up bending his ear for over half an hour, reeling off a litany of woes against her girls. When she finally left his office, he had slumped in his chair, drained of energy like a balloon deflating from a slow leak. During her harangue he had considered saying, "don't you know there's a war on?" but couldn't be bothered.

Head buzzing from the demands of the senior WAAF, he decided to bolster his strength with some lunch. He found Everett in the Mess tucking into sponge and custard and went over to him.

"Where have you been?" Carter asked.

"Group," Everett said round a mouthful of custard.

"Mind if I join you?" Everett waved to the empty chair across the table.

"Feel free, old man."

Carter settled himself at the table. One of the white jacketed stewards came over and asked him what he wanted. Carter pointed to Everett's plate.

"Same please."

Everett saw the weary look on Carter's face.

"How goes the war?"

"With who?" Carter asked. "The Germans or the senior WAAF?"

Everett grinned.

"I'd heard she was on the prowl. What did *she* want?"

"A litany of crimes. The usual moans and to cap it all," Carter threw up his hands, "a complaint about joyriding."

Everett grunted. He ran the spoon around the bowl, gathering up custard.

"Not on this station."

"I know. I've not heard a dickybird either."

"What did you tell her?" Everett asked.

"That I'd look into it." Carter leaned forward on the table, resting his chin on his forearms.

"Why do you think I disappeared to Group?" Everett said.

Carter's eyes opened wide, his mouth forming a silent, 'oh'. Clearly there were a few administrative tricks he needed to learn a bit faster.

"What are you going to do?"

Carter shrugged.

"I figured I'd sit on it for a few days till things calm down."

Everett licked his spoon. Finished, he stood up. He leaned on the back of his chair as he slid it against the table.

"That's one way of dealing with it," he admitted. "There is another way of course…" his voice trailed off. Carter bit.

"Which is?"

"The Germans might settle the matter for us. See you later."

Carter just stared and watched Everett walk away as the steward brought him a bowl and set it down in front of him.

Afterwards; he went along to Ops and was going through some admin when the teletype started chattering away. Stuttgart would be the target for tonight. Nestled in among a group of valleys, the city was nowhere near any rivers or lakes or other specific feature that would provide a good navigational pinpoint. The lead elements would use Gee to help locate the target and the main force would follow them in ten minutes later. Even allowing for the industrial smog which was persistent over the factory towns, Stuttgart was not an easy target to find.

This time, 363 was going for something specific. At the north end of the city surrounded by woodland was the Bosch factory which made pumps, magnetos and other engine parts, a bottleneck of the German war machine. Carter poured over the target maps. As Stuttgart was at the bottom end of Happy Valley, rather than fly all the way over the flak, they were routed to go beyond the Ruhr and then turn south, coming in from the north east. Once they bombed, they were to run west, out over France towards home.

Linkletter spent hours scrutinising the meteorological reports, updating his charts. At briefing, he predicted clear skies aided by bright moonlight but there was a good chance of heavy cloud on the return with the possibility of some fog. It might clear as a low pressure front moved in.

The raid was a shambles, they fought headwinds all the way there to find the area blanketed in 10/10ths cloud. Large fires and searchlights made the clouds glow and Flak guns fired blind at them through the clag. They never saw a sniff of the target so they released their bombs on a cluster of red flares and struggled home.

On such a bright night, the nightfighters were active and claimed a number of easy victims. Todd and Murphy spent a tense few hours, straining to see in the dark. Vos kept watch from the astrodome while Flynn froze in the front turret.

363 had one early return and lost two aircraft that night. Neither of the casualties were from his Flight. One was shot down not long after crossing the Dutch coast. The other was caught by flak over the target.

Carter had five hours restless sleep then got up. He had a frank discussion with Pullen then took a Lanc up for a test. After lunch he summoned Pilot Officer Lambeth. He'd come to the squadron just after they converted onto Lancs but he only had a handful of ops to his name due to a number of early returns. The subject of some gossip in the Mess, Lambeth was becoming labelled a fringe merchant. He'd come back early last night as well and Carter decided that something needed to be done.

There was a nasty phrase that could be used for this, LMF; Lack of Moral Fibre. LMF was the bogey man that stalked squadrons and claimed victims in the night like Jack the Ripper. It wasn't something that could be defined very easily.

A chap might be fine one night and then on the next op, it just became one too many. The spark would be gone and pressing on regardless of risk no longer held any attractions. There were other names for it like *Twitch*. Men who lost their nerve were shuffled off a station quickly before the sickness spread to others. Their files were stamped with a big red W, for Waverer. Officers lost their commissions and were booted out of the service. NCO's were reduced in the ranks and given menial tasks for the remainder of their service life, forever reviled and whispered about.

Carter had seen some decent men sacrificed on the altar of necessity because the stress and strains had become too much. He also knew that it was not such a cut and dried issue as some might think. Someone might have just had a child and suddenly started worrying about whether or not they would live to see them grow up. A chap might have just seen his best friend get his head blown off, or not return from an op. There was lot to play on a man's mind. A gunner on Carter's last squadron had walked into the CO's office one day and torn off his Air Gunners brevet badge and quit, just like that. He'd done twenty trips. He had never been wounded but he'd reached his limit and that was it.

Applying his instructor rationale, Carter was not prepared to make a snap judgement; but it didn't look good for Lambeth. He wanted to talk to him about it first to see what he had to say.

There was a knock on the door and he came in, a tall figure with rounded shoulders. A shock of ginger hair topped a pale nervous face.

Lambeth remained at attention and Carter did not invite him to sit down which spoke volumes in itself.

"I have a decision to make, Lambeth. It's not a pleasant one and it will be the hardest decision I've had to make since I took up command of the Flight."

Lambeth swallowed hard, his adam's apple bobbing up and down. Carter closed the training record and put the file to one side. He shot a look at Lambeth, conscious of the fact he was looking at himself as he had been eighteen months ago, fresh and untainted.

"You returned early last night," he said directly.

"Yes sir."

"And it's not the first time," Carter said, his tone accusatory.

"Yes, sir," Lambeth replied, his voice flat.

"What do you have to say?"

"I had engine problems," Lambeth said simply, as if those four words were explanation enough.

"And last night?" he asked, pushing for more detail.

"I couldn't get above nine thousand, sir. The starboard engines weren't giving full power. I wasn't about to risk my crew at that height, I'd have been a sitting duck."

That was a reasonable explanation. A year ago, nine thousand was just about okay. Today, the flak would blow you out of the sky. Carter just had one problem with what Lambeth said.

"It might interest you to know that I flew your aircraft this morning." Carter stared hard at him, looking for a discernible reaction. "Squadron Leader Pullen checked it out as well. He couldn't find anything wrong and neither could I."

"I'm not making this up, sir," Lambeth protested. "I couldn't get any power to climb last night."

Carter nodded slowly. Little things could make all the difference. One or two things could dent your confidence and all of a sudden, a little fault became a bigger issue.

"I know there are teething problems. I also know that you seem to have had more than your fair share of them. People are starting to talk." Lambeth flinched at that. "Do you *really* want LMF stamped on your service jacket?"

"No, sir," said Lambeth, his voice quiet as his composure cracked. He shuffled on his feet and his chin dropped.

"Then get a grip man!" Carter shouted. "I've seen nineteen year old boys shaking with fear but it didn't stop them going out there and going off to war. You've got mens lives in your hands. They're relying on *you* to lead them. If you don't do this, you're going to regret it the rest of your life."

The silence grew heavy as Carter let that sink in. He leaned back in his chair and looked at Lambeth, unimpressed.

"So, there it is. You have two options. You're either going to go on the next op; or your going to be posted from here. I need crews that will press on despite the difficulties but not take foolhardy risks."

An image of Archer flashed into Carter's head when he said that. Archer, the man who had pushed his luck just once too often. At that moment, Carter softened ever so slightly.

"There's a fine line between caution and cowardice," he said softly.

"I'm not a coward…sir," Lambeth replied immediately, finally stung into a response. For a moment, his eyes flashed defiance, nostrils flaring, his face flushed.

"Then I look forward to seeing that. You can go, Lambeth."

Dismissed, Lambeth left the office. Carter turned to his paperwork. Before he could even get started there was a hard knock on the door and Everett poked his head round.

"We're on again for tonight. Op orders coming through now."

Carter almost shot out of his seat; the admin forgotten in an instant. It looked like Lambeth was going to have to show his mettle sooner than he thought.

Church led the squadron that night while Everett took a turn in Ops. Still smarting from the earlier rebuke, Lambeth was surprised to see Carter waiting for him at dispersal. He came out of the ramshackle hut the erks used, a mug of tea in his hand.

"Bright night, mister Lambeth," he said cordially.

"If you say so, sir," Lambeth replied stiffly.

"Let's have a walk around shall we?"

Carter passed no comment as he watched Lambeth go through his pre-flight checks. He got into his aircraft to get settled before start up. Carter went back into the erks hut and emerged a few minutes later with his flying kit on.

Woods had thought he was mad when he first mentioned this idea in the afternoon.

"Don't do it, skipper," he pleaded. "We can't lose you now."

"You're not going to lose me," Carter had assured him although they both knew that was an empty sentiment. "Todd's extending his tour," he said in his defence. Woods had snorted.

"That's different. Skipper, if you do this, you'll just be a passenger waiting for the chop."

It had seemed like an inspired piece of leadership earlier. Now, climbing up the ladder into the nose, Woods words came back to haunt him. Carter would be exactly that tonight; a passenger.

"Don't mind me," he said as he came into the cockpit. "Just pretend I'm not here," he suggested.

They took off and Lambeth was cautious, nursing the engines.

During the climb, the crew bantered on the R/T, chatting freely, very relaxed even with the extra passenger on board who could hear everything. The talk continued after they crossed the coast and were on their way. Carter had promised himself he wouldn't do this, but finally, he had enough. He cut in on the R/T and demanded silence.

"Accidents waiting to happen, the lot of you!" he raged. "God knows how you've survived so far. How can you do your jobs if you're constantly jabbering."

He looked around the cockpit, taking in the airspace. He saw another Lanc above them to port about half a mile away.

"Was anyone going to report seeing that?" his voice flayed them. "Wake up gunners! That's your job!"

He did the rounds of each station, giving them something to do. Carter lashed them all the way there and back. They were slow getting to height and he nagged at Lambeth.

"Height is life. You know that. A few extra thousand over the target makes all the difference. You should be climbing hard all the way there."

Lambeth nodded curtly and increased their angle of climb. After staring at the sky through the astrodome, Carter was bored and his legs were aching from standing. He had never been such a spare part before. Even when White and Jensen had been flying, he would be right there, watching them and evaluating their performance. As an OTU instructor he had stood watching but never for this amount of time.

After another hour he went down into the nose to have a look see. The bomb aimer got up and shouted in his ear, "I need to go to the loo." Carter nodded and the man squeezed past him.

Carter lay down and looked out of the bomb aimers bubble. He had never been in the nose before during an op. The moon was bright and the tops of the clouds were almost glowing.

The flak started not long after that. A constant scatter of explosions above and below the clouds. Carter could feel the pock, pock, pock, as a cluster of shells went off near by. There was a flash ahead of them and then a long streak of flame heading for the ground.

"Kite going down in front of us, about three miles on track," he reported.

"Navigator, note that please," Lambeth ordered crisply.

The flak continued to jolt them around and Carter hung on, a mere spectator. There was a tap on his shoulder. The bomb aimer was back. He checked his watch; half an hour had gone by. They swapped places and Carter lingered for a few more minutes, looking over his shoulder before going back up to the cockpit.

He went back to the navigator's station and looked at the chart. He went up to the astrodome and looked around. Either side of him was the great sweep of the wings, the yellow tipped spinning discs of the props glittering as they caught the moonlight.

The big bomber undulated along. Carter always thought it was eerie. It was black as far as the eye could see but he knew that there were over one hundred other aircraft out there, all heading in the same direction.

The undulations turned into heavy bouncing and buffeting. Lambeth leaned over the yoke, peering forward. Carters eyes went wide with sudden realisation.

"Take her down, NOW!" he shouted into the R/T

To his credit, Lambeth didn't question. He reacted on instinct and the Lancaster plunged down. Carter clung on as a Handley Page Halifax loomed out of the darkness above them. They missed each other by a few feet.

"Jesus, that must have given their tail gunner a scare," said Lambeths' engineer.

"What about me?" shouted the bomb aimer. When he saw the twin tail of the Halifax appear in front of him, he really thought that was it.

Carter blew out his cheeks. That had been too close. That was another one of his lives gone. The crew chattered for a few minutes, getting the surge of adrenalin out of their system. Lambeth let them talk and then called them to heel, getting them to settle down and focus.

"Lunatic. Raving lunatic, that's what you are!" Church shouted. He strode back and forth in Etheridge's office in agitation. He was still in his flying gear and his eyes were wild. He stopped pacing and stood in front of Carter. "Are you out of your mind? What on earth possessed you to do it?"

"I felt I needed to lead by example, sir. Show them I believed in them."

Church almost laughed. He shrugged off his flying jacket and dumped it on the chair in front of Etheridge's desk.

"There are other ways to do that."

"Maybe. But Lambeth is in my flight. I wanted him to see he had my trust. I'm not prepared to tar someone as LMF until I'm sure."

"And what do you think now?"

"Lambeth just needed some confidence in the kite and his own abilities. He'll be okay I think." All the anger and frustration seeped out of Church. He turned to the station commander. "Do you want to add anything, sir"

Etheridge scratched his cheek slowly and stared at Carter.

"No. I think you've covered everything. That's all, Carter; just don't do it again."

After he left, Church looked at Etheridge.
"How do we go about getting the silly sod a medal?"

53 - Unreasonable Haste Is The Direct Road To Error

The early morning recce photos showed the Bosch factory was untouched. Harris sent them back to Stuttgart for the third night in a row. It was Rostock all over again but there was no great fire this time, no great pall of smoke to mark where they had been.

Ground haze foxed them and decoy fires drew the main force north, with most of the bombs falling around Heilbronn twenty miles away. The Ruhr remained a problem to be solved.

After three nights on the trot, there were no ops the next night. The beer flowed in the Mess and the squadron let its hair down. Two bicycles were produced and the sofas were moved around to create a space. The men divided into two teams for a relay race. Each rider had to do a lap of the room while drinking from a pint pot. The Flight Commanders went first.

Everett had the lead until he tipped his head back to finish his pint off. He couldn't see where he was going and missed turning the corner. He ploughed into a knot of men and was thrown over the handlebars. He ended in a tangle of limbs and by the time he struggled free he was well behind. He also had to pay a penalty and drink an extra pint for dropping his own.

Carter got back to the start, finished off his pint and then handed the bike over to Harding who promptly shot off round the course with a comfortable lead. Despite the early advantage, 'B' Flight lost after it turned out the middle runners didn't know how to ride a bicycle. They fell, crashed, got up, fell again and straggled round the circuit before getting back to the start.

The party went into the night and for once, Carter didn't leave early. After three busy days he needed to relax. At around one, things were starting to wind down and Carter decided he'd had enough.

He staggered along with Woods as they supported each other on the way back to their billet. Halfway there they stopped at a bench and collapsed onto it. Woods finished off a bottle of beer he had been carrying. He banged the bottle and peered at the spout, seeing if any more would come out. When he was sure it was empty, he chucked it over his shoulder.

"Are you planning any more joyrides, skipper?"

"Not in the near future, no," Carter slurred.

"Good." Woods fished in his pockets for a cigarette and came up empty. "Don't do it again, please."

"What are you, my mother?"

"Yes, I bloody am," Woods said shortly. "At this moment? I am. You know I'm the poor sod who would have to tell, Georgette if something happened to you. What would I tell her?"

"Yeah, well….," Carter said guiltily. Woods levered himself up.

"Come on, let's get to bed."

Merlin was waiting for them. As the door opened, a furry blonde missile shot towards them and bowled them over. They lay on the ground seeing stars while the Labrador went from one to the other, tail wagging as he licked their faces. Woods hauled himself up and took the dog for a walk while Carter poured himself into bed.

He woke up refreshed and went for a walk. When he got back, Woods bed was empty. He fussed Merlin for a few minutes, shaved, put on a fresh uniform and went for breakfast, his stomach growling.

He found Vos and Woods in the Mess, hunched over their food. Neither of them looked very energetic. Carter had a tough time deciding which of them was more green around the gills. Woods was nibbling on toast, while Vos was struggling to cope with a bowl of porridge. He left them to it and went to dispersal. Latimer was there as usual.

"Morning, sir."

"Everything okay?"

"Top notch, sir."

"How are the men holding up?" he asked.

"Some of them are pretty tired," the NCO said. "Three days on the trot is asking a lot."

Carter nodded in understanding. It was no mean feat getting a Lancaster ready for war. Kites had to be serviced and tested. An engine change could add hours to a working day. In good weather, that wasn't so bad, but Carter remembered the winter months when the crews had worked on the kites in all weathers.

Latimer felt sorry for the armourers. He was content keeping one aircraft in top condition. The armourers had to clean and service all the guns and each Lancaster had eight .303 Browning machine guns. All of the ammunition had to be belted up and that was thousands of rounds.

Finally, before every op, the bombs had to be made ready. That was a detail job. You couldn't rush something like that. Personally, Latimer considered anyone who mucked about with explosives to be mentally unstable.

After lunch, the gates to Amber Hill were closed and the

teleprinter machines started chattering as the Operational Order started coming through. One of the early instructions was the loadout, specifying the bombload. Everyone would be carrying a 4,000lb Cookie with a mix of 500lb GP bombs and incendiary cannisters. Wheeler rang the bomb dump to let them know as the armourers got to work.

Each bomb had to be fused with a pistol detonator. Some had a long delay fuse set. Then they were fitted with a detachable tail unit and hooked up to a bomb rack before being put on a trolley. Cannisters were filled with bundles of 4lb incendiaries.

As soon as the airtests were done, the armourers drove out to dispersal and positioned the trolleys under each aircraft so the bombs and incendiaries could be winched up into the long bomb bays. Do that fifteen or sixteen times per aircraft and you were good to go.

Corporal Dennison was halfway through bombing up a Lanc on the south side of the field. The wind was whipping around his ankles and he was chilled to the bone. Numb fingers fiddled with the rack as he locked it into place. He leaned against the ladder and wiped his nose against the back of his sleeve.

He felt grotty, he was dog tired, his eyes were itchy and irritated and he had a terrible blocked nose and sore throat. Despite his room mates badgering he'd not reported sick as perhaps he should have done. There was a flap on, he just wanted to push through and get it finished and then he could have a hot bath.

"Get a move on, Dennison," shouted Sergeant Lowery. "You've got two more to load up after this. Pull your finger out."

"Yes, Sarge," replied Dennison glumly. Lowery spent most of the time in an agitated mood as he flew around the armament sections, driving the men to do more. At least at the bomb dump you could normally spot him coming and tidy up before he arrived. He was worse when ops were on. He watched as Lowery sped off on his bicycle towards the Lancaster opposite, chivvying the men there to work faster.

Dennison turned back to the task in hand. He checked the rack fitted to the bomb, making sure it was hooked into the bombs lug and the fuse was correct. Four more 500lb bombs and then it was back to the dump to pick up the load for the next aircraft.

What happened next was always going to be a mystery. Perhaps Dennison sneezed at the wrong moment. Perhaps he knocked the bomb as he was attaching the rack to the bay. Whatever the reason, the grips on the rack sprang open and the bomb fell towards the ground. Dennison just had time to stare in wonder before there was a massive bang.

That explosion started off a chain reaction that obliterated four aircraft and damaged five others. All that was left of N-Nuts and the other three Lancasters was a series of overlapping stinking craters. Debris was thrown two thousand feet in the air and windows rattled across the station and surrounding farms from the force of the blast.

Dazed personnel peered out from behind walls while smoke drifted into the sky. Carter worked his jaw to pop his ears. The windows of the briefing room had been blown out and everyone was covered in shards of glass. The station stirred itself and the fire trucks and ambulances sped out to dispersal, onlookers following on foot.

Ten men were killed in the blast but they only ever found two of them. Lowery and an aircraftman were located two hundred yards from the explosion with not a mark on them. The shockwave from the blast had killed them outright and Lowery lay on his back with a surprised expression on his face.

The post mortem would have to come later; the war waited for no man. Seven undamaged Lancs including L-Lady were bombed up and ready to go. They went. Carter picked six crews to go with him. Harding, Wright, Higgins, Lambeth, Biggs and Duquene took off for Warnemunde.

54 - One Of Our Aircraft Is Missing

For once, Headquarters got it badly wrong; or the Germans just guessed right for once. Two hundred aircraft went out to Warenmunde, twenty failed to come back. Ten percent. Ten percent gone in one night. A few more like that and Bomber Command would be lucky to still exist.

363 lost four and all those who made it back had damage of one kind or another. Carter came back on three engines with a fetching collection of 20mm holes. He landed gingerly, keeping it light on the port side as he touched down.

Things had gone wrong for Carter and his crew almost from the beginning. He had picked up on their mood in the truck when they rode out to dispersal. Murphy and Flynn were not their usual chatty selves and there were no tales of their latest sexual conquests. Vos stared moodily into the distance and even Woods seemed dour.

All of them gave the big cookie a wary look before getting on board. Even Latimer was not as upbeat as he normally was. The days earlier events had unnerved all of them more than they cared to admit. Through the startup, Byron's voice was a flat monotone, lacking in any life or enthusiasm.

"Let's just get this over with," he told them as they taxied out. "Drinks are on me when we get back."

Over the North Sea, he let them talk about the earlier explosion for a while. Conversation turned to their own bomb load and the majority of them were in favour of dumping the Cookie after what had happened.

Carter would have gladly done so, but he knew the target camera was activated when that was released. If they dropped it early, all they'd have was a photograph of the ocean. They were stuck with it, but none of them could wait to get to Warnemunde so they could get rid of the thing.

Crossing the coast at Esbjerg, flak chased them all the way along the route to Flensburg. It exploded harmlessly below but it was a taste of things to come. Winds shoved them off track and they strayed too close to a Luftwaffe airfield. They were tense after that. Pushing the engines as hard as they dared, Carter climbed, wanting to put as much height as possible between them and trouble.

Suddenly, death leapt at them out of the darkness. Todd shouted a warning as the 110 came charging in from the rear starboard quarter. He must have been a rookie because he fired from way back. The cannon shells were as big as golf balls as they trailed behind.

"Call it," said Carter. He leaned over the yoke, ready to go. Byron left his panel and hovered next to Carter, his hand on the throttle levers.

The 110 continued to charge in, still firing in a long continuous burst. The pilot was trying to walk his cannon fire onto the Lancaster.

"Corkscrew starboard! GO!" shouted Todd. Carter pulled the yoke back and rolled right, turning into the nightfighters path of approach.

Realising their error, the 110 reversed their turn, trying to follow the big bomber round. At that moment, Todd and Murphy opened up and six streams of tracer laced out, reaching for the 110. *The Lady* jumped as cannon shells slammed into the outer port wing. Carter could feel the hits go in, but he also felt the vibrations as Todd and Murphy fired back.

The yoke jumped in his hands and he gripped it tight, steering the Lancaster through the climbing turn. The Merlins were screaming at maximum revs as Byron shoved the throttles through the gate, screwing every ounce of power out of the engines.

"He overshot! He overshot!" shouted Murphy as the grey 110 screamed past. He craned his neck, trying to see where they went. "He went to port! To port!"

"Find the bastard," said Todd.

"Now!" Carter shouted to Byron. The Flight Engineer chopped the throttles on the port engines. Carter rolled left and then booted the rudder to haul them round and down. In the nose, Flynn clung on like a boy on a rollercoaster at the fair as the Lancaster plunged and then bottomed out of its diving turn and climbed back up again.

The 110 broke left and climbed. The pilot wiped the back of his hand across his brow. His mouth was dry and sweat beaded on his face. He thought he'd made a perfect approach and the Lancaster was a pigeon, ripe for plucking. He hadn't expected such a spirited defence.

He checked his crew were still with him and then with the bit between his teeth, he turned to make another attack. He dodged in and out of the wisps of clouds and stayed low, keeping the Lancaster above the line of the horizon so they would be highlighted against the background of the starlit sky. He peered intently, looking for the stab of blue flame from the engine exhausts.

"He's still back there," said Todd. He panned his turret to the right and kept a careful eye on it as the 110 stalked them. He watched as it slowly climbed to their altitude and began to draw level on their left.

Todd grinned behind his oxygen mask. That was an old trick. Going alongside and feigning they hadn't seen the bomber. If he stuck to the script, he would just about come level before turning hard to make a slashing attack, guns blazing. Carter held it steady, every sense tuned, ready to react in a moment.

"Get ready, Spud." Todd gripped the gun controls and settled in his seat.

"I'm ready." Murphy pressed the oxygen mask to his face and breathed deep.

The 110 stood on its starboard wingtip and came in. This time they held their fire, wanting to get closer and make sure.

"Corkscrew to port! GO!" Murphy shouted.

The port wing dipped and Murphy's world tilted as Carter dived the big bomber to cut into the 110's attack. Murphy traversed his turret and fired in short controlled bursts. Todd could only wait. Even at full traverse, the 110 was beyond his firing arc and he would have to hang on for his chance.

The 110 opened fire as the Lancaster crossed in front of him. He placed the dot of his gunsight on the big fat fuselage. Sparks went flying as rounds went through the thin skin.

Murphy adjusted his deflection and gave them both barrels. The fighter staggered and then reared up. Murphy carried on pouring it on, pumping round after round into the 110. The nightfighter drunkenly rolled right, exposing their vulnerable belly. Fire streamed from the starboard wing as it dived away out of sight.

"Got him! I got him!" Murphy exclaimed fizzing with excitement. It had all happened so fast. Blink and they were gone.

"He got us as well," muttered Carter as he levelled off. The yoke had juddered in his hands and he could feel the air tugging on something.

Byron looked at his board of instruments. The temperature on the port outer was starting to climb. He tapped the glass but the needle continued to go round the dial into the red.

"Port outer caught a packet."

Carter glanced left and then back to his instruments. Murphy reported a thin white trail streaming back from the engine. Vos crawled around the fuselage in the dark with a flashlight, looking for other damage.

The port outer started to labour and Byron shut it down, feathering the prop. Carter edged the throttles forward on the remaining engines but it soon became apparent they'd be unable to maintain their current airspeed.

"How long to go, Woody?"

Woods played with his maps and did some fast calculations. The loss of one engine wasn't too serious. They could maintain height on three easily and once they let the bombs go they would have reserve power to spare.

"About an hour. East to the island of Fehmarn and then the final run in to Warnemunde."

"Eyes open everyone. If there's one fighter out there, there's more. Let's see if we can't make it two for the night."

Warnemunde was right on the coast, just north of Rostock. There was no trouble finding it but it was a far harder proposition than that sleepy little town. Unlike the really big industrial targets, the town and the city itself were only a quarter of a mile wide along the waterfront, it was easy to miss. The Heinkel aircraft factory was ringed by guns and searchlights as were the docks and warehouses.

The guns sent up a wall of flak. Carter saw a Wellington coned by the blue white beam of a master searchlight. More lights pinned it and no matter how much it twisted and turned; it was only a matter of time. The flak walked upwards, boxed it in and then blotted it from the sky.

A searchlight passed over them and for a moment, the inside of the cockpit was as bright as day. Carter dived and blinked to clear the spots from his eyes. Flynn couldn't see a thing either.

"Get us out of this," he screamed, his voice shrill.

Carter was suddenly reminded of what he had drummed into Harding. This was no time to be delicate, they had to get out of the beam. If they pulled the wings off, so be it. The Lancaster twisted and dived. Carter finally broke free after he turned right for the umpteenth time. The searchlight anticipated that they would twist left again but Carter continued his turn. They went one way; the light went the other and they were free.

Blinking and wiping his eyes, Carter shook his head. He was knackered and his arms felt like they were coming out of their sockets. He levelled off and pressed on.

Almost blinded by the glare, Flynn got a sighting on something and let the bombs go. Carter waited for the photo and then turned for home, diving for the ground and the safety of the dark.

Interrogation was short. As only three crews had made it back, it wasn't long before Kent went back to his office to ring the results through to Group. Lambeth, Biggs, Higgins and Duquene were missing.

"Just one of those nights, chaps. New day tomorrow," said Church, trying to gee the men up. Tired eyes stared back at him.

Yvonne had sighed with relief when Woods walked through the door. She had listened with her heart in her mouth when Murphy relayed the details of the fighter attack.

The following morning, Carter was noodling with some admin but his heart wasn't in it. He was waiting for a phone call and was growing impatient. One of their missing Lancs had pancaked on a field on the south coast but there was no information on who it was or if there had been any casualties.
"If Mohammed won't come to the mountain…" said a voice at the door. Carter jumped.
"Good lord."
"Here I am," said Wilkinson.
"Cuppa?" Carter asked, about to call the admin staff outside his office. Wilkinson shook his head.
"Flying visit, old boy. Official business after yesterdays conflagration. Just saying hello. You'll be around later?"
"Of course."
Wilkinson disappeared as fast as he had come. Carter closed his office door and went back to waiting for the phone to ring.
The word came through an hour later. It was Biggs who had made it back. He'd come down hard on an emergency field with two engines out. Two of his crew had been wounded and Biggs broke his left leg on landing. All of them had been taken to the local hospital to be checked out. Carter rang Saunderson so he could start packing up the personal effects of the missing.

Wilkinson and the Group Armaments Officer went round Amber Hill conducting an enquiry of sorts. It was short and sweet. It was hard to hold a detailed investigation when there were no living witnesses. They questioned the remaining armourers about their knowledge of procedures and the squadrons current work practises.
There was always the possibility of a handling error but other causes were considered as well. Pullen speculated that stray static could have activated the release mechanism. Strictly speaking that shouldn't have been possible as the bomb release system was supposed to be isolated before they started loading up, but tired men made mistakes. There was also the chance it could have been a faulty detonating pistol or a defective long delay fuse.
With no definitive proof one way or another to provide a convincing conclusion, Wilkinson was not about to sully dead mens reputations. In the end, the report left an open judgement.
Replacement aircraft were flown in and life returned to normal. Civilians who had property damaged by the blast were compensated. The explosion made the local newspapers. It was too big a thing to be

ignored but the reports were scant on detail, the censor doing their best to limit what was known.

Within a week, the holes would be filled in and fresh concrete laid. The only sign anything had occurred would be the scorched grass and even that would grow over. In the end, the only reminder would be a brass plaque Etheridge had commissioned. It listed the date and the names of the dead and was put up in the admin block. After two weeks it was a mere footnote in the squadron histories. Wheeler noted the names of the dead and the serial numbers of the aircraft written off in the Squadron record book.

The funeral for the victims of the accident was three days later. No one was explicitly ordered to go but enough nods, winks and suggestions were made over the intervening days that there was a good turnout at the service.

The village church was a quaint little eighteenth century stone building with a neat graveyard. The Priest was a wizened old figure who shared the service with the station Chaplain. The hymns were suitably solemn and the elderly organ player churned out music that was not far off nails being dragged down a blackboard. Only two of the ten flag draped coffins actually contained anything. The rest were there for show after the explosion had wiped the men from the face of the earth.

Carter stood near the back of the church with Georgette. He knelt and stood when required but he just went through the motions. Seeing war up close had bludgeoned what little faith he had out of him.

Sitting with Etheridge in the front pew was Sergeant Lowery's grieving widow. Clad head to toe in black, she would have come down on the train from Sheffield, but Etheridge had sent his car and driver to collect her as a guest of the squadron. She was put up in a hotel in Lincoln. Considering what had happened it was the least the RAF could do.

The coffins were lowered into the ground and the episode was brought to a close. Church escorted the widow to the wake back at the station. She was a timid little thing, with big tear streaked eyes. She sat with a cup of tea while people stood around offering condolences and tried not to look too awkward.

Depressed by the service and the stark reminder of deaths proximity, Carter needed to see some life. He took Georgette for a drive and drove off in a random direction, stopping a few miles away from the village where a sign pointed the way down to the river. Carter parked the car at a layby and they went for a walk.

Georgette was subdued and quiet and walked slowly alongside him. They got to a dry stone wall with a stile built into it. Carter stepped over and turned back, offering his hand to help her across. She gripped his hand tightly and climbed over the wall, doing her best to maintain her dignity which was not easy in a knee length skirt. The path was well worn this side of the wall and the going was easier as they got closer to the river.

It was a warm day. The sun shone brightly and as they walked, Carter took off his tunic and rolled his shirt sleeves up.

"When do you need to get back?" he asked her.

"Not for a while yet. I'm not on duty until tomorrow but I do want to get back in time to do my hair."

"I think we can manage that," he said as he smiled for the first time today.

The end of the path was shaded by trees that lined both sides of the river bank. A footpath wended its way amongst the trees that leaned out over the water. The river was about twenty feet across, but the water was low and the current was quite weak. Here and there the bank had subsided, offering a gentle way to get down to the edge of the water.

They sat down on a fallen log surrounded by long grass. Georgette stared at the water, watching it flow over and around rocks that stood proud of the surface.

"Funerals," she said. She shuddered and rubbed her hands together. "Our parents didn't let us go to funerals," she told him. "We didn't even go to our grandparents service even though we wanted to." Her mouth twisted in a small moue of annoyance, the past hurt resurfacing for a moment. "They said it was too upsetting for us. I just remember a bunch of people who came to the house, talking in hushed whispers; lots of black." Carter remained quiet and let her talk. "You know, this is only the second funeral I've been to?"

Carter mentally kicked himself.

"I'm sorry," he apologised. "I should have realised."

"It's all right, darling," she gave him a weak smile. "That was another life, a long time ago."

"Still-" she put a finger on his lips.

"It's all right."

The mood passed as suddenly as it came. Georgette looked around to make sure there was no one else around. When she was sure the coast was clear, she stood up and slipped off her shoes. She hitched her skirt up and rolled her stockings down.

"What are you doing?" Carter asked, surprised. He grasped her hand to steady her while she took them off. She turned to him and pulled him to his feet.

"Come on. It's too hot to just sit in the sun."

Her laugh drifting on the breeze, she navigated the slope down to the water. Rolling the hem of her skirt higher, she walked into the stream, picking her way forwards. The water only came up to her ankles, but it was nice and cooling on such a warm day.

Carter stood watching on the bank, pleased to see the gloom lift as she paddled around. He went down to the waters edge and rummaged around in the fine clay soil. He selected a few smooth flat stones and crouched low, skipping them off the water. He got one to bounce three times before making the far bank. He sent another one skittering through a cloud of midges that clung to the surface under the shade of a weeping willow.

"Come in," she called to him. Taken by the same impulse, he kicked off his shoes and socks and rolled up his trouser legs.

"Ya bugger," he said as he waded out, surprised at how cold the water was. He gingerly edged out towards her, his feet feeling the way through the sand and silt and pebbles.

"Come on silly," she chided him, laughing. "You're not going to drown."

She kicked water at him and he dodged out of the way. For a few moments they were like children, the cares of the world washed away. She chased him around, kicking water as she held her skirt up. Carter gave up, his trouser legs soaking. Finally, he ran out of breath and he held up a hand.

"Stop; enough."

Georgette giggled. She closed the distance between him and he gathered her into his arms and kissed her. She leaned into him and they stood there, in the shade with the water rushing around their ankles.

55 - Hold Them By The Hand

After such a concentrated burst of operations, 363 settled down to a more normal pace. Training continued as usual and new crews came in to replace the losses over Warnemunde. After a few days, three crews went minelaying in the Baltic. Some more went the next night off Heligoland. Four went out, three came back. Lord HawHaw took great delight in citing the serial number of the missing aircraft and boasting that a flak ship got them.

On the Sunday, there was a station sports competition. Etheridge had arranged for teams from Waddington to come across. Lunch was laid on and the men spent the afternoon hacking at each others ankles while they chased a football around the pitch.

Woods moaned the following morning when he saw the bruises come up on his shins. He lay on his bed staring at the lurid purple marks. He hobbled around the Mess at breakfast and he was not the only one.

Once a week, Etheridge had got into the habit of having a meeting with the ground staff and squadron staff. Church, Everett and Carter attended as did Pullen and other specialists as and when required by whatever agenda the Group Captain was working to. Etheridge found it an excellent way to have discussions about morale and any other issues that cropped up on the station.

A directive came from Group regarding adherence to bomb loading procedures. Particular emphasis was laid on isolating the release mechanisms before bombs were loaded. There was no specific finger pointing that it was because of their accident, but they could all read the hidden message.

After the meeting broke up, Carter was nearly back to his office when Saunderson slid smoothly alongside him.

"All right, sir?" he asked pleasantly; too pleasantly and Carter could feel his antennae twitching.

"Not bad, what I can do for you?" he replied. Saunderson paused and looked around.

"I need to talk to you about something," he said, his voice evasive, a little mysterious.

"Er…okay." Carter waited. Saunderson hesitated. "Spit it out."

"Gambling, sir."

"Gambling?"

"More specifically, your lot gambling."

Carter started to have a germ of an idea where this conversation was going. They went straight to his office. Carter dumped his peaked cap on his desk. He flopped down into his seat and indicated for Saunderson to sit.

"I've noticed an increase lately in people complaining about being skint in letters home." Carter motioned for him to continue. "A few of them made some oblique references to being unlucky. Then they said their luck would turn."

Carter leaned back and frowned. He was waiting for Saunderson to join the dots.

"It's pretty much an open secret that there's a regular game in one of the Flight Sergeant huts and all of your bods live there." Bingo. "I just thought a quiet word might be better than doing something official."

Carter sighed.

"I'll sort it out."

Saunderson looked relieved and bobbed his head in thanks. Ordinarily, he would have dealt with something like this himself, but he felt it was better coming from Carter.

During the walk to the billets, Carter thought about this and the host of other things that crossed his desk. This was the other side of squadron life most people never saw. It certainly wasn't something that had bothered him on his first tour. Running a crew was about as far as most people got. Mothering 'B' Flight, shepherding a squadron with a guiding hand was another thing entirely.

This was why Adjutants were so important. They were the glue that held everything together. They were a shoulder to cry on. The good ones anticipated problems and had the knack to recognise needs before you were really aware of it. In this instance, Saunderson had shown his value yet again, adroitly raising a potential problem and putting the good of the squadron ahead of process. Carter wished Saunderson could pull a similar trick with the senior WAAF. She had rung him earlier pestering him for an update on her representations.

He had been able to deflect her with the events of the last few days but he knew it was just putting off the inevitable. The thing was, there really wasn't very much to tell her. The SP's were nowhere with the great WAAFery break in. As to illegal joyrides, that was a complete non starter as he and Everett knew it would be.

Regarding the pregnancy thing, she would have a fight on her hands. One of the alleged fathers was the best engine mechanic on the squadron. There was no way Church was posting him elsewhere. There would be words of advice and some serious hints would be dropped about being a gentleman and doing the right thing but that would be it. Five minutes of fun in the armoury had earned the Corporal a posting to Saint Athan in soggy Wales and a reprimand. Carter had a feeling Hakes wouldn't be happy with that.

That internal tussle took him to the billets. He knocked on the door and waited a moment until Murphy opened it.

"Boss."

"Can I come in?" he asked. A little surprised, Murphy stepped back and Carter entered. He looked around. The billet was the same as before. The only difference was the pile of tins was gone like he had told them and the heap of wood and coal was a more normal proportion.

As expected, the Poker game was running and Carter stepped over. Flynn was sitting on an upturned vegetable crate. A cigarette hung from his lips. He riffled a pile of shillings in front of him. Murphy resumed his seat next to him and Carter watched while they played a few hands. Byron was by the window, reading a technical manual on Merlin engines. Todd was elsewhere. A Canadian gunner did quite well. Flynn did better, clearing three hands in a row. Carter watched carefully. There were no strategically placed mirrors and no underhand manipulation of the cards.

During a tea break, Carter picked up the pack and riffled them. It was a worn pack, but there were no bent corners, nothing obvious to give certain cards away. He split the pack in two and shuffled them together again.

"Shall we deal you in, sir?" Flynn asked, flashing him his best smile while he sipped from a tin mug. Carter handed him the pack.

"Too rich for me." He gestured to the pile of coins. "You'd have the shirt off my back in no time."

He remembered his early flying training, losing heavily in the dorms as he was introduced to five card stud Poker. Carter could follow the game all right, he just wasn't very good at figuring odds and predicting who had what. He could have a little fun, but there was no future in it.

The thing was, some people didn't know when to quit. They would start chasing bad hands and follow that with bad play and stupid bets trying to win their money back. Young lads, away from home for the first time with money burning a hole in their pocket were an easy mark to a seasoned player.

"I'll tell you what," he said, addressing himself to Murphy and Flynn. "Let's go for a walk, shall we?" The tone was friendly but his face said otherwise. His mouth was fixed in a rictus grin, the scar twitching. Murphy knew that look.

"Time for a break lads. Come back in an hour," Murphy told the rest of them. Murphy and Flynn grabbed their forage caps and crammed them on their heads. Flynn picked up his winnings and shoved the coins in a jar on the shelf by his bed. Carter waited until they were a good distance from the billets before speaking again.

"I think it's good for a chap to have hobbies outside of work," he said simply.

"Everyone needs an outlet," agreed Flynn.

"I'm not one to cramp a man's style. When you're not flying, you can entertain yourselves doing whatever you like best. Smoke, drink, shag whoever you want. As long as you don't get into punch ups in town in which case you've made a rod for your own back. Get in trouble financially…" He left the unspoken threat hanging.

Flynn and Murphy could see the metaphorical club hanging over them. Murphy found the grass fascinating. He kicked at a clump of dandelions and watched as the seed head exploded in a cloud of white fluff.

"You might want to think about making the games shorter and for smaller stakes. Not everyone can afford it."

"That's a bit harsh, Boss," complained Flynn. "Everyone's a big boy. We're not holding a gun to anyone's head either-"

"I know," interrupted Carter. "But it's no longer an innocent game. It's been noticed. If I were you, I'd be thankful it's just me having this conversation and not someone else. Next time it might be the SP's knocking. They'll make it official, then the CO will have no option but to take action. Just be a little more discreet, okay?" he warned them.

Pullen used the lull to sort all the little mechanical niggles that had built up recently. *The Lady* was put to rights. The damaged engine was replaced. The holes in the fuselage were patched and the outer part of the port wing was scrapped and changed. Every day, Carter went out to the hangar to watch the progress.

As *The Lady* wasn't ready, Carter took one of the Manchester's up for a flip. It wasn't just a nostalgia trip. As it was dual control, Carter used the opportunity to give Byron some stick time. It was nothing fancy of course, but it was better than nothing. He finished by deliberately trimming nose down and getting Byron to keep them level. It was as close as they could get to simulating damage.

"Just remember," Carter told him. "Once you've been damaged, it's a matter of finesse. Yanking the things around might cause more problems."

Byron just nodded and concentrated as he wrestled with the controls.

On the way back to Amber Hill, there was some chatter about plans for the evening.

"Do we have to go to *The Tarleton?*" asked Byron.

"And what's wrong with it?" demanded Todd.

"We always go there."

"So?" replied the Aussie, a hint of challenge in his voice.

"Tradition, Mister Byron," said Carter. "If there's a particular pub you have in mind, I'm open to suggestions, but we always start at *The Tarleton*."

"Anyone decided what to do with their leave?" asked Woods. There was a stony silence for a moment. Their next leave was when their tour was over. Talking about that felt like tempting fate.

"Sleep," responded Todd.

"Shagging," said Murphy.

"How original," said Carter, deadpan.

"I thought we could all go to London before we scatter to the four winds," Woods suggested. "We might not see each other for a while after that."

"I'm game," said Vos.

"And me," echoed Flynn, already thinking about the lovelies around Piccadilly Circus he could bestow his favours on.

On the truck back to the equipment room, the banter continued. Flynn was describing a brunette who was his latest conquest.

"Like an older Olivia de Havilland," he enthused. "With curves in all the right places." He moved his hands up and down in an hourglass shape.

Todd was unimpressed. He had yet to see Flynn with one of these girls and he had his suspicions regarding their existence. Then again, he had thought the same thing about Murphy and look how wrong he had been about that.

Todd was still quietly seeing Muriel. It had taken a few weeks of him seeing her at the pub before the frost had thawed. They had gone to the pictures since and one Sunday they had spent the day together, walking in the ornamental gardens in Lincoln and finishing with tea back in her flat. It was slow going but he was happy to go at whatever pace Muriel wanted. She was still brittle but relations between them were a lot better than they had been.

"Have I mentioned my kill?" Murphy asked casually. Everyone groaned in good humour. It had become the running joke on the ride back in the truck.

"What about mine," Todd countered. "I don't think I've mentioned it for a while."

"I'm not surprised," chided Murphy as he blew a raspberry. "Bagging a sitter was too easy."

"Hey!" Todd protested.

"How about a slap up dinner before we go on leave?" suggested Woods, changing the subject. "Anyone can bring a guest if they want."

There was little enthusiasm for that.

"Bit formal for me," said Byron nervously. He still felt a little bit of an outsider when things like this were discussed. Murphy said yes, Flynn was non-committal. Todd said no. He would have loved to bring Muriel but he doubted she'd want to come. The idea fizzled out.

"Well it was just a thought," Woods said moodily.

Back in their billet they got changed to go out. Another letter from White had come and Carter read out bits aloud to Walsh as they dressed.

Progress had been slow. A skin graft to his neck had gone well but McIndoe had yet to have a go on his hands. Elaine still visited when she could and they had gotten engaged. There was no date for a wedding yet. White wanted to be in better shape, but he wanted as many of the crew to come if possible once the date was set.

"Remarkable," said Woods. He was in awe of the strength it took for White to keep going in the face of so many challenges.

He looked in the mirror and ran a hand over his chin, contemplating a shave. He decided he was good enough and shrugged his shirt on.

"Talking of dates," said Carter. "How about dinner at the weekend? You, me, Vos, our girls and I've got a friend and his wife who might be able to come."

"Sounds like a good idea," agreed Woods.

Carter asked Vos about it on the way into Lincoln. The Belgian said yes and he mentioned it to Denise later in the evening. She looked down at her changing figure. She felt fat and dowdy, but Vos talked her round.

"It'll be good for you to get out." Denise was still unsure. "I'll buy you a new dress," he said in good humour.

"Shoes?" she asked with a smile.

"And shoes," he agreed, laughing.

The date was set for the following Saturday, ops permitting of course. Carter rang Wilkinson and asked him.

"Helen will be thrilled," he said. "I've been trying to get her out of the house for weeks."

"Tell her it's a mission of mercy," Carter told him. "My Wireless Ops girl is pregnant, a few months along and she's just a slip of a girl. She could do with some words of wisdom."

"We'll see you then," he assured him.

"So we'll be free that day?" Carter asked pointedly, fishing for information.

"You know everything I do, old chap," Wilkinson replied, dodging the question and put the phone down.

56 - Command Decisions

Located at High Wycombe in Buckinghamshire, Bomber Command Headquarters had been built away from London to avoid the expected enemy raids. Located amongst thick Beech trees, it was more like a village than an RAF station. The Air Staff Block was built in the style of a town hall. The Officers Mess looked like a country manor. All of the buildings were interconnected by underground tunnels. The key building was the Operations block. Fifty five feet underground, it was protected from bombs by three layers of reinforced concrete with a cushion of earth between them.

The Operations room was not hugely different from the briefing room at Amber Hill, it was just bigger. On the far wall was a huge map of Europe with the known flak belts marked out and key targets highlighted. Other large map boards stood either side of it and it was from here that Harris would sit and direct Bomber Commands efforts. Each day, Harris would be given the results of the previous nights operations. He would hear a precis of the raids, what went right, what went wrong and would be shown recce photos of bomb damage.

The meteorologist would report on the expected weather for that night. Harris was always concerned with two things, how clear things would be over the target, but also, what the weather would be like on the return. There was no point sending his squadrons out if England was blanketed in fog when they got back making landing impossible.

Of course, forecasting the weather was not an exact science. The weather over England could be predicted with a high degree of accuracy, but the weather forecast for Europe was more subjective. Sometimes the wind did what you least expected and created problems, but Harris didn't like risking his men unnecessarily. As much as he was driven by results, he was also careful to husband his force strength as much as possible for future operations.

When deciding on each night's operations, Harris had a number of competing demands. Air Ministry Directives listed his priorities. Sometimes, he had to go for what he called 'panacea' targets, a sop to political reactions or the other services requirements. Harris avoided them whenever he could but it was not always possible. He would hear the weather report, consider the list then issue orders for ops, sending his force to places with codenames like Grayling, Chubb, Trout and Spratt.

A keen fly fisherman, Air Vice Marshal Saundby, had used the names of types of fish for each target. Hannover was Eel, Cologne was Trout. Berlin was Whitebait which Harris found amusing. The capital of Nazi Germany and Saundby had called it after the immature fry of fish that were small and insignificant.

Lately, Harris had been wanting to expand operations. There had been great hopes for Gee to assist in that regard, but the early raids had produced mixed results. Rostock had shown what could be achieved, but as a coastal target, it was not the same proposition as one of the big industrial cities.

Having flown extensively at night himself during the Great War, Harris knew how difficult it was to find your way. Add in decoy targets, blackout, wind, adverse weather, flak and nightfighters, it was a wonder any of his boys made it to a target at all; and they were *his* boys. Harris felt losses keenly and had to balance his natural urge to protect his men against the tactical and strategic requirements of Bomber Command's role.

Harris' thoughts often turned to casualties. On an average raid, the loss rate usually ran between three and five percent. Harris disliked turning anything into a numbers game but three to five percent was a manageable, acceptable rate. He was pained when he heard the butchers bill at morning prayers. Five of our aircraft are missing might not sound so bad on the radio, but each one was five, six, seven men; never to return. Raids like the recent one on Warnemunde had caused palpitations. It had required a fraught phone call with Portal to smooth things over and assure him that it was a fluke.

His mind turned, as it often did, to reducing that figure. The problem was that the German defences were growing stronger in parallel with the incremental improvements in aircraft, heavier bombloads and better techniques. If the defences could be overwhelmed, it would be a different story.

The German had built themselves a defensive line of radar controlled nightfighters. Intelligence said it was called the Kammhuber Line. The sky was divided into boxes and inside each box was a nightfighter that was directed to its target by ground controlled radar. Any bomber crossing the box was like a fly getting caught in a web. It was very clever, Teutonically efficient and deadly in the right hands.

What they needed to do was flood the system; so that so many aircraft crossed a box that one nightfighter couldn't cope. Similarly, if lots of aircraft went over the target together, the searchlights couldn't be everywhere. There would be a risk of collision of course, but the boffins could figure out the odds on that one.

Since he had taken command, he had begun to lay the

groundwork to achieve that, but he knew it was only a matter of time before the Luftwaffe responded. He pondered the idea of some kind of knockout blow.

Harris went to London in bullish mood. After months of being under a cloud, Bomber Command was moving forward. He had good headlines and with the new Lancaster starting to come into service in greater numbers, he finally had the weapon he needed to win the war.

He went to London and argued for more aircraft and a buildup of strength. The Minister of Aircraft Production was away touring some aircraft factories up north so Harris had to content himself with a mere deputy of department. The man dug his heels in.

"Bomber Command has hardly covered itself in glory," he said with that nasal air of disdain that civil servants do so well.

"With inadequate aircraft, inadequate numbers," Harris shot back.

"Last autumn, you lost the equivalent of your entire first line strength in a few months."

Harris snorted. Second guessing other people's decisions was easy. He was not about to rubbish his predecessors and play armchair general on tactical decisions to satisfy some civil servant.

"I wasn't in charge then," he snapped. "We're delivering results *now*. Bomber Command can win the war, but not without proper aircraft and *not* without aircraft in numbers."

"I understand," said Llewellin's deputy smoothly. He steepled his hands in front of him, "empire building," he murmured. Harris almost exploded. He leaned forward on the desk, anger rising.

"I couldn't give a fig for power," he said hotly. "I spent *years* before the war advocating for better aircraft, better training and better navigational aids when everyone else's eye was off the ball! Miracles don't happen overnight." He stepped back and clamped down on his temper. "My boys are going up night after night on a wing and a prayer. The Navy get the best ships, the army get their tanks. I will not let my boys go off with yesterdays cast offs."

Harris went for the door, but a final remark made him stop.

"You can't wish for the moon."

"No; just the stars," he bit out as he slammed the door.

A few days later he was invited to dine at Chequers. A few miles from High Wycombe, Chequers was northwest of London and had been the countryside home of the Prime Ministers of England since 1921. As Downing Street was a cramped, terraced house in the middle of London, it lacked the grandeur and space to lavishly entertain foreign dignitaries, Chequers provided that.

Harris had driven over there in his Bentley and talked into the night with Churchill. The Prime Minister had been his usual garrulous self and Harris sparred with him verbally, their conversation sweeping across a vast range of subjects. Harris used the opportunity to expound on his idea of breaking Germany with bombing, advocating his theory of total war.

Harris argued there was no need for an invasion; bombing could win the war on its own. If Bomber Command could put their cities to the sword, it would weaken the morale of the German people and destroy their industrial infrastructure. Their armies would be starved of weapons and the tools to wage war.

Churchill was not oblivious to the arguments. Bombing Germany would destroy factories, displace the population and at the very least force the Nazis to divert guns, planes and men from the front to defend their homeland. He was also well aware that the Russians had been calling for some time to relieve the pressure on their own forces, advocating a second front.

"We *are* the second front," Harris insisted. "Forget the invasion. There's no need to risk hundreds of thousands; *millions* of men in a land invasion if I can break the Nazi at home."

Churchill looked at him, his eyes slitted in shrewd appraisal.

"How long would it take?" he asked finally.

"If I get the aircraft I want, I could finish the war in a year," Harris replied with crisp certainty.

"With the Americans on board?" Churchill asked pointedly.

Harris paused to consider his answer.

"Bombing around the clock, them by day, me by night; six months," he said with confidence.

The Prime Minister sat by the fire, cigar in one hand, brandy in the other. He swirled the dark liquid around in the glass, watching it catch the light of the flames. There was some appeal in what Harris was saying. The slaughter of the Great War was not something Churchill wanted to see repeated. The Somme, Gallipoli, First and Second Ypres were all battles that were going to win the war and instead they had become a slaughter. He pondered the conflicts that were to come. A land invasion of Europe could be risky, the casualties could be frightful.

He had people from every theater of war clamouring for bombers. Japan was running rampant like a toddler in a nursery and knocking on the gates of India and Australia. Rommel was yet to be beaten in North Africa. Malta was still besieged and the Russians needed as much help as could be given.

Churchill knew the Dehousing paper provided some support for Harris' arguments and he agreed with the general principal. He had seen first hand the effect heavy bombing could have on civilian morale and infrastructure when he visited Coventry and London's East End. To do the same thing to the Germans would be poetic justice indeed.

Sir Archibald Sinclair, Secretary of State for Air also approved of the Dehousing Paper, but Churchill knew there were others who were opposed to it. Portal had voiced concern as Bomber Command were not likely to get ten thousand bombers any time in the near future. More vocal was Sir Henry Tizard on the Air Council. He was pressing very strongly for Bomber Command to concentrate specifically on shipyards and the submarine pens to support the Navy. The Admiralty had seized on that and added their own voice to the growing noise. As inter-departmental bunfights went, it was a classic.

"Prove it to me," Churchill said quietly. "Show me Bomber Command can do it. Show me you can do it to some big target, not some grubby little town on the coast. Give me a knockout blow."

"Give me a little time, Prime Minister."

"Go to it, Bomber."

During the drive back to High Wycombe, Harris' mind was whirring with plans and possibilities. The following day, after morning prayers, he called his senior staff to his office and explained what he wanted. Saundby went off to do some sums. Harris had known Saundby since the 1920's when they had flown together in Iraq. He was one of the few men who had his ear and could talk to him frankly. He reported back in the afternoon with the bald figures.

"If we put everything on the line in the Groups, we can scrape up over five hundred aircraft," Saundby told him.

Harris was impressed and at the same time disgruntled. It was an impressive number to be sure, but it lacked sparkle. He needed something that would grab headlines, something that would put everyone on notice that Bomber Command meant business. They needed a magic number.

"A thousand. Get me one thousand aircraft, Sandy," he told Saundby. "I don't care how you do it. Twist arms, bully, sweet talk, whatever it takes."

Saundby blinked, the only outward sign of reaction. Inside, his brain ran a million miles an hour while it did some rapid mathematics.

"It won't be easy, sir. We could take aircraft and men from the OTU's," he suggested, "but it would mean interrupting training schedules. If we could have some aircraft from Coastal Command as well, I think we can do it."

"I'll sort that out," Harris assured him. "God knows, the Navy have nabbed enough of my squadrons, the least the fish heads can do is loan some of them back for a few trips."

Harris went to see Portal and put forward his idea of a knockout blow and pressed for a contribution from Coastal Command. Portal made enquiries and reported back that the Prime Minister warmly approved of the plan and had received the Admiralty's support in principal. With that assurance, Harris got to work. He wanted to take advantage of the next moon period so there was little time to get ready. He signalled all Groups to prepare for a massive attack on a scale previously unseen from the 28th May onwards as soon as the weather was suitable.

57 - The Measure Of A Man

While Bomber Command moved into gear, normal operations continued. On the 19th, the squadron was sent to Mannheim and did well. The press lauded the raid as another precision effort. 'Knocking the Hun for six!" one headline had read. Carter read the article, it was the same old fluff, upbeat and heroic; it turned his stomach.

The Lady ran sweet as a nut and took them there and back without any fuss. All but two aircraft reported bombing the city and losses were light. One gunner was killed and one aircraft was missing. Two others had bailed out of B-Bravo during an attack by a nightfighter. Carter heard the story during interrogation. With one engine on fire, the Lancaster had dived over six thousand feet almost straight down before shaking off the pursuit. Under those circumstances, Carter wasn't surprised they'd bailed out. He would have done the same.

Etheridge gathered the station staff for a meeting after lunch. Something big was brewing because Group had passed the word that 363 needed to make sure they could provide every available aircraft when required at some unconfirmed future date. If it had wings, an engine and could carry bombs, it was to be made operational. Pullen had scowled when Etheridge announced the requirement. His workload had just increased exponentially with no set end date in sight.

Regarding personnel, a glance at the squadron roster showed that they had enough spare odds and sods and people recovering to make up another three crews. That was the easy part, but they still needed aircraft for them to fly. They were stuck with what to do about that until Carter remembered they still had the four Manchester's they'd been using for training. Two were down for maintenance but it wouldn't take much to get them on the line. Church reluctantly agreed that they could be made ready to make up the numbers.

Carter had no idea what it was about, just that it would be soon. He had visions of going after the *Tirpitz* again and shuddered at the thought of fumbling around Norway trying to find the right fjord she was berthed in.

As was usual, nothing stayed secret for long and the squadron was soon buzzing that something was going on. In the Mess, Woods and Vos collared Carter when he put in an appearance.

"What's it all about, skipper?" asked the Canadian. Carter looked at them over the top of his pint and shrugged.

"Beats me," he replied. "I've told you lot before not to listen to idle gossip. It beats me how these rumours get started in the first place."

Busy men would have less time to gossip, so in the afternoon, Church had the squadron assemble for parade in PT gear. During the football games on the Sunday, he felt the men had been a bit flabby. He told them they lacked some zip and needed perking up a bit. He had them run round the perimeter track twice.

The next day, he had them paraded after breakfast to do it again. Nine of the men decided to chance their hand and stay in bed. Once everyone else had done their run, Church had the offenders turfed out of their pits. Stood to attention in their vests and underwear, Church tore them off a strip for being slackers and then had them do the run in full flying kitn. To his dismay, he had Carter follow them to make sure they went all the way round. Carter borrowed a bicycle as there was no way he was going to do that run twice.

Carter was stiff as a board the following morning. The backs of his legs were tight and he groaned when he sat up in bed. It was murder just to lift his legs and get his socks on. Woods felt no better. He'd not ached like this since basic training.

This time, there was no run but they had tug of war, short sprints and an hour of calisthenics, bouncing up and down on the grass doing star jumps, squat thrusts, sit ups and press ups. Church finished them off with another game of football. That seemed to satisfy him and the men were allowed to slink off and die for the afternoon.

On the Saturday morning, Carter went to the station church. The chapel at Amber Hill was nothing special; it was just another Nissen hut. Inside, it could have doubled up as the briefing room on a smaller scale. There was a central aisle with rows of chairs either side of it. Instead of propaganda posters on the wall there were quotes from scripture, painted in a flowing script. The altar at the end was on a raised dais with the cross standing on top of a snowy white cloth draped over it.

Carter went halfway down the aisle and stopped. He eyed the altar, started to genuflect and then stopped himself, feeling a bit of a hypocrite. He slid onto a chair to his left. The silence hung heavy and Carter wondered why he had bothered coming in. He was about to leave when a voice stopped him.

"Hullo, a visitor."

It was the Padre. A short man, he wore a normal RAF blue

uniform and had eschewed wearing the black bib and white dog collar. In his early forties, he had VR flashes on his lapels. The three medal ribbons of Pip, Squeak and Wilfred from the Great War were on his chest.

Carter sank back onto his chair. The Padre came over in a measured tread and took the chair next to him. He pulled his trousers up slightly as he did so to stop his legs getting knees in the fabric.

"I've not seen you in here before," he said softly. He regarded Carter carefully with a measured stare.

"No. I'm afraid I've not really thought it worthwhile, Padre."

The priest grunted. It was not the first time he'd heard that or something similar. It had been like that in the first war as well. He'd lost count of how many young men who had believed themselves beyond gods reach, only to come seeking advice, or solace, or absolution when the moment of crisis presented itself.

He took a very long view when it came to faith. Each man was on a journey and some just made it to the end before some of the others. In the last show he had lived alongside the men at the front, shivering in the mud and sharing shelter with rats and other vermin. In the winter, he had stood around a brazier, reading from the bible to lads from the slums who could barely write their own names.

He had often asked himself how a loving God could let such carnage happen but, in the end, he decided it was too big a question. His role was to guide his flock and give them sustenance in the face of difficulty. The worst of it had been at the Somme, seeing them cut to pieces in that slow walk across No Mans Land. He had crawled across the mud, giving final absolution to boys who lay in the slime, eyes wide as they stared at the sky taking their last breath.

"The Lord is patient," he told Carter. "You need to open yourself to His calm and in time, your role will be revealed to you."

Carter stifled a snort. He knew his role; it was dropping tons of high explosive and to keep on doing it until he was told to stop. He made to move when the Padre placed a hand on his wrist.

"It's not too late to unburden yourself, my son. God is patient."

"I-," Carter's mouth had gone dry. The Padre's eyes seemed to pierce him and he found his cynical reserve crumbling. "I'll think about it," he managed. He paused at the door and looked back, seeing the Padre looking at him with such incredible calm.

In the early afternoon, Wilkinson, Vos, Woods and Carter and their respective halves met at *The Madison*. Wilkinson had borrowed a Humber and picked up Vos, Denise and Helen. Carter had brought the others, squeezed into his car.

As it was a nice day, the doors in the dining room had been opened and fresh air blew in from the grounds. They had a light lunch and afterwards, they went down to the lake.

Carter carried a wicker basket with some bottles of beer and some apples. Wilkinson carried a few blankets provided by the hotel. On the way there, they walked past the summer house. Carter and Georgette shared a look and laughed, remembering their winter fumblings.

The lake was a good size with a small island in the middle covered in thick shrubs and trees. A big weeping willow was on one side of the island, hanging over the water. A row of Birch trees created a shaded area on one side of the lake. Old trees, they were about fifty feet high with a light canopy and drooping branches. At the edge of the lake was a punt and he could see a small jetty on the island. Off to the right on the other side of the lake was a wooden hut built on the waters edge and he could just make out the bow of some sort of boat sticking out from it.

Wilkinson spread out the blankets by the trees and kneeled down, looking around. The lake was hidden from the big house and it was a nice secluded spot. They relaxed for a while, letting their lunch settle. Carter found it hard to relax. Ever since that order had come from Group about being at maximum readiness, it felt like there was something big looming on the horizon. He tried to prise some information out of Wilkinson but his friend remained tight lipped.

Wilkinson asked Carter about the Lancaster. Apart from sitting in one in a hangar, he'd not had a chance to go up in one yet. Helen's ears twitched at that. She knew he was desperate to fly a Lancaster and if he managed that, he was one step closer to going back on ops. She was happy where he was at the moment and wanted it to stay that way. Yvonne and Georgette talked about their respective jobs, two halves of the same coin almost.

Helen sat down next to Denise and the two of them talked quietly about what was to come. She answered the girl's questions as honestly as she could. It was obvious to see Denise was scared and she took her under her wing, extending an open invitation for her to visit whenever she wanted.

Denise brightened appreciably after that. As much as there were other women in her office at work, she had little in common with them. Georgette had been nice to her, but Helen was the first person she could really talk to about the situation she found herself in.

Afterwards, she moved with Vos under one of the trees. He propped himself up against the trunk and Denise snuggled up to him, one of the blankets draped around them while he read her selections of poetry.

Helen looked over her shoulder to make sure they were far enough away before saying anything.

"That poor girl," she said. "All on her own. Her Doctor's told her next to nothing."

"I'm glad you were able to help, old girl," said Carter.

"Don't you, old girl me, Alex Carter," she told him. "You're older than me."

"My dear, Helen, do forgive me."

"I'll think about it," she said, giggling with an impish smile on her face.

They talked about the previous summer for a while, comparing this year with the last. A whole year had gone by but so much had happened in that time.

"You know, I can't believe this place hasn't been requisitioned," Carter said suddenly.

"It still might," Wilkinson responded. He popped the top off one of the beer bottles and handed it to Carter. "The Yanks are coming. Did you know there's been a few of them floating around Group the last few weeks having a look at how we do things." Carters eyebrows went up in interest at that little titbit of gossip.

"Gosh, Americans," commented Yvonne with some enthusiasm. "Could you get us some nylons do you think?" she asked archly, batting her eyelids. Wilkinson laughed.

"I might be able to manage some chocolate bars, will that do?"

Yvonne wrinkled her nose.

"Got some of those already," she pouted.

"They're going to need a lot of airfields and buildings for their infrastructure once they come over in force with their heavies," Wilkinson continued. *The Madison* would be ideal as a headquarters he thought. It had plenty of space and was close enough to 5 Group HQ at Saint Vincents Hall to ensure good cooperation.

"Are they any good?" Carter asked. He'd seen propaganda film about Liberators in Coastal Command but knew little about American aircraft beyond that.

"I've seen one," said Wilkinson. "We went down to Farnborough to look them over. Flying Fortresses, they call them. Bristling with guns but they've got a tiny bomb bay."

On first impressions, Wilkinson had thought the B17's were an impressive bit of kit. The blended wing and rounded fuselage made them an attractive aircraft. What concerned him was their cocksure confidence that they'd be able to fight their way through to a target in broad daylight without any escorting fighters.

"The Yanks I spoke to said they could lob a bomb into a pickle barrel, whatever that is, from twenty thousand feet in good conditions. They're very keen to try their hand at daylight bombing."

Woods and Carter snorted in derision.

"Huh, good luck," said Carter. Wilkinson agreed with them.

"I'm sorry to be a bore, darling, but I think we might have to push off," Helen interjected. She had seen the time and as much as she'd liked getting out for a while, she was beginning to fret about being away from Martha for so long. She got her things together and slipped her shoes back on. Carter called over to Vos and Denise and they stirred themselves. Wilkinson helped his wife up and they said their goodbyes. Helen hugged Carter close.

"Take care of yourself, Alex. It's not long to go now."

"I will."

They walked back up the slope towards the house. Woods watched them go and then crooked his arm for Yvonne.

"Shall we take a turn around the lake? I'd like to explore before we go."

They headed off, leaving Carter and Georgette on their own. Carter finished his beer and stowed the empty bottle back into the basket.

He stretched out on the blanket and Georgette leaned next to him. They watched the Canadian and his girl walk into the distance around the lake. Soon they disappeared into the wood on the far side.

"Yvonne's nice," Georgette said.

"She is," Carter agreed. "I thought he was never going to ask her out."

"I think it's sweet." They listened to the normal sounds for a few minutes. A bee buzzed nearby, prowling for some flowers. Faintly, she could hear an aero engine in the distance and she frowned. She wondered if there would ever be a day when such things were no longer heard as ever present background noise. Curious, she walked down to the edge of the lake. Carter watched her as she went over to the punt and looked it over.

"Come on," she told him. "I want to go for a ride."

He levered himself up, drowsy from the sun and beer. He shook his head and joined her by the water. She got into the punt, and settled herself on the bench seat in bow. Carter dug his heels in and pushed the punt out into the water, jumping on board at the last second. He picked up the pole and shoved it into the mud, having to pull hard to get it back before he fell in.

She leaned back seductively on the seat and looked up at him through hooded eyes and smiled. She liked the bulge of his arms in his shirt as he moved the pole around. He moved it with practised ease, having mucked about with punts when he had been at university.

"I could get used to this," she laughed, almost purring.

She braced herself on one elbow and looked over her shoulder. She waved her free hand towards the island.

"Thattaway my good man."

"All I ask is a tall ship-" he whispered.

"- and a star to steer by." She finished for him, remembering

New Years in the middle of nowhere stood next to a broken car.

A few more shoves got them to the island and the bow of the punt nudged the bank. Carter went to the bow to grasp the jetty. There was a bit of rope and he used it to stop the punt from drifting away and stranding them there. Georgette went ashore and he followed her.

The island was a kidney shaped spit of land, about sixty yards long, covered in trees and wild undergrowth. The big Willow tree was at the other end. A rough path led from the jetty to the summit. Here there was a natural break among the trees to provide a small cleared area, no more than five or six yards long and a few yards wide, sheltered on all sides.

Georgette lay down on the grass and stretched. Carter took off his jacket and rolled it into a bit of a pillow, joining her. In the shade of the trees and bushes it was quite peaceful here, their own private island.

She turned onto her side and propped her head up with her left hand as she looked down at him. He had his eyes closed and appeared quite peaceful. He tilted his head towards her and she could feel his breath on her arm.

"When do you get your next leave?" she asked him.

"When I finish my tour" he told her, his voice drowsy. "Well, when I get to thirty anyway," he corrected, almost as an afterthought. That throwaway remark caught her attention. Second tours were supposed to be no more than thirty ops, even she knew that.

"That sounds ominous," she said, failing to keep an edge of concern out of her voice. "You are finishing your tour, aren't you?"

Carter opened one eye, suddenly aware how that had sounded. He looked up at her and gave her a reassuring smile.

"Four to go. Then who knows."

"What does that mean," she asked, more alarmed now.

"The Group Captain said he might have a job for me," he said carefully, remembering how his own heart had hammered when Etheridge had first asked him if he wanted to do another job. His mind had reeled at the thought of extending his tour or being detailed for some kind of special mission.

"Not ops," she said, her stomach clenching into knots. "You've done your share."

"No, not ops," he said, his voice soothing. He stroked her left arm, seeing the goosepimples on her skin as she shivered to his touch. "More squadrons are getting Lanc's. They're thinking of forming a Heavy Conversion Unit to get the chaps on the squadrons flying quickly. They want a few experienced hands to show people the ropes. He muttered about a promotion if I'm good enough at it."

Georgette's mood changed immediately.

"But darling, that's wonderful," she almost cooed in relief. "You'll still be in 5 Group so we can still see each other."

She had been waiting in hope for his tour to be over but dreading that he'd be posted back to Scotland or some other faraway place. This was an entirely different prospect.

"Four to go," he repeated, "then we'll see what happens. I love you."

She leaned in to kiss him, her hand resting on his jaw, fingers running down his neck to his shoulder. She hooked her right leg over him and he responded by pulling her over so she shifted, straddling him.

"I love you too," she said against his mouth, her eyes clamped shut. "Alex, make love to me."

"Wha-here? Now?"

She laughed.

"Don't you want to?" she asked. She sat up, her weight on his hips. She started unbuttoning his shirt, sliding her hands under the material.

"Yes, but-" he was suddenly shy.

"Alex Carter, I do believe you're blushing." She put her index finger against her lips. "Kiss," she told him.

"Someone might see."

She made an exaggerated show of looking around them while at the same time grinding her pelvis against him. He groaned. She undid the buttons on her blouse and pulled it off her shoulders.

"We're on an island," she told him. "Come on, stop stalling. I *have* done this before. I don't need protecting, I *was* married you know," she chided.

"Goodgie."

She kissed him while her hands went lower, undoing the belt on his trousers and tugging the zip down. That did it and he yielded to her demands and his own. He hitched his pants down and she guided him in.

"Just…oh!"

She held herself very still as he moved slowly up and down in small measured movements. She shivered and collapsed onto him, her breasts pressed against his chest, her breath warm on his neck.

He spiralled down the rabbit hole. For every thrust, she responded. Her tongue darted into his mouth, running around his teeth. Her lips were slick against his. Her perfume overwhelmed him; her hair tickled his neck.

The pace of their movements increased. He drove into her more frantically and she ground down to meet him with equal measure. She fixed him with her eyes, staring into his soul. He kissed her, welding himself to her as she went over the edge and he went with her. She clamped down on him and held him there as he shuddered, the stars exploding behind his eyes and his blood roaring in his ears. He floated after that, clinging to her like a rock in the ocean. She nestled in his arms, her hands tracing the line of scars on his rib cage, going from one to the next, up and down.

Finally, they gathered themselves together, putting themselves to rights. Georgette pinned her hair back and reapplied her lipstick. She smiled to herself, basking in his adoring gaze.

Right at this moment he was at peace. All his fears were distant mirages, things to worry about another day as they flickered at the edges of his world. This was a day to think about himself, his hearts desire and what he wanted. He took her hand in his and kissed the knuckles before turning it over and kissing her palm.

"Goodgie?"

"Mmmm?"

"Will you marry me?"

That surprised her.

"Darling! You don't have to propose just because we've done it."

"True. We have done it before," he demurred. He kissed her hand again and then stroked the back of it with his thumb. "I'm serious. When my tours up, let's get married."

She looked at him, barely blinking, her face frozen. For a moment, Carter thought he had ruined everything. Then her eyes softened, those little crinkles at the corners he loved so much, that broad smile he had showered with kisses.

"All right," she said finally. "I do." She put her left hand flat against his chest. She could feel his heart hammering. "I hope you realise I'm going to hold you to this. I love you."

He kissed her.

"I love you too."

58 - The Politics Of War

Planning for the raid continued in meticulous detail. Photographs of the target had to be assembled. Maps needed to be updated with the latest intelligence information regarding the locations of flak batteries, barrage balloons and searchlights. Calculations would be made to optimise the fuel and bomb loads. 2 Group were requested to lay on intruders to go for the enemy airfields and provide cover for the bombers on the way out and coming back. On the 23rd May, Operation Order 147 was sent to the Groups. The primary target was specified as Hamburg with Cologne as the alternate if the conditions were not favourable.

Two days later, the Admiralty upset the apple cart. Harris was in his office when Saundby broke the news that the Admiralty had ordered Coastal Command to withdraw its cooperation. That left them two hundred fifty aircraft short, a quarter of the total force. Harris turned slitted eyes on his subordinate and exploded.

"But they're ours," he said, his anger building. "They were ours before they were ever theirs. It's not like we're asking to keep the bloody things, only borrow them. They are aware I want to bomb Hamburg; where they make U-boats and other things that are sinking their little ships?"

"I did explain that, sir," Saundby said, keeping his voice neutral. Harris clenched his hands in his lap, his knuckles going white.

He knew what this was; dirty politics, plain and simple. Beyond spite, there was no reason why they should have changed their minds at this late hour, especially after they had been two faced enough to assure the Prime Minister of cooperating. Harris knew he could force their hand by going to the Prime Minister but the Navy had timed it well. Sorting this mess out would take time and it was time he didn't have. He knew he would win the argument in the end, but once their hand had been turned, the Navy would say there was insufficient time to get ready and Harris would miss his chance for this moon period.

"Right. Well there's nothing we can do about it now. I'm not going begging to the fish heads and I'm not running to Portal or the PM telling tales in school."

As soon as he was informed of this development, Saundby had gathered the latest availability figures which the Groups were reporting daily. Despite the assurances given, Saundby was an old campaigner. He had seen the RAF struggle on throughout the twenties and the service infighting that had denied them needed aircraft and resources. He had anticipated this possibility and you didn't climb the ranks without knowing a few ways the system could be made to work in your favour.

He knew that most squadrons had one or two aircraft available as ready spares. When aircraft were unserviceable, they could be called upon to fill in the gap or make up for losses on operations. Surreptitiously he had ordered all of the squadrons to indent the supply chain to provide two new spare aircraft from the factories and air parks. That would give them nearly one hundred more aircraft right off the bat. Crews to man them could be made up from spares every station had lying around and there were always some screened crews who'd just completed their tours who could be pressed into doing one more trip.

In the three days since the requirement had gone out, Saundby had the Groups reporting daily availability figures. In that time, the squadrons had already made nearly fifty extra aircraft available and there would be more to come.

Even with this contribution, Harris knew they were still short and without outside help, there was only really one other option left but it carried an enormous risk with it. They would have to send raw crews that were just beginning their training to make up the remaining numbers.

In the past, they had always sent trainee crews on nickeling jobs and minelaying. It was seen as a good way to give them a bit of experience and seasoning. It also freed up the main force for operations, but these were normally crews close to the end of their training. It was a big difference asking raw trainees to go on a raid.

If things went badly wrong, it could cripple the training system, perhaps catastrophically. Churchill had told him at Chequers that he was willing to lose up to one hundred aircraft or more. Harris wasn't, but he was also realistic enough to admit that it *could* happen.

"Get me the AOC's of 91 and 92 Group and the head of Training Command. If I'm going to be, Oliver Twist, the least I can do is make the call personally to explain the situation."

Training Command promised to supply forty nine extra aircraft. They were clapped out Hampden's and Whitley's, but every aircraft counted. By scraping the barrel and including every training and conversion flight, 91 and 92 Group could raise another eighty or so. Even three Wellington's 109 squadron had sent to 26 Signals Group were borrowed back to make up the number. When the final tally was made, Harris had his magic number.

The following day, a revised Operational Order went out to the

Groups, bringing the planned date forward by twenty four hours. With the weather being so unsettled over the last few days, Harris wanted to give himself some more flexibility as the operation depended on a clear moonlit night.

Security was paramount. If the Germans caught one whiff that a load of additional aircraft were being used for operations it could be a disaster. As a result, on the 27th May, when the aircraft from 91 and 92 Group and Training Command deployed to forward airfields it was done under the guise of a training exercise called Operation Banquet. Banquet was a response to a German invasion on the south coast where all available bombers would be deployed to counter it.

Eight Hampdens from 91 Group flew in to Amber Hill. Pullen had the erks check them out and found some of them lacked items of equipment they would need. Stores were pillaged and the groundcrew slaved to prepare the aircraft.

Confined to camp, everyone was encouraged to enter into the spirit of things and prepare as if an invasion was imminent. Taking that sentiment to heart, some of the crews wanted to draw sidearms from the armoury and take potshots at bottles on the range. Appalled at the prospect of aircrew filling themselves with holes, Church said no. When someone noticed the OTU aircraft were loaded with incendiaries, even the dimmest bulbs in the box knew something special was going on.

Berths were found for the newcomers and the Mess was cramped that evening as the new men speculated how long they would be there. Some of the veterans delighted in telling lurid tales of operations in front of the greenhorns to provoke a reaction.

Of course, after going to all the trouble to get things ready, they had to wait on the weather to oblige them. With such a large raid, the conditions would play a critical part in the operations success. Harris knew that the weather over central Europe was always questionable. He could hope for good weather on perhaps one day in three. Now, when he needed it the most, it seemed like the gods were conspiring against him.

A persistent front of heavy cloud moved in, covering Hamburg and the surrounding countryside. There was no point going, only to drop blind because they couldn't see the target. Hamburg was the preferred choice. Like Lübeck and Rostock, Hamburg was on the coast making it an easy navigation problem. The alternate target was Cologne. Well within Gee range, Cologne had been attacked before with mixed results. A large raid could be the knockout blow to make the difference.

Harris became increasingly agitated as the days went by. He had ordered there be no operations the day before the big raid so that his crews could be fresh and rested but by the 29th, the situation had still not improved. He became very conscious that the Germans might suspect something was up if there were no operations at all during a clear moon period.

Reluctantly, with the weather clear over the Channel and France, he sent a modest force after the Gnome et Rhone aircraft factory on the outskirts of Paris. Other spoiling attacks were sent to Dieppe and Cherbourg and there was the usual gardening around the Frisian Islands and the Baltic to grab the Germans attention.

Finally, things came to a head. Portal had been asking for progress and Harris knew he couldn't keep the aircraft in reserve for much longer. Everything came down to that day's weather. At morning prayers, the forecast for northwest Germany was far from ideal. Thundery cloud was hovering over north west Germany but the prediction was that it would clear southwards during the night. This was far from ideal but it was the most promising forecast of the last few days.

The Meteorologist, Magnus Spence, blinked while he waited for Harris' response. Morning Prayers was always a brisk affair. Harris would breeze into the room and sit down at a natty little chair that looked like it had come from a servant's room. Smoking heavily, he would ask sharp questions concerning casualties, aircraft availability and the results of the previous nights operations. The staff were always prepared and had the answers to hand. The light relief usually came at the end, when Harris jousted with Spence, challenging his predictions and pushing the Met man as far as he would go.

Today, the boss had listened to a summary of the raids on France with his usual attention to detail but everyone was aware of the elephant in the room. Harris fished in his pocket and produced a carton of American Lucky Strike cigarettes. He tapped the pack with his thumb and extracted one. He lit it and jammed it into a short cigarette holder. He studied a map of Europe on the desk in front of him. All eyes were on him as he ruminated in silence. He traced a finger over the map, resting it on Germany. It moved down and pressed hard on Cologne.

"Cologne," he said, "tonight."

Like that, ops were on.

59 - Trout

The orders went out to the Groups and from there on to the squadrons. At Amber Hill the aircraft were air tested and by the early afternoon, every member of aircrew on the station was called to briefing. The stage was full when they took their seats. Church went first and grabbed their attention from the get go.

"Since the Germans started this war, they've bombed Rotterdam, Warsaw, Coventry. They blitzed London and a whole host of other places. Herman Goering once made a speech. He said this in 1939, I'll read it to you." He pulled a piece of paper from his pocket. He looked at it although he knew the words by heart. "No enemy bomber can reach the Ruhr. If one reaches the Ruhr, my name is not, Goering, you may call me, Meyer." A throaty chuckle rippled around the room. "I'm not the kind of person to let an opportunity pass us by. Tonight, is the night Bomber Command delivers a knockout blow to the Nazi war machine," he said, his voice full of vim. He was positively crackling with energy. "Tonight, is history in the making. We are going to be part of the largest airborne raid ever mounted."

"Every single aircraft Bomber Command has is going. It's a maximum effort in the true meaning of the word. Over one thousand aircraft are going to burn the black heart out of Cologne and deliver the biggest blow to German morale since the war began."

That rocked the room into a hushed silence. The number was mesmerising. One thousand bombers.

"The entire force will go over the city in ninety minutes." That caused a further sensation and Church did his best to play down the risks. "I am assured that the chances of collision are very low, perhaps only two aircraft" he said, which brought a laugh. The room erupted when some wag at the back asked, "which two?"

The briefing room buzzed with excitement, something Carter had not seen since the early days of his first tour. Each specialist took their place on the stage. The gunnery officer warned them against shooting each other down.

Church waited a moment for them to settle down. He told them the route they would be going in. There would be no wandering back and forth over the target like the old days. Any idiot doing that tonight would blunder into someone else and make a very bright flash in the sky. 1 and 3 Group would go in first, using Gee to locate the target and mark with flares. Everyone else would follow them in.

"There skies are going to be crowded tonight, so watch it you gunners. Only shoot if you're sure of your target." Murphy and Todd shared a look. They knew where he could stick that.

Kent went into detail of the nightfighters based near Cologne and the defences. The rumour was over four hundred guns ringed the city but Kent assured them that tonight, the flak gunners would be overwhelmed by the numbers of aircraft.

The weather forecast was mixed. The Navigator's paid particular attention when emergency fields were mentioned. If the weather changed, the skies were going to get awfully crowded when they got back with everyone hunting for somewhere to land.

Etheridge took the stage at the end to round things up. He looked across the crowded room and cleared his throat. The noise echoed in the hush.

"I have here, a signal from the CinC, which I'm going to read to you."

He smoothed out the piece of paper in front of him and began reading.

"The force of which you are about to take part tonight is at least twice the size and more than four times the carrying capacity of the largest Air Force ever before concentrated on one objective. You have the opportunity therefore to strike a blow at the enemy which will resound, not only throughout Germany, but throughout the world. In your hands be the means of destroying a major part of he resources by which the enemy's war effort is maintained. It depends, however, upon each individual crew whether full concentration is achieved."

"Press home your attack to your precise objectives with the utmost determination and resolution in the full knowledge that, if you individually succeed, the most shattering and devastating blow will have been delivered against the very vitals of the enemy. Let him have it, right on the chin."

He looked up, every eye was fixed on him, the atmosphere electric.

"Good luck gentlemen."

The chairs scraped back, everyone stood and Etheridge walked from the briefing room.

Each man got ready in their own way. Woods took Merlin for a walk, throwing a ball and watching the Labrador streak after it. Todd had a snooze before dinner, he wanted to be properly rested before getting into that cold turret. Byron wrote a letter and left it on his bed, a strong sense of foreboding hanging over him.

Carters response was a little more measured. He thought about having four more to go, the prospect of getting off ops. He knew he was chasing the odds now and was on borrowed time. The closer the end got, the more nervous he became. He had more to lose now. He thought about Georgette and for a moment, he was back at the lake with her under the afternoon sun, remembering that perfect moment of holding her in his arms.

At nine he went to get changed. Sitting on the bench seat in the equipment room he pulled on his flying boots. He glanced up and caught Todd looking at him. He nodded slightly and the Australian gave him a lopsided smile in return. He remembered that Todd had already finished his tour. He could be sitting this one out, but here he was, going again, like it was a walk in the park.

On the way out to the kite, Carter steeled himself for the raid ahead. The lads talked quietly amongst themselves, conscious they were part of something really big. They went through the start up routine with practised ease. The tanks, pumps and brakes were checked. Byron edged the throttles forward and set the radiator and supercharger controls. Carter and Byron went back and forth, their voices a constant like a metronome.

"Ready to go, skipper."

Carter slid back the cockpit window and gave a thumbs up.

"Contact! Starboard inner!" he called. He flicked the cover off the starter button and jammed it down hard. A big flash of flame belched from the engine exhaust stacks. It caught straight away with a throaty roar. *The Lady* thrummed with the power of the Merlin engine.

Within five minutes, all four engines were running. Carter disengaged the booster coil and waved from the window. He watched the battery cart get pulled away and he waited until Latimer reappeared and waved back to tell him it was clear.

The engines idled as they warmed up. Byron watched the oil and coolant temps like a hawk. They checked the superchargers and the prop controls, ears tuned listening for the slightest deviation from the norm. Tonight, was not the night to have a problem. Byron eased the throttles forward to the stops while Carter checked boost and revs.

The starboard outer showed a slight drop on the magneto test but it was within normal limits. He told Byron to make a note of it. They were ready. He checked his watch. He nodded to Byron and the engineer slipped out of sight. He resumed his position a few minutes later.

"Hatches secure, boss. Okay to taxi."

Carter leaned out of the cockpit window and banged his bunched fists together. Latimer nodded and gestured to some erks. They dashed underneath the big wings and tugged and pulled on the big wooden chocks. Latimer held two hands in the air once they had been pulled away.

Carter released the brakes and Byron edged the throttles for the two inner engines forward. The Lancaster started to move, wobbling on her undercarriage. At the end of the peri track, two aircraft were ahead of them and Carter slowed down, not wanting to stand idle and have the engines overheat. The Lancaster went, then the Hampden and then it was their turn. Byron gunned the starboard throttles and Carter kicked the rudder to swing the nose round. He dabbed the brakes to stop the swing and then released it, letting the Lancaster roll slowly foward until they were lined up on the runway.

He double checked the trim controls, giving it a bit of nose down. He dropped the flaps fifteen degrees and rattled through the checklist for the prop controls, the fuel tank selection and superchargers. Pulling the brakes on, he checked the crew. Everyone was ready.

"Here we go," he said on the R/T. He eased the throttles forward. As he felt the Lancaster lean against the brakes, he released them and she started rolling. The airspeed picked up quickly. The tail lifted and Carter kept her there, balanced on the main wheels as they rolled along the runway. Byron took over the throttles and called out the increasing speed.

"Seventy five, eighty." He pushed the throttles the rest of the way, hard up against the gate.

"Ninety, ninety five."

Carter kept the nose down. Flame stabbed from the exhausts as the Merlins screamed at full power.

"One oh five. One ten."

Carter moved the yoke ever so slightly and the Lancaster flew. Byron put the throttles through the gate and the Lancaster surged forward. Carter kept the nose level, letting the speed build up for a few more seconds before climbing away. The undercarriage came up and there was a slight bump as they locked into their nacelles.

Woods noted their take off time in his log. 2359 hours. It was a forty minute run to the coast. They steered one four five to dog leg around the wash and crossed on track between Southwold and Orfordness in Norfolk. As England slid into the darkness behind them, Carter laid down the law.

"Forget all that shit, Ackroyd said in briefing," he told Todd and Murphy. "If you see something, you shoot. Anyone who hesitates gets killed."

"Don't worry, boss," replied Todd. "We already decided to do that. I haven't come this far to get my arse shot off."

Carter had to smile.

"I'm glad to hear it. All right, let's focus from now on. Test your guns once we clear the coast."

A few minutes later, Flynn traversed the nose turret left and right and fired the guns. Carter felt more vibrations as Todd and

Murphy loosed off some rounds from their turrets in the rear.

Not long after that they encountered dense banks of cloud that went up to eight and nine thousand feet. They climbed hard to keep clear of that. With so many aircraft in the air tonight, there was no way Carter was groping his way through thick clouds.

On such a clear night, with white clouds below, Carter could see a lot of aircraft around them. To starboard were a few Hampdens. A number of Lancasters were ahead both above and below. Ridiculous as it sounded, Carter felt a little hemmed in and he asked Todd to shout out if anyone was behind them. The Australian craned his neck, looking everywhere to make sure there were no hidden surprises.

It was a short hop across the Channel and they passed over the Haringvliet, south of Rotterdam a little north of track. From here, it was a straight run to Cologne. The cloud started to thin out, revealing the land below.

At fifteen thousand feet, the air was crystal clear. Carter sucked down on the oxygen and he grimaced at the rubbery taste he was getting in his mouth. He mimed drinking from a cup to Byron and the Flight Engineer nodded. He poured a cup of tea from the flask in his bag and handed it to Carter. His pilot nodded his thanks and sipped slowly. He swilled it around his mouth, letting the heat penetrate, washing his tongue.

He did an R/T check to make sure everyone was still awake. They responded quickly.

"Check your hoses," he warned. "Run your hand up and down the hose to make sure there's no buildup in ice crystals."

Apart from the occasional call from Todd or Murphy as a bomber strayed near them, it was quiet in the Lanc as everyone focused on their tasks. Flynn called out a sighting as they passed Eindhoven and Woods updated his chart. They were still a little north of track and he gave Carter a correction.

As intended, the German nightfighter defences were overwhelmed. Only twenty five fighters were sent up to meet the intruding force. Many waited on the ground for scramble orders that never came.

The bombers didn't get away entirely scot free. They passed a few burning pyres on the ground along their route, testament to the lethality of the enemies defences when they caught the unwary.

The starboard outer started running rough. Power was down and Byron thought about the mag drop they'd had before take off. He tried juggling the throttles, trying to find a setting the engine was comfortable with. The fuselage vibrated as the power continued to surge and then fall back.

They could see the glow from all the fires over fifty miles away. Carter called Woods and Vos up to the cockpit to take a look. The

Belgian looked on with cruel pleasure. Maybe with a few more raids like this the war would end.

"My god," said Woods. He'd not seen anything like this before. The sky was dotted by little pricks of light as flak detonated above the city. One glimpse was enough for him and he went back to his station.

Flynn left the front turret and got ready in the nose. He settled himself on the padding and checked his selector switches. He'd heard the story about one bomb aimer who had come back to Amber Hill with a full load because he forgot to set his bomb selector switches properly. When he'd pressed the release, nothing had actually fallen out of the aircraft. Flynn wasn't going to make that mistake.

A few minutes later, the starboard outer went into its death throes. The oil temperatures shot up and it was clearly on borrowed time.

"Sorry, skipper, we're going to have to shut it down."

"Okay. Pilot to crew, we're going to feather the starboard outer. Nothing to worry about," he told them, keeping his voice businesslike. They cut the fuel, closed the throttle and feathered the engine. The needle blade propellers rotated into the airflow and stopped spinning.

"Feathered!" Byron announced. Carter edged the remaining throttles forward slightly to compensate for the dead engine and fed in some trim to keep the nose straight.

On the final run in to the city there was very little cloud. The forecast that the cloud would disperse south had been bang on and they had an unobstructed view of the destruction below them. Coming in from the north west; their cockpit was bathed in orange light from the hundreds of fires all over the place.

Outside the city the Germans had lit a number of dummy fires trying to draw the main force off. It was a common tactic and on one of their normal raids, it might have worked. Tonight, the raid was just too big, everyone ignored them and went straight in.

On the ground, it seemed like the raid went on and on, with no respite, no let up to give them a chance to organise. The air raid sirens wailed, their strident dirge the cry of a wounded animal, writhing in pain.

Cookies rained down, the blast of the big bombs blowing off the roofs of buildings. The incendiaries burned the contents. Whole rows of streets were put to the torch and there was little the firemen could do. Well trained from previous raids, they knew that this would go on for hours, but they always managed to get to the fires and put them out before they could take hold. This time, the fires were everywhere.

As each successive wave crossed over the city, bombs rained down in different districts. The first wave had bombed the centre of Cologne to get things started. The aiming point for the second wave was one mile north, the third, one mile to the south. Roads were blocked by rubble. Gas mains fractured and added to the conflagrations.

"Bomb doors open!" said Flynn. This was terrific. There was none of the usual haze or cloud to make things difficult. He didn't bother setting for wind tonight. It was a big city and there were plenty of things to hit.

Ahead of them, a Lancaster staggered right, blown bodily sideways by a flak burst. A bright yellow streak trailed back on the port side, then it lurched as the wing folded and it went straight down. Two white bundles fell away from it and then it was out of sight.

Carter gripped the yoke hard, his jaw grinding. *The Lady* bounced on a pocket of hot air and he wrestled to keep her level. He looked around, slightly confused. Every briefing and report said Cologne was crawling with over four hundred flak guns. Searchlights weaved left and right but there was little flak. For a moment, he wondered if they had run out of ammunition.

The response to that thought was a burst of flak off to port, a few hundred yards away. Carter checked his altimeter. They were at thirteen thousand feet, well above the range of all the light flak. He eased back on the yoke slightly and took it up another five hundred feet.

"Keep an eye out for fighters," he warned. "They could be hunting over the city."

"Roger, skipper."

Todd span his turret left and right, scanning the sky. In the mid upper, Murphy did slow circles, flinching when some shrapnel pinged off his turret. There was a stab of blue above him and he saw a Lancaster sliding into position almost directly overhead.

"We're under another Lanc, boss."

Carter paled. The last thing they needed was copping a packet from a stray bomb crashing through the fuselage. He flat turned to the right ten degrees off track to put a bit of distance between him and the other bomber.

"Keep an eye on him," Carter ordered. "Left. Left," Flynn's voice droned. He'd spotted a long straight boulevard on the south side running roughly south east to north west. That would do perfectly. Beyond that boulevard was a big area of densely packed tenement buildings. He put the crosshairs on that. Flak exploded in front of them and the Lancaster jumped up, dropped and Flynn's stomach lurched. He clung on tightly.

"Steady. Steady. Ten seconds."

Carter found himself leaning forward in his seat. They were over the city. This was not one of those occasions where Flynn needed to be precise. Go! Go! Go!

"Five seconds." Flynn counted down and hit the release. "Bombs away!"

The cookie released; a big tumbling dustbin. Incendiaries fell around it. Flynn closed the bomb doors.

Carter turned away to the south. He let the speed build up, keeping a firm grip of the controls. As they peeled off, the cockpit lit up a bright white as a searchlight passed over them. The light dazzled him, destroying his night vision. Seeing spots, he hauled back on the yoke, translating the speed built up in the dive into a climb to try and throw off the searchlight. It stayed locked on them, like a Bulldog with its teeth wrapped around your leg.

The flak came up, a box barrage the likes of which Carter had never seen. The explosion when it came hit him like a hammer and everything went dark and there was a roaring in his ears.

60 - Crucible

Time slowed down and his brain felt like treacle. Everything around him was shaking. His hands were being shaken and the vibrations went up his arms. It was dark and Carter screamed, convinced he'd been blinded. He shouted for Byron to help him but he heard nothing. Something hit his shoulder and his head flopped about like a rag doll. He flailed his arm to get it to stop. At least he thought he did, he wasn't sure.

His vision came back in stages. It started in the centre as if he was looking down a telescope from far away. Gradually the dark receded and he became aware of Byrons face looming over him; he was fighting him for the controls. Glacially slow, Carter looked down. His left hand was on the yoke, his right was in his lap. That wasn't right.

They were diving. They were diving! Everything snapped back into focus in a rush, sharp and crystal clear. He snatched at the yoke and it flopped around. The rudder pedals were soft. They were still descending. He centred the yoke and tried again and he found if he moved it more slowly, then he got a bite.

He pulled back, gritting his teeth at the strain. The nose started to move but it was painfully slow. Carter reached down for the elevator trim wheel and turned it full. That helped, but even then, it took an age for them to level off.

The Lancaster was wallowing and Carter found he had to make frequent control inputs to keep them going. He was sweating. He had no idea what altitude they were at as the gauge had gone. There were holes in the instrument panel and there were holes in the canopy. The front windscreen panel was cracked and wind howled by his ear. Something banged behind him, he could feel it flapping around, the vibration coming up through his seat.

The tang of burnt wiring and cordite stung his nostrils and made his eyes water. He tried the R/T but heard nothing, not even a hiss in his earphones. He looked over at the Engineers station and saw Byron was pale, his face clammy, his eyes wide. Carter tapped the ear of his flying helmet and Byron understood. He came close and cupped his hands to shout in Carters ear.

"Thank god you're okay, skipper."

"Are you all right?" Byron nodded. "We took a big hit. Aft I think."

"There's a hell of a draught," Byron agreed.

"Get Vos to have a look. See if you can sort out the R/T."

Byron disappeared leaving Carter to commune with the Lanc and keep her going. Something was obviously wrong back there because he had a devil of a job keeping the wings level. Normally, he could fly almost hands off. With one engine out it needed a bit more work, but now, she was all over the shop. He had to constantly move the yoke and due to the slack, he had to anticipate things to a large degree. He would put a correction in but it would take a few seconds before anything seemed to happen in response.

He glanced down at the instruments. The panel was a mess but at least he had his artificial horizon and airspeed indicator. Some of the engine instruments were smashed but the engines themselves seemed to be okay.

Vos had been listening on his radio set when the flak caught them. One minute he was sitting at his operators' desk, the next, he was flung forward and plunged into darkness as the small light by his panel went out. There was a massive rush of air behind him as he fumbled around in the dark. He tried the switch but it didn't come back on. Either the bulb had gone or the circuit had blown.

They were diving and he froze at his desk. This was it; they were going down for the final time. Fear gripped him and he glanced up at the escape hatch. He thought about the time they had ditched in the lake, the struggle it had been to get out. He reached for his parachute pack and blanched when his hand was met with empty air. He scrabbled around on his hands and knees but couldn't locate it.

When they levelled off, he sat back down, his heart thumping in his chest and it took him some time to gather himself together. Byron appeared out of the dark and shouted in his ear. Vos cast an anxious glance down the dark pit of fuselage. Light flickered in a weird kaleidoscope back there. Byron gave him a little shove and Vos swallowed hard as he squirmed over the main spar.

A huge gale tugged at him. It looked like the left side of the fuselage was gone. There was a huge gash in the skin and he could see the stars outside. The flickers of light were flashes of flak and glimmers of searchlight shining through the gaping hole in the thin skin. The slipstream tore at the gap, scrabbling for a purchase. Bits of torn metal flapped and banged against each other.

Clinging to the right side, he fumbled his way along. He tripped over something on the floor and screamed as he fell, thinking he was going out the hole. He crawled forward on his hands and knees; his hands slick from some viscous liquid on the floor. He came to the mid upper turret and looked up. Murphy was slumped in the sling seat, his arms dangling down by his side. Vos stood up, using Murphy's legs to get his balance.

He tugged on the gunners clothing but he didn't stir at all. Turbulent air battered at Vos's face. He unhooked the safety belt and Murphy flopped into his arms. They crashed to the fuselage floor, Murphy on top of Vos, a dead weight. Vos rolled him off him to the side and kept a firm grip of his jacket, to stop him falling out. It would be along way down without a parachute.

Gingerly getting to his feet, he dragged Murphy back to the rear of the main spar and propped him up against it. He felt around his clothing but there were no obvious tears or gashes. Vos shook him by the shoulders but Murphy remained stubbornly unconscious. Cursing, Vos fumbled around for a first aid kit. It wasn't where it was supposed to be, and he was feeling around on the floor of the fuselage for it when he was kicked hard in the back.

Oberleutnant Fischer was amazed. The numbers were simply incredible. When the first reports were coming in, it had seemed like a fantasy. Ground control had reported an enormous armada that just kept on coming. Bomber after bomber had flown over Cologne and put the city to the torch.

Like many other nightfighters, he had been on the ground, engines running, waiting to be given the order to take off. The raid had been going on for over an hour before he was finally given permission to intercept them.

Engines screaming, he had climbed hard, desperate to gain height and infiltrate the enemy route home before they got away. Ground control had alerted him to the bombers going south of the city before turning northwest, back the way they had come. Circling to the south, he used the glow from the fires to silhouette the bombers below him and his radar operator directed him in.

He had already killed tonight. He had swooped on a Wellington as it turned away from the city and turned it into a funeral pyre for its crew. The wing tanks ignited and it blew up, scattering bits of itself all over Germany.

Seated behind him, his operator fiddled with his radar set. The Lichtenstein radar had a range of no more than three kilometers but tonight, there were so many aircraft in the air it was picking up targets all over the place. Three small screens glowed in the dark. One gave range, the other azimuth, the other elevation. He picked up a target a short distance away below them to port. He communed with the screens and called out directions until his pilot could visually acquire the target.

Fischer saw it. The big bomber was weaving gently left and right as it went along. He stalked them, gaining some height as he drew closer on their starboard side. He grew more confident when he saw the mid upper turret wasn't moving at all. Either their hydraulics were out or something was wrong with the gunner. Settling himself in his seat, the pilot pressed the oxygen mask to his face and flicked the safety off.

He dived towards the Lancaster, putting the reticle of his gunsight on the fat fuselage, right behind the wing. Underneath the middle turret he could see the roundel; the big circle of red, blue and white ringed in yellow. He bore in, hunched forwards, both hands gripping the stick.

The tail turret opened fire and four lines of tracer headed his way. Glowing balls whipped past his cockpit and he felt the thud as some hit the port wing. He squeezed the triggers and the nose flashed as the 20mm shells reached out. He exulted as he saw the rounds go in. The hits flashed sparks on the fuselage.

There was another jolt as the bomber scored on him again. He tightened his turn and carried on firing, raking the tail of the bomber as he broke off the attack. He climbed away, translating the speed from the dive to gain some altitude. He came around in a lazy circle and blinked, rubbing his eyes. The flashes from the guns in the nose had messed with his night vision and it would take a minute or two to get it back.

"Where is he, Becker?" he asked his operator.

Becker looked at his non functioning set. Two of his screens were dead. He told his pilot they were blind. Fischer was not happy. With no radar set, he would have to do this the old fashioned way.

He advanced the throttles and dived. He would go lower, letting the bright moonlight silhouette the bombers against the sky. Their black painted undersides would stand out perfectly. He turned right to insert himself into the bomber stream heading for home.

In the tail, with the R/T out, there was little warning Todd could give. The only thing he could do was to open fire early to prompt the boss into taking evasive action. As it was, nothing much happened. They must have been asleep up front because they just plodded along straight and level while the 110 raked the fuselage.

The first burst from the 110 took Vos in the back and tore through his stomach. He collapsed in a heap with a shocked look on his face. He had just enough time to register the pain before he died.

Todd adjusted deflection and carried on firing, giving as good as he got. The four .303's flashed as round after round spat out of the guns at the 110 as it rolled right. He traversed right and was still firing when the world came apart around him. Perspex splintered and there was a sharp pain in his arm that jerked his hand off the controls.

Up front, Carter felt the vibrations as the tail turret opened fire but there was little he could do in the way of evading action. The controls were so mushy, he thought if he tried anything drastic, they would fall out of the sky. He shoved the throttles forward to get more power. He could feel the tugs as they were hit and he did his best to stop the wing flicking over as he turned left. The rudder pedals juddered as more hits went in and then the yoke was snatched out of his hand and the nose went down.

The stricken Lancaster dropped like a pebble down a well, engines roaring. The dive steepened and Carter gingerly pulled back on the yoke, convinced it would come away in his hand like some stupid cartoon film. A solid wall of air came in from the nose and took his breathe away, a hurricane that ripped and tore at him. They continued to dive, and Carter railed against his fate. It wasn't supposed to end like this.

"Come on you, bitch!" he shouted. "Up! UPPPP!"

He closed the throttles and fed in some trim again. His teeth rattled in his head as the bomber shook and vibrated. The gale battered Carter and he shivered as he leaned over the yoke. They continued down and he shot a glance at the airspeed indicator. The gauge must have been broken because the needle showed them going over three hundred miles an hour. If they carried on diving like this, it would be even money the wings ripped off before they hit the ground.

Carter closed his eyes and prayed. He closed the throttles and then pushed the yoke forward and pulled back again, trying to coax something out of the elevators. Unbelievably, the nose began to come up, inch by miserable inch. Shuddering, vibrating fit to the bust, the Lancaster eventually bottomed out of the dive at about a thousand feet.

When they levelled off, Byron went forward to find out what was going on in the nose. He expected to see a hole in the blister and what was left of Flynn smeared all over the place. What he found instead was an empty space. There was a hole in the floor where the escape hatch had been and Flynn was nowhere to be seen. Panicked by the dive, he had clipped on his parachute and slithered out of the hatch while there was still height to do so. Byron went back to the cockpit to report.

"Flynn's gone," he told Carter.

"What do you mean he's gone?"

"Gone. Bailed out. Jumped."

"The daft bugger," said Carter through gritted teeth as he fought the controls. "You stay with me and try and sort the R/T out. Get Woods to go and find out what's going on back there."

Woods clambered over the spar shining a torch. He found Murphy and Vos slumped on the floor. It looked like a slaughterhouse.

493

One glance at Vos was enough to know there was nothing he could do for him. The Belgian lay on his side, eyes wide open, staring off into the distance, blood puddle underneath him. Woods knelt down next to him and closed his eyes.

He moved onto Murphy. Blood was splashed all over his clothes and it took a few minutes of checking before he was sure there were no holes in him. The only thing he found was a cut to his left cheek. Woods tried to find a pulse, but his hands were shaking so much, he couldn't tell if it was his or Murphy's. He was warm to the touch though, so he propped him up against the main spar.

Woods moved gingerly down the fuselage. There were a number of holes punched in the starboard side but that was nothing in comparison to the ripped open skin on the port side. When he got to the mid upper turret, he pulled himself up inside it and had a look. The guns were pointing skywards and there were gaping holes in the perspex.

He carried on, shining the torch to find his way. One of the long trays that fed the rear turret was broken and loose cartridges of ammunition rolled around, swimming in liquid from the Elsan chemical toilet.

He crawled over the tail to the rear turret. It moved slowly from left to right and he breathed a sigh of relief. He opened the doors to the back of the turret and Todd jumped in shock. His eyes were wide behind his goggles as he stared at Woods like he was some apparition. Woods clapped him on the shoulder and gripped him hard.

"Murphy's caught a packet and the R/T's out!" he shouted. "So you're it."

Todd bobbed his head in understanding. Woods closed the turret doors and went forward again. He took his time, shuffling slowly and keeping well away from the port side.

Back in his turret, Todd took stock. The perspex to his left was smashed, and the slipstream whipped around him but the turret still worked as did his guns. His arm stung like hell but there was no point mentioning anything now. He had to man the turret and with Murphy gone he was their sole defence. He opened a first aid kit and shoved some bandages inside his flying gear, pressing it on the wound to staunch the bleeding.

As they soldiered on, Carter's head was ringing from the constant barrage. The engines roared, the air shrieked through the nose and the holes in the canopy. His scalp felt tight, like he'd had one drink too many. His eyes were two hot ball bearings in his skull and his face was frozen into a rigid block. He thanked god he had goggles on or it would have been impossible to see anything.

Woods reappeared at his shoulder.

"Do you want the good news, or the bad news?" his navigator bellowed.

"What the hell; in for a penny...good news."

"Todd isn't dead and he's still playing tail end charley."

There was a pause and Carter waited for the next bit, there wasn't one.

"That's it?"

Woods decided there was no way to soften the blow so he just came out with it.

"Vos is dead. I'm not sure about, Murphy. I've made him comfortable but his turret is U/S."

Carter's jaw tensed. Flynn gone, Vos dead and Murphy injured. Not a very good scorecard.

"Do you know why we're wallowing around?" he asked.

"Flak's burst open the fuselage down the port side and I don't mean a small hole. It's like leaving the front door open when a hurricanes blowing. There's all sorts flapping around back there."

"Christ," Carter cursed.

"Oh, and I've got no charts," Woods finished. "They've all got sucked away god knows where. Apart from that, we're fine," he said, beaming maniacally.

"Super."

Carter faced a dilemma. The engines were untouched and now they were on their way home they could get some altitude in case they needed to bail out. But the higher they went; the more likely fighters or flak might take a shot at them. With no R/T they were in a real jam.

He decided to stay low and trust to luck. Out of the stream, they might attract less attention. If it all went wrong, he would just have to put her down fast and dirty any way he could.

Woods gave Carter the course for home off the top of his head and went back to Murphy to keep an eye on him. Twenty minutes later, the R/T crackled into life.

"Excellent, well done, Byron."

"Piece of cake, skip," replied the Engineer. He kept himself busy, doing his best to ignore the raging gale twisting down the fuselage.

"Todd, how're you doing back there?"

Todd's reply sounded like he was at the bottom of a well, but at least they could talk to him again.

"I'm in rough shape, boss, but I'm still here."

"Keep an eye out, we're not home yet."

"Remind me why I extended my tour again?" said the Australian and Carter had to laugh at the situation they were in.

They were crawling along, barely above stalling speed. Due to the missing nose hatch and the hole in the side, they were about as aerodynamic as a barn door. A long way from home, in a crippled bomber, it was a good two hours or more to get back to Amber Hill. Carter decided there was no way they were hanging on to get home. Granted, it would be bravado and sheer bloody mindedness to get back, but it would be a stupid risk. With Murphy injured and *The Lady* shot to bits, Carter was going to put down on the first airfield they came across as soon as they crossed the south coast.

With no maps, it might have been difficult getting home but in this instance, it was just parallel to the way in. The only bit of the route he was concerned about was when they went past Saint Trond. There was a nightfighter field there. God help them if a fighter found them then.

Carter dropped down to five hundred feet for a while, trying to blend into the background. Overhead, he saw a bright streamer of flame as another bomber went down. Then the sky flickered on the horizon with beams of searchlights going back and forth. Carter drifted starboard to try and skirt round it.

The village of Hasselen was a sleepy Belgian village west of Sint Truiden. It had a mill, a bakery, a cobblers and a small church. Nothing much happened there until the Germans came. A supply depot was built on the big field next to the mill and a German detachment moved in, building wooden huts to house the men. Trucks regularly came and went carrying supplies and life settled down into its new pattern. The bakery provided bread to the barracks; the cobblers did a roaring trade fixing worn out jackboots.

When the British started making intruder raids on the continent, someone decided a supply depot would make a tempting target for fast low flying bombers so a flak detachment was moved into the village. It wasn't much, just some 3.7cm mounts but enough to scare off any Blenheim or Boston that wanted to chance their arm. Tonight, the flak gunners had been roused out of bed and they had manned their guns, staring up at the sky while they heard the drone of one thousand bombers going south east. They heard them coming back not long afterwards.

They were bored and just about to go back to bed when the Feldwebel in charge of the gun to the south of the depot heard the deep rumble of aero engines coming towards them. He perked up immediately and had his single barrelled gun traversed to face the sound. He peered over the parapet of the gun emplacement and cocked his ear, listening.

The bomber was on them before they knew it. They lost precious seconds getting over the shock of something so big being so low before they opened fire. It snarled overhead, almost brushing over the trees. They loosed off eight rounds into the night sky and before the loader could insert a new clip, the bomber was gone.

One shell hit the port inner in the radiator, another hit the bomb bay doors and exploded sending splinters lancing upwards. Carter screamed as shrapnel ripped into his left arm and nicked his thigh. The controls jerked and he caught the Lancaster before she nosed in. He advanced the throttles and clawed for height.

Just like that, they were out of range but the damage had been done. Carter held onto the yoke with his right hand. His left hand was numb, the blood dripping down his arm.

"Byron!" he shouted. The Flight Engineer came over. "Help me," Carter said through gritted teeth. Byron grabbed the yoke with one hand and helped Carter keep it back. Between the two of them they kept the Lancaster level but Carter found it difficult to concentrate as the pain crashed over him in waves.

He glanced down and winced. His leather jacket had been ripped open and a piece of shrapnel had torn through his bicep and into his shoulder deltoid muscle. Another bit of metal had torn across the top of his hand. He tried moving his fingers but it was difficult, they didn't want to do what they were told.

Byron got a first aid kit and squeezed behind the pilots seat and tended to Carter's arm. He wadded up a bandage and held it in place with another one. All it did was slow down the bleeding. It was crude, but there wasn't much he could do. The wound was too far up his arm to put a tourniquet on and he didn't want to give Carter any morphine because he wouldn't be able to fly.

Carter used his teeth to hold one end of another bandage while Byron wrapped it around his palm.

"That okay, skipper?" Byron asked as he tied it off.

"Would it make a difference if I said no?"

"I guess not. What do you want me to do?"

"If you can handle the throttles and help with the stick."

"Will do, boss."

They carried on, somehow managing between them to keep *The Lady* in the air. The Lancaster undulated up and down, never holding level for more than a few seconds at a time. Chilled to the bone, Carter found it hard to concentrate for long as his mind began to drift. It was like being tired on a Sunday afternoon after a big roast dinner. Your head started going, your eyes closed for a second and then your head dropped and you jerked awake, your senses focusing for a moment before you started to drift again.

Byron steadied the yoke, getting the hang of anticipating Carter's movements as they both fought the wounded bomber. Woods came forward.

"I think, Murphy's had it. There's not a mark on him but I can't find a pulse and he's going cold."

"*I'm* going cold," said Byron.

"I think the blast did for him," said Woods.

"Poor sod," said Carter, shaking his head, his voice slurred. "At least it was quick." He closed one eye and focused on the compass. "How long to home?"

Woods glanced at the instrument panel.

"At this speed? Hour and a half, maybe more."

"I won't last that," said Carter.

"Forty minutes to get across the channel then."

"That'll do,"

Todd warned them there was a stream of something trailing back from the starboard wing. Byron checked the fuel tank gauges on his engineer's panels and thought they were leaking fuel from the one of the starboard tanks. They ignored it. So close to home there couldn't have been much left anyway.

The temperature started to climb on the port inner. They debated shutting it down.

"Can we fly on two like this?" Woods asked, genuinely concerned. In their old Manchester they would have had no chance at this height.

"Piece of cake," said Carter, half smiling. He felt light headed and he was blinking rapidly, trying to stay focused. Byron suggested restarting the starboard outer but Carter said he would rather wait. The port inner was still running even if it was a bit hot.

They steered around Antwerp. At this height, the towns flak gunners would have gobbled them up in seconds. They roared over the dykes and out over the Schelde estuary. Carter took them low. A searchlight flicked on but they left it far behind while their slipstream stirred up the surface of the water. Once they cleared the coast, they went back up to five hundred feet.

This was the worst part of the entire trip. They listened to the engines and watched the gauges. The slightest twitch of the needles gave them kittens as they expected the engines to conk out at any moment. None of them relished ditching in the black forbidding waters, remembering their landing in the pond.

They crossed the coast just south of Felixstowe and Harwich, threading delicately between the port and Colchester. Their eyes went in a thousand directions at once, keeping a keen lookout for barrage balloons.

Woods took them north and within a few minutes they were over RAF Wattisham. At one thousand feet, Carter circled once to get the lay of the land. Wattisham was a day bomber field, home to Blenheims from 2 Group. There were two runways and to the east of them were the airfields buildings, four type C hangars and the usual cluster of Nissen huts. Carter was grateful that the surrounding land was quite flat as he circled north to setup for the approach. In their condition he wanted a straight run in with no hills to worry about.

"Do you want to try the wheels?" asked Byron.

Carter thought about that. Most of the damage was to the rear so it was a good chance the undercarriage was alright. He didn't relish the idea of coming in on their belly.

"We'll give it a go. Give me some flap to see if we've got any hydraulic pressure. We can always blow the wheels down if we have to."

Byron set for fifteen degrees of flap and Carter could feel them bite into the air as they came down. The nose lifted slightly and Carter left the trim alone, using what little elevator authority he had to keep them level.

He had trouble focusing on the instruments and he shook his head to clear it as his vision swam. He asked Byron to call out their altitude as they descended. They dropped the wheels and Carter felt the thump as they extended and locked home. The Lancaster staggered over the boundary fence. Carter kept the speed up in case they had to go round again.

"We're high, we're too high, skipper," Byron shouted.

Carter made no reply and Byron shot him a look. Carter's head lolled, his eyes almost rolling into the back of his head.

"Skipper!" Byron shouted. The voice came from far away, echoing in his head. Carter suddenly snapped forward, eyes wide, his brow knotted as he concentrated on these last few seconds. His vision swam, going light and dark.

He tightened his grip on the yoke with both hands, but his left hand refused to work and he hissed as pain shot up his arm. He told Byron to close the throttles. Byron edged them back, hearing the engine note dip.

The ground rushed up to meet them. *The Lady* thumped down once, twice to a squeal of rubber and then stayed down, squashing on her wheels.

"We're down! Cut the switches," said Carter, his senses swimming. His hands went slack on the controls and Byron pulled back on the yoke to keep the tail down. The engines cut and the sudden silence was almost deafening after five hours in the air.

As their speed dropped off, Byron stretched his leg over to push on the right rudder pedal to steer off the runway. They bumped across the grass and finally came to a stop.

"We made it, skipper!" shouted Byron.

"That's good," Carter whispered, so quiet they almost missed it. "Think I'll sleep for a while." His voice trailed off as his chin rested on his chest.

Byron turned on him, his voice stricken.

"Skipper?" He shook Carter by the shoulder. "Skipper!"

He saw the lights of some cars approaching across the field. He went down into the nose and dropped through the hatch, running towards them, waving his arms.

Helping hands got Carter down from the Lancaster and straight into a waiting ambulance. Todd joined him.

"Why didn't you say anything, Digger?" asked Woods as he stuck a cigarette between the Australians lips.

"Somebody had to do it," Todd replied quietly. Woods lit the cigarette, then the doors of the ambulance were closed and they were whisked away. The ambulance also carried the blanket shrouded bodies of Vos and Murphy. Byron and Woods were watching it drive off into the distance when a studious looking Squadron Leader came over to them.

"You chaps look done in." He put a friendly hand on Woods shoulder. "Let's get this over with so you can get some rest."

"Will someone tell our squadron where we are?" asked Woods, his head ringing. Suddenly it all seemed so unreal. Adrenalin was surging through his veins and his eyes were wide, his pulse throbbing.

"Don't you worry about that. We'll take care of everything, old chap," said the Squadron Leader. "I've got a nice hot cup of tea with a nip of something stronger in waiting for you."

61 - World Enough And Time

Initial reports of the raid were highly favourable. Some of the new Mosquitoes flew over Cologne early in the morning only a few hours after the main force had left, but heavy smoke blanketing the city stopped them getting photographs of the damage.

Losses had been light and despite Harris' fears, were no worse than any other raid. 3.9% had been lost and the third wave suffered only 1.9% casualties, well below the figure Churchill would have been prepared to accept. Nearly nine hundred aircraft had reported bombing the city and very few had turned back early. More tonnage had been dropped on Cologne in one night than in all the other raids that had taken place since the war began. It was a roaring success by any standard. There had been no sea of fire like there had been at Rostock. Cologne was a modern city with wide avenues and open spaces but the damage was still extensive. Later estimates thought that up to fifty thousand people had been bombed out. Hundreds of factories had been damaged and there had been a major loss of production.

The CinC was not one to miss an opportunity. While the moon was with him, it made sense to go again before the OTU aircraft had to disperse back to their airfields. The day the newspapers shouted the news that the greatest bomber raid in history had taken place, Bomber Command went to Essen. The weather had foxed Harris again and Hamburg would have to wait for now. Regardless, he had his headline and silenced his most vocal critics. There would be no more talk of breaking up Bomber Command now.

Late in the morning, Woods and Byron went down to see *The Lady* while they were waiting for transport to take them back to Amber Hill. In daylight, the full extent of her injuries were clearly evident. Going from the joint of the mid section to nearly the entire length of the tail, the port side was blown out. The metal skin curled outwards like it had been attacked by a tin opener. Only the inherent toughness of Roy Chadwicks design and Carter's deft handling had seen them home.

To the untrained eye, she was a write off, but to the repair crews, they knew better. Lancaster fuselages were assembled at the factory in three sections, the nose and cockpit, the main spar and the rear fuselage. L-Lady was disassembled where she stood at Wattisham, loaded onto the transporters and packed off to a reconditioning workshop. The damaged section was scrapped and replaced. Within five weeks she was airworthy again with a new tail and sent to 97 squadron at Waddington as a replacement. She served for another four missions before falling on a raid over Duisburg.

An Oxford picked up Woods and Byron and they were flown up to Amber Hill in the afternoon to find the station getting ready to go again to Essen. The station was buzzing as the erks worked to get the kites ready. Kent took a quick report off them and Church had the MO put them straight to bed, they were wrung out and in no shape to do anything for a day or two.

Todd and Carter were whisked off to hospital, suffering from shock and blood loss in addition to their wounds. Tucked up in a soft warm bed, the hell over Cologne seemed a million miles away as they talked about the struggle to get home and the nightfighter attack. Reading about it and the later attack on Essen in the newspapers didn't seem real somehow.

Todd was back flying within a month. The bullet had gone straight through his arm and soon healed and he had another scar to go with the one on his scalp. Despite the offer, he still stubbornly refused to be screened and remained a committed ops man. He was left to carry on, one of those incorrigibles that warmed Harris' heart and he fondly referred to as his 'old lags'.

Carter's recovery was more drawn out. Aside from concussion, the damage to his arm and hand were more extensive than anyone first thought. They managed to save his arm but had to remove some of the muscle which had been torn by the shrapnel. It took two operations before they were happy with his hand.

The doctors had explained to him that there'd been some nerve damage and it would take a while to settle down before they knew how much function would return. For a long while he found it difficult to manipulate objects with his fingers and he had no grip strength at all. They also warned him that the pain and numbness may never completely go away. Carter considered it a small price to pay considering the bill plenty of others had paid, Church, Archer, Salmon, Dickinson, Murphy and Vos.

It was the beginning of August before he was released from hospital and went back to Amber Hill on light duties. He found a new man waiting for him in the CO's office. Wing Commander Forrester had taken over the squadron after Church failed to return from the third thousand plane raid at the end of June.

He wasted no time on niceties and got straight to the point.

Forrester told Carter he was done; his tour was up and he was being sent on recuperative leave. Carter argued to stay until he was fit to fly so he could finish his tour but his appeal fell on deaf ears. The decision had been made from on high and once his leave was up, Group would decide where he went after that. Saunderson had his leave papers waiting for him when he came out of the office.

Now that he was off ops, Georgette wangled some leave and they were married in a small service at the registry office in Grantham. Woods and Yvonne, Wilkinson and Helen were there as witness, best man and bridesmaids respectively. They visited his mother in Harrogate and then had five intense days near Lake Windermere before returning to Grantham. He got a room at a boarding house in town and spent the days sleeping, reading and enjoying a slower pace of life for once while his arm continued to heal.

During his time in hospital he'd started to piece things together in his head. As near as Carter could figure, one shell had exploded close to the rear fuselage, blowing out the thin metal skin and killing Murphy instantly. Another shell must have gone up between the port inner and the fuselage and exploded almost directly above the cockpit, most of the force going upwards and away. It was the hammer blow of the blast that had knocked him silly for a few seconds.

Woods filled in the remaining blanks for him when they got together for drinks after the wedding service. When he saw a photograph of their badly damaged Lanc, Carter was amazed they'd made it back at all. He felt foolish for taking such a chance landing her when they could have just bailed out.

Vos and Murphy were buried in a sombre service on a rainy day in the first week of June. Denise attended the funeral, a pale figure dressed in black, sobbing her heart out as she clung to Woods arm for support. Breaking the news to her was the hardest thing Woods had ever done. Saunderson had gone with him and Yvonne had offered to come along as well. Woods was glad she did.

They went round in the early evening on the 1st June. When Denise opened the door, she knew. When a colleague of your man came to the door wearing sorrow as a mask, there was only one thing it could be. Fighting back tears, she had gestured into the room with a dead hand and they'd filed in.

She walked slowly to one of the armchairs by the fire and sank into it. Woods took the seat across from her. He hitched forward, resting his elbows on his knees. Yvonne sat on the bed while Saunderson did his best to disappear. Feeling surplus to requirements, he went downstairs to see if he could get Mrs Peck to make some tea and avoid having to observe this little tableau.

The girl had stared into the fire, her gaze fixed, eyes glittering with tears. Everything about her was frozen perfectly still, like a sculpture. The silence hung thick in the air and then Woods started telling the story. He skipped some bits, glossed over others and all while he talked, he could feel the gap between himself and the French girl grow. Finally, he ran out of words at a loss for what to say next.

Yvonne came over to Denise and crouched down next to her. It was only when she gathered her into her arms that the girls composure finally cracked and the great wailing sobs came out of her, rolling like waves on a beach, one after another as her life fell apart. Yvonne looked over her shoulder and nodded to the door and Woods took the hint.

Downstairs in the parlour, the two men stood glum while Mrs Peck poured them another cup of tea with a disapproving scowl on her face. Saunderson stared at the ceiling as more wailing could be heard. Grim indeed. This was not his thing. He packed personal effects and wrote letters for the CO to sign. Calling on girls of the deceased to deliver bad news was outside of his experience. Eventually, the cries stopped and Yvonne came downstairs. Her own eyes were red rimmed as she stood next to Woods, clasping his hand for strength.

"She's sleeping now, the poor thing. This news has broken her."

Mrs Peck looked up at the ceiling.

"I'll go up," she said.

"I'd leave it for a bit," cautioned Yvonne.

"Is there any hope?" Mrs Peck asked, her voice trailing off.

"None, I'm afraid," Woods said quietly.

They'd left then, promising to come and see her the following day.

After the funeral she withdrew from from life and Mrs Peck became a surrogate mother, fussing over her and making sure she looked after herself. Woods, Yvonne and Helen would call on her when they could but the French girl became a hollow shell of her former self, devastated by her loss.

One day, she disappeared, never to be seen again. Helen Wilkinson had gone round to check on her to find the room empty of all her things and no note saying where she'd gone or what she intended to do.

Mrs Peck was in pieces, worried sick for Denise and the baby. Enquiries were made with the Police and the local hospitals but Helen felt they made a half hearted effort. One missing French girl in the middle of a war just wasn't a priority. It was a sad end to a sad story.

Flynn was dead. After bailing out at dangerously low level during that mad dive, he had landed heavily in a ploughed field and hurt his ankle. Abandoning his parachute, he had hobbled along for two miles across the countryside before the Police found him. Flynn contemplated running, but he wouldn't get far on a gammy leg. He stuck his hands in the air and gave himself up. They searched him, relieving him of a silk scarf and some chocolate before shoving him in front of them while they cycled behind, prodding him with a stick to keep him moving.

The entire time, the Police officers had nervously looked upwards at the never ending drone of aero engines passing overhead. The noise was terrific. On the horizon, the sky glowed orange where Cologne burned.

When they got to a small village, they were met by an angry knot of people. Harsh words were exchanged, then the Police officers were shoved out of the way and Flynn was taken hold of. Rushed across the street, a placard tied with a loop of string was put over his head. Crude letters had been painted on it to spell *Terfforfleiger*. Protesting at being roughly handled, he was still struggling when his arms were pinned to his side and a noose was put around his neck.

He was strung up from a lamp post in the street, his feet thrashing; hands scrabbling at the rope. The crowd cheered and stood there watching as he slowly suffocated to death. Before he was cut down, one enterprising soul helped themselves to his flying boots. The authorities were given a bland account that he'd died from injuries sustained while bailing out and his remaining personal effects were sent home via the Red Cross.

The big Canadian went on to finish out his tour with a friend. Commissioned as a Pilot Officer, Jensen returned to Amber Hill and gathered up what was left of his old crew. Byron and Todd continued to fly with him as he held them all to the standard Carter had shown him all those months before.

When his tour was over, there was a massive party in the Mess to send Woods on his way. Ten months after he first arrived at Amber Hill, there were few familiar faces to help him celebrate, a stark reminder of the human cost of a tour of operations.

He managed a few days away with Yvonne and asked her to marry him. She readily accepted and he spent the remainder of his special leave on the station to be close to her. They had a tearful farewell on the platform at Lincoln train station when he left to teach budding navigator's in Wales.

When his leave was over, Carter was nervous when he went to Group in his best uniform to find out what fate had in store for him. He needn't have worried too much. 5 Group was not about to let such an experienced man go too far affield. He was posted to take command of a new HCU at New Haven, a satellite field near Bassingham, south of Lincoln.

The months that followed were a blur. Forming a unit from scratch was hard work, but he threw himself into it. He managed to get a good adjutant who was a whizz at paperwork and Carter came to rely on him a great deal. He gathered a core of experienced men to be instructors and drew up a training program that would get squadrons converted and operational as quickly as possible. To start with, they went to the squadrons to do the work, but once New Haven was ready, crews came to them. He built extras into the program to encompass all the lessons that had been so dearly earned in blood.

In the middle of it all, he returned to Amber Hill at the end of September to have his second DFC pinned to his chest by Group Captain Etheridge. Todd received the DFM for remaining in his turret while wounded and driving off the nightfighter. It was one of the few occasions Carter had seen the Australian lost for words. Cullen was there to record the event with a photographer. He still considered Carter to be the centrepiece of his story of the bomber war.

Another medal recipient was White, awarded the DFC for his devotion to duty that night over Norfolk. He made the journey from East Grinstead to stand in his uniform, weathering the pain to be with his peers. Carter promised him a place as an instructor when he was cleared to fly again. White emphasised the *when*, rather than the unspoken *if*. Stubborn determination blazed in his eyes to make that a reality.

The one thing he missed during the fuss of setting up the HCU was Wilkinson. By the time he'd returned to Group, his friend was long gone. At the beginning of July, Wilkinson had been posted as an RAF liaison officer to the newly formed American 8th Air Force headquarters. Helen and their new daughter went with him, setting up house in a nice little cottage, not far from the HQ. He was kept busy, smoothing ruffled local feathers as new airfields sprang up all over the place in Norfolk. The air was filled with the noisy thunder of Wright Cyclone engines as B17's and B24's started to arrive from across the Atlantic.

He still thought the Americans were mad to try daylight bombing. All the same, that didn't stop him from going on some of the early missions over Lorient and other French targets as a waist gunner to see them in action. Helen would have killed him if she had known her husband was risking his neck over France so he told her he'd gone up on training flights. Wilkinson wrote Carter a letter about it all, telling him about the tight box formations the Americans flew and the B17's that bristled with guns like some porcupine.

As 1942 drew to a close, Carter settled into life at New Haven. He went up regularly to see that the trainees were coming up to his standard but he never flew himself. With a gammy arm, the Flight Surgeon had pronounced his flying days were over. Carter had strong opinions about that. If Douglas bloody Bader could fly with no legs and some other fighter johnny could fly a Spit with one hand missing and a hook in its place, then Carter felt he should be allowed to go back on ops.

One day he managed to wangle a flip in one of the new Mosquitoes. Fast and nimble, she was responsive on the controls and his weak hand was not the impediment he thought it would be. Despite everything that had happened, he still felt the pull to be part of an operational squadron again. He knew he wasn't ready yet, but one day he would be. It was just going to take perseverance and a lot of hard work to get back.

He thought about that as he got changed in his office one drab autumn morning. He knew what Georgette would say. Part of him thought he was crazy to contemplate going back on ops, but he knew deep down that if he was ever given the chance he'd jump at the opportunity.

His arm twinged and his fingers tingled with pins and needles as he took off his tunic and draped it over the back of his chair. He flexed his fingers as he looked at his hand, turning it front to back, seeing the zig zag of scars in the skin. He shrugged on his leather flying jacket and went outside, the straps on his flying boots flapping, the Mae West draped over his shoulder. He got into the waiting Tilly and the Corporal drove him out to dispersal to put another crew through their paces.

"Right chaps, let's get cracking," he said as he climbed up into the cockpit. "Maximum effort!"

The pilot slid the side window open and gave the groundcrew a thumbs up. The Sergeant pointed to the starboard inner. The propeller started turning, the cylinders banged and then there was a throaty roar as the Merlin engine caught.

THE END

Printed in Great Britain
by Amazon